BRAVE NEW WORLD

AND

BRAVE NEW WORLD REVISITED

BOOKS BY ALDOUS HUXLEY

NOVELS

The Genius and the Goddess
Ape and Essence
Time Must Have a Stop
After Many a Summer Dies the Swan
Eyeless in Gaza
Point Counter Point
Those Barren Leaves
Antic Hay
Crome Yellow
Brave New World
Island

ESSAYS AND BELLES LETTRES

Brave New World Revisited
Tomorrow and Tomorrow and Tomorrow
Heaven and Hell
The Doors of Perception
The Devils of Loudon
Themes and Variations
Ends and Means
Texts and Pretexts
The Olive Tree
Music at Night
Vulgarity in Literature
Do What You Will
Proper Studies
Jesting Pilate
Along the Round
On the Margin
Essays New and Old
The Art of Seeing
The Perennial Philosophy
Science, Liberty and Peace

SHORT STORIES

Collected Short Stories
Brief Candles
Two or Three Graces
Limbo
Little Mexican
Mortal Coils

BIOGRAPHY

Grey Eminence

POETRY

The Cicadas
Leda

TRAVEL

Beyond the Mexique Bay

DRAMA

Mortal Coils—A Play
The World of Light
The Discovery, Adapted from Francis Sheridan

SELECTED WORKS

Rotunda
The World of Aldous Huxley

BRAVE NEW WORLD

AND

BRAVE NEW WORLD REVISITED

ALDOUS HUXLEY

FOREWORD BY
CHRISTOPHER HITCHENS

HARPER PERENNIAL

NEW YORK • LONDON • TORONTO • SYDNEY

HARPER PERENNIAL

A hardcover edition of *Brave New World* was published in 1932 by Harper & Brothers, Publishers.

Most of the material in *Brave New World Revisited* was published by *Newsday* under the title *Tyranny over the Mind*. A hardcover edition of *Brave New World Revisited* was published in 1958 by Harper & Row, Publishers.

A hardcover edition of this book was published in 2004 by HarperCollins Publishers.

P.S.™ is a trademark of HarperCollins Publishers Inc.

First Perennial Library edition of *Brave New World* published 1969. Reset 1989.
First Perennial Classics edition of *Brave New World* published 1998.
First Perennial Library edition of *Brave New World Revisited* published 1965. Reset 1989.
First Perennial Classics edition of *Brave New World Revisited* published 2000.
First Harper Perennial Modern Classics edition of *Brave New World and Brave New World Revisited* published 2005.

Designed by Joseph Rutt

The Library of Congress has catalogued the hardcover edition as follows:
Huxley, Aldous, 1894–1963.
[Brave new world]
Brave new world and Brave new world revisited / Aldous Huxley ; foreword by Christopher Hitchens.—1st ed.
p. cm.
ISBN 0-06-053526-1
1. Passivity (Psychology)—Fiction. 2. Genetic engineering—Fiction. 3. Totalitarianism—Fiction. 4. Collectivism—Fiction. I. Title: Brave new world and Brave new world revisited. II. Huxley, Aldous, 1894–1963. Brave new world revisited. III. Title: Brave new world revisited. IV. Title.

ISBN-10: 0-06-077609-9 (pbk.)
ISBN-13: 978-0-06-0776091 (pbk.)

13 ❖/RRD 30 29 28 27 26 25 24

CONTENTS

FOREWORD

Aldous Huxley absolutely detested mass culture and popular entertainment, and many of his toughest critical essays, as well as several intense passages in his fiction, consist of sneers and jeers at the cheapness of the cinematic ethic and the vulgarity of commercial music. He chanced to die on the same day as the assassination of President Kennedy in November 1963 (being cheated of a proper obituary notice as a result, and sharing the date of decease with C. S. Lewis, chronicler of Narnia) so he missed the televisual event which once and for all confirmed the "global village." But if he were able to return to us, and cast his scornful and lofty gaze on our hedonistic society, he would probably be relatively unsurprised at the way things are going. Sex has been divorced from procreation to a degree hard to imagine even in 1963, and the current great debates in the moral sciences concern the implications of reproductive cloning and of the employment of fetal stem-cells in medicine. The study of history is everywhere, but especially in the United States, in steep decline. Public life in the richer societies is routinely compared to the rhythms of spectacle and entertainment. A flickering hunger for authenticity pushes many people to explore the peripheral and shrinking worlds of the "indigenous." This was all prefigured in *Brave New World*. So, in a way, was the "one child" policy now followed in Communist China, where to the extent that the program is successful we will not only see a formerly clannish society where everyone is an only child but a formerly Marxist one that has no real cognate word for "brotherhood." Intercontinental rocket travel has not become the commonplace Huxley anticipated but its equivalents have become a cliché: jumbo jets do the same work of abolishing distance for the masses even though, in a strange moment of refusal, the developed world has stepped back from the supersonic Concorde and reverted to the days of voyaging comfortably below the speed of sound.

No, what would astonish laconic old Aldous would be the discovery that his photograph is among those on the album cover of *Sergeant Pepper's Lonely Hearts Club Band*—perhaps the least cacophonous of the signature records of pop and rock—and that Jim Morrison of The Doors had named his group after Huxley's later and proto-psychedelic book *The Doors of Perception*. In America, as Joan Didion once wrote, people who say "No Man Is An Island" think that they are quoting Ernest Hemingway: the fans who still make a shrine of Morrison's grave in Paris probably don't appreciate that Huxley was himself borrowing from William Blake. Nonetheless, literary immortality often depends on such vague but durable misunderstandings, and the three words "Brave New World" (themselves annexed from Miranda's speech in Shakespeare's *Tempest*) are as well known as "Catch-22" or "Nineteen Eighty-Four"—virtual hieroglyphics which almost automatically summon a universe of images and associations.

English literary society in the twentieth century was a fairly small pond, and the English class system tended to mean in any case that a limited number of people kept running into each other. (This is one of the bonding yet realistic elements in the splendid novel sequence written by Anthony Powell.) However, that Aldous Huxley should have taught George Orwell at Eton, which was also Anthony Powell's old school, seems to strain the natural serendipity of coincidence. Having originally hoped to become a physician, Huxley contracted a serious eye infection as an adolescent, lost a good deal of his sight, and until he could launch himself as a writer was compelled to be a rather diffident and reluctant teacher of French. In his class were Stephen Runciman, later to become the grand historian of Byzantium and the Crusades, and Eric Blair, later to metamorphose into George Orwell. Runciman remembers that "Blair" admired Huxley's command of French culture and that he detested those boys who took advantage of the schoolmaster's myopia.

Orwell never referred to this personal connection in print, as far as I know, when *Brave New World* was published in 1931 and when its dystopic metaphors entered the conversational and social bloodstream. He suggested at one point that Huxley had "plagiarized" from an earlier anti-Utopian novel, Evgeny Zamyatin's *We*. But since he acknowledged that work as an inspiration of his own, the allegation may have been no insult. He didn't get around to reviewing *Brave New World* until July 1940, when Britain seemed to have more urgent problems than the supposed nightmare of too much free sex and narcosis:

> Here the hedonistic principle is pushed to its utmost, the whole world has turned into a Riviera hotel. But though *Brave New World* was a brilliant caricature of the present (the present of 1930), it probably casts no light on the future. No society of that kind would last more than a couple of generations, because a ruling class that thought principally of a "good time" would soon lose its vitality. A ruling class has got to have a strict morality, a quasi-religious belief in itself, a *mystique*.

For some decades after this review was written, many people might have been inclined to say that Orwell was right, and that the "true" threat was one of jackboots, tanks, bombs, and bullies. Nonetheless, Huxley never went out of style. Something about his work seemed to tug at our consciousness.

One could also point out that, in the picture of Mustapha Mond with which Huxley opens the work, we are in fact introduced to a self-conscious ruling class with ideas of its own. Mond is not represented as wanting a "good time" for himself, after all. He is the chilly, objective theorist of the idea that social engineering and the wide distribution of easy pleasure will keep the masses in line. And two further things are made plain at once, both of which may have influenced Orwell more than he knew. We are told quite early on, in the flashbacks that occur during Mond's address to the awe-struck students, that the brave new epoch began after the "Nine Years War," in which weapons of mass destruction (including "anthrax bombs": a superbly modern detail) had been employed. And we are also reminded of the crucial role played by amnesia in the maintenance of power. Mond takes the great capitalist Henry Ford at his word:

> "History," he repeated slowly, "is bunk."
>
> He waved his hand; and it was as though, with an invisible feather whisk, he had brushed away a little dust, and the dust was Harappa, was Ur of the Chaldees; some spider-webs, and they were Thebes and Babylon and Cnossos and Mycenae. Whisk. Whisk—and where was Odysseus, where was Job, where were Jupiter and Gotama and Jesus? Whisk—and those specks of antique dirt called Athens and Rome, Jerusalem and the Middle Kingdom—all were gone. Whisk—the place where Italy had been was empty. Whisk, the cathedrals; whisk, whisk, King Lear and the Thoughts of Pascal. Whisk, Passion; whisk, Requiem; whisk, Symphony; whisk. . . .

This combination, of annihilating war and the subsequent obliteration and erasure of cultural and historical memory, is almost exactly what Orwell later relied upon to set the scene for his *Nineteen Eighty-Four*. But he was writing about the forbidding, part-alien experience of Nazism and Stalinism, whereas Huxley was locating disgust and menace in the very things—the new toys of materialism, from cars to contraceptives—that were becoming everyday pursuits. Perhaps that is why his book still operates on our subconscious.

There must indeed be an explanation for this, because I have to say that the fine passage quoted above is not completely typical. Huxley was thought rather snobbish even in his own generation, and often tended to condescend to the reader, as much of the dialogue in *Brave New World* also tends to do. It is didactic and pedagogic and faintly superior: indeed you might say it was the tone of voice of an Etonian schoolmaster. It is also somewhat contradictory and even self-defeating. Clearly, Huxley disdained socialism and the idea of equality: why then give the name of Bernard Marx to the only dissident in his awful system? And why call one of the few natural and spontaneous girls Lenina? This is stodgy and heavy rather than ironic, and it becomes absurd when we meet a sexy little child named Polly Trotsky in the opening chapters. (It's elsewhere stated that all citizens must be named from a pool of officially authorized surnames: the hedonistic regime either wants to abolish interest in history or it does not, and in neither case will it tempt fate by naming millions of its subjects after revolutionaries.)

Huxley came from revolutionary stock, but of a different kind. His grandfather was T. H. Huxley, a celebrated naturalist, who was a partisan and friend of Charles Darwin. It was the elder Huxley who first coined the term "agnostic" and who vanquished the Victorian Bishop Wilberforce in the famous debate between evolution and creationism at Oxford University. On his mother's side, Aldous could claim Matthew Arnold, author of *Culture and Anarchy*, as a maternal uncle. His own views were to fluctuate between the affirmative importance of high culture and the necessity of skepticism. His favorite philosopher was the ancient Hellenic thinker Pyrrho, who argued that judgment be suspended on any matter concerning the truth. Every position may be held to be equally right as well as equally wrong.

It's worth knowing this about Huxley, who often held and expressed diametrically opposite opinions, and who described himself as an "amused Pyrrhonic aesthete" in the introduction he wrote to the twentieth-anniversary edition of *Brave New World.* In the novel itself, one can often detect strong hints of a vicarious approval of what is ostensibly being satirized. For example, when Mustapha Mond invites the medical students to "try to imagine what 'living with one's family' meant," he goes on:

> Home, home—a few small rooms, stiflingly over-inhabited by a man, by a periodically teeming woman, by a rabble of boys and girls of all ages. No air, no space; an understerilized prison; darkness, disease and smells.

Huxley was never at all impoverished as a boy (and in any case we can recognize the denunciation above from any study of Victorian or now "Third World" domestic conditions), but his mother died of cancer when he was fourteen and his brother committed suicide two years later, so he knew that even upper-class family life could be distraught. The above passage combines this insight with a fastidious disdain for the masses.

The study of eugenics was popular among the governing and intellectual classes of Britain in the Victorian epoch and subsequently (indeed it was an aspect of what has been termed "Social Darwinism"), and we learn from his biographer Nicholas Murray that Aldous Huxley was highly interested in "breeding," in both the aristocratic and the scientific sense of the term. I know from Huxley's own essays that he fell straight for the early theorists of IQ, who believed in its distribution by heredity. To this he added that it was important to encourage "the normal and supernormal members of the population to have large families," while preventing the subnormal "from having any children at all." So it was very clever of him—as well as quite Pyrrhonic—both to mobilize his own feelings on this subject, and then to harness them for a satire on the planned economy. One need not object to his having things both ways, as long as one notices the trick being performed.

In rather the same way, Huxley thought that free love and infidelity were all very well for people like himself (he and his first wife had an open marriage and even shared the bed of the same female lover, Mary Hutchinson). But still, when he came to describe the mindless and amoral sex lives of the men and women in *Brave New World*, he wrote with a curled lip. In an article describing the "jazz age" in California in the late 1920s, he had relished the profusion of nubile young girls and wrote that: "Plumply ravishing, they give, as T. S. Eliot has phrased it, 'a promise of pneumatic bliss.'" Eliot spent his critical and poetic energy in the attempt to revive, in a more specifically Christian and conservative form, the values of Matthew Arnold. So it is again amusing to note that the coarse word "pneumatic," used throughout *Brave New World* by both its male and female characters as a cheap synonym for good sex, derives from this rather disapproving source, as well as expressing Huxley's own divided view of the subject.

The influence of T. S. Eliot can also be felt in the depiction of "World Controller" Mustapha Mond, described as possessing "a hooked nose, full red lips, and eyes very piercing and dark." Martin Green has drawn attention to the resemblance to Mustapha Kemal, better known as Ataturk, who was a commanding figure when Huxley was writing. Sir Alfred Mond, the founder of the giant chemical multinational known as ICI (Imperial Chemical Industries), was also a power-celebrity of the period, and Eliot often alluded to him as the prototypical cosmopolitan Jew. (Huxley's few references to Jews were also often disobliging: he blamed them for the mercantile sleaziness of Hollywood, among other things. As if to rub this in, there's also a somewhat repellent character in *Brave New World* named Morgana Rothschild.) And we catch another prefiguration of *Nineteen Eighty-Four*, when the Director of Hatcheries and Conditioning finds himself nervous in Mond's presence, because "there were those strange rumors of old forbidden books hidden in a safe in the Controller's study. Bibles, poetry—Ford knew what." Did Orwell half-remember this when he created the looming figure of O'Brien and the Inner Party's secret book? If so, his review of *Brave New World* was again unfair to Huxley.

I find the tracing of these contemporary influences to be valuable, because Huxley was composing *Brave New World* at a time when modernity as we know it was just coming into full view. He later reproached himself for not mentioning nuclear fission, about which he was quite well informed, but this element of the literal hardly matters. Readers then and since have filled in many gaps for themselves: they knew and they know what Huxley was driving at. Can the human being be designed and controlled, from uterus to grave, "for its own good"? And would this version of super-utilitarianism bring real happiness?

Huxley himself conceded that his fictional characters were no more than puppets to illustrate his points, and this lack of characterization (truly a drawback in his earlier and later novels, most especially in *Island,* his last and most self-consciously Utopian effort) is paradoxically rather a help in *Brave New World.* The marionettes do their stuff, giving us a very rapid and complete picture of mindless bliss and its usefulness to power. Then they begin, or some of them are authorized by their carpenter to begin, to experience vague but definite feelings of discontent. They find themselves asking: Is this all there is? The three deficiencies they feel, often without knowing how to name them, are Nature, Religion, and Literature. With only chemical and mechanical and sexual comforts provided to them, they sense the absence of challenge and drama and they fall prey to *ennui.* With no concept of a cosmos beyond the immediately human, they are deprived of the chance to feel awed or alienated. And with nothing but sensory entertainment (Huxley might not have been the best of movie critics, given his near-blindness, but he used this disadvantage to imagine "the feelies" as the culmination of "talkies" and "movies) they have no appreciation for words.

Huxley's expression of this dilemma, and of its resolution, is again very didactic. He allows some of his prefabricated figures to feel the stirrings of sexual jealousy and its two accompaniments: the yearning for monogamy and the desire to bear one's own child. He permits them the aspiration to experience the wilderness, even if it is only a reservation, and to take the requisite risks. And he leaves a tattered copy of Shakespeare lying around. (I'm sorry to keep doing this, but when Winston Smith in *Nineteen Eighty-Four* awakes from a haunting dream of a lost pastoral England, he does so to his own surprise "with the word Shakespeare on his lips.")

The possessor of the Shakespeare edition is The Savage, and it is he who wreaks revenge on the overprotected and superinsulated creatures who stumble upon his existence. This revenge is partly accidental, in that his own need for authentic emotion is enough in itself to cause convulsions in the society that adopts him as a fearful curiosity or freak. Huxley later said that if he could rewrite the novel he would have given The Savage more warning of what to expect. This shows that fiction writers do well to leave their creations alone and spare them from second thoughts: it is the effect of The Savage upon others that makes the dramatic difference, and it is his very naïveté and simplicity that make a quasi-Calvary out of the final chapter. Huxley was fairly indifferent to Christianity as a religion (and his satire on the Church of England and the "Arch-Community-Songster of Canterbury" has since been easily surpassed by the fatuous degeneration of that Church itself), but he was not immune to its metaphors, and the seeker for reality in the wilderness is only one of these. We can always be sure of one thing—that the messengers of discomfort and sacrifice will be stoned and pelted by those who wish to preserve at all costs their own contentment. This is not a lesson that is confined to the Testaments.

In a way, I have been arguing that *Brave New World* was both ahead of, and behind, its time. And Huxley was—shall we say?—a reactionary modernist. He had this quality in common with Evelyn Waugh, who also took his tone from Eliot's "Waste Land" and who dilated about eugenics and euthanasia while carrying a burden of unpurged religious guilt. The disguised presence of original sin is reimagined in *Brave New World* when Huxley, in the most absurd of his scenarios, shows us little children being sleep-conditioned to consume, and to use up material goods and opportunities with as much abandon as possible. Here one must ask, who but a member of the comfortable or agnostic classes imagines that people need to be brainwashed into being greedy? The acquisitive instinct, perhaps initially supplied by Satan himself in one interpretation, is after all fairly easily engaged. It was Karl Marx and not Bernard Marx who wrote that, in relation to his victims, the capitalist "therefore searches for all possible ways of stimulating them to consume, by making his commodities more attractive and by filling their ears with babble about new needs." Marx also thought, as is usually forgotten or overlooked, that this impulse led to innovation and experiment and to the liberating process of what has sometimes been called "creative destruction." In other words, it is a means of arousing discontent with the *status quo*, not a mere means of stupefying the masses. Our own contemporary world suggests that the energy of capital is not easily compatible with *stasis*.

Having never wanted for much himself, Huxley was quicker to miss this point than he might have been. And, in his Pyrrhonic way, he was also quicker to surrender to the blandishments of Nirvana, in its consumer-capitalist form, than most. This is what makes *Brave New World Revisited* into a disappointment. Once again, the clue is to be found in an exchange with Orwell, who sent Huxley an advance copy of *Nineteen Eighty-Four*. In late 1949, Huxley wrote back to say "how fine and profoundly important" the book was. However, he was convinced that future rulers would discover that:

> infant-conditioning and narco-hypnosis are more efficient, as instruments of government, than clubs and prisons, and that the lust for power can be just as completely satisfied by suggesting people into loving their servitude as by flogging and kicking them into obedience . . . the nightmare of *Nine-*

> *teen Eighty-Four* is destined to modulate into the nightmare of a world having more resemblances to that which I imagined in *Brave New World*. The change will be brought about as a result of a felt need for increased efficiency.

Perhaps it is partly Orwell's fault, since his descriptions of the Thought Police and Room 101 are so annihilatingly and memorably ghastly, but it does deserve to be said that his own fictionalization of absolutism does not depend exclusively upon the power of fear and violence. The masses are not handed *soma* to tranquilize them, but they are given plentiful cheap gin. Lotteries are staged for their amusement and excitement, and cheap pornographic literature is freely available to all proles. The cinema is depicted as an orgy of distraction and propaganda, on Colosseum lines, admittedly, rather than of exquisite sensation. The *Nineteen Eighty-Four* regime is one of scarcity rather than abundance, but the traditional bribes of materialism and indeed of conditioning cannot be said to have been overlooked.

When he came to publish *Brave New World Revisited* almost a decade later, in 1958, Huxley nonetheless opened with a long contrast between his own vision and the Orwellian one; a contrast very similar to the one he had sketched in his letter of 1949. He rightly pointed out that in the Soviet Union the need for rationalization of the economy had produced some alleviation of the totalitarian system. However, his general obsession with eugenics once again caused him to replace the emphasis elsewhere:

> The United States is not at present an over-populated country. If, however, the population continues to increase at the present rate (which is higher than that of India's increase, though happily a good deal lower than the rate now current in Mexico or Guatemala), the problem of numbers in relation to available resources might well become troublesome by the beginning of the twenty-first century. For the moment

> over-population is not a direct threat to the personal freedom of Americans. It remains, however, an indirect threat, a menace at one remove. If over-population should drive the underdeveloped countries into totalitarianism, and if these new dictatorships should ally themselves with Russia, then the military position of the United States would become less secure and the preparations for defense and retaliation would have to be intensified. But liberty, as we all know, cannot flourish in a country that is permanently on a war-footing, or even a near-war footing. Permanent crisis justifies permanent control of everybody and everything by the agencies of the central government. And permanent crisis is what we have to expect in a world in which over-population is producing a state of things, in which dictatorship under Communist auspices becomes almost inevitable.

In no respect is this a paragraph of prescience. The geopolitical sentences are both too detailed and too vague. One might note, also, that the chief demographic problem of the United States in 2003 is its ageing population, with the "graying" process somewhat delayed or postponed by legal and illegal immigration. Scholars, such as Amartya Sen in particular, have come up with multiple refutations of Malthus. "Population bomb" theorists, most notably Paul Ehrlich, have seen their extrapolated predictions repeatedly fail to come true—at least partly because they are extrapolations. Finally, it would appear from his remarks about Mexico and Guatemala that Huxley suddenly isn't all that much in love with the primitive adobe and cactus natives, or not as much in love as he affected to be in *Brave New World*.

One element of that ancestral culture had, however, quite bewitched him in the years that separate the writing of *Brave New World* and *Brave New World Revisited*. His Lawrentian sojourns in California, New Mexico, and elsewhere—he was the editor of D. H. Lawrence's letters—had exposed him to the psychedelic properties of peyote and mescaline and their derivatives, such as LSD (the "Lucy in the Sky with Diamonds" of the *Sergeant Pepper* smash hit). I don't mean to be too "judgmental" about this: Huxley was almost blind and was entitled to any colorful voyage of the imagination that he could get his hands on. But there is something almost promiscuously uncritical in his *Brave New World Revisited* recommendation:

> In LSD-25 (lysergic acid diethylamide) the pharmacologists have recently created another aspect of *soma*—a perception-improver and vision-producer that is, physiologically speaking, almost costless. This extraordinary drug, which is effective in doses as small as fifty or even twenty-five millionths of a gram, has power (like peyote) to transport people into the other world. In the majority of cases, the other world to which LSD-25 gives access is heavenly; alternatively it may be purgatorial or even infernal. But, positive or negative, the lysergic acid experience is felt by almost everyone who undergoes it to be profoundly significant and enlightening. In any event, the fact that minds can be changed so radically at so little cost to the body is altogether astonishing.

Huxley became a friend of Dr. Timothy Leary, a man of great charm and wit (as I can testify from experience) and a truant Harvard scientist whose advocacy of LSD trips made him an emblem of the "Sixties." It was this comradeship that attracted the attention of the Beatles and Jim Morrison. But again one must pause and notice a contradiction. Leary believed that the use of mind-altering drugs was essentially subversive, and would help individuals both to evade and erode "the system." The authorities appear to have agreed with him on this, pursuing and imprisoning him (at one point in a cell adjacent to Charles Manson) and making it highly illegal to follow his advice, not just concerning LSD but also cocaine and marijuana. What becomes, then, of Huxley's belief that such hallucinogens, analgesics, and stimulants are the ideal instrument of state control?

The "war on drugs" is now being extended to a state-sponsored campaign against tobacco and alcohol and painkillers: if the ruling class wants people to be blissed-out it has a strange way of pursuing this elementary goal. In our time, the symbol of state intrusion into the private life is the mandatory urine test.

A map of the world that does not show Utopia, said Oscar Wilde, is not worth glancing at. In *Brave New World,* and in his closing novel *Island,* Huxley tried to fix Utopian cartography in our minds. In the first setting, sex and drugs and the conditioning of the young are the symptoms of un-freedom and the roots of alienation and anomie, while in the second they are the tools of emancipation and the keys to happiness. The inhabitants of *Brave New World* have no external enemies to keep them afraid and in line; the *Island*-people of Pala have to contend with an aggressive neighboring dictatorship led by Colonel Dipa, a Saddam/Milosevic type who seems to think, and with good reason, that the traditional methods of club and boot and gun are still pretty serviceable. We should, I think, be grateful that Aldous Huxley was such a mass of internal contradictions. These enabled him to register the splendors and miseries, not just of modernity, but of the human condition. In his essay "Ravens and Writing Desks," written for *Vanity Fair* in 1928, he said:

> God is, but at the same time God also is not. The Universe is governed by blind chance and at the same time by a providence with ethical preoccupations. Suffering is gratuitous and pointless, but also valuable and necessary. The universe is an imbecile sadist, but also, simultaneously, the most benevolent of parents. Everything is rigidly predetermined, but the will is perfectly free. This list of contradictions could be lengthened so as to include all problems that have ever vexed the philosopher and the theologian.

Aware perhaps that this teetered on the edge of tautology, the old Pyrrhonist wrote elsewhere in his essay on the great Spinoza:

> "Homer was wrong," wrote Heracleitus of Ephesus, "Homer was wrong in saying: 'Would that strife might perish from among gods and men!' He did not see that he was praying for the destruction of the universe; for if his prayer was heard, all things would pass away."

The search for Nirvana, like the search for Utopia or the end of history or the classless society, is ultimately a futile and dangerous one. It involves, if it does not necessitate, the sleep of reason. There is no escape from anxiety and struggle, and Huxley assists us in attaining this valuable glimpse of the obvious, precisely because it was a conclusion that was in many ways unwelcome to him.

Christopher Hitchens
Washington, D.C.
November 28, 2003

Les utopies apparaissent comme bien plus réalisables qu'on ne le croyait autrefois. Et nous nous trouvons actuellement devant une question bien autrement angoissante: Comment éviter leur réalisation définitive? . . . Les utopies sont réalisables. La vie marche vers les utopies. Et peut-être un siècle nouveau commence-t-il, un siècle où les intellectuels et la classe cultivée rêveront aux moyens d'éviter les utopies et de retourner à une société non utopique, moins "parfaite" et plus libre.

—NICOLAS BERDIAEFF

BRAVE NEW WORLD

Preface

Chronic remorse, as all the moralists are agreed, is a most undesirable sentiment. If you have behaved badly, repent, make what amends you can and address yourself to the task of behaving better next time. On no account brood over your wrong-doing. Rolling in the muck is not the best way of getting clean.

Art also has its morality, and many of the rules of this morality are the same as, or at least analogous to, the rules of ordinary ethics. Remorse, for example, is as undesirable in relation to our bad art as it is in relation to our bad behaviour. The badness should be hunted out, acknowledged and, if possible, avoided in the future. To pore over the literary shortcomings of twenty years ago, to attempt to patch a faulty work into the perfection it missed at its first execution, to spend one's middle age in trying to mend the artistic sins committed and bequeathed by that different person who was oneself in youth—all this is surely vain and futile. And that is why this new *Brave New World* is the same as the old one. Its defects as a work of art are considerable; but in order to correct them I should have to rewrite the book—and in the process of rewriting, as an older, other person, I should probably get rid not only of some of the faults of the story, but also of such merits as it originally possessed. And so, resisting the temptation to wallow in artistic remorse, I prefer to leave both well and ill alone and to think about something else.

In the meantime, however, it seems worth while at least to mention the most serious defect in the story, which is this. The Savage is offered only two alternatives, an insane life in Utopia, or the life of a primitive in an Indian village, a life more human in some respects, but in others hardly less queer and abnormal. At the time the book was written this idea, that human beings are given free will in order to choose between insanity on the one hand and lunacy on the other, was one that I found amusing and regarded as quite possibly true. For the sake, however, of dramatic effect, the Savage is often permitted to speak more rationally than his upbringing among the practitioners of a religion that is half fertility cult and half *Penitente* ferocity would actually warrant. Even his acquaintance with Shakespeare would not in reality justify such utterances. And at the close, of course, he is made to retreat from sanity; his native *Penitente*-ism reasserts its authority and he ends in maniacal self-torture and despairing suicide. "And so they died miserably ever after"—much to the reassurance of the amused, Pyrrhonic aesthete who was the author of the fable.

Today I feel no wish to demonstrate that sanity is impossible. On the contrary, though I remain no less sadly certain than in the past that sanity is a rather rare phenomenon, I am convinced that it can be achieved and would like to see more of it. For having said so in several recent books and, above all, for having compiled an anthology of what the sane have said about sanity and the means whereby it can be achieved, I have been told by an eminent academic critic that I am a sad symptom of the failure of an intellectual class in time of crisis. The implication being, I suppose, that the professor and his colleagues are hilarious symptoms of success. The benefactors of humanity deserve due honour and commemoration. Let us build a Pantheon for professors. It should be located among the ruins of one of the gutted cities of Europe or Japan, and over the entrance to the ossuary I would inscribe, in letters six or seven feet high, the simple words: SACRED TO THE MEMORY OF THE WORLD'S EDUCATORS. SI MONUMENTUM REQUIRIS CIRCUMSPICE.

But to return to the future . . . If I were now to rewrite the book, I would offer the Savage a third alternative. Between the utopian and the primitive horns of his dilemma would lie the possibility of sanity—a possibility already actualized, to some extent, in a community of exiles and refugees from the Brave New World, living within the borders of the Reservation. In this community economics would be decentralist and Henry-Georgian, politics Kropotkinesque co-operative. Science and technology would be used as though, like the Sabbath, they had been made for man, not (as at present and still more so in the Brave New World) as though man were to be adapted and enslaved to them. Religion would be the conscious and intelligent pursuit of man's Final End, the unitive knowledge of the immanent Tao or Logos, the transcendent Godhead or Brahman. And the prevailing philosophy of life would be a kind of Higher Utilitarianism, in which the Greatest Happiness principle would be secondary to the Final End principle—the first question to be asked and answered in every contingency of life being: "How will this thought or action contribute to, or interfere with, the achievement, by me and the greatest possible number of other individuals, of man's Final End?"

Brought up among the primitives, the Savage (in this hypothetical new version of the book) would not be transported to Utopia until he had had an opportunity of learning something at first hand about the nature of a society composed of freely co-operating individuals devoted to the pursuit of sanity. Thus altered, *Brave New World* would possess artistic and (if it is permissible to use so large a word in connection with a work of fiction) a philosophical completeness, which in its present form it evidently lacks.

But *Brave New World* is a book about the future and, whatever its artistic or philosophical qualities, a book about the future can interest us only if its prophecies look as though they might conceivably come true. From our present vantage point, fifteen years further down the inclined plane of modern history, how plausible do its prognostications seem? What has happened in the painful interval to confirm or invalidate the forecasts of 1931?

One vast and obvious failure of foresight is immediately apparent. *Brave New World* contains no reference to nuclear fission. That it does not is actually rather odd, for the possibilities of atomic energy had been a popular topic of conversation for years before the book was written. My old friend, Robert Nichols, had even written a successful play about the subject, and I recall that I myself had casually mentioned it in a novel published in the late twenties. So it seems, as I say, very odd that the rockets and helicopters of the seventh century of Our Ford should not have been powered by disintegrating nuclei. The oversight may not be excusable; but at least it can be easily explained. The theme of *Brave New World* is not the advancement of science as such; it is the advancement of science as it affects human individuals. The triumphs of physics, chemistry and engineering are tacitly taken for granted. The only scientific advances to be specifically described are those involving the application to human beings of the results of future research in biology, physiology and psychology. It is only by means of the sciences of life that the quality of life can be radically changed. The sciences of matter can be applied in such a way that they will destroy life or make the living of it impossibly complex and uncomfortable; but, unless used as instruments by the biologists and psychologists, they can do nothing to modify the natural forms and expressions of life itself. The release of atomic energy marks a great revolution in human history, but not (unless we blow ourselves to bits and so put an end to history) the final and most searching revolution.

This really revolutionary revolution is to be achieved, not in the external world, but in the souls and flesh of human beings. Living as he did in a revolutionary period, the Marquis de Sade very naturally made use of this theory of revolutions in order to rationalize his peculiar brand of insanity. Robespierre had achieved the most superficial kind of revolution, the political. Going a little deeper, Babeuf had attempted the economic revolution. Sade regarded himself as the apostle of the truly revolutionary revolution, beyond mere politics and economics—the revolution in individual men, women and children, whose bodies were henceforward to become the common sexual property of all and whose minds were to be purged of all the natural decencies, all the laboriously acquired inhibitions of traditional civilization. Between sadism and the really revolutionary revolution there is, of course, no necessary or inevitable connection. Sade was a lunatic and the more or less conscious goal of his revolution was universal chaos and destruction. The people who govern the Brave New World may not be sane (in what may be called the absolute sense of the word); but they are not madmen, and their aim is not anarchy but social stability. It is in order to achieve stability that they carry out, by scientific means, the ultimate, personal, really revolutionary revolution.

But meanwhile we are in the first phase of what is perhaps the penultimate revolution. Its next phase may be atomic warfare, in which case we do not have to bother with prophecies about the future. But it is conceivable that we may have enough sense, if not to stop fighting altogether, at least to behave as rationally as did our eighteenth-century ancestors. The unimaginable horrors of the Thirty Years War actually taught men a lesson, and for more than a hundred years the politicians and generals of Europe consciously resisted the temptation to use their military resources to the limits of destructiveness or (in the majority of conflicts) to go on fighting until the enemy was totally annihilated. They were aggressors, of course, greedy for profit and glory; but they were also conservatives, determined at all costs to keep their world intact, as a going concern. For the last thirty years there have been no conservatives; there have been only nationalistic radicals of the right and nationalistic radicals of the left. The last conservative statesman was the fifth Marquess of Lansdowne; and when he wrote a letter to the *Times*, suggesting that the First World War should be concluded with a compromise, as most of the wars of the eighteenth century had been, the editor of that once conservative journal refused to print it. The nationalistic radicals had their way, with the consequences that we all know—Bolshevism, Fascism, inflation, depression, Hitler, the Second World War, the ruin of Europe and all but universal famine.

Assuming, then, that we are capable of learning as much from Hiroshima as our forefathers learned from Magdeburg, we may look forward to a period, not indeed of peace, but of limited and only partially ruinous warfare. During that period it may be assumed that nuclear energy will be harnessed to industrial uses. The result, pretty obviously, will be a series of economic and social changes unprecedented in rapidity and completeness. All the existing patterns of human life will be disrupted and new patterns will have to be improvised to conform with the nonhuman fact of atomic power. Procrustes in modern dress, the nuclear scientist will prepare the bed on which mankind must lie; and if mankind doesn't fit—well, that will be just too bad for mankind. There will have to be some stretching and a bit of amputation—the same sort of stretching and amputations as have been going on ever since applied science really got into its stride, only this time they will be a good deal more drastic than in the past. These far from painless operations will be directed by highly centralized totalitarian governments. Inevitably so; for the immediate future is likely to resemble the immediate past, and in the immediate past rapid technological changes, taking place in a mass-producing economy and among a population predominantly propertyless, have always tended to produce economic and social confusion. To deal with confusion, power has been centralized and government control increased. It is probable that all the world's governments will be more or less completely totalitarian even before the harnessing of atomic energy; that they will be totalitarian during and after the harnessing seems almost certain. Only a large-scale popular movement toward decentralization and self-help can arrest the present tendency toward statism. At present there is no sign that such a movement will take place.

There is, of course, no reason why the new totalitarianisms should resemble the old. Government by clubs and firing squads, by artificial famine, mass imprisonment and mass deportation, is not merely inhumane (nobody cares much about that nowadays), it is demonstrably inefficient and in an age of advanced technology, inefficiency is the sin against the Holy Ghost. A really efficient totalitarian state would be one in which the all-powerful executive of political bosses and their army of managers control a population of slaves who do not have to be coerced, because they love their servitude. To make them love it is the task assigned, in present-day totalitarian states, to ministries of propaganda, newspaper editors and schoolteachers. But their methods are still crude and unscientific. The old Jesuits' boast that, if they were given the schooling of the child, they could answer for the man's religious opinions, was a product of wishful thinking. And the modern pedagogue is probably rather less efficient at conditioning his pupils' reflexes than were the reverend fathers who educated Voltaire. The greatest triumphs of propaganda have been accomplished, not by doing something, but by refraining from doing. Great is truth, but still greater, from a practical point of view, is silence about truth. By simply not mentioning certain subjects, by lowering what Mr. Churchill calls an "iron curtain" between the masses and such facts or arguments as the local political bosses regard as undesirable, totalitarian propagandists have influenced opinion much more effectively than they could have done by the most eloquent denunciations, the most compelling of logical rebuttals. But silence is not enough. If persecution, liquidation and the other symptoms of social friction are to be avoided, the positive sides of propaganda must be made as effective as the negative. The most important Manhattan Projects of the future will be vast government-sponsored enquiries into what the politicians and the participating scientists will call "the problem of happiness"—in other words, the problem of making people love their servitude. Without economic security, the love of servitude cannot possibly come into existence; for the sake of brevity, I assume that the all-powerful executive and its managers will succeed in solving the problem of permanent security. But security tends very quickly to be taken for granted. Its achievement is merely a superficial, external revolution. The love of servitude cannot be established except as the result of a deep, personal revolution in human minds and bodies. To bring about that revolution we require, among others, the following discoveries and inventions. First, a greatly improved technique of suggestion—through infant conditioning and, later, with the aid of drugs, such as scopolamine. Second, a fully developed science of human differences, enabling government managers to assign any given individual to his or her proper place in the social and economic hierarchy. (Round pegs in square holes tend to have dangerous thoughts about the social system and to infect others with their discontents.) Third (since reality, however utopian, is something from which people feel the need of taking pretty frequent holidays), a substitute for alcohol and the other narcotics, something at once less harmful and more pleasure-giving than gin or heroin. And fourth (but this would be a long-term project, which it would take generations of totalitarian control to bring to a successful conclusion), a foolproof system of eugenics, designed to standardize the human product and so to facilitate the task of the managers. In *Brave New World* this standardization of the human product has been pushed to fantastic, though not perhaps impossible, extremes. Technically and ideologically we are still a long way from bottled babies and Bokanovsky groups of semi-morons. But by A.F. 600, who knows what may not be happening? Meanwhile the other characteristic features of that happier and more stable world—the equivalents of soma and hypnopaedia and the scientific caste system—are probably not more than three or four generations away. Nor does the sexual promiscuity of *Brave New World* seem so very distant. There are already certain American cities in which the number of divorces is equal to the number of marriages. In a few years, no doubt, marriage licenses will be sold like dog licenses, good for a period of twelve months, with no law against changing dogs or keeping more than one animal at a time. As political and economic freedom diminishes, sexual freedom tends compensatingly to increase. And the dictator (unless he needs cannon fodder and families with which to colonize empty or conquered territories) will do well to encourage that freedom. In conjunction with the freedom to daydream under the influence of dope and movies and the radio, it will help to reconcile his subjects to the servitude which is their fate.

All things considered it looks as though Utopia were far closer to us than anyone, only fifteen years ago, could have imagined. Then, I projected it six hundred years into the future. Today it seems quite possible that the horror may be upon us within a single century. That is, if we refrain from blowing ourselves to smithereens in the interval. Indeed, unless we choose to decentralize and to use applied science, not as the end to which human beings are to be made the means, but as the means to producing a race of free individuals, we have only two alternatives to choose from: either a number of national, militarized totalitarianisms, having as their root the terror of the atomic bomb and as their consequence the destruction of civilization (or, if the warfare is limited, the perpetuation of militarism); or else one supranational totalitarianism, called into existence by the social chaos resulting from rapid technological progress in general and the atomic revolution in particular, and developing, under the need for efficiency and stability, into the welfare-tyranny of Utopia. You pays your money and you takes your choice.

I

A squat grey building of only thirty-four stories. Over the main entrance the words, CENTRAL LONDON HATCHERY AND CONDITIONING CENTRE, and, in a shield, the World State's motto, COMMUNITY, IDENTITY, STABILITY.

The enormous room on the ground floor faced towards the north. Cold for all the summer beyond the panes, for all the tropical heat of the room itself, a harsh thin light glared through the windows, hungrily seeking some draped lay figure, some pallid shape of academic goose-flesh, but finding only the glass and nickel and bleakly shining porcelain of a laboratory. Wintriness responded to wintriness. The overalls of the workers were white, their hands gloved with a pale corpse-coloured rubber. The light was frozen, dead, a ghost. Only from the yellow barrels of the microscopes did it borrow a certain rich and living substance, lying along the polished tubes like butter, streak after luscious streak in long recession down the work tables.

"And this," said the Director opening the door, "is the Fertilizing Room."

Bent over their instruments, three hundred Fertilizers were plunged, as the Director of Hatcheries and Conditioning entered the room, in the scarcely breathing silence, the absent-minded, soliloquizing hum or whistle, of absorbed concentration. A troop of newly arrived students, very young, pink and callow, followed nervously, rather abjectly, at the Director's heels. Each of them carried a notebook, in which, whenever the great man spoke, he desperately scribbled. Straight from the horse's mouth. It was a rare privilege. The D.H.C. for Central London always made a point of personally conducting his new students round the various departments.

"Just to give you a general idea," he would explain to them. For of course some sort of general idea they must have, if they were to do their work intelligently—though as little of one, if they were to be good and happy members of society, as possible. For particulars, as every one knows, make for virtue and happiness; generalities are intellectually necessary evils. Not philosophers but fretsawyers and stamp collectors compose the backbone of society.

"To-morrow," he would add, smiling at them with a slightly menacing geniality, "you'll be settling down to serious work. You won't have time for generalities. Meanwhile . . ."

Meanwhile, it was a privilege. Straight from the horse's mouth into the notebook. The boys scribbled like mad.

Tall and rather thin but upright, the Director advanced into the room. He had a long chin and big rather prominent teeth, just covered, when he was not talking, by his full, floridly curved lips. Old, young? Thirty? Fifty? Fifty-five? It was hard to say. And anyhow the question didn't arise; in this year of stability, A.F. 632, it didn't occur to you to ask it.

"I shall begin at the beginning," said the D.H.C. and the more zealous students recorded his intention in their notebooks: *Begin at the beginning.* "These," he waved his hand, "are the incubators." And opening an insulated door he showed them racks upon racks of numbered test-tubes. "The week's supply of ova. Kept," he explained, "at blood heat; whereas the male gametes," and here he opened another door, "they have to be kept at thirty-five instead of thirty-seven. Full blood heat sterilizes." Rams wrapped in theremogene beget no lambs.

Still leaning against the incubators he gave them, while the pencils scurried illegibly across the pages, a brief description of the modern fertilizing process; spoke first, of course, of its surgical introduction—"the operation undergone voluntarily for the good of Society, not to mention the fact that it carries a bonus amounting to six months' salary"; continued with some account of the technique for preserving the excised ovary alive and actively developing; passed on to a consideration of optimum temperature, salinity, viscosity; referred to the liquor in which the detached and ripened eggs were kept; and, leading his charges to the work tables, actually showed them how this liquor was drawn off from the test-tubes; how it was let out drop by drop onto the specially warmed slides of the microscopes; how the eggs which it contained were inspected for abnormalities, counted and transferred to a porous receptacle; how (and he now took them to watch the operation) this receptacle was immersed in a warm bouillon containing free-swimming spermatozoa—at a minimum concentration of one hundred thousand per cubic centimetre, he insisted; and how, after ten minutes, the container was lifted out of the liquor and its contents reexamined; how, if any of the eggs remained unfertilized, it was again immersed, and, if necessary, yet again; how the fertilized ova went back to the incubators; where the Alphas and Betas remained until definitely bottled; while the Gammas, Deltas and Epsilons were brought out again, after only thirty-six hours, to undergo Bokanovsky's Process.

"Bokanovsky's Process," repeated the Director, and the students underlined the words in their little notebooks.

One egg, one embryo, one adult—normality. But a bokanovskified egg will bud, will proliferate, will divide. From eight to ninety-six buds, and every bud will grow into a perfectly formed embryo, and every embryo into a full-sized adult. Making ninety-six human beings grow where only one grew before. Progress.

"Essentially," the D.H.C. concluded, "bokanovskification consists of a series of arrests of development. We check the normal growth and, paradoxically enough, the egg responds by budding."

Responds by budding. The pencils were busy.

He pointed. On a very slowly moving band a rack-full of test-tubes was entering a large metal box, another rack-full was emerging. Machinery faintly purred. It took eight minutes for the tubes to go through, he told them. Eight minutes of hard X-rays being about as much as an egg can stand. A few died; of the rest, the least susceptible divided into two; most put out four buds; some eight; all were returned to the incubators, where the buds began to develop; then, after two days, were suddenly chilled, chilled and checked. Two, four, eight, the buds in their turn budded; and having budded were dosed almost to death with alcohol; consequently burgeoned again and having budded—bud out of bud out of bud—were thereafter—further arrest being generally fatal—left to develop in peace. By which time the original egg was in a fair way to becoming anything from eight to ninety-six embryos—a prodigious improvement, you will agree, on nature. Identical twins—but not in piddling twos and threes as in the old viviparous days, when an egg would sometimes accidentally divide; actually by dozens, by scores at a time.

"Scores," the Director repeated and flung out his arms, as though he were distributing largesse. "Scores."

But one of the students was fool enough to ask where the advantage lay.

"My good boy!" The Director wheeled sharply round on him. "Can't you see? Can't you *see*?" He raised a hand; his expression was solemn. "Bokanovsky's Process is one of the major instruments of social stability!"

Major instruments of social stability.

Standard men and women; in uniform batches. The whole of a small factory staffed with the products of a single bokanovskified egg.

"Ninety-six identical twins working ninety-six identical machines!" The voice was almost tremulous with enthusiasm. "You really know where you are. For the first time in history." He quoted the planetary motto. "Community, Identity, Stability." Grand words.

"If we could bokanovskify indefinitely the whole problem would be solved."

Solved by standard Gammas, unvarying Deltas, uniform Epsilons. Millions of identical twins. The principle of mass production at last applied to biology.

"But, alas," the Director shook his head, "we can't bokanovskify indefinitely."

Ninety-six seemed to be the limit; seventy-two a good average. From the same ovary and with gametes of the same male to manufacture as many batches of identical twins as possible—that was the best (sadly a second best) that they could do. And even that was difficult.

"For in nature it takes thirty years for two hundred eggs to reach maturity. But our business is to stabilize the population at this moment, here and now. Dribbling out twins over a quarter of a century—what would be the use of that?"

Obviously, no use at all. But Podsnap's Technique had immensely accelerated the process of ripening. They could make sure of at least a hundred and fifty mature eggs within two years. Fertilize and bokanovskify—in other words, multiply by seventy-two—and you get an average of nearly eleven thousand brothers and sisters in a hundred and fifty batches of identical twins, all within two years of the same age.

"And in exceptional cases we can make one ovary yield us over fifteen thousand adult individuals."

Beckoning to a fair-haired, ruddy young man who happened to be passing at the moment. "Mr. Foster," he called. The ruddy young man approached. "Can you tell us the record for a single ovary, Mr. Foster?"

"Sixteen thousand and twelve in this Centre," Mr. Foster replied without hesitation. He spoke very quickly, had a vivacious blue eye, and took an evident pleasure in quoting figures. "Sixteen thousand and twelve; in one hundred and eighty-nine batches of identicals.

But of course they've done much better," he rattled on, "in some of the tropical Centres. Singapore has often produced over sixteen thousand five hundred; and Mombasa has actually touched the seventeen thousand mark. But then they have unfair advantages. You should see the way a negro ovary responds to pituitary! It's quite astonishing, when you're used to working with European material. Still," he added, with a laugh (but the light of combat was in his eyes and the lift of his chin was challenging), "still, we mean to beat them if we can. I'm working on a wonderful Delta-Minus ovary at this moment. Only just eighteen months old. Over twelve thousand seven hundred children already, either decanted or in embryo. And still going strong. We'll beat them yet."

"That's the spirit I like!" cried the Director, and clapped Mr. Foster on the shoulder. "Come along with us, and give these boys the benefit of your expert knowledge."

Mr. Foster smiled modestly. "With pleasure." They went.

In the Bottling Room all was harmonious bustle and ordered activity. Flaps of fresh sow's peritoneum ready cut to the proper size came shooting up in little lifts from the Organ Store in the sub-basement. Whizz and then, click! the lift-hatches flew open; the bottle-liner had only to reach out a hand, take the flap, insert, smooth-down, and before the lined bottle had had time to travel out of reach along the endless band, whizz, click! another flap of peritoneum had shot up from the depths, ready to be slipped into yet another bottle, the next of that slow interminable procession on the band.

Next to the Liners stood the Matriculators. The procession advanced; one by one the eggs were transferred from their test-tubes to the larger containers; deftly the peritoneal lining was slit, the morula dropped into place, the saline solution poured in . . . and already the bottle had passed, and it was the turn of the labellers. Heredity, date of fertilization, membership of Bokanovsky Group—details were transferred from test-tube to bottle. No longer anonymous, but named, identified, the procession marched slowly on; on through an opening in the wall, slowly on into the Social Predestination Room.

"Eighty-eight cubic metres of card-index," said Mr. Foster with relish, as they entered.

"Containing all the relevant information," added the Director.

"Brought up to date every morning."

"And co-ordinated every afternoon."

"On the basis of which they make their calculations."

"So many individuals, of such and such quality," said Mr. Foster.

"Distributed in such and such quantities."

"The optimum Decanting Rate at any given moment."

"Unforeseen wastages promptly made good."

"Promptly," repeated Mr. Foster. "If you knew the amount of overtime I had to put in after the last Japanese earthquake!" He laughed goodhumouredly and shook his head.

"The Predestinators send in their figures to the Fertilizers."

"Who give them the embryos they ask for."

"And the bottles come in here to be predestined in detail."

"After which they are sent down to the Embryo Store."

"Where we now proceed ourselves."

And opening a door Mr. Foster led the way down a staircase into the basement.

The temperature was still tropical. They descended into a thickening twilight. Two doors and a passage with a double turn insured the cellar against any possible infiltration of the day.

"Embryos are like photograph film," said Mr. Foster waggishly, as he pushed open the second door. "They can only stand red light."

And in effect the sultry darkness into which the students now followed him was visible and crimson, like the darkness of closed eyes on a summer's afternoon. The bulging flanks of row on receding row and tier above tier of bottles glinted with innumerable rubies, and among the rubies moved the dim red spectres of men and women with purple eyes and all the symptoms of lupus. The hum and rattle of machinery faintly stirred the air.

"Give them a few figures, Mr. Foster," said the Director, who was tired of talking.

Mr. Foster was only too happy to give them a few figures.

Two hundred and twenty metres long, two hundred wide, ten high. He pointed upwards. Like chickens drinking, the students lifted their eyes towards the distant ceiling.

Three tiers of racks: ground floor level, first gallery, second gallery.

The spidery steel-work of gallery above gallery faded away in all directions into the dark. Near them three red ghosts were busily unloading demijohns from a moving staircase.

The escalator from the Social Predestination Room.

Each bottle could be placed on one of fifteen racks, each rack, though you couldn't see it, was a conveyor traveling at the rate of thirty-three and a third centimetres an hour. Two hundred and sixty-seven days at eight metres a day. Two thousand one hundred and thirty-six metres in all. One circuit of the cellar at ground level, one on the first gallery, half on the second, and on the two hundred and sixty-seventh morning, daylight in the Decanting Room. Independent existence—so called.

"But in the interval," Mr. Foster concluded, "we've managed to do a lot to them. Oh, a very great deal." His laugh was knowing and triumphant.

"That's the spirit I like," said the Director once more. "Let's walk around. You tell them everything, Mr. Foster."

Mr. Foster duly told them.

Told them of the growing embryo on its bed of peritoneum. Made them taste the rich blood surrogate on which it fed. Explained why it had to be stimulated with placentin and thyroxin. Told them of the *corpus luteum* extract. Showed them the jets through which at every twelfth metre from zero to 2040 it was automatically injected. Spoke of those gradually increasing doses of pituitary administered during the final ninety-six metres of their course. Described the artificial maternal circulation installed in every bottle at Metre

112; showed them the reservoir of blood-surrogate, the centrifugal pump that kept the liquid moving over the placenta and drove it through the synthetic lung and waste product filter. Referred to the embryo's troublesome tendency to anæmia, to the massive doses of hog's stomach extract and foetal foal's liver with which, in consequence, it had to be supplied.

Showed them the simple mechanism by means of which, during the last two metres out of every eight, all the embryos were simultaneously shaken into familiarity with movement. Hinted at the gravity of the so-called "trauma of decanting," and enumerated the precautions taken to minimize, by a suitable training of the bottled embryo, that dangerous shock. Told them of the test for sex carried out in the neighborhood of Metre 200. Explained the system of labelling—a T for the males, a circle for the females and for those who were destined to become freemartins a question mark, black on a white ground.

"For of course," said Mr. Foster, "in the vast majority of cases, fertility is merely a nuisance. One fertile ovary in twelve hundred—that would really be quite sufficient for our purposes. But we want to have a good choice. And of course one must always have an enormous margin of safety. So we allow as many as thirty per cent of the female embryos to develop normally. The others get a dose of male sex-hormone every twenty-four metres for the rest of the course. Result: they're decanted as freemartins—structurally quite normal (except," he had to admit, "that they *do* have the slightest tendency to grow beards), but sterile. Guaranteed sterile. Which brings us at last," continued Mr. Foster, "out of the realm of mere slavish imitation of nature into the much more interesting world of human invention."

He rubbed his hands. For of course, they didn't content themselves with merely hatching out embryos: any cow could do that.

"We also predestine and condition. We decant our babies as socialized human beings, as Alphas or Epsilons, as future sewage workers or future . . ." He was going to say "future World controllers," but correcting himself, said "future Directors of Hatcheries," instead.

The D.H.C. acknowledged the compliment with a smile.

They were passing Metre 320 on Rack 11. A young Beta-Minus mechanic was busy with screwdriver and spanner on the blood-surrogate pump of a passing bottle. The hum of the electric motor deepened by fractions of a tone as he turned the nuts. Down, down . . . A final twist, a glance at the revolution counter, and he was done. He moved two paces down the line and began the same process on the next pump.

"Reducing the number of revolutions per minute," Mr. Foster explained. "The surrogate goes round slower; therefore passes through the lung at longer intervals; therefore gives the embryo less oxygen. Nothing like oxygen-shortage for keeping an embryo below par." Again he rubbed his hands.

"But why do you want to keep the embryo below par?" asked an ingenuous student.

"Ass!" said the Director, breaking a long silence. "Hasn't it occurred to you that an Epsilon embryo must have an Epsilon environment as well as an Epsilon heredity?"

It evidently hadn't occurred to him. He was covered with confusion.

"The lower the caste," said Mr. Foster, "the shorter the oxygen." The first organ affected was the brain. After that the skeleton. At seventy per cent of normal oxygen you got dwarfs. At less than seventy eyeless monsters.

"Who are no use at all," concluded Mr. Foster.

Whereas (his voice became confidential and eager), if they could discover a technique for shortening the period of maturation what a triumph, what a benefaction to Society!

"Consider the horse."

They considered it.

Mature at six; the elephant at ten. While at thirteen a man is not yet sexually mature; and is only full-grown at twenty. Hence, of course, that fruit of delayed development, the human intelligence.

"But in Epsilons," said Mr. Foster very justly, "we don't need human intelligence."

Didn't need and didn't get it. But though the Epsilon mind was mature at ten, the Epsilon body was not fit to work till eighteen. Long years of superfluous and wasted immaturity. If the physical development could be speeded up till it was as quick, say, as a cow's, what an enormous saving to the Community!

"Enormous!" murmured the students. Mr. Foster's enthusiasm was infectious.

He became rather technical; spoke of the abnormal endocrine co-ordination which made men grow so slowly; postulated a germinal mutation to account for it. Could the effects of this germinal mutation be undone? Could the individual Epsilon embryo be made a revert, by a suitable technique, to the normality of dogs and cows? That was the problem. And it was all but solved.

Pilkington, at Mombasa, had produced individuals who were sexually mature at four and full-grown at six and a half. A scientific triumph. But socially useless. Six-year-old men and women were too stupid to do even Epsilon work. And the process was an all-or-nothing one; either you failed to modify at all, or else you modified the whole way. They were still trying to find the ideal compromise between adults of twenty and adults of six. So far without success. Mr. Foster sighed and shook his head.

Their wanderings through the crimson twilight had brought them to the neighborhood of Metre 170 on Rack 9. From this point onwards Rack 9 was enclosed and the bottles performed the remainder of their journey in a kind of tunnel, interrupted here and there by openings two or three metres wide.

"Heat conditioning," said Mr. Foster.

Hot tunnels alternated with cool tunnels. Coolness was wedded to discomfort in the form of hard X-rays. By the time they were decanted the embryos had a horror of cold. They were predestined to emigrate to the tropics, to be miners and acetate silk spinners and steel workers. Later on their minds would be made to endorse the judgment of their bodies. "We condition them to thrive on heat," concluded Mr. Foster. "Our colleagues upstairs will teach them to love it."

"And that," put in the Director sententiously, "that is the secret of happiness and virtue—liking what you've got to do. All conditioning aims at that: making people like their unescapable social destiny."

In a gap between two tunnels, a nurse was delicately probing with a long fine syringe into the gelatinous contents of a passing bottle. The students and their guides stood watching her for a few moments in silence.

"Well, Lenina," said Mr. Foster, when at last she withdrew the syringe and straightened herself up.

The girl turned with a start. One could see that, for all the lupus and the purple eyes, she was uncommonly pretty.

"Henry!" Her smile flashed redly at him—a row of coral teeth.

"Charming, charming," murmured the Director and, giving her two or three little pats, received in exchange a rather deferential smile for himself.

"What are you giving them?" asked Mr. Foster, making his tone very professional.

"Oh, the usual typhoid and sleeping sickness."

"Tropical workers start being inoculated at Metre 150," Mr. Foster explained to the students. "The embryos still have gills. We immunize the fish against the future man's diseases." Then, turning back to Lenina, "Ten to five on the roof this afternoon," he said, "as usual."

"Charming," said the Director once more, and, with a final pat, moved away after the others.

On Rack 10 rows of next generation's chemical workers were being trained in the toleration of lead, caustic soda, tar, chlorine.

The first of a batch of two hundred and fifty embryonic rocket-plane engineers was just passing the eleven hundred metre mark on Rack 3. A special mechanism kept their containers in constant rotation. "To improve their sense of balance," Mr. Foster explained. "Doing repairs on the outside of a rocket in mid-air is a ticklish job. We slacken off the circulation when they're right way up, so that they're half starved, and double the flow of surrogate when they're upside down. They learn to associate topsy-turvydom with well-being; in fact, they're only truly happy when they're standing on their heads.

"And now," Mr. Foster went on, "I'd like to show you some very interesting conditioning for Alpha Plus Intellectuals. We have a big batch of them on Rack 5. First Gallery level," he called to two boys who had started to go down to the ground floor.

"They're round about Metre 900," he explained. "You can't really do any useful intellectual conditioning till the foetuses have lost their tails. Follow me."

But the Director had looked at his watch. "Ten to three," he said. "No time for the intellectual embryos, I'm afraid. We must go up to the Nurseries before the children have finished their afternoon sleep."

Mr. Foster was disappointed. "At least one glance at the Decanting Room," he pleaded.

"Very well then." The Director smiled indulgently. "Just one glance."

2

Mr. Foster was left in the Decanting Room. The D.H.C. and his students stepped into the nearest lift and were carried up to the fifth floor.

INFANT NURSERIES. NEO-PAVLOVIAN CONDITIONING ROOMS, announced the notice board.

The Director opened a door. They were in a large bare room, very bright and sunny; for the whole of the southern wall was a single window. Half a dozen nurses, trousered and jacketed in the regulation white viscose-linen uniform, their hair aseptically hidden under white caps, were engaged in setting out bowls of roses in a long row across the floor. Big bowls, packed tight with blossom. Thousands of petals, ripe-blown and silkily smooth, like the cheeks of innumerable little cherubs, but of cherubs, in that bright light, not exclusively pink and Aryan, but also luminously Chinese, also Mexican, also apoplectic with too much blowing of celestial trumpets, also pale as death, pale with the posthumous whiteness of marble.

The nurses stiffened to attention as the D.H.C. came in.

"Set out the books," he said curtly.

In silence the nurses obeyed his command. Between the rose bowls the books were duly set out—a row of nursery quartos opened invitingly each at some gaily coloured image of beast or fish or bird.

"Now bring in the children."

They hurried out of the room and returned in a minute or two, each pushing a kind of tall dumb-waiter laden, on all its four wire-netted shelves, with eight-month-old babies, all exactly alike (a Bokanovsky Group, it was evident) and all (since their caste was Delta) dressed in khaki.

"Put them down on the floor."

The infants were unloaded.

"Now turn them so that they can see the flowers and books."

Turned, the babies at once fell silent, then began to crawl towards those clusters of sleek colours, those shapes so gay and brilliant on the white pages. As they approached, the sun came out of a momentary eclipse behind a cloud. The roses flamed up as though with a sudden passion from within; a new and profound significance seemed to suffuse the shining pages of the books. From the ranks of the crawling babies came little squeals of excitement, gurgles and twitterings of pleasure.

The Director rubbed his hands. "Excellent!" he said. "It might almost have been done on purpose."

The swiftest crawlers were already at their goal. Small hands reached out uncertainly, touched, grasped, unpetaling the transfigured roses, crumpling the illuminated pages of the books. The Director waited until all were happily busy. Then, "Watch carefully," he said. And, lifting his hand, he gave the signal.

The Head Nurse, who was standing by a switchboard at the other end of the room, pressed down a little lever.

There was a violent explosion. Shriller and ever shriller, a siren shrieked. Alarm bells maddeningly sounded.

The children started, screamed; their faces were distorted with terror.

"And now," the Director shouted (for the noise was deafening), "now we proceed to rub in the lesson with a mild electric shock."

He waved his hand again, and the Head Nurse pressed a second lever. The screaming of the babies suddenly changed its tone. There was something desperate, almost insane, about the sharp spasmodic yelps to which they now gave utterance. Their little bodies twitched and stiffened; their limbs moved jerkily as if to the tug of unseen wires.

"We can electrify that whole strip of floor," bawled the Director in explanation. "But that's enough," he signalled to the nurse.

The explosions ceased, the bells stopped ringing, the shriek of the siren died down from tone to tone into silence. The stiffly twitching bodies relaxed, and what had become the sob and yelp of infant maniacs broadened out once more into a normal howl of ordinary terror.

"Offer them the flowers and the books again."

The nurses obeyed; but at the approach of the roses, at the mere sight of those gaily-coloured images of pussy and cock-a-doodle-doo and baa-baa black sheep, the infants shrank away in horror; the volume of their howling suddenly increased.

"Observe," said the Director triumphantly, "observe."

Books and loud noises, flowers and electric shocks—already in the infant mind these couples were compromisingly linked; and after two hundred repetitions of the same or a similar lesson would be wedded indissolubly. What man has joined, nature is powerless to put asunder.

"They'll grow up with what the psychologists used to call an 'instinctive' hatred of books and flowers. Reflexes unalterably conditioned. They'll be safe from books and botany all their lives." The Director turned to his nurses. "Take them away again."

Still yelling, the khaki babies were loaded on to their dumb-waiters and wheeled out, leaving behind them the smell of sour milk and a most welcome silence.

One of the students held up his hand; and though he could see quite well why you couldn't have lower-caste people wasting the Community's time over books, and that there was always the risk of their reading something which might undesirably decondition one of their reflexes, yet . . . well, he couldn't understand about the flowers. Why go to the trouble of making it psychologically impossible for Deltas to like flowers?

Patiently the D.H.C. explained. If the children were made to scream at the sight of a rose, that was on grounds of high economic policy. Not so very long ago (a century or thereabouts), Gammas, Deltas, even Epsilons, had been conditioned to like flowers—flowers in particular and wild nature in general. The idea was to make them want to be going out into the country at every available opportunity, and so compel them to consume transport.

"And didn't they consume transport?" asked the student.

"Quite a lot," the D.H.C. replied. "But nothing else."

Primroses and landscapes, he pointed out, have one grave defect: they are gratuitous. A love of nature keeps no factories busy. It was decided to abolish the love of nature, at any rate among the lower classes; to abolish the love of nature, but *not* the tendency to consume transport. For of course it was essential that they should keep on going to the country, even though they hated it. The problem was to find an economically sounder reason for consuming transport than a mere affection for primroses and landscapes. It was duly found.

"We condition the masses to hate the country," concluded the Director. "But simultaneously we condition them to love all country sports. At the same time, we see to it that all country sports shall entail the use of elaborate apparatus. So that they consume manufactured articles as well as transport. Hence those electric shocks."

"I see," said the student, and was silent, lost in admiration.

There was a silence; then, clearing his throat, "Once upon a time," the Director began, "while our Ford was still on earth, there was a little boy called Reuben Rabinovitch. Reuben was the child of Polish-speaking parents." The Director interrupted himself. "You know what Polish is, I suppose?"

"A dead language."

"Like French and German," added another student, officiously showing off his learning.

"And 'parent'?" questioned the D.H.C.

There was an uneasy silence. Several of the boys blushed. They had not yet learned to draw the significant but often very fine distinction between smut and pure science. One, at last, had the courage to raise a hand.

"Human beings used to be . . ." he hesitated; the blood rushed to his cheeks. "Well they used to be viviparous."

"Quite right." The Director nodded approvingly.

"And when the babies were decanted . . ."

" 'Born,' " came the correction.

"Well, then they were the parents—I mean, not the babies, of course; the other ones." The poor boy was overwhelmed with confusion.

"In brief," the Director summed up, "the parents were the father and the mother." The smut that was really science fell with a crash into the boys' eye-avoiding silence. "Mother," he repeated loudly rubbing in the science; and, leaning back in his chair, "These," he said gravely, "are unpleasant facts; I know it. But then most historical facts *are* unpleasant."

He returned to Little Reuben—to Little Reuben, in whose room, one evening, by an oversight, his father and mother (crash, crash!) happened to leave the radio turned on.

("For you must remember that in those days of gross viviparous reproduction, children were always brought up by their parents and not in State Conditioning Centres.")

While the child was asleep, a broadcast programme from London suddenly started to come through; and the next morning, to the astonishment of his crash and crash (the more daring of the boys ventured to grin at one another), Little Reuben woke up repeating word for word a long lecture by that curious old writer ("one of the very few whose works have been permitted to come down to us"),

George Bernard Shaw, who was speaking, according to a well-authenticated tradition, about his own genius. To Little Reuben's wink and snigger, this lecture was, of course, perfectly incomprehensible and, imagining that their child had suddenly gone mad, they sent for a doctor. He, fortunately, understood English, recognized the discourse as that which Shaw had broadcasted the previous evening, realized the significance of what had happened, and sent a letter to the medical press about it.

"The principle of sleep-teaching, or hypnopædia, had been discovered." The D.H.C. made an impressive pause.

The principle had been discovered; but many, many years were to elapse before that principle was usefully applied.

"The case of Little Reuben occurred only twenty-three years after Our Ford's first T-Model was put on the market." (Here the Director made a sign of the T on his stomach and all the students reverently followed suit.) "And yet . . ."

Furiously the students scribbled. *"Hypnopædia, first used officially in A.F. 214. Why not before? Two reasons. (a) . . ."*

"These early experimenters," the D.H.C. was saying, "were on the wrong track. They thought that hypnopædia could be made an instrument of intellectual education . . ."

(A small boy asleep on his right side, the right arm stuck out, the right hand hanging limp over the edge of the bed. Through a round grating in the side of a box a voice speaks softly.

"The Nile is the longest river in Africa and the second in length of all the rivers of the globe. Although falling short of the length of the Mississippi-Missouri, the Nile is at the head of all rivers as regards the length of its basin, which extends through 35 degrees of latitude . . ."

At breakfast the next morning, "Tommy," some one says, "do you know which is the longest river in Africa?" A shaking of the head. "But don't you remember something that begins: The Nile is the . . ."

"The - Nile - is - the - longest - river - in - Africa - and - the -

second - in - length - of - all - the - rivers - of - the - globe . . ." The words come rushing out. "Although - falling - short - of . . ."

"Well now, which is the longest river in Africa?"

The eyes are blank. "I don't know."

"But the Nile, Tommy."

"The - Nile - is - the - longest - river - in - Africa - and - second . . ."

"Then which river is the longest, Tommy?"

Tommy bursts into tears. "I don't know," he howls.)

That howl, the Director made it plain, discouraged the earliest investigators. The experiments were abandoned. No further attempt was made to teach children the length of the Nile in their sleep. Quite rightly. You can't learn a science unless you know what it's all about.

"Whereas, if they'd only started on *moral* education," said the Director, leading the way towards the door. The students followed him, desperately scribbling as they walked and all the way up in the lift. "Moral education, which ought never, in any circumstances, to be rational."

"Silence, silence," whispered a loud speaker as they stepped out at the fourteenth floor, and "Silence, silence," the trumpet mouths indefatigably repeated at intervals down every corridor. The students and even the Director himself rose automatically to the tips of their toes. They were Alphas, of course; but even Alphas have been well conditioned. "Silence, silence." All the air of the fourteenth floor was sibilant with the categorical imperative.

Fifty yards of tiptoeing brought them to a door which the Director cautiously opened. They stepped over the threshold into the twilight of a shuttered dormitory. Eighty cots stood in a row against the wall. There was a sound of light regular breathing and a continuous murmur, as of very faint voices remotely whispering.

A nurse rose as they entered and came to attention before the Director.

"What's the lesson this afternoon?" he asked.

"We had Elementary Sex for the first forty minutes," she answered. "But now it's switched over to Elementary Class Consciousness."

The Director walked slowly down the long line of cots. Rosy and relaxed with sleep, eighty little boys and girls lay softly breathing. There was a whisper under every pillow. The D.H.C. halted and, bending over one of the little beds, listened attentively.

"Elementary Class Consciousness, did you say? Let's have it repeated a little louder by the trumpet."

At the end of the room a loud speaker projected from the wall. The Director walked up to it and pressed a switch.

". . . all wear green," said a soft but very distinct voice, beginning in the middle of a sentence, "and Delta Children wear khaki. Oh no, I don't want to play with Delta children. And Epsilons are still worse. They're too stupid to be able to read or write. Besides they wear black, which is such a beastly colour. I'm *so* glad I'm a Beta."

There was a pause; then the voice began again.

"Alpha children wear grey. They work much harder than we do, because they're so frightfully clever. I'm really awfully glad I'm a Beta, because I don't work so hard. And then we are much better than the Gammas and Deltas. Gammas are stupid. They all wear green, and Delta children wear khaki. Oh no, I *don't* want to play with Delta children. And Epsilons are still worse. They're too stupid to be able . . ."

The Director pushed back the switch. The voice was silent. Only its thin ghost continued to mutter from beneath the eighty pillows.

"They'll have that repeated forty or fifty times more before they wake; then again on Thursday, and again on Saturday. A hundred and twenty times three times a week for thirty months. After which they go on to a more advanced lesson."

Roses and electric shocks, the khaki of Deltas and a whiff of asafœtida—wedded indissolubly before the child can speak. But wordless conditioning is crude and wholesale; cannot bring home the finer distinctions, cannot inculcate the more complex courses of behaviour. For that there must be words, but words without reason. In brief, hypnopædia.

"The greatest moralizing and socializing force of all time."

The students took it down in their little books. Straight from the horse's mouth.

Once more the Director touched the switch.

". . . so frightfully clever," the soft, insinuating, indefatigable voice was saying, "I'm really awfully glad I'm a Beta, because . . ."

Not so much like drops of water, though water, it is true, can wear holes in the hardest granite; rather, drops of liquid sealing-wax, drops that adhere, incrust, incorporate themselves with what they fall on, till finally the rock is all one scarlet blob.

"Till at last the child's mind *is* these suggestions, and the sum of the suggestions *is* the child's mind. And not the child's mind only. The adult's mind too—all his life long. The mind that judges and desires and decides—made up of these suggestions. But all these suggestions are *our* suggestions!" The Director almost shouted in his triumph. "Suggestions from the State." He banged the nearest table. "It therefore follows . . ."

A noise made him turn round.

"Oh, Ford!" he said in another tone, "I've gone and woken the children."

3

Outside, in the garden, it was playtime. Naked in the warm June sunshine, six or seven hundred little boys and girls were running with shrill yells over the lawns, or playing ball games, or squatting silently in twos and threes among the flowering shrubs. The roses were in bloom, two nightingales soliloquized in the boskage, a cuckoo was just going out of tune among the lime trees. The air was drowsy with the murmur of bees and helicopters.

The Director and his students stood for a short time watching a game of Centrifugal Bumble-puppy. Twenty children were grouped in a circle round a chrome steel tower. A ball thrown up so as to land on the platform at the top of the tower rolled down into the interior, fell on a rapidly revolving disk, was hurled through one or other of the numerous apertures pierced in the cylindrical casing, and had to be caught.

"Strange," mused the Director, as they turned away, "strange to think that even in Our Ford's day most games were played without more apparatus than a ball or two and a few sticks and perhaps a bit of netting. Imagine the folly of allowing people to play elaborate games which do nothing whatever to increase consumption. It's madness. Nowadays the Controllers won't approve of any new game unless it can be shown that it requires at least as much apparatus as the most complicated of existing games." He interrupted himself.

"That's a charming little group," he said, pointing.

In a little grassy bay between tall clumps of Mediterranean heather, two children, a little boy of about seven and a little girl who might have been a year older, were playing, very gravely and with all the focussed attention of scientists intent on a labour of discovery, a rudimentary sexual game.

"Charming, charming!" the D.H.C. repeated sentimentally.

"Charming," the boys politely agreed. But their smile was rather patronizing. They had put aside similar childish amusements too recently to be able to watch them now without a touch of contempt. Charming? but it was just a pair of kids fooling about; that was all. Just kids.

"I always think," the Director was continuing in the same rather maudlin tone, when he was interrupted by a loud boo-hooing.

From a neighbouring shrubbery emerged a nurse, leading by the hand a small boy, who howled as he went. An anxious-looking little girl trotted at her heels.

"What's the matter?" asked the Director.

The nurse shrugged her shoulders. "Nothing much," she answered. "It's just that this little boy seems rather reluctant to join in the ordinary erotic play. I'd noticed it once or twice before. And now again to-day. He started yelling just now . . ."

"Honestly," put in the anxious-looking little girl, "I didn't mean to hurt him or anything. Honestly."

"Of course you didn't, dear," said the nurse reassuringly. "And so," she went on, turning back to the Director, "I'm taking him in to see the Assistant Superintendent of Psychology. Just to see if anything's at all abnormal."

"Quite right," said the Director. "Take him in. You stay here, little girl," he added, as the nurse moved away with her still howling charge. "What's your name?"

"Polly Trotsky."

"And a very good name too," said the Director. "Run away now and see if you can find some other little boy to play with."

The child scampered off into the bushes and was lost to sight.

"Exquisite little creature!" said the Director, looking after her. Then, turning to his students, "What I'm going to tell you now," he said, "may sound incredible. But then, when you're not accustomed to history, most facts about the past *do* sound incredible."

He let out the amazing truth. For a very long period before the time of Our Ford, and even for some generations afterwards, erotic play between children had been regarded as abnormal (there was a roar of laughter); and not only abnormal, actually immoral (no!): and had therefore been rigorously suppressed.

A look of astonished incredulity appeared on the faces of his listeners. Poor little kids not allowed to amuse themselves? They could not believe it.

"Even adolescents," the D.H.C. was saying, "even adolescents like yourselves . . ."

"Not possible!"

"Barring a little surreptitious auto-erotism and homosexuality—absolutely nothing."

"Nothing?"

"In most cases, till they were over twenty years old."

"Twenty years old?" echoed the students in a chorus of loud disbelief.

"Twenty," the Director repeated. "I told you that you'd find it incredible."

"But what happened?" they asked. "What were the results?"

"The results were terrible." A deep resonant voice broke startlingly into the dialogue.

They looked around. On the fringe of the little group stood a stranger—a man of middle height, black-haired, with a hooked nose, full red lips, eyes very piercing and dark. "Terrible," he repeated.

The D.H.C. had at that moment sat down on one of the steel and rubber benches conveniently scattered through the gardens; but at the sight of the stranger, he sprang to his feet and darted forward, his hand outstretched, smiling with all his teeth, effusive.

"Controller! What an unexpected pleasure! Boys, what are you thinking of? This is the Controller; this is his ford-ship, Mustapha Mond."

In the four thousand rooms of the Centre the four thousand electric clocks simultaneously struck four. Discarnate voices called from the trumpet mouths.

"Main Day-shift off duty. Second Day-shift take over. Main Day-shift off . . ."

In the lift, on their way up to the changing rooms, Henry Foster and the Assistant Director of Predestination rather pointedly turned their backs on Bernard Marx from the Psychology Bureau: averted themselves from that unsavoury reputation.

The faint hum and rattle of machinery still stirred the crimson air in the Embryo Store. Shifts might come and go, one lupus-coloured face give place to another; majestically and for ever the conveyors crept forward with their load of future men and women.

Lenina Crowne walked briskly towards the door.

His fordship Mustapha Mond! The eyes of the saluting students almost popped out of their heads. Mustapha Mond! The Resident Controller for Western Europe! One of the Ten World Controllers. One of the Ten . . . and he sat down on the bench with the D.H.C., he was going to stay, to stay, yes, and actually talk to them . . . straight from the horse's mouth. Straight from the mouth of Ford himself.

Two shrimp-brown children emerged from a neighbouring shrubbery, stared at them for a moment with large, astonished eyes, then returned to their amusements among the leaves.

"You all remember," said the Controller, in his strong deep voice, "you all remember, I suppose, that beautiful and inspired saying of Our Ford's: History is bunk. History," he repeated slowly, "is bunk."

He waved his hand; and it was as though, with an invisible feather wisk, he had brushed away a little dust, and the dust was Harappa, was Ur of the Chaldees; some spider-webs, and they were Thebes and Babylon and Cnossos and Mycenae. Whisk. Whisk—and where was Odysseus, where was Job, where were Jupiter and Gotama and Jesus? Whisk—and those specks of antique dirt called Athens and Rome, Jerusalem and the Middle Kingdom—all were gone. Whisk—the place where Italy had been was empty. Whisk, the cathedrals; whisk, whisk, King Lear and the Thoughts of Pascal. Whisk, Passion; whisk, Requiem; whisk, Symphony; whisk . . .

"Going to the Feelies this evening, Henry?" enquired the Assistant Predestinator. "I hear the new one at the Alhambra is first-rate. There's a love scene on a bearskin rug; they say it's marvellous. Every hair of the bear reproduced. The most amazing tactual effects."

"That's why you're taught no history," the Controller was saying. "But now the time has come . . ."

The D.H.C. looked at him nervously. There were those strange rumours of old forbidden books hidden in a safe in the Controller's study. Bibles, poetry—Ford knew what.

Mustapha Mond intercepted his anxious glance and the corners of his red lips twitched ironically.

"It's all right, Director," he said in a tone of faint derision, "I won't corrupt them."

The D.H.C. was overwhelmed with confusion.

Those who feel themselves despised do well to look despising. The smile on Bernard Marx's face was contemptuous. Every hair on the bear indeed!

"I shall make a point of going," said Henry Foster.

* * *

Mustapha Mond leaned forward, shook a finger at them. "Just try to realize it," he said, and his voice sent a strange thrill quivering along their diaphragms. "Try to realize what it was like to have a viviparous mother."

That smutty word again. But none of them dreamed, this time, of smiling.

"Try to imagine what 'living with one's family' meant."

They tried; but obviously without the smallest success.

"And do you know what a 'home' was?"

They shook their heads.

From her dim crimson cellar Lenina Crowne shot up seventeen stories, turned to the right as she stepped out of the lift, walked down a long corridor and, opening the door marked GIRLS' DRESSING-ROOM, plunged into a deafening chaos of arms and bosoms and underclothing. Torrents of hot water were splashing into or gurgling out of a hundred baths. Rumbling and hissing, eighty vibro-vacuum massage machines were simultaneously kneading and sucking the firm and sunburnt flesh of eighty superb female specimens. Every one was talking at the top of her voice. A Synthetic Music machine was warbling out a super-cornet solo.

"Hullo, Fanny," said Lenina to the young woman who had the pegs and locker next to hers.

Fanny worked in the Bottling Room, and her surname was also Crowne. But as the two thousand million inhabitants of the planet had only ten thousand names between them, the coincidence was not particularly surprising.

Lenina pulled at her zippers—downwards on the jacket, downwards with a double-handed gesture at the two that held trousers, downwards again to loosen her undergarment. Still wearing her shoes and stockings, she walked off towards the bathrooms.

* * *

Home, home—a few small rooms, stiflingly over-inhabited by a man, by a periodically teeming woman, by a rabble of boys and girls of all ages. No air, no space; an understerilized prison; darkness, disease, and smells.

(The Controller's evocation was so vivid that one of the boys, more sensitive than the rest, turned pale at the mere description and was on the point of being sick.)

Lenina got out of the bath, toweled herself dry, took hold of a long flexible tube plugged into the wall, presented the nozzle to her breast, as though she meant to commit suicide, pressed down the trigger. A blast of warmed air dusted her with the finest talcum powder. Eight different scents and eau-de-Cologne were laid on in little taps over the wash-basin. She turned on the third from the left, dabbed herself with chypre and, carrying her shoes and stockings in her hand, went out to see if one of the vibro-vacuum machines were free.

And home was as squalid psychically as physically. Psychically, it was a rabbit hole, a midden, hot with the frictions of tightly packed life, reeking with emotion. What suffocating intimacies, what dangerous, insane, obscene relationships between the members of the family group! Maniacally, the mother brooded over her children (*her* children) . . . brooded over them like a cat over its kittens; but a cat that could talk, a cat that could say, "My baby, my baby," over and over again. "My baby, and oh, oh, at my breast, the little hands, the hunger, and that unspeakable agonizing pleasure! Till at last my baby sleeps, my baby sleeps with a bubble of white milk at the corner of his mouth. My little baby sleeps . . ."

"Yes," said Mustapha Mond, nodding his head, "you may well shudder."

* * *

"Who are you going out with to-night?" Lenina asked, returning from the vibro-vac like a pearl illuminated from within, pinkly glowing.

"Nobody."

Lenina raised her eyebrows in astonishment.

"I've been feeling rather out of sorts lately," Fanny explained. "Dr. Wells advised me to have a Pregnancy Substitute."

"But, my dear, you're only nineteen. The first Pregnancy Substitute isn't compulsory till twenty-one."

"I know, dear. But some people are better if they begin earlier. Dr. Wells told me that brunettes with wide pelvises, like me, ought to have their first Pregnancy Substitute at seventeen. So I'm really two years late, not two years early." She opened the door of her locker and pointed to the row of boxes and labelled phials on the upper shelf.

"SYRUP OF CORPUS LUTEUM," Lenina read the names aloud. "OVARIN, GUARANTEED FRESH: NOT TO BE USED AFTER AUGUST 1ST, A.F. 632. MAMMARY GLAND EXTRACT: TO BE TAKEN THREE TIMES DAILY, BEFORE MEALS, WITH A LITTLE WATER. PLACENTIN: 5CC TO BE INJECTED INTRAVENALLY EVERY THIRD DAY . . . Ugh!" Lenina shuddered. "How I loathe intravenals, don't you?"

"Yes. But when they do one good . . ." Fanny was a particularly sensible girl.

Our Ford—or Our Freud, as, for some inscrutable reason, he chose to call himself whenever he spoke of psychological matters—Our Freud had been the first to reveal the appalling dangers of family life. The world was full of fathers—was therefore full of misery; full of mothers—therefore of every kind of perversion from sadism to chastity; full of brothers, sisters, uncles, aunts—full of madness and suicide.

"And yet, among the savages of Samoa, in certain islands off the coast of New Guinea . . ."

The tropical sunshine lay like warm honey on the naked bodies of children tumbling promiscuously among the hibiscus blossoms. Home was in any one of twenty palm-thatched houses. In the Trobriands conception was the work of ancestral ghosts; nobody had ever heard of a father.

"Extremes," said the Controller, "meet. For the good reason that they were made to meet."

"Dr. Wells says that a three months' Pregnancy Substitute now will make all the difference to my health for the next three or four years."

"Well, I hope he's right," said Lenina. "But, Fanny, do you really mean to say that for the next three months you're not supposed to . . ."

"Oh no, dear. Only for a week or two, that's all. I shall spend the evening at the Club playing Musical Bridge. I suppose you're going out?"

Lenina nodded.

"Who with?"

"Henry Foster."

"Again?" Fanny's kind, rather moon-like face took on an incongruous expression of pained and disapproving astonishment. "Do you mean to tell me you're *still* going out with Henry Foster?"

Mothers and fathers, brothers and sisters. But there were also husbands, wives, lovers. There were also monogamy and romance.

"Though you probably don't know what those are," said Mustapha Mond.

They shook their heads.

Family, monogamy, romance. Everywhere exclusiveness, a narrow channelling of impulse and energy.

"But every one belongs to every one else," he concluded, citing the hypnopædic proverb.

The students nodded, emphatically agreeing with a statement which upwards of sixty-two thousand repetitions in the dark had made them accept, not merely as true, but as axiomatic, self-evident, utterly indisputable.

"But after all," Lenina was protesting, "it's only about four months now since I've been having Henry."

"*Only* four months! I like that. And what's more," Fanny went on, pointing an accusing finger, "there's been nobody else except Henry all that time. Has there?"

Lenina blushed scarlet; but her eyes, the tone of her voice remained defiant. "No, there hasn't been any one else," she answered almost truculently. "And I jolly well don't see why there should have been."

"Oh, she jolly well doesn't see why there should have been," Fanny repeated, as though to an invisible listener behind Lenina's left shoulder. Then, with a sudden change of tone, "But seriously," she said, "I really do think you ought to be careful. It's such horribly bad form to go on and on like this with one man. At forty, or thirty-five, it wouldn't be so bad. But at *your* age, Lenina! No, it really won't do. And you know how strongly the D.H.C. objects to anything intense or long-drawn. Four months of Henry Foster, without having another man—why, he'd be furious if he knew . . ."

"Think of water under pressure in a pipe." They thought of it. "I pierce it once," said the Controller. "What a jet!"

He pierced it twenty times. There were twenty piddling little fountains.

"My baby. My baby . . . !"

"Mother!" The madness is infectious.

"My love, my one and only, precious, precious . . ."

Mother, monogamy, romance. High spurts the fountain; fierce and foamy the wild jet. The urge has but a single outlet. My love, my baby. No wonder these poor pre-moderns were mad and wicked and miserable. Their world didn't allow them to take things easily, didn't allow them to be sane, virtuous, happy. What with mothers and lovers, what with the prohibitions they were not conditioned to obey, what with the temptations and the lonely remorses, what with all the diseases and the endless isolating pain, what with the uncertainties and the poverty—they were forced to feel strongly. And feeling strongly (and strongly, what was more, in solitude, in hopelessly individual isolation), how could they be stable?

"Of course there's no need to give him up. Have somebody else from time to time, that's all. He has other girls, doesn't he?"

Lenina admitted it.

"Of course he does. Trust Henry Foster to be the perfect gentleman—always correct. And then there's the Director to think of. You know what a stickler . . ."

Nodding, "He patted me on the behind this afternoon," said Lenina.

"There, you see!" Fanny was triumphant. "That shows what *he* stands for. The strictest conventionality."

"Stability," said the Controller, "stability. No civilization without social stability. No social stability without individual stability." His voice was a trumpet. Listening they felt larger, warmer.

The machine turns, turns and must keep on turning—for ever. It is death if it stands still. A thousand millions scrabbled the crust of the earth. The wheels began to turn. In a hundred and fifty years there were two thousand millions. Stop all the wheels. In a hundred and fifty weeks there are once more only a thousand millions; a thousand thousand thousand men and women have starved to death.

Wheels must turn steadily, but cannot turn untended. There must be men to tend them, men as steady as the wheels upon their axles, sane men, obedient men, stable in contentment.

Crying: My baby, my mother, my only, only love; groaning: My sin, my terrible God; screaming with pain, muttering with fever, bemoaning old age and poverty—how can they tend the wheels? And if they cannot tend the wheels . . . The corpses of a thousand thousand thousand men and women would be hard to bury or burn.

"And after all," Fanny's tone was coaxing, "it's not as though there were anything painful or disagreeable about having one or two men besides Henry. And seeing that you *ought* to be a little more promiscuous . . ."

"Stability," insisted the Controller, "stability. The primal and the ultimate need. Stability. Hence all this."

With a wave of his hand he indicated the gardens, the huge building of the Conditioning Centre, the naked children furtive in the undergrowth or running across the lawns.

Lenina shook her head. "Somehow," she mused, "I hadn't been feeling very keen on promiscuity lately. There are times when one doesn't. Haven't you found that too, Fanny?"

Fanny nodded her sympathy and understanding. "But one's got to make the effort," she said, sententiously, "one's got to play the game. After all, every one belongs to every one else."

"Yes, every one belongs to every one else," Lenina repeated

slowly and, sighing, was silent for a moment; then, taking Fanny's hand, gave it a little squeeze. "You're quite right, Fanny. As usual. I'll make the effort."

Impulse arrested spills over, and the flood is feeling, the flood is passion, the flood is even madness: it depends on the force of the current, the height and strength of the barrier. The unchecked stream flows smoothly down its appointed channels into a calm well-being. The embryo is hungry; day in, day out, the blood-surrogate pump unceasingly turns its eight hundred revolutions a minute. The decanted infant howls; at once a nurse appears with a bottle of external secretion. Feeling lurks in that interval of time between desire and its consummation. Shorten that interval, break down all those old unnecessary barriers.

"Fortunate boys!" said the Controller. "No pains have been spared to make your lives emotionally easy—to preserve you, so far as that is possible, from having emotions at all."

"Ford's in his flivver," murmured the D.H.C. "All's well with the world."

"Lenina Crowne?" said Henry Foster, echoing the Assistant Predestinator's question as he zipped up his trousers. "Oh, she's a splendid girl. Wonderfully pneumatic. I'm surprised you haven't had her."

"I can't think how it is I haven't," said the Assistant Predestinator. "I certainly will. At the first opportunity."

From his place on the opposite side of the changing-room aisle, Bernard Marx overheard what they were saying and turned pale.

"And to tell the truth," said Lenina, "I'm beginning to get just a tiny bit bored with nothing but Henry every day." She pulled on her left stocking. "Do you know Bernard Marx?" she asked in a tone whose excessive casualness was evidently forced.

Fanny looked startled. "You don't mean to say . . . ?"

"Why not? Bernard's an Alpha Plus. Besides, he asked me to go to one of the Savage Reservations with him. I've always wanted to see a Savage Reservation."

"But his reputation?"

"What do I care about his reputation?"

"They say he doesn't like Obstacle Golf."

"They say, they say," mocked Lenina.

"And then he spends most of his time by himself—*alone*." There was horror in Fanny's voice.

"Well, he won't be alone when he's with me. And anyhow, why are people so beastly to him? I think he's rather sweet." She smiled to herself; how absurdly shy he had been! Frightened almost—as though she were a World Controller and he a Gamma-Minus machine minder.

"Consider your own lives," said Mustapha Mond. "Has any of you ever encountered an insurmountable obstacle?"

The question was answered by a negative silence.

"Has any of you been compelled to live through a long time-interval between the consciousness of a desire and its fulfilment?"

"Well," began one of the boys, and hesitated.

"Speak up," said the D.H.C. "Don't keep his fordship waiting."

"I once had to wait nearly four weeks before a girl I wanted would let me have her."

"And you felt a strong emotion in consequence?"

"Horrible!"

"Horrible; precisely," said the Controller. "Our ancestors were so stupid and short-sighted that when the first reformers came along and offered to deliver them from those horrible emotions, they wouldn't have anything to do with them."

* * *

"Talking about her as though she were a bit of meat." Bernard ground his teeth. "Have her here, have her there. Like mutton. Degrading her to so much mutton. She said she'd think it over, she said she'd give me an answer this week. Oh, Ford, Ford, Ford." He would have liked to go up to them and hit them in the face—hard, again and again.

"Yes, I really do advise you to try her," Henry Foster was saying.

"Take Ectogenesis. Pfitzner and Kawaguchi had got the whole technique worked out. But would the Governments look at it? No. There was something called Christianity. Women were forced to go on being viviparous."

"He's so ugly!" said Fanny.

"But I rather like his looks."

"And then so *small*." Fanny made a grimace; smallness was so horribly and typically low-caste.

"I think that's rather sweet," said Lenina. "One feels one would like to pet him. You know. Like a cat."

Fanny was shocked. "They say somebody made a mistake when he was still in the bottle—thought he was a Gamma and put alcohol into his blood-surrogate. That's why he's so stunted."

"What nonsense!" Lenina was indignant.

"Sleep teaching was actually prohibited in England. There was something called liberalism. Parliament, if you know what that was, passed a law against it. The records survive. Speeches about liberty of the subject. Liberty to be inefficient and miserable. Freedom to be a round peg in a square hole."

* * *

"But, my dear chap, you're welcome, I assure you. You're welcome." Henry Foster patted the Assistant Predestinator on the shoulder. "Every one belongs to every one else, after all."

One hundred repetitions three nights a week for four years, thought Bernard Marx, who was a specialist on hypnopædia. Sixty-two thousand four hundred repetitions make one truth. Idiots!

"Or the Caste System. Constantly proposed, constantly rejected. There was something called democracy. As though men were more than physico-chemically equal."

"Well, all I can say is that I'm going to accept his invitation."

Bernard hated them, hated them. But they were two, they were large, they were strong.

"Then the Nine Years' War began in A.F. 141."

"Not even if it *were* true about the alcohol in his blood-surrogate."

"Phosgene, chloropicrin, ethyl iodoacetate, diphenylcyanarsine, trichlormethyl, chloroformate, dichlorethyl sulphide. Not to mention hydrocyanic acid."

"Which I simply don't believe," Lenina concluded.

* * *

"The noise of fourteen thousand aeroplanes advancing in open order. But in the Kurfurstendamm and the Eighth Arrondissement, the explosion of the anthrax bombs is hardly louder than the popping of a paper bag."

"Because I *do* want to see a Savage Reservation."

$Ch_8C_6H_2(NO_2)8 + Hg(CNO)_2$ = well, what? An enormous hole in the ground, a pile of masonry, some bits of flesh and mucus, a foot, with the boot still on it, flying through the air and landing, flop, in the middle of the geraniums—the scarlet ones; such a splendid show that summer!

"You're hopeless, Lenina, I give you up."

"The Russian technique for infecting water supplies was particularly ingenious."

Back turned to back, Fanny and Lenina continued their changing in silence.

"The Nine Years' War, the great Economic Collapse. There was a choice between World Control and destruction. Between stability and . . ."

* * *

"Fanny Crowne's a nice girl too," said the Assistant Predestinator.

In the nurseries, the Elementary Class Consciousness lesson was over, the voices were adapting future demand to future industrial supply. "I do love flying," they whispered, "I do love flying, I do love having new clothes, I do love . . ."

"Liberalism, of course, was dead of anthrax, but all the same you couldn't do things by force."

"Not nearly so pneumatic as Lenina. Oh, not nearly."

"But old clothes are beastly," continued the untiring whisper. "We always throw away old clothes. Ending is better than mending, ending is better than mending, ending is better . . ."

"Government's an affair of sitting, not hitting. You rule with the brains and the buttocks, never with the fists. For example, there was the conscription of consumption."

"There, I'm ready," said Lenina, but Fanny remained speechless and averted. "Let's make peace, Fanny darling."

"Every man, woman and child compelled to consume so much a year. In the interests of industry. The sole result . . ."

* * *

"Ending is better than mending. The more stitches, the less riches; the more stitches . . ."

"One of these days," said Fanny, with dismal emphasis, "you'll get into trouble."

"Conscientious objection on an enormous scale. Anything not to consume. Back to nature."

"I do love flying. I do love flying."

"Back to culture. Yes, actually to culture. You can't consume much if you sit still and read books."

"Do I look all right?" Lenina asked. Her jacket was made of bottle green acetate cloth with green viscose fur at the cuffs and collar.

"Eight hundred Simple Lifers were mowed down by machine guns at Golders Green."

"Ending is better than mending, ending is better than mending."

Green corduroy shorts and white viscose-woollen stockings turned down below the knee.

* * *

"Then came the famous British Museum Massacre. Two thousand culture fans gassed with dichlorethyl sulphide."

A green-and-white jockey cap shaded Lenina's eyes; her shoes were bright green and highly polished.

"In the end," said Mustapha Mond, "the Controllers realized that force was no good. The slower but infinitely surer methods of ectogenesis, neo-Pavlovian conditioning and hypnopædia . . ."

And round her waist she wore a silver-mounted green morocco-surrogate cartridge belt, bulging (for Lenina was not a freemartin) with the regulation supply of contraceptives.

"The discoveries of Pfitzner and Kawaguchi were at last made use of. An intensive propaganda against viviparous reproduction . . ."

"Perfect!" cried Fanny enthusiastically. She could never resist Lenina's charm for long. "And what a perfectly *sweet* Malthusian belt!"

"Accompanied by a campaign against the Past; by the closing of museums, the blowing up of historical monuments (luckily most of them had already been destroyed during the Nine Years' War); by the suppression of all books published before A.F. 150."

"I simply must get one like it," said Fanny.

* * *

"There were some things called the pyramids, for example."

"My old black-patent bandolier . . ."

"And a man called Shakespeare. You've never heard of them of course."

"It's an absolute disgrace—that bandolier of mine."

"Such are the advantages of a really scientific education."

"The more stitches the less riches; the more stitches the less . . ."

"The introduction of Our Ford's first T-Model . . ."

"I've had it nearly three months."

"Chosen as the opening date of the new era."

"Ending is better than mending; ending is better . . ."

"There was a thing, as I've said before, called Christianity."

* * *

"Ending is better than mending."

"The ethics and philosophy of under-consumption . . ."

"I love new clothes, I love new clothes, I love . . ."

"So essential when there was under-production; but in an age of machines and the fixation of nitrogen—positively a crime against society."

"Henry Foster gave it me."

"All crosses had their tops cut and became T's. There was also a thing called God."

"It's real morocco-surrogate."

"We have the World State now. And Ford's Day celebrations, and Community Sings, and Solidarity Services."

"Ford, how I hate them!" Bernard Marx was thinking.

"There was a thing called Heaven; but all the same they used to drink enormous quantities of alcohol."

* * *

"Like meat, like so much meat."

"There was a thing called the soul and a thing called immortality."

"Do ask Henry where he got it."

"But they used to take morphia and cocaine."

"And what makes it worse, she thinks of herself as meat."

"Two thousand pharmacologists and bio-chemists were subsidized in A.F. 178."

"He does look glum," said the Assistant Predestinator, pointing at Bernard Marx.

"Six years later it was being produced commercially. The perfect drug."

"Let's bait him."

"Euphoric, narcotic, pleasantly hallucinant."

* * *

"Glum, Marx, glum." The clap on the shoulder made him start, look up. It was that brute Henry Foster. "What you need is a gramme of *soma*."

"All the advantages of Christianity and alcohol; none of their defects."

"Ford, I should like to kill him!" But all he did was to say, "No, thank you," and fend off the proffered tube of tablets.

"Take a holiday from reality whenever you like, and come back without so much as a headache or a mythology."

"Take it," insisted Henry Foster, "take it."

"Stability was practically assured."

"One cubic centimetre cures ten gloomy sentiments," said the Assistant Predestinator citing a piece of homely hypnopædic wisdom.

"It only remained to conquer old age."

"Damn you, damn you!" shouted Bernard Marx.

* * *

"Hoity-toity."

"Gonadal hormones, transfusion of young blood, magnesium salts . . ."

"And do remember that a gramme is better than a damn." They went out, laughing.

"All the physiological stigmata of old age have been abolished. And along with them, of course . . ."

"Don't forget to ask him about that Malthusian belt," said Fanny.

"Along with them all the old man's mental peculiarities. Characters remain constant throughout a whole lifetime."

". . . two rounds of Obstacle Golf to get through before dark. I must fly."

"Work, play—at sixty our powers and tastes are what they were at seventeen. Old men in the bad old days used to renounce, retire, take to religion, spend their time reading, thinking—*thinking!*"

"Idiots, swine!" Bernard Marx was saying to himself, as he walked down the corridor to the lift.

* * *

"Now—such is progress—the old men work, the old men copulate, the old men have no time, no leisure from pleasure, not a moment to sit down and think—or if ever by some unlucky chance such a crevice of time should yawn in the solid substance of their distractions, there is always *soma*, delicious *soma*, half a gramme for a half-holiday, a gramme for a week-end, two grammes for a trip to the gorgeous East, three for a dark eternity on the moon; returning whence they find themselves on the other side of the crevice, safe on the solid ground of daily labour and distraction, scampering from feely to feely, from girl to pneumatic girl, from Electromagnetic Golf course to . . ."

"Go away, little girl," shouted the D.H.C. angrily. "Go away, little boy! Can't you see that his fordship's busy? Go and do your erotic play somewhere else."

"Suffer little children," said the Controller.

Slowly, majestically, with a faint humming of machinery, the Conveyors moved forward, thirty-three centimetres an hour. In the red darkness glinted innumerable rubies.

4

PART 1

The lift was crowded with men from the Alpha Changing Rooms, and Lenina's entry was greeted by many friendly nods and smiles. She was a popular girl and, at one time or another, had spent a night with almost all of them.

They were dear boys, she thought, as she returned their salutations. Charming boys! Still, she did wish that George Edzel's ears weren't quite so big (perhaps he'd been given just a spot too much parathyroid at Metre 328?). And looking at Benito Hoover, she couldn't help remembering that he was really *too* hairy when he took his clothes off.

Turning, with eyes a little saddened by the recollection of Benito's curly blackness, she saw in a corner the small thin body, the melancholy face of Bernard Marx.

"Bernard!" she stepped up to him. "I was looking for you." Her voice rang clear above the hum of the mounting lift. The others looked round curiously. "I wanted to talk to you about our New Mexico plan." Out of the tail of her eye she could see Benito Hoover gaping with astonishment. The gape annoyed her. "Surprised I shouldn't be begging to go with *him* again!" she said to herself. Then aloud, and more warmly than ever, "I'd simply *love* to come with you for a week in July," she went on. (Anyhow, she was publicly proving her unfaithfulness to Henry. Fanny ought to be pleased, even though it was Bernard.) "That is," Lenina gave him her most deliciously significant smile, "if you still want to have me."

Bernard's pale face flushed. "What on earth for?" she wondered, astonished, but at the same time touched by this strange tribute to her power.

"Hadn't we better talk about it somewhere else?" he stammered, looking horribly uncomfortable.

"As though I'd been saying something shocking," thought Lenina. "He couldn't look more upset if I'd made a dirty joke—asked him who his mother was, or something like that."

"I mean, with all these people about . . ." He was choked with confusion.

Lenina's laugh was frank and wholly unmalicious. "How funny you are!" she said; and she quite genuinely did think him funny. "You'll give me at least a week's warning, won't you," she went on in another tone. "I suppose we take the Blue Pacific Rocket? Does it start from the Charing-T Tower? Or is it from Hampstead?"

Before Bernard could answer, the lift came to a standstill.

"Roof!" called a creaking voice.

The liftman was a small simian creature, dressed in the black tunic of an Epsilon-Minus Semi-Moron.

"Roof!"

He flung open the gates. The warm glory of afternoon sunlight made him start and blink his eyes. "Oh, roof!" he repeated in a voice of rapture. He was as though suddenly and joyfully awakened from a dark annihilating stupor. "Roof!"

He smiled up with a kind of doggily expectant adoration into the faces of his passengers. Talking and laughing together, they stepped out into the light. The liftman looked after them.

"Roof?" he said once more, questioningly.

Then a bell rang, and from the ceiling of the lift a loud speaker began, very softly and yet very imperiously, to issue its commands.

"Go down," it said, "go down. Floor Eighteen. Go down, go down. Floor Eighteen. Go down, go . . ."

The liftman slammed the gates, touched a button and instantly dropped back into the droning twilight of the well, the twilight of his own habitual stupor.

It was warm and bright on the roof. The summer afternoon was drowsy with the hum of passing helicopters; and the deeper drone of the rocket-planes hastening, invisible, through the bright sky five or six miles overhead was like a caress on the soft air. Bernard Marx drew a deep breath. He looked up into the sky and round the blue horizon and finally down into Lenina's face.

"Isn't it beautiful!" His voice trembled a little.

She smiled at him with an expression of the most sympathetic understanding. "Simply perfect for Obstacle Golf," she answered rapturously. "And now I must fly, Bernard. Henry gets cross if I keep him waiting. Let me know in good time about the date." And waving her hand, she ran away across the wide flat roof towards the hangars. Bernard stood watching the retreating twinkle of the white stockings, the sunburnt knees vivaciously bending and unbending again, again, and the softer rolling of those well-fitted corduroy shorts beneath the bottle green jacket. His face wore an expression of pain.

"I should say she was pretty," said a loud and cheery voice just behind him.

Bernard started and looked around. The chubby red face of Benito Hoover was beaming down at him—beaming with manifest cordiality. Benito was notoriously good-natured. People said of him that he could have got through life without ever touching *soma*. The malice and bad tempers from which other people had to take holidays never afflicted him. Reality for Benito was always sunny.

"Pneumatic too. And how!" Then, in another tone: "But, I say," he went on, "you look glum! What you need is a gramme of *soma*."

Diving into his right-hand trouser-pocket, Benito produced a phial. "One cubic centimetre cures ten gloomy . . . But, I say!"

Bernard had suddenly turned and rushed away.

Benito stared after him. "What can be the matter with the fellow?" he wondered, and, shaking his head, decided that the story about the alcohol having been put into the poor chap's blood-surrogate must be true. "Touched his brain, I suppose."

He put away the *soma* bottle, and taking out a packet of sex-hormone chewing-gum, stuffed a plug into his cheek and walked slowly away towards the hangars, ruminating.

Henry Foster had had his machine wheeled out of its lockup and, when Lenina arrived, was already seated in the cockpit, waiting.

"Four minutes late," was all his comment, as she climbed in beside him. He started the engines and threw the helicopter screws into gear. The machine shot vertically into the air. Henry accelerated; the humming of the propeller shrilled from hornet to wasp, from wasp to mosquito; the speedometer showed that they were rising at the best part of two kilometres a minute. London diminished beneath them. The huge table-topped buildings were no more, in a few seconds, than a bed of geometrical mushrooms sprouting from the green of park and garden. In the midst of them, thin-stalked, a taller, slenderer fungus, the Charing-T Tower lifted towards the sky a disk of shining concrete.

Like the vague torsos of fabulous athletes, huge fleshy clouds lolled on the blue air above their heads. Out of one of them suddenly dropped a small scarlet insect, buzzing as it fell.

"There's the Red Rocket," said Henry, "just come in from New York." Looking at his watch. "Seven minutes behind time," he added, and shook his head. "These Atlantic services—they're really scandalously unpunctual."

He took his foot off the accelerator. The humming of the screws overhead dropped an octave and a half, back through wasp and hornet to bumble bee, to cockchafer, to stag-beetle. The upward rush of the machine slackened off; a moment later they were hanging motionless in the air. Henry pushed at a lever; there was a click. Slowly at first, then faster and faster, till it was a circular mist before their eyes, the propeller in front of them began to revolve. The wind of a horizontal speed whistled ever more shrilly in the stays. Henry kept his eye on the revolution-counter; when the needle touched the twelve hundred mark, he threw the helicopter screws out of gear. The machine had enough forward momentum to be able to fly on its planes.

Lenina looked down through the window in the floor between her feet. They were flying over the six kilometre zone of park-land that separated Central London from its first ring of satellite suburbs. The green was maggoty with fore-shortened life. Forests of Centrifugal Bumble-puppy towers gleamed between the trees. Near Shepherd's Bush two thousand Beta-Minus mixed doubles were playing Riemann-surface tennis. A double row of Escalator Fives Courts lined the main road from Notting Hill to Willesden. In the Ealing stadium a Delta gymnastic display and community sing was in progress.

"What a hideous colour khaki is," remarked Lenina, voicing the hypnopædic prejudices of her caste.

The buildings of the Hounslow Feely Studio covered seven and a half hectares. Near them a black and khaki army of labourers was busy revitrifying the surface of the Great West Road. One of the huge travelling crucibles was being tapped as they flew over. The molten stone poured out in a stream of dazzling incandescence across the road; the asbestos rollers came and went; at the tail of an insulated watering cart the steam rose in white clouds.

At Brentford the Television Corporation's factory was like a small town.

"They must be changing the shift," said Lenina.

Like aphides and ants, the leaf-green Gamma girls, the black Semi-Morons swarmed round the entrances, or stood in queues to take their places in the monorail tram-cars. Mulberry-coloured Beta-Minuses came and went among the crowd. The roof of the main building was alive with the alighting and departure of helicopters.

"My word," said Lenina, "I'm glad I'm not a Gamma."

Ten minutes later they were at Stoke Poges and had started their first round of Obstacle Golf.

PART 2

With eyes for the most part downcast and, if ever they lighted on a fellow creature, at once and furtively averted, Bernard hastened across the roof. He was like a man pursued, but pursued by enemies he does not wish to see, lest they should seem more hostile even than he had supposed, and he himself be made to feel guiltier and even more helplessly alone.

"That horrible Benito Hoover!" And yet the man had meant well enough. Which only made it, in a way, much worse. Those who meant well behaved in the same way as those who meant badly. Even Lenina was making him suffer. He remembered those weeks of timid indecision, during which he had looked and longed and despaired of ever having the courage to ask her. Dared he face the risk of being humiliated by a contemptuous refusal? But if she were to say yes, what rapture! Well, now she had said it and he was still wretched—wretched that she should have thought it such a perfect afternoon for Obstacle Golf, that she should have trotted away to join Henry Foster, that she should have found him funny for not wanting to talk of their most private affairs in public. Wretched, in a word, because she had behaved as any healthy and virtuous English girl ought to behave and not in some other, abnormal, extraordinary way.

He opened the door of his lock-up and called to a lounging couple of Delta-Minus attendants to come and push his machine out on to the roof. The hangars were staffed by a single Bokanovsky Group, and the men were twins, identically small, black and hideous. Bernard gave his orders in the sharp, rather arrogant and even offensive tone of one who does not feel himself too secure in his superiority. To have dealings with members of the lower castes was always, for Bernard, a most distressing experience. For whatever the cause (and the current gossip about the alcohol in his blood-surrogate may very likely—for accidents will happen—have been true) Bernard's physique was hardly better than that of the average Gamma. He stood eight centimetres short of the standard Alpha height and was slender in proportion. Contact with members of the lower castes always reminded him painfully of this physical inadequacy. "I am I, and wish I wasn't"; his self-consciousness was acute and distressing. Each time he found himself looking on the level, instead of downward, into a Delta's face, he felt humiliated. Would the creature treat him with the respect due to his caste? The question haunted him. Not without reason. For Gammas, Deltas and Epsilons had been to some extent conditioned to associate corporeal mass with social superiority. Indeed, a faint hypnopædic prejudice in favour of size was universal. Hence the laughter of the women to whom he made proposals, the practical joking of his equals among the men. The mockery made him feel an outsider; and feeling an outsider he behaved like one, which increased the prejudice against him and intensified the contempt and hostility aroused by his physical defects. Which in turn increased his sense of being alien and alone. A chronic fear of being slighted made him avoid his equals, made him stand, where his inferiors were concerned, self-consciously on his dignity. How bitterly he envied men like Henry Foster and Benito Hoover! Men who never had to shout at an Epsilon to get an order obeyed; men who took their position for granted; men who moved through the caste system as a fish through water—so utterly at home as to be unaware either of themselves or of the beneficent and comfortable element in which they had their being.

Slackly, it seemed to him, and with reluctance, the twin attendants wheeled his plane out on the roof.

"Hurry up!" said Bernard irritably. One of them glanced at him. Was that a kind of bestial derision that he detected in those blank grey eyes? "Hurry up!" he shouted more loudly, and there was an ugly rasp in his voice.

He climbed into the plane and, a minute later, was flying southwards, towards the river.

The various Bureaux of Propaganda and the College of Emotional Engineering were housed in a single sixty-story building in Fleet Street. In the basement and on the lower floors were the presses and offices of the three great London newspapers—*The Hourly Radio*, an upper-caste sheet, in pale green *Gamma Gazette*, and, on khaki paper and in words exclusively of one syllable, *The Delta Mirror*. Then came the Bureaux of Propaganda by Television, by Feeling Picture, and by Synthetic Voice and Music respectively—twenty-two floors of them. Above were the research laboratories and the padded rooms in which the Sound-Track Writers and Synthetic Composers did their delicate work. The top eighteen floors were occupied by the College of Emotional Engineering.

Bernard landed on the roof of Propaganda House and stepped out.

"Ring down to Mr. Helmholtz Watson," he ordered the Gamma-Plus porter, "and tell him that Mr. Bernard Marx is waiting for him on the roof."

He sat down and lit a cigarette.

Helmholtz Watson was writing when the message came down.

"Tell him I'm coming at once," he said and hung up the receiver. Then, turning to his secretary, "I'll leave you to put my things away," he went on in the same official and impersonal tone; and, ignoring her lustrous smile, got up and walked briskly to the door.

He was a powerfully built man, deep-chested, broad-shouldered, massive, and yet quick in his movements, springly and agile. The round strong pillar of his neck supported a beautifully shaped head. His hair was dark and curly, his features strongly marked. In a forcible emphatic way, he was handsome and looked, as his secretary was never tired of repeating, every centimetre an Alpha-Plus. By profession he was a lecturer at the College of Emotional Engineering (Department of Writing) and in the intervals of his educational activities, a working Emotional Engineer. He wrote regularly for *The Hourly Radio*, composed feely scenarios, and had the happiest knack for slogans and hypnopædic rhymes.

"Able," was the verdict of his superiors. "Perhaps," (and they would shake their heads, would significantly lower their voices) "a little *too* able."

Yes, a little too able; they were right. A mental excess had produced in Helmholtz Watson effects very similar to those which, in Bernard Marx, were the result of a physical defect. Too little bone and brawn had isolated Bernard from his fellow men, and the sense of this apartness, being, by all the current standards, a mental excess, became in its turn a cause of wider separation. That which had made Helmholtz so uncomfortably aware of being himself and all alone was too much ability. What the two men shared was the knowledge that they were individuals. But whereas the physically defective Bernard had suffered all his life from the consciousness of being separate, it was only quite recently that, grown aware of his mental excess, Helmholtz Watson had also become aware of his difference from the people who surrounded him. This Escalator-Squash champion, this indefatigable lover (it was said that he had had six hundred and forty different girls in under four years), this admirable committee man and best mixer had realized quite suddenly that sport, women, communal activities were only, so far as he was concerned, second bests. Really, and at the bottom, he was interested in something else. But in what? In what? That was the problem which Bernard had come to discuss with him—or rather, since it was always Helmholtz who did all the talking, to listen to his friend discussing, yet once more.

Three charming girls from the Bureaux of Propaganda by Synthetic Voice waylaid him as he stepped out of the lift.

"Oh, Helmholtz, darling, *do* come and have a picnic supper with us on Exmoor." They clung round him imploringly.

He shook his head, he pushed his way through them. "No, no."

"We're not inviting any other man."

But Helmholtz remained unshaken even by this delightful promise. "No," he repeated, "I'm busy." And he held resolutely on his course. The girls trailed after him. It was not till he had actually climbed into Bernard's plane and slammed the door that they gave up pursuit. Not without reproaches.

"These women!" he said, as the machine rose into the air. "These women!" And he shook his head, he frowned. "Too awful," Bernard hypocritically agreed, wishing, as he spoke the words, that he could have as many girls as Helmholtz did, and with as little trouble. He was seized with a sudden urgent need to boast. "I'm taking Lenina Crowne to New Mexico with me," he said in a tone as casual as he could make it.

"Are you?" said Helmholtz, with a total absense of interest. Then after a little pause, "This last week or two," he went on, "I've been cutting all my committees and all my girls. You can't imagine what a hullabaloo they've been making about it at the College. Still, it's been worth it, I think. The effects . . ." He hesitated. "Well, they're odd, they're very odd."

A physical shortcoming could produce a kind of mental excess. The process, it seemed, was reversible. Mental excess could produce, for its own purposes, the voluntary blindness and deafness of deliberate solitude, the artificial impotence of asceticism.

The rest of the short flight was accomplished in silence. When they had arrived and were comfortably stretched out on the pneumatic sofas in Bernard's room, Helmholtz began again.

Speaking very slowly, "Did you ever feel," he asked, "as though you had something inside you that was only waiting for you to give it a chance to come out? Some sort of extra power that you aren't using—you know, like all the water that goes down the falls instead of through the turbines?" He looked at Bernard questioningly.

"You mean all the emotions one might be feeling if things were different?"

Helmholtz shook his head. "Not quite. I'm thinking of a queer feeling I sometimes get, a feeling that I've got something important to say and the power to say it—only I don't know what it is, and I can't make any use of the power. If there was some different way of writing . . . Or else something else to write about . . ." He was silent; then, "You see," he went on at last, "I'm pretty good at inventing phrases—you know, the sort of words that suddenly make you jump, almost as though you'd sat on a pin, they seem so new and exciting even though they're about something hypnopædically obvious. But that doesn't seem enough. It's not enough for the phrases to be good; what you make with them ought to be good too."

"But your things are good, Helmholtz."

"Oh, as far as they go." Helmholtz shrugged his shoulders. "But they go such a little way. They aren't important enough, somehow. I feel I could do something much more important. Yes, and more intense, more violent. But what? What is there more important ' say? And how can one be violent about the sort of things one's pected to write about? Words can be like X-rays, if you use properly—they'll go through anything. You read and you're That's one of the things I try to teach my students—ho piercingly. But what on earth's the good of being pierce cle about a Community Sing, or the latest improveme gans? Besides, can you make words really piercing the very hardest X-rays—when you're writing thing? Can you say something about nothing? boils down to. I try and I try . . ."

"Hush!" said Bernard suddenly, and lif listened. "I believe there's somebody at

Helmholtz got up, tiptoed acros quick movement flung the door w nobody there.

"I'm sorry," said Bernard, feeling a

foolish. "I suppose I've got things on my nerves a bit. When people are suspicious with you, you start being suspicious with them."

He passed his hand across his eyes, he sighed, his voice became plaintive. He was justifying himself. "If you knew what I'd had to put up with recently," he said almost tearfully—and the uprush of his self-pity was like a fountain suddenly released. "If you only knew!"

Helmholtz Watson listened with a certain sense of discomfort. "Poor little Bernard!" he said to himself. But at the same time he felt rather ashamed for his friend. He wished Bernard would show a little more pride.

5

PART 1

By eight o'clock the light was failing. The loud speakers in the tower of the Stoke Poges Club House began, in a more than human tenor, to announce the closing of the courses. Lenina and Henry abandoned their game and walked back towards the Club. From the grounds of the Internal and External Secretion Trust came the lowing of those thousands of cattle which provided, with their hormones and their milk, the raw materials for the great factory at Farnham Royal.

An incessant buzzing of helicopters filled the twilight. Every two and a half minutes a bell and the screech of whistles announced the departure of one of the light monorail trains which carried the lower-caste golfers back from their separate course to the metropolis.

Lenina and Henry climbed into their machine and started off. At eight hundred feet Henry slowed down the helicopter screws, and they hung for a minute or two poised above the fading landscape. The forest of Burnham Beeches stretched like a great pool of darkness towards the bright shore of the western sky. Crimson at the horizon, the last of the sunset faded, through orange, upwards into yellow and a pale watery green. Northwards, beyond and above the trees, the Internal and External Secretions factory glared with a fierce electric brilliance from every window of its twenty stories. Beneath them lay the buildings of the Golf Club—the huge Lower Caste barracks and, on the other side of a dividing wall, the smaller houses reserved for Alpha and Beta members. The approaches to the monorail station were black with the ant-like pullulation of lower-caste activity. From under the glass vault a lighted train shot out into the open. Following its south-easterly course across the dark plain their eyes were drawn to the majestic buildings of the Slough Crematorium. For the safety of night-flying planes, its four tall chimneys were flood-lighted and tipped with crimson danger signals. It was a landmark.

"Why do the smoke-stacks have those things like balconies around them?" enquired Lenina.

"Phosphorous recovery," explained Henry telegraphically. "On their way up the chimney the gases go through four separate treatments. P_2O_5 used to go right out of circulation every time they cremated some one. Now they recover over ninety-eight per cent of it. More than a kilo and a half per adult corpse. Which makes the best part of four hundred tons of phosphorous every year from England alone." Henry spoke with a happy pride, rejoicing wholeheartedly in the achievement, as though it had been his own. "Fine to think we can go on being socially useful even after we're dead. Making plants grow."

Lenina, meanwhile, had turned her eyes away and was looking perpendicularly downwards at the monorail station. "Fine," she agreed. "But queer that Alphas and Betas won't make any more plants grow than those nasty little Gammas and Deltas and Epsilons down there."

"All men are physico-chemically equal," said Henry sententiously. "Besides, even Epsilons perform indispensable services."

"Even an Epsilon . . ." Lenina suddenly remembered an occasion when, as a little girl at school, she had woken up in the middle of the night and become aware, for the first time, of the whispering that

had haunted all her sleeps. She saw again the beam of moonlight, the row of small white beds; heard once more the soft, soft voice that said (the words were there, unforgotten, unforgettable after so many night-long repetitions): "Every one works for every one else. We can't do without any one. Even Epsilons are useful. We couldn't do without Epsilons. Every one works for every one else. We can't do without any one . . ." Lenina remembered her first shock of fear and surprise; her speculations through half a wakeful hour; and then, under the influence of those endless repetitions, the gradual soothing of her mind, the soothing, the smoothing, the stealthy creeping of sleep. . . .

"I suppose Epsilons don't really mind being Epsilons," she said aloud.

"Of course they don't. How can they? They don't know what it's like being anything else. We'd mind, of course. But then we've been differently conditioned. Besides, we start with a different heredity."

"I'm glad I'm not an Epsilon," said Lenina, with conviction.

"And if you were an Epsilon," said Henry, "your conditioning would have made you no less thankful that you weren't a Beta or an Alpha." He put his forward propeller into gear and headed the machine towards London. Behind them, in the west, the crimson and orange were almost faded; a dark bank of cloud had crept into the zenith. As they flew over the Crematorium, the plane shot upwards on the column of hot air rising from the chimneys, only to fall as suddenly when it passed into the descending chill beyond.

"What a marvellous switchback!" Lenina laughed delightedly.

But Henry's tone was almost, for a moment, melancholy. "Do you know what that switchback was?" he said. "It was some human being finally and definitely disappearing. Going up in a squirt of hot gas. It would be curious to know who it was—a man or a woman, an Alpha or an Epsilon. . . ." He sighed. Then, in a resolutely cheerful voice, "Anyhow," he concluded, "there's one thing we can be certain of; whoever he may have been, he was happy when he was alive. Everybody's happy now."

"Yes, everybody's happy now," echoed Lenina. They had heard the words repeated a hundred and fifty times every night for twelve years.

Landing on the roof of Henry's forty-story apartment house in Westminster, they went straight down to the dining-hall. There, in a loud and cheerful company, they ate an excellent meal. *Soma* was served with the coffee. Lenina took two half-gramme tablets and Henry three. At twenty past nine they walked across the street to the newly opened Westminster Abbey Cabaret. It was a night almost without clouds, moonless and starry; but of this on the whole depressing fact Lenina and Henry were fortunately unaware. The electric sky-signs effectively shut off the outer darkness. "CALVIN STOPES AND HIS SIXTEEN SEXOPHONISTS." From the façade of the new Abbey the giant letters invitingly glared. "LONDON'S FINEST SCENT AND COLOUR ORGAN. ALL THE LATEST SYNTHETIC MUSIC."

They entered. The air seemed hot and somehow breathless with the scent of ambergris and sandalwood. On the domed ceiling of the hall, the colour organ had momentarily painted a tropical sunset. The Sixteen Sexophonists were playing an old favourite: "There ain't no Bottle in all the world like that dear little Bottle of mine." Four hundred couples were five-stepping round the polished floor. Lenina and Henry were soon the four hundred and first. The sexophones wailed like melodious cats under the moon, moaned in the alto and tenor registers as though the little death were upon them. Rich with a wealth of harmonics, their tremulous chorus mounted towards a climax, louder and ever louder—until at last, with a wave of his hand, the conductor let loose the final shattering note of ether-music and blew the sixteen merely human blowers clean out of existence. Thunder in A flat major. And then, in all but silence, in all but darkness, there followed a gradual deturgescence, a *diminuendo* sliding gradually, through quarter tones, down, down to a faintly whispered dominant chord that lingered on (while the five-four rhythms still pulsed below) charging the darkened seconds with an intense expectancy. And at last expectancy was fulfilled. There was a sudden explosive sunrise, and simultaneously, the Sixteen burst into song:

"Bottle of mine, it's you I've always wanted!
Bottle of mine, why was I ever decanted?
Skies are blue inside of you,
The weather's always fine;
For
There ain't no Bottle in all the world
Like that dear little Bottle of mine."

Five-stepping with the other four hundred round and round Westminster Abbey, Lenina and Henry were yet dancing in another world—the warm, the richly coloured, the infinitely friendly world of *soma*-holiday. How kind, how good-looking, how delightfully amusing every one was! "Bottle of mine, it's you I've always wanted . . ." But Lenina and Henry had what they wanted . . . They were inside, here and now—safely inside with the fine weather, the perennially blue sky. And when, exhausted, the Sixteen had laid by their sexophones and the Synthetic Music apparatus was producing the very latest in slow Malthusian Blues, they might have been twin embryos gently rocking together on the waves of a bottled ocean of blood-surrogate.

"Good-night, dear friends. Good-night, dear friends." The loud speakers veiled their commands in a genial and musical politeness. "Good-night, dear friends . . ."

Obediently, with all the others, Lenina and Henry left the building. The depressing stars had travelled quite some way across the heavens. But though the separating screen of the sky-signs had now to a great extent dissolved, the two young people still retained their happy ignorance of the night.

Swallowing half an hour before closing time, that second dose of *soma* had raised a quite impenetrable wall between the actual universe and their minds. Bottled, they crossed the street; bottled, they took the lift up to Henry's room on the twenty-eighth floor. And yet, bottled as she was, and in spite of that second gramme of *soma*, Lenina did not forget to take all the contraceptive precautions prescribed by the regulations. Years of intensive hypnopædia and, from twelve to seventeen, Malthusian drill three times a week had made the taking of these precautions almost as automatic and inevitable as blinking.

"Oh, and that reminds me," she said, as she came back from the bathroom, "Fanny Crowne wants to know where you found that lovely green morocco-surrogate cartridge belt you gave me."

PART 2

Alternate Thursdays were Bernard's Solidarity Service days. After an early dinner at the Aphroditæum (to which Helmholtz had recently been elected under Rule Two) he took leave of his friend and, hailing a taxi on the roof, told the man to fly to the Fordson Community Singery. The machine rose a couple of hundred metres, then headed eastwards, and as it turned, there before Bernard's eyes, gigantically beautiful, was the Singery. Flood-lighted, its three hundred and twenty metres of white Carrara-surrogate gleamed with a snowy incandescence over Ludgate Hill; at each of the four corners of its helicopter platform an immense T shone crimson against the night, and from the mouths of twenty-four vast golden trumpets rumbled a solemn synthetic music.

"Damn, I'm late," Bernard said to himself as he first caught sight of Big Henry, the Singery clock. And sure enough, as he was paying off his cab, Big Henry sounded the hour. "Ford," sang out an immense bass voice from all the golden trumpets. "Ford, Ford, Ford . . ." Nine times. Bernard ran for the lift.

The great auditorium for Ford's Day celebrations and other massed Community Sings was at the bottom of the building. Above it, a hundred to each floor, were the seven thousand rooms used by Solidarity Groups for their fortnight services. Bernard dropped down to floor thirty-three, hurried along the corridor, stood hesitating for a moment outside Room 3210, then, having wound himself up, opened the door and walked in.

Thank Ford! he was not the last. Three chairs of the twelve arranged round the circular table were still unoccupied. He slipped into the nearest of them as inconspicuously as he could and prepared to frown at the yet later comers whenever they should arrive.

Turning towards him, "What were you playing this afternoon?" the girl on his left enquired. "Obstacle, or Electro-magnetic?"

Bernard looked at her (Ford! it was Morgana Rothschild) and blushingly had to admit that he had been playing neither. Morgana stared at him with astonishment. There was an awkward silence.

Then pointedly she turned away and addressed herself to the more sporting man on her left.

"A good beginning for a Solidarity Service," thought Bernard miserably, and foresaw for himself yet another failure to achieve atonement. If only he had given himself time to look around instead of scuttling for the nearest chair! He could have sat between Fifi Bradlaugh and Joanna Diesel. Instead of which he had gone and blindly planted himself next to Morgana. *Morgana!* Ford! Those black eyebrows of hers—that eyebrow, rather—for they met above the nose. Ford! And on his right was Clara Deterding. True, Clara's eyebrows didn't meet. But she was really *too* pneumatic. Whereas Fifi and Joanna were absolutely right. Plump, blonde, not too large . . . And it was that great lout, Tom Kawaguchi, who now took the seat between them.

The last arrival was Sarojini Engels.

"You're late," said the President of the Group severely. "Don't let it happen again."

Sarojini apologized and slid into her place between Jim Bokanovsky and Herbert Bakunin. The group was now complete, the solidarity circle perfect and without flaw. Man, woman, man, in a ring of endless alternation round the table. Twelve of them ready to be made one, waiting to come together, to be fused, to lose their twelve separate identities in a larger being.

The President stood up, made the sign of the T and, switching on the synthetic music, let loose the soft indefatigable beating of drums and a choir of instruments—near-wind and super-string—that plangently repeated and repeated the brief and unescapably haunting melody of the first Solidarity Hymn. Again, again—and it was not the ear that heard the pulsing rhythm, it was the midriff; the wail and clang of those recurring harmonies haunted, not the mind, but the yearning bowels of compassion.

The President made another sign of the T and sat down. The service had begun. The dedicated *soma* tablets were placed in the centre of the table. The loving cup of strawberry ice-cream *soma* was passed from hand to hand and, with the formula, "I drink to my annihilation," twelve times quaffed. Then to the accompaniment of the synthetic orchestra the First Solidarity Hymn was sung.

"Ford, we are twelve; oh, make us one,
Like drops within the Social River;
Oh, make us now together run
As swiftly as thy shining Flivver."

Twelve yearning stanzas. And then the loving cup was passed a second time. "I drink to the Greater Being" was now the formula. All drank. Tirelessly the music played. The drums beat. The crying and clashing of the harmonies were an obsession in the melted bowels. The Second Solidarity Hymn was sung.

"Come, Greater Being, Social Friend,
Annihilating Twelve-in-One!
We long to die, for when we end,
Our larger life has but begun."

Again twelve stanzas. By this time the soma had begun to work. Eyes shone, cheeks were flushed, the inner light of universal benevolence broke out on every face in happy, friendly smiles. Even Bernard felt himself a little melted. When Morgana Rothschild turned and beamed at him, he did his best to beam back. But the eyebrow, that black two-in-one—alas, it was still there; he couldn't ignore it, couldn't, however hard he tried. The melting hadn't gone far enough. Perhaps if he had been sitting between Fifi and Joanna . . . For the third time the loving cup went round. "I drink to the imminence of His Coming," said Morgana Rothschild, whose turn it happened to be to initiate the circular rite. Her tone was loud, exultant. She drank and passed the cup to Bernard. "I drink to the imminence of His Coming," he repeated, with a sincere attempt to feel that the coming was imminent; but the eyebrow continued to haunt him, and the Coming, so far as he was concerned, was horribly remote. He drank and handed the cup to Clara Deterding. "It'll be a failure again," he said to himself. "I know it will." But he went on doing his best to beam.

The loving cup had made its circuit. Lifting his hand, the President gave a signal; the chorus broke out into the third Solidarity Hymn.

"Feel how the Greater Being comes!
Rejoice and, in rejoicings, die!
Melt in the music of the drums!
For I am you and you are I."

As verse succeeded verse the voices thrilled with an ever intenser excitement. The sense of the Coming's imminence was like an electric tension in the air. The President switched off the music and, with the final note of the final stanza, there was absolute silence—the silence of stretched expectancy, quivering and creeping with a galvanic life. The President reached out his hand; and suddenly a Voice, a deep strong Voice, more musical than any merely human voice, richer, warmer, more vibrant with love and yearning and compassion, a wonderful, mysterious, supernatural Voice spoke from above their heads. Very slowly, "Oh, Ford, Ford, Ford," it said diminishingly and on a descending scale. A sensation of warmth radiated thrillingly out from the solar plexus to every extremity of the bodies of those who listened; tears came into their eyes; their hearts, their bowels seemed to move within them, as though with an independent life. "Ford!" they were melting, "Ford!" dissolved, dissolved. Then, in another tone, suddenly, startlingly. "Listen!" trumpeted the voice. "Listen!" They listened. After a pause, sunk to a whisper, but a whisper, somehow, more penetrating than the loudest cry. "The feet of the Greater Being," it went on, and repeated the words: "The feet of the Greater Being." The whisper almost expired. "The feet of the Greater Being are on the stairs." And once more there was silence; and the expectancy, momentarily relaxed, was stretched again, tauter, tauter, almost to the tearing point. The feet of the Greater Being—oh, they heard them, they heard them, coming softly down the stairs, coming nearer and nearer down the invisible stairs. The feet of the Greater Being. And suddenly the tearing point was reached. Her eyes staring, her lips parted. Morgana Rothschild sprang to her feet.

"I hear him," she cried. "I hear him."

"He's coming," shouted Sarojini Engels.

"Yes, he's coming, I hear him." Fifi Bradlaugh and Tom Kawaguchi rose simultaneously to their feet.

"Oh, oh, oh!" Joanna inarticulately testified.

"He's coming!" yelled Jim Bokanovsky.

The President leaned foward and, with a touch, released a delirium of cymbals and blown brass, a fever of tom-tomming.

"Oh, he's coming!" screamed Clara Deterding. "Aie!" and it was as though she were having her throat cut.

Feeling that it was time for him to do something, Bernard also jumped up and shouted: "I hear him; He's coming." But it wasn't true. He heard nothing and, for him, nobody was coming. Nobody—

in spite of the music, in spite of the mounting excitement. But he waved his arms, he shouted with the best of them; and when the others began to jig and stamp and shuffle, he also jigged and shuffled.

Round they went, a circular procession of dancers, each with hands on the hips of the dancer preceding, round and round, shouting in unison, stamping to the rhythm of the music with their feet, beating it, beating it out with hands on the buttocks in front; twelve pairs of hands beating as one; as one, twelve buttocks slabbily resounding. Twelve as one, twelve as one. "I hear Him, I hear Him coming." The music quickened; faster beat the feet, faster, faster fell the rhythmic hands. And all at once a great synthetic bass boomed out the words which announced the approaching atonement and final consummation of solidarity, the coming of the Twelve-in-One, the incarnation of the Greater Being. "Orgy-porgy," it sang, while the tom-toms continued to beat their feverish tattoo:

"Orgy-porgy, Ford and fun,
Kiss the girls and make them One.
Boys at one with girls at peace;
Orgy-porgy gives release."

"Orgy-porgy," the dancers caught up the liturgical refrain, "Orgy-porgy, Ford and fun, kiss the girls . . ." And as they sang, the lights began slowly to fade—to fade and at the same time to grow warmer, richer, redder, until at last they were dancing in the crimson twilight of an Embryo Store. "Orgy-porgy . . ." In their blood-coloured and foetal darkness the dancers continued for a while to circulate, to beat and beat out the indefatigable rhythm. "Orgy-porgy . . ." Then the circle wavered, broke, fell in partial disintegration on the ring of couches which surrounded—circle enclosing circle—the table and its planetary chairs. "Orgy-porgy . . ." Tenderly the deep Voice crooned and cooed; in the red twilight it was as though some enormous negro dove were hovering benevolently over the now prone or supine dancers.

* * *

They were standing on the roof; Big Henry had just sung eleven. The night was calm and warm.

"Wasn't it wonderful?" said Fifi Bradlaugh. "Wasn't it simply wonderful?" She looked at Bernard with an expression of rapture, but of rapture in which there was no trace of agitation or excitement—for to be excited is still to be unsatisfied. Hers was the calm ecstasy of achieved consummation, the peace, not of mere vacant satiety and nothingness, but of balanced life, of energies at rest and in equilibrium. A rich and living peace. For the Solidarity Service had given as well as taken, drawn off only to replenish. She was full, she was made perfect, she was still more than merely herself. "Didn't you think it was wonderful?" she insisted, looking into Bernard's face with those supernaturally shining eyes.

"Yes, I thought it was wonderful," he lied and looked away; the sight of her transfigured face was at once an accusation and an ironical reminder of his own separateness. He was as miserably isolated now as he had been when the service began—more isolated by reason of his unreplenished emptiness, his dead satiety. Separate and unatoned, while the others were being fused into the Greater Being; alone even in Morgana's embrace—much more alone, indeed, more hopelessly himself than he had ever been in his life before. He had emerged from that crimson twilight into the common electric glare with a self-consciousness intensified to the pitch of agony. He was utterly miserable, and perhaps (her shining eyes accused him), perhaps it was his own fault. "Quite wonderful," he repeated; but the only thing he could think of was Morgana's eyebrow.

6

PART 1

Odd, odd, *odd*, was Lenina's verdict on Bernard Marx. So odd, indeed, that in the course of the succeeding weeks she had wondered more than once whether she shouldn't change her mind about the New Mexico holiday, and go instead to the North Pole with Benito Hoover. The trouble was that she knew the North Pole, had been there with George Edzel only last summer, and what was more, found it pretty grim. Nothing to do, and the hotel too hopelessly old-fashioned—no television laid on in the bedrooms, no scent organ, only the most putrid synthetic music, and not more than twenty-five Escalator-Squash Courts for over two hundred guests. No, decidedly she couldn't face the North Pole again. Added to which, she had only been to America once before. And even then, how inadequately! A cheap week-end in New York—had it been with Jean-Jacques Habibullah or Bokanovsky Jones? She couldn't remember. Anyhow, it was of absolutely no importance. The prospect of flying West again, and for a whole week, was very inviting. Moreover, for at least three days of that week they would be in the Savage Reservation. Not more than half a dozen people in the whole Centre had ever been inside a Savage Reservation. As an Alpha-Plus psychologist, Bernard was one of the few men she knew entitled to a permit. For Lenina, the opportunity was unique. And yet, so unique also was Bernard's oddness that she had hesitated to take it, had actually thought of risking the Pole again with funny old Benito. At least Benito was normal. Whereas Bernard . . .

"Alcohol in his blood-surrogate," was Fanny's explanation of every eccentricity. But Henry, with whom, one evening when they were in bed together, Lenina had rather anxiously discussed her new lover, Henry had compared poor Bernard to a rhinoceros.

"You can't teach a rhinoceros tricks," he had explained in his brief and vigorous style. "Some men are almost rhinoceroses; they don't respond properly to conditioning. Poor Devils! Bernard's one of them. Luckily for him, he's pretty good at his job. Otherwise the Director would never have kept him. However," he added consolingly, "I think he's pretty harmless."

Pretty harmless, perhaps; but also pretty disquieting. That mania, to start with, for doing things in private. Which meant, in practice, not doing anything at all. For what was there that one *could* do in private. (Apart, of course, from going to bed: but one couldn't do that all the time.) Yes, what *was* there? Precious little. The first afternoon they went out together was particularly fine. Lenina had suggested a swim at Toquay Country Club followed by dinner at the Oxford Union. But Bernard thought there would be too much of a crowd. Then what about a round of Electro-magnetic Golf at St. Andrew's? But again, no: Bernard considered that Electro-magnetic Golf was a waste of time.

"Then what's time for?" asked Lenina in some astonishment.

Apparently, for going on walks in the Lake District; for that was what he now proposed. Land on the top of Skiddaw and walk for a couple of hours in the heather. "Alone with you, Lenina."

"But, Bernard, we shall be alone all night."

Bernard blushed and looked away. "I meant, alone for talking," he mumbled.

"Talking? But what about?" Walking and talking—that seemed a very odd way of spending an afternoon.

In the end she persuaded him, much against his will, to fly over to Amsterdam to see the Semi-Demi-Finals of the Women's Heavyweight Wrestling Championship.

"In a crowd," he grumbled. "As usual." He remained obstinately gloomy the whole afternoon; wouldn't talk to Lenina's friends (of whom they met dozens in the ice-cream *soma* bar between the wrestling bouts); and in spite of his misery absolutely refused to take the half-gramme raspberry sundae which she pressed upon him. "I'd rather be myself," he said. "Myself and nasty. Not somebody else, however jolly."

"A gramme in time saves nine," said Lenina, producing a bright treasure of sleep-taught wisdom.

Bernard pushed away the proffered glass impatiently.

"Now, don't lose your temper," she said. "Remember one cubic centimetre cures ten gloomy sentiments."

"Oh, for Ford's sake, be quiet!" he shouted.

Lenina shrugged her shoulders. "A gramme is always better than a damn," she concluded with dignity, and drank the sundae herself.

On their way back across the Channel, Bernard insisted on stopping his propeller and hovering on his helicopter screws within a hundred feet of the waves. The weather had taken a change for the worse; a south-westerly wind had sprung up, the sky was cloudy.

"Look," he commanded.

"But it's horrible," said Lenina, shrinking back from the window. She was appalled by the rushing emptiness of the night, by the black foam-flecked water heaving beneath them, by the pale face of the moon, so haggard and distracted among the hastening clouds. "Let's turn on the radio. Quick!" She reached for the dialling knob on the dashboard and turned it at random.

". . . skies are blue inside of you," sang sixteen tremoloing falsettos, "the weather's always . . ."

Then a hiccough and silence. Bernard had switched off the current.

"I want to look at the sea in peace," he said. "One can't even look with that beastly noise going on."

"But it's lovely. And I don't want to look."

"But I do," he insisted. "It makes me feel as though . . ." he hesitated, searching for words with which to express himself, "as though I were more *me*, if you see what I mean. More on my own, not so completely a part of something else. Not just a cell in the social body. Doesn't it make you feel like that, Lenina?"

But Lenina was crying. "It's horrible, it's horrible," she kept repeating. "And how can you talk like that about not wanting to be a part of the social body? After all, every one works for every one else. We can't do without any one. Even Epsilons . . ."

"Yes, I know," said Bernard derisively. " 'Even Epsilons are useful'! So am I. And I damned well wish I weren't!"

Lenina was shocked by his blasphemy. "Bernard!" She protested in a voice of amazed distress. "How can you?"

In a different key, "How can I?" he repeated meditatively. "No, the real problem is: How is it that I can't, or rather—because, after all, I know quite well why I can't—what would it be like if I could, if I were free—not enslaved by my conditioning."

"But, Bernard, you're saying the most awful things."

"Don't you wish you were free, Lenina?"

"I don't know what you mean. I am free. Free to have the most wonderful time. Everybody's happy nowadays."

He laughed, "Yes, 'Everybody's happy nowadays.' We begin giving the children that at five. But wouldn't you like to be free to be happy in some other way, Lenina? In your own way, for example; not in everybody else's way."

"I don't know what you mean," she repeated. Then, turning to him, "Oh, do let's go back, Bernard," she besought; "I do so hate it here."

"Don't you like being with me?"

"But of course, Bernard. It's this horrible place."

"I thought we'd be more . . . more *together* here—with nothing but the sea and moon. More together than in that crowd, or even in my rooms. Don't you understand that?"

"I don't understand anything," she said with decision, determined to preserve her incomprehension intact. "Nothing. Least of all," she continued in another tone, "why you don't take *soma* when you have these dreadful ideas of yours. You'd forget all about them. And instead of feeling miserable, you'd be jolly. *So* jolly," she repeated and smiled, for all the puzzled anxiety in her eyes, with what was meant to be an inviting and voluptuous cajolery.

He looked at her in silence, his face unresponsive and very grave—looked at her intently. After a few seconds Lenina's eyes flinched away; she uttered a nervous little laugh, tried to think of something to say and couldn't. The silence prolonged itself.

When Bernard spoke at last, it was in a small tired voice. "All right then," he said, "we'll go back." And stepping hard on the accelerator, he sent the machine rocketing up into the sky. At four thousand he started his propeller. They flew in silence for a minute or two. Then, suddenly, Bernard began to laugh. Rather oddly, Lenina thought; but still, it was laughter.

"Feeling better?" she ventured to ask.

For answer, he lifted one hand from the controls and, slipping his arm around her, began to fondle her breasts.

"Thank Ford," she said to herself, "he's all right again."

Half an hour later they were back in his rooms. Bernard swallowed four tablets of *soma* at a gulp, turned on the radio and television and began to undress.

"Well," Lenina enquired, with significant archness when they met next afternoon on the roof, "did you think it was fun yesterday?"

Bernard nodded. They climbed into the plane. A little jolt, and they were off.

"Every one says I'm awfully pneumatic," said Lenina reflectively, patting her own legs.

"Awfully." But there was an expression of pain in Bernard's eyes. "Like meat," he was thinking.

She looked up with a certain anxiety. "But you don't think I'm *too* plump, do you?"

He shook his head. Like so much meat.

"You think I'm all right." Another nod. "In every way?"

"Perfect," he said aloud. And inwardly. "She thinks of herself that way. She doesn't mind being meat."

Lenina smiled triumphantly. But her satisfaction was premature.

"All the same," he went on, after a little pause, "I still rather wish it had all ended differently."

"Differently?" Were there other endings?

"I didn't want it to end with our going to bed," he specified.

Lenina was astonished.

"Not at once, not the first day."

"But then what . . . ?"

He began to talk a lot of incomprehensible and dangerous nonsense. Lenina did her best to stop the ears of her mind; but every now and then a phrase would insist on becoming audible. ". . . to try the effect of arresting my impulses," she heard him say. The words seemed to touch a spring in her mind.

"Never put off till to-morrow the fun you can have today," she said gravely.

"Two hundred repetitions, twice a week from fourteen to sixteen and a half," was all his comment. The mad bad talk rambled on. "I want to know what passion is," she heard him saying. "I want to feel something strongly."

"When the individual feels, the community reels," Lenina pronounced.

"Well, why shouldn't it reel a bit?"

"Bernard!"

But Bernard remained unabashed.

"Adults intellectually and during working hours," he went on. "Infants where feeling and desire are concerned."

"Our Ford loved infants."

Ignoring the interruption. "It suddenly struck me the other day," continued Bernard, "that it might be possible to be an adult all the time."

"I don't understand." Lenina's tone was firm.

"I know you don't. And that's why we went to bed together yesterday—like infants—instead of being adults and waiting."

"But it was fun," Lenina insisted. "Wasn't it?"

"Oh, the greatest fun," he answered, but in a voice so mournful, with an expression so profoundly miserable, that Lenina felt all her triumph suddenly evaporate. Perhaps he had found her too plump, after all.

"I told you so," was all that Fanny said, when Lenina came and made her confidences. "It's the alcohol they put in his surrogate."

"All the same," Lenina insisted. "I do like him. He has such awfully nice hands. And the way he moves his shoulders—that's very attractive." She sighed. "But I wish he weren't so odd."

PART 2

Halting for a moment outside the door of the Director's room, Bernard drew a deep breath and squared his shoulders, bracing himself to meet the dislike and disapproval which he was certain of finding within. He knocked and entered.

"A permit for you to initial, Director," he said as airily as possible, and laid the paper on the writing-table.

The Director glanced at him sourly. But the stamp of the World Controller's Office was at the head of the paper and the signature of Mustapha Mond, bold and black, across the bottom. Everything was perfectly in order. The Director had no choice. He pencilled his initials—two small pale letters abject at the feet of Mustapha Mond—

and was about to return the paper without a word of comment or genial Ford-speed, when his eye was caught by something written in the body of the permit.

"For the New Mexican Reservation?" he said, and his tone, the face he lifted to Bernard, expressed a kind of agitated astonishment.

Surprised by his surprise, Bernard nodded. There was a silence.

The Director leaned back in his chair, frowning. "How long ago was it?" he said, speaking more to himself than to Bernard. "Twenty years, I suppose. Nearer twenty-five. I must have been your age . . ." He sighed and shook his head.

Bernard felt extremely uncomfortable. A man so conventional, so scrupulously correct as the Director—and to commit so gross a solecism! It made him want to hide his face, to run out of the room. Not that he himself saw anything intrinsically objectionable in people talking about the remote past; that was one of those hypnopædic prejudices he had (so he imagined) completely got rid of. What made him feel shy was the knowledge that the Director disapproved—disapproved and yet had been betrayed into doing the forbidden thing. Under what inward compulsion? Through his discomfort Bernard eagerly listened.

"I had the same idea as you," the Director was saying. "Wanted to have a look at the savages. Got a permit for New Mexico and went there for my summer holiday. With the girl I was having at the moment. She was a Beta-Minus, and I think" (he shut his eyes), "I think she had yellow hair. Anyhow she was pneumatic, particularly pneumatic; I remember that. Well, we went there, and we looked at the savages, and we rode about on horses and all that. And then—it was almost the last day of my leave—then . . . well, she got lost. We'd gone riding up one of those revolting mountains, and it was horribly hot and oppressive, and after lunch we went to sleep. Or at least I did. She must have gone for a walk, alone. At any rate, when I woke up, she wasn't there. And the most frightful thunderstorm I've ever seen was just bursting on us. And it poured and roared and flashed; and the horses broke loose and ran away; and I fell down, trying to catch them, and hurt my knee, so that I could hardly walk. Still, I searched and I shouted and I searched. But there was no sign of her. Then I thought she must have gone back to the rest-house by herself. So I crawled down into the valley by the way we had come. My knee was agonizingly painful, and I'd lost my *soma*. It took me hours. I didn't get back to the rest-house till after midnight. And she wasn't there; she wasn't there," the Director repeated. There was a silence. "Well," he resumed at last, "the next day there was a search. But we couldn't find her. She must have fallen into a gully somewhere; or been eaten by a mountain lion. Ford knows. Anyhow it was horrible. It upset me very much at the time. More than it ought to have done, I dare say. Because, after all, it's the sort of accident that might have happened to any one; and, of course, the social body persists although the component cells may change." But this sleep-taught consolation did not seem to be very effective. Shaking his head, "I actually dream about it sometimes," the Director went on in a low voice. "Dream of being woken up by that peal of thunder and finding her gone; dream of searching and searching for her under the trees." He lapsed into the silence of reminiscence.

"You must have had a terrible shock," said Bernard, almost enviously.

At the sound of his voice the Director started into a guilty realization of where he was; shot a glance at Bernard, and averting his eyes, blushed darkly; looked at him again with sudden suspicion and, angrily on his dignity, "Don't imagine," he said, "that I'd had any indecorous relation with the girl. Nothing emotional, nothing longdrawn. It was all perfectly healthy and normal." He handed Bernard the permit. "I really don't know why I bored you with this trivial anecdote." Furious with himself for having given away a discreditable secret, he vented his rage on Bernard. The look in his eyes was now frankly malignant. "And I should like to take this opportunity, Mr. Marx," he went on, "of saying that I'm not at all pleased with the reports I receive of your behaviour outside working hours. You may say that this is not my business. But it is. I have the good name of the Centre to think of. My workers must be above suspicion, particularly those of the highest castes. Alphas are so conditioned that they do not *have* to be infantile in their emotional behaviour. But that is all the more reason for their making a special effort to conform. It is their duty to be infantile, even against their inclination. And so, Mr. Marx, I give you fair warning." The Director's voice vibrated with an indignation that had now become wholly righteous and impersonal—was the expression of the disapproval of Society itself. "If ever I hear again of any lapse from a proper standard of infantile decorum, I shall ask for your transference to a Sub-Centre—preferably to Iceland. Good morning." And swivelling round in his chair, he picked up his pen and began to write.

"That'll teach him," he said to himself. But he was mistaken. For Bernard left the room with a swagger, exulting, as he banged the door behind him, in the thought that he stood alone, embattled against the order of things; elated by the intoxicating consciousness of his individual significance and importance. Even the thought of persecution left him undismayed, was rather tonic than depressing. He felt strong enough to meet and overcome affliction, strong enough to face even Iceland. And this confidence was the greater for his not for a moment really believing that he would be called upon to face anything at all. People simply weren't transferred for things like that. Iceland was just a threat. A most stimulating and life-giving threat. Walking along the corridor, he actually whistled.

Heroic was the account he gave that evening of his interview with the D.H.C. "Whereupon," it concluded, "I simply told him to go to the Bottomless Past and marched out of the room. And that was that." He looked at Helmholtz Watson expectantly, awaiting his due reward of sympathy, encouragement, admiration. But no word came. Helmholtz sat silent, staring at the floor.

He liked Bernard; he was grateful to him for being the only man of his acquaintance with whom he could talk about the subjects he felt to be important. Nevertheless, there were things in

Bernard which he hated. This boasting, for example. And the outbursts of an abject self-pity with which it alternated. And his deplorable habit of being bold after the event, and full, in absence, of the most extraordinary presence of mind. He hated these things—just because he liked Bernard. The seconds passed. Helmholtz continued to stare at the floor. And suddenly Bernard blushed and turned away.

PART 3

The journey was quite uneventful. The Blue Pacific Rocket was two and a half minutes early at New Orleans, lost four minutes in a tornado over Texas, but flew into a favourable air current at Longitude 95 West, and was able to land at Santa Fé less than forty seconds behind schedule time.

"Forty seconds on a six and a half hour flight. Not so bad," Lenina conceded.

They slept that night at Santa Fé. The hotel was excellent—incomparably better, for example, than that horrible Aurora Bora Palace in which Lenina had suffered so much the previous summer. Liquid air, television, vibro-vacuum massage, radio, boiling caffeine solution, hot contraceptives, and eight different kinds of scent were laid on in every bedroom. The synthetic music plant was working as they entered the hall and left nothing to be desired. A notice in the lift announced that there were sixty Escalator-Squash Racket Courts in the hotel, and that Obstacle and Electro-magnetic Golf could both be played in the park.

"But it sounds simply too lovely," cried Lenina. "I almost wish we could stay here. Sixty Escalator-Squash Courts . . ."

"There won't be any in the Reservation," Bernard warned her. "And no scent, no television, no hot water even. If you feel you can't stand it, stay here till I come back."

Lenina was quite offended. "Of course I can stand it. I only said it was lovely here because . . . well, because progress *is* lovely, isn't it?"

"Five hundred repetitions once a week from thirteen to seventeen," said Bernard wearily, as though to himself.

"What did you say?"

"I said that progress was lovely. That's why you mustn't come to the Reservation unless you really want to."

"But I do want to."

"Very well, then," said Bernard; and it was almost a threat.

Their permit required the signature of the Warden of the Reservation, at whose office next morning they duly presented themselves. An Epsilon-Plus negro porter took in Bernard's card, and they were admitted almost immediately.

The Warden was a blond and brachycephalic Alpha-Minus, short, red, moon-faced, and broad-shouldered, with a loud booming voice, very well adapted to the utterance of hypnopædic wisdom. He was a mine of irrelevant information and unasked-for good advice. Once started, he went on and on—boomingly.

". . . five hundred and sixty thousand square kilometers, divided into four distinct Sub-Reservations, each surrounded by a high-tension wire fence."

At this moment, and for no apparent reason, Bernard suddenly remembered that he had left the Eau-de-Cologne tap in his bathroom wide open and running.

". . . supplied with current from the Grand Canyon hydroelectric station."

"Cost me a fortune by the time I get back." With his mind's eye, Bernard saw the needle on the scent meter creeping round and round, antlike, indefatigable. "Quickly telephone to Helmholtz Watson."

". . . upwards of five thousand kilometres of fencing at sixty thousand volts."

"You don't say so," said Lenina politely, not knowing in the least what the Warden had said, but taking her cue from his dramatic pause. When the Warden started booming, she had inconspicuously swallowed half a gramme of *soma*, with the result that she could now sit, serenely not listening, thinking of nothing at all, but with her large blue eyes fixed on the Warden's face in an expression of rapt attention.

"To touch the fence is instant death," pronounced the Warden solemnly. "There is no escape from a Savage Reservation."

The word "escape" was suggestive. "Perhaps," said Bernard, half rising, "we ought to think of going." The little black needle was scurrying, an insect, nibbling through time, eating into his money.

"No escape," repeated the Warden, waving him back into his chair; and as the permit was not yet countersigned, Bernard had no choice but to obey. "Those who are born in the Reservation—and remember, my dear young lady," he added, leering obscenely at Lenina, and speaking in an improper whisper, "remember that, in the Reservation, children still *are* born, yes, actually born, revolting as that may seem . . ." (He hoped that this reference to a shameful subject would make Lenina blush; but she only smiled with simulated intelligence and said, "You don't say so!" Disappointed, the Warden began again.) "Those, I repeat, who are born in the Reservation are destined to die there."

Destined to die . . . A decilitre of Eau de Cologne every minute. Six litres an hour. "Perhaps," Bernard tried again, "we ought . . ."

Leaning forward, the Warden tapped the table with his forefinger. "You ask me how many people live in the Reservation. And I reply"—triumphantly—"I reply that we do not know. We can only guess."

"You don't say so."

"My dear young lady, I do say so."

Six times twenty-four—no, it would be nearer six times thirty-six. Bernard was pale and trembling with impatience. But inexorably the booming continued.

". . . about sixty thousand Indians and half-breeds . . . absolute savages . . . our inspectors occasionally visit . . . otherwise, no communication whatever with the civilized world . . . still preserve their repulsive habits and customs . . . marriage, if you know what that is, my dear young lady; families . . . no conditioning . . . monstrous superstitions . . . Christianity and totemism and ancestor worship . . . extinct languages, such as Zuñi and Spanish and Athapascan . . . pumas, porcupines and other ferocious animals . . . infectious diseases . . . priests . . . venomous lizards . . ."

"You don't say so?"

They got away at last. Bernard dashed to the telephone. Quick, quick; but it took him nearly three minutes to get on to Helmholtz Watson. "We might be among the savages already," he complained. "Damned incompetence!"

"Have a gramme," suggested Lenina.

He refused, preferring his anger. And at last, thank Ford, he was through and, yes, it was Helmholtz; Helmholtz, to whom he explained what had happened, and who promised to go round at once, at once, and turn off the tap, yes, at once, but took this opportunity to tell him what the D.H.C. had said, in public, yesterday evening . . .

"What? He's looking out for some one to take my place?" Bernard's voice was agonized. "So it's actually decided? Did he mention Iceland? You say he did? Ford! Iceland . . ." He hung up the receiver and turned back to Lenina. His face was pale, his expression utterly dejected.

"What's the matter?" she asked.

"The matter?" He dropped heavily into a chair. "I'm going to be sent to Iceland."

Often in the past he had wondered what it would be like to be subjected (*soma*-less and with nothing but his own inward resources to rely on) to some great trial, some pain, some persecution; he had even longed for affliction. As recently as a week ago, in the Director's office, he had imagined himself courageously resisting, stoically accepting suffering without a word. The Director's threats had actually elated him, made him feel larger than life. But that, as he now realized, was because he had not taken the threats quite seriously; he had not believed that, when it came to the point, the D.H.C. would ever do anything. Now that it looked as though the threats were really to be fulfilled, Bernard was appalled. Of that imagined stoicism, that theoretical courage, not a trace was left.

He raged against himself—what a fool!—against the Director—how unfair not to give him that other chance, that other chance which, he now had no doubt at all, he had always intended to take. And Iceland, Iceland . . .

Lenina shook her head. "Was and will make me ill," she quoted, "I take a gramme and only am."

In the end she persuaded him to swallow four tablets of *soma*. Five minutes later roots and fruits were abolished; the flower of the present rosily blossomed. A message from the porter announced that, at the Warden's orders, a Reservation Guard had come round with a plane and was waiting on the roof of the hotel. They went up at once. An octoroon in Gamma-green uniform saluted and proceeded to recite the morning's programme.

A bird's-eye view of ten or a dozen of the principal pueblos, then a landing for lunch in the valley of Malpais. The rest-house was comfortable there, and up at the pueblo the savages would probably be celebrating their summer festival. It would be the best place to spend the night.

They took their seats in the plane and set off. Ten minutes later they were crossing the frontier that separated civilization from savagery. Uphill and down, across the deserts of salt or sand, through forests, into the violet depth of canyons, over crag and peak and table-topped mesa, the fence marched on and on, irresistibly the straight line, the geometrical symbol of triumphant human purpose. And at its foot, here and there, a mosaic of white bones, a still unrotted carcase dark on the tawny ground marked the place where deer or steer, puma or porcupine or coyote, or the greedy turkey buzzards drawn down by the whiff of carrion and fulminated as though by a poetic justice, had come too close to the destroying wires.

"They never learn," said the green-uniformed pilot, pointing down at the skeletons on the ground below them. "And they never will learn," he added and laughed, as though he had somehow scored a personal triumph over the electrocuted animals.

Bernard also laughed; after two grammes of *soma* the joke seemed, for some reason, good. Laughed and then, almost immediately, dropped off to sleep, and sleeping was carried over Taos and Tesuque; over Nambe and Picuris and Pojoaque, over Sia and Cochiti, over Laguna and Acoma and the Enchanted Mesa, over Zuñi and Cibola and Ojo Caliente, and woke at last to find the machine standing on the ground, Lenina carrying the suit-cases into a small square house, and the Gamma-green octoroon talking incomprehensibly with a young Indian.

"Malpais," explained the pilot, as Bernard stepped out. "This is the rest-house. And there's a dance this afternoon at the pueblo. He'll take you there." He pointed to the sullen young savage. "Funny, I expect." He grinned. "Everything they do is funny." And with that he climbed into the plane and started up the engines. "Back to-morrow. And remember," he added reassuringly to Lenina, "they're perfectly tame; savages won't do you any harm. They've got enough experience of gas bombs to know that they mustn't play any tricks." Still laughing, he threw the helicopter screws into gear, accelerated, and was gone.

7

The mesa was like a ship becalmed in a strait of lion-coloured dust. The channel wound between precipitous banks, and slanting from one wall to the other across the valley ran a streak of green—the river and its fields. On the prow of that stone ship in the centre of the strait, and seemingly a part of it, a shaped and geometrical outcrop of the naked rock, stood the pueblo of Malpais. Block above block, each story smaller than the one below, the tall houses rose like stepped and amputated pyramids into the blue sky. At their feet lay a straggle of low buildings, a criss-cross of walls; and on three sides the precipices fell sheer into the plain. A few columns of smoke mounted perpendicularly into the windless air and were lost.

"Queer," said Lenina. "Very queer." It was her ordinary word of condemnation. "I don't like it. And I don't like that man." She pointed to the Indian guide who had been appointed to take them up to the pueblo. Her feeling was evidently reciprocated; the very back of the man, as he walked along before them, was hostile, sullenly contemptuous.

"Besides," she lowered her voice, "he smells."

Bernard did not attempt to deny it. They walked on.

Suddenly it was as though the whole air had come alive and were pulsing, pulsing with the indefatigable movement of blood. Up there, in Malpais, the drums were being beaten. Their feet fell in with the rhythm of that mysterious heart; they quickened their pace. Their path led them to the foot of the precipice. The sides of the great mesa ship towered over them, three hundred feet to the gunwale.

"I wish we could have brought the plane," said Lenina, looking up resentfully at the blank impending rock-face. "I hate walking. And you feel so small when you're on the ground at the bottom of a hill."

They walked along for some way in the shadow of the mesa, rounded a projection, and there, in a water-worn ravine, was the way up the companion ladder. They climbed. It was a very steep path that zigzagged from side to side of the gully. Sometimes the pulsing of the drums was all but inaudible, at others they seemed to be beating only just round the corner.

When they were half-way up, an eagle flew past so close to them that the wind of his wings blew chill on their faces. In a crevice of the rock lay a pile of bones. It was all oppressively queer, and the Indian smelt stronger and stronger. They emerged at last from the ravine into the full sunlight. The top of the mesa was a flat deck of stone.

"Like the Charing-T Tower," was Lenina's comment. But she was not allowed to enjoy her discovery of this reassuring resemblance for long. A padding of soft feet made them turn round. Naked from throat to navel, their dark brown bodies painted with white lines ("like asphalt tennis courts," Lenina was later to explain), their faces inhuman with daubings of scarlet, black and ochre, two Indians came running along the path. Their black hair was braided with fox fur and red flannel. Cloaks of turkey feathers fluttered from their shoulders; huge feather diadems exploded gaudily round their heads. With every step they took came the clink and rattle of their silver bracelets, their heavy necklaces of bone and turquoise beads. They came on without a word, running quietly in their deerskin moccasins. One of them was holding a feather brush;

the other carried, in either hand, what looked at a distance like three or four pieces of thick rope. One of the ropes writhed uneasily, and suddenly Lenina saw that they were snakes.

The men came nearer and nearer; their dark eyes looked at her, but without giving any sign of recognition, any smallest sign that they had seen her or were aware of her existence. The writhing snake hung limp again with the rest. The men passed.

"I don't like it," said Lenina. "I don't like it."

She liked even less what awaited her at the entrance to the pueblo, where their guide had left them while he went inside for instructions. The dirt, to start with, the piles of rubbish, the dust, the dogs, the flies. Her face wrinkled up into a grimace of disgust. She held her handkerchief to her nose.

"But how can they live like this?" she broke out in a voice of indignant incredulity. (It wasn't possible.)

Bernard shrugged his shoulders philosophically. "Anyhow," he said, "they've been doing it for the last five or six thousand years. So I suppose they must be used to it by now."

"But cleanliness is next to fordliness," she insisted.

"Yes, and civilization is sterilization," Bernard went on, concluding on a tone of irony the second hypnopædic lesson in elementary hygiene. "But these people have never heard of Our Ford, and they aren't civilized. So there's no point in . . ."

"Oh!" She gripped his arm. "Look."

An almost naked Indian was very slowly climbing down the ladder from the first-floor terrace of a neighboring house—rung after rung, with the tremulous caution of extreme old age. His face was profoundly wrinkled and black, like a mask of obsidian. The toothless mouth had fallen in. At the corners of the lips, and on each side of the chin, a few long bristles gleamed almost white against the dark skin. The long unbraided hair hung down in grey wisps round his face. His body was bent and emaciated to the bone, almost fleshless. Very slowly he came down, pausing at each rung before he ventured another step.

"What's the matter with him?" whispered Lenina. Her eyes were wide with horror and amazement.

"He's old, that's all," Bernard answered as carelessly as he could. He too was startled; but he made an effort to seem unmoved.

"Old?" she repeated. "But the Director's old; lots of people are old; they're not like that."

"That's because we don't allow them to be like that. We preserve them from diseases. We keep their internal secretions artificially balanced at a youthful equilibrium. We don't permit their magnesium-calcium ratio to fall below what it was at thirty. We give them transfusions of young blood. We keep their metabolism permanently stimulated. So, of course, they don't look like that. Partly," he added, "because most of them die long before they reach this old creature's age. Youth almost unimpaired till sixty, and then, crack! the end."

But Lenina was not listening. She was watching the old man. Slowly, slowly he came down. His feet touched the ground. He turned. In their deep-sunken orbits his eyes were still extraordinarily bright. They looked at her for a long moment expressionlessly, without surprise, as though she had not been there at all. Then slowly, with bent back, the old man hobbled past them and was gone.

"But it's terrible," Lenina whispered. "It's awful. We ought not to have come here." She felt in her pocket for her *soma*—only to discover that, by some unprecedented oversight, she had left the bottle down at the rest-house. Bernard's pockets were also empty.

Lenina was left to face the horrors of Malpais unaided. They came crowding in on her thick and fast. The spectacle of two young women giving breast to their babies made her blush and turn away her face. She had never seen anything so indecent in her life. And what made it worse was that, instead of tactfully ignoring it, Bernard proceeded to make open comments on this revoltingly viviparous scene. Ashamed, now that the effects of the *soma* had worn off, of the weakness he had displayed that morning in the hotel, he went out of his way to show himself strong and unorthodox.

"What a wonderfully intimate relationship," he said, deliberately outrageous. "And what an intensity of feeling it must generate! I often think one may have missed something in not having had a mother. And perhaps you've missed something in not *being* a mother, Lenina. Imagine yourself sitting there with a little baby of your own. . . ."

"Bernard! How can you?" The passage of an old woman with ophthalmia and a disease of the skin distracted her from her indignation.

"Let's go away," she begged. "I don't like it."

But at this moment their guide came back and, beckoning them to follow, led the way down the narrow street between the houses. They rounded a corner. A dead dog was lying on a rubbish heap; a woman with a goitre was looking for lice in the hair of a small girl. Their guide halted at the foot of a ladder, raised his hand perpendicularly, then darted it horizontally forward. They did what he mutely commanded—climbed the ladder and walked through the doorway, to which it gave access, into a long narrow room, rather dark and smelling of smoke and cooked grease and long-worn, long-unwashed clothes. At the further end of the room was another doorway, through which came a shaft of sunlight and the noise, very loud and close, of the drums.

They stepped across the threshold and found themselves on a wide terrace. Below them, shut in by the tall houses, was the village square, crowded with Indians. Bright blankets, and feathers in black hair, and the glint of turquoise, and dark skins shining with heat. Lenina put her handkerchief to her nose again. In the open space at the centre of the square were two circular platforms of masonry and trampled clay—the roofs, it was evident, of underground chambers; for in the centre of each platform was an open hatchway, with a ladder emerging from the lower darkness. A sound of subterranean flute playing came up and was almost lost in the steady remorseless persistence of the drums.

Lenina liked the drums. Shutting her eyes she abandoned herself to their soft repeated thunder, allowed it to invade her consciousness more and more completely, till at last there was nothing left in the world but that one deep pulse of sound. It reminded her reassuringly of the synthetic noises made at Solidarity Services and Ford's Day celebrations. "Orgy-porgy," she whispered to herself. These drums beat out just the same rhythms.

There was a sudden startling burst of singing—hundreds of male voices crying out fiercely in harsh metallic unison. A few long notes and silence, the thunderous silence of the drums; then shrill, in a neighing treble, the women's answer. Then again the drums; and once more the men's deep savage affirmation of their manhood.

Queer—yes. The place was queer, so was the music, so were the clothes and the goitres and the skin diseases and the old people. But the performance itself—there seemed to be nothing specially queer about that.

"It reminds me of a lower-caste Community Sing," she told Bernard.

But a little later it was reminding her a good deal less of that innocuous function. For suddenly there had swarmed up from those round chambers underground a ghastly troop of monsters. Hideously masked or painted out of all semblance of humanity, they had tramped out a strange limping dance round the square; round and again round, singing as they went, round and round—each time a little faster; and the drums had changed and quickened their rhythm, so that it became like the pulsing of fever in the ears; and the crowd had begun to sing with the dancers, louder and louder; and first one woman had shrieked, and then another and another, as though they were being killed; and then suddenly the leader of the dancers broke out of the line, ran to a big wooden chest which was standing at one end of the square, raised the lid and pulled out a pair of black snakes. A great yell went up from the crowd, and all the other dancers ran towards him with out-stretched hands. He tossed the snakes to the first-comers, then dipped back into the chest for more. More and more, black snakes and brown and mottled—he flung them out. And then the dance began again on a different rhythm. Round and round they went with their snakes, snakily, with a soft undulating movement at the knees and hips. Round and round. Then the leader gave a signal, and one after another, all the snakes were flung down in the middle of the square; an old man came up from underground and sprinkled them with corn meal, and from the other hatchway came a woman and sprinkled them with water from a black jar. Then the old man lifted his hand and, startlingly, terrifyingly, there was absolute silence. The drums stopped beating, life seemed to have come to an end. The old man pointed towards the two hatchways that gave entrance to the lower world. And slowly, raised by invisible hands from below, there emerged from the one a painted image of an eagle, from the other that of a man, naked, and nailed to a cross. They hung there, seemingly self-sustained, as though watching. The old man clapped his hands. Naked but for a white cotton breech-cloth, a boy of about eighteen stepped out of the crowd and stood before him, his hands crossed over his chest, his head bowed. The old man made the sign of the cross over him and turned away. Slowly, the boy began to walk round the writhing heap of snakes. He had completed the first circuit and was half-way through the second when, from among the dancers, a tall man wearing the mask of a coyote and holding in his hand a whip of plaited leather, advanced towards him. The boy moved on as though unaware of the other's existence. The coyote-man raised his whip; there was a long moment of expectancy, then a swift movement, the whistle of the lash and its loud flat-sounding impact on the flesh. The boy's body quivered; but he made no sound, he walked on at the same slow, steady pace. The coyote struck again, again; and at every blow at first a gasp, and then a deep groan went up from the crowd. The boy walked. Twice, thrice, four times round he went. The blood was streaming. Five times round, six times round. Suddenly Lenina covered her face with her hands and began to sob. "Oh, stop them, stop them!" she implored. But the whip fell and fell inexorably. Seven times round. Then all at once the boy staggered and, still without a sound, pitched forward on to his face.

Bending over him, the old man touched his back with a long white feather, held it up for a moment, crimson, for the people to see, then shook it thrice over the snakes. A few drops fell, and suddenly the drums broke out again into a panic of hurrying notes; there was a great shout. The dancers rushed forward, picked up the snakes and ran out of the square. Men, women, children, all the crowd ran after them. A minute later the square was empty, only the boy remained, prone where he had fallen, quite still. Three old women came out of one of the houses, and with some difficulty lifted him and carried him in. The eagle and the man on the cross kept guard for a little while over the empty pueblo; then, as though they had seen enough, sank slowly down through their hatchways, out of sight, into the nether world.

Lenina was still sobbing. "Too awful," she kept repeating, and all Bernard's consolations were in vain. "Too awful! That blood!" She shuddered. "Oh, I wish I had my *soma.*"

There was the sound of feet in the inner room.

Lenina did not move, but sat with her face in her hands, unseeing, apart. Only Bernard turned round.

The dress of the young man who now stepped out on to the terrace was Indian; but his plaited hair was straw-coloured, his eyes a pale blue, and his skin a white skin, bronzed.

"Hullo. Good-morrow," said the stranger, in faultless but peculiar English. "You're civilized, aren't you? You come from the Other Place, outside the Reservation?"

"Who on earth . . . ?" Bernard began in astonishment.

The young man sighed and shook his head. "A most unhappy gentleman." And, pointing to the bloodstains in the centre of the square, "Do you see that damned spot?" he asked in a voice that trembled with emotion.

"A gramme is better than a damn," said Lenina mechanically from behind her hands. "I wish I had my *soma!*"

"*I* ought to have been there," the young man went on. "Why wouldn't they let me be the sacrifice? I'd have gone round ten times—twelve, fifteen. Palowhtiwa only got as far as seven. They could have had twice as much blood from me. The multitudinous seas incarnadine." He flung out his arms in a lavish gesture; then, despairingly, let them fall again. "But they wouldn't let me. They disliked me for my complexion. It's always been like that. Always." Tears stood in the young man's eyes; he was ashamed and turned away.

Astonishment made Lenina forget the deprivation of *soma*. She uncovered her face and, for the first time, looked at the stranger. "Do you mean to say that you *wanted* to be hit with that whip?"

Still averted from her, the young man made a sign of affirmation. "For the sake of the pueblo—to make the rain come and the corn grow. And to please Pookong and Jesus. And then to show that I can bear pain without crying out. Yes," and his voice suddenly took on a new resonance, he turned with a proud squaring of the shoulders, a proud, defiant lifting of the chin, "to show that I'm a man . . . Oh!" He gave a gasp and was silent, gaping. He had seen, for the first time in his life, the face of a girl whose cheeks were not the colour of chocolate or dogskin, whose hair was auburn and permanently waved, and whose expression (amazing novelty!) was one of benevolent interest. Lenina was smiling at him; such a nice-looking boy, she was thinking, and a really beautiful body. The blood rushed up into the young man's face; he dropped his eyes, raised them again for a moment only to find her still smiling at him, and was so much overcome that he had to turn away and pretend to be looking very hard at something on the other side of the square.

Bernard's questions made a diversion. Who? How? When? From where? Keeping his eyes fixed on Bernard's face (for so passionately did he long to see Lenina smiling that he simply dared not look at her), the young man tried to explain himself. Linda and he—Linda was his mother (the word made Lenina look uncomfortable)—were strangers in the Reservation. Linda had come from the Other Place long ago, before he was born, with a man who was his father. (Bernard pricked up his ears.) She had gone walking alone in those mountains over there to the North, had fallen down a steep place and hurt her head. ("Go on, go on," said Bernard excitedly.) Some hunters from Malpais had found her and brought her to the pueblo. As for the man who was his father, Linda had never seen him again. His name was Tomakin. (Yes, "Thomas" was the D.H.C.'s first name.) He must have flown away, back to the Other Place, away without her—a bad, unkind, unnatural man.

"And so I was born in Malpais," he concluded. "In Malpais." And he shook his head.

The squalor of that little house on the outskirts of the pueblo!

A space of dust and rubbish separated it from the village. Two famine-stricken dogs were nosing obscenely in the garbage at its door. Inside, when they entered, the twilight stank and was loud with flies.

"Linda!" the young man called.

From the inner room a rather hoarse female voice said, "Coming."

They waited. In bowls on the floor were the remains of a meal, perhaps of several meals.

The door opened. A very stout blonde squaw stepped across the threshold and stood looking at the strangers, staring incredulously, her mouth open. Lenina noticed with disgust that two of the front teeth were missing. And the colour of the ones that remained... She shuddered. It was worse than the old man. So fat. And all the lines in her face, the flabbiness, the wrinkles. And the sagging cheeks, with those purplish blotches. And the red veins on her nose, the bloodshot eyes. And that neck—that neck; and the blanket she wore over her head—ragged and filthy. And under the brown sack-shaped tunic those enormous breasts, the bulge of the stomach, the hips. Oh, much worse than the old man, much worse! And suddenly the creature burst out in a torrent of speech, rushed at her with outstretched arms and—Ford! Ford! it was too revolting, in another moment she'd be sick—pressed her against the bulge, the bosom, and began to kiss her. Ford! to *kiss,* slobberingly, and smelt too horrible, obviously never had a bath, and simply reeked of that beastly stuff that was put into Delta and Epsilon bottles (no, it wasn't true about Bernard), positively stank of alcohol. She broke away as quickly as she could.

A blubbered and distorted face confronted her; the creature was crying.

"Oh, my dear, my dear." The torrent of words flowed sobbingly. "If you knew how glad—after all these years! A civilized face. Yes, and civilized clothes. Because I thought I should never see a piece of real acetate silk again." She fingered the sleeve of Lenina's shirt. The nails were black. "And those adorable viscose velveteen shorts! Do you know, dear, I've still got my old clothes, the ones I came in, put away in a box. I'll show them to you afterwards. Though, of course, the acetate has all gone into holes. But such a lovely white bandolier—though I must say your green morocco is even lovelier. Not that it did *me* much good, that bandolier." Her tears began to flow again. "I suppose John told you. What I had to suffer—and not a gramme of *soma* to be had. Only a drink of *mescal* every now and then, when Popé used to bring it. Popé is a boy I used to know. But it makes you feel so bad afterwards, the *mescal* does, and you're sick with the *peyotl*; besides it always made that awful feeling of being ashamed much worse the next day. And I *was* so ashamed. Just think of it: me, a Beta—having a baby: put yourself in my place." (The mere suggestion made Lenina shudder.) "Though it wasn't my fault, I swear; because I still don't know how it happened, seeing that I did all the Malthusian Drill—you know, by numbers, One, two, three, four, always, I swear it; but all the same it happened; and of course there wasn't anything like an Abortion Centre here. Is it still down in Chelsea, by the way?" she asked. Lenina nodded. "And still floodlighted on Tuesdays and Fridays?" Lenina nodded again. "That lovely pink glass tower!" Poor Linda lifted her face and with closed eyes ecstatically contemplated the bright remembered image. "And the river at night," she whispered. Great tears oozed slowly out from behind her tight-shut eyelids. "And flying back in the evening from Stoke Poges. And then a hot bath and vibro-vacuum massage . . . But there." She drew a deep breath, shook her head, opened her eyes again, sniffed once or twice, then blew her nose on her fingers and wiped them on the skirt of her tunic. "Oh, I'm so sorry," she said in response to Lenina's involuntary grimace of disgust. "I oughtn't to have done that. I'm sorry. But what *are* you to do when there aren't any handkerchiefs? I remember how it used to upset me, all that dirt, and nothing being aseptic. I had an awful cut on my head when they first brought me here. You can't imagine what they used to put on it. Filth, just filth. 'Civilization is Sterilization,' I used to say to them. And 'Streptocock-Gee to Banbury-T, to see a fine bathroom and W.C.' as though they were children. But of course they didn't understand. How should they? And in the end I suppose I got used to it. And anyhow, how *can* you keep things clean when there isn't hot water laid on? And look at these clothes. This beastly wool isn't like acetate. It lasts and lasts. And you're supposed to mend it if it gets torn. But I'm a Beta; I worked in the Fertilizing Room; nobody ever taught me to do anything like that. It wasn't my business. Besides, it never used to be right to mend clothes. Throw them away when they've got holes in them and buy new. 'The more stitches, the less riches.' Isn't that right? Mending's anti-social. But it's all different here. It's like living with lunatics. Everything they do is mad." She looked round; saw John and Bernard had left them and were walking up and down in the dust and garbage outside the house; but, none the less confidentially lowering her voice, and leaning, while Lenina stiffened and shrank, so close that the blown reek of embryo-poison stirred the hair on her cheek. "For instance," she hoarsely whispered, "take the way they have one another here. Mad, I tell you, absolutely mad. Everybody belongs to every one else—don't they? don't they?" she insisted, tugging at Lenina's sleeve. Lenina nodded her averted head, let out the breath she had been holding and managed to draw another one, relatively untainted. "Well, here," the other went on, "nobody's supposed to belong to more than one person. And if you have people in the ordinary way, the others think you're wicked and anti-social. They hate and despise you. Once a lot of women came and made a scene because their men came to see me. Well, why not? And then they rushed at me . . . No, it was too awful. I can't tell you about it." Linda covered her face with her hands and shuddered. "They're so hateful, the women here. Mad, mad and cruel. And of course they don't know anything about Malthusian Drill, or bottles, or decanting, or anything of that sort. So they're having children all the time—like dogs. It's too revolting. And to think that I . . . Oh, Ford, Ford, Ford! And yet John *was* a great comfort to me. I don't know what I should have done without him. Even though he did get so upset whenever a man . . . Quite as a tiny boy, even. Once (but that was when he was bigger) he tried to kill poor Waihusiwa—or was it Popé?—just because I used to have them sometimes. Because I never *could* make him understand that that was what civilized people ought to do. Being mad's infectious, I believe. Anyhow, John seems to have caught it from the Indians. Because, of course, he was with them a lot. Even though they always were so beastly to him and wouldn't let him do all the things the other boys did. Which was a good thing in a way, because it made it easier for me to condition him a little. Though you've no idea how difficult that is. There's so much one doesn't know; it wasn't my business to know. I mean, when a child asks you how a helicopter works or who made the world—well, what are you to answer if you're a Beta and have always worked in the Fertilizing Room? What *are* you to answer?"

8

Outside, in the dust and among the garbage (there were four dogs now), Bernard and John were walking slowly up and down.

"So hard for me to realize," Bernard was saying, "to reconstruct. As though we were living on different planets, in different centuries. A mother, and all this dirt, and gods, and old age, and disease . . ." He shook his head. "It's almost inconceivable. I shall never understand, unless you explain."

"Explain what?"

"This." He indicated the pueblo. "That." And it was the little house outside the village. "Everything. All your life."

"But what is there to say?"

"From the beginning. As far back as you can remember."

"As far back as I can remember." John frowned. There was a long silence.

It was very hot. They had eaten a lot of tortillas and sweet corn. Linda said, "Come and lie down, Baby." They lay down together in the big bed. "Sing," and Linda sang. Sang "Streptocock-Gee to Banbury-T" and "Bye Baby Banting, soon you'll need decanting." Her voice got fainter and fainter . . .

There was a loud noise, and he woke with a start. A man was saying something to Linda, and Linda was laughing. She had pulled the blanket up to her chin, but the man pulled it down again. His hair was like two black ropes, and round his arm was a lovely silver bracelet with blue stones in it. He liked the bracelet; but all the same, he was frightened; he hid his face against Linda's body. Linda put her hand on him and he felt safer. In those other words he did not understand so well, she said to the man, "Not with John here." The man looked at him, then again at Linda, and said a few words in a soft voice. Linda said, "No." But the man bent over the bed towards him and his face was huge, terrible; the black ropes of hair touched the blanket. "No," Linda said again, and he felt her hand squeezing him more tightly. "No, no!" But the man took hold of one of his arms, and it hurt. He screamed. The man put up his other hand and lifted him up. Linda was still holding him, still saying, "No, no." The man said something short and angry, and suddenly her hands were gone. "Linda, Linda." He kicked and wriggled; but the man carried him across to the door, opened it, put him down on the floor in the middle of the other room, and went away, shutting the door behind him. He got up, he ran to the door. Standing on tiptoe he could just reach the big wooden latch. He lifted it and pushed; but the door wouldn't open. "Linda," he shouted. She didn't answer.

He remembered a huge room, rather dark; and there were big wooden things with strings fastened to them, and lots of women standing round them—making blankets, Linda said. Linda told him to sit in the corner with the other children, while she went and helped the women. He played with the little boys for a long time. Suddenly people started talking very loud, and there were the women pushing Linda away, and Linda was crying. She went to the door and he ran after her. He asked her why they were angry. "Because I broke something," she said. And then she got angry too. "How should I know how to do their beastly weaving?" she said. "Beastly savages." He asked her what savages were. When they got back to their house, Popé was waiting at the door, and he came in with them. He had a big gourd full of stuff that looked like water; only it wasn't water, but something with a bad smell that burnt your mouth and made you cough. Linda drank some and Popé drank some, and then Linda laughed a lot and talked very loud; and then she and Popé went into the other room. When Popé went away, he went into the room. Linda was in bed and so fast asleep that he couldn't wake her.

Popé used to come often. He said the stuff in the gourd was called *mescal*; but Linda said it ought to be called *soma*; only it made you feel ill afterwards. He hated Popé. He hated them all—all the men who came to see Linda. One afternoon, when he had been playing with the other children—it was cold, he remembered, and there was snow on the mountains—he came back to the house and heard angry voices in the bedroom. They were women's voices, and they said words he didn't understand; but he knew they were dreadful words. Then suddenly, crash! something was upset; he heard people moving about quickly, and there was another crash and then a noise like hitting a mule, only not so bony; then Linda screamed. "Oh, don't, don't, don't!" she said. He ran in. There were three women in dark blankets. Linda was on the bed. One of the women was holding her wrists. Another was lying across her legs, so that she couldn't kick. The third was hitting her with a whip. Once, twice, three times; and each time Linda screamed. Crying, he tugged at the fringe of the woman's blanket. "Please, please." With her free hand she held him away. The whip came down again, and again Linda screamed. He caught hold of the woman's enormous brown hand between his own and bit it with all his might. She cried out, wrenched her hand free, and gave him such a push that he fell down. While he was lying on the ground she hit him three times with the whip. It hurt more than anything he had ever felt—like fire. The whip whistled again, fell. But this time it was Linda who screamed.

"But why did they want to hurt you, Linda?" he asked that night. He was crying, because the red marks of the whip on his back still hurt so terribly. But he was also crying because people were so beastly and unfair, and because he was only a little boy and couldn't do anything against them. Linda was crying too. She was grown up, but she wasn't big enough to fight against three of them. It wasn't fair for her either. "Why did they want to hurt you, Linda?"

"I don't know. How should I know?" It was difficult to hear what she said, because she was lying on her stomach and her face was in the pillow. "They say those men are *their* men," she went on; and she did not seem to be talking to him at all; she seemed to be talking with some one inside herself. A long talk which she didn't understand; and in the end she started crying louder than ever.

"Oh, don't cry, Linda. Don't cry."

He pressed himself against her. He put his arm round her neck. Linda cried out. "Oh, be careful. My shoulder! Oh!" and she pushed him away, hard. His head banged against the wall. "Little idiot!" she shouted; and then, suddenly, she began to slap him. Slap, slap . . .

"Linda," he cried out. "Oh, mother, don't!"

"I'm not your mother. I won't be your mother."

"But, Linda . . . Oh!" She slapped him on the cheek.

"Turned into a savage," she shouted. "Having young ones like an animal . . . If it hadn't been for you, I might have gone to the Inspector, I might have got away. But not with a baby. That would have been too shameful."

He saw that she was going to hit him again, and lifted his arm to guard his face. "Oh, don't, Linda, please don't."

"Little beast!" She pulled down his arm; his face was uncovered.

"Don't, Linda." He shut his eyes, expecting the blow.

But she didn't hit him. After a little time, he opened his eyes again and saw that she was looking at him. He tried to smile at her. Suddenly she put her arms round him and kissed him again and again.

Sometimes, for several days, Linda didn't get up at all. She lay in bed and was sad. Or else she drank the stuff that Popé brought and laughed a great deal and went to sleep. Sometimes she was sick. Often she forgot to wash him, and there was nothing to eat except cold tortillas. He remembered the first time she found those little animals in his hair, how she screamed and screamed.

* * *

The happiest times were when she told him about the Other Place. "And you really can go flying, whenever you like?"

"Whenever you like." And she would tell him about the lovely music that came out of a box, and all the nice games you could play, and the delicious things to eat and drink, and the light that came when you pressed a little thing in the wall, and the pictures that you could hear and feel and smell, as well as see, and another box for making nice smells, and the pink and green and blue and silver houses as high as mountains, and everybody happy and no one ever sad or angry, and every one belonging to every one else, and the boxes where you could see and hear what was happening at the other side of the world, and babies in lovely clean bottles—everything so clean, and no nasty smells, no dirt at all—and people never lonely, but living together and being so jolly and happy, like the summer dances here in Malpais, but much happier, and the happiness being there every day, every day. . . . He listened by the hour. And sometimes, when he and the other children were tired with too much playing, one of the old men of the pueblo would talk to them, in those other words, of the great Transformer of the World, and of the long fight between Right Hand and Left Hand, between Wet and Dry; of Awonawilona, who made a great fog by thinking in the night, and then made the whole world out of the fog; of Earth Mother and Sky Father; of Ahaiyuta and Marsailema, the twins of War and Chance; of Jesus and Pookong; of Mary and Etsanatlehi, the woman who makes herself young again; of the Black Stone at Laguna and the Great Eagle and Our Lady of Acoma. Strange stories, all the more wonderful to him for being told in the other words and so not fully understood. Lying in bed, he would think of Heaven and London and Our Lady of Acoma and the rows and rows of babies in clean bottles and Jesus flying up and Linda flying up and the great Director of World hatcheries and Awonawilona.

* * *

Lots of men came to see Linda. The boys began to point their fingers at him. In the strange other words they said that Linda was bad; they called her names he did not understand, but that he knew were bad names. One day they sang a song about her, again and again. He threw stones at them. They threw back; a sharp stone cut his cheek. The blood wouldn't stop; he was covered with blood.

Linda taught him to read. With a piece of charcoal she drew pictures on the wall—an animal sitting down, a baby inside a bottle; then she wrote letters. THE CAT IS ON THE MAT. THE TOT IS IN THE POT. He learned quickly and easily. When he knew how to read all the words she wrote on the wall, Linda opened her big wooden box and pulled out from under those funny little red trousers she never wore a thin little book. He had often seen it before. "When you're bigger," she had said, "you can read it." Well, now he was big enough. He was proud. "I'm afraid you won't find it very exciting," she said. "But it's the only thing I have." She sighed. "If only you could see the lovely reading machines we used to have in London!" He began reading. *The Chemical and Bacteriological Conditioning of the Embryo. Practical Instructions for Beta Embryo-Store Workers.* It took him a quarter of an hour to read the title alone. He threw the book on the floor. "Beastly, beastly book!" he said, and began to cry.

The boys still sang their horrible song about Linda. Sometimes, too, they laughed at him for being so ragged. When he tore his clothes, Linda did not know how to mend them. In the Other Place, she told him, people threw away clothes with holes in them and got new ones. "Rags, rags!" the boys used to shout at him. "But I can read," he said to himself, "and they can't. They don't even know what reading is." It was fairly easy, if he thought hard enough about the reading, to pretend that he didn't mind when they made fun of him. He asked Linda to give him the book again.

The more the boys pointed and sang, the harder he read. Soon he could read all the words quite well. Even the longest. But what did they mean? He asked Linda; but even when she could answer it didn't seem to make it very clear. And generally she couldn't answer at all.

"What are chemicals?" he would ask.

"Oh, stuff like magnesium salts, and alcohol for keeping the Deltas and Epsilons small and backward, and calcium carbonate for bones, and all that sort of thing."

"But how do you make chemicals, Linda? Where do they come from?"

"Well, I don't know. You get them out of bottles. And when the bottles are empty, you send up to the Chemical Store for more. It's the Chemical Store people who make them, I suppose. Or else they send to the factory for them. I don't know. I never did any chemistry. My job was always with the embryos."

It was the same with everything else he asked about. Linda never seemed to know. The old men of the pueblo had much more definite answers.

"The seed of men and all creatures, the seed of the sun and the seed of earth and the seed of the sky—Awonawilona made them all out of the Fog of Increase. Now the world has four wombs; and he laid the seeds in the lowest of the four wombs. And gradually the seeds began to grow . . ."

One day (John calculated later that it must have been soon after his twelfth birthday) he came home and found a book that he had never seen before lying on the floor in the bedroom. It was a thick book and looked very old. The binding had been eaten by mice; some of its pages were loose and crumpled. He picked it up, looked at the title-page: the book was called *The Complete Works of William Shakespeare*.

Linda was lying on the bed, sipping that horrible stinking *mescal* out of a cup. "Popé brought it," she said. Her voice was thick and hoarse like somebody else's voice. "It was lying in one of the chests

of the Antelope Kiva. It's supposed to have been there for hundreds of years. I expect it's true, because I looked at it, and it seemed to be full of nonsense. Uncivilized. Still, it'll be good enough for you to practise your reading on." She took a last sip, set the cup down on the floor beside the bed, turned over on her side, hiccoughed once or twice and went to sleep.

He opened the book at random.

Nay, but to live
In the rank sweat of an enseamed bed,
Stew'd in corruption, honeying and making love
Over the nasty sty . . .

The strange words rolled through his mind; rumbled, like the drums at the summer dances, if the drums could have spoken; like the men singing the Corn Song, beautiful, beautiful, so that you cried; like old Mitsima saying magic over his feathers and his carved sticks and his bits of bone and stone—*kiathla tsílu sílokwe sílokwe sílokwe. Kiai sílu sílu, tsithl*—but better than Mitsima's magic, because it meant more, because it talked to *him*; talked wonderfully and only half-understandably, a terrible beautiful magic, about Linda; about Linda lying there snoring, with the empty cup on the floor beside the bed; about Linda and Popé, Linda and Popé.

He hated Popé more and more. A man can smile and smile and be a villain. Remorseless, treacherous, lecherous, kindless villain. What did the words exactly mean? He only half knew. But their magic was strong and went on rumbling in his head, and somehow it was as though he had never really hated Popé before; never really hated him because he had never been able to say how much he hated him. But now he had these words, these words like drums and singing and magic. These words and the strange, strange story out of which they were taken (he couldn't make head or tail of it, but it was wonderful, wonderful all the same)—they gave him a reason for hating Popé; and they made his hatred more real; they even made Popé himself more real.

One day, when he came in from playing, the door of the inner room was open, and he saw them lying together on the bed, asleep—white Linda and Popé almost black beside her, with one arm under her shoulders and the other dark hand on her breast, and one of the plaits of his long hair lying across her throat, like a black snake trying to strangle her. Popé's gourd and a cup were standing on the floor near the bed. Linda was snoring.

His heart seemed to have disappeared and left a hole. He was empty. Empty, and cold, and rather sick, and giddy. He leaned against the wall to steady himself. Remorseless, treacherous, lecherous . . . Like drums, like the men singing for the corn, like magic, the words repeated and repeated themselves in his head. From being cold he was suddenly hot. His cheeks burnt with the rush of blood, the room swam and darkened before his eyes. He ground his teeth. "I'll kill him, I'll kill him, I'll kill him," he kept saying. And suddenly there were more words.

When he is drunk asleep, or in his rage
Or in the incestuous pleasure of his bed . . .

The magic was on his side, the magic explained and gave orders. He stepped back in the outer room. "When he is drunk asleep . . ." The knife for the meat was lying on the floor near the fireplace. He picked it up and tiptoed to the door again. "When he is drunk asleep, drunk asleep . . ." He ran across the room and stabbed—oh, the blood!—stabbed again, as Popé heaved out of his sleep, lifted his hand to stab once more, but found his wrist caught, held and—oh, oh!—twisted. He couldn't move, he was trapped, and there were Popé's small black eyes, very close, staring into his own. He looked away. There were two cuts on Popé's left shoulder. "Oh, look at the blood!" Linda was crying. "Look at the blood!" She had never been able to bear the sight of blood. Popé lifted his other hand—to strike him, he thought. He stiffened to receive the blow. But the hand only took him under the chin and turned his face, so that he had to look again into Popé's eyes. For a long time, for hours and hours. And suddenly—he couldn't help it—he began to cry. Popé burst out laughing. "Go," he said, in the other Indian words. "Go, my brave Ahaiyuta." He ran out into the other room to hide his tears.

"You are fifteen," said old Mitsima, in the Indian words. "Now I may teach you to work the clay."

Squatting by the river, they worked together.

"First of all," said Mitsima, taking a lump of the wetted clay between his hands, "we make a little moon." The old man squeezed the lump into a disk, then bent up the edges; the moon became a shallow cup.

Slowly and unskilfully he imitated the old man's delicate gestures.

"A moon, a cup, and now a snake." Mitsima rolled out another piece of clay into a long flexible cylinder, hooped it into a circle and pressed it on to the rim of the cup. "Then another snake. And another. And another." Round by round, Mitsima built up the sides of the pot; it was narrow, it bulged, it narrowed again towards the neck. Mitsima squeezed and patted, stroked and scraped; and there at last it stood, in shape the familiar water pot of Malpais, but creamy white instead of black, and still soft to the touch. The crooked parody of Mitsima's, his own stood beside it. Looking at the two pots, he had to laugh.

"But the next one will be better," he said, and began to moisten another piece of clay.

To fashion, to give form, to feel his fingers gaining in skill and power—this gave him an extraordinary pleasure. "A, B, C, Vitamin D," he sang to himself as he worked. "The fat's in the liver, the cod's in the sea." And Mitsima also sang—a song about killing a bear. They worked all day, and all day he was filled with an intense, absorbing happiness.

"Next winter," said old Mitsima, "I will teach you to make the bow."

He stood for a long time outside the house, and at last the ceremonies within were finished. The door opened; they came out. Kothlu came first, his right hand outstretched and tightly closed, as though over some precious jewel. Her clenched hand similarly outstretched, Kiakimé followed. They walked in silence, and in silence, behind them, came the brothers and sisters and cousins and all the troop of old people.

They walked out of the pueblo, across the mesa. At the edge of the cliff they halted, facing the early morning sun. Kothlu opened his hand. A pinch of corn meal lay white on the palm; he breathed on it, murmured a few words, then threw it, a handful of white dust, towards the sun. Kiakimé did the same. Then Kiakimé's father stepped forward, and holding up a feathered prayer stick, made a long prayer, then threw the stick after the corn meal.

"It is finished," said old Mitsima in a loud voice. "They are married."

"Well," said Linda, as they turned away, "all I can say is, it does seem a lot of fuss to make about so little. In civilized countries, when a boy wants to have a girl, he just . . . But where *are* you going, John?"

He paid no attention to her calling, but ran on, away, away, anywhere to be by himself.

It is finished. Old Mitsima's words repeated themselves in his mind. Finished, finished . . . In silence and from a long way off, but violently, desperately, hopelessly, he had loved Kiakimé. And now it was finished. He was sixteen.

At the full moon, in the Antelope Kiva, secrets would be told, secrets would be done and borne. They would go down, boys, into the kiva and come out again, men. The boys were all afraid and at the same time impatient. And at last it was the day. The sun went down, the moon rose. He went with the others. Men were standing, dark, at the entrance to the kiva; the ladder went down into the red lighted depths. Already the leading boys had begun to climb down. Suddenly, one of the men stepped forward, caught him by the arm, and pulled him out of the ranks. He broke free and dodged back into his place among the others. This time the man struck him, pulled his hair. "Not for you, white-hair!" "Not for the son of the she-dog," said one of the other men. The boys laughed. "Go!" And as he still hovered on the fringes of the group, "Go!" the men shouted again. One of them bent down, took a stone, threw it. "Go, go, go!" There was a shower of stones. Bleeding, he ran away into the darkness. From the red-lit kiva came the noise of singing. The last of the boys had climbed down the ladder. He was all alone.

All alone, outside the pueblo, on the bare plain of the mesa. The rock was like bleached bones in the moonlight. Down in the valley, the coyotes were howling at the moon. The bruises hurt him, the cuts were still bleeding; but it was not for pain that he sobbed; it was because he was all alone, because he had been driven out, alone, into this skeleton world of rocks and moonlight. At the edge of the precipice he sat down. The moon was behind him; he looked down into the black shadow of the mesa, into the black shadow of death. He had only to take one step, one little jump. . . . He held out his right hand in the moonlight. From the cut on his wrist the blood was still oozing. Every few seconds a drop fell, dark, almost colourless in the dead light. Drop, drop, drop. To-morrow and to-morrow and to-morrow . . .

He had discovered Time and Death and God.

* * *

"Alone, always alone," the young man was saying.

The words awoke a plaintive echo in Bernard's mind. Alone, alone . . . "So am I," he said, on a gush of confidingness. "Terribly alone."

"Are you?" John looked surprised. "I thought that in the Other Place . . . I mean, Linda always said that nobody was ever alone there."

Bernard blushed uncomfortably. "You see," he said, mumbling and with averted eyes, "I'm rather different from most people, I suppose. If one happens to be decanted different . . ."

"Yes, that's just it." The young man nodded. "If one's different, one's bound to be lonely. They're beastly to one. Do you know, they shut me out of absolutely everything? When the other boys were sent out to spend the night on the mountains—you know, when you have to dream which your sacred animal is—they wouldn't let me go with the others; they wouldn't tell me any of the secrets. I did it by myself, though," he added. "Didn't eat anything for five days and then went out one night alone into those mountains there." He pointed.

Patronizingly, Bernard smiled. "And did you dream of anything?" he asked.

The other nodded. "But I mustn't tell you what." He was silent for a little; then, in a low voice, "Once," he went on, "I did something that none of the others did: I stood against a rock in the middle of the day, in summer, with my arms out, like Jesus on the Cross."

"What on earth for?"

"I wanted to know what it was like being crucified. Hanging there in the sun . . ."

"But why?"

"Why? Well . . ." He hesitated. "Because I felt I ought to. If Jesus could stand it. And then, if one has done something wrong . . . Besides, I was unhappy; that was another reason."

"It seems a funny way of curing your unhappiness," said Bernard. But on second thoughts he decided that there was, after all, some sense in it. Better than taking *soma* . . .

"I fainted after a time," said the young man. "Fell down on my face. Do you see the mark where I cut myself?" He lifted the thick yellow hair from his forehead. The scar showed, pale and puckered, on his right temple.

Bernard looked, and then quickly, with a little shudder, averted his eyes. His conditioning had made him not so much pitiful as profoundly squeamish. The mere suggestion of illness or wounds was to him not only horrifying, but even repulsive and rather disgusting. Like dirt, or deformity, or old age. Hastily he changed the subject.

"I wonder if you'd like to come back to London with us?" he asked, making the first move in a campaign whose strategy he had been secretly elaborating ever since, in the little house, he had realized who the "father" of this young savage must be. "Would you like that?"

The young man's face lit up. "Do you really mean it?"

"Of course; if I can get permission, that is."

"Linda too?"

"Well . . ." He hesitated doubtfully. That revolting creature! No, it was impossible. Unless, unless . . . It suddenly occurred to Bernard that her very revoltingness might prove an enormous asset. "But of course!" he cried, making up for his first hesitations with an excess of noisy cordiality.

The young man drew a deep breath. "To think it should be coming true—what I've dreamt of all my life. Do you remember what Miranda says?"

"Who's Miranda?"

But the young man had evidently not heard the question. "O wonder!" he was saying; and his eyes shone, his face was brightly flushed. "How many goodly creatures are there here! How beauteous mankind is!" The flush suddenly deepened; he was thinking of Lenina, of an angel in bottle-green viscose, lustrous with youth and skin food, plump, benevolently smiling. His voice faltered. "O brave new world," he began, then suddenly interrupted himself; the blood had left his cheeks; he was as pale as paper. "Are you married to her?" he asked.

"Am I what?"

"Married. You know—for ever. They say 'for ever' in the Indian words; it can't be broken."

"Ford, no!" Bernard couldn't help laughing.

John also laughed, but for another reason—laughed for pure joy. "O brave new world," he repeated. "O brave new world that has such people in it. Let's start at once."

"You have a most peculiar way of talking sometimes," said Bernard, staring at the young man in perplexed astonishment. "And, anyhow, hadn't you better wait till you actually see the new world?"

9

Lenina felt herself entitled, after this day of queerness and horror, to a complete and absolute holiday. As soon as they got back to the rest-house, she swallowed six half-gramme tablets of *soma*, lay down on her bed, and within ten minutes had embarked for lunar eternity. It would be eighteen hours at the least before she was in time again.

Bernard meanwhile lay pensive and wide-eyed in the dark. It was long after midnight before he fell asleep. Long after midnight; but his insomnia had not been fruitless; he had a plan.

Punctually, on the following morning, at ten o'clock, the green-uniformed octoroon stepped out of his helicopter. Bernard was waiting for him among the agaves.

"Miss Crowne's gone on *soma*-holiday," he explained. "Can hardly be back before five. Which leaves us seven hours."

He could fly to Santa Fé, do all the business he had to do, and be in Malpais again long before she woke up.

"She'll be quite safe here by herself?"

"Safe as helicopters," the octoroon assured him.

They climbed into the machine and started off at once. At ten thirty-four they landed on the roof of the Santa Fé Post Office; at ten thirty-seven Bernard had got through to the World Controller's Office in Whitehall; at ten thirty-nine he was speaking to his fordship's fourth personal secretary; at ten forty-four he was repeating his story to the first secretary, and at ten forty-seven and a half it was the deep, resonant voice of Mustapha Mond himself that sounded in his ears.

"I ventured to think," stammered Bernard, "that your fordship might find the matter of sufficient scientific interest . . ."

"Yes, I do find it of sufficient scientific interest," said the deep voice. "Bring these two individuals back to London with you."

"Your fordship is aware that I shall need a special permit . . ."

"The necessary orders," said Mustapha Mond, "are being sent to the Warden of the Reservation at this moment. You will proceed at once to the Warden's Office. Good-morning, Mr. Marx."

There was silence. Bernard hung up the receiver and hurried up to the roof.

"Warden's Office," he said to the Gamma-green octoroon.

At ten fifty-four Bernard was shaking hands with the Warden.

"Delighted, Mr. Marx, delighted." His boom was deferential. "We have just received special orders . . ."

"I know," said Bernard, interrupting him. "I was talking to his fordship on the phone a moment ago." His bored tone implied that he was in the habit of talking to his fordship every day of the week. He dropped into a chair. "If you'll kindly take all the necessary steps as soon as possible. As soon as possible," he emphatically repeated. He was thoroughly enjoying himself.

At eleven three he had all the necessary papers in his pocket.

"So long," he said patronizingly to the Warden, who had accompanied him as far as the lift gates. "So long."

He walked across to the hotel, had a bath, a vibro-vac massage, and an electrolytic shave, listened in to the morning's news, looked in for half an hour on the televisor, ate a leisured luncheon, and at half-past two flew back with the octoroon to Malpais.

The young man stood outside the rest-house.

"Bernard," he called. "Bernard!" There was no answer.

Noiseless on his deerskin moccasins, he ran up the steps and tried the door. The door was locked.

They were gone! Gone! It was the most terrible thing that had ever happened to him. She had asked him to come and see them, and now they were gone. He sat down on the steps and cried.

Half an hour later it occurred to him to look through the window. The first thing he saw was a green suit-case, with the initials L.C. painted on the lid. Joy flared up like fire within him. He picked up a stone. The smashed glass tinkled on the floor. A moment later he was inside the room. He opened the green suit-case; and all at once he was breathing Lenina's perfume, filling his lungs with her essential being. His heart beat wildly; for a moment he was almost faint. Then, bending over the precious box, he touched, he lifted into the light, he examined. The zippers on Lenina's spare pair of viscose velveteen shorts were at first a puzzle, then solved, a delight. Zip, and then zip; zip, and then zip; he was enchanted. Her green slippers were the most beautiful things he had ever seen. He unfolded a pair of zippicamiknicks, blushed, put them hastily away again; but kissed a perfumed acetate handkerchief and wound a scarf round his neck. Opening a box, he spilt a cloud of scented powder. His hands were floury with the stuff. He wiped them on his chest, on his shoulders, on his bare arms. Delicious perfume! He shut his eyes; he rubbed his cheek against his own powdered arm. Touch of smooth skin against his face, scent in his nostrils of musky dust—her real presence. "Lenina," he whispered. "Lenina!"

A noise made him start, made him guiltily turn. He crammed up his thieveries into the suit-case and shut the lid; then listened again, looked. Not a sign of life, not a sound. And yet he had certainly heard something—something like a sigh, something like the creak of a board. He tiptoed to the door and, cautiously opening it, found himself looking on to a broad landing. On the opposite side of the landing was another door, ajar. He stepped out, pushed, peeped.

There, on a low bed, the sheet flung back, dressed in a pair of pink one-piece zippyjamas, lay Lenina, fast asleep and so beautiful in the midst of her curls, so touchingly childish with her pink toes and her grave sleeping face, so trustful in the helplessness of her limp hands and melted limbs, that the tears came to his eyes.

With an infinity of quite unnecessary precautions—for nothing short of a pistol shot could have called Lenina back from her *soma*-holiday before the appointed time—he entered the room, he knelt on the floor beside the bed. He gazed, he clasped his hands, his lips moved. "Her eyes," he murmured,

"Her eyes, her hair, her cheek, her gait, her voice;
Handlest in thy discourse O! that her hand,
In whose comparison all whites are ink
Writing their own reproach; to whose soft seizure
The cygnet's down is harsh . . ."

A fly buzzed round her; he waved it away. "Flies," he remembered,

"On the white wonder of dear Juliet's hand, may seize
And steal immortal blessing from her lips,
Who, even in pure and vestal modesty,
Still blush, as thinking their own kisses sin."

Very slowly, with the hesitating gesture of one who reaches forward to stroke a shy and possibly rather dangerous bird, he put out his hand. It hung there trembling, within an inch of those limp fingers, on the verge of contact. Did he dare? Dare to profane with his unworthiest hand that . . . No, he didn't. The bird was too dangerous. His hand dropped back. How beautiful she was! How beautiful!

Then suddenly he found himself reflecting that he had only to take hold of the zipper at her neck and give one long, strong pull . . . He shut his eyes, he shook his head with the gesture of a dog shaking its ears as it emerges from the water. Detestable thought! He was ashamed of himself. Pure and vestal modesty . . .

There was a humming in the air. Another fly trying to steal immortal blessings? A wasp? He looked, saw nothing. The humming grew louder and louder, localized itself as being outside the shuttered windows. The plane! In a panic, he scrambled to his feet and ran into the other room, vaulted through the open window, and hurrying along the path between the tall agaves was in time to receive Bernard Marx as he climbed out of the helicopter.

10

The hands of all the four thousand electric clocks in all the Bloomsbury Centre's four thousand rooms marked twenty-seven minutes past two. "This hive of industry," as the Director was fond of calling it, was in the full buzz of work. Every one was busy, everything in ordered motion. Under the microscopes, their long tails furiously lashing, spermatozoa were burrowing head first into eggs; and, fertilized, the eggs were expanding, dividing, or if bokanovskified, budding and breaking up into whole populations of separate embryos. From the Social Predestination Room the escalators went rumbling down into the basement, and there, in the crimson darkness, stewing warm on their cushion of peritoneum and gorged with blood-surrogate and hormones, the foetuses grew and grew or, poisoned, languished into a stunted Epsilonhood. With a faint hum and rattle the moving racks crawled imperceptibly through the weeks and the recapitulated aeons to where, in the Decanting Room, the newly-unbottled babes uttered their first yell of horror and amazement.

The dynamos purred in the sub-basement, the lifts rushed up and down. On all the eleven floors of Nurseries it was feeding time. From eighteen hundred bottles eighteen hundred carefully labelled infants were simultaneously sucking down their pint of pasteurized external secretion.

Above them, in ten successive layers of dormitory, the little boys and girls who were still young enough to need an afternoon sleep were as busy as every one else, though they did not know it, listening unconsciously to hypnopædic lessons in hygiene and sociability, in class-consciousness and the toddler's love-life. Above these again were the playrooms where, the weather having turned to rain, nine hundred older children were amusing themselves with bricks and clay modelling, hunt-the-zipper, and erotic play.

Buzz, buzz! the hive was humming, busily, joyfully. Blithe was the singing of the young girls over their test-tubes, the Predestinators whistled as they worked, and in the Decanting Room what glorious jokes were cracked above the empty bottles! But the Director's face, as he entered the Fertilizing Room with Henry Foster, was grave, wooden with severity.

"A public example," he was saying. "In this room, because it contains more high-caste workers than any other in the Centre. I have told him to meet me here at half-past two."

"He does his work very well," put in Henry, with hypocritical generosity.

"I know. But that's all the more reason for severity. His intellectual eminence carries with it corresponding moral responsibilities. The greater a man's talents, the greater his power to lead astray. It is better that one should suffer than that many should be corrupted. Consider the matter dispassionately, Mr. Foster, and you will see that no offence is so heinous as unorthodoxy of behaviour. Murder kills only the individual—and, after all, what is an individual?" With a sweeping gesture he indicated the rows of microscopes, the test-tubes, the incubators. "We can make a new one with the greatest ease—as many as we like. Unorthodoxy threatens more than the life of a mere individual; it strikes at Society itself. Yes, at Society itself," he repeated. "Ah, but here he comes."

Bernard had entered the room and was advancing between the rows of fertilizers toward them. A veneer of jaunty self-confidence thinly concealed his nervousness. The voice in which he said,

"Good-morning, Director," was absurdly too loud; that in which, correcting his mistake, he said, "You asked me to come and speak to you here," ridiculously soft, a squeak.

"Yes, Mr. Marx," said the Director portentously. "I did ask you to come to me here. You returned from your holiday last night, I understand."

"Yes," Bernard answered.

"Yes-s," repeated the Director, lingering, a serpent, on the "s." Then, suddenly raising his voice, "Ladies and gentlemen," he trumpeted, "ladies and gentlemen."

The singing of the girls over their test-tubes, the preoccupied whistling of the Microscopists, suddenly ceased. There was a profound silence; every one looked round.

"Ladies and gentlemen," the Director repeated once more, "excuse me for thus interrupting your labours. A painful duty constrains me. The security and stability of Society are in danger. Yes, in danger, ladies and gentlemen. This man," he pointed accusingly at Bernard, "this man who stands before you here, this Alpha-Plus to whom so much has been given, and from whom, in consequence, so much must be expected, this colleague of yours—or should I anticipate and say this ex-colleague?—has grossly betrayed the trust imposed in him. By his heretical views on sport and *soma*, by the scandalous unorthodoxy of his sexlife, by his refusal to obey the teachings of Our Ford and behave out of office hours, 'even as a little infant,'" (here the Director made the sign of the T), "he has proved himself an enemy of Society, a subverter, ladies and gentlemen, of all Order and Stability, a conspirator against Civilization itself. For this reason I propose to dismiss him, to dismiss him with ignominy from the post he has held in this Centre; I propose forthwith to apply for his transference to a Sub-Centre of the lowest order and, that his punishment may serve the best interest of Society, as far as possible removed from any important Centre of population. In Iceland he will have small opportunity to lead others astray

by his unfordly example." The Director paused; then, folding his arms, he turned impressively to Bernard. "Marx," he said, "can you show any reason why I should not now execute the judgment passed upon you?"

"Yes, I can," Bernard answered in a very loud voice.

Somewhat taken aback, but still majestically, "Then show it," said the Director.

"Certainly. But it's in the passage. One moment." Bernard hurried to the door and threw it open. "Come in," he commanded, and the reason came in and showed itself.

There was a gasp, a murmur of astonishment and horror; a young girl screamed; standing on a chair to get a better view some one upset two test-tubes full of spermatozoa. Bloated, sagging, and among those firm youthful bodies, those undistorted faces, a strange and terrifying monster of middle-agedness, Linda advanced into the room, coquettishly smiling her broken and discoloured smile, and rolling as she walked, with what was meant to be a voluptuous undulation, her enormous haunches. Bernard walked beside her.

"There he is," he said, pointing at the Director.

"Did you think I didn't recognize him?" Linda asked indignantly; then, turning to the Director, "Of course I knew you; Tomakin, I should have known you anywhere, among a thousand. But perhaps you've forgotten me. Don't you remember? Don't you remember, Tomakin? Your Linda." She stood looking at him, her head on one side, still smiling, but with a smile that became progressively, in face of the Director's expression of petrified disgust, less and less self-confident, that wavered and finally went out. "Don't you remember, Tomakin?" she repeated in a voice that trembled. Her eyes were anxious, agonized. The blotched and sagging face twisted grotesquely into the grimace of extreme grief. "Tomakin!" She held out her arms. Some one began to titter.

"What's the meaning," began the Director, "of this monstrous . . ."

"Tomakin!" She ran forward, her blanket trailing behind her, threw her arms round his neck, hid her face on his chest.

A howl of laughter went up irrepressibly.

". . . this monstrous practical joke," the Director shouted.

Red in the face, he tried to disengage himself from her embrace. Desperately she clung. "But I'm Linda, I'm Linda." The laughter drowned her voice. "You made me have a baby," she screamed above the uproar. There was a sudden and appalling hush; eyes floated uncomfortably, not knowing where to look. The Director went suddenly pale, stopped struggling and stood, his hands on her wrists, staring down at her, horrified. "Yes, a baby—and I was its mother." She flung the obscenity like a challenge into the outraged silence; then, suddenly breaking away from him, ashamed, ashamed, covered her face with her hands, sobbing. "It wasn't my fault, Tomakin. Because I always did my drill, didn't I? Didn't I? Always . . . I don't know how . . . If you knew how awful, Tomakin . . . But he was a comfort to me, all the same." Turning towards the door, "John!" she called. "John!"

He came in at once, paused for a moment just inside the door, looked round, then soft on his moccasined feet strode quickly across the room, fell on his knees in front of the Director, and said in a clear voice: "My father!"

The word (for "father" was not so much obscene as—with its connotation of something at one remove from the loathsomeness and moral obliquity of child-bearing—merely gross, a scatological rather than a pornographic impropriety); the comically smutty word relieved what had become a quite intolerable tension. Laughter broke out, enormous, almost hysterical, peal after peal, as though it would never stop. My father—and it was the Director! My *father!* Oh Ford, oh Ford! That was really too good. The whooping and the roaring renewed themselves, faces seemed on the point of disintegration, tears were streaming. Six more test-tubes of spermatozoa were upset. My *father!*

Pale, wild-eyed, the Director glared about him in an agony of bewildered humiliation.

My *father!* The laughter, which had shown signs of dying away, broke out again more loudly than ever. He put his hands over his ears and rushed out of the room.

II

After the scene in the Fertilizing Room, all upper-caste London was wild to see this delicious creature who had fallen on his knees before the Director of Hatcheries and Conditioning—or rather the ex-Director, for the poor man had resigned immediately afterwards and never set foot inside the Centre again—had flopped down and called him (the joke was almost too good to be true!) "my father." Linda, on the contrary, cut no ice; nobody had the smallest desire to see Linda. To say one was a mother—that was past a joke: it was an obscenity. Moreover, she wasn't a real savage, had been hatched out of a bottle and conditioned like any one else: so couldn't have really quaint ideas. Finally—and this was by far the strongest reason for people's not wanting to see poor Linda—there was her appearance. Fat; having lost her youth; with bad teeth, and a blotched complexion, and that figure (Ford!)—you simply couldn't look at her without feeling sick, yes, positively sick. So the best people were quite determined *not* to see Linda. And Linda, for her part, had no desire to see them. The return to civilization was for her the return to *soma*, was the possibility of lying in bed and taking holiday after holiday, without ever having to come back to a headache or a fit of vomiting, without ever being made to feel as you always felt after *peyotl*, as though you'd done something so shamefully anti-social that you could never hold up your head again. *Soma* played none of these unpleasant tricks. The holiday it gave was perfect and, if the morning after was disagreeable, it was so, not intrinsically, but only by comparison with the joys of the holiday. The remedy was to make the holiday continuous. Greedily she clamoured for ever larger, ever more frequent doses. Dr. Shaw at first demurred; then let her have what she wanted. She took as much as twenty grammes a day.

"Which will finish her off in a month or two," the doctor confided to Bernard. "One day the respiratory centre will be paralyzed. No more breathing. Finished. And a good thing too. If we could rejuvenate, of course it would be different. But we can't."

Surprisingly, as every one thought (for on *soma*-holiday Linda was most conveniently out of the way), John raised objections.

"But aren't you shortening her life by giving her so much?"

"In one sense, yes," Dr. Shaw admitted. "But in another we're actually lengthening it." The young man stared, uncomprehending. "*Soma* may make you lose a few years in time," the doctor went on. "But think of the enormous, immeasurable durations it can give you out of time. Every *soma*-holiday is a bit of what our ancestors used to call eternity."

John began to understand. "Eternity was in our lips and eyes," he murmured.

"Eh?"

"Nothing."

"Of course," Dr. Shaw went on, "you can't allow people to go popping off into eternity if they've got any serious work to do. But as she hasn't got any serious work . . ."

"All the same," John persisted, "I don't believe it's right."

The doctor shrugged his shoulders. "Well, of course, if you prefer to have her screaming mad all the time . . ."

In the end John was forced to give in. Linda got her *soma*. Thenceforward she remained in her little room on the thirty-seventh floor of Bernard's apartment house, in bed, with the radio and television always on, and the patchouli tap just dripping, and the *soma* tablets within reach of her hand—there she remained; and yet wasn't there at all, was all the time away, infinitely far away, on holiday; on holiday in some other world, where the music of the radio was a labyrinth of sonorous colours, a sliding, palpitating labyrinth, that led (by what beautifully inevitable windings) to a bright centre of absolute conviction; where the dancing images of the television box were the performers in some indescribably delicious all-singing feely; where the dripping patchouli was more than scent—was the sun, was a million sexophones, was Popé making love, only much more so, incomparably more, and without end.

"No, we can't rejuvenate. But I'm very glad," Dr. Shaw had concluded, "to have had this opportunity to see an example of senility in a human being. Thank you so much for calling me in." He shook Bernard warmly by the hand.

It was John, then, they were all after. And as it was only through Bernard, his accredited guardian, that John could be seen, Bernard now found himself, for the first time in his life, treated not merely normally, but as a person of outstanding importance. There was no more talk of the alcohol in his blood-surrogate, no gibes at his personal appearance. Henry Foster went out of his way to be friendly; Benito Hoover made him a present of six packets of sex-hormone chewing-gum; the Assistant Predestinator came out and cadged almost abjectly for an invitation to one of Bernard's evening parties. As for the women, Bernard had only to hint at the possibility of an invitation, and he could have whichever of them he liked.

"Bernard's asked me to meet the Savage next Wednesday," Fanny announced triumphantly.

"I'm so glad," said Lenina. "And now you must admit that you were wrong about Bernard. Don't you think he's really rather sweet?"

Fanny nodded. "And I must say," she said, "I was quite agreeably surprised."

The Chief Bottler, the Director of Predestination, three Deputy Assistant Fertilizer-Generals, the Professor of Feelies in the College of Emotional Engineering, the Dean of the Westminster Community Singery, the Supervisor of Bokanovskification—the list of Bernard's notabilities was interminable.

"And I had six girls last week," he confided to Helmholtz Watson. "One on Monday, two on Tuesday, two more on Friday, and one on Saturday. And if I'd had the time or the inclination, there were at least a dozen more who were only too anxious . . ."

Helmholtz listened to his boastings in a silence so gloomily disapproving that Bernard was offended.

"You're envious," he said.

Helmholtz shook his head. "I'm rather sad, that's all," he answered.

Bernard went off in a huff. Never, he told himself, never would he speak to Helmholtz again.

The days passed. Success went fizzily to Bernard's head, and in the process completely reconciled him (as any good intoxicant should do) to a world which, up till then, he had found very unsatisfactory. In so far as it recognized him as important, the order of things was good. But, reconciled by his success, he yet refused to forego the privilege of criticizing this order. For the act of criticizing heightened his sense of importance, made him feel larger. Moreover, he did genuinely believe that there were things to criticize. (At the same time, he genuinely liked being a success and having all the girls he wanted.) Before those who now, for the sake of the Savage, paid their court to him, Bernard would parade a carping unorthodoxy. He was politely listened to. But behind his back people shook their heads. "That young man will come to a bad end," they said, prophesying the more confidently in that they themselves would in due course personally see to it that the end was bad. "He won't find another Savage to help him out a second time," they said. Meanwhile, however, there was the first Savage; they were polite. And because they were polite, Bernard felt positively gigantic—gigantic and at the same time light with elation, lighter than air.

"Lighter than air," said Bernard, pointing upwards.

Like a pearl in the sky, high, high above them, the Weather Department's captive balloon shone rosily in the sunshine.

". . . the said Savage," so ran Bernard's instructions, "to be shown civilized life in all its aspects. . . ."

He was being shown a bird's-eye view of it at present, a bird's-eye view from the platform of the Charing-T Tower. The Station Master and the Resident Meteorologist were acting as guides. But it was Bernard who did most of the talking. Intoxicated, he was behaving as though, at the very least, he were a visiting World Controller. Lighter than air.

The Bombay Green Rocket dropped out of the sky. The passengers alighted. Eight identical Dravidian twins in khaki looked out of the eight portholes of the cabin—the stewards.

"Twelve hundred and fifty kilometres an hour," said the Station Master impressively. "What do you think of that, Mr. Savage?"

John thought it very nice. "Still," he said, "Ariel could put a girdle round the earth in forty minutes."

"The Savage," wrote Bernard in his report to Mustapha Mond, "shows surprisingly little astonishment at, or awe of, civilized inventions. This is partly due, no doubt, to the fact that he has heard them talked about by the woman Linda, his m—."

(Mustapha Mond frowned. "Does the fool think I'm too squeamish to see the word written out at full length?")

"Partly on his interest being focussed on what he calls 'the soul,' which he persists in regarding as an entity independent of the physical environment, whereas, as I tried to point out to him . . ."

The Controller skipped the next sentences and was just about to turn the page in search of something more interestingly concrete, when his eye was caught by a series of quite extraordinary phrases. ". . . though I must admit," he read, "that I agree with the Savage in finding civilized infantility too easy or, as he put it, not expensive enough; and I would like to take this opportunity of drawing your fordship's attention to . . ."

Mustapha Mond's anger gave place almost at once to mirth. The idea of this creature solemnly lecturing him—*him*—about the social order was really too grotesque. The man must have gone mad. "I ought to give him a lesson," he said to himself; then threw back his head and laughed aloud. For the moment, at any rate, the lesson would not be given.

It was a small factory of lighting-sets for helicopters, a branch of the Electrical Equipment Corporation. They were met on the roof itself (for that circular letter of recommendation from the Controller was magical in its effects) by the Chief Technician and the Human Element Manager. They walked downstairs into the factory.

"Each process," explained the Human Element Manager, "is carried out, so far as possible, by a single Bokanovsky Group."

And, in effect, eighty-three almost noseless black brachycephalic Deltas were cold-pressing. The fifty-six four-spindle chucking and turning machines were being manipulated by fifty-six aquiline and ginger Gammas. One hundred and seven heat-conditioned Epsilon Senegalese were working in the foundry. Thirty-three Delta females, long-headed, sandy, with narrow pelvises, and all within 20 millimetres of 1 metre 69 centimetres tall, were cutting screws. In the assembling room, the dynamos were being put together by two sets of Gamma-Plus dwarfs. The two low work-tables faced one another; between them crawled the conveyor with its load of separate parts; forty-seven blonde heads were confronted by forty-seven brown ones. Forty-seven snubs by forty-seven hooks; forty-seven receding by forty-seven prognathous chins. The completed mechanisms were inspected by eighteen identical curly auburn girls in Gamma green, packed in crates by thirty-four short-legged, left-handed male Delta-Minuses, and loaded into the waiting trucks and lorries by sixty-three blue-eyed, flaxen and freckled Epsilon Semi-Morons.

"O brave new world . . ." By some malice of his memory the Savage found himself repeating Miranda's words. "O brave new world that has such people in it."

"And I assure you," the Human Element Manager concluded, as they left the factory, "we hardly ever have any trouble with our workers. We always find . . ."

But the Savage had suddenly broken away from his companions and was violently retching, behind a clump of laurels, as though the solid earth had been a helicopter in an air pocket.

"The Savage," wrote Bernard, "refuses to take *soma*, and seems much distressed because the woman Linda, his m——, remains permanently on holiday. It is worthy of note that, in spite of his m——'s senility and the extreme repulsiveness of her appearance, the Savage frequently goes to see her and appears to be much attracted to her—an interesting example of the way in which early conditioning can be made to modify and even run counter to natural impulses (in this case, the impulse to recoil from an unpleasant object)."

At Eton they alighted on the roof of Upper School. On the opposite side of School Yard, the fifty-two stories of Lupton's Tower gleamed white in the sunshine. College on their left and, on their right, the School Community Singery reared their venerable piles of ferro-concrete and vita-glass. In the centre of the quadrangle stood the quaint old chrome-steel statue of Our Ford.

Dr. Gaffney, the Provost, and Miss Keate, the Head Mistress, received them as they stepped out of the plane.

"Do you have many twins here?" the Savage asked rather apprehensively, as they set out on their tour of inspection.

"Oh, no," the Provost answered. "Eton is reserved exclusively for upper-caste boys and girls. One egg, one adult. It makes education more difficult of course. But as they'll be called upon to take responsibilities and deal with unexpected emergencies, it can't be helped." He sighed.

Bernard, meanwhile, had taken a strong fancy to Miss Keate. "If you're free any Monday, Wednesday, or Friday evening," he was saying. Jerking his thumb towards the Savage, "He's curious, you know," Bernard added. "Quaint."

Miss Keate smiled (and her smile was really charming, he thought); said Thank you; would be delighted to come to one of his parties. The Provost opened a door.

Five minutes in that Alpha Double Plus classroom left John a trifle bewildered.

"What *is* elementary relativity?" he whispered to Bernard. Bernard tried to explain, then thought better of it and suggested that they should go to some other classroom.

From behind a door in the corridor leading to the Beta-Minus geography room, a ringing soprano voice called, "One, two, three, four," and then, with a weary impatience, "As you were."

"Malthusian Drill," explained the Head Mistress. "Most of our girls are freemartins, of course. I'm a freemartin myself." She smiled at Bernard. "But we have about eight hundred unsterilized ones who need constant drilling."

In the Beta-Minus geography room John learnt that "a savage reservation is a place which, owing to unfavourable climatic or geological conditions, or poverty of natural resources, has not been worth the expense of civilizing." A click; the room was darkened; and suddenly, on the screen above the Master's head, there were the *Penitentes* of Acoma prostrating themselves before Our Lady, and wailing as John had heard them wail, confessing their sins before Jesus on the Cross, before the eagle image of Pookong. The young Etonians fairly shouted with laughter. Still wailing, the *Penitentes* rose to their feet, stripped off their upper garments and, with knotted whips, began to beat themselves, blow after blow. Redoubled, the laughter drowned even the amplified record of their groans.

"But why do they laugh?" asked the Savage in a pained bewilderment.

"Why?" The Provost turned towards him a still broadly grinning face. "*Why?* But because it's so extraordinarily funny."

In the cinematographic twilight, Bernard risked a gesture which, in the past, even total darkness would hardly have emboldened him to make. Strong in his new importance, he put his arm around the Head Mistress's waist. It yielded, willowily. He was just about to snatch a kiss or two and perhaps a gentle pinch, when the shutters clicked open again.

"Perhaps we had better go on," said Miss Keate, and moved towards the door.

"And this," said the Provost a moment later, "is the Hypnopædic Control Room."

Hundreds of synthetic music boxes, one for each dormitory, stood ranged in shelves round three sides of the room; pigeon-holed on the fourth were the paper soundtrack rolls on which the various hypnopædic lessons were printed.

"You slip the roll in here," explained Bernard, interrupting Dr. Gaffney, "press down this switch . . ."

"No, that one," corrected the Provost, annoyed.

"That one, then. The roll unwinds. The selenium cells transform the light impulses into sound waves, and . . ."

"And there you are," Dr. Gaffney concluded.

"Do they read Shakespeare?" asked the Savage as they walked, on their way to the Bio-chemical Laboratories, past the School Library.

"Certainly not," said the Head Mistress, blushing.

"Our library," said Dr. Gaffney, "contains only books of reference. If our young people need distraction, they can get it at the feelies. We don't encourage them to indulge in any solitary amusements."

Five bus-loads of boys and girls, singing or in a silent embracement, rolled past them over the vitrified highway.

"Just returned," explained Dr. Gaffney, while Bernard, whispering, made an appointment with the Head Mistress for that very evening, "from the Slough Crematorium. Death conditioning begins at eighteen months. Every tot spends two mornings a week in a Hospital for the Dying. All the best toys are kept there, and they get chocolate cream on death days. They learn to take dying as a matter of course."

"Like any other physiological process," put in the Head Mistress professionally.

Eight o'clock at the Savoy. It was all arranged.

On their way back to London they stopped at the Television Corporation's factory at Brentford.

"Do you mind waiting here a moment while I go and telephone?" asked Bernard.

The Savage waited and watched. The Main Day-Shift was just going off duty. Crowds of lower-caste workers were queued up in front of the monorail station—seven or eight hundred Gamma, Delta and Epsilon men and women, with not more than a dozen faces and statures between them. To each of them, with his or her ticket, the booking clerk pushed over a little cardboard pillbox. The long caterpillar of men and women moved slowly forward.

"What's in those" (remembering *The Merchant of Venice*) "those caskets?" the Savage enquired when Bernard had rejoined him.

"The day's *soma* ration," Bernard answered rather indistinctly; for he was masticating a piece of Benito Hoover's chewing-gum. "They get it after their work's over. Four half-gramme tablets. Six on Saturdays."

He took John's arm affectionately and they walked back towards the helicopter.

Lenina came singing into the Changing Room.

"You seem very pleased with yourself," said Fanny.

"I *am* pleased," she answered. Zip! "Bernard rang up half an hour ago." Zip, zip! She stepped out of her shorts. "He has an unexpected engagement." Zip! "Asked me if I'd take the Savage to the feelies this evening. I must fly." She hurried away towards the bathroom.

"She's a lucky girl," Fanny said to herself as she watched Lenina go.

There was no envy in the comment; good-natured Fanny was merely stating a fact. Lenina *was* lucky; lucky in having shared with Bernard a generous portion of the Savage's immense celebrity, lucky in reflecting from her insignificant person the moment's supremely fashionable glory. Had not the Secretary of the Young Women's Fordian Association asked her to give a lecture about her experiences? Had she not been invited to the Annual Dinner of the Aphroditeum Club? Had she not already appeared in the Feelytone News—visibly, audibly and tactually appeared to countless millions all over the planet?

Hardly less flattering had been the attentions paid her by conspicuous individuals. The Resident World Controller's Second Secretary had asked her to dinner and breakfast. She had spent one week-end with the Ford Chief-Justice, and another with the Arch-Community-Songster of Canterbury. The President of the Internal and External Secretions Corporation was perpetually on the phone, and she had been to Deauville with the Deputy-Governor of the Bank of Europe.

"It's wonderful, of course. And yet in a way," she had confessed to Fanny, "I feel as though I were getting something on false pretences. Because, of course, the first thing they all want to know is what it's like to make love to a Savage. And I have to say I don't know." She shook her head. "Most of the men don't believe me, of course. But it's true. I wish it weren't," she added sadly and sighed. "He's terribly good-looking; don't you think so?"

"But doesn't he like you?" asked Fanny.

"Sometimes I think he does and sometimes I think he doesn't. He always does his best to avoid me; goes out of the room when I come in; won't touch me; won't even look at me. But sometimes if I turn round suddenly, I catch him staring; and then—well, you know how men look when they like you."

Yes, Fanny knew.

"I can't make it out," said Lenina.

She couldn't make it out; and not only was bewildered; was also rather upset.

"Because, you see, Fanny, *I* like him."

Liked him more and more. Well, now there'd be a real chance, she thought, as she scented herself after her bath. Dab, dab, dab—a real chance. Her high spirits overflowed in song.

"Hug me till you drug me, honey;
Kiss me till I'm in a coma:
Hug me, honey, snuggly bunny;
Love's as good as soma."

The secret organ was playing a delightfully refreshing Herbal Capriccio—rippling arpeggios of thyme and lavender, of rosemary, basil, myrtle, tarragon; a series of daring modulations through the spice keys into ambergris; and a slow return through sandalwood, camphor, cedar and new-mown hay (with occasional subtle touches of discord—a whiff of kidney pudding, the faintest suspicion of pig's dung) back to the simple aromatics with which the piece began. The final blast of thyme died away; there was a round of applause; the lights went up. In the synthetic music machine the soundtrack roll began to unwind. It was a trio for hyper-violin, super-cello and oboe-surrogate that now filled the air with its agreeable languor. Thirty or forty bars—and then, against this instrumental background, a much more than human voice began to warble; now throaty, now from the head, now hollow as a flute, now charged with yearning harmonics, it effortlessly passed from Gaspard's Forster's low record on the very frontiers of musical tone to a trilled bat-note high above the highest C to which (in 1770, at the ducal opera of

Parma, and to the astonishment of Mozart) Lucrezia Ajugari, alone of all the singers in history, once piercingly gave utterance.

Sunk in their pneumatic stalls, Lenina and the Savage sniffed and listened. It was now the turn also for eyes and skin.

The house lights went down; fiery letters stood out solid and as though self-supported in the darkness. THREE WEEKS IN A HELICOPTER. AN ALL-SUPER-SINGING, SYNTHETIC-TALKING, COLOURED, STEREOSCOPIC FEELY. WITH SYNCHRONIZED SCENT-ORGAN ACCOMPANIMENT.

"Take hold of those metal knobs on the arms of your chair," whispered Lenina. "Otherwise you won't get any of the feely effects."

The Savage did as he was told.

Those fiery letters, meanwhile, had disappeared; there were ten seconds of complete darkness; then suddenly, dazzling and incomparably more solid-looking than they would have seemed in actual flesh and blood, far more real than reality, there stood the stereoscopic images, locked in one another's arms, of a gigantic negro and a golden-haired young brachycephalic Beta-Plus female.

The Savage started. That sensation on his lips! He lifted a hand to his mouth; the titillation ceased; let his hand fall back on the metal knob; it began again. The scent organ, meanwhile, breathed pure musk. Expiringly, a sound-track super-dove cooed "Oo-ooh"; and vibrating only thirty-two times a second, a deeper than African bass made answer: "Aa-aah." "Ooh-ah! Ooh-ah!" the stereoscopic lips came together again, and once more the facial erogenous zones of the six thousand spectators in the Alhambra tingled with almost intolerable galvanic pleasure. "Ooh . . ."

The plot of the film was extremely simple. A few minutes after the first Oohs and Aahs (a duet having been sung and a little love made on that famous bearskin, every hair of which—the Assistant Predestinator was perfectly right—could be separately and distinctly felt), the negro had a helicopter accident, fell on his head. Thump! what a twinge through the forehead! A chorus of *ow's* and *aie's* went up from the audience.

The concussion knocked all the negro's conditioning into a cocked hat. He developed for the Beta blonde an exclusive and maniacal passion. She protested. He persisted. There were struggles, pursuits, an assault on a rival, finally a sensational kidnapping. The Beta blonde was ravished away into the sky and kept there, hovering, for three weeks in a wildly anti-social *têta-à-tête* with the black madman. Finally, after a whole series of adventures and much aerial acrobacy three handsome young Alphas succeeded in rescuing her. The negro was packed off to an Adult Re-conditioning Centre and the film ended happily and decorously, with the Beta blonde becoming the mistress of all her three rescuers. They interrupted themselves for a moment to sing a synthetic quartet, with full super-orchestral accompaniment and gardenias on the scent organ. Then the bearskin made a final appearance and, amid a blare of sexophones, the last stereoscopic kiss faded into darkness, the last electric titillation died on the lips like a dying moth that quivers, quivers, ever more feebly, ever more faintly, and at last is quite, quite still.

But for Lenina the moth did not completely die. Even after the lights had gone up, while they were shuffling slowly along with the crowd towards the lifts, its ghost still fluttered against her lips, still traced fine shuddering roads of anxiety and pleasure across her skin. Her cheeks were flushed. She caught hold of the Savage's arm and pressed it, limp, against her side. He looked down at her for a moment, pale, pained, desiring, and ashamed of his desire. He was not worthy, not . . . Their eyes for a moment met. What treasures hers promised! A queen's ransom of temperament. Hastily he looked away, disengaged his imprisoned arm. He was obscurely terrified lest she should cease to be something he could feel himself unworthy of.

"I don't think you ought to see things like that," he said, making haste to transfer from Lenina herself to the surrounding circumstances the blame for any past or possible future lapse from perfection.

"Things like what, John?"

"Like this horrible film."

"Horrible?" Lenina was genuinely astonished. "But I thought it was lovely."

"It was base," he said indignantly, "it was ignoble."

She shook her head. "I don't know what you mean." Why was he so queer? Why did he go out of his way to spoil things?

In the taxicopter he hardly even looked at her. Bound by strong vows that had never been pronounced, obedient to laws that had long since ceased to run, he sat averted and in silence. Sometimes, as though a finger had plucked at some taut, almost breaking string, his whole body would shake with a sudden nervous start.

The taxicopter landed on the roof of Lenina's apartment house. "At last," she thought exultantly as she stepped out of the cab. At last—even though he *had* been so queer just now. Standing under a lamp, she peered into her hand mirror. At last. Yes, her nose *was* a bit shiny. She shook the loose powder from her puff. While he was paying off the taxi—there would just be time. She rubbed at the shininess, thinking: "He's terribly good-looking. No need for him to be shy like Bernard. And yet . . . Any other man would have done it long ago. Well, now at last." That fragment of a face in the little round mirror suddenly smiled at her.

"Good-night," said a strangled voice behind her. Lenina wheeled round. He was standing in the doorway of the cab, his eyes fixed, staring; had evidently been staring all this time while she was powdering her nose, waiting—but what for? or hesitating, trying to make up his mind, and all the time thinking, thinking—she could not imagine what extraordinary thoughts. "Good-night, Lenina," he repeated, and made a strange grimacing attempt to smile.

"But, John . . . I thought you were . . . I mean, aren't you? . . ."

He shut the door and bent forward to say something to the driver. The cab shot up into the air.

Looking down through the window in the floor, the Savage could see Lenina's upturned face, pale in the bluish light of the

lamps. The mouth was open, she was calling. Her foreshortened figure rushed away from him; the diminishing square of the roof seemed to be falling through the darkness.

Five minutes later he was back in his room. From its hiding-place he took out his mouse-nibbled volume, turned with religious care its stained and crumbled pages, and began to read *Othello*. Othello, he remembered, was like the hero of *Three Weeks in a Helicopter*—a black man.

Drying her eyes, Lenina walked across the roof to the lift. On her way down to the twenty-seventh floor she pulled out her *soma* bottle. One gramme, she decided, would not be enough; hers had been more than a one-gramme affliction. But if she took two grammes, she ran the risk of not waking up in time to-morrow morning. She compromised and, into her cupped left palm, shook out three half-gramme tablets.

12

Bernard had to shout through the locked door; the Savage would not open.

"But everybody's there, waiting for you."

"Let them wait," came back the muffled voice through the door.

"But you know quite well, John" (how difficult it is to sound persuasive at the top of one's voice!) "I asked them on purpose to meet you."

"You ought to have asked *me* first whether I wanted to meet *them*."

"But you always came before, John."

"That's precisely why I don't want to come again."

"Just to please me," Bernard bellowingly wheedled. "Won't you come to please me?"

"No."

"Do you seriously mean it?"

"Yes."

Despairingly, "But what shall I do?" Bernard wailed.

"Go to hell!" bawled the exasperated voice from within.

"But the Arch-Community-Songster of Canterbury is there tonight." Bernard was almost in tears.

"Ai yaa tákwa!" It was only in Zuñi that the Savage could ade-

quately express what he felt about the Arch-Community-Songster. *"Háni!"* he added as an afterthought; and then (with what derisive ferocity!): *"Sons éso tse-ná."* And he spat on the ground, as Popé might have done.

In the end Bernard had to slink back, diminished, to his rooms and inform the impatient assembly that the Savage would not be appearing that evening. The news was received with indignation. The men were furious at having been tricked into behaving politely to this insignificant fellow with the unsavoury reputation and the heretical opinions. The higher their position in the hierarchy, the deeper their resentment.

"To play such a joke on me," the Arch-Songster kept repeating, "on *me!*"

As for the women, they indignantly felt that they had been had on false pretences—had by a wretched little man who had had alcohol poured into his bottle by mistake—by a creature with a Gamma-Minus physique. It was an outrage, and they said so, more and more loudly. The Head Mistress of Eton was particularly scathing.

Lenina alone said nothing. Pale, her blue eyes clouded with an unwonted melancholy, she sat in a corner, cut off from those who surrounded her by an emotion which they did not share. She had come to the party filled with a strange feeling of anxious exultation. "In a few minutes," she had said to herself, as she entered the room, "I shall be seeing him, talking to him, telling him" (for she had come with her mind made up) "that I like him—more than anybody I've ever known. And then perhaps he'll say . . ."

What would he say? The blood had rushed to her cheeks.

"Why was he so strange the other night, after the feelies? So queer. And yet I'm absolutely sure he really does rather like me. I'm sure . . ."

It was at this moment that Bernard had made his announcement; the Savage wasn't coming to the party.

Lenina suddenly felt all the sensations normally experienced at the beginning of a Violent Passion Surrogate treatment—a sense of dreadful emptiness, a breathless apprehension, a nausea. Her heart seemed to stop beating.

"Perhaps it's because he doesn't like me," she said to herself. And at once this possibility became an established certainty: John had refused to come because he didn't like her. He didn't like her. . . .

"It really is a bit *too* thick," the Head Mistress of Eton was saying to the Director of Crematoria and Phosphorous Reclamation. "When I think that I actually . . ."

"Yes," came the voice of Fanny Crowne, "it's absolutely true about the alcohol. Some one I know knew some one who was working in the Embryo Store at the time. She said to my friend, and my friend said to me . . ."

"Too bad, too bad," said Henry Foster, sympathizing with the Arch-Community-Songster. "It may interest you to know that our ex-Director was on the point of transferring him to Iceland."

Pierced by every word that was spoken, the tight balloon of Bernard's happy self-confidence was leaking from a thousand wounds. Pale, distraught, abject and agitated, he moved among his guests stammering incoherent apologies, assuring them that next time the Savage would certainly be there, begging them to sit down and take a carotene sandwich, a slice of vitamin A *pâté,* a glass of champagne-surrogate. They duly ate, but ignored him; drank and were either rude to his face or talked to one another about him, loudly and offensively, as though he had not been there.

"And now, my friends," said the Arch-Community-Songster of Canterbury, in that beautiful ringing voice with which he led the proceedings at Ford's Day Celebrations, "Now, my friends, I think perhaps the time has come . . ." He rose, put down his glass, brushed from his purple viscose waistcoat the crumbs of a considerable collation, and walked towards the door.

Bernard darted forward to intercept him.

"Must you really, Arch-Songster? . . . It's very early still. I'd hoped you would . . ."

Yes, what hadn't he hoped, when Lenina confidentially told him that the Arch-Community-Songster would accept an invitation if it were sent. "He's really rather sweet, you know." And she had shown Bernard the little golden zipper-fastening in the form of a T which the Arch-Songster had given her as a memento of the week-end she had spent at Lambeth. *To meet the Arch-Community-Songster of Canterbury and Mr. Savage.* Bernard had proclaimed his triumph on every invitation card. But the Savage had chosen this evening of all evenings to lock himself up in his room, to shout *"Háni!"* and even (it was lucky that Bernard didn't understand Zuñi) *"Sons éso tse-ná!"* What should have been the crowning moment of Bernard's whole career had turned out to be the moment of his greatest humiliation.

"I'd so much hoped . . ." he stammeringly repeated, looking up at the great dignitary with pleading and distracted eyes.

"My young friend," said the Arch-Community-Songster in a tone of loud and solemn severity; there was a general silence. "Let me give you a word of advice." He wagged his finger at Bernard. "Before it's too late. A word of good advice." (His voice became sepulchral.) "Mend your ways, my young friend, mend your ways." He made the sign of the T over him and turned away. "Lenina, my dear," he called in another tone. "Come with me."

Obediently, but unsmiling and (wholly insensible of the honour done to her) without elation, Lenina walked after him, out of the room. The other guests followed at a respectful interval. The last of them slammed the door. Bernard was all alone.

Punctured, utterly deflated, he dropped into a chair and, covering his face with his hands, began to weep. A few minutes later, however, he thought better of it and took four tablets of *soma*.

Upstairs in his room the Savage was reading *Romeo and Juliet*.

Lenina and the Arch-Community-Songster stepped out on to the roof of Lambeth Palace. "Hurry up, my young friend—I mean,

Lenina," called the Arch-Songster impatiently from the lift gates. Lenina, who had lingered for a moment to look at the moon, dropped her eyes and came hurrying across the roof to rejoin him.

"A New Theory of Biology," was the title of the paper which Mustapha Mond had just finished reading. He sat for some time, meditatively frowning, then picked up his pen and wrote across the title-page: "The author's mathematical treatment of the conception of purpose is novel and highly ingenious, but heretical and, so far as the present social order is concerned, dangerous and potentially subversive. *Not to be published.*" He underlined the words. "The author will be kept under supervision. His transference to the Marine Biological Station of St. Helena may become necessary." A pity, he thought, as he signed his name. It was a masterly piece of work. But once you began admitting explanations in terms of purpose—well, you didn't know what the result might be. It was the sort of idea that might easily decondition the more unsettled minds among the higher castes—make them lose their faith in happiness as the Sovereign Good and take to believing, instead, that the goal was somewhere beyond, somewhere outside the present human sphere; that the purpose of life was not the maintenance of well-being, but some intensification and refining of consciousness, some enlargement of knowledge. Which was, the Controller reflected, quite possibly true. But not, in the present circumstance, admissible. He picked up his pen again, and under the words *"Not to be published"* drew a second line, thicker and blacker than the first; then sighed, "What fun it would be," he thought, "if one didn't have to think about happiness!"

With closed eyes, his face shining with rapture, John was softly declaiming to vacancy:

"Oh! she doth teach the torches to burn bright.
It seems she hangs upon the cheek of night,
Like a rich jewel in an Ethiop's ear;
Beauty too rich for use, for earth too dear . . ."

The golden T lay shining on Lenina's bosom. Sportively, the Arch-Community-Songster caught hold of it, sportively he pulled, pulled. "I think," said Lenina suddenly, breaking a long silence, "I'd better take a couple of grammes of *soma*."

Bernard, by this time, was fast asleep and smiling at the private paradise of his dreams. Smiling, smiling. But inexorably, every thirty seconds, the minute hand of the electric clock above his bed jumped forward with an almost imperceptible click. Click, click, click, click . . . And it was morning. Bernard was back among the miseries of space and time. It was in the lowest spirits that he taxied across to his work at the Conditioning Centre. The intoxication of success had evaporated; he was soberly his old self; and by contrast with the temporary balloon of these last weeks, the old self seemed unprecedentedly heavier than the surrounding atmosphere.

To this deflated Bernard the Savage showed himself unexpectedly sympathetic.

"You're more like what you were at Malpais," he said, when Bernard had told him his plaintive story. "Do you remember when we first talked together? Outside the little house. You're like what you were then."

"Because I'm unhappy again; that's why."

"Well, I'd rather be unhappy than have the sort of false, lying happiness you were having here."

"I like that," said Bernard bitterly. "When it's you who were the cause of it all. Refusing to come to my party and so turning them all against me!" He knew that what he was saying was absurd in its injustice; he admitted inwardly, and at last even aloud, the truth of all that the Savage now said about the worthlessness of friends who could be turned upon so slight a provocation into persecuting enemies. But in spite of this knowledge and these admissions, in spite of the fact that his friend's support and sympathy were now his only comfort, Bernard continued perversely to nourish, along with his quite genuine affection, a secret grievance against the Savage, to meditate a campaign of small revenges to be wreaked upon him. Nourishing a grievance against the Arch-Community-Songster was useless; there was no possibility of being revenged on the Chief Bottler or the Assistant Predestinator. As a victim, the Savage possessed, for Bernard, this enormous superiority over the others: that he was accessible. One of the principal functions of a friend is to suffer (in a milder and symbolic form) the punishments that we should like, but are unable, to inflict upon our enemies.

Bernard's other victim-friend was Helmholtz. When, discomfited, he came and asked once more for the friendship which, in his prosperity, he had not thought it worth his while to preserve, Helmholtz gave it; and gave it without a reproach, without a comment, as though he had forgotten that there had ever been a quarrel. Touched, Bernard felt himself at the same time humiliated by this magnanimity—a magnanimity the more extraordinary and therefore the more humiliating in that it owed nothing to *soma* and everything to Helmholtz's character. It was the Helmholtz of daily life who forgot and forgave, not the Helmholtz of a half-gramme holiday. Bernard was duly grateful (it was an enormous comfort to have his friend again) and also duly resentful (it would be a pleasure to take some revenge on Helmholtz for his generosity).

At their first meeting after the estrangement, Bernard poured out the tale of his miseries and accepted consolation. It was not till some days later that he learned, to his surprise and with a twinge of shame, that he was not the only one who had been in trouble. Helmholtz had also come into conflict with Authority.

"It was over some rhymes," he explained. "I was giving my usual course of Advanced Emotional Engineering for Third Year Students. Twelve lectures, of which the seventh is about rhymes. 'On the Use of Rhymes in Moral Propaganda and Advertisement,' to be precise. I always illustrate my lecture with a lot of technical examples. This time I thought I'd give them one I'd just written myself. Pure madness, of course; but I couldn't resist it." He laughed. "I was curious to see what their reactions would be. Besides," he added more gravely, "I wanted to do a bit of propaganda; I was trying to engineer them into feeling as I'd felt when I wrote the rhymes. Ford!" He laughed again. "What an outcry there was! The Principal had me up and threatened to hand me the immediate sack. I'm a marked man."

"But what were your rhymes?" Bernard asked.

"They were about being alone."

Bernard's eyebrows went up.

"I'll recite them to you, if you like." And Helmholtz began:

"Yesterday's committee,
Sticks, but a broken drum,
Midnight in the City,
Flutes in a vacuum,
Shut lips, sleeping faces,
Every stopped machine,
The dumb and littered places
Where crowds have been: . . .
All silences rejoice,
Weep (loudly or low),
Speak—but with the voice
Of whom, I do not know.
Absence, say, of Susan's,
Absence of Egeria's
Arms and respective bosoms,
Lips and, ah, posteriors,
Slowly form a presence;
Whose? and, I ask, of what

So absurd an essence,
That something, which is not,
Nevertheless should populate
Empty night more solidly
Than that with which we copulate,
Why should it seem so squalidly?

"Well, I gave them that as an example, and they reported me to the Principal."

"I'm not surprised," said Bernard. "It's flatly against all their sleep-teaching. Remember, they've had at least a quarter of a million warnings against solitude."

"I know. But I thought I'd like to see what the effect would be."

"Well, you've seen now."

Helmholtz only laughed. "I feel," he said, after a silence, "as though I were just beginning to have something to write about. As though I were beginning to be able to use that power I feel I've got inside me—that extra, latent power. Something seems to be coming to me." In spite of all his troubles, he seemed, Bernard thought, profoundly happy.

Helmholtz and the Savage took to one another at once. So cordially indeed that Bernard felt a sharp pang of jealousy. In all these weeks he had never come to so close an intimacy with the Savage as Helmholtz immediately achieved. Watching them, listening to their talk, he found himself sometimes resentfully wishing that he had never brought them together. He was ashamed of his jealousy and alternately made efforts of will and took *soma* to keep himself from feeling it. But the efforts were not very successful; and between the *soma*-holidays there were, of necessity, intervals. The odious sentiment kept on returning.

At his third meeting with the Savage, Helmholtz recited his rhymes on Solitude.

"What do you think of them?" he asked when he had done.

The Savage shook his head. "Listen to *this*," was his answer; and unlocking the drawer in which he kept his mouse-eaten book, he opened and read:

"Let the bird of loudest lay
On the sole Arabian tree,
Herald sad and trumpet be . . ."

Helmholtz listened with a growing excitement. At "sole Arabian tree" he started; at "thou shrieking harbinger" he smiled with sudden pleasure; at "every fowl of tyrant wing" the blood rushed up into his cheeks; but at "defunctive music" he turned pale and trembled with an unprecedented emotion. The Savage read on:

"Property was thus appall'd,
That the self was not the same;
Single nature's double name
Neither two nor one was call'd
Reason in itself confounded
Saw division grow together . . ."

"Orgy-porgy!" said Bernard, interrupting the reading with a loud, unpleasant laugh. "It's just a Solidarity Service hymn." He was revenging himself on his two friends for liking one another more than they liked him.

In the course of their next two or three meetings he frequently repeated this little act of vengeance. It was simple and, since both Helmholtz and the Savage were dreadfully pained by the shattering and defilement of a favourite poetic crystal, extremely effective. In the end, Helmholtz threatened to kick him out of the room if he dared to interrupt again. And yet, strangely enough, the next interruption, the most disgraceful of all, came from Helmholtz himself.

The Savage was reading *Romeo and Juliet* aloud—reading (for all the time he was seeing himself as Romeo and Lenina as Juliet) with an intense and quivering passion. Helmholtz had listened to the scene of the lovers' first meeting with a puzzled interest. The scene in the orchard had delighted him with its poetry; but the sentiments expressed had made him smile. Getting into such a state about having a girl—it seemed rather ridiculous. But, taken detail by verbal detail, what a superb piece of emotional engineering! "That old fellow," he said, "he makes our best propaganda technicians look absolutely silly." The Savage smiled triumphantly and resumed his reading. All went tolerably well until, in the last scene of the third act, Capulet and Lady Capulet began to bully Juliet to marry Paris. Helmholtz had been restless throughout the entire scene; but when, pathetically mimed by the Savage, Juliet cried out:

"Is there no pity sitting in the clouds,
That sees into the bottom of my grief?
O sweet my mother, cast me not away:
Delay this marriage for a month, a week;
Or, if you do not, make the bridal bed
In that dim monument where Tybalt lies . . ."

when Juliet said this, Helmholtz broke out in an explosion of uncontrollable guffawing.

The mother and father (grotesque obscenity) forcing the daughter to have some one she didn't want! And the idiotic girl not saying that she was having some one else whom (for the moment, at any rate) she preferred! In its smutty absurdity the situation was irresistibly comical. He had managed, with a heroic effort, to hold down the mounting pressure of his hilarity; but "sweet mother" (in the Savage's tremulous tone of anguish) and the reference to Tybalt lying dead, but evidently uncremated and wasting his phosphorous on a dim monument, were too much for him. He laughed and laughed till the tears streamed down his face—quenchlessly laughed while, pale with a sense of outrage, the Savage looked at him over the top of his book and then, as the laughter still continued, closed it indignantly, got up and, with the gesture of one who removes his pearl from before swine, locked it away in its drawer.

"And yet," said Helmholtz when, having recovered breath enough to apologize, he had mollified the Savage into listening to his explanations, "I know quite well that one needs ridiculous, mad situations like that; one can't write really well about anything else. Why was that old fellow such a marvellous propaganda technician? Because he had so many insane, excruciating things to get excited about. You've got to be hurt and upset; otherwise you can't think of the really good, penetrating, X-rayish phrases. But fathers and mothers!" He shook his head. "You can't expect me to keep a straight face about fathers and mothers. And who's going to get excited about a boy having a girl or not having her?" (The Savage winced; but Helmholtz, who was staring pensively at the floor, saw nothing.) "No," he concluded, with a sigh, "it won't do. We need some other kind of madness and violence. But what? What? Where can one find it?" He was silent; then, shaking his head, "I don't know," he said at last, "I don't know."

13

Henry Foster loomed up through the twilight of the Embryo Store.

"Like to come to a feely this evening?"

Lenina shook her head without speaking.

"Going out with some one else?" It interested him to know which of his friends was being had by which other. "Is it Benito?" he questioned.

She shook her head again.

Henry detected the weariness in those purple eyes, the pallor beneath that glaze of lupus, the sadness at the corners of the unsmiling crimson mouth. "You're not feeling ill, are you?" he asked, a trifle anxiously, afraid that she might be suffering from one of the few remaining infectious diseases.

Yet once more Lenina shook her head.

"Anyhow, you ought to go and see the doctor," said Henry. "A doctor a day keeps the jim-jams away," he added heartily, driving home his hypnopædic adage with a clap on the shoulder. "Perhaps you need a Pregnancy Substitute," he suggested. "Or else an extra-strong V.P.S. treatment. Sometimes, you know, the standard passion surrogate isn't quite . . ."

"Oh, for Ford's sake," said Lenina, breaking her stubborn silence, "shut up!" And she turned back to her neglected embryos.

A V.P.S. treatment indeed! She would have laughed, if she hadn't been on the point of crying. As though she hadn't got enough V.P. of her own! She sighed profoundly as she refilled her syringe. "John," she murmured to herself, "John . . ." Then "My Ford," she wondered, "have I given this one its sleeping sickness injection, or haven't I?" She simply couldn't remember. In the end, she decided not to run the risk of letting it have a second dose, and moved down the line to the next bottle.

Twenty-two years, eight months, and four days from that moment, a promising young Alpha-Minus administrator at Mwanza-Mwanza was to die of trypanosomiasis—the first case for over half a century. Sighing, Lenina went on with her work.

An hour later, in the Changing Room, Fanny was energetically protesting. "But it's absurd to let yourself get into a state like this. Simply absurd," she repeated "And what about? A man—*one* man."

"But he's the one I want."

"As though there weren't millions of other men in the world."

"But I don't want them."

"How can you know till you've tried?"

"I have tried."

"But how many?" asked Fanny, shrugging her shoulders contemptuously. "One, two?"

"Dozens. But," shaking her head, "it wasn't any good," she added.

"Well, you must persevere," said Fanny sententiously. But it was obvious that her confidence in her own prescriptions had been shaken. "Nothing can be achieved without perseverance."

"But meanwhile . . ."

"Don't think of him."

"I can't help it."

"Take *soma*, then."

"I do."

"Well, go on."

"But in the intervals I still like him. I shall always like him."

"Well, if that's the case," said Fanny, with decision, "why don't you just go and take him. Whether he wants it or no."

"But if you knew how terribly *queer* he was!"

"All the more reason for taking a firm line."

"It's all very well to *say* that."

"Don't stand any nonsense. Act." Fanny's voice was a trumpet; she might have been a Y.W.F.A. lecturer giving an evening talk to adolescent Beta-Minuses. "Yes, act—at once. Do it now."

"I'd be scared," said Lenina.

"Well, you've only got to take half a gramme of *soma* first. And now I'm going to have my bath." She marched off, trailing her towel.

The bell rang, and the Savage, who was impatiently hoping that Helmholtz would come that afternoon (for having at last made up his mind to talk to Helmholtz about Lenina, he could not bear to postpone his confidences a moment longer), jumped up and ran to the door.

"I had a premonition it was you, Helmholtz," he shouted as he opened.

On the threshold, in a white acetate-satin sailor suit, and with a round white cap rakishly tilted over her left ear, stood Lenina.

"Oh!" said the Savage, as though some one had struck him a heavy blow.

Half a gramme had been enough to make Lenina forget her fears and her embarrassments. "Hullo, John," she said, smiling, and walked past him into the room. Automatically he closed the door and followed her. Lenina sat down. There was a long silence.

"You don't seem very glad to see me, John," she said at last.

"Not glad?" The Savage looked at her reproachfully; then suddenly fell on his knees before her and, taking Lenina's hand, reverently kissed it. "Not glad? Oh, if you only knew," he whispered and, venturing to raise his eyes to her face, "Admired Lenina," he went on, "indeed the top of admiration, worth what's dearest in the world." She smiled at him with a luscious tenderness. "Oh, you so perfect" (she was leaning towards him with parted lips), "so perfect and so peerless are created" (nearer and nearer) "of every creature's best." Still nearer. The Savage suddenly scrambled to his feet. "That's why," he said speaking with averted face, "I wanted to *do* something first . . . I mean, to show I was worthy of you. Not that I could ever really be that. But at any rate to show I wasn't absolutely *un*-worthy. I wanted to do *something*."

"Why should you think it necessary . . ." Lenina began, but left the sentence unfinished. There was a note of irritation in her voice. When one has leant forward, nearer and nearer, with parted lips—only to find oneself, quite suddenly, as a clumsy oaf scrambles to his feet, leaning towards nothing at all—well, there is a reason, even with half a gramme of *soma* circulating in one's blood-stream, a genuine reason for annoyance.

"At Malpais," the Savage was incoherently mumbling, "you had to bring her the skin of a mountain lion—I mean, when you wanted to marry some one. Or else a wolf."

"There aren't any lions in England," Lenina almost snapped.

"And even if there were," the Savage added, with sudden contemptuous resentment, "people would kill them out of helicopters, I suppose, with poison gas or something. I wouldn't do *that*, Lenina." He squared his shoulders, he ventured to look at her and was met with a stare of annoyed incomprehension. Confused, "I'll do anything," he went on, more and more incoherently. "Anything you tell me. There be some sports are painful—you know. But their labour delight in them sets off. That's what I feel. I mean I'd sweep the floor if you wanted."

"But we've got vacuum cleaners here," said Lenina in bewilderment. "It isn't necessary."

"No, of course it isn't *necessary*. But some kinds of baseness are nobly undergone. I'd like to undergo something nobly. Don't you see?"

"But if there *are* vacuum cleaners . . ."

"That's not the point."

"And Epsilon Semi-Morons to work them," she went on, "well, really, *why?*"

"Why? But for you, for *you*. Just to show that I . . ."

"And what on earth vacuum cleaners have got to do with lions . . ."

"To show how much . . ."

"Or lions with being glad to see *me* . . ." She was getting more and more exasperated.

"How much I love you, Lenina," he brought out almost desperately.

An emblem of the inner tide of startled elation, the blood rushed up into Lenina's cheeks. "Do you mean it, John?"

"But I hadn't meant to say so," cried the Savage, clasping his hands in a kind of agony. "Not until . . . Listen, Lenina; in Malpais people get married."

"Get what?" The irritation had begun to creep back into her voice. What was he talking about now?

"For always. They make a promise to live together for always."

"What a horrible idea!" Lenina was genuinely shocked.

"Outliving beauty's outward with a mind that doth renew swifter than blood decays."

"What?"

"It's like that in Shakespeare too. 'If thou dost break her virgin knot before all sanctimonious ceremonies may with full and holy rite . . .' "

"For Ford's sake, John, talk sense. I can't understand a word you say. First it's vacuum cleaners; then it's knots. You're driving me crazy." She jumped up and, as though afraid that he might run away from her physically, as well as with his mind, caught him by the wrist. "Answer me this question: do you really like me, or don't you?"

There was a moment's silence; then, in a very low voice, "I love you more than anything in the world," he said.

"Then why on earth didn't you say so?" she cried, and so intense was her exasperation that she drove her sharp nails into the skin of his wrist. "Instead of drivelling away about knots and vacuum cleaners and lions, and making me miserable for weeks and weeks."

She released his hand and flung it angrily away from her.

"If I didn't like you so much," she said, "I'd be furious with you."

And suddenly her arms were round his neck; he felt her lips soft against his own. So deliciously soft, so warm and electric that inevitably he found himself thinking of the embraces in *Three Weeks in a Helicopter*. Ooh! ooh! the stereoscopic blonde and aah! the more than real blackamoor. Horror, horror, horror . . . he tried to disengage himself; but Lenina tightened her embrace.

"Why didn't you say so?" she whispered, drawing back her face to look at him. Her eyes were tenderly reproachful.

"The murkiest den, the most opportune place" (the voice of conscience thundered poetically), "the strongest suggestion our worser genius can, shall never melt mine honour into lust. Never, never!" he resolved.

"You silly boy!" she was saying. "I wanted you so much. And if you wanted me too, why didn't you? . . ."

"But, Lenina . . ." he began protesting; and as she immediately untwined her arms, as she stepped away from him, he thought, for a moment, that she had taken his unspoken hint. But when she unbuckled her white patent cartridge belt and hung it carefully over the back of a chair, he began to suspect that he had been mistaken.

"Lenina!" he repeated apprehensively.

She put her hand to her neck and gave a long vertical pull; her white sailor's blouse was ripped to the hem; suspicion condensed into a too, too solid certainty. "Lenina, what *are* you doing?"

Zip, zip! Her answer was wordless. She stepped out of her bell-bottomed trousers. Her zippicamiknicks were a pale shell pink. The Arch-Community-Songster's golden T dangled at her breast.

"For those milk paps that through the window bars bore at men's eyes. . . ." The singing, thundering, magical words made her seem doubly dangerous, doubly alluring. Soft, soft, but how piercing! boring and drilling into reason, tunnelling through resolution. "The strongest oaths are straw to the fire i' the blood. Be more abstemious, or else . . ."

Zip! The rounded pinkness fell apart like a neatly divided apple. A wriggle of the arms, a lifting first of the right foot, then the left: the zippicamiknicks were lying lifeless and as though deflated on the floor.

Still wearing her shoes and socks, and her rakishly tilted round white cap, she advanced towards him. "Darling. *Darling!* If only you'd said so before!" She held out her arms.

But instead of also saying "Darling!" and holding out *his* arms, the Savage retreated in terror, flapping his hands at her as though he were trying to scare away some intruding and dangerous animal. Four backwards steps, and he was brought to bay against the wall.

"Sweet!" said Lenina and, laying her hands on his shoulders, pressed herself against him. "Put your arms round me," she commanded. "Hug me till you drug me, honey." She too had poetry at her command, knew words that sang and were spells and beat drums. "Kiss me"; she closed her eyes, she let her voice sink to a sleepy murmur, "kiss me till I'm in a coma. Hug me, honey, snuggly . . ."

The Savage caught her by the wrists, tore her hands from his shoulders, thrust her roughly away at arm's length.

"Ow, you're hurting me, you're . . . oh!" She was suddenly silent. Terror had made her forget the pain. Opening her eyes, she had seen his face—no, not *his* face, a ferocious stranger's, pale, distorted, twitching with some insane, inexplicable fury. Aghast, "But what is it, John?" she whispered. He did not answer, but only stared into her face with those mad eyes. The hands that held her wrists were trembling. He breathed deeply and irregularly. Faint almost to imperceptibility, but appalling, she suddenly heard the grinding of his teeth. "What is it?" she almost screamed.

And as though awakened by her cry he caught her by the shoulders and shook her. "Whore!" he shouted. "Whore! Impudent strumpet!"

"Oh, don't, do-on't," she protested in a voice made grotesquely tremulous by his shaking.

"Whore!"

"Ple-ease."

"Damned whore!"

"A gra-amme is be-etter . . ." she began.

The Savage pushed her away with such force that she staggered and fell. "Go," he shouted, standing over her menacingly, "get out of my sight or I'll kill you." He clenched his fists.

Lenina raised her arm to cover her face. "No, please don't, John . . ."

"Hurry up. Quick!"

One arm still raised, and following his every movement with a terrified eye, she scrambled to her feet and still crouching, still covering her head, made a dash for the bathroom.

The noise of that prodigious slap by which her departure was accelerated was like a pistol shot.

"Ow!" Lenina bounded forward.

Safely locked into the bathroom, she had leisure to take stock of her injuries. Standing with her back to the mirror, she twisted her head. Looking over her left shoulder she could see the imprint of an open hand standing out distinct and crimson on the pearly flesh. Gingerly she rubbed the wounded spot.

Outside, in the other room, the Savage was striding up and down, marching, marching to the drums and music of magical words. "The wren goes to't and the small gilded fly does lecher in my sight." Maddeningly they rumbled in his ears. "The fitchew nor the soiled horse goes to't with a more riotous appetite. Down from the waist they are Centaurs, though women all above. But to the girdle do the gods inherit. Beneath is all the fiend's. There's hell, there's darkness, there is the sulphurous pit, burning, scalding, stench, consumption; fie, fie, fie, pah, pah! Give me an ounce of civet, good apothecary, to sweeten my imagination."

"John!" ventured a small ingratiating voice from the bathroom. "John!"

"O thou weed, who are so lovely fair and smell'st so sweet that the sense aches at thee. Was this most goodly book made to write 'whore' upon? Heaven stops the nose at it . . ."

But her perfume still hung about him, his jacket was white with the powder that had scented her velvety body. "Impudent strumpet, impudent strumpet, impudent strumpet." The inexorable rhythm beat itself out. "Impudent . . ."

"John, do you think I might have my clothes?"

He picked up the bell-bottomed trousers, the blouse, the zippicamiknicks.

"Open!" he ordered, kicking the door.

"No, I won't." The voice was frightened and defiant.

"Well, how do you expect me to give them to you?"

"Push them through the ventilator over the door."

He did what she suggested and returned to his uneasy pacing of the room. "Impudent strumpet, impudent strumpet. The devil Luxury with his fat rump and potato finger . . ."

"John."

He would not answer. "Fat rump and potato finger."

"John."

"What is it?" he asked gruffly.

"I wonder if you'd mind giving me my Malthusian belt."

Lenina sat, listening to the footsteps in the other room, wondering, as she listened, how long he was likely to go tramping up and down like that; whether she would have to wait until he left the flat; or if it would be safe, after allowing his madness a reasonable time to subside, to open the bathroom door and make a dash for it.

She was interrupted in the midst of these uneasy speculations by the sound of the telephone bell ringing in the other room. Abruptly the tramping ceased. She heard the voice of the Savage parleying with silence.

"Hullo."

. . . .

"Yes."

. . . .

"If I do not usurp myself, I am."

. . . .

"Yes, didn't you hear me say so? Mr. Savage speaking."

. . . .

"What? Who's ill? Of course it interests me."

. . . .

"But is it serious? Is she really bad? I'll go at once . . ."

. . . .

"Not in her rooms any more? Where has she been taken?"

. . . .

"Oh, my God! What's the address?"

. . . .

"Three Park Lane—is that it? Three? Thanks."

Lenina heard the click of the replaced receiver, then hurrying steps. A door slammed. There was silence. Was he really gone?

With an infinity of precautions she opened the door a quarter of an inch; peeped through the crack; was encouraged by the view of emptiness; opened a little further; and put her whole head out; finally tiptoed into the room; stood for a few seconds with strongly beating heart, listening, listening; then darted to the front door, opened, slipped through, slammed, ran. It was not till she was in the lift and actually dropping down the well that she began to feel herself secure.

14

The Park Lane Hospital for the Dying was a sixty-story tower of primrose tiles. As the Savage stepped out of his taxicopter a convoy of gaily-coloured aerial hearses rose whirring from the roof and darted away across the Park, westwards, bound for the Slough Crematorium. At the lift gates the presiding porter gave him the information he required, and he dropped down to Ward 81 (a Galloping Senility ward, the porter explained) on the seventeenth floor.

It was a large room bright with sunshine and yellow paint, and containing twenty beds, all occupied. Linda was dying in company—in company and with all the modern conveniences. The air was continuously alive with gay synthetic melodies. At the foot of every bed, confronting its moribund occupant, was a television box. Television was left on, a running tap, from morning till night. Every quarter of an hour the prevailing perfume of the room was automatically changed. "We try," explained the nurse, who had taken charge of the Savage at the door, "we try to create a thoroughly pleasant atmosphere here, something between a first-class hotel and a feely-palace, if you take my meaning."

"Where is she?" asked the Savage, ignoring these polite explanations.

The nurse was offended. "You *are* in a hurry," she said.

"Is there any hope?" he asked.

"You mean, of her not dying?" (He nodded.) "No, of course there isn't. When somebody's sent here, there's no . . ." Startled by the expression of distress on his pale face, she suddenly broke off. "Why, whatever is the matter?" she asked. She was not accustomed to this kind of thing in visitors. (Not that there were many visitors anyhow: or any reason why there should be many visitors.) "You're not feeling ill, are you?"

He shook his head. "She's my mother," he said in a scarcely audible voice.

The nurse glanced at him with startled, horrified eyes; then quickly looked away. From throat to temple she was all one hot blush.

"Take me to her," said the Savage, making an effort to speak in an ordinary tone.

Still blushing, she led the way down the ward. Faces still fresh and unwithered (for senility galloped so hard that it had no time to age the cheeks, only the heart and brain) turned as they passed. Their progress was followed by the blank, incurious eyes of second infancy. The Savage shuddered as he looked.

Linda was lying in the last of the long row of beds, next to the wall. Propped up on pillows, she was watching the Semi-finals of the South American Riemann-Surface Tennis Championship, which were being played in silent and diminished reproduction on the screen of the television box at the foot of the bed. Hither and thither across their square of illuminated glass the little figures noiselessly darted, like fish in an aquarium—the silent but agitated inhabitants of another world.

Linda looked on, vaguely and uncomprehendingly smiling. Her pale, bloated face wore an expression of imbecile happiness. Every now and then her eyelids closed, and for a few seconds she seemed to be dozing. Then with a little start she would wake up again—wake up to the aquarium antics of the Tennis Champions, to the Super-Vox-Wurlitzeriana rendering of "Hug me till you drug me, honey," to the warm draught of verbena that came blowing through the ventilator above her head—would wake to these things, or rather to a dream of which these things, transformed and embellished by the *soma* in her blood, were the marvellous constituents, and smile once more her broken and discoloured smile of infantile contentment.

"Well, I must go," said the nurse. "I've got my batch of children coming. Besides, there's Number 3." She pointed up the ward. "Might go off any minute now. Well, make yourself comfortable." She walked briskly away.

The Savage sat down beside the bed.

"Linda," he whispered, taking her hand.

At the sound of her name, she turned. Her vague eyes brightened with recognition. She squeezed his hand, she smiled, her lips moved, then quite suddenly her head fell forward. She was asleep. He sat watching her—seeking through the tired flesh, seeking and finding that young, bright face which had stooped over his childhood in Malpais, remembering (and he closed his eyes) her voice, her movements, all the events of their life together. "Streptocock-Gee to Banbury T . . ." How beautiful her singing had been! And those childish rhymes, how magically strange and mysterious!

A, B, C, vitamin D:
The fat's in the liver, the cod's in the sea.

He felt the hot tears welling up behind his eyelids as he recalled the words and Linda's voice as she repeated them. And then the reading lessons: The tot is in the pot, the cat is on the mat; and the Elementary Instructions for Beta Workers in the Embryo Store. And long evenings by the fire or, in summertime, on the roof of the little house, when she told him those stories about the Other Place, outside the Reservation: that beautiful, beautiful Other Place, whose memory, as of a heaven, a paradise of goodness and loveliness, he still kept whole and intact, undefiled by contact with the reality of this real London, these actual civilized men and women.

A sudden noise of shrill voices made him open his eyes and, after hastily brushing away the tears, look round. What seemed an interminable stream of identical eight-year-old male twins was pouring into the room. Twin after twin, twin after twin, they came—a nightmare. Their faces, their repeated face—for there was only one between the lot of them—puggishly stared, all nostrils and pale goggling eyes. Their uniform was khaki. All their mouths hung open. Squealing and chattering they entered. In a moment, it seemed, the ward was maggoty with them. They swarmed between the beds, clambered over, crawled under, peeped into the television boxes, made faces at the patients.

Linda astonished and rather alarmed them. A group stood clustered at the foot of her bed, staring with the frightened and stupid curiosity of animals suddenly confronted by the unknown.

"Oh, look, look!" They spoke in low, scared voices. "Whatever is the matter with her? Why is she so fat?"

They had never seen a face like hers before—had never seen a face that was not youthful and taut-skinned, a body that had ceased to be slim and upright. All these moribund sexagenarians had the appearance of childish girls. At forty-four, Linda seemed, by contrast, a monster of flaccid and distorted senility.

"Isn't she awful?" came the whispered comments. "Look at her teeth!"

Suddenly from under the bed a pug-faced twin popped up between John's chair and the wall, and began peering into Linda's sleeping face.

"I say . . ." he began; but the sentence ended prematurely in a squeal. The Savage had seized him by the collar, lifted him clear over the chair and, with a smart box on the ears, sent him howling away.

His yells brought the Head Nurse hurrying to the rescue.

"What have you been doing to him?" she demanded fiercely. "I won't have you striking the children."

"Well then, keep them away from this bed." The Savage's voice was trembling with indignation. "What are these filthy little brats doing here at all? It's disgraceful!"

"Disgraceful? But what do you mean? They're being death-conditioned. And I tell you," she warned him truculently, "if I have any more of your interference with their conditioning, I'll send for the porters and have you thrown out."

The Savage rose to his feet and took a couple of steps towards her. His movements and the expression on his face were so menacing that the nurse fell back in terror. With a great effort he checked himself and, without speaking, turned away and sat down again by the bed.

Reassured, but with a dignity that was a trifle shrill and uncertain, "I've warned you," said the nurse, "so mind." Still, she led the too inquisitive twins away and made them join in the game of hunt-the-zipper, which had been organized by one of her colleagues at the other end of the room.

"Run along now and have your cup of caffeine solution, dear," she said to the other nurse. The exercise of authority restored her confidence, made her feel better. "Now children!" she called.

Linda had stirred uneasily, had opened her eyes for a moment, looked vaguely around, and then once more dropped off to sleep. Sitting beside her, the Savage tried hard to recapture his mood of a few minutes before. "A, B, C, vitamin D," he repeated to himself, as though the words were a spell that would restore the dead past to life. But the spell was ineffective. Obstinately the beautiful memories refused to rise; there was only a hateful resurrection of jealousies and uglinesses and miseries. Popé with the blood trickling down from his cut shoulder; and Linda hideously asleep, and the flies buzzing round the spilt *mescal* on the floor beside the bed; and the boys calling those names as she passed. . . . Ah, no, no! He shut his eyes, he shook his head in strenuous denial of these memories. "A, B, C, vitamin D . . ." He tried to think of those times when he sat on her knees and she put her arms about him and sang, over and over again, rocking him, rocking him to sleep. "A, B, C, vitamin D, vitamin D, vitamin D . . ."

The Super-Vox-Wurlitzeriana had risen to a sobbing crescendo; and suddenly the verbena gave place, in the scent-circulating system, to an intense patchouli. Linda stirred, woke up, stared for a few seconds bewilderedly at the Semi-finalists, then, lifting her face, sniffed once or twice at the newly perfumed air and suddenly smiled—a smile of childish ecstasy.

"Popé!" she murmured, and closed her eyes. "Oh, I do so like it, I do . . ." She sighed and let herself sink back into the pillows.

"But, Linda!" The Savage spoke imploringly, "Don't you know me?" He had tried so hard, had done his very best; why wouldn't she allow him to forget? He squeezed her limp hand almost with violence, as though he would force her to come back from this dream of ignoble pleasures, from these base and hateful memories—back into the present, back into reality; the appalling present, the awful reality—but sublime, but significant, but desperately important precisely because of the imminence of that which made them so fearful. "Don't you know me, Linda?"

He felt the faint answering pressure of her hand. The tears started into his eyes. He bent over her and kissed her.

Her lips moved. "Popé!" she whispered again, and it was as though he had had a pailful of ordure thrown in his face.

Anger suddenly boiled up in him. Balked for the second time, the passion of his grief had found another outlet, was transformed into a passion of agonized rage.

"But I'm John!" he shouted. "I'm John!" And in his furious misery he actually caught her by the shoulder and shook her.

Linda's eyes fluttered open; she saw him, knew him—"John!"—but situated the real face, the real and violent hands, in an imaginary world—among the inward and private equivalents of patchouli and the Super-Wurlitzer, among the transfigured memories and the strangely transposed sensations that constituted the universe of her dream. She knew him for John, her son, but fancied him an intruder into that paradisal Malpais where she had been spending her *soma*-holiday with Popé. He was angry because she liked Popé, he was shaking her because Popé was there in the bed—as though there were something wrong, as though all civilized people didn't do the same. "Every one belongs to every . . ." Her voice suddenly died into an almost inaudible breathless croaking. Her mouth fell open: she made a desperate effort to fill her lungs with air. But it was as though she had forgotten how to breathe. She tried to cry out—but no sound came; only the terror of her staring eyes revealed what she was suffering. Her hands went to her throat, then clawed at the air—the air she could no longer breathe, the air that, for her, had ceased to exist.

The Savage was on his feet, bent over her. "What is it, Linda? What is it?" His voice was imploring; it was as though he were begging to be reassured.

The look she gave him was charged with an unspeakable terror—with terror and, it seemed to him, reproach. She tried to raise herself in bed, but fell back on to the pillows. Her face was horribly distorted, her lips blue.

The Savage turned and ran up the ward.

"Quick, quick!" he shouted. "Quick!"

Standing in the center of a ring of zipper-hunting twins, the Head Nurse looked round. The first moment's astonishment gave place almost instantly to disapproval. "Don't shout! Think of the little ones," she said, frowning. "You might decondition . . . But what are you doing?" He had broken through the ring. "Be careful!" A child was yelling.

"Quick, quick!" He caught her by the sleeve, dragged her after him. "Quick! Something's happened. I've killed her."

By the time they were back at the end of the ward Linda was dead.

The Savage stood for a moment in frozen silence, then fell on his knees beside the bed and, covering his face with his hands, sobbed uncontrollably.

The nurse stood irresolute, looking now at the kneeling figure by the bed (the scandalous exhibition!) and now (poor children!) at the twins who had stopped their hunting of the zipper and were staring from the other end of the ward, staring with all their eyes and nostrils at the shocking scene that was being enacted round Bed 20. Should she speak to him? try to bring him back to a sense of decency? remind him of where he was? of what fatal mischief he might do to these poor innocents? Undoing all their wholesome death-conditioning with this disgusting outcry—as though death were something terrible, as though any one mattered as much as all that! It might give them the most disastrous ideas about the subject, might upset them into reacting in the entirely wrong, the utterly antisocial way.

She stepped forward, she touched him on the shoulder. "Can't you behave?" she said in a low, angry voice. But, looking around, she saw that half a dozen twins were already on their feet and advancing down the ward. The circle was disintegrating. In another moment . . . No, the risk was too great; the whole Group might be put back six or seven months in its conditioning. She hurried back towards her menaced charges.

"Now, who wants a chocolate éclair?" she asked in a loud, cheerful tone.

"Me!" yelled the entire Bokanovsky Group in chorus. Bed 20 was completely forgotten.

"Oh, God, God, God . . ." the Savage kept repeating to himself. In the chaos of grief and remorse that filled his mind it was the one articulate word. "God!" he whispered it aloud. "God . . ."

"Whatever *is* he saying?" said a voice, very near, distinct and shrill through the warblings of the Super-Wurlitzer.

The Savage violently started and, uncovering his face, looked round. Five khaki twins, each with the stump of a long éclair in his right hand, and their identical faces variously smeared with liquid chocolate, were standing in a row, puggily goggling at him.

They met his eyes and simultaneously grinned. One of them pointed with his éclair butt.

"Is she dead?" he asked.

The Savage stared at them for a moment in silence. Then in silence he rose to his feet, in silence slowly walked towards the door.

"Is she dead?" repeated the inquisitive twin trotting at his side.

The Savage looked down at him and still without speaking pushed him away. The twin fell on the floor and at once began to howl. The Savage did not even look round.

15

The menial staff of the Park Lane Hospital for the Dying consisted of one hundred and sixty-two Deltas divided into two Bokanovsky Groups of eighty-four red-headed female and seventy-eight dark dolychocephalic male twins, respectively. At six, when their working day was over, the two Groups assembled in the vestibule of the Hospital and were served by the Deputy Sub-Bursar with their *soma* ration.

From the lift the Savage stepped out into the midst of them. But his mind was elsewhere—with death, with his grief, and his remorse; mechanically, without consciousness of what he was doing, he began to shoulder his way through the crowd.

"Who are you pushing? Where do you think you're going?"

High, low, from a multitude of separate throats, only two voices squeaked or growled. Repeated indefinitely, as though by a train of mirrors, two faces, one a hairless and freckled moon haloed in orange, the other a thin, beaked bird-mask, stubbly with two days' beard, turned angrily towards him. Their words and, in his ribs, the sharp nudging of elbows, broke through his unawareness. He woke once more to external reality, looked round him, knew what he saw—knew it, with a sinking sense of horror and disgust, for the recurrent delirium of his days and nights, the nightmare of swarming indistinguishable sameness. Twins, twins. . . . Like maggots they had swarmed defilingly over the mystery of Linda's death. Maggots again, but larger, full grown, they now crawled across his grief and his repentance. He halted and, with bewildered and horrified eyes, stared round him at the khaki mob, in the midst of which, overtopping it by a full head, he stood. "How many goodly creatures are there here!" The singing words mocked him derisively. "How beauteous mankind is! O brave new world . . ."

"*Soma* distribution!" shouted a loud voice. "In good order, please. Hurry up there."

A door had been opened, a table and chair carried into the vestibule. The voice was that of a jaunty young Alpha, who had entered carrying a black iron cash-box. A murmur of satisfaction went up from the expectant twins. They forgot all about the Savage. Their attention was now focused on the black cash-box, which the young man had placed on the table, and was now in process of unlocking. The lid was lifted.

"Oo-oh!" said all the hundred and sixty-two simultaneously, as though they were looking at fireworks.

The young man took out a handful of tiny pill-boxes. "Now," he said peremptorily, "step forward, please. One at a time, and no shoving."

One at a time, with no shoving, the twins stepped forward. First two males, then a female, then another male, then three females, then . . .

The Savage stood looking on. "O brave new world, O brave new world . . ." In his mind the singing words seemed to change their tone. They had mocked him through his misery and remorse, mocked him with how hideous a note of cynical derision! Fiendishly laughing, they had insisted on the low squalor, the nauseous ugliness of the nightmare. Now, suddenly, they trumpeted a call to arms. "O brave new world!" Miranda was proclaiming the possibility of loveliness, the possibility of transforming even the nightmare into something fine and noble. "O brave new world!" It was a challenge, a command.

"No shoving there now!" shouted the Deputy Sub-Bursar in a fury. He slammed down the lid of his cash-box. "I shall stop the distribution unless I have good behaviour."

The Deltas muttered, jostled one another a little, and then were still. The threat had been effective. Deprivation of *soma*—appalling thought!

"That's better," said the young man, and reopened his cash-box.

Linda had been a slave, Linda had died; others should live in freedom, and the world be made beautiful. A reparation, a duty. And suddenly it was luminously clear to the Savage what he must do; it was as though a shutter had been opened, a curtain drawn back.

"Now," said the Deputy Sub-Bursar.

Another khaki female stepped forward.

"Stop!" called the Savage in a loud and ringing voice. "Stop!"

He pushed his way to the table; the Deltas stared at him with astonishment.

"Ford!" said the Deputy Sub-Bursar, below his breath. "It's the Savage." He felt scared.

"Listen, I beg of you," cried the Savage earnestly. "Lend me your ears . . ." He had never spoken in public before, and found it very difficult to express what he wanted to say. "Don't take that horrible stuff. It's poison, it's poison."

"I say, Mr. Savage," said the Deputy Sub-Bursar, smiling propitiatingly. "Would you mind letting me . . ."

"Poison to soul as well as body."

"Yes, but let me get on with my distribution, won't you? There's a good fellow." With the cautious tenderness of one who strokes a notoriously vicious animal, he patted the Savage's arm. "Just let me . . ."

"Never!" cried the Savage.

"But look here, old man . . ."

"Throw it all away, that horrible poison."

The words "Throw it all away" pierced through the enfolding layers of incomprehension to the quick of the Deltas' consciousness. An angry murmur went up from the crowd.

"I come to bring you freedom," said the Savage, turning back towards the twins. "I come . . ."

The Deputy Sub-Bursar heard no more; he had slipped out of the vestibule and was looking up a number in the telephone book.

"Not in his own rooms," Bernard summed up. "Not in mine, not in yours. Not at the Aphroditæum; not at the Centre or the College. Where can he have got to?"

Helmholtz shrugged his shoulders. They had come back from their work expecting to find the Savage waiting for them at one or other of the usual meeting-places, and there was no sign of the fellow. Which was annoying, as they had meant to nip across to Biarritz in Helmholtz's four-seater sporticopter. They'd be late for dinner if he didn't come soon.

"We'll give him five more minutes," said Helmholtz. "If he doesn't turn up by then we'll . . ."

The ringing of the telephone bell interrupted him. He picked up the receiver. "Hullo. Speaking." Then, after a long interval of listening, "Ford in Flivver!" he swore. "I'll come at once."

"What is it?" Bernard asked.

"A fellow I know at the Park Lane Hospital," said Helmholtz. "The Savage is there. Seems to have gone mad. Anyhow, it's urgent. Will you come with me?"

Together they hurried along the corridor to the lifts.

"But do you like being slaves?" the Savage was saying as they entered the Hospital. His face was flushed, his eyes bright with ardour and indignation. "Do you like being babies? Yes, babies. Mewling and puking," he added, exasperated by their bestial stupidity into throwing insults at those he had come to save. The insults bounced off their carapace of thick stupidity; they stared at him with a blank expression of dull and sullen resentment in their eyes. "Yes, puking!" he fairly shouted. Grief and remorse, compassion and duty—all were forgotten now and, as it were, absorbed into an intense overpowering hatred of these less than human monsters. "Don't you want to be free and men? Don't you even understand what manhood and freedom are?" Rage was making him fluent; the words came easily, in a rush. "Don't you?" he repeated, but got no answer to his question. "Very well then," he went on grimly. "I'll teach you; I'll *make* you be free whether you want to or not." And pushing open a window that looked on to the inner court of the Hospital, he began to throw the little pill-boxes of *soma* tablets in handfuls out into the area.

For a moment the khaki mob was silent, petrified, at the spectacle of this wanton sacrilege, with amazement and horror.

"He's mad," whispered Bernard, staring with wide open eyes. "They'll kill him. They'll . . ." A great shout suddenly went up from the mob; a wave of movement drove it menacingly towards the Savage. "Ford help him!" said Bernard, and averted his eyes.

"Ford helps those who help themselves." And with a laugh, actually a laugh of exultation, Helmholtz Watson pushed his way through the crowd.

"Free, free!" the Savage shouted, and with one hand continued to throw the *soma* into the area while, with the other, he punched the indistinguishable faces of his assailants. "Free!" And suddenly there was Helmholtz at his side—"Good old Helmholtz!"—also punching—"Men at last!"—and in the interval also throwing the poison out by handfuls through the open window. "Yes, men! men!" and there was no more poison left. He picked up the cash-box and showed them its black emptiness. "You're free!"

Howling, the Deltas charged with a redoubled fury.

Hesitant on the fringes of the battle. "They're done for," said Bernard and, urged by a sudden impulse, ran forward to help them; then thought better of it and halted; then, ashamed, stepped forward again; then again thought better of it, and was standing in an agony of humiliated indecision—thinking that *they* might be killed if he didn't help them, and that *he* might be killed if he did—when (Ford be praised!), goggle-eyed and swine-snouted in their gas-masks, in ran the police.

Bernard dashed to meet them. He waved his arms; and it was action, he was doing something. He shouted "Help!" several times, more and more loudly so as to give himself the illusion of helping. "Help! *Help!* HELP!"

The policemen pushed him out of the way and got on with their work. Three men with spraying machines buckled to their shoulders pumped thick clouds of *soma* vapour into the air. Two more were busy round the portable Synthetic Music Box. Carrying water pistols charged with a powerful anæsthetic, four others had pushed their way into the crowd and were methodically laying out, squirt by squirt, the more ferocious of the fighters.

"Quick, quick!" yelled Bernard. "They'll be killed if you don't hurry. They'll . . . Oh!" Annoyed by his chatter, one of the policemen had given him a shot from his water pistol. Bernard stood for a second or two wambling unsteadily on legs that seemed to have lost their bones, their tendons, their muscles, to have become mere sticks of jelly, and at last not even jelly—water: he tumbled in a heap on the floor.

Suddenly, from out of the Synthetic Music Box a Voice began to speak. The Voice of Reason, the Voice of Good Feeling. The sound-track roll was unwinding itself in Synthetic Anti-Riot Speech Number Two (Medium Strength). Straight from the depths of a non-existent heart, "My friends, my friends!" said the Voice so pathetically, with a note of such infinitely tender reproach that, behind their gas masks, even the policemen's eyes were momentarily dimmed with tears, "what is the meaning of this? Why aren't you all being happy and good together? Happy and good," the Voice repeated. "At peace, at peace." It trembled, sank into a whisper and momentarily expired. "Oh, I do want you to be happy," it began, with a yearning earnestness. "I do so want you to be good! Please, please be good and . . ."

Two minutes later the Voice and the *soma* vapour had produced their effect. In tears, the Deltas were kissing and hugging one another—half a dozen twins at a time in a comprehensive embrace. Even Helmholtz and the Savage were almost crying. A fresh supply of pill-boxes was brought in from the Bursary; a new distribution was hastily made and, to the sound of the Voice's richly affectionate, baritone valedictions, the twins dispersed, blubbering as though their hearts would break. "Good-bye, my dearest, dearest friends, Ford keep you! Good-bye, my dearest, dearest friends, Ford keep you. Good-bye my dearest, dearest . . ."

When the last of the Deltas had gone the policeman switched off the current. The angelic Voice fell silent.

"Will you come quietly?" asked the Sergeant, "or must we anæsthetize?" He pointed his water pistol menacingly.

"Oh, we'll come quietly," the Savage answered, dabbing alternately a cut lip, a scratched neck, and a bitten left hand.

Still keeping his handkerchief to his bleeding nose Helmholtz nodded in confirmation.

Awake and having recovered the use of his legs, Bernard had chosen this moment to move as inconspicuously as he could towards the door.

"Hi, you there," called the Sergeant, and a swine-masked policeman hurried across the room and laid a hand on the young man's shoulder.

Bernard turned with an expression of indignant innocence. Escaping? He hadn't dreamed of such a thing. "Though what on earth you want *me* for," he said to the Sergeant, "I really can't imagine."

"You're a friend of the prisoner's, aren't you?"

"Well . . ." said Bernard, and hesitated. No, he really couldn't deny it. "Why shouldn't I be?" he asked.

"Come on then," said the Sergeant, and led the way towards the door and the waiting police car.

16

The room into which the three were ushered was the Controller's study.

"His fordship will be down in a moment." The Gamma butler left them to themselves.

Helmholtz laughed aloud.

"It's more like a caffeine-solution party than a trial," he said, and let himself fall into the most luxurious of the pneumatic armchairs. "Cheer up, Bernard," he added, catching sight of his friend's green unhappy face. But Bernard would not be cheered; without answering, without even looking at Helmholtz, he went and sat down on the most uncomfortable chair in the room, carefully chosen in the obscure hope of somehow deprecating the wrath of the higher powers.

The Savage meanwhile wandered restlessly round the room, peering with a vague superficial inquisitiveness at the books in the shelves, at the sound-track rolls and reading machine bobbins in their numbered pigeon-holes. On the table under the window lay a massive volume bound in limp black leather-surrogate, and stamped with large golden T's. He picked it up and opened it. MY LIFE AND WORK, BY OUR FORD. The book had been published at Detroit by the Society for the Propagation of Fordian Knowledge. Idly he turned the pages, read a sentence here, a paragraph there, and had just come to the conclusion that the book didn't interest him, when the door opened, and the Resident World Controller for Western Europe walked briskly into the room.

Mustapha Mond shook hands with all three of them; but it was to the Savage that he addressed himself. "So you don't much like civilization, Mr. Savage," he said.

The Savage looked at him. He had been prepared to lie, to bluster, to remain sullenly unresponsive; but, reassured by the good-humoured intelligence of the Controller's face, he decided to tell the truth, straightforwardly. "No." He shook his head.

Bernard started and looked horrified. What would the Controller think? To be labelled as the friend of a man who said that he didn't like civilization—said it openly and, of all people, to the Controller—it was terrible. "But, John," he began. A look from Mustapha Mond reduced him to an abject silence.

"Of course," the Savage went on to admit, "there are some very nice things. All that music in the air, for instance . . ."

"Sometimes a thousand twangling instruments will hum about my ears and sometimes voices."

The Savage's face lit up with a sudden pleasure. "Have you read it too?" he asked. "I thought nobody knew about that book here, in England."

"Almost nobody. I'm one of the very few. It's prohibited, you see. But as I make the laws here, I can also break them. With impunity, Mr. Marx," he added, turning to Bernard. "Which I'm afraid you *can't* do."

Bernard sank into a yet more hopeless misery.

"But why is it prohibited?" asked the Savage. In the excitement of meeting a man who had read Shakespeare he had momentarily forgotten everything else.

The Controller shrugged his shoulders. "Because it's old; that's the chief reason. We haven't any use for old things here."

"Even when they're beautiful?"

"Particularly when they're beautiful. Beauty's attractive, and we don't want people to be attracted by old things. We want them to like the new ones."

"But the new ones are so stupid and horrible. Those plays, where there's nothing but helicopters flying about and you *feel* the people kissing." He made a grimace. "Goats and monkeys!" Only in Othello's words could he find an adequate vehicle for his contempt and hatred.

"Nice tame animals, anyhow," the Controller murmured parenthetically.

"Why don't you let them see *Othello* instead?"

"I've told you; it's old. Besides, they couldn't understand it."

Yes, that was true. He remembered how Helmholtz had laughed at *Romeo and Juliet*. "Well then," he said, after a pause, "something new that's like *Othello*, and that they could understand."

"That's what we've all been wanting to write," said Helmholtz, breaking a long silence.

"And it's what you never will write," said the Controller. "Because, if it were really like *Othello* nobody could understand it, however new it might be. And if it were new, it couldn't possibly be like *Othello*."

"Why not?"

"Yes, why not?" Helmholtz repeated. He too was forgetting the unpleasant realities of the situation. Green with anxiety and apprehension, only Bernard remembered them; the others ignored him. "Why not?"

"Because our world is not the same as Othello's world. You can't make flivvers without steel—and you can't make tragedies without social instability. The world's stable now. People are happy; they get what they want, and they never want what they can't get. They're well off; they're safe; they're never ill; they're not afraid of death; they're blissfully ignorant of passion and old age; they're plagued with no mothers or fathers; they've got no wives, or children, or lovers to feel strongly about; they're so conditioned that they practically can't help behaving as they ought to behave. And if anything should go wrong, there's *soma*. Which you go and chuck out of the window in the name of liberty, Mr. Savage. *Liberty!*" He laughed. "Expecting Deltas to know what liberty is! And now expecting them to understand *Othello!* My good boy!"

The Savage was silent for a little. "All the same," he insisted obstinately, "*Othello's* good, *Othello's* better than those feelies."

"Of course it is," the Controller agreed. "But that's the price we have to pay for stability. You've got to choose between happiness and what people used to call high art. We've sacrificed the high art. We have the feelies and the scent organ instead."

"But they don't mean anything."

"They mean themselves; they mean a lot of agreeable sensations to the audience."

"But they're . . . they're told by an idiot."

The Controller laughed. "You're not being very polite to your friend, Mr. Watson. One of our most distinguished Emotional Engineers . . ."

"But he's right," said Helmholtz gloomily. "Because it *is* idiotic. Writing when there's nothing to say . . ."

"Precisely. But that requires the most enormous ingenuity. You're making flivvers out of the absolute minimum of steel—works of art out of practically nothing but pure sensation."

The Savage shook his head. "It all seems to me quite horrible."

"Of course it does. Actual happiness always looks pretty squalid in comparison with the overcompensations for misery. And, of course, stability isn't nearly so spectacular as instability. And being contented has none of the glamour of a good fight against misfortune, none of the picturesqueness of a struggle with temptation, or a fatal overthrow by passion or doubt. Happiness is never grand."

"I suppose not," said the Savage after a silence. "But need it be quite so bad as those twins?" He passed his hand over his eyes as though he were trying to wipe away the remembered image of those long rows of identical midgets at the assembling tables, those queued-up twin-herds at the entrance to the Brentford monorail station, those human maggots swarming round Linda's bed of death, the endlessly repeated face of his assailants. He looked at his bandaged left hand and shuddered. "Horrible!"

"But how useful! I see you don't like our Bokanovsky Groups; but, I assure you, they're the foundation on which everything else is built. They're the gyroscope that stabilizes the rocket plane of state on its unswerving course." The deep voice thrillingly vibrated; the gesticulating hand implied all space and the onrush of the irresistible machine. Mustapha Mond's oratory was almost up to synthetic standards.

"I was wondering," said the Savage, "why you had them at all—seeing that you can get whatever you want out of those bottles. Why don't you make everybody an Alpha Double Plus while you're about it?"

Mustapha Mond laughed. "Because we have no wish to have our throats cut," he answered. "We believe in happiness and stability. A society of Alphas couldn't fail to be unstable and miserable. Imagine a factory staffed by Alphas—that is to say by separate and unrelated individuals of good heredity and conditioned so as to be capable (within limits) of making a free choice and assuming responsibilities. Imagine it!" he repeated.

The Savage tried to imagine it, not very successfully.

"It's an absurdity. An Alpha-decanted, Alpha-conditioned man would go mad if he had to do Epsilon Semi-Moron work—go mad, or start smashing things up. Alphas can be completely socialized—but only on condition that you make them do Alpha work. Only an Epsilon can be expected to make Epsilon sacrifices, for the good reason that for him they aren't sacrifices; they're the line of least resistance. His conditioning has laid down rails along which he's got to run. He can't help himself; he's foredoomed. Even after decanting, he's still inside a bottle—an invisible bottle of infantile and embryonic fixations. Each one of us, of course," the Controller meditatively continued, "goes through life inside a bottle. But if we happen to be Alphas, our bottles are, relatively speaking, enormous. We should suffer acutely if we were confined in a narrower space. You cannot pour upper-caste champagne-surrogate into lower-caste bottles. It's obvious theoretically. But it has also been proved in actual practice. The result of the Cyprus experiment was convincing."

"What was that?" asked the Savage.

Mustapha Mond smiled. "Well, you can call it an experiment in rebottling if you like. It began in A.F. 473. The Controllers had the island of Cyprus cleared of all its existing inhabitants and re-colonized with a specially prepared batch of twenty-two thousand Alphas. All agricultural and industrial equipment was handed over to them and they were left to manage their own affairs. The result exactly fulfilled all the theoretical predictions. The land wasn't properly worked; there were strikes in all the factories; the laws were set at naught, orders disobeyed; all the people detailed for a spell of low-grade work were perpetually intriguing for high-grade jobs, and all the people with high-grade jobs were counter-intriguing at all costs to stay where they were. Within six years they were having a first-class civil war. When nineteen out of the twenty-two thousand had been killed, the survivors unanimously petitioned the World Controllers to resume the government of the island. Which they did. And that was the end of the only society of Alphas that the world has ever seen."

The Savage sighed, profoundly.

"The optimum population," said Mustapha Mond, "is modelled on the iceberg—eight-ninths below the water line, one-ninth above."

"And they're happy below the water line?"

"Happier than above it. Happier than your friend here, for example." He pointed.

"In spite of that awful work?"

"Awful? *They* don't find it so. On the contrary, they like it. It's light, it's childishly simple. No strain on the mind or the muscles. Seven and a half hours of mild, unexhausting labour, and then the *soma* ration and games and unrestricted copulation and the feelies. What more can they ask for? True," he added, "they might ask for shorter hours. And of course we could give them shorter hours. Technically, it would be perfectly simple to reduce all lower-caste working hours to three or four a day. But would they be any the happier for that? No, they wouldn't. The experiment was tried, more than a century and a half ago. The whole of Ireland was put on to the four-hour day. What was the result? Unrest and a large increase in the consumption of *soma*; that was all. Those three and a half hours of extra leisure were so far from being a source of happiness, that people felt constrained to take a holiday from them. The Inventions Office is stuffed with plans for labour-saving processes. Thousands of them." Mustapha Mond made a lavish gesture. "And why don't we put them into execution? For the sake of the labourers; it would be sheer cruelty to afflict them with excessive leisure. It's the same with agriculture. We could synthesize every morsel of food, if we wanted to. But we don't. We prefer to keep a third of the population on the land. For their own sakes—because it takes *longer* to get food out of the land than out of a factory. Besides, we have our stability to think of. We don't want to change. Every change is a menace to stability. That's another reason why we're so chary of applying new inventions. Every discovery in pure science is potentially subversive; even science must sometimes be treated as a possible enemy. Yes, even science."

Science? The Savage frowned. He knew the word. But what it exactly signified he could not say. Shakespeare and the old men of the pueblo had never mentioned science, and from Linda he had only gathered the vaguest hints: science was something you made helicopters with, something that caused you to laugh at the Corn Dances, something that prevented you from being wrinkled and losing your teeth. He made a desperate effort to take the Controller's meaning.

"Yes," Mustapha Mond was saying, "that's another item in the cost of stability. It isn't only art that's incompatible with happiness;

it's also science. Science is dangerous; we have to keep it most carefully chained and muzzled."

"What?" said Helmholtz, in astonishment. "But we're always saying that science is everything. It's a hypnopædic platitude."

"Three times a week between thirteen and seventeen," put in Bernard.

"And all the science propaganda we do at the College . . ."

"Yes; but what sort of science?" asked Mustapha Mond sarcastically. "You've had no scientific training, so you can't judge. I was a pretty good physicist in my time. Too good—good enough to realize that all our science is just a cookery book, with an orthodox theory of cooking that nobody's allowed to question, and a list of recipes that mustn't be added to except by special permission from the head cook. I'm the head cook now. But I was an inquisitive young scullion once. I started doing a bit of cooking on my own. Unorthodox cooking, illicit cooking. A bit of real science, in fact." He was silent.

"What happened?" asked Helmholtz Watson.

The Controller sighed. "Very nearly what's going to happen to you young men. I was on the point of being sent to an island."

The words galvanized Bernard into violent and unseemly activity. "Send *me* to an island?" He jumped up, ran across the room, and stood gesticulating in front of the Controller. "You can't send *me*. I haven't done anything. It was the others. I swear it was the others." He pointed accusingly to Helmholtz and the Savage. "Oh, please don't send me to Iceland. I promise I'll do what I ought to do. Give me another chance. Please give me another chance." The tears began to flow. "I tell you, it's their fault," he sobbed. "And not to Iceland. Oh please, your fordship, please . . ." And in a paroxysm of abjection he threw himself on his knees before the Controller. Mustapha Mond tried to make him get up; but Bernard persisted in his grovelling; the stream of words poured out inexhaustibly. In the end the Controller had to ring for his fourth secretary.

"Bring three men," he ordered, "and take Mr. Marx into a bedroom. Give him a good *soma* vaporization and then put him to bed and leave him."

The fourth secretary went out and returned with three green-uniformed twin footmen. Still shouting and sobbing, Bernard was carried out.

"One would think he was going to have his throat cut," said the Controller, as the door closed. "Whereas, if he had the smallest sense, he'd understand that his punishment is really a reward. He's being sent to an island. That's to say, he's being sent to a place where he'll meet the most interesting set of men and women to be found anywhere in the world. All the people who, for one reason or another, have got too self-consciously individual to fit into community-life. All the people who aren't satisfied with orthodoxy, who've got independent ideas of their own. Every one, in a word, who's any one. I almost envy you, Mr. Watson."

Helmholtz laughed. "Then why aren't you on an island yourself?"

"Because, finally, I preferred this," the Controller answered. "I was given the choice; to be sent to an island, where I could have got on with my pure science, or to be taken on to the Controllers' Council with the prospect of succeeding in due course to an actual Controllership. I chose this and let the science go." After a little silence, "Sometimes," he added, "I rather regret the science. Happiness is a hard master—particularly other people's happiness. A much harder master, if one isn't conditioned to accept it unquestioningly, than truth." He sighed, fell silent again, then continued in a brisker tone, "Well, duty's duty. One can't consult one's own preference. I'm interested in truth, I like science. But truth's a menace, science is a public danger. As dangerous as it's been beneficent. It has given us the stablest equilibrium in history. China's was hopelessly insecure by comparison; even the primitive matriarchies weren't steadier than we are. Thanks, I repeat, to science. But we can't allow science to undo its own good work. That's why we so carefully limit the scope of its researches—that's why I almost got sent to an island. We don't allow it to deal with any but the most immediate problems of the moment. All other enquiries are most sedulously discouraged. It's curious," he went on after a little pause, "to read what people in the time of Our Ford used to write about scientific progress. They seemed to have imagined that it could be allowed to go on indefinitely, regardless of everything else. Knowledge was the highest good, truth the supreme value; all the rest was secondary and subordinate. True, ideas were beginning to change even then. Our Ford himself did a great deal to shift the emphasis from truth and beauty to comfort and happiness. Mass production demanded the shift. Universal happiness keeps the wheels steadily turning; truth and beauty can't. And, of course, whenever the masses seized political power, then it was happiness rather than truth and beauty that mattered. Still, in spite of everything, unrestricted scientific research was still permitted. People still went on talking about truth and beauty as though they were the sovereign goods. Right up to the time of the Nine Years' War. *That* made them change their tune all right. What's the point of truth or beauty or knowledge when the anthrax bombs are popping all around you? That was when science first began to be controlled—after the Nine Years' War. People were ready to have even their appetites controlled then. Anything for a quiet life. We've gone on controlling ever since. It hasn't been very good for truth, of course. But it's been very good for happiness. One can't have something for nothing. Happiness has got to be paid for. You're paying for it, Mr. Watson—paying because you happen to be too much interested in beauty. I was too much interested in truth; I paid too."

"But *you* didn't go to an island," said the Savage, breaking a long silence.

The Controller smiled. "That's how I paid. By choosing to serve happiness. Other people's—not mine. It's lucky," he added, after a pause, "that there are such a lot of islands in the world. I don't know what we should do without them. Put you all in the lethal chamber,

I suppose. By the way, Mr. Watson, would you like a tropical climate? The Marquesas, for example; or Samoa? Or something rather more bracing?"

Helmholtz rose from his pneumatic chair. "I should like a thoroughly bad climate," he answered. "I believe one would write better if the climate were bad. If there were a lot of wind and storms, for example . . ."

The Controller nodded his approbation. "I like your spirit, Mr. Watson. I like it very much indeed. As much as I officially disapprove of it." He smiled. "What about the Falkland Islands?"

"Yes, I think that will do," Helmholtz answered. "And now, if you don't mind, I'll go and see how poor Bernard's getting on."

17

"Art, science—you seem to have paid a fairly high price for your happiness," said the Savage, when they were alone. "Anything else?"

"Well, religion, of course," replied the Controller. "There used to be something called God—before the Nine Years' War. But I was forgetting; you know all about God, I suppose."

"Well . . ." The Savage hesitated. He would have liked to say something about solitude, about night, about the mesa lying pale under the moon, about the precipice, the plunge into shadowy darkness, about death. He would have liked to speak; but there were no words. Not even in Shakespeare.

The Controller, meanwhile, had crossed to the other side of the room and was unlocking a large safe set into the wall between the bookshelves. The heavy door swung open. Rummaging in the darkness within, "It's a subject," he said, "that has always had a great interest for me." He pulled out a thick black volume. "You've never read this, for example."

The Savage took it. *"The Holy Bible, containing the Old and New Testaments,"* he read aloud from the title-page.

"Nor this." It was a small book and had lost its cover.

"The Imitation of Christ."

"Nor this." He handed out another volume.

"*The Varieties of Religious Experience*. By William James."

"And I've got plenty more," Mustapha Mond continued, resuming his seat. "A whole collection of pornographic old books. God in the safe and Ford on the shelves." He pointed with a laugh to his avowed library—to the shelves of books, the rack full of reading-machine bobbins and sound-track rolls.

"But if you know about God, why don't you tell them?" asked the Savage indignantly. "Why don't you give them these books about God?"

"For the same reason as we don't give them *Othello*: they're old; they're about God hundreds of years ago. Not about God now."

"But God doesn't change."

"Men do, though."

"What difference does that make?"

"All the difference in the world," said Mustapha Mond. He got up again and walked to the safe. "There was a man called Cardinal Newman," he said. "A cardinal," he exclaimed parenthetically, "was a kind of Arch-Community-Songster."

"'I Pandulph, of fair Milan, cardinal.' I've read about them in Shakespeare."

"Of course you have. Well, as I was saying, there was a man called Cardinal Newman. Ah, here's the book." He pulled it out. "And while I'm about it I'll take this one too. It's by a man called Maine de Biran. He was a philosopher, if you know what that was."

"A man who dreams of fewer things than there are in heaven and earth," said the Savage promptly.

"Quite so. I'll read you one of the things he *did* dream of in a moment. Meanwhile, listen to what this old Arch-Community-Songster said." He opened the book at the place marked by a slip of paper and began to read. "'We are not our own any more than what we possess is our own. We did not make ourselves, we cannot be supreme over ourselves. We are not our own masters. We are God's property. Is it not our happiness thus to view the matter? Is it any happiness or any comfort, to consider that we *are* our own? It may be thought so by the young and prosperous. These may think it a great thing to have everything, as they suppose, their own way—to depend on no one—to have to think of nothing out of sight, to be without the irksomeness of continual acknowledgment, continual prayer, continual reference of what they do to the will of another. But as time goes on, they, as all men, will find that independence was not made for man—that it is an unnatural state—will do for a while, but will not carry us on safely to the end . . .'" Mustapha Mond paused, put down the first book and, picking up the other, turned over the pages. "Take this, for example," he said, and in his deep voice once more began to read: "'A man grows old; he feels in himself that radical sense of weakness, of listlessness, of discomfort, which accompanies the advance of age; and, feeling thus, imagines himself merely sick, lulling his fears with the notion that this distressing condition is due to some particular cause, from which, as from an illness, he hopes to recover. Vain imaginings! That sickness is old age; and a horrible disease it is. They say that it is the fear of death and of what comes after death that makes men turn to religion as they advance in years. But my own experience has given me the conviction that, quite apart from any such terrors or imaginings, the religious sentiment tends to develop as we grow older; to develop because, as the passions grow calm, as the fancy and sensibilities are less excited and less excitable, our reason becomes less troubled in its working, less obscured by the images, desires and distractions, in which it used to be absorbed; whereupon God emerges as from behind a cloud; our soul feels, sees, turns towards the source of all light; turns naturally and inevitably; for now that all that gave to the world of sensations its life and charms has begun to leak away from us, now that phenomenal existence is no more bolstered up by impressions from within or from without, we feel the need to lean on something that abides, something that will never play us false—a reality, an absolute and everlasting truth. Yes, we inevitably turn to God; for this religious sentiment is of its nature so pure, so delightful to the soul that experiences it, that it makes up to us for all our other losses.'" Mustapha Mond shut the book and leaned back in his chair. "One of the numerous things in heaven and earth that these philosophers didn't dream about was this" (he waved his hand), "us, the modern world. 'You can only be independent of God while you've got youth and prosperity; independence won't take you safely to the end.' Well, we've now got youth and prosperity right up to the end. What follows? Evidently, that we can be independent of God. 'The religious sentiment will compensate us for all our losses.' But there aren't any losses for us to compensate; religious sentiment is superfluous. And why should we go hunting for a substitute for youthful desires, when youthful desires never fail? A substitute for distractions, when we go on enjoying all the old fooleries to the very last? What need have we of repose when our minds and bodies continue to delight in activity? of consolation, when we have *soma?* of something immovable, when there is the social order?"

"Then you think there is no God?"

"No, I think there quite probably is one."

"Then why? . . ."

Mustapha Mond checked him. "But he manifests himself in different ways to different men. In premodern times he manifested himself as the being that's described in these books. Now . . ."

"How does he manifest himself now?" asked the Savage.

"Well, he manifests himself as an absence; as though he weren't there at all."

"That's your fault."

"Call it the fault of civilization. God isn't compatible with machinery and scientific medicine and universal happiness. You must make your choice. Our civilization has chosen machinery and medicine and happiness. That's why I have to keep these books locked up in the safe. They're smut. People would be shocked if . . ."

The Savage interrupted him. "But isn't it *natural* to feel there's a God?"

"You might as well ask if it's natural to do up one's trousers with zippers," said the Controller sarcastically. "You remind me of another of those old fellows called Bradley. He defined philosophy as the finding of bad reason for what one believes by instinct. As if one believed anything by instinct! One believes things because one has been conditioned to believe them. Finding bad reasons for what one believes for other bad reasons—that's philosophy. People believe in God because they've been conditioned to believe in God."

"But all the same," insisted the Savage, "it is natural to believe in God when you're alone—quite alone, in the night, thinking about death . . ."

"But people never are alone now," said Mustapha Mond. "We make them hate solitude; and we arrange their lives so that it's almost impossible for them ever to have it."

The Savage nodded gloomily. At Malpais he had suffered because they had shut him out from the communal activities of the pueblo, in civilized London he was suffering because he could never escape from those communal activities, never be quietly alone.

"Do you remember that bit in *King Lear?*" said the Savage at last. "'The gods are just and of our pleasant vices make instruments to plague us; the dark and vicious place where thee he got cost him his eyes,' and Edmund answers—you remember, he's wounded, he's dying—'Thou hast spoken right; 'tis true. The wheel has come full circle; I am here.' What about that now? Doesn't there seem to be a God managing things, punishing, rewarding?"

"Well, does there?" questioned the Controller in his turn. "You can indulge in any number of pleasant vices with a freemartin and run no risks of having your eyes put out by your son's mistress. 'The wheel has come full circle; I am here.' But where would Edmund be nowadays? Sitting in a pneumatic chair, with his arm round a girl's waist, sucking away at his sex-hormone chewing-gum and looking at the feelies. The gods are just. No doubt. But their code of law is dictated, in the last resort, by the people who organize society; Providence takes its cue from men."

"Are you sure?" asked the Savage. "Are you quite sure that the Edmund in that pneumatic chair hasn't been just as heavily punished as the Edmund who's wounded and bleeding to death? The gods are just. Haven't they used his pleasant vices as an instrument to degrade him?"

"Degrade him from what position? As a happy, hardworking, goods-consuming citizen he's perfect. Of course, if you choose some other standard than ours, then perhaps you might say he was degraded. But you've got to stick to one set of postulates. You can't play Electro-magnetic Golf according to the rules of Centrifugal Bumble-puppy."

"But value dwells not in particular will," said the Savage. "It holds his estimate and dignity as well wherein 'tis precious of itself as in the prizer."

"Come, come," protested Mustapha Mond, "that's going rather far, isn't it?"

"If you allowed yourselves to think of God, you wouldn't allow yourselves to be degraded by pleasant vices. You'd have a reason for bearing things patiently, for doing things with courage. I've seen it with the Indians."

"I'm sure you have," said Mustapha Mond. "But then we aren't Indians. There isn't any need for a civilized man to bear anything that's seriously unpleasant. And as for doing things—Ford forbid that he should get the idea into his head. It would upset the whole social order if men started doing things on their own."

"What about self-denial, then? If you had a God, you'd have a reason for self-denial."

"But industrial civilization is only possible when there's no self-denial. Self-indulgence up to the very limits imposed by hygiene and economics. Otherwise the wheels stop turning."

"You'd have a reason for chastity!" said the Savage, blushing a little as he spoke the words.

"But chastity means passion, chastity means neurasthenia. And passion and neurasthenia mean instability. And instability means the end of civilization. You can't have a lasting civilization without plenty of pleasant vices."

"But God's the reason for everything noble and fine and heroic. If you had a God . . ."

"My dear young friend," said Mustapha Mond, "civilization has absolutely no need of nobility or heroism. These things are symptoms of political inefficiency. In a properly organized society like ours, nobody has any opportunities for being noble or heroic. Conditions have got to be thoroughly unstable before the occasion can arise. Where there are wars, where there are divided allegiances, where there are temptations to be resisted, objects of love to be fought for or defended—there, obviously, nobility and heroism have some sense. But there aren't any wars nowadays. The greatest care is taken to prevent you from loving any one too much. There's no such thing as a divided allegiance; you're so conditioned that you can't help doing what you ought to do. And what you ought to do is on the whole so pleasant, so many of the natural impulses are allowed free play, that there really aren't any temptations to resist. And if ever, by some unlucky chance, anything unpleasant should somehow happen, why, there's always *soma* to give you a holiday from the facts. And there's always *soma* to calm your anger, to reconcile you to your enemies, to make you patient and long-suffering. In the past you could only accomplish these things by making a great effort and after years of hard moral training. Now, you swallow two or three half-gramme tablets, and there you are. Anybody can be virtuous now. You can carry at least half your mortality about in a bottle. Christianity without tears—that's what *soma* is."

"But the tears are necessary. Don't you remember what Othello said? 'If after every tempest came such calms, may the winds blow till they have wakened death.' There's a story one of the old Indians used to tell us, about the Girl of Mátaski. The young men who wanted to marry her had to do a morning's hoeing in her garden. It seemed easy; but there were flies and mosquitoes, magic ones. Most of the young men simply couldn't stand the biting and stinging. But the one that could—he got the girl."

"Charming! But in civilized countries," said the Controller, "you can have girls without hoeing for them; and there aren't any flies or mosquitoes to sting you. We got rid of them all centuries ago."

The Savage nodded, frowning. "You got rid of them. Yes, that's just like you. Getting rid of everything unpleasant instead of learning to put up with it. Whether 'tis better in the mind to suffer the slings and arrows of outrageous fortune, or to take arms against a sea of troubles and by opposing end them . . . But you don't do either. Neither suffer nor oppose. You just abolish the slings and arrows. It's too easy."

He was suddenly silent, thinking of his mother. In her room on the thirty-seventh floor, Linda had floated in a sea of singing lights and perfumed caresses—floated away, out of space, out of time, out of the prison of her memories, her habits, her aged and bloated body. And Tomakin, ex-Director of Hatcheries and Conditioning, Tomakin was still on holiday—on holiday from humiliation and pain, in a world where he could not hear those words, that derisive laughter, could not see that hideous face, feel those moist and flabby arms round his neck, in a beautiful world . . .

"What you need," the Savage went on, "is something *with* tears for a change. Nothing costs enough here."

("Twelve and a half million dollars," Henry Foster had protested when the Savage told him that. "Twelve and a half million—that's what the new Conditioning Centre cost. Not a cent less.")

"Exposing what is mortal and unsure to all that fortune, death and danger dare, even for an eggshell. Isn't there something in that?" he asked, looking up at Mustapha Mond. "Quite apart from God—though of course God would be a reason for it. Isn't there something in living dangerously?"

"There's a great deal in it," the Controller replied. "Men and women must have their adrenals stimulated from time to time."

"What?" questioned the Savage, uncomprehending.

"It's one of the conditions of perfect health. That's why we've made the V.P.S. treatments compulsory."

"V.P.S.?"

"Violent Passion Surrogate. Regularly once a month. We flood the whole system with adrenin. It's the complete physiological equivalent of fear and rage. All the tonic effects of murdering Desdemona and being murdered by Othello, without any of the inconveniences."

"But I like the inconveniences."

"We don't," said the Controller. "We prefer to do things comfortably."

"But I don't want comfort. I want God, I want poetry, I want real danger, I want freedom, I want goodness. I want sin."

"In fact," said Mustapha Mond, "you're claiming the right to be unhappy."

"All right then," said the Savage defiantly, "I'm claiming the right to be unhappy."

"Not to mention the right to grow old and ugly and impotent; the right to have syphilis and cancer; the right to have too little to eat; the right to be lousy; the right to live in constant apprehension of what may happen tomorrow; the right to catch typhoid; the right to be tortured by unspeakable pains of every kind." There was a long silence.

"I claim them all," said the Savage at last.

Mustapha Mond shrugged his shoulders. "You're welcome," he said.

18

The door was ajar; they entered.

"John!"

From the bathroom came an unpleasant and characteristic sound.

"Is there anything the matter?" Helmholtz called.

There was no answer. The unpleasant sound was repeated, twice; there was silence. Then, with a click the bathroom door opened and, very pale, the Savage emerged.

"I say," Helmholtz exclaimed solicitously, "you *do* look ill, John!"

"Did you eat something that didn't agree with you?" asked Bernard.

The Savage nodded. "I ate civilization."

"What?"

"It poisoned me; I was defiled. And then," he added, in a lower tone, "I ate my own wickedness."

"Yes, but what exactly? . . . I mean, just now you were . . ."

"Now I am purified," said the Savage. "I drank some mustard and warm water."

The others stared at him in astonishment. "Do you mean to say that you were doing it on purpose?" asked Bernard.

"That's how the Indians always purify themselves." He sat down and, sighing, passed his hand across his forehead. "I shall rest for a few minutes," he said. "I'm rather tired."

"Well, I'm not surprised," said Helmholtz. After a silence, "We've come to say good-bye," he went on in another tone. "We're off to-morrow morning."

"Yes, we're off to-morrow," said Bernard on whose face the Savage remarked a new expression of determined resignation. "And by the way, John," he continued, leaning forward in his chair and laying a hand on the Savage's knee, "I want to say how sorry I am about everything that happened yesterday." He blushed. "How ashamed," he went on, in spite of the unsteadiness of his voice, "how really . . ."

The Savage cut him short and, taking his hand, affectionately pressed it.

"Helmholtz was wonderful to me," Bernard resumed, after a little pause. "If it hadn't been for him, I should . . ."

"Now, now," Helmholtz protested.

There was a silence. In spite of their sadness—because of it, even; for their sadness was the symptom of their love for one another—the three young men were happy.

"I went to see the Controller this morning," said the Savage at last.

"What for?"

"To ask if I mightn't go to the islands with you."

"And what did he say?" asked Helmholtz eagerly.

The Savage shook his head. "He wouldn't let me."

"Why not?"

"He said he wanted to go on with the experiment. But I'm damned," the Savage added, with sudden fury, "I'm damned if I'll go on being experimented with. Not for all the Controllers in the world. *I* shall go away to-morrow too."

"But where?" the others asked in unison.

The Savage shrugged his shoulders. "Anywhere. I don't care. So long as I can be alone."

* * *

From Guildford the down-line followed the Wey valley to Godalming, then, over Milford and Witley, proceeded to Haslemere and on through Petersfield towards Portsmouth. Roughly parallel to it, the upline passed over Worplesden, Tongham, Puttenham, Elstead and Grayshott. Between the Hog's Back and Hindhead there were points where the two lines were not more than six or seven kilometres apart. The distance was too small for careless flyers—particularly at night and when they had taken half a gramme too much. There had been accidents. Serious ones. It had been decided to deflect the upline a few kilometres to the west. Between Grayshott and Tongham four abandoned air-lighthouses marked the course of the old Portsmouth-to-London road. The skies above them were silent and deserted. It was over Selborne, Bordon and Farnham that the helicopters now ceaselessly hummed and roared.

The Savage had chosen as his hermitage the old lighthouse which stood on the crest of the hill between Puttenham and Elstead. The building was of ferro-concrete and in excellent condition—almost too comfortable the Savage had thought when he first explored the place, almost too civilizedly luxurious. He pacified his conscience by promising himself a compensatingly harder self-discipline, purifications the more complete and thorough. His first night in the hermitage was, deliberately, a sleepless one. He spent the hours on his knees praying, now to that Heaven from which the guilty Claudius had begged forgiveness, now in Zuñi to Awonawilona, now to Jesus and Pookong, now to his own guardian animal, the eagle. From time to time he stretched out his arms as though he were on the Cross, and held them thus through long minutes of an ache that gradually increased till it became a tremulous and excruciating agony; held them, in voluntary crucifixion, while he repeated, through clenched teeth, (the sweat, meanwhile, pouring down his face), "Oh, forgive me! Oh, make me pure! Oh, help me to be good!" again and again, till he was on the point of fainting from the pain.

When morning came, he felt he had earned the right to inhabit the lighthouse; yet, even though there still *was* glass in most of the windows, even though the view from the platform *was* so fine. For the very reason why he had chosen the lighthouse had become almost instantly a reason for going somewhere else. He had decided to live there because the view was so beautiful, because, from his vantage point, he seemed to be looking out on to the incarnation of a divine being. But who was he to be pampered with the daily and hourly sight of loveliness? Who was he to be living in the visible presence of God? All he deserved to live in was some filthy sty, some blind hole in the ground. Stiff and still aching after his long night of pain, but for that very reason inwardly reassured, he climbed up to the platform of his tower, he looked out over the bright sunrise world which he had regained the right to inhabit. On the north the view was bounded by the long chalk ridge of the Hog's Back, from behind whose eastern extremity rose the towers of the seven skyscrapers which constituted Guildford. Seeing them, the Savage made a grimace; but he was to become reconciled to them in course of time; for at night they twinkled gaily with geometrical constellations, or else, flood-lighted, pointed their luminous fingers (with a gesture whose significance nobody in England but the Savage now understood) solemnly towards the plumbless mysteries of heaven.

In the valley which separated the Hog's Back from the sandy hill on which the lighthouse stood, Puttenham was a modest little village nine stories high, with silos, a poultry farm, and a small vitamin-D factory. On the other side of the lighthouse, towards the South, the ground fell away in long slopes of heather to a chain of ponds.

Beyond them, above the intervening woods, rose the fourteen-story tower of Elstead. Dim in the hazy English air, Hindhead and Selborne invited the eye into a blue romantic distance. But it was not alone the distance that had attracted the Savage to his lighthouse; the near was as seductive as the far. The woods, the open stretches of heather and yellow gorse, the clumps of Scotch firs, the shining ponds with their overhanging birch trees, their water lilies, their beds of rushes—these were beautiful and, to an eye accustomed to the aridities of the American desert, astonishing. And then the solitude! Whole days passed during which he never saw a human being. The lighthouse was only a quarter of an hour's flight from the Charing-T Tower; but the hills of Malpais were hardly more deserted than this Surrey heath. The crowds that daily left London, left it only to play Electro-magnetic Golf or Tennis. Puttenham possessed no links; the nearest Riemann-surfaces were at Guildford. Flowers and a landscape were the only attractions here. And so, as there was no good reason for coming, nobody came. During the first days the Savage lived alone and undisturbed.

Of the money which, on his first arrival, John had received for his personal expenses, most had been spent on his equipment. Before leaving London he had bought four viscose-woollen blankets, rope and string, nails, glue, a few tools, matches (though he intended in due course to make a fire drill), some pots and pans, two dozen packets of seeds, and ten kilogrammes of wheat flour. "No, *not* synthetic starch and cotton-waste flour-substitute," he had insisted. "Even though it is more nourishing." But when it came to pan-glandular biscuits and vitaminized beef-surrogate, he had not been able to resist the shopman's persuasion. Looking at the tins now, he bitterly reproached himself for his weakness. Loathsome civilized stuff! He had made up his mind that he would never eat it, even if he were starving. "That'll teach them," he thought vindictively. It would also teach him.

He counted his money. The little that remained would be enough, he hoped, to tide him over the winter. By next spring, his garden would be producing enough to make him independent of the outside world. Meanwhile, there would always be game. He had seen plenty of rabbits, and there were waterfowl on the ponds. He set to work at once to make a bow and arrows.

There were ash trees near the lighthouse and, for arrow shafts, a whole copse full of beautifully straight hazel saplings. He began by felling a young ash, cut out six feet of unbranched stem, stripped off the bark and, paring by paring, shaved away the white wood, as old

Mitsima had taught him, until he had a stave of his own height, stiff at the thickened centre, lively and quick at the slender tips. The work gave him an intense pleasure. After those weeks of idleness in London, with nothing to do, whenever he wanted anything, but to press a switch or turn a handle, it was pure delight to be doing something that demanded skill and patience.

He had almost finished whittling the stave into shape, when he realized with a start that he was singing—*singing!* It was as though, stumbling upon himself from the outside, he had suddenly caught himself out, taken himself flagrantly at fault. Guiltily he blushed. After all, it was not to sing and enjoy himself that he had come here. It was to escape further contamination by the filth of civilized life; it was to be purified and made good; it was actively to make amends. He realized to his dismay that, absorbed in the whittling of his bow, he had forgotten what he had sworn to himself he would constantly remember—poor Linda, and his own murderous unkindness to her, and those loathsome twins, swarming like lice across the mystery of her death, insulting, with their presence, not merely his own grief and repentance, but the very gods themselves. He had sworn to remember, he had sworn unceasingly to make amends. And there was he, sitting happily over his bow-stave, singing, actually singing. . . .

He went indoors, opened the box of mustard, and put some water to boil on the fire.

Half an hour later, three Delta-Minus land-workers from one of the Puttenham Bokanovsky Groups happened to be driving to Elstead and, at the top of the hill, were astonished to see a young man standing outside the abandoned lighthouse stripped to the waist and hitting himself with a whip of knotted cords. His back was horizontally streaked with crimson, and from weal to weal ran thin trickles of blood. The driver of the lorry pulled up at the side of the road and, with his two companions, stared open-mouthed at the extraordinary spectacle. One, two three—they counted the strokes. After the eighth, the young man interrupted his self-punishment to run to the wood's edge and there be violently sick. When he had finished, he picked up the whip and began hitting himself again. Nine, ten, eleven, twelve . . .

"Ford!" whispered the driver. And his twins were of the same opinion.

"Fordey!" they said.

Three days later, like turkey buzzards settling on a corpse, the reporters came.

Dried and hardened over a slow fire of green wood, the bow was ready. The Savage was busy on his arrows. Thirty hazel sticks had been whittled and dried, tipped with sharp nails, carefully nocked. He had made a raid one night on the Puttenham poultry farm, and now had feathers enough to equip a whole armoury. It was at work upon the feathering of his shafts that the first of the reporters found him. Noiseless on his pneumatic shoes, the man came up behind him.

"Good-morning, Mr. Savage," he said. "I am the representative of *The Hourly Radio.*"

Startled as though by the bite of a snake, the Savage sprang to his feet, scattering arrows, feathers, glue-pot and brush in all directions.

"I beg your pardon," said the reporter, with genuine compunction. "I had no intention . . ." He touched his hat—the aluminum stove-pipe hat in which he carried his wireless receiver and transmitter. "Excuse my not taking it off," he said. "It's a bit heavy. Well, as I was saying, I am the representative of *The Hourly* . . ."

"What do you want?" asked the Savage, scowling. The reporter returned his most ingratiating smile.

"Well, of course, our readers would be profoundly interested . . ." He put his head on one side, his smile became almost coquettish. "Just a few words from you, Mr. Savage." And rapidly, with a series of ritual gestures, he uncoiled two wires connected to the portable battery buckled round his waist; plugged them simultaneously into the sides of his aluminum hat; touched a spring on the crown—and antennæ shot up into the air; touched another spring on the peak of the brim—and, like a jack-in-the-box, out jumped a microphone and hung there, quivering, six inches in front of his nose; pulled down a pair of receivers over his ears; pressed a switch on the left side of the hat—and from within came a faint waspy buzzing; turned a knob on the right—and the buzzing was interrupted by a stethoscopic wheeze and cackle, by hiccoughs and sudden squeaks. "Hullo," he said to the microphone, "hullo, hullo . . ." A bell suddenly rang inside his hat. "Is that you, Edzel? Primo Mellon speaking. Yes, I've got hold of him. Mr. Savage will now take the microphone and say a few words. Won't you, Mr. Savage?" He looked up at the Savage with another of those winning smiles of his. "Just tell our readers why you came here. What made you leave London (hold on, Edzel!) so very suddenly. And, of course, that whip." (The Savage started. How did they know about the whip?) "We're all crazy to know about the whip. And then something about Civilization. You know the sort of stuff. 'What I think of the Civilized Girl.' Just a few words, a very few . . ."

The Savage obeyed with a disconcerting literalness. Five words he uttered and no more—five words, the same as those he had said to Bernard about the Arch-Community-Songster of Canterbury. *"Háni! Sons éso tse-ná!"* And seizing the reporter by the shoulder, he spun him round (the young man revealed himself invitingly well-covered), aimed and, with all the force and accuracy of a champion foot-and-mouth-baller, delivered a most prodigious kick.

Eight minutes later, a new edition of *The Hourly Radio* was on sale in the streets of London. "HOURLY RADIO REPORTER HAS COCCYX KICKED BY MYSTERY SAVAGE," ran the headlines on the front page. "SENSATION IN SURREY."

"Sensation even in London," thought the reporter when, on his return, he read the words. And a very painful sensation, what was more. He sat down gingerly to his luncheon.

Undeterred by that cautionary bruise on their colleague's coccyx, four other reporters, representing the New York *Times*, the

Frankfurt *Four-Dimensional Continuum, The Fordian Science Monitor*, and *The Delta Mirror*, called that afternoon at the lighthouse and met with receptions of progressively increasing violence.

From a safe distance and still rubbing his buttocks, "Benighted fool!" shouted the man from *The Fordian Science Monitor*, "why don't you take *soma*?"

"Get away!" The Savage shook his fist.

The other retreated a few steps then turned round again. "Evil's an unreality if you take a couple of grammes."

"Kohakwa iyathtokyai!" The tone was menacingly derisive.

"Pain's a delusion."

"Oh, is it?" said the Savage and, picking up a thick hazel switch, strode forward.

The man from *The Fordian Science Monitor* made a dash for his helicopter.

After that the Savage was left for a time in peace. A few helicopters came and hovered inquisitively round the tower. He shot an arrow into the importunately nearest of them. It pierced the aluminum floor of the cabin; there was a shrill yell, and the machine went rocketing up into the air with all the acceleration that its super-charger could give it. The others, in future, kept their distance respectfully. Ignoring their tiresome humming (he likened himself in his imagination to one of the suitors of the Maiden of Mátsaki, unmoved and persistent among the winged vermin), the Savage dug at what was to be his garden. After a time the vermin evidently became bored and flew away; for hours at a stretch the sky above his head was empty and, but for the larks, silent.

The weather was breathlessly hot, there was thunder in the air. He had dug all the morning and was resting, stretched out along the floor. And suddenly the thought of Lenina was a real presence, naked and tangible, saying "Sweet!" and "Put your arms round me!"—in shoes and socks, perfumed. Impudent strumpet! But oh, oh, her arms round his neck, the lifting of her breasts, her mouth! Eternity was in our lips and eyes. Lenina . . . No, no, no, no! He sprang to his feet and, half naked as he was, ran out of the house. At the edge of the heath stood a clump of hoary juniper bushes. He flung himself against them, he embraced, not the smooth body of his desires, but an armful of green spikes. Sharp, with a thousand points, they pricked him. He tried to think of poor Linda, breathless and dumb, with her clutching hands and the unutterable terror in her eyes. Poor Linda whom he had sworn to remember. But it was still the presence of Lenina that haunted him. Lenina whom he had promised to forget. Even through the stab and sting of the juniper needles, his wincing flesh was aware of her, unescapably real. "Sweet, sweet . . . And if you wanted me too, why didn't you . . ."

The whip was hanging on a nail by the door, ready to hand against the arrival of reporters. In a frenzy the Savage ran back to the house, seized it, whirled it. The knotted cords bit into his flesh.

"Strumpet! Strumpet!" he shouted at every blow as though it were Lenina (and how frantically, without knowing it, he wished it were), white, warm, scented, infamous Lenina that he was flogging thus. "Strumpet!" And then, in a voice of despair, "Oh, Linda, forgive me. Forgive me, God. I'm bad. I'm wicked. I'm . . . No, no, you strumpet, you strumpet!"

From his carefully constructed hide in the wood three hundred metres away, Darwin Bonaparte, the Feely Corporation's most expert big game photographer had watched the whole proceedings. Patience and skill had been rewarded. He had spent three days sitting inside the bole of an artificial oak tree, three nights crawling on his belly through the heather, hiding microphones in gorse bushes, burying wires in the soft grey sand. Seventy-two hours of profound discomfort. But now the great moment had come—the greatest, Darwin Bonaparte had time to reflect, as he moved among his instruments, the greatest since his taking of the famous all-howling stereoscopic feely of the gorillas' wedding. "Splendid," he said to himself as the Savage started his astonishing performance. "Splendid!" He kept his telescopic cameras carefully aimed—glued to their moving objective; clapped on a higher power to get a close-up of the frantic and distorted face (admirable!); switched over, for half a minute, to slow motion (an exquisitely comical effect, he promised himself); listened in, meanwhile, to the blows, the groans, the wild and raving words that were being recorded on the sound-track at the edge of his film, tried the effect of a little amplification (yes, that was decidedly better); was delighted to hear, in a momentary lull, the shrill singing of a lark; wished the Savage would turn round so that he could get a good close-up of the blood on his back—and almost instantly (what astonishing luck!) the accommodating fellow did turn round, and he was able to take a perfect close-up.

"Well, that was grand!" he said to himself when it was all over. "Really grand!" He mopped his face. When they had put in the feely effects at the studio, it would be a wonderful film. Almost as good, thought Darwin Bonaparte, as the *Sperm Whale's Love-Life*—and that, by Ford, was saying a good deal!

Twelve days later *The Savage of Surrey* had been released and could be seen, heard and felt in every first-class feely-palace in Western Europe.

The effect of Darwin Bonaparte's film was immediate and enormous. On the afternoon which followed the evening of its release John's rustic solitude was suddenly broken by the arrival overhead of a great swarm of helicopters.

He was digging in his garden—digging, too, in his own mind, laboriously turning up the substance of his thought. Death—and he drove in his spade once, and again, and yet again. And all our yesterdays have lighted fools the way to dusty death. A convincing thunder rumbled through the words. He lifted another spadeful of earth. Why had Linda died? Why had she been allowed to become gradually less than human and at last . . . He shuddered. A good kissing carrion. He planted his foot on his spade and stamped it fiercely into the tough ground. As flies to wanton boys are we to the gods; they kill us for their sport. Thunder again; words that proclaimed themselves true—truer somehow than truth itself. And yet that same Gloucester had called them ever-gentle gods. Besides, thy best of rest is sleep and that thou oft provok'st; yet grossly fear'st thy death which is no more. No more than sleep. Sleep. Perchance to dream. His spade struck against a stone; he stooped to pick it up. For in that sleep of death, what dreams? . . .

A humming overhead had become a roar; and suddenly he was in shadow, there was something between the sun and him. He looked up, startled, from his digging, from his thoughts; looked up in a dazzled bewilderment, his mind still wandering in that other world of truer-than-truth, still focused on the immensities of death and deity; looked up and saw, close above him, the swarm of hovering machines. Like locusts they came, hung poised, descended all around him on the heather. And from out of the bellies of these giant grasshoppers stepped men in white viscose-flannels, women (for the weather was hot) in acetate-shantung pyjamas or velveteen shorts and sleeveless, half-unzippered singlets—one couple from each. In a few minutes there were dozens of them, standing in a wide circle round the lighthouse, staring, laughing, clicking their cameras, throwing (as to an ape) peanuts, packets of sex-hormone chewing-gum, pan-glandular *petits beurres*. And every moment—for across the Hog's Back the stream of traffic now flowed unceasingly—their numbers increased. As in a nightmare, the dozens became scores, the scores hundreds.

The Savage had retreated towards cover, and now, in the posture of an animal at bay, stood with his back to the wall of the lighthouse, staring from face to face in speechless horror, like a man out of his senses.

From this stupor he was aroused to a more immediate sense of reality by the impact on his cheek of a well-aimed packet of chewing-gum. A shock of startling pain—and he was broad awake, awake and fiercely angry.

"Go away!" he shouted.

The ape had spoken; there was a burst of laughter and hand-clapping. "Good old Savage! Hurrah, hurrah!" And through the babel he heard cries of: "Whip, whip, the whip!"

Acting on the word's suggestion, he seized the bunch of knotted cords from its nail behind the door and shook it at his tormentors.

There was a yell of ironical applause.

Menacingly he advanced towards them. A woman cried out in fear. The line wavered at its most immediately threatened point, then stiffened again, stood firm. The consciousness of being in overwhelming force had given these sightseers a courage which the Savage had not expected of them. Taken aback, he halted and looked round.

"Why don't you leave me alone?" There was an almost plaintive note in his anger.

"Have a few magnesium-salted almonds!" said the man who, if the Savage were to advance, would be the first to be attacked. He held out a packet. "They're really very good, you know," he added, with a rather nervous smile of propitiation. "And the magnesium salts will help to keep you young."

The Savage ignored his offer. "What do you want with me?" he asked, turning from one grinning face to another. "What do you want with me?"

"The whip," answered a hundred voices confusedly. "Do the whipping stunt. Let's see the whipping stunt."

Then, in unison, and on a slow, heavy rhythm, "We—want—the whip," shouted a group at the end of the line. "We—want—the whip."

Others at once took up the cry, and the phrase was repeated, parrot-fashion, again and again, with an ever-growing volume of sound, until, by the seventh or eighth reiteration, no other word was being spoken. "We—want—the whip."

They were all crying together; and, intoxicated by the noise, the unanimity, the sense of rhythmical atonement, they might, it seemed, have gone on for hours—almost indefinitely. But at about the twenty-fifth repetition the proceedings were startlingly interrupted. Yet another helicopter had arrived from across the Hog's Back, hung poised above the crowd, then dropped within a few yards of where the Savage was standing, in the open space between the line of sightseers and the lighthouse. The roar of the air screws momentarily drowned the shouting; then, as the machine touched the ground and the engines were turned off: "We—want—the whip; we—want—the whip," broke out again in the same loud, insistent monotone.

The door of the helicopter opened, and out stepped, first a fair and ruddy-faced young man, then, in green velveteen shorts, white shirt, and jockey cap, a young woman.

At the sight of the young woman, the Savage started, recoiled, turned pale.

The young woman stood, smiling at him—an uncertain, imploring, almost abject smile. The seconds passed. Her lips moved, she was saying something; but the sound of her voice was covered by the loud reiterated refrain of the sightseers.

"We—want—the whip! We—want—the whip!"

The young woman pressed both hands to her left side, and on that peach-bright, doll-beautiful face of hers appeared a strangely incongruous expression of yearning distress. Her blue eyes seemed to grow larger, brighter; and suddenly two tears rolled down her cheeks. Inaudibly, she spoke again; then, with a quick, impassioned gesture stretched out her arms towards the Savage, stepped forward.

"We—want—the whip! We—want . . ."

And all of a sudden they had what they wanted.

"Strumpet!" The Savage had rushed at her like a madman. "Fitchew!" Like a madman, he was slashing at her with his whip of small cords.

Terrified, she had turned to flee, had tripped and fallen in the heather. "Henry, Henry!" she shouted. But her ruddy-faced companion had bolted out of harm's way behind the helicopter.

With a whoop of delighted excitement the line broke; there was a convergent stampede towards that magnetic centre of attraction. Pain was a fascinating horror.

"Fry, lechery, fry!" Frenzied, the Savage slashed again.

Hungrily they gathered round, pushing and scrambling like swine about the trough.

"Oh, the flesh!" The Savage ground his teeth. This time it was on his shoulders that the whip descended. "Kill it, kill it!"

Drawn by the fascination of the horror of pain and, from within, impelled by that habit of cooperation, that desire for unanimity and atonement, which their conditioning had so ineradicably implanted in them, they began to mime the frenzy of his gestures, striking at one another as the Savage struck at his own rebellious flesh, or at that plump incarnation of turpitude writhing in the heather at his feet.

"Kill it, kill it, kill it . . ." The Savage went on shouting.

Then suddenly somebody started singing "Orgy-porgy" and, in a moment, they had all caught up the refrain and, singing, had begun to dance. Orgy-porgy, round and round and round, beating one another in six-eight time. Orgy-porgy . . .

It was after midnight when the last of the helicopters took its flight. Stupefied by *soma*, and exhausted by a long-drawn frenzy of sensuality, the Savage lay sleeping in the heather. The sun was already high when he awoke. He lay for a moment, blinking in owlish incomprehension at the light; then suddenly remembered—everything.

"Oh, my God, my God!" He covered his eyes with his hand.

That evening the swarm of helicopters that came buzzing across the Hog's Back was a dark cloud ten kilometres long. The description of last night's orgy of atonement had been in all the papers.

"Savage!" called the first arrivals, as they alighted from their machine. "Mr. Savage!"

There was no answer.

The door of the lighthouse was ajar. They pushed it open and walked into a shuttered twilight. Through an archway on the further side of the room they could see the bottom of the staircase that led up to the higher floors. Just under the crown of the arch dangled a pair of feet.

"Mr. Savage!"

Slowly, very slowly, like two unhurried compass needles, the feet turned towards the right; north, north-east, east, south-east, south, south-south-west; then paused, and, after a few seconds, turned as unhurriedly back towards the left. South-south-west, south, south-east, east. . . .

BRAVE NEW WORLD REVISITED

Preface

The soul of wit may become the very body of untruth. However elegant and memorable, brevity can never, in the nature of things, do justice to all the facts of a complex situation. On such a theme one can be brief only by omission and simplification. Omission and simplification help us to understand—but help us, in many cases, to understand the wrong thing; for our comprehension may be only of the abbreviator's neatly formulated notions, not of the vast, ramifying reality from which these notions have been so arbitrarily abstracted.

But life is short and information endless: nobody has time for everything. In practice we are generally forced to choose between an unduly brief exposition and no exposition at all. Abbreviation is a necessary evil and the abbreviator's business is to make the best of a job which, though intrinsically bad, is still better than nothing. He must learn to simplify, but not to the point of falsification. He must learn to concentrate upon the essentials of a situation, but without ignoring too many of reality's qualifying side issues. In this way he may be able to tell, not indeed the whole truth (for the whole truth about almost any important subject is incompatible with brevity), but considerably more than the dangerous quarter-truths and half-truths which have always been the current coin of thought.

The subject of freedom and its enemies is enormous, and what I have written is certainly too short to do it full justice; but at least I have touched on many aspects of the problem. Each aspect may have been somewhat over-simplified in the exposition; but these successive over-simplifications add up to a picture that, I hope, gives some hint of the vastness and complexity of the original.

Omitted from the picture (not as being unimportant, but merely for convenience and because I have discussed them on earlier occasions) are the mechanical and military enemies of freedom—the weapons and "hardware" which have so powerfully strengthened the hands of the world's rulers against their subjects, and the ever more ruinously costly preparations for ever more senseless and suicidal wars. The chapters that follow should be read against a background of thoughts about the Hungarian uprising and its repression, about H-bombs, about the cost of what every nation refers to as "defense," and about those endless columns of uniformed boys, white, black, brown, yellow, marching obediently toward the common grave.

I

OVER-POPULATION

In 1931, when Brave New World was being written, I was convinced that there was still plenty of time. The completely organized society, the scientific caste system, the abolition of free will by methodical conditioning, the servitude made acceptable by regular doses of chemically induced happiness, the orthodoxies drummed in by nightly courses of sleep-teaching—these things were coming all right, but not in my time, not even in the time of my grandchildren. I forget the exact date of the events recorded in *Brave New World*; but it was somewhere in the sixth or seventh century A.F. (After Ford). We who were living in the second quarter of the twentieth century A.D. were the inhabitants, admittedly, of a gruesome kind of universe; but the nightmare of those depression years was radically different from the nightmare of the future, described in *Brave New World*. Ours was a nightmare of too little order; theirs, in the seventh century A.F., of too much. In the passing from one extreme to the other, there would be a long interval, so I imagined, during which the more fortunate third of the human race would make the best of both worlds—the disorderly world of liberalism and the much too orderly Brave New World where perfect efficiency left no room for freedom or personal initiative.

Twenty-seven years later, in this third quarter of the twentieth century A.D., and long before the end of the first century A.F., I feel a good deal less optimistic than I did when I was writing *Brave New World*. The prophecies made in 1931 are coming true much sooner than I thought they would. The blessed interval between too little order and the nightmare of too much has not begun and shows no sign of beginning. In the West, it is true, individual men and women still enjoy a large measure of freedom. But even in those countries that have a tradition of democratic government, this freedom and even the desire for this freedom seem to be on the wane. In the rest of the world freedom for individuals has already gone, or is manifestly about to go. The nightmare of total organization, which I had situated in the seventh century After Ford, has emerged from the safe, remote future and is now awaiting us, just around the next corner.

George Orwell's *1984* was a magnified projection into the future of a present that had contained Stalinism and an immediate past that had witnessed the flowering of Nazism. *Brave New World* was written before the rise of Hitler to supreme power in Germany and when the Russian tyrant had not yet got into his stride. In 1931 systematic terrorism was not the obsessive contemporary fact which it had become in 1948, and the future dictatorship of my imaginary world was a good deal less brutal than the future dictatorship so brilliantly portrayed by Orwell. In the context of 1948, *1984* seemed dreadfully convincing. But tyrants, after all, are mortal and circumstances change. Recent developments in Russia and recent advances in science and technology have robbed Orwell's book of some of its gruesome verisimilitude. A nuclear war will, of course, make nonsense of everybody's predictions. But, assuming for the moment that the Great Powers can somehow refrain from destroying us, we can say that it now looks as though the odds were more in favor of something like *Brave New World* than of something like *1984*.

In the light of what we have recently learned about animal behavior in general, and human behavior in particular, it has become clear that control through the punishment of undesirable behavior is less effective, in the long run, than control through the reinforcement of desirable behavior by rewards, and that government through terror works on the whole less well than government through the non-violent manipulation of the environment and of the thoughts and feelings of individual men, women and children. Punishment temporarily puts a stop to undesirable behavior, but does not permanently reduce the victim's tendency to indulge in it. Moreover, the psychophysical by-products of punishment may be just as undesirable as the behavior for which an individual has been punished. Psychotherapy is largely concerned with the debilitating or anti-social consequences of past punishments.

The society described in *1984* is a society controlled almost exclusively by punishment and the fear of punishment. In the imaginary world of my own fable punishment is infrequent and generally mild. The nearly perfect control exercised by the government is achieved by systematic reinforcement of desirable behavior, by many kinds of nearly non-violent manipulation, both physical and psychological, and by genetic standardization. Babies in bottles and the centralized control of reproduction are not perhaps impossible; but it is quite clear that for a long time to come we shall remain a viviparous species breeding at random. For practical purposes genetic standardization may be ruled out. Societies will continue to be controlled post-natally—by punishment, as in the past, and to an ever increasing extent by the more effective methods of reward and scientific manipulation.

In Russia the old-fashioned, *1984*-style dictatorship of Stalin has begun to give way to a more up-to-date form of tyranny. In the upper levels of the Soviets' hierarchical society the reinforcement of desirable behavior has begun to replace the older methods of control through the punishment of undesirable behavior. Engineers and scientists, teachers and administrators, are handsomely paid for good work and so moderately taxed that they are under a constant incentive to do better and so be more highly rewarded. In certain areas they are at liberty to think and do more or less what they like. Punishment awaits them only when they stray beyond their prescribed limits into the realms of ideology and politics. It is because they have been granted a measure of professional freedom that Russian teachers, scientists and technicians have achieved such remarkable successes. Those who live near the base of the Soviet pyramid enjoy none of the privileges accorded to the lucky or specially gifted minority. Their wages are meager and they pay, in the form of high prices, a disproportionately large share of the taxes. The area in which they can do as they please is extremely restricted, and their rulers control them more by punishment and the threat of punishment than through non-violent manipulation or the reinforcement of desirable behavior by reward. The Soviet system combines elements of *1984* with elements that are prophetic of what went on among higher castes in *Brave New World*.

Meanwhile impersonal forces over which we have almost no control seem to be pushing us all in the direction of the Brave New Worldian nightmare; and this impersonal pushing is being consciously accelerated by representatives of commercial and political organizations who have developed a number of new techniques for manipulating, in the interest of some minority, the thoughts and feelings of the masses. The techniques of manipulation will be discussed in later chapters. For the moment let us confine our attention to those impersonal forces which are now making the world so extremely unsafe for democracy, so very inhospitable to individual freedom. What are these forces? And why has the nightmare, which I had projected into the seventh century A.F., made so swift an advance in our direction? The answer to these questions must begin where the life of even the most highly civilized society has its beginnings—on the level of biology.

On the first Christmas Day the population of our planet was about two hundred and fifty millions—less than half the population of modern China. Sixteen centuries later, when the Pilgrim Fathers landed at Plymouth Rock, human numbers had climbed to a little more than five hundred millions. By the time of the signing of the Declaration of Independence, world population had passed the seven hundred million mark. In 1931, when I was writing *Brave New World*, it stood at just under two billions. Today, only twenty-seven years later, there are two billion eight hundred million of us. And tomorrow—what? Penicillin, DDT and clean water are cheap commodities, whose effects on public health are out of all proportion to their cost. Even the poorest government is rich enough to provide its subjects with a substantial measure of death control. Birth control is a very different matter. Death control is something which can be provided for a whole people by a few technicians working in the pay of a benevolent government. Birth control depends on the co-operation of an entire people. It must be practiced by countless individuals, from whom it demands more intelligence and will power than most of the world's teeming illiterates possess, and (where chemical or mechanical methods of contraception are used) an expenditure of more money than most of these millions can now afford. Moreover, there are nowhere any religious traditions in favor of unrestricted death, whereas religious and social traditions in favor of unrestricted reproduction are widespread. For all these reasons, death control is achieved very easily, birth control is achieved with great difficulty. Death rates have therefore fallen in recent years with startling suddenness. But birth rates have either remained at their old high level or, if they have fallen, have fallen very little and at a very slow rate. In consequence, human numbers are now increasing more rapidly than at any time in the history of the species.

Moreover, the yearly increases are themselves increasing. They increase regularly, according to the rules of compound interest; and they also increase irregularly with every application, by a technologically backward society of the principles of Public Health. At the present time the annual increase in world population runs to about forty-three millions. This means that every four years mankind adds to its numbers the equivalent of the present population of India. At the rate of increase prevailing between the birth of Christ and the death of Queen Elizabeth I, it took sixteen centuries for the population of the earth to double. At the present rate it will double in less than half a century. And this fantastically rapid doubling of our numbers will be taking place on a planet whose most desirable and productive areas are already densely populated, whose soils are being eroded by the frantic efforts of bad farmers to raise more food, and whose easily available mineral capital is being squandered with the reckless extravagance of a drunken sailor getting rid of his accumulated pay.

In the Brave New World of my fable, the problem of human numbers in their relation to natural resources had been effectively solved. An optimum figure for world population had been calculated and numbers were maintained at this figure (a little under two billions, if I remember rightly) generation after generation. In the real contemporary world, the population problem has not been solved. On the contrary it is becoming graver and more formidable with every passing year. It is against this grim biological background that all the political, economic, cultural and psychological dramas of our time are being played out. As the twentieth century wears on, as the new billions are added to the existing billions (there will be more than five and a half billions of us by the time my granddaughter is fifty), this biological background will advance, ever more insistently, ever more menacingly, toward the front and center of the historical stage. The problem of rapidly increasing numbers in relation to natural resources, to social stability and to the well-being of individuals—this is now the central problem of mankind; and it will remain the central problem certainly for another century, and perhaps for several centuries thereafter. A new age is supposed to have begun on October 4, 1957. But actually, in the present context, all our exuberant post-Sputnik talk is irrelevant and even nonsensical. So far the masses of mankind are concerned, the coming time will not be the Space Age; it will be the

Age of Over-population. We can parody the words of the old song and ask,

Will the space that you're so rich in
Light a fire in the kitchen,
Or the little god of space turn the spit, spit, spit?

The answer, it is obvious, is in the negative. A settlement on the moon may be of some military advantage to the nation that does the settling. But it will do nothing whatever to make life more tolerable, during the fifty years that it will take our present population to double, for the earth's undernourished and proliferating billions. And even if, at some future date, emigration to Mars should become feasible, even if any considerable number of men and women were desperate enough to choose a new life under conditions comparable to those prevailing on a mountain twice as high as Mount Everest, what difference would that make? In the course of the last four centuries quite a number of people sailed from the Old World to the New. But neither their departure nor the returning flow of food and raw materials could solve the problems of the Old World. Similarly the shipping of a few surplus humans to Mars (at a cost, for transportation and development, of several million dollars a head) will do nothing to solve the problem of mounting population pressures on our own planet. Unsolved, that problem will render insoluble all our other problems. Worse still, it will create conditions in which individual freedom and the social decencies of the democratic way of life will become impossible, almost unthinkable. Not all dictatorships arise in the same way. There are many roads to Brave New World; but perhaps the straightest and the broadest of them is the road we are traveling today, the road that leads through gigantic numbers and accelerating increases. Let us briefly review the reasons for this close correlation between too many people, too rapidly multiplying, and the formulation of authoritarian philosophies, the rise of totalitarian systems of government.

As large and increasing numbers press more heavily upon available resources, the economic position of the society undergoing this ordeal becomes ever more precarious. This is especially true of those underdeveloped regions, where a sudden lowering of the death rate by means of DDT, penicillin and clean water has not been accompanied by a corresponding fall in the birth rate. In parts of Asia and in most of Central and South America populations are increasing so fast that they will double themselves in little more than twenty years. If the production of food and manufactured articles, of houses, schools and teachers, could be increased at a greater rate than human numbers, it would be possible to improve the wretched lot of those who live in these underdeveloped and overpopulated countries. But unfortunately these countries lack not merely agricultural machinery and an industrial plant capable of turning out this machinery, but also the capital required to create such a plant. Capital is what is left over after the primary needs of a population have been satisfied. But the primary needs of most of the people in underdeveloped countries are never fully satisfied. At the end of each year almost nothing is left over, and there is therefore almost no capital available for creating the industrial and agricultural plant, by means of which the people's needs might be satisfied. Moreover, there is, in all these underdeveloped countries, a serious shortage of the trained manpower without which a modern industrial and agricultural plant cannot be operated. The present educational facilities are inadequate; so are the resources, financial and cultural, for improving the existing facilities as fast as the situation demands. Meanwhile the population of some of these underdeveloped countries is increasing at the rate of 3 per cent per annum.

Their tragic situation is discussed in an important book, published in 1957—*The Next Hundred Years,* by Professors Harrison Brown, James Bonner and John Weir of the California Institute of Technology. How is mankind coping with the problem of rapidly increasing numbers? Not very successfully. "The evidence suggests rather strongly that in most underdeveloped countries the lot of the average individual has worsened appreciably in the last half century. People have become more poorly fed. There are fewer available goods per person. And practically every attempt to improve the situation has been nullified by the relentless pressure of continued population growth."

Whenever the economic life of a nation becomes precarious, the central government is forced to assume additional responsibilities for the general welfare. It must work out elaborate plans for dealing with a critical situation; it must impose ever greater restrictions upon the activities of its subjects; and if, as is very likely, worsening economic conditions result in political unrest, or open rebellion, the central government must intervene to preserve public order and its own authority. More and more power is thus concentrated in the hands of the executives and their bureaucratic managers. But the nature of power is such that even those who have not sought it, but have had it forced upon them, tend to acquire a taste for more. "Lead us not into temptation," we pray—and with good reason; for when human beings are tempted too enticingly or too long, they generally yield. A democratic constitution is a device for preventing the local rulers from yielding to those particularly dangerous temptations that arise when too much power is concentrated in too few hands. Such a constitution works pretty well where, as in Britain or the United States, there is a traditional respect for constitutional procedures. Where the republican or limited monarchical tradition is weak, the best of constitutions will not prevent ambitious politicians from succuming with glee and gusto to the temptation of power. And in any country where numbers have begun to press heavily upon available resources, these temptations cannot fail to arise. Over-population leads to economic insecurity and social unrest. Unrest and insecurity lead to more control by central governments and an increase of their power. In the absence of a constitutional tradition, this increased power will probably be exercised in a dictatorial fashion. Even if Communism had never been invented, this would be likely to happen. But Communism has been invented. Given this fact, the probability of over-population leading through unrest to dictatorship becomes a virtual certainty. It is a pretty safe bet that, twenty years from now, all the world's over-populated and underdeveloped countries will be under some form of totalitarian rule—probably by the Communist party.

How will this development affect the over-populated, but highly industrialized and still democratic countries of Europe? If the newly formed dictatorships were hostile to them, and if the normal flow of raw materials from the underdeveloped countries were deliberately interrupted, the nations of the West would find themselves in a very bad way indeed. Their industrial system would break down, and the highly developed technology, which up till now has permitted them to sustain a population much greater than that which could be supported by locally available resources, would no longer protect them against the consequences of having too many people in too small a territory. If this should happen, the enormous powers forced by unfavorable conditions upon central governments may come to be used in the spirit of totalitarian dictatorship.

The United States is not at present an over-populated country. If, however, the population continues to increase at the present rate (which is higher than that of India's increase, though happily a good deal lower than the rate now current in Mexico or Guatemala), the problem of numbers in relation to available resources might well become troublesome by the beginning of the twenty-first century. For the moment over-population is not a direct threat to the personal freedom of Americans. It remains, however, an indirect threat, a menace at one remove. If over-population should drive the underdeveloped countries into totalitarianism, and if these new dictatorships should ally themselves with Russia, then the military position of the United States would become less secure and the preparations for defense and retaliation would have to be intensified. But liberty, as we all know, cannot flourish in a country that is permanently on a war footing, or even a near-war footing. Permanent crisis justifies permanent control of everybody and everything by the agencies of the central government. And permanent crisis is what we have to expect in a world in which over-population is producing a state of things, in which dictatorship under Communist auspices becomes almost inevitable.

II

QUANTITY, QUALITY, MORALITY

In the Brave New World of my fantasy eugenics and dysgenics were practiced systematically. In one set of bottles biologically superior ova, fertilized by biologically superior sperm, were given the best possible prenatal treatment and were finally decanted as Betas, Alphas and even Alpha Pluses. In another, much more numerous set of bottles, biologically inferior ova, fertilized by biologically inferior sperm, were subjected to the Bokanovsky Process (ninety-six identical twins out of a single egg) and treated prenatally with alcohol and other protein poisons. The creatures finally decanted were almost subhuman; but they were capable of performing unskilled work and, when properly conditioned, detensioned by free and frequent access to the opposite sex, constantly distracted by gratuitous entertainment and reinforced in their good behavior patterns by daily doses of soma, would be counted on to give no trouble to their superiors.

In this second half of the twentieth century we do nothing systematic about our breeding; but in our random and unregulated way we are not only over-populating our planet, we are also, it would seem, making sure that these greater numbers shall be of biologically poorer quality. In the bad old days children with considerable, or even with slight, hereditary defects rarely survived. Today, thanks to sanitation, modern pharmacology and the social conscience, most of the children born with hereditary defects reach maturity and multiply their kind. Under the conditions now prevailing, every advance in medicine will tend to be offset by a corresponding advance in the survival rate of individuals cursed by some genetic insufficiency. In spite of new wonder drugs and better treatment (indeed, in a certain sense, precisely because of these things), the physical health of the general population will show no improvement, and may even deteriorate. And along with a decline of average healthiness there may well go a decline in average intelligence. Indeed, some competent authorities are convinced that such a decline has already taken place and is continuing. "Under conditions that are both soft and unregulated," writes Dr. W. H. Sheldon, "our best stock tends to be outbred by stock that is inferior to it in every respect.... It is the fashion in some academic circles to assure students that the alarm over differential birthrates is unfounded; that these problems are merely economic, or merely educational, or merely religious, or merely cultural or something of the sort. This is Pollyanna optimism. Reproductive delinquency is biological and basic." And he adds that "nobody knows just how far the average IQ in this country [the U.S.A.] has declined since 1916, when Terman attempted to standardize the meaning of IQ 100."

In an undeveloped and over-populated country, where four-fifths of the people get less than two thousand calories a day and one-fifth enjoys an adequate diet, can democratic institutions arise spontaneously? Or if they should be imposed from outside or from above, can they possibly survive?

And now let us consider the case of the rich, industrialized and democratic society, in which, owing to the random but effective practice of dysgenics, IQ's and physical vigor are on the decline. For how long can such a society maintain its traditions of individual liberty and democratic government? Fifty or a hundred years from now our children will learn the answer to this question.

Meanwhile we find ourselves confronted by a most disturbing

moral problem. We know that the pursuit of good ends does not justify the employment of bad means. But what about those situations, now of such frequent occurrence, in which good means have end results which turn out to be bad?

For example, we go to a tropical island and with the aid of DDT we stamp out malaria and, in two or three years, save hundreds of thousands of lives. This is obviously good. But the hundreds of thousands of human beings thus saved, and the millions whom they beget and bring to birth, cannot be adequately clothed, housed, educated or even fed out of the island's available resources. Quick death by malaria has been abolished; but life made miserable by undernourishment and over-crowding is now the rule, and slow death by outright starvation threatens ever greater numbers.

And what about the congenitally insufficient organisms, whom our medicine and our social services now preserve so that they may propagate their kind? To help the unfortunate is obviously good. But the wholesale transmission to our descendants of the results of unfavorable mutations, and the progressive contamination of the genetic pool from which the members of our species will have to draw, are no less obviously bad. We are on the horns of an ethical dilemma, and to find the middle way will require all our intelligence and all our good will.

III

OVER-ORGANIZATION

The shortest and broadest road to the nightmare of Brave New World leads, as I have pointed out, through over-population and the accelerating increase of human numbers—twenty-eight hundred millions today, fifty-five hundred millions by the turn of the century, with most of humanity facing the choice between anarchy and totalitarian control. But the increasing pressure of numbers upon available resources is not the only force propelling us in the direction of totalitarianism. This blind biological enemy of freedom is allied with immensely powerful forces generated by the very advances in technology of which we are most proud. Justifiably proud, it may be added; for these advances are the fruits of genius and persistent hard work, of logic, imagination and self-denial—in a word, of moral and intellectual virtues for which one can feel nothing but admiration. But the Nature of Things is such that nobody in this world ever gets anything for nothing. These amazing and admirable advances have had to be paid for. Indeed, like last year's washing machine, they are still being paid for—and each installment is higher than the last. Many historians, many sociologists and psychologists have written at length, and with a deep concern, about the price that Western man has had to pay and will go on paying for technological progress. They point out, for example, that democracy can hardly be expected to flourish in societies where political and economic power is being progressively concentrated and centralized. But the progress of technology has led and is still leading to just such a concentration and centralization of power. As the machinery of mass production is made more efficient it tends to become more complex and more expensive—and so less available to the enterpriser of limited means. Moreover, mass production cannot work without mass distribution; but mass distribution raises problems which only the largest producers can satisfactorily solve. In a world of mass production and mass distribution the Little Man, with his inadequate stock of working capital, is at a grave disadvantage. In competition with the Big Man, he loses his money and finally his very existence as an independent producer; the Big Man has gobbled him up. As the Little Men disappear, more and more economic power comes to be wielded by fewer and fewer people. Under a dictatorship the Big Business, made possible by advancing technology and the consequent ruin of Little Business, is controlled by the State—that is to say, by a small group of party leaders and the soldiers, policemen and civil servants who carry out their orders. In a capitalist democracy, such as the United States, it is controlled by what Professor C. Wright Mills has called the Power Elite. This Power Elite directly employs several millions of the country's working force in its factories, offices and stores, controls many millions more by lending them the money to buy its products, and, through its ownership of the media of mass communication, influences the thoughts, the feelings and the actions of virtually everybody. To parody the words of Winston Churchill, never have so many been manipulated so much by so few. We are far indeed from Jefferson's ideal of a genuinely free society composed of a hierarchy of self-governing units—"the elementary republics of the wards, the county republics, the State republics and the Republic of the Union, forming a gradation of authorities."

We see, then, that modern technology has led to the concentration of economic and political power, and to the development of a society controlled (ruthlessly in the totalitarian states, politely and inconspicuously in the democracies) by Big Business and Big Government. But societies are composed of individuals and are good only insofar as they help individuals to realize their potentialities and to lead a happy and creative life. How have individuals been affected by the technological advances of recent years? Here is the answer to this question given by a philosopher-psychiatrist, Dr. Erich Fromm:

> Our contemporary Western society, in spite of its material, intellectual and political progress, is increasingly less conducive to mental health, and tends to undermine the inner security, happiness, reason and the capacity for love in the individual; it tends to turn him into an automaton who pays for his human failure with increasing mental sickness, and with despair hidden under a frantic drive for work and so-called pleasure.

Our "increasing mental sickness" may find expression in neurotic symptoms. These symptoms are conspicuous and extremely distressing. But "let us beware," says Dr. Fromm, "of defining mental hygiene as the prevention of symptoms. Symptoms as such are not our enemy, but our friend; where there are symptoms there is conflict, and conflict always indicates that the forces of life which strive for integration and happiness are still fighting." The really hopeless victims of mental illness are to be found among those who appear to be most normal. "Many of them are normal because they are so well adjusted to our mode of existence, because their human voice has been silenced so early in their lives, that they do not even struggle or suffer or develop symptoms as the neurotic does." They are normal not in what may be called the absolute sense of the word; they are normal only in relation to a profoundly abnormal society. Their perfect adjustment to that abnormal society is a measure of their mental sickness. These millions of abnormally normal people, living without fuss in a society to which, if they were fully human beings, they ought not to be adjusted, still cherish "the illusion of individuality," but in fact they have been to a great extent deindividualized. Their conformity is developing into something like uniformity. But "uniformity and freedom are incompatible. Uniformity and mental health are incompatible too. . . . Man is not made to be an automaton, and if he becomes one, the basis for mental health is destroyed."

In the course of evolution nature has gone to endless trouble to see that every individual is unlike every other individual. We reproduce our kind by bringing the father's genes into contact with the mother's. These hereditary factors may be combined in an almost infinite number of ways. Physically and mentally, each one of us is unique. Any culture which, in the interests of efficiency or in the name of some political or religious dogma, seeks to standardize the human individual, commits an outrage against man's biological nature.

Science may be defined as the reduction of multiplicity to unity. It seeks to explain the endlessly diverse phenomena of nature by ignoring the uniqueness of particular events, concentrating on what they have in common and finally abstracting some kind of "law," in terms of which they make sense and can be effectively dealt with. For examples, apples fall from the tree and the moon moves across the sky. People had been observing these facts from time immemorial. With Gertrude Stein they were convinced that an apple is an apple is an apple, whereas the moon is the moon is the moon. It remained for Isaac Newton to perceive what these very dissimilar phenomena had in common, and to formulate a theory of gravitation in terms of which certain aspects of the behavior of apples, of the heavenly bodies and indeed of everything else in the phyical universe could be explained and dealt with in terms of a single system of ideas. In the same spirit the artist takes the innumerable diversities and uniquenesses of the outer world and his own imagination and gives them meaning within an orderly system of plastic, literary or musical patterns. The wish to impose order upon confusion, to bring harmony out of dissonance and unity out of multiplicity is a kind of intellectual instinct, a primary and fundamental urge of the mind. Within the realms of science, art and philosophy the workings of what I may call this "Will to Order" are mainly beneficent. True, the Will to Order has produced many premature syntheses based upon insufficient evidence, many absurd systems of metaphysics and theology, much pedantic mistaking of notions for realities, of symbols and abstractions for the data of immediate experience. But these errors, however regrettable, do not do much harm, at any rate directly—though it sometimes happens that a bad philosophical system may do harm indirectly, by being used as a justification for senseless and inhuman actions. It is in the social sphere, in the realm of politics and economics, that the Will to Order becomes really dangerous.

Here the theoretical reduction of unmanageable multiplicity to comprehensible unity becomes the practical reduction of human diversity to subhuman uniformity, of freedom to servitude. In politics the equivalent of a fully developed scientific theory or philosophical system is a totalitarian dictatorship. In economics, the equivalent of a beautifully composed work of art is the smoothly running factory in which the workers are perfectly adjusted to the machines. The Will to Order can make tyrants out of those who merely aspire to clear up a mess. The beauty of tidiness is used as a justification for despotism.

Organization is indispensable; for liberty arises and has meaning only within a self-regulating community of freely cooperating individuals. But, though indispensable, organization can also be fatal. Too much organization transforms men and women into automata, suffocates the creative spirit and abolishes the very possibility of freedom. As usual, the only safe course is in the middle, between the extremes of *laissez-faire* at one end of the scale and of total control at the other.

During the past century the successive advances in technology have been accompanied by corresponding advances in organization. Complicated machinery has had to be matched by complicated social arrangements, designed to work as smoothly and efficiently as the new instruments of production. In order to fit into these organizations, individuals have had to deindividualize themselves, have had to deny their native diversity and conform to a standard pattern, have had to do their best to become automata.

The dehumanizing effects of over-organization are reinforced by the dehumanizing effects of over-population. Industry, as it expands, draws an ever greater proportion of humanity's increasing numbers into large cities. But life in large cities is not conducive to mental health (the highest incidence of schizophrenia, we are told, occurs among the swarming inhabitants of industrial slums); nor does it foster the kind of responsible freedom within small self-governing groups, which is the first condition of a genuine democracy. City life is anonymous and, as it were, abstract. People are related to one another, not as total personalities, but as the embodiments of economic functions or, when they are not at work, as irresponsible seekers of entertainment. Subjected to this kind of life, individuals tend to feel lonely and insignificant. Their existence ceases to have any point or meaning.

Biologically speaking, man is a moderately gregarious, not a completely social animal—a creature more like a wolf, let us say, or an elephant, than like a bee or an ant. In their original form human societies bore no resemblance to the hive or the ant heap; they were merely packs. Civilization is, among other things, the process by which primitive packs are transformed into an analogue, crude and mechanical, of the social insects' organic communities. At the present time the pressures of over-population and technological change are accelerating this process. The termitary has come to seem a realizable and even, in some eyes, a desirable ideal. Needless to say, the ideal will never in fact be realized. A great gulf separates the social insect from the not too gregarious, big-brained mammal; and even though the mammal should do his best to imitate the insect, the gulf would remain. However hard they try, men cannot create a social organism, they can only create an organization. In the process of trying to create an organism they will merely create a totalitarian despotism.

Brave New World presents a fanciful and somewhat ribald picture of a society, in which the attempt to recreate human beings in the likeness of termites has been pushed almost to the limits of the possible. That we are being propelled in the direction of Brave New World is obvious. But no less obvious is the fact that we can, if we so desire, refuse to co-operate with the blind forces that are propelling us. For the moment, however, the wish to resist does not seem to be very strong or very widespread. As Mr. William Whyte has shown in his remarkable book, *The Organization Man,* a new Social Ethic is replacing our traditional ethical system—the system in which the individual is primary. The key words in this Social Ethic are "adjustment," "adaptation," "socially orientated behavior," "belongingness," "acquisition of social skills," "team work," "group living," "group loyalty," "group dynamics," "group thinking," "group creativity." Its basic assumption is that the social whole has greater worth and significance than its individual parts, that inborn biological differences should be sacrificed to cultural uniformity, that the rights of the collectivity take precedence over what the eighteenth century called the Rights of Man. According to the Social Ethic, Jesus was competely wrong in asserting that the Sabbath was made for man. On the contrary, man was made for the Sabbath, and must sacrifice his inherited idiosyncrasies and pretend to be the kind of standardized good mixer that organizers of group activity regard as ideal for their purposes. This ideal man is the man who displays "dynamic conformity" (delicious phrase!) and an intense loyalty to the group, an unflagging desire to subordinate himself, to belong. And the ideal man must have an ideal wife, highly gregarious, infintely adaptable and not merely resigned to the fact that her husband's first loyalty is to the Corporation, but actively loyal on her own account. "He for God only," as Milton said of Adam and Eve, "she for

God in him." And in one important respect the wife of the ideal organization man is a good deal worse off than our First Mother. She and Adam were permitted by the Lord to be completely uninhibited in the matter of "youthful dalliance."

> *Nor turned, I ween,*
> *Adam from his fair spouse, nor Eve the rites*
> *Mysterious of connubial love refused.*

Today, according to a writer in the *Harvard Business Review*, the wife of the man who is trying to live up to the ideal proposed by the Social Ethic, "must not demand too much of her husband's time and interest. Because of his single-minded concentration on his job, even his sexual activity must be relegated to a secondary place." The monk makes vows of poverty, obedience and chastity. The organization man is allowed to be rich, but promises obedience ("he accepts authority without resentment, he looks up to his superiors"—*Mussolini ha sempre ragione*) and he must be prepared, for the greater glory of the organization that employs him, to forswear even conjugal love.

It is worth remarking that, in *1984*, the members of the Party are compelled to conform to a sexual ethic of more than Puritan severity. In *Brave New World*, on the other hand, all are permitted to indulge their sexual impulses without let or hindrance. The society described in Orwell's fable is a society permanently at war, and the aim of its rulers is first, of course, to exercise power for its own delightful sake and, second, to keep their subjects in that state of constant tension which a state of constant war demands of those who wage it. By crusading against sexuality the bosses are able to maintain the required tension in their followers and at the same time can satisfy their lust for power in a most gratifying way. The society described in *Brave New World* is a world-state, in which war has been eliminated and where the first aim of the rulers is at all costs to keep their subjects from making trouble. This they achieve by (among other methods) legalizing a degree of sexual freedom (made possible by the abolition of the family) that practically guarantees the Brave New Worlders against any form of destructive (or creative) emotional tension. In *1984* the lust for power is satisfied by inflicting pain; in *Brave New World*, by inflicting a hardly less humiliating pleasure.

The current Social Ethic, it is obvious, is merely a justification after the fact of the less desirable consequences of over-organization. It represents a pathetic attempt to make a virtue of necessity, to extract a positive value from an unpleasant datum. It is a very unrealistic, and therefore very dangerous, system of morality. The social whole, whose value is assumed to be greater than that of its component parts, is not an organism in the sense that a hive or a termitary may be thought of as an organism. It is merely an organization, a piece of social machinery. There can be no value except in relation to life and awareness. An organization is neither conscious nor alive. Its value is instrumental and derivative. It is not good in itself; it is good only to the extent that it promotes the good of the individuals who are the parts of the collective whole. To give organizations precedence over persons is to subordinate ends to means. What happens when ends are subordinated to means was clearly demonstrated by Hitler and Stalin. Under their hideous rule personal ends were subordinated to organizational means by a mixture of violence and propaganda, systematic terror and the systematic manipulation of minds. In the more efficient dictatorships of tomorrow there will probably be much less violence than under Hitler and Stalin. The future dictator's subjects will be painlessly regimented by a corps of highly trained social engineers. "The challenge of social engineering in our time," writes an enthusiastic advocate of this new science, "is like the challenge of technical engineering fifty years ago. If the first half of the twentieth century was the era of the technical engineers, the second half may well be the era of the social engineers"—and the twenty-first century, I suppose, will be the era of World Controllers, the scientific caste system and Brave New World. To the question *quis custodiet custodes?*—Who will mount guard over our guardians, who will engineer the engineers?—the answer is a bland denial that they need any supervision. There seems to be a touching belief among certain Ph.D.'s in sociology that Ph.D.'s in sociology will never be corrupted by power. Like Sir Galahad's, their strength is as the strength of ten because their heart is pure—and their heart is pure because they are scientists and have taken six thousand hours of social studies.

Alas, higher education is not necessarily a guarantee of higher virtue, or higher political wisdom. And to these misgivings on ethical and psychological grounds must be added misgivings of a purely scientific character. Can we accept the theories on which the social engineers base their practice, and in terms of which they justify their manipulations of human beings? For example, Professor Elton Mayo tells us categorically that "man's desire to be continuously associated in work with his fellows is a strong, if not the strongest human characteristic." This, I would say, is manifestly untrue. Some people have the kind of desire described by Mayo; others do not. It is a matter of temperament and inherited constitution. Any social organization based upon the assumption that "man" (whoever "man" may be) desires to be continuously associated with his fellows would be, for many individual men and women, a bed of Procrustes. Only by being amputated or stretched upon the rack could they be adjusted to it.

Again, how romantically misleading are the lyrical accounts of the Middle Ages with which many contemporary theorists of social relations adorn their works! "Membership in a guild, manorial estate or village protected medieval man throughout his life and gave him peace and serenity." Protected him from what, we may ask. Certainly not from remorseless bullying at the hands of his superiors. And along with all that "peace and serenity" there was, throughout the Middle Ages, an enormous amount of chronic frustration, acute unhappiness and a passionate resentment against the rigid, hierarchical system that permitted no vertical movement up the social ladder and, for those who were bound to the land, very little horizontal movement in space. The impersonal forces of over-population and over-organization, and the social engineers who are trying to direct these forces, are pushing us in the direction of a new medieval system. This revival will be made more acceptable than the original by such Brave-New-Worldian amenities as infant conditioning, sleep-teaching and drug-induced euphoria; but, for the majority of men and women, it will still be a kind of servitude.

IV

PROPAGANDA IN A DEMOCRATIC SOCIETY

"The doctrines of Europe," Jefferson wrote, "were that men in numerous associations cannot be restrained within the limit of order and justice, except by forces physical and moral wielded over them by authorities independent of their will. . . . We (the founders of the new American democracy) believe that man was a rational animal, endowed by nature with rights, and with an innate sense of justice, and that he could be restrained from wrong, and protected in right, by moderate powers, confided to persons of his own choice and held to their duties by dependence on his own will." To post-Freudian ears, this kind of language seems touchingly quaint and ingenuous. Human beings are a good deal less rational and innately just than the optimists of the eighteenth century supposed. On the other hand they are neither so morally blind nor so hopelessly unreasonable as the pessimists of the twentieth would have us believe. In spite of the Id and the Unconscious, in spite of endemic neurosis and the prevalence of low IQ's, most men and women are probably decent enough and sensible enough to be trusted with the direction of their own destinies.

Democratic institutions are devices for reconciling social order with individual freedom and initiative, and for making the immediate power of a country's rulers subject to the ultimate power of the ruled. The fact that, in Western Europe and America, these devices have worked, all things considered, not too badly is proof enough that the eighteenth-century optimists were not entirely wrong. Given a fair chance, human beings can govern themselves, and govern themselves better, though perhaps with less mechanical efficiency, than they can be governed by "authorities independent of their will." Given a fair chance, I repeat; for the fair chance is an indispensable prerequisite. No people that passes abruptly from a state of subservience under the rule of a despot to the completely unfamiliar state of political independence can be said to have a fair chance of making democratic institutions work. Again, no people in a precarious economic condition has a fair chance of being able to govern itself democratically. Liberalism flourishes in an atmosphere of prosperity and declines as declining prosperity makes it necessary for the government to intervene ever more frequently and drastically in the affairs of its subjects. Over-population and over-organization are two conditions which, as I have already pointed out, deprive a society of a fair chance of making democratic institutions work effectively. We see, then, that there are certain historical, economic, demographic and technological conditions which make it very hard for Jefferson's rational animals, endowed by nature with inalienable rights and an innate sense of justice, to exercise their reason, claim their rights and act justly within a democratically organized society. We in the West have been supremely fortunate in having been given our fair chance of making the great experiment in self-government. Unfortunately it now looks as though, owing to recent changes in our circumstances, this infinitely precious fair chance were being, little by little, taken away from us. And this, of course, is not the whole story. These blind impersonal forces are not the only enemies of individual liberty and democratic institutions. There are also forces of another, less abstract character, forces that can be deliberately used by power-seeking individuals whose aim is to establish partial or complete control over their fellows. Fifty years ago, when I was a boy, it seemed completely self-evident that the bad old days were over, that torture and massacre, slavery, and the persecution of heretics, were things of the past. Among people who wore top hats, traveled in trains, and took a bath every morning such horrors were simply out of the question. After all, we were living in the twentieth century. A few years later these people who took daily baths and went to church in top hats were committing atrocities on a scale undreamed of by the benighted Africans and Asiatics. In the light of recent history it would be foolish to suppose that this sort of thing cannot happen again. It can and, no doubt, it will. But in the immediate future there is some reason to believe that the punitive methods of *1984* will give place to the reinforcements and manipulations of *Brave New World.*

There are two kinds of propaganda—rational propaganda in favor of action that is consonant with the enlightened self-interest of those who make it and those to whom it is addressed, and nonrational propaganda that is not consonant with anybody's enlightened self-interest, but is dictated by, and appeals to, passion. Where the actions of individuals are concerned there are motives more exalted than enlightened self-interest, but where collective action has to be taken in the field of politics and economics, enlightened self-interest is probably the highest of effective motives. If politicians and their constituents always acted to promote their own or their country's long-range self-interest, this world would be an earthly paradise. As it is, they often act against their own interests, merely to gratify their least creditable passions; the world, in consequence, is a place of misery. Propaganda in favor of action that is consonant with enlightened self-interest appeals to reason by means of logical arguments based upon the best available evidence fully and honestly set forth. Propaganda in favor of action dictated by the impulses that are below self-interest offers false, garbled or incomplete evidence, avoids logical argument and seeks to influence its victims by the mere repetition of catchwords, by the furious denunciation of foreign or domestic scapegoats, and by cunningly associating the lowest passions with the highest ideals, so that atrocities come to be perpetrated in the name of God and the most cynical kind of *Realpolitik* is treated as a matter of religious principle and patriotic duty.

In John Dewey's words, "a renewal of faith in common human nature, in its potentialities in general, and in its power in particular to respond to reason and truth, is a surer bulwark against totalitarianism than a demonstration of material success or a devout worship of special legal and political forms." The power to respond to reason and truth exists in all of us. But so, unfortunately, does the tendency to respond to unreason and falsehood—particularly in those cases where the falsehood evokes some enjoyable emotion, or where the appeal to unreason strikes some answering chord in the primitive, subhuman depths of our being. In certain fields of activity men have learned to respond to reason and truth pretty consistently. The authors of learned articles do not appeal to the passions of their fellow scientists and technologists. They set forth what, to the best of their knowledge, is the truth about some particular aspect of reality, they use reason to explain the facts they have observed and they support their point of view with arguments that appeal to reason in other people. All this is fairly easy in the fields of physical science and technology. It is much more difficult in the fields of politics and religion and ethics. Here the relevant facts often elude us. As for the meaning of the facts, that of course depends upon the particular system of ideas, in terms of which you choose to interpret them. And these are not the only difficulties that confront the rational truth-seeker. In public and in private life, it often happens that there is simply no time to collect the relevant facts or to weigh their significance. We are forced to act on insufficient evidence and by a light considerably less steady than that of logic. With the best will in the world, we cannot always be completely truthful or consistently rational. All that is in our power is to be as truthful and rational as circumstances permit us to be, and to respond as well as we can to the limited truth and imperfect reasonings offered for our consideration by others.

"If a nation expects to be ignorant and free," said Jefferson, "it expects what never was and never will be. . . . The people cannot be safe without information. Where the press is free, and every man able to read, all is safe." Across the Atlantic another passionate believer in reason was thinking about the same time, in almost precisely similar terms. Here is what John Stuart Mill wrote of his father, the utilitarian philosopher, James Mill: "So complete was his reliance upon the influence of reason over the minds of mankind, whenever it is allowed to reach them, that he felt as if all would be gained, if the whole population were able to read, and if all sorts of opinions were allowed to be addressed to them by word or in writing, and if by the suffrage they could nominate a legislature to give effect to the opinions they had adopted." *All is safe, all would be gained!* Once more we hear the note of eighteenth-century optimism. Jefferson, it is true, was a realist as well as an optimist. He knew by bitter experience that the freedom of the press can be shamefully abused. "Nothing," he declared, "can now be believed which is seen in a newspaper." And yet, he insisted (and we can only agree with him), "within the pale of truth, the press is a noble institution, equally the friend of science and civil liberty." Mass communication, in a word, is neither good nor bad ; it is simply a force and, like any other force, it can be used either well or ill. Used in one way, the press, the radio and the cinema are indispensable to the survival of democracy. Used in another way, they are among the most powerful weapons in the dictator's armory. In the field of mass communications as in almost every other field of enterprise, technological progress has hurt the Little Man and helped the Big Man. As lately as fifty years ago, every democratic country could boast of a great number of small journals and local newspapers. Thousands of country editors expressed thousands of independent opinions. Somewhere or other almost anybody could get almost anything printed. Today the press is still legally free; but most of the little papers have disappeared. The cost of wood-pulp, of modern printing machinery and of syndicated news is too high for the Little Man. In the totalitarian East there is political censorship, and the media of mass communication are controlled by the State. In the democratic West there is economic censorship and the media of mass communication are controlled by members of the Power Elite. Censorship by rising costs and the concentration of communication power in the hands of a few big concerns is less objectionable than State ownership and government propaganda; but certainly it is not something of which a Jeffersonian democrat could possibly approve.

In regard to propaganda the early advocates of universal literacy and a free press envisaged only two possibilities: the propaganda might be true, or it might be false. They did not foresee what in fact has happened, above all in our Western capitalist democracies—the development of a vast mass communications industry, concerned in the main neither with the true nor the false, but with the unreal, the more or less totally irrelevant. In a word, they failed to take into account man's almost infinite appetite for distractions.

In the past most people never got a chance of fully satisfying this appetite. They might long for distractions, but the distractions were not provided. Christmas came but once a year, feasts were "solemn and rare," there were few readers and very little to read, and the nearest approach to a neighborhood movie theater was the parish church, where the performances, though frequent, were somewhat monotonous. For conditions even remotely comparable to those now prevailing we must return to imperial Rome, where the populace was kept in good humor by frequent, gratuitous doses of many kinds of entertainment—from poetical dramas to gladiatorial fights, from recitations of Virgil to all-out boxing, from concerts to military reviews and public executions. But even in Rome there was nothing like the non-stop distraction now provided by newspapers and magazines, by radio, television and the cinema. In *Brave New World* non-stop distractions of the most fascinating nature (the feelies, orgy-porgy, centrifugal bumble-puppy) are deliberately used as instruments of policy, for the purpose of preventing people from paying too much attention to the realities of the social and political situation. The other world of religion is different from the other world of entertainment; but they resemble one another in being most decidedly "not of this world." Both are distractions and, if lived in too continuously, both can become, in Marx's phrase, "the opium of the people" and so a threat to freedom. Only the vigilant can maintain their liberties, and only those who are constantly and intelligently on the spot can hope to govern themselves effectively by democratic procedures. A society, most of whose members spend a great part of their time, not on the spot, not here and now and in the calculable future, but somewhere else, in the irrelevant other worlds of sport and soap opera, of mythology and metaphysical fantasy, will find it hard to resist the encroachments of those who would manipulate and control it.

In their propaganda today's dictators rely for the most part on repetition, suppression and rationalization—the repetition of catchwords which they wish to be accepted as true, the suppression of facts which they wish to be ignored, the arousal and rationalization of passions which may be used in the interests of the Party or the State. As the art and science of manipulation come to be better understood, the dictators of the future will doubtless learn to combine these techniques with the non-stop distractions which, in the West, are now threatening to drown in a sea of irrelevance the rational propaganda essential to the maintenance of individual liberty and the survival of democratic institutions.

V

PROPAGANDA UNDER A DICTATORSHIP

At his trial after the Second World War, Hitler's Minister for Armaments, Albert Speer, delivered a long speech in which, with remarkable acuteness, he described the Nazi tyranny and analyzed its methods. "Hitler's dictatorship," he said, "differed in one fundamental point from all its predecessors in history. It was the first dictatorship in the present period of modern technical development, a dictatorship which made complete use of all technical means for the domination of its own country. Through technical devices like the radio and the loudspeaker, eighty million people were deprived of independent thought. It was thereby possible to subject them to the will of one man. . . . Earlier dictators needed highly qualified assistants even at the lowest level—men who could think and act independently. The totalitarian system in the period of modern technical development can dispense with such men; thanks to modern methods of communication, it is possible to mechanize the lower leadership. As a result of this there has arisen the new type of the uncritical recipient of orders."

In the Brave New World of my prophetic fable technology had advanced far beyond the point it had reached in Hitler's day; consequently the recipients of orders were far less critical than their Nazi counterparts, far more obedient to the order-giving elite. Moreover, they had been genetically standardized and postnatally conditioned to perform their subordinate functions, and could therefore be depended upon to behave almost as predictably as machines. As we shall see in a later chapter, this conditioning of "the lower leadership" is already going on under the Communist dictatorships. The Chinese and the Russians are not relying merely on the indirect efforts of advancing technology; they are working directly on the psychophysical organisms of their lower leaders, subjecting minds and bodies to a system of ruthless and, from all accounts, highly effective conditioning. "Many a man," said Speer, "has been haunted by the nightmare that one day nations might be dominated by technical means. That nightmare was almost realized in Hitler's totalitarian system." Almost, but not quite. The Nazis did not have time—and perhaps did not have the intelligence and the necessary knowledge—to brainwash and condition their lower leadership. This, it may be, is one of the reasons why they failed.

Since Hitler's day the armory of technical devices at the disposal of the would-be dictator has been considerably enlarged. As well as the radio, the loudspeaker, the moving picture camera and the rotary press, the contemporary propagandist can make use of television to broadcast the image as well as the voice of his client, and can record both image and voice on spools of magnetic tape. Thanks to technological progress, Big Brother can now be almost as omnipresent as God. Nor is it only on the technical front that the hand of the would-be dictator has been strengthened. Since Hitler's day a great deal of work has been carried out in those fields of applied psychology and neurology which are the special province of the propagandist, the indoctrinator and the brainwasher. In the past these specialists in the art of changing people's minds were empiricists. By a method of trial and error they had worked out a number of techniques and procedures, which they used very effectively without, however, knowing precisely why they were effective. Today the art of mind-control is in the process of becoming a science. The practitioners of this science know what they are doing and why. They are guided in their work by theories and hypotheses solidly established on a massive foundation of experimental evidence. Thanks to the new insights and the new techniques made possible by these insights, the nightmare that was "all but realized in Hitler's totalitarian system" may soon be completely realizable.

But before we discuss these new insights and techniques let us take a look at the nightmare that so nearly came true in Nazi Germany. What were the methods used by Hitler and Goebbels for "depriving eighty million people of independent thought and subjecting them to the will of one man"? And what was the theory of human nature upon which those terrifyingly successful methods were based? These questions can be answered, for the most part, in Hitler's own words. And what remarkably clear and astute words they are! When he writes about such vast abstractions as Race and History and Providence, Hitler is strictly unreadable. But when he writes about the German masses and the methods he used for dominating and directing them, his style changes. Nonsense gives place to sense, bombast to a hard-boiled and cynical lucidity. In his philosophical lucubrations Hitler was either cloudily daydreaming or reproducing other people's half-baked notions. In his comments on crowds and propaganda he was writing of things he knew by first-hand experience. In the words of his ablest biographer, Mr. Alan Bullock, "Hitler was the greatest demagogue in history." Those who add, "only a demagogue," fail to appreciate the nature of political power in an age of mass politics. As he himself said, "To be a leader means to be able to move the masses." Hitler's aim was first to move the masses and then, having pried them loose from their traditional loyalties and moralities, to impose upon them (with the hypnotized consent of the majority) a new authoritarian order of his own devising. "Hitler," wrote Hermann Rauschning in 1939, "has a deep respect for the Catholic church and the Jesuit order; not because of their Christian doctrine, but because of the 'machinery' they have elaborated and controlled, their hierarchical system, their extremely clever tactics, their knowledge of human nature and their wise use of human weaknesses in ruling over believers." Ecclesiasticism without Christianity, the discipline of a monastic rule, not for God's sake or in order to achieve personal salvation, but for the sake of the State and for the greater glory and power of the demagogue turned Leader—this was the goal toward which the systematic moving of the masses was to lead.

Let us see what Hitler thought of the masses he moved and how he did the moving. The first principle from which he started was a value judgment: the masses are utterly contemptible. They are incapable of abstract thinking and uninterested in any fact outside the circle of their immediate experience. Their behavior is determined, not by knowledge and reason, but by feelings and unconscious drives. It is in these drives and feelings that "the roots of their positive as well as their negative attitudes are implanted." To be successful a propagandist must learn how to manipulate these instincts and emotions. "The driving force which has brought about the most tremendous revolutions on this earth has never been a body of scientific teaching which has gained power over the masses, but always a devotion which has inspired them, and often a kind of hysteria which has urged them into action. Whoever wishes to win over the masses must know the key that will open the door of their hearts." . . . In post-Freudian jargon, of their unconscious.

Hitler made his strongest appeal to those members of the lower middle classes who had been ruined by the inflation of 1923, and then ruined all over again by the depression of 1929 and the following years. "The masses" of whom he speaks were these bewildered, frustrated and chronically anxious millions. To make them more masslike, more homogeneously subhuman, he assembled them, by the thousands and the tens of thousands, in vast halls and arenas, where individuals could lose their personal identity, even their elementary humanity, and be merged with the crowd. A man or woman makes direct contact with society in two ways: as a member of some familial, professional or religious group, or as a member of a crowd. Groups are capable of being as moral and intelligent as the individuals who form them; a crowd is chaotic, has no purpose of its own and is capable of anything except intelligent action and realistic thinking. Assembled in a crowd, people lose their powers of reasoning and their capacity for moral choice. Their suggestibility is increased to the point where they cease to have any judgment or will of their own. They become very excitable, they lose all sense of individual or collective responsibility, they are subject to sudden accesses of rage, enthusiasm and panic. In a word, a man in a crowd behaves as though he had swallowed a large dose of some powerful intoxicant. He is a victim of what I have called "herd-poisoning." Like alcohol, herd-poison is an active, extraverted drug. The crowd-intoxicated individual escapes from responsibility, intelligence and morality into a kind of frantic, animal mindlessness.

During his long career as an agitator, Hitler had studied the effects of herd-poison and had learned how to exploit them for his own purposes. He had discovered that the orator can appeal to those "hidden forces" which motivate men's actions, much more effectively than can the writer. Reading is a private, not a collective activity. The writer speaks only to individuals, sitting by themselves in a state of normal sobriety. The orator speaks to masses of individuals, already well primed with herd-poison. They are at his mercy and, if he knows his business, he can do what he likes with them. As an orator, Hitler knew his business supremely well. He was able, in his own words, "to follow the lead of the great mass in such a way that from the living emotion of his hearers the apt word which he needed would be suggested to him and in its turn this would go straight to the heart of his hearers." Otto Strasser called him "a loud-speaker, proclaiming the most secret desires, the least admissible instincts, the sufferings and personal revolts of a whole nation." Twenty years before Madison Avenue embarked upon "Motivational Research," Hitler was systematically exploring and exploiting the secret fears and hopes, the cravings, anxieties and frustrations of the German masses. It is by manipulating "hidden forces" that the advertising experts induce us to buy their wares—a toothpaste, a brand of cigarettes, a political candidate. And it is by appealing to the same hidden forces—and to others too dangerous for Madison Avenue to meddle with—that Hitler induced the German masses to buy themselves a Fuehrer, an insane philosophy and the Second World War.

Unlike the masses, intellectuals have a taste for rationality and an interest in facts. Their critical habit of mind makes them resistant to the kind of propaganda that works so well on the majority. Among the masses "instinct is supreme, and from instinct comes faith. . . . While the healthy common folk instinctively close their ranks to form a community of the people" (under a Leader, it goes without saying) "intellectuals run this way and that, like hens in a poultry yard. With them one cannot make history; they cannot be used as elements composing a community." Intellectuals are the kind of people who demand evidence and are shocked by logical inconsistencies and fallacies. They regard over-simplification as the original sin of the mind and have no use for the slogans, the unqualified assertions and sweeping generalizations which are the propagandist's stock in trade. "All effective propaganda," Hitler wrote, "must be confined to a few bare necessities and then must be expressed in a few stereotyped formulas." These stereotyped formulas must be constantly repeated, for "only constant repetition will finally succeed in imprinting an idea upon the memory of a crowd." Philosophy teaches us to feel uncertain about the things that seem to us self-evident. Propaganda, on the other hand, teaches us to accept as self-evident matters about which it would be reasonable to suspend our judgment or to feel doubt. The aim of the demagogue is to create social coherence under his own leadership. But, as Bertrand Russell has pointed out, "systems of dogma without empirical foundations, such as scholasticism, Marxism and fascism, have the advantage of producing a great deal of social coherence among their disciples." The demagogic propagandist must therefore be consistently dogmatic. All his statements are made without qualification. There are no grays in his picture of the world; everything is either diabolically black or celestially white. In Hitler's words, the propagandist should adopt "a systematically one-sided attitude towards every problem that has to be dealt with." He must never admit that he might be wrong or that people with a different point of view might be even partially right. Opponents should not be argued with; they should be attacked, shouted down, or, if they become too much of a nuisance, liquidated. The morally squeamish intellectual may be shocked by this kind of thing. But the masses are always convinced that "right is on the side of the active aggressor."

Such, then, was Hitler's opinion of humanity in the mass. It was a very low opinion. Was it also an incorrect opinion? The tree is known by its fruits, and a theory of human nature which inspired the kind of techniques that proved so horribly effective must contain at least an element of truth. Virtue and intelligence belong to human beings as individuals freely associating with other individuals in small groups. So do sin and stupidity. But the subhuman mindlessness to which the demogogue makes his appeal, the moral imbecility on which he relies when he goads his victims into action, are characteristic not of men and women as individuals, but of men and women in masses. Mindlessness and moral idiocy are not characteristically human attributes; they are symptoms of herd-poisoning. In all the world's higher religions, salvation and enlightenment are for individuals. The kingdom of heaven is within the mind of a person, not within the collective mindlessness of a crowd. Christ promised to be present where two or three are gathered together. He did not say anything about being present where thousands are intoxicating one another with herd-poison. Under the Nazis enormous numbers of people were compelled to spend an enormous amount of time marching in serried ranks from point A to point B and back again to point A. "This keeping of the whole population on the march seemed to be a senseless waste of time and energy. Only much later," adds Hermann Rauschning, "was there revealed in it a subtle intention based on a well-judged adjustment of ends and means. Marching diverts men's thoughts. Marching kills thought. Marching makes an end of individuality. Marching is the indispensable magic stroke performed in order to accustom the people to a mechanical, quasi-ritualistic activity until it becomes second nature."

From his point of view and at the level where he had chosen to do his dreadful work, Hitler was perfectly correct in his estimate of human nature. To those of us who look at men and women as individuals rather than as members of crowds, or of regimented collectives, he seems hideously wrong. In an age of accelerating over-population, of accelerating over-organization and ever more efficient means of mass communication, how can we preserve the integrity and reassert the value of the human individual? This is a question that can still be asked and perhaps effectively answered. A generation from now it may be too late to find an answer and perhaps impossible, in the stifling collective climate of that future time, even to ask the question.

VI

THE ARTS OF SELLING

The survival of democracy depends on the ability of large numbers of people to make realistic choices in the light of adequate information. A dictatorship, on the other hand, maintains itself by censoring or distorting the facts, and by appealing, not to reason, not to enlightened self-interest, but to passion and prejudice, to the powerful "hidden forces," as Hitler called them, present in the unconscious depths of every human mind.

In the West, democratic principles are proclaimed and many able and conscientious publicists do their best to supply electors with adequate information and to persuade them, by rational argument, to make realistic choices in the light of that information. All this is greatly to the good. But unfortunately propaganda in the Western democracies, above all in America, has two faces and a divided personality. In charge of the editorial department there is often a democratic Dr. Jekyll—a propagandist who would be very happy to prove that John Dewey had been right about the ability of human nature to respond to truth and reason. But this worthy man controls only a part of the machinery of mass communication. In charge of advertising we find an anti-democratic, because anti-rational, Mr. Hyde—or rather a Dr. Hyde, for Hyde is now a Ph.D. in psychology and has a master's degree as well in the social sciences.

This Dr. Hyde would be very unhappy indeed if everybody always lived up to John Dewey's faith in human nature. Truth and reason are Jekyll's affair, not his. Hyde is a motivation analyst, and his business is to study human weaknesses and failings, to investigate those unconscious desires and fears by which so much of men's conscious thinking and overt doing is determined. And he does this, not in the spirit of the moralist who would like to make people better, or of the physician who would like to improve their health, but simply in order to find out the best way to take advantage of their ignorance and to exploit their irrationality for the pecuniary benefit of his employers. But after all, it may be argued, "capitalism is dead, consumerism is king"—and consumerism requires the services of expert salesmen versed in all the arts (including the more insidious arts) of persuasion. Under a free enterprise system commercial propaganda by any and every means is absolutely indispensable. But the indispensable is not necessarily the desirable. What is demonstrably good in the sphere of economics may be far from good for men and women as voters or even as human beings. An earlier, more moralistic generation would have been profoundly shocked by the bland cynicism of the motivation analysts. Today we read a book like Mr. Vance Packard's *The Hidden Persuaders*, and are more amused than horrified, more resigned than indignant. Given Freud, given Behaviorism, given the mass producer's chronically desperate need for mass consumption, this is the sort of thing that is only to be expected. But what, we may ask, is the sort of thing that is to be expected in the future? Are Hyde's activities compatible in the long run with Jekyll's? Can a campaign in favor of rationality be successful in the teeth of another and even more vigorous campaign in favor of irrationality? These are questions which, for the moment, I shall not attempt to answer, but shall leave hanging, so to speak, as a backdrop to our discussion of the methods of mass persuasion in a technologically advanced democratic society.

The task of the commercial propagandist in a democracy is in some ways easier and in some ways more difficult than that of a political propagandist employed by an established dictator or a dictator in the making. It is easier inasmuch as almost everyone starts out with a prejudice in favor of beer, cigarettes and iceboxes, whereas almost nobody starts out with a prejudice in favor of tyrants. It is more difficult inasmuch as the commercial propagandist is not permitted, by the rules of his particular game, to appeal to the more savage instincts of his public. The advertiser of dairy products would dearly love to tell his readers and listeners that all their troubles are caused by the machinations of a gang of godless international margarine manufacturers, and that it is their patriotic duty to march out and burn the oppressors' factories. This sort of thing, however, is ruled out, and he must be content with a milder approach. But the mild approach is less exciting than the approach through verbal and physical violence. In the long run, anger and hatred are self-defeating emotions. But in the short run they pay high dividends in the form of psychological and even (since they release large quantities of adrenalin and noradrenalin) physiological satisfaction. People may start out with an initial prejudice against tyrants; but when tyrants or would-be tyrants treat them to adrenalin-releasing propaganda about the wickedness of their enemies—particularly of enemies weak enough to be persecuted—they are ready to follow him with enthusiasm. In his speeches Hitler kept repeating such words as "hatred," "force," "ruthless," "crush," "smash"; and he would accompany these violent words with even more violent gestures. He would yell, he would scream, his veins would swell, his face would turn purple. Strong emotion (as every actor and dramatist knows) is in the highest degree contagious. Infected by the malignant frenzy of the orator, the audience would groan and sob and scream in an orgy of uninhibited passion. And these orgies were so enjoyable that most of those who had experienced them eagerly came back for more. Almost all of us long for peace and freedom; but very few of us have much enthusiasm for the thoughts, feelings and actions that make for peace and freedom. Conversely almost nobody wants war or tyranny; but a great many people find an intense pleasure in the thoughts, feelings and actions that make for war and tyranny. These thoughts, feelings and actions are too dangerous to be exploited for commercial purposes. Accepting this handicap, the advertising man must do the best he can with the less intoxicating emotions, the quieter forms of irrationality.

Effective rational propaganda becomes possible only when there is a clear understanding, on the part of all concerned, of the nature of symbols and of their relations to the things and events symbolized. Irrational propaganda depends for its effectiveness on the general failure to understand the nature of symbols. Simple-minded people tend to equate the symbol with what it stands for, to attribute to things and events some of the qualities expressed by the words in terms of which the propagandist has chosen, for his own purposes, to talk about them. Consider a simple example. Most cosmetics are made of lanolin, which is a mixture of purified wool fat and water beaten up into an emulsion. This emulsion has many valuable properties: it penetrates the skin, it does not become rancid, it is mildly antiseptic and so forth. But the commercial propagandists do not speak about the genuine virtues of the emulsion. They give it some picturesquely voluptuous name, talk ecstatically and misleadingly about feminine beauty and show pictures of gorgeous blondes nourishing their tissues with skin food. "The cosmetic manufacturers," one of their number has written, "are not selling lanolin, they are selling hope." For this hope, this fraudulent implication of a promise that they will be transfigured, women will pay ten or twenty times the value of the emulsion which the propagandists have so skillfully related, by means of misleading symbols, to a deep-seated and almost universal feminine wish—the wish to be more attractive to members of the opposite sex. The principles underlying this kind of propaganda are extremely simple. Find some common desire, some widespread unconscious fear or anxiety; think out some way to relate this wish or fear to the product you have to sell; then build a bridge of verbal or pictorial symbols over which your customer can pass from fact to compensatory dream, and from the dream to the illusion that your product, when purchased, will make the dream come true. "We no longer buy oranges, we buy vitality. We do not buy just an auto, we buy prestige." And so with all the rest. In toothpaste, for example, we buy, not a mere cleanser and antiseptic, but release from the fear of being sexually repulsive. In vodka and whisky we are not buying a protoplasmic poison which in small doses, may depress the nervous system in a psychologically valuable way; we are buying friendliness and good fellowship, the warmth of Dingley Dell and the brilliance of the Mermaid Tavern. With our laxatives we buy the health of a Greek god, the radiance of one of Diana's nymphs. With the monthly best seller we acquire culture, the envy of our less literate neighbors and the respect of the sophisticated. In every case the motivation analyst has found some deep-seated wish or fear, whose energy can be used to move the customer to part with cash and so, indirectly, to turn the wheels of industry. Stored in the minds and bodies of countless individuals, this potential energy is released by, and transmitted along, a line of symbols carefully laid out so as to bypass rationality and obscure the real issue.

Sometimes the symbols take effect by being disproportionately impressive, haunting and fascinating in their own right. Of this kind are the rites and pomps of religion. These "beauties of holiness" strengthen faith where it already exists and, where there is no faith, contribute to conversion. Appealing, as they do, only to the aesthetic sense, they guarantee neither the truth nor the ethical value of the doctrines with which they have been, quite arbitrarily, associated. As a matter of plain historical fact, the beauties of holiness have often been matched and indeed surpassed by the beauties of unholiness. Under Hitler, for example, the yearly Nuremberg rallies were masterpieces of ritual and theatrical art. "I had spent six years in St. Petersburg before the war in the best days of the old Russian ballet," writes Sir Nevile Henderson, the British ambassador to Hitler's Germany, "but for grandiose beauty I have never seen any ballet to compare with the Nuremberg rally." One thinks of Keats—

"beauty is truth, truth beauty." Alas, the identity exists only on some ultimate, supramundane level. On the levels of politics and theology, beauty is perfectly compatible with nonsense and tyranny. Which is very fortunate; for if beauty were incompatible with nonsense and tyranny, there would be precious little art in the world. The masterpieces of painting, sculpture and architecture were produced as religious or political propaganda, for the greater glory of a god, a government or a priesthood. But most kings and priests have been despotic and all religions have been riddled with superstition. Genius has been the servant of tyranny and art has advertised the merits of the local cult. Time, as it passes, separates the good art from the bad metaphysics. Can we learn to make this separation, not after the event, but while it is actually taking place? That is the question.

In commercial propaganda the principle of the disproportionately fascinating symbol is clearly understood. Every propagandist has his Art Department, and attempts are constantly being made to beautify the billboards with striking posters, the advertising pages of magazines with lively drawings and photographs. There are no masterpieces; for masterpieces appeal only to a limited audience, and the commercial propagandist is out to captivate the majority. For him, the ideal is a moderate excellence. Those who like this not too good, but sufficiently striking, art may be expected to like the products with which it has been associated and for which it symbolically stands.

Another disproportionately fascinating symbol is the Singing Commercial. Singing Commercials are a recent invention; but the Singing Theological and the Singing Devotional—the hymn and the psalm—are as old as religion itself. Singing Militaries, or marching songs, are coeval with war and Singing Patriotics, the precursors of our national anthems, were doubtless used to promote group solidarity, to emphasize the distinction between "us" and "them," by the wandering bands of paleolithic hunters and food gatherers. To most people music is intrinsically attractive. Moreover, melodies tend to ingrain themselves in the listener's mind. A tune will haunt the memory during the whole of a lifetime. Here, for example, is a quite uninteresting statement or value judgment. As it stands nobody will pay attention to it. But now set the words to a catchy and easily remembered tune. Immediately they become words of power. Moreover, the words will tend automatically to repeat themselves every time the melody is heard or spontaneously remembered. Orpheus has entered into an alliance with Pavlov—the power of sound with the conditioned reflex. For the commercial propagandist, as for his colleagues in the fields of politics and religion, music possesses yet another advantage. Nonsense which it would be shameful for a reasonable being to write, speak or hear spoken can be sung or listened to by that same rational being with pleasure and even with a kind of intellectual conviction. Can we learn to separate the pleasure of singing or of listening to song from the all too human tendency to believe in the propaganda which the song is putting over? That again is the question.

Thanks to compulsory education and the rotary press, the propagandist has been able, for many years past, to convey his messages to virtually every adult in every civilized country. Today, thanks to radio and television, he is in the happy position of being able to communicate even with unschooled adults and not yet literate children.

Children, as might be expected, are highly susceptible to propaganda. They are ignorant of the world and its ways, and therefore completely unsuspecting. Their critical faculties are undeveloped. The youngest of them have not yet reached the age of reason and the older ones lack the experience on which their newfound rationality can effectively work. In Europe, conscripts used to be playfully referred to as "cannon fodder." Their little brothers and sisters have now become radio fodder and television fodder. In my childhood we were taught to sing nursery rhymes and, in pious households, hymns. Today the little ones warble the Singing Commercials. Which is better—"Rheingold is my beer, the dry beer," or "Hey diddle-diddle, the cat and the fiddle"? "Abide with me" or "You'll wonder where the yellow went, when you brush your teeth with Pepsodent"? Who knows?

"I don't say that children should be forced to harass their parents into buying products they've seen advertised on television, but at the same time I cannot close my eyes to the fact that it's being done every day." So writes the star of one of the many programs beamed to a juvenile audience. "Children," he adds, "are living, talking records of what we tell them every day." And in due course these living, talking records of television commercials will grow up, earn money and buy the products of industry. "Think," writes Mr. Clyde Miller ecstatically, "think of what it can mean to your firm in profits if you can condition a million or ten million children, who will grow up into adults trained to buy your product, as soldiers are trained in advance when they hear the trigger words, Forward March!" Yes, just think of it! And at the same time remember that the dictators and the would-be dictators have been thinking about this sort of thing for years, and that millions, tens of millions, hundreds of millions of children are in the process of growing up to buy the local despot's ideological product and, like well-trained soldiers, to respond with appropriate behavior to the trigger words implanted in those young minds by the despot's propagandists.

Self-government is in inverse ratio to numbers. The larger the constituency, the less the value of any particular vote. When he is merely one of millions, the individual elector feels himself to be impotent, a negligible quantity. The candidates he has voted into office are far away, at the top of the pyramid of power. Theoretically they are the servants of the people; but in fact it is the servants who give orders and the people, far off at the base of the great pyramid, who must obey. Increasing population and advancing technology have resulted in an increase in the number and complexity of organizations, an increase in the amount of power concentrated in the hands of officials and a corresponding decrease in the amount of control exercised by electors, coupled with a decrease in the public's regard for democratic procedures. Already weakened by the vast impersonal forces at work in the modern world, democratic institutions are now being undermined from within by the politicians and their propagandists.

Human beings act in a great variety of irrational ways, but all of them seem to be capable, if given a fair chance, of making a reasonable choice in the light of available evidence. Democratic institutions can be made to work only if all concerned do their best to impart knowledge and to encourage rationality. But today, in the world's most powerful democracy, the politicians and their propagandists prefer to make nonsense of democratic procedures by appealing almost exclusively to the ignorance and irrationality of the electors. "Both parties," we were told in 1956 by the editor of a leading business journal, "will merchandize their candidates and issues by the same methods that business had developed to sell goods. These include scientific selection of appeals and planned repetition. . . . Radio spot announcements and ads will repeat phrases with a planned intensity. Billboards will push slogans of proven power. . . . Candidates need, in addition to rich voices and good diction, to be able to look 'sincerely' at the TV camera."

The political merchandisers appeal only to the weaknesses of voters, never to their potential strength. They make no attempt to educate the masses into becoming fit for self-government; they are content merely to manipulate and exploit them. For this purpose all the resources of psychology and the social sciences are mobilized and set to work. Carefully selected samples of the electorate are given "interviews in depth." These interviews in depth reveal the unconscious fears and wishes most prevalent in a given society at the time of an election. Phrases and images aimed at allaying or, if necessary, enhancing these fears, at satisfying these wishes, at least symbolically, are then chosen by the experts, tried out on readers and audiences, changed or improved in the light of the information thus obtained. After which the political campaign is ready for the mass communicators. All that is now needed is money and a candidate who can be coached to look "sincere." Under the new dispensation, political principles and plans for specific action have come to lose most of their importance. The personality of the candidate and the way he is projected by the advertising experts are the things that really matter.

In one way or another, as vigorous he-man or kindly father, the candidate must be glamorous. He must also be an entertainer who never bores his audience. Inured to television and radio, that audience is accustomed to being distracted and does not like to be asked to concentrate or make a prolonged intellectual effort. All speeches by the entertainer-candidate must therefore be short and snappy. The great issues of the day must be dealt with in five minutes at the most—and preferably (since the audience will be eager to pass on to something a little livelier than inflation or the H-bomb) in sixty seconds flat. The nature of oratory is such that there has always been a tendency among politicians and clergymen to over-simplify complex issues. From a pulpit or a platform even the most conscientious of speakers finds it very difficult to tell the whole truth. The methods now being used to merchandise the political candidate as though he were a deodorant positively guarantee the electorate against ever hearing the truth about anything.

VII

BRAINWASHING

In the two preceding chapters I have described the techniques of what may be called wholesale mind-manipulation, as practiced by the greatest demagogue and the most successful salesmen in recorded history. But no human problem can be solved by wholesale methods alone. The shotgun has its place, but so has the hypodermic syringe. In the chapters that follow I shall describe some of the more effective techniques for manipulating not crowds, not entire publics, but isolated individuals.

In the course of his epoch-making experiments on the conditioned reflex, Ivan Pavlov observed that, when subjected to prolonged physical or psychic stress, laboratory animals exhibit all the symptoms of a nervous breakdown. Refusing to cope any longer with the intolerable situation, their brains go on strike, so to speak, and either stop working altogether (the dog loses consciousness), or else resort to slowdowns and sabotage (the dog behaves unrealistically, or develops the kind of physical symptoms which, in a human being, we would call hysterical). Some animals are more resistant to stress than others. Dogs possessing what Pavlov called a "strong excitatory" constitution break down much more quickly than dogs of a merely "lively" (as opposed to a choleric or agitated) temperament. Similarly "weak inhibitory" dogs reach the end of their tether much sooner than do "calm imperturbable" dogs. But even the most stoical dog is unable to resist indefinitely. If the stress to which he is subjected is sufficiently intense or sufficiently prolonged, he will end by breaking down as abjectly and as completely as the weakest of his kind.

Pavlov's findings were confirmed in the most distressing manner, and on a very large scale, during the two World Wars. As the result of a single catastrophic experience, or of a succession of terrors less appalling but frequently repeated, soldiers develop a number of disabling psychophysical symptoms. Temporary unconsciousness, extreme agitation, lethargy, functional blindness or paralysis, completely unrealistic responses to the challenge of events, strange reversals of lifelong patterns of behavior—all the symptoms, which Pavlov observed in his dogs, reappeared among the victims of what in the First World War was called "shell shock," in the Second, "battle fatigue." Every man, like every dog, has his own individual limit of endurance. Most men reach their limit after about thirty days of more or less continuous stress under the conditions of modern combat. The more than averagely susceptible succumb in only fifteen days. The more than averagely tough can resist for forty-five or even fifty days. Strong or weak, in the long run all of them break down. All, that is to say, of those who are initially sane. For, ironically enough, the only people who can hold up indefinitely under the stress of modern war are psychotics. Individual insanity is immune to the consequences of collective insanity.

The fact that every individual has his breaking point has been known and, in a crude unscientific way, exploited from time immemorial. In some cases man's dreadful inhumanity to man has been inspired by the love of cruelty for its own horrible and fascinating sake. More often, however, pure sadism was tempered by utilitarianism, theology or reasons of state. Physical torture and other forms of stress were inflicted by lawyers in order to loosen the tongues of reluctant witnesses; by clergymen in order to punish the unorthodox and induce them to change their opinions; by the secret police to extract confessions from persons suspected of being hostile to the government. Under Hitler, torture, followed by mass extermination, was used on those biological heretics, the Jews. For a young Nazi, a tour of duty in the Extermination Camps was (in Himmler's words) "the best indoctrination on inferior beings and the subhuman races." Given the obsessional quality of the anti-Semitism which Hitler had picked up as a young man in the slums of Vienna, this revival of the methods employed by the Holy Office against heretics and witches was inevitable. But in the light of the findings of Pavlov and of the knowledge gained by psychiatrists in the treatment of war neuroses, it seems a hideous and grotesque anachronism. Stresses amply sufficient to cause a complete cerebral breakdown can be induced by methods which, though hatefully inhuman, fall short of physical torture.

Whatever may have happened in earlier years, it seems fairly certain that torture is not extensively used by the Communist police today. They draw their inspiration, not from the Inquisitor or the SS man, but from the physiologist and his methodically conditioned laboratory animals. For the dictator and his policemen, Pavlov's findings have important practical implications. If the central nervous system of dogs can be broken down, so can the central nervous system of political prisoners. It is simply a matter of applying the right amount of stress for the right length of time. At the end of the treatment, the prisoner will be in a state of neurosis or hysteria, and will be ready to confess whatever his captors want him to confess.

But confession is not enough. A hopeless neurotic is no use to anyone. What the intelligent and practical dictator needs is not a patient to be institutionalized, or a victim to be shot, but a convert who will work for the Cause. Turning once again to Pavlov, he learns that, on their way to the point of final breakdown, dogs become more than normally suggestible. New behavior patterns can easily be installed while the dog is at or near the limit of its cerebral endurance, and these new behavior patterns seem to be ineradicable. The animal in which they have been implanted cannot be deconditioned; that which it has learned under stress will remain an integral part of its make-up.

Psychological stresses can be produced in many ways. Dogs become disturbed when stimuli are unusually strong; when the interval between a stimulus and the customary response is unduly prolonged and the animal is left in a state of suspense; when the brain is confused by stimuli that run counter to what the dog has learned to expect; when stimuli make no sense within the victim's established frame of reference. Furthermore, it has been found that the deliberate induction of fear, rage or anxiety markedly heightens the dog's suggestibility. If these emotions are kept at a high pitch of intensity for a long enough time, the brain goes "on strike." When this happens, new behavior patterns may be installed with the greatest of ease.

Among the physical stresses that increase a dog's suggestibility are fatigue, wounds and every form of sickness.

For the would-be dictator these findings possess important practical implications. They prove, for example, that Hitler was quite right in maintaining that mass meetings at night were more effective than mass meetings in the daytime. During the day, he wrote, "man's will power revolts with highest energy against any attempt at being forced under another's will and another's opinion. In the evening, however, they succumb more easily to the dominating force of a stronger will."

Pavlov would have agreed with him; fatigue increases suggestibility. (That is why, among other reasons, the commercial sponsors of television programs prefer the evening hours and are ready to back their preference with hard cash.)

Illness is even more effective than fatigue as an intensifier of suggestibility. In the past, sickrooms were the scene of countless religious conversions. The scientifically trained dictator of the future will have all the hospitals in his dominions wired for sound and equipped with pillow speakers. Canned persuasion will be on the air twenty-four hours a day, and the more important patients will be visited by political soul-savers and mind-changers just as, in the past, their ancestors were visited by priests, nuns and pious laymen.

The fact that strong negative emotions tend to heighten suggestibility and so facilitate a change of heart had been observed and exploited long before the days of Pavlov. As Dr. William Sargant has pointed out in his enlightening book, *Battle for the Mind*, John Wesley's enormous success as a preacher was based upon an intuitive understanding of the central nervous system. He would open his sermon with a long and detailed description of the torments to which, unless they underwent conversion, his hearers would undoubtedly be condemned for all eternity. Then, when terror and an agonizing sense of guilt had brought his audience to the verge, or in some cases over the verge, of a complete cerebral breakdown, he would change his tone and promise salvation to those who believed and repented. By this kind of preaching, Wesley converted thousands of men, women and children. Intense, prolonged fear broke them down and produced a state of greatly intensified suggestibility. In this state they were able to accept the preacher's theological pronouncements without question. After which they were reintegrated by words of comfort, and emerged from their ordeal with new and generally better behavior patterns ineradicably implanted in their minds and nervous systems.

The effectiveness of political and religious propaganda depends upon the methods employed, not upon the doctrines taught. These doctrines may be true or false, wholesome or pernicious—it makes little or no difference. If the indoctrination is given in the right way at the proper stage of nervous exhaustion, it will work. Under favorable conditions, practically everybody can be converted to practically anything.

We possess detailed descriptions of the methods used by the Communist police for dealing with political prisoners. From the moment he is taken into custody, the victim is subjected systematically to many kinds of physical and psychological stress. He is badly fed, he is made extremely uncomfortable, he is not allowed to sleep for more than a few hours each night. And all the time he is kept in a state of suspense, uncertainty and acute apprehension. Day after day—or rather night after night, for these Pavlovian policemen understand the value of fatigue as an intensifier of suggestibility—he is questioned, often for many hours at a stretch, by interrogators who do their best to frighten, confuse and bewilder him. After a few weeks or months of such treatment, his brain goes on strike and he confesses whatever it is that his captors want him to confess. Then, if he is to be converted rather than shot, he is offered the comfort of hope. If he will but accept the true faith, he can yet be saved—not, of course, in the next life (for, officially, there is no next life), but in this.

Similar but rather less drastic methods were used during the Korean War on military prisoners. In their Chinese camps the young Western captives were systematically subjected to stress. Thus, for the most trivial breaches of the rules, offenders would be summoned to the commandant's office, there to be questioned, browbeaten and publicly humiliated. And the process would be repeated, again and again, at any hour of the day or night. This continuous harassment produced in its victims a sense of bewilderment and chronic anxiety. To intensify their sense of guilt, prisoners were made to write and rewrite, in ever more intimate detail, long autobiographical accounts of their shortcomings. And after having confessed their own sins, they were required to confess the sins of their companions. The aim was to create within the camp a nightmarish society, in which everybody was spying on, and informing against, everyone else. To these mental stresses were added the physical stresses of malnutrition, discomfort and illness. The increased suggestibility thus induced was skillfully exploited by the Chinese, who poured into these abnormally receptive minds large doses of pro-Communist and anti-capitalist literature. These Pavlovian techniques were remarkably successful. One out of every seven American prisoners was guilty, we are officially told, of grave collaboration with the Chinese authorities, one out of three of technical collaboration.

It must not be supposed that this kind of treatment is reserved by the Communists exclusively for their enemies. The young field workers, whose business it was, during the first years of the new regime, to act as Communist missionaries and organizers in China's innumerable towns and villages were made to take a course of indoctrination far more intense than that to which any prisoner of war was ever subjected. In his *China under Communism* R. L. Walker describes the methods by which the party leaders are able to fabricate out of ordinary men and women the thousands of selfless fanatics required for spreading the Communist gospel and for enforcing Communist policies. Under this system of training, the human raw material is shipped to special camps, where the trainees are completely isolated from their friends, families and the outside world in general. In these camps they are made to perform exhausting physical and mental work; they are never alone, always in groups; they are encouraged to spy on one another; they are required to write self-accusatory autobiographies; they live in chronic fear of the dreadful fate that may befall them on account of what has been said about them by informers or of what they themselves have confessed. In this state of heightened suggestibility they are given an intensive course in theoretical and applied Marxism—a course in which failure to pass examinations may mean anything from ignominious expulsion to a term in a forced labor camp or even liquidation. After about six months of this kind of thing, prolonged mental and physical stress produces the results which Pavlov's findings would lead one to expect. One after another, or in whole groups, the trainees break down. Neurotic and hysterical symptoms make their appearance. Some of the victims commit suicide, others (as many, we are told, as 20 per cent of the total) develop a severe mental illness. Those who survive the rigors of the conversion process emerge with new and ineradicable behavior patterns. All their ties with the past—friends, family, traditional decencies and pieties—have been severed. They are new men, re-created in the image of their new god and totally dedicated to his service.

Throughout the Communist world tens of thousands of these disciplined and devoted young men are being turned out every year from hundreds of conditioning centers. What the Jesuits did for the Roman Church of the Counter Reformation, these products of a more scientific and even harsher training are now doing, and will doubtless continue to do, for the Communist parties of Europe, Asia and Africa.

In politics Pavlov seems to have been an old-fashioned liberal. But, by a strange irony of fate, his researches and the theories he based upon them have called into existence a great army of fanatics dedicated heart and soul, reflex and nervous system, to the destruction of old-fashioned liberalism, wherever it can be found.

Brainwashing, as it is now practiced, is a hybrid technique, depending for its effectiveness partly on the systematic use of violence, partly on skillful psychological manipulation. It represents the tradition of *1984* on its way to becoming the tradition of *Brave New World.* Under a long-established and well-regulated dictatorship our current methods of semiviolent manipulation will seem, no doubt, absurdly crude. Conditioned from earliest infancy (and perhaps also biologically predestined), the average middle- or lower-caste individual will never require conversion or even a refresher course in the true faith. The members of the highest caste will have to be able to think new thoughts in response to new situations; consequently their training will be much less rigid than the training imposed upon those whose business is not to reason why, but merely to do and die with the minimum of fuss. These upper-caste individuals will be members, still, of a wild species—the trainers and guardians, themselves only slightly conditioned, of a breed of completely domesticated animals. Their wildness will make it possible for them to become heretical and rebellious. When this happens, they will have to be either liquidated, or brainwashed back into orthodoxy, or (as in *Brave New World*) exiled to some island, where they can give no further trouble, except of course to one another. But universal infant conditioning and the other techniques of manipulation and control are still a few generations away in the future. On the road to the Brave New World our rulers will have to rely on the transitional and provisional techniques of brainwashing.

VIII

CHEMICAL PERSUASION

In the Brave New World of my fable there was no whisky, no tobacco, no illicit heroin, no bootlegged cocaine. People neither smoked, nor drank, nor sniffed, nor gave themselves injections. Whenever anyone felt depressed or below par, he would swallow a tablet or two of a chemical compound called soma. The original soma, from which I took the name of this hypothetical drug, was an unknown plant (possibly *Asclepias acida*) used by the ancient Aryan invaders of India in one of the most solemn of their religious rites. The intoxicating juice expressed from the stems of this plant was drunk by the priests and nobles in the course of an elaborate ceremony. In the Vedic hymns we are told that the drinkers of soma were blessed in many ways. Their bodies were strengthened, their hearts were filled with courage, joy and enthusiasm, their minds were enlightened and in an immediate experience of eternal life they received the assurance of their immortality. But the sacred juice had its drawbacks. Soma was a dangerous drug—so dangerous that even the great sky-god, Indra, was sometimes made ill by drinking it. Ordinary mortals might even die of an overdose. But the experience was so transcendently blissful and enlightening that soma drinking was regarded as a high privilege. For this privilege no price was too great.

The soma of *Brave New World* had none of the drawbacks of its Indian original. In small doses it brought a sense of bliss, in larger doses it made you see visions and, if you took three tablets, you would sink in a few minutes into refreshing sleep. And all at no physiological or mental cost. The Brave New Worlders could take holidays from their black moods, or from the familiar annoyances of everyday life, without sacrificing their health or permanently reducing their efficiency.

In the Brave New World the soma habit was not a private vice, it was a political institution, it was the very essence of the Life, Liberty and Pursuit of Happiness guaranteed by the Bill of Rights. But this most previous of the subjects' inalienable privileges was at the same time one of the most powerful instruments of rule in the dictator's armory. The systematic drugging of individuals for the benefit of the State (and incidentally, of course, for their own delight) was a main plank in the policy of the World Controllers. The daily soma ration was an insurance against personal maladjustment, social unrest and the spread of subversive ideas. Religion, Karl Marx declared, is the opium of the people. In the Brave New World this situation was reversed. Opium, or rather soma, was the people's religion. Like religion, the drug had power to console and compensate, it called up visions of another, better world, it offered hope, strengthened faith and promoted charity. Beer, a poet has written,

. . . does more than Milton can
To justify God's ways to man.

And let us remember that, compared with soma, beer is a drug of the crudest and most unreliable kind. In this matter of justifying God's ways to man, soma is to alcohol as alcohol is to the theological arguments of Milton.

In 1931, when I was writing about the imaginary synthetic by means of which future generations would be made both happy and docile, the well-known American biochemist, Dr. Irvine Page, was preparing to leave Germany, where he had spent the three preceding years at the Kaiser Wilhelm Institute, working on the chemistry of the brain. "It is hard to understand," Dr. Page has written in a recent article, "why it took so long for scientists to get around to investigating the chemical reactions in their own brains. I speak," he adds, "from acute personal experience. When I came home in 1931 . . . I could not get a job in this field (the field of brain chemistry) or stir a ripple of interest in it." Today, twenty-seven years later, the nonexistent ripple of 1931 has become a tidal wave of biochemical and psychopharmacological research. The enzymes which regulate the workings of the brain are being studied. Within the body, hitherto unknown chemical substances such as adrenochrome and serotonin (of which Dr. Page was a co-discoverer) have been isolated and their far-reaching effects on our mental and physical functions are now being investigated. Meanwhile new drugs are being synthesized—drugs that reinforce or correct or interfere with the actions of the various chemicals, by means of which the nervous system performs its daily and hourly miracles as the controller of the body, the instrument and mediator of consciousness. From our present point of view, the most interesting fact about these new drugs is that they temporarily alter the chemistry of the brain and the associated state of the mind without doing any permanent damage to the organism as a whole. In this respect they are like soma—and profoundly unlike the mind-changing drugs of the past. For example, the classical tranquillizer is opium. But opium is a dangerous drug which, from neolithic times down to the present day, has been making addicts and ruining health. The same is true of the classical euphoric, alcohol—the drug which, in the words of the Psalmist, "maketh glad the heart of man." But unfortunately alcohol not only maketh glad the heart of man; it also, in excessive doses, causes illness and addiction, and has been a main source, for the last eight or ten thousand years, of crime, domestic unhappiness, moral degradation and avoidable accidents.

Among the classical stimulants, tea, coffee and maté are, thank goodness, almost completely harmless. They are also very weak stimulants. Unlike these "cups that cheer but not inebriate," cocaine is a very powerful and a very dangerous drug. Those who make use of it must pay for their ecstasies, their sense of unlimited physical and mental power, by spells of agonizing depression, by such horrible physical symptoms as the sensation of being infested by myriads of crawling insects and by paranoid delusions that may lead to crimes of violence. Another stimulant of more recent vintage is amphetamine, better known under its trade name of Benzedrine. Amphetamine works very effectively—but works, if abused, at the expense of mental and physical health. It has been reported that, in Japan, there are now about one million amphetamine addicts.

Of the classical vision-producers the best known are the peyote of Mexico and the southwestern United States and *Cannabis sativa*, consumed all over the world under such names as hashish, bhang, kif and marihuana. According to the best medical and anthropological evidence, peyote is far less harmful than the White Man's gin or whisky. It permits the Indians who use it in their religious rites to enter paradise, and to feel at one with the beloved community, without making them pay for the privilege by anything worse than the ordeal of having to chew on something with a revolting flavor and of feeling somewhat nauseated for an hour or two. *Cannabis sativa* is a less innocuous drug—though not nearly so harmful as the sensation-mongers would have us believe. The Medical Committee, appointed in 1944 by the Mayor of New York to investigate the problem of marihuana, came to the conclusion, after careful investigation, that *Cannabis sativa* is not a serious menace to society, or even to those who indulge in it. It is merely a nuisance.

From these classical mind-changes we pass to the latest products of psychopharmacological research. Most highly publicized of these are the three new tranquillizers, reserpine, chlorpromazine and meprobamate. Administered to certain classes of psychotics, the first two have proved to be remarkably effective, not in curing mental illnesses, but at least in temporarily abolishing their more distressing symptoms. Meprobamate (alias Miltown) produces similar effects in persons suffering from various forms of neurosis. None of these drugs is perfectly harmless; but their cost, in terms of physical health and mental efficiency, is extraordinarily low. In a world where nobody gets anything for nothing tranquillizers offer a great deal for very little. Miltown and chlorpromazine are not yet soma; but they come fairly near to being one of the aspects of that mythical drug. They provide temporary relief from nervous tension without, in the great majority of cases, inflicting permanent organic harm, and without causing more than a rather slight impairment, while the drug is working, of intellectual and physical efficiency. Except as narcotics, they are probably to be preferred to the barbiturates, which blunt the mind's cutting edge and, in large doses, cause a number of undesirable psychophysical symptoms and may result in a full-blown addiction.

In LSD-25 (lysergic acid diethylamide) the pharmacologists have recently created another aspect of soma—a perception-improver and vision-producer that is, physiologically speaking, almost costless. This extraordinary drug, which is effective in doses as small as fifty or even twenty-five millionths of a gram, has power (like peyote) to transport people into the other world. In the majority of cases, the other world to which LSD-25 gives access is heavenly; alternatively it may be purgatorial or even infernal. But, positive, or negative, the lysergic acid experience is felt by almost everyone who undergoes it to be profoundly significant and enlightening. In any event, the fact that minds can be changed so radically at so little cost to the body is altogether astonishing.

Soma was not only a vision-producer and a tranquillizer; it was also (and no doubt impossibly) a stimulant of mind and body, a creator of active euphoria as well as of the negative happiness that follows the release from anxiety and tension.

The ideal stimulant—powerful but innocuous—still awaits discovery. Amphetamine, as we have seen, was far from satisfactory; it exacted too high a price for what it gave. A more promising candidate for the role of soma in its third aspect is Iproniazid, which is now being used to lift depressed patients out of their misery, to enliven the apathetic and in general to increase the amount of available psychic energy. Still more promising, according to a distinguished pharmacologist of my acquaintance, is a new compound, still in the testing stage, to be known as Deaner. Deaner is an amino-alcohol and is thought to increase the production of acetyl-choline within the body, and thereby to increase the activity and effectiveness of the nervous system. The man who takes the new pill needs less sleep, feels more alert and cheerful, thinks faster and better—and all at next to no organic cost, at any rate in the short run. It sounds almost too good to be true.

We see then that, though soma does not yet exist (and will probably never exist), fairly good substitutes for the various aspects of soma have already been discovered. There are now physiologically cheap tranquillizers, physiologically cheap vision-producers and physiologically cheap stimulants.

That a dictator could, if he so desired, make use of these drugs for political purposes is obvious. He could ensure himself against political unrest by changing the chemistry of his subjects' brains and so making them content with their servile condition. He could use tranquillizers to calm the excited, stimulants to arouse enthusiasm in the indifferent, hallucinants to distract the attention of the wretched from their miseries. But how, it may be asked, will the dictator get his subjects to take the pills that will make them think, feel and behave in the ways he finds desirable? In all probability it will be enough merely to make the pills available. Today alcohol and tobacco are available, and people spend considerably more on these very unsatisfactory euphorics, pseudo-stimulants and sedatives than they are ready to spend on the education of their children. Or consider the barbiturates and the tranquillizers. In the United States these drugs can be obtained only on a doctor's prescription. But the demand of the American public for something that will make life in an urban-industrial environment a little more tolerable is so great that doctors are now writing prescriptions for the various tranquillizers at the rate of forty-eight millions a year. Moreover, a majority of these prescriptions are refilled. A hundred doses of happiness are not enough: send to the drugstore for another bottle—and, when that is finished, for another. . . . There can be no doubt that, if tranquillizers could be bought as easily and cheaply as aspirin, they would be consumed, not by the billions, as they are at present, but by the scores and hundreds of billions. And a good, cheap stimulant would be almost as popular.

Under a dictatorship pharmacists would be instructed to change their tune with every change of circumstances. In times of national crisis it would be their business to push the sale of stimulants. Between crises, too much alertness and energy on the part of his subjects might prove embarrassing to the tyrant. At such times the masses would be urged to buy tranquillizers and vision-producers. Under the influence of these soothing syrups they could be relied upon to give their master no trouble.

As things now stand, the tranquillizers may prevent some people from giving enough trouble, not only to their rulers, but even to themselves. Too much tension is a disease; but so is too little. There are certain occasions when we *ought* to be tense, when an excess of tranquillity (and especially of tranquillity imposed from the outside, by a chemical) is entirely inappropriate.

At a recent symposium on meprobamate, in which I was a participant, an eminent biochemist playfully suggested that the United States government should make a free gift to the Soviet people of fifty billion doses of this most popular of the tranquillizers. The joke had a serious point to it. In a contest between two populations, one of which is being constantly stimulated by threats and promises, constantly directed by one-pointed propaganda, while the other is no less constantly being distracted by television and tranquillized by Miltown, which of the opponents is more likely to come out on top?

As well as tranquillizing, hallucinating and stimulating, the soma of my fable had the power of heightening suggestibility, and so could be used to reinforce the effects of governmental propaganda.

Less effectively and at a higher physiological cost, several drugs already in the pharmacopoeia can be used for the same purpose. There is scopolamine, for example, the active principle of henbane and, in large doses, a powerful poison; there are pentothal and sodium amytal. Nicknamed for some odd reason "the truth serum," pentothal has been used by the police of various countries for the purpose of extracting confessions from (or perhaps suggesting confessions to) reluctant criminals. Pentothal and sodium amytal lower the barrier between the conscious and the subconscious mind and are of great value in the treatment of "battle fatigue" by the process known in England as "abreaction therapy," in America as "narcosynthesis." It is said that these drugs are sometimes employed by the Communists, when preparing important prisoners for their public appearance in court.

Meanwhile pharmacology, biochemistry and neurology are on the march, and we can be quite certain that, in the course of the next few years, new and better chemical methods for increasing suggestibility and lowering psychological resistance will be discovered. Like everything else, these discoveries may be used well or badly. They may help the psychiatrist in his battle against mental illness, or they may help the dictator in his battle against freedom. More probably (since science is divinely impartial) they will both enslave and make free, heal and at the same time destroy.

IX

SUBCONSCIOUS PERSUASION

In a footnote appended to the 1919 edition of his book, *The Interpretation of Dreams*, Sigmund Freud called attention to the work of Dr. Poetzl, an Austrian neurologist, who had recently published a paper describing his experiments with the tachistoscope. (The tachistoscope is an instrument that comes in two forms—a viewing box, into which the subject looks at an image that is exposed for a small fraction of a second; a magic lantern with a high-speed shutter, capable of projecting an image very briefly upon a screen.) In these experiments "Poetzl required the subjects to make a drawing of what they had consciously noted of a picture exposed to their view in a tachistoscope. . . . He then turned his attention to the dreams dreamed by the subjects during the following night and required them once more to make drawings of appropriate portions of these dreams. It was shown unmistakably that those details of the exposed picture which had *not* been noted by the subject provided material for the construction of the dream."

With various modifications and refinements Poetzl's experiments have been repeated several times, most recently by Dr. Charles Fisher, who has contributed three excellent papers on the subject of dreams and "preconscious perception" to the *Journal of the American Psychoanalytic Association*. Meanwhile the academic psychologists have not been idle. Confirming Poetzl's findings, their studies have shown that people actually see and hear a great deal more than they consciously know they see and hear, and that what they see and hear without knowing it is recorded by the subconscious mind and may affect their conscious thoughts, feelings and behavior.

Pure science does not remain pure indefinitely. Sooner or later it is apt to turn into applied science and finally into technology. Theory modulates into industrial practice, knowledge becomes power, formulas and laboratory experiments undergo a metamorphosis, and emerge as the H-bomb. In the present case, Poetzl's nice little piece of pure science, and all the other nice little pieces of pure science in the field of preconscious perception, retained their pristine purity for a surprisingly long time. Then, in the early autumn of 1957, exactly forty years after the publication of Poetzl's original paper, it was announced that their purity was a thing of the past; they had been applied, they had entered the realm of technology. The announcement made a considerable stir, and was talked and written about all over the civilized world. And no wonder; for the new techniques of "subliminal projection," as it was called, was intimately associated with mass entertainment, and in the life of civilized human beings mass entertainment now plays a part comparable to that played in the Middle Ages by religion. Our epoch has been given many nicknames—the Age of Anxiety, the Atomic Age, the Space Age. It might, with equally good reason, be called the Age of Television Addiction, the Age of Soap Opera, the Age of the Disk Jockey. In such an age the announcement that Poetzl's pure science had been applied in the form of a technique of subliminal projection could not fail to arouse the most intense interest among the world's mass entertainees. For the new technique was aimed directly at them, and its purpose was to manipulate their minds without their being aware of what was being done to them. By means of specially designed tachistoscopes words or images were to be flashed for a millisecond or less upon the screens of television sets and motion picture theaters *during* (not before or after) the program. "Drink Coca-Cola" or "Light up a Camel" would be superimposed upon the lovers' embrace, the tears of the broken-hearted mother, and the optic nerves of the viewers would record these secret messages, their subconscious minds would respond to them and in due course they would consciously feel a craving for soda pop and tobacco. And meanwhile other secret messages would be whispered too softly, or squeaked too shrilly, for conscious hearing. Consciously the listener might be paying attention to some phrase as "Darling, I love you"; but subliminally, beneath the threshold of awareness, his incredibly sensitive ears and his subconscious mind would be taking in the latest good news about deodorants and laxatives.

Does this kind of commercial propaganda really work? The evidence produced by the commercial firm that first unveiled a technique for subliminal projection was vague and, from a scientific point of view, very unsatisfactory. Repeated at regular intervals during the showing of a picture in a movie theater, the command to buy more popcorn was said to have resulted in a 50 per cent increase in popcorn sales during the intermission. But a single experiment proves very little. Moreover, this particular experiment was poorly set up. There were no controls and no attempt was made to allow for the many variables that undoubtedly affect the consumption of popcorn by a theater audience. And anyhow was this the most effective way of applying the knowledge accumulated over the years by the scientific investigators of subconscious perception? Was it intrinsically probable that, by merely flashing the name of a product and a command to buy it, you would be able to break down sales resistance and recruit new customers? The answer to both these questions is pretty obviously in the negative. But this does not mean, of course, that the findings of the neurologists and psychologists are without any practical importance. Skillfully applied, Poetzl's nice little piece of pure science might well become a powerful instrument for the manipulation of unsuspecting minds.

For a few suggestive hints let us now turn from the popcorn

vendors to those who, with less noise but more imagination and better methods, have been experimenting in the same field. In Britain, where the process of manipulating minds below the level of consciousness is known as "strobonic injection," investigators have stressed the practical importance of creating the right psychological conditions for subconscious persuasion. A suggestion above the threshold of awareness is more likely to take effect when the recipient is in a light hypnotic trance, under the influence of certain drugs, or has been debilitated by illness, starvation, or any kind of physical or emotional stress. But what is true for suggestions above the threshold of consciousness is also true for suggestions beneath that threshold. In a word, the lower the level of a person's psychological resistance, the greater will be the effectiveness of strobonically injected suggestions. The scientific dictator of tomorrow will set up his whispering machines and subliminal projectors in schools and hospitals (children and the sick are highly suggestible), and in all public places where audiences can be given a preliminary softening up by suggestibility-increasing oratory or rituals.

From the conditions under which we may expect subliminal suggestion to be effective we now pass to the suggestions themselves. In what terms should the propagandist address himself to his victims' subconscious minds? Direct commands ("Buy popcorn" or "Vote for Jones") and unqualified statements ("Socialism stinks" or "X's toothpaste cures halitosis") are likely to take effect only upon those minds that are already partial to Jones and popcorn, already alive to the dangers of body odors and the public ownership of the means of production. But to strengthen existing faith is not enough; the propagandist, if he is worth his salt, must create new faith, must know how to bring the indifferent and the undecided over to his side, must be able to mollify and perhaps even convert the hostile. To subliminal assertion and command he knows that he must add subliminal persuasion.

Above the threshold of awareness, one of the most effective methods of non-rational persuasion is what may be called persuasion-by-association. The propagandist arbitrarily associates his chosen product, candidate or cause with some idea, some image of a person or thing which most people, in a given culture, unquestioningly regard as good. Thus, in a selling campaign female beauty may be arbitrarily associated with anything from a bulldozer to a diuretic; in a political campaign patriotism may be associated with any cause from *apartheid* to integration, and with any kind of person, from a Mahatma Gandhi to a Senator McCarthy. Years ago, in Central America, I observed an example of persuasion-by-association which filled me with an appalled admiration for the men who had devised it. In the mountains of Guatemala the only imported art works are the colored calendars distributed free of charge by the foreign companies whose products are sold to the Indians. The American calendars showed pictures of dogs, of landscapes, of young women in a state of partial nudity. But to the Indian, dogs are merely utilitarian objects, landscapes are what he sees only too much of, every day of his life, and half-naked blondes are uninteresting, perhaps a little repulsive. American calendars were, in consequence, far less popular than German calendars; for the German advertisers had taken the trouble to find out what the Indians valued and were interested in. I remember in particular one masterpiece of commercial propaganda. It was a calendar put out by a manufacturer of aspirin. At the bottom of the picture one saw the familiar trademark on the familiar bottle of white tablets. Above it were no snow scenes or autumnal woods, no cocker spaniels or bosomy chorus girls. No—the wily Germans had associated their pain-relievers with a brightly colored and extremely lifelike picture of the Holy Trinity sitting on a cumulus cloud and surrounded by St. Joseph, the Virgin Mary, assorted saints and a large number of angels. The miraculous virtues of acetyl salicylic acid were thus guaranteed, in the Indians' simple and deeply religious minds, by God the Father and the entire heavenly host.

This kind of persuasion-by-association is something to which the techniques of subliminal projection seem to lend themselves particularly well. In a series of experiments carried out at New York University, under the auspices of the National Institute of Health, it was found that a person's feelings about some consciously seen image could be modified by associating it, on the subconscious level, with another image, or, better still, with value-bearing words. Thus, when associated, on the subconscious level, with the word "happy," a blank expressionless face would seem to the observer to smile, to look friendly, amiable, outgoing. When the same face was associated, also on the subconscious level, with the word "angry," it took on a forbidding expression, and seemed to the observer to have become hostile and disagreeable. (To a group of young women, it also came to seem very masculine—whereas when it was associated with "happy," they saw the face as belonging to a member of their own sex. Fathers and husbands, please take note.) For the commercial and political propagandist, these findings, it is obvious, are highly significant. If he can put his victims into a state of abnormally high suggestibility, if he can show them, while they are in that state, the thing, the person or, through a symbol, the cause he has to sell, and if, on the subconscious level, he can associate this thing, person or symbol with some value-bearing word or image, he may be able to modify their feelings and opinions without their having any idea of what he is doing. It should be possible, according to an enterprising commercial group in New Orleans, to enhance the entertainment value of films and television plays by using this technique. People like to feel strong emotions and therefore enjoy tragedies, thrillers, murder mysteries and tales of passion. The dramatization of a fight or an embrace produces strong emotions in the spectators. It might produce even stronger emotions if it were associated, on the subconscious level, with appropriate words or symbols. For example, in the film version of *A Farewell to Arms*, the death of the heroine in childbirth might be made even more distressing than it already is by subliminally flashing upon the screen, again and again, during the playing of the scene, such ominous words as "pain," "blood" and "death." Consciously, the words would not be seen; but their effect upon the subconscious mind might be very great and these effects might powerfully reinforce the emotions evoked, on the conscious level, by the acting and the dialogue. If, as seems pretty certain, subliminal projection can consistently intensify the emotions felt by moviegoers, the motion picture industry may yet be saved from bankruptcy—that is, if the producers of television plays don't get there first.

In the light of what has been said about persuasion-by-association and the enhancement of emotions by subliminal suggestion, let us try to imagine what the political meeting of tomorrow will be like. The candidate (if there is still a question of candidates), or the appointed representative of the ruling oligarchy, will make his speech for all to hear. Meanwhile the tachistoscopes, the whispering and squeaking machines, the projectors of images so dim that only the subconscious mind can respond to them, will be reinforcing what he says by systematically associating the man and his cause with positively charged words and hallowed images, and by strobonically injecting negatively charged words and odious symbols whenever he mentions the enemies of the State or the Party. In the United State brief flashes of Abraham Lincoln and the words "government by the people" will be projected upon the rostrum. In Russia the speaker will, of course, be associated with glimpses of Lenin, with the words "people's democracy," with the prophetic beard of Father Marx. Because all this is still safely in the future, we can afford to smile. Ten or twenty years from now, it will probably seem a good deal less amusing. For what is now merely science fiction will have become everyday political fact.

Poetzl was one of the portents which, when writing *Brave New World*, I somehow overlooked. There is no reference in my fable to subliminal projection. It is a mistake of omission which, if I were to rewrite the book today, I should most certainly correct.

X

HYPNOPAEDIA

In the late autumn of 1957 the Woodland Road Camp, a penal institution in Tulare County, California, became the scene of a curious and interesting experiment. Miniature loud-speakers were placed under the pillows of a group of prisoners who had volunteered to act as psychological guinea pigs. Each of these pillow speakers was hooked up to a phonograph in the Warden's office. Every hour throughout the night an inspirational whisper repeated a brief homily on "the principles of moral living." Waking at midnight, a prisoner might hear this still small voice extolling the cardinal virtues or murmuring, on behalf of his own Better Self, "I am filled with love and compassion for all, so help me God."

After reading about the Woodland Road Camp, I turned to the second chapter of *Brave New World*. In that chapter the Director of Hatcheries and Conditioning for Western Europe explains to a group of freshman conditioners and hatchers the workings of that state-controlled system of ethical education, known in the seventh century After Ford as hypnopaedia. The earliest attempts at sleep-teaching, the Director told his audience, had been misguided, and therefore unsuccessful. Educators had tried to give intellectual training to their slumbering pupils. But intellectual activity is incompatible with sleep. Hypnopaedia became successful only when it was used for *moral* training—in other words, for the conditioning of behavior through verbal suggestion at a time of lowered psychological resistance. "Wordless conditioning is crude and wholesale, cannot inculcate the more complex courses of behavior required by the State. For that there must be words, but words without reason"... the kind of words that require no analysis for their comprehension, but can be swallowed whole by the sleeping brain. This is true hypnopaedia, "the greatest moralizing and socializing force of all time." In the Brave New World, no citizens belonging to the lower castes ever gave any trouble. Why? Because, from the moment he could speak and understand what was said to him, every lower-caste child was exposed to endlessly repeated suggestions, night after night, during the hours of drowsiness and sleep. These suggestions were "like drops of liquid sealing wax, drops that adhere, incrust, incorporate themselves with what they fall on, till finally the rock is all one scarlet blob. Till at last the child's mind *is* these suggestions and the sum of these suggestions *is* the child's mind. And not the child's mind only. The adult's mind too—all his life long. The mind that judges and desires and decides—made up of these suggestions. But these suggestions are *our* suggestions—suggestions from the State...."

To date, so far as I know, hypnopaedic suggestions have been given by no state more formidable than Tulare County, and the nature of Tulare's hypnopaedic suggestions to lawbreakers is unexceptionable. If only all of us, and not only the inmates of the Woodland Road Camp, could be effectively filled, during our sleep, with love and compassion for all! No, it is not the message conveyed by the inspirational whisper that one objects to; it is the principle of sleep teaching by governmental agencies. Is hypnopaedia the sort of instrument that officials, delegated to exercise authority in a democratic society, ought to be allowed to use at their discretion? In the present instance they are using it only on volunteers and with the best intentions. But there is no guarantee that in other cases the intentions will be good or the indoctrination on a voluntary basis. Any law or social arrangement which makes it possible for officials to be led into temptation is bad. Any law or arrangement which preserves them from being tempted to abuse their delegated power for their own advantage, or for the benefit of the State or of some political, economic or ecclesiastical organization, is good. Hypnopaedia, if it is effective, would be a tremendously powerful instrument in the hands of anyone in a position to impose suggestions upon a captive audience. A democratic society is a society dedicated to the proposition that power is often abused and should therefore be entrusted to officials only in limited amounts and for limited periods of time. In such a society, the use of hypnopaedia by officials should be regulated by law—that is, of course, if hypnopaedia is genuinely an instrument of power. But is it in fact an instrument of power? Will it work now as well as I imagined it working in the seventh century A.F.? Let us examine the evidence.

In the *Psychological Bulletin* for July, 1955, Charles W. Simon and William H. Emmons have analyzed and evaluated the ten most important studies in the field. All these studies were concerned with memory. Does sleep-teaching help the pupil in his task of learning by rote? And to what extent is material whispered into the ear of a sleeping person remembered next morning when he wakes? Simon and Emmons answer as follows: "Ten sleep-learning studies were reviewed. Many of these have been cited uncritically by commercial firms or in popular magazines and news articles as evidence in support of the feasibility of learning during sleep. A critical analysis was made of their experimental design, statistics, methodology and criteria of sleep. All the studies had weaknesses in one or more of these areas. The studies do not make it unequivocally clear that learning during *sleep* actually takes place. But some learning appears to take place in a special kind of waking state wherein the subjects do not remember later on if they had been awake. This may be of great practical importance from the standpoint of economy in study time, but it cannot be construed as *sleep learning*. . . . The problem is partially confounded by an inadequate definition of sleep."

Meanwhile the fact remains that in the American Army during the Second World War (and even, experimentally, during the First) daytime instructions in the Morse Code and in foreign languages was supplemented by instruction during sleep—apparently with satisfactory results. Since the end of World War II several commercial firms in the United States and elsewhere have sold large numbers of pillow speakers and clock-controlled phonographs and tape recorders for the use of actors in a hurry to learn their parts, of politicians and preachers who want to give the illusion of being extemporaneously eloquent, of students preparing for examinations and, finally and most profitably, of the countless people who are dissatisfied with themselves as they are and would like to be suggested or autosuggested into becoming something else. Self-administered suggestion can easily be recorded on magnetic tape and listened to, over and over again, by day and during sleep. Suggestions from the outside may be bought in the form of records carrying a wide variety of helpful messages. There are on the market records for the release of tension and the induction of deep relaxation, records for promoting self-confidence (much used by salesmen), records for increasing one's charm and making one's personality more magnetic. Among the best sellers are records for the achievement of sexual harmony and records for those who wish to lose weight. ("I am cold to chocolate, insensible to the lure of potatoes, utterly unmoved by muffins.") There are records for improved health and even records for making more money. And the remarkable thing is that, according to the unsolicited testimonials sent in by grateful purchasers of these records, many people actually do make more money after listening to hypnopaedic suggestions to that effect, many obese ladies do lose weight and many couples on the verge of divorce achieve sexual harmony and live happily ever after.

In this context an article by Theodore X. Barber, "Sleep and Hypnosis," which appeared in *The Journal of Clinical and Experimental Hypnosis* for October, 1956, is most enlightening. Mr. Barber points out that there is a significant difference between light sleep and deep sleep. In deep sleep the electroencephalograph records no alpha waves; in light sleep alpha waves make their appearance. In this respect light sleep is closer to the waking and hypnotic states (in both of which alpha waves are present) than it is to deep sleep. A loud noise will cause a person in deep sleep to awaken. A less violent stimulus will not arouse him, but will cause the reappearance of alpha waves. Deep sleep has given place for the time being to light sleep.

A person in deep sleep is unsuggestible. But when subjects in light sleep are given suggestions, they will respond to them, Mr. Barber found, in the same way that they respond to suggestions when in the hypnotic trance.

Many of the earlier investigators of hypnotism made similar experiments. In his classical *History, Practice and Theory of Hypnotism*, first published in 1903, Milne Bramwell records that "many authorities claim to have changed natural sleep into hypnotic sleep. According to Wetterstrand, it is often very easy to put oneself *en rapport* with sleeping persons, especially children. . . . Wetterstrand thinks this method of inducing hypnosis of much practical value and claims to have often used it successfully." Bramwell cites many other experienced hypnotists (including such eminent authorities as Bernheim, Moll and Forel) to the same effect. Today an experimenter would not speak of "changing natural into hypnotic sleep." All he is prepared to say is that light sleep (as opposed to deep sleep without alpha waves) is a state in which many subjects will accept suggestions as readily as they do when under hypnosis. For example, after being told, when lightly asleep, that they will wake up in a little while, feeling extremely thirsty, many subjects will duly wake up with a dry throat and a craving for water. The cortex may be too inactive to think straight; but it is alert enough to respond to suggestions and to pass them on to the autonomic nervous system.

As we have already seen, the well-known Swedish physician and experimenter, Wetterstrand, was especially successful in the hypnotic treatment of sleeping children. In our own day Wetterstrand's methods are followed by a number of pediatricians, who instruct young mothers in the art of giving helpful suggestions to their children during the hours of light sleep. By this kind of hypnopaedia children can be cured of bed wetting and nail biting, can be prepared to go into surgery without apprehension, can be given confidence and reassurance when, for any reason, the circumstances of their life have become distressing. I myself have seen remarkable results achieved by the therapeutic sleep-teaching of small children. Comparable results could probably be achieved with many adults.

For a would-be dictator, the moral of all this is plain. Under proper conditions, hypnopaedia actually works—works, it would seem, about as well as hypnosis. Most of the things that can be done with and to a person in hypnotic trance can be done with and to a person in light sleep. Verbal suggestions can be passed through the somnolent cortext to the mid-brain, the brain stem and the autonomic nervous system. If these suggestions are well conceived and frequently repeated, the bodily functions of the sleeper can be improved or interfered with, new patterns of feeling can be installed and old ones modified, posthypnotic commands can be given, slogans, formulas and trigger words deeply ingrained in the memory. Children are better hypnopaedic subjects than adults, and the would-be dictator will take full advantage of the fact. Children of nursery-school and kindergarten age will be treated to hypnopaedic suggestions during their afternoon nap. For older children and particularly the children of party members—the boys and girls who will grow up to be leaders, administrators and teachers—there will be boarding schools, in which an excellent day-time education will be supplemented by nightly sleep-teaching. In the case of adults, special attention will be paid to the sick. As Pavlov demonstrated many years ago, strong-minded and resistant dogs become completely suggestible after an operation or when suffering from some debilitating illness. Our dictator will therefore see that every hospital ward is wired for sound. An appendectomy, an accouchement, a bout of pneumonia or hepatitis, can be made the occasion for an intensive course in loyalty and the true faith, a refresher in the principles of the local ideology. Other captive audiences can be found in prisons, in labor camps, in military barracks, on ships at sea, on trains and airplanes in the night, in the dismal waiting rooms of bus terminals and railway stations. Even if the hypnopaedic suggestions given to these captive audiences were no more than 10 percent effective, the results would still be impressive and, for a dictator, highly desirable.

From the heightened suggestibility associated with light sleep and hypnosis let us pass to the normal suggestibility of those who are awake—or at least who think they are awake. (In fact, as the Buddhists insist, most of us are half asleep all the time and go through life as somnambulists obeying somebody else's suggestions. Enlightenment is total awakeness. The word "Buddha" can be translated as "The Wake.")

Genetically, every human being is unique and in many ways unlike every other human being. The range of individual variation from the statistical norm is amazingly wide. And the statistical norm, let us remember, is useful only in actuarial calculations, not in real life. In real life there is no such person as the average man. There are only particular men, women and children, each with his or her inborn idiosyncrasies of mind and body, and all trying (or being compelled) to squeeze their biological diversities into the uniformity of some cultural mold.

Suggestibility is one of the qualities that vary significantly from individual to individual. Environmental factors certainly play their part in making one person more responsive to suggestion than another; but there are also, no less certainly, constitutional differences in the suggestibility of individuals. Extreme resistance to suggestion is rather rare. Fortunately so. For if everyone were as unsuggestible as some people are, social life would be impossible. Societies can function with a reasonable degree of efficiency because, in varying degrees, most people are fairly suggestible. Extreme suggestibility is probably about as rare as extreme unsuggestibility. And this also is fortunate. For if most people were as responsive to outside suggestions as the men and women at the extreme limits of suggestibility, free, rational choice would become, for the majority of the electorate, virtually impossible, and democratic institutions could not survive, or even come into existence.

A few years ago, at the Massachusetts General Hospital, a group of researchers carried out a most illuminating experiment on the pain-relieving effects of placebos. (A placebo is anything which the patient believes to be an active drug, but which in fact is pharmacologically inactive.) In this experiment the subjects were one hundred and sixty-two patients who had just come out of surgery and were all in considerable pain. Whenever a patient asked for medication to relieve pain, he or she was given an injection, either of morphine or of distilled water. All the patients received some injections of morphine and some of the placebo. About 30 percent of the patients never obtained relief from the placebo. On the other hand 14 per cent obtained relief after *every* injection of distilled water. The remaining 55 per cent of the group were relieved by the placebo on some occasions, but not on others.

In what respects did the suggestible reactors differ from the unsuggestible non-reactors? Careful study and testing revealed that neither age nor sex was a significant factor. Men reacted to placebo as frequently as did women, and young people as often as old ones. Nor did intelligence, as measured by the standard tests, seem to be important. The average IQ of the two groups was about the same. It was above all in temperament, in the way they felt about themselves and other people that the members of the two groups were significantly different. The reactors were more co-operative than the non-reactors, less critical and suspicious. They gave the nurses no trouble and thought that the care they were receiving in the hospital was simply "wonderful." But though less unfriendly toward others than the non-reactors, the reactors were generally much more anxious about themselves. Under stress, this anxiety tended to translate itself into various psychosomatic symptoms, such as stomach upsets, diarrhea and headaches. In spite of or because of their anxiety, most of the reactors were more uninhibited in the display of emotion than were the nonreactors, and more voluble. They were also much more religious, much more active in the affairs of their church and much more preoccupied, on a subconscious level, with their pelvic and abdominal organs.

It is interesting to compare these figures for reaction to placebos with the estimates made in their own special field, by writers on hypnosis. About a fifth of the population, they tell us, can be hypnotized very easily. Another fifth cannot be hypnotized at all, or can be hypnotized only when drugs or fatigue have lowered psychological resistance. The remaining three-fifths can be hypnotized somewhat less easily than the first group, but considerably more easily than the second. A manufacturer of hypnopaedic records has told me that about 20 per cent of his customers are enthusiastic and report striking results in a very short time. At the other end of the spectrum of suggestibility there is an 8 per cent minority that regularly asks for its money back. Between these two extremes are the people who fail to get quick results, but are suggestible enough to be affected in the long run. If they listen perseveringly to the appropriate hypnopaedic instructions they will end by getting what they want—self-confidence or sexual harmony, less weight or more money.

The ideals of democracy and freedom confront the brute fact of human suggestibility. One-fifth of every electorate can be hypnotized almost in the twinkling of an eye, one-seventh can be relieved of pain by injections of water, one-quarter will respond promptly and enthusiastically to hypnopaedia. And to these all too co-operative minorities must be added the slow-starting majorities, whose less extreme suggestibility can be effectually exploited by anyone who knows his business and is prepared to take the necessary time and trouble.

Is individual freedom compatible with a high degree of individual suggestibility? Can democratic institutions survive the subversion from within of skilled mind-manipulators trained in the science and art of exploiting the suggestibility both of individuals and of crowds? To what extent can the inborn tendency to be too suggestible for one's own good or the good of a democratic society be neutralized by education? How far can the exploitation of inordinate suggestibility by businessmen and ecclesiastics, by politicians in and out of power, be controlled by law? Explicitly or implicitly, the first two questions have been discussed in earlier articles. In what follows I shall consider the problems of prevention and cure.

XI

EDUCATION FOR FREEDOM

Education for freedom must begin by stating facts and enunciating values, and must go on to develop appropriate techniques for realizing the values and for combating those who, for whatever reason, choose to ignore the facts or deny the values.

In an earlier chapter I have discussed the Social Ethic, in terms of which the evils resulting from over-organization and over-population are justified and made to seem good. Is such a system of values consonant with what we know about human physique and temperament? The Social Ethic assumes that nurture is all-important in determining human behavior and that nature—the psychophysical equipment with which individuals are born—is a negligible factor. But is this true? Is it true that human beings are nothing but the products of their social environment? And if it is not true, what justification can there be for maintaining that the individual is less important than the group of which he is a member?

All the available evidence points to the conclusion that in the life of individuals and societies heredity is no less significant than culture. Every individual is biologically unique and unlike all other individuals. Freedom is therefore a great good, tolerance a great virtue and regimentation a great misfortune. For practical or theoretical reasons, dictators, organization men and certain scientists are anxious to reduce the maddening diversity of men's natures to some kind of manageable uniformity. In the first flush of his Behavioristic fervor, J. B. Watson roundly declared that he could find "no support for hereditary patterns of behavior, nor for special abilities (musical, art, etc.) which are supposed to run in families." And even today we find a distinguished psychologist, Professor B. F. Skinner of Harvard, insisting that, "as scientific explanation becomes more and more comprehensive, the contribution which may be claimed by the individual himself appears to approach zero. Man's vaunted creative powers, his achievements in art, science and morals, his capacity to choose and our right to hold him responsible for the consequences of his choice—none of these is conspicuous in the new scientific self-portrait." In a word, Shakespeare's plays were not written by Shakespeare, not even by Bacon or the Earl of Oxford; they were written by Elizabethan England.

More than sixty years ago William James wrote an essay on "Great Men and Their Environment," in which he set out to defend the outstanding individual against the assaults of Herbert Spencer. Spencer had proclaimed that "Science" (that wonderfully convenient personification of the opinions, at a given date, of Professors X, Y, and Z) had completely abolished the Great Man. "The great man," he had written, "must be classed with all other phenomena in the society that gave him birth, as a product of its antecedents." The great man may be (or seem to be) "the proximate initiator of changes. . . . But if there is to be anything like a real explanation of these changes, it must be sought in that aggregate of conditions out of which both he and they have arisen." This is one of those empty profundities to which no operational meaning can possibly be attached. What our philosopher is saying is that we must know everything before we can fully understand anything. No doubt. But in fact we shall never know everything. We must therefore be content with partial understanding and proximate causes—including the influence of great men. "If anything is humanly certain," writes William James, "it is that the great man's society, properly so called, does not make him before he can remake it. Physiological forces, with which the social, political, geographical and to a great extent anthropological conditions have just as much and just as little to do as the crater of Vesuvius has to do with the flickering of this gas by which I write, are what make him. Can it be that Mr. Spencer holds the convergence of sociological pressures to have so impinged upon Stratford-upon-Avon about the twenty-sixth of April, 1564, that a W. Shakespeare, with all his mental peculiarities, had to be born there? . . . And does he mean to say that if the aforesaid W. Shakespeare had died of cholera infantum, another mother at Stratford-upon-Avon would need have engendered a duplicate copy of him, to restore the sociologic equilibrium?"

Professor Skinner is an experimental psychologist, and his treatise on "Science and Human Behavior" is solidly based upon facts. But unfortunately the facts belong to so limited a class that when at last he ventures upon a generalization, his conclusions are as sweepingly unrealistic as those of the Victorian theorizer. Inevitably so; for Professor Skinner's indifference to what James calls the "physiological forces" is almost as complete as Herbert Spencer's. The genetic factors determining human behavior are dismissed by him in less than a page. There is no reference in his book to the findings of constitutional medicine, nor any hint of that constitutional psychology, in terms of which (and in terms of which alone, so far as I can judge) it might be possible to write a complete and realistic biography of an individual in relation to the relevant facts of his existence—his body, his temperament, his intellectual endowments, his immediate environment from moment to moment, his time, place and culture. A science of human behavior is like a science of motion in the abstract—necessary, but, by itself, wholly inadequate to the facts. Consider a dragonfly, a rocket and a breaking wave. All three of them illustrate the same fundamental laws of motion; but they illustrate these laws in different ways, and the differences are at least as important as the identities. By itself, a study of motion can tell us almost nothing about that which, in any given instance, is being moved. Similarly a study of behavior can, by itself, tell us almost nothing about the individual mind-body that, in any particular instance, is exhibiting the behavior. But to us who are mind-bodies, a knowledge of mind-bodies is of paramount importance. Moreover, we know by observation and experience that the differences between individual mind-bodies are enormously great, and that some mind-bodies can and do profoundly affect their social environment. On this last point Mr. Bertrand Russell is in full agreement with William James—and with practically everyone, I would add, except the proponents of Spencerian or Behavioristic scientism. In Russell's view the causes of historical change are of three kinds—economic change, political theory and important individuals. "I do not believe," says Mr. Russell, "that any of these can be ignored, or wholly explained away as the effect of causes of another kind." Thus, if Bismarck and Lenin had died in infancy, our world would be very different from what, thanks in part to Bismarck and Lenin, it now is. "History is not yet a science, and can only be made to seem scientific by falsifications and omissions." In real life, life as it is lived from day to day, the individual can never be explained away. It is only in theory that his contributions appear to approach zero; in practice they are all-important. When a piece of work gets done in the world, who actually does it? Whose eyes and ears do the perceiving, whose cortex does the thinking, who has the feelings that motivate, the will that overcomes obstacles? Certainly not the social environment; for a group is not an organism, but only a blind unconscious organization. Everything that is done within a society is done by individuals. These individuals are, of course, profoundly influenced by the local culture, the taboos and moralities, the information and misinformation handed down from the past and preserved in a body of spoken traditions or written literature; but whatever each individual takes from society (or, to be more accurate, whatever he takes from other individuals associated in groups, or from the symbolic records compiled by other individuals, living or dead) will be used by him in his own unique way—with *his* special senses, *his* biochemical make-up, *his* physique and temperament, and nobody else's. No amount of scientific explanation, however comprehensive, can explain away these self-evident facts. And let us remember that Professor Skinner's scientific portrait of man as the product of the social environment is not the only scientific portrait. There are other, more realistic likenesses. Consider, for example, Professor Roger Williams' portrait. What he paints is not behavior in the abstract, but mind-bodies behaving—mind-bodies that are the products partly of the environment they share with other mind-bodies, partly of their own private heredity. In *The Human Frontier* and *Free but Unequal* Professor Williams has expatiated, with a wealth of detailed evidence, on those innate differences between individuals, for which Dr. Watson could find no support and whose importance, in Professor Skinner's eyes, approaches zero. Among animals, biological variability within a given species becomes more and more conspicuous as we move up the evolutionary scale. This biological variability is highest in man, and human beings display a greater degree of biochemical, structural and temperamental diversity than do the members of any other species. This is a plain observable fact. But what I have called the Will to Order, the desire to impose a comprehensible uniformity upon the bewildering manifoldness of things and events, has led many people to ignore this fact. They have minimized biological uniqueness and have concentrated all their attention upon the simpler and, in the present state of knowledge, more understandable environmental factors involved in human behavior. "As a result of this environmentally centered thinking and investigation," writes Professor Williams, "the doctrine of the essential uniformity of human infants has been widely accepted and is held by a great body of social psychologists, sociologists, social anthropologists, and many others, including historians, economists, educationalists, legal scholars and men in public life. This doctrine has been incorporated into the prevailing mode of thought of many who have had to do with shaping educational and governmental policies and is often accepted unquestioningly by those who do little critical thinking of their own."

An ethical system that is based upon a fairly realistic appraisal of the data of experience is likely to do more good than harm. But many ethical systems have been based upon an appraisal of experience, a view of the nature of things, that is hopelessly unrealistic. Such an ethic is likely to do more harm than good. Thus, until quite recent times, it was universally believed that bad weather, diseases of cattle and sexual impotence could be, and in many cases actually were, caused by the malevolent operations of magicians. To catch and kill magicians was therefore a duty—and this duty, moreover, had been divinely ordained in the second Book of Moses: "Thou shalt not suffer a witch to live." The systems of ethics and law that were based upon this erroneous view of the nature of things were the cause (during the centuries when they were taken most seriously by men in authority) of the most appalling evils. The orgy of spying, lynching and judicial murder, which these wrong views about magic made logical and mandatory, was not matched until our own days, when the Communist ethic, based upon erroneous views about economics, and the Nazi ethic, based upon erroneous views about race, commanded and justified atrocities on an even greater scale. Consequences hardly less undesirable are likely to follow the general adoption of a Social Ethic, based upon the erroneous view that ours is a fully social species, that human infants are born uniform and that individuals are the product of conditioning by and within the collective environment. If these views were correct, if human beings were in fact the members of a truly social species, and if their individual differences were trifling and could be completely ironed out by appropriate conditioning, then, obviously, there would be no need for liberty and the State would be justified in persecuting the heretics who demanded it. For the individual termite, service to the termitary is perfect freedom. But human beings are not completely social; they are only moderately gregarious. Their societies are not organisms, like the hive or the anthill; they are organizations, in other words *ad hoc* machines for collective living. Moreover, the differences between individuals are so great that, in spite of the most intensive cultural ironing, an extreme endomorph (to use W. H.

Sheldon's terminology) will retain his sociable viscerotonic characteristics, an extreme mesomorph will remain energetically somatotonic through thick and thin and an extreme ectomorph will always be cerebrotonic, introverted and oversensitive. In the Brave New World of my fable socially desirable behavior was insured by a double process of genetic manipulation and postnatal conditioning. Babies were cultivated in bottles and a high degree of uniformity in the human product was assured by using ova from a limited number of mothers and by treating each ovum in such a way that it would split and split again, producing identical twins in batches of a hundred or more. In this way it was possible to produce standardized machine-minders for standardized machines. And the standardization of the machine-minders was perfected, after birth, by infant conditioning, hypnopaedia and chemically induced euphoria as a substitute for the satisfaction of feeling oneself free and creative. In the world we live in, as has been pointed out in earlier chapters, vast impersonal forces are making for the centralization of power and a regimented society. The genetic standardization of individuals is still impossible; but Big Government and Big Business already possess, or will very soon possess, all the techniques for mind-manipulation described in *Brave New World*, along with others of which I was too unimaginative to dream. Lacking the ability to impose genetic uniformity upon embryos, the rulers of tomorrow's over-populated and over-organized world will try to impose social and cultural uniformity upon adults and their children. To achieve this end, they will (unless prevented) make use of all the mind-manipulating techniques at their disposal and will not hesitate to reinforce these methods of non-rational persuasion by economic coercion and threats of physical violence. If this kind of tyranny is to be avoided, we must begin without delay to educate ourselves and our children for freedom and self-government.

Such an education for freedom should be, as I have said, an education first of all in facts and in values—the fact of individual diversity and genetic uniqueness and the values of freedom, tolerance and mutual charity which are the ethical corollaries of these facts. But unfortunately correct knowledge and sound principles are not enough. An unexciting truth may be eclipsed by a thrilling falsehood. A skillful appeal to passion is often too strong for the best of good resolutions. The effects of false and pernicious propaganda cannot be neutralized except by a thorough training in the art of analyzing its techniques and seeing through its sophistries. Language has made possible man's progress from animality to civilization. But language has also inspired that sustained folly and that systematic, that genuinely diabolic wickedness which are no less characteristic of human behavior than are the language-inspired virtues of systematic forethought and sustained angelic benevolence. Language permits its users to pay attention to things, persons and events, even when the things and persons are absent and the events are not taking place. Language gives definition to our memories and, by translating experiences into symbols, converts the immediacy of craving or abhorrence, of hatred or love, into fixed principles of feeling and conduct. In some way of which we are wholly unconscious, the reticular system of the brain selects from a countless host of stimuli those few experiences which are of practical importance to us. From these unconsciously selected experiences we more or less consciously select and abstract a smaller number, which we label with words from our vocabulary and then classify within a system at once metaphysical, scientific and ethical, made up of other words on a higher level of abstraction. In cases where the selecting and abstracting have been dictated by a system that is not too erroneous as a view of the nature of things, and where the verbal labels have been intelligently chosen and their symbolic nature clearly understood, our behavior is apt to be realistic and tolerably decent. But under the influence of badly chosen words, applied, without any understanding of their merely symbolic character, to experiences that have been selected and abstracted in the light of a system of erroneous ideas, we are apt to behave with a fiendishness and an organized stupidity, of which dumb animals (precisely because they *are* dumb and cannot speak) are blessedly incapable.

In their anti-rational propaganda the enemies of freedom systematically pervert the resources of language in order to wheedle or stampede their victims into thinking, feeling and acting as they, the mind-manipulators, want them to think, feel and act. An education for freedom (and for the love and intelligence which are at once the conditions and the results of freedom) must be, among other things, an education in the proper uses of language. For the last two or three generations philosophers have devoted a great deal of time and thought to the analysis of symbols and the meaning of meaning. How are the words and sentences which we speak related to the things, persons and events, with which we have to deal in our day-to-day living? To discuss this problem would take too long and lead us too far afield. Suffice it to say that all the intellectual materials for a sound education in the proper use of language—an education on every level from the kindergarten to the postgraduate school—are now available. Such an education in the art of distinguishing between the proper and the improper use of symbols could be inaugurated immediately. Indeed it might have been inaugurated at any time during the last thirty or forty years. And yet children are nowhere taught, in any systematic way, to distinguish true from false, or meaningful from meaningless, statements. Why is this so? Because their elders, even in the democratic countries, do not want them to be given this kind of education. In this context the brief, sad history of the Institute for Propaganda Analysis is highly significant. The Institute was founded in 1937, when Nazi propaganda was at its noisiest and most effective, by Mr. Filene, the New England philanthropist. Under its auspices analyses of non-rational propaganda were made and several texts for the instruction of high school and university students were prepared. Then came the war—a total war on all the fronts, the mental no less than the physical. With all the Allied governments engaging in "psychological warfare," an insistence upon the desirability of analyzing propaganda seemed a bit tactless. The Institute was closed in 1941. But even before the outbreak of hostilities, there were many persons to whom its activities seemed profoundly objectionable. Certain educators, for example, disapproved of the teaching of propaganda analysis on the grounds that it would make adolescents unduly cynical. Nor was it welcomed by the military authorities, who were afraid that recruits might start to analyze the utterances of drill sergeants. And then there were the clergymen and the advertisers. The clergymen were against propaganda analysis as tending to undermine belief and diminish churchgoing; the advertisers objected on the grounds that it might undermine brand loyalty and reduce sales.

These fears and dislikes were not unfounded. Too searching a scrutiny by too many of the common folk of what is said by their pastors and masters might prove to be profoundly subversive. In its present form, the social order depends for its continued existence on the acceptance, without too many embarrassing questions, of the propaganda put forth by those in authority and the propaganda hallowed by the local traditions. The problem, once more, is to find the happy mean. Individuals must be suggestible enough to be willing and able to make their society work, but not so suggestible as to fall helplessly under the spell of professional mind-manipulators. Similarly, they should be taught enough about propaganda analysis to preserve them from an uncritical belief in sheer nonsense, but not so much as to make them reject outright the not always rational outpourings of the well-meaning guardians of tradition. Probably the happy mean between gullibility and a total skepticism can never be discovered and maintained by analysis alone. This rather negative approach to the problem will have to be supplemented by something more positive—the enunciation of a set of generally acceptable values based upon a solid foundation of facts. The value, first of all, of individual freedom, based upon the facts of human diversity and genetic uniqueness; the value of charity and compassion, based upon the old familiar fact, lately rediscovered by modern psychiatry—the fact that, whatever their mental and physical diversity, love is as necessary to human beings as food and shelter; and finally the value of intelligence, without which love is impotent and freedom unattainable. This set of values will provide us with a criterion by which propaganda may be judged. The propaganda that is found to be both nonsensical and immoral may be rejected out of hand. That which is merely irrational, but compatible with love and freedom, and not on principle opposed to the exercise of intelligence, may be provisionally accepted for what it is worth.

XII

WHAT CAN BE DONE?

We can be educated for freedom—much better educated for it than we are at present. But freedom, as I have tried to show, is threatened from many directions, and these threats are of many different kinds—demographic, social, political, psychological. Our disease has a multiplicity of co-operating causes and is not to be cured except by a multiplicity of co-operating remedies. In coping with any complex human situation, we must take account of all the relevant factors, not merely of a single factor. Nothing short of everything is ever really enough. Freedom is menaced, and education for freedom is urgently needed. But so are many other things—for example, social organization for freedom, birth control for freedom, legislation for freedom. Let us begin with the last of these items.

From the time of Magna Carta and even earlier, the makers of English law have been concerned to protect the physical freedom of the individual. A person who is being kept in prison on grounds of doubtful legality has the right, under the Common Law as clarified by the statute of 1679, to appeal to one of the higher courts of justice for a writ of *habeas corpus*. This writ is addressed by a judge of the high court to a sheriff or jailer, and commands him, within a specified period of time, to bring the person he is holding in custody to the court for an examination of his case—to bring, be it noted, not the person's written complaint, nor his legal representatives, but his *corpus*, his body, the too too solid flesh which has been made to sleep on boards, to smell the fetid prison air, to eat the revolting prison food. This concern with the basic condition of freedom—the absence of physical constraint—is unquestionably necessary, but is not all that is necessary. It is perfectly possible for a man to be out of prison, and yet not free—to be under no physical constraint and yet to be a psychological captive, compelled to think, feel and act as the representatives of the national State, or of some private interest within the nation, want him to think, feel and act. There will never be such a thing as a writ of *habeas mentem*; for no sheriff or jailer can bring an illegally imprisoned mind into court, and no person whose mind has been made captive by the methods outlined in earlier articles would be in a position to complain of his captivity. The nature of psychological compulsion is such that those who act under constraint remain under the impression that they are acting on their own initiative. The victim of mind-manipulation does not know that he is a victim. To him, the walls of his prison are invisible, and he believes and the good laws will remain on the statute book; but these liberal forms will merely serve to mask and adorn a profoundly illiberal substance. Given unchecked over-population and over-organization, we may expect to see in the democratic countries a reversal of the process which transformed England into a democracy, while retaining all the outward forms of a monarchy. Under the relentless thrust of accelerating over-population and increasing over-organization, and by means of ever more effective methods of mind-manipulation, the democracies will change their nature; the quaint old forms—elections, parliaments, Supreme Courts and all the rest—will remain. The underlying substance will be a new kind of non-violent totalitarianism. All the traditional names, all the hallowed slogans will remain exactly what they were in the good old days. Democracy and freedom will be the theme of every broadcast and editorial—but democracy and freedom in a strictly Pickwickian sense. Meanwhile the ruling oligarchy and its highly trained elite of soldiers, policemen, thought-manufacturers and mind-manipulators will quietly run the show as they see fit.

How can we control the vast impersonal forces that now menace our hard-won freedoms? On the verbal level and in general terms, the question may be answered with the utmost ease. Consider the problem of over-population. Rapidly mounting human numbers are pressing ever more heavily on natural resources. What is to be done? Obviously we must, with all possible speed, reduce the birth rate to the point where it does not exceed the death rate. At the same time we must, with all possible speed, increase food production, we must institute and implement a world-wide policy for conserving our soils and our forests, we must develop practical substitutes, preferably less dangerous and less rapidly exhaustible than uranium, for our present fuels; and, while husbanding our dwindling resources of easily available minerals, we must work out new and not too costly methods for extracting these minerals from ever poorer and poorer ores—the poorest ore of all being sea water. But all this, needless to say, is almost infinitely easier said than done. The annual increase of numbers should be reduced. But how? We are given two choices—famine, pestilence and war on the one hand, birth control on the other. Most of us choose birth control—and immediately find ourselves confronted by a problem that is simultaneously a puzzle in physiology, pharmacology, sociology, psychology and even theology. "The Pill" has not yet been invented. When and if it is invented, how can it be distributed to the many hundreds of millions of potential mothers (or, if it is a pill that works upon the male, potential fathers) who will have to take it if the birth rate of the species is to be reduced? And, given existing social customs and the forces of cultural and psychological inertia, how can those who ought to take the pill, but don't want to, be persuaded to change their minds? And what about the objections on the part of the Roman Catholic Church, to any form of birth control except the so-called Rhythm Method—a method, incidentally, which has proved, hitherto, to be almost completely ineffective in reducing the birth rate of those industrially backward societies where such a reduction is most urgently necessary? And these questions about the future, hypothetical Pill must be asked, with as little prospect of eliciting satisfactory answers, about the chemical and mechanical methods of birth control already available.

When we pass from the problems of birth control to the problems of increasing the available food supply and conserving our natural resources, we find ourselves confronted by difficulties not perhaps quite so great, but still enormous. There is the problem, first of all, of education. How soon can the innumerable peasants and farmers, who are now responsible for raising most of the world's supply of food, be educated into improving their methods? And when and if they are educated, where will they find the capital to provide them with the machines, the fuel and lubricants, the electric power, the fertilizers and the improved strains of food plants and domestic animals, without which the best agricultural education is useless? Similarly, who is going to educate the human race in the principles and practice of conservation? And how are the hungry peasant-citizens of a country whose population and demands for food are rapidly rising to be prevented from "mining the soil"? And, if they can be prevented, who will pay for their support while the wounded and exhausted earth is being gradually nursed back, if that is still feasible, to health and restored fertility? Or consider the backward societies that are now trying to industrialize. If they succeed, who is to prevent them, in their desperate efforts to catch up and keep up, from squandering the planet's irreplaceable resources as stupidly and wantonly as was done, and is still being done, by their forerunners in the race. And when the day of reckoning comes, where, in the poorer countries, will anyone find the scientific manpower and the huge amounts of capital that will be required to extract the indispensable minerals from ores in which their concentration is too low, under existing circumstances, to make extraction technically feasible or economically justifiable? It may be that, in time, a practical answer to all these questions can be found. But in how much time? In any race between human numbers and natural resources, time is against us. By the end of the present century, there may, if we try very hard, be twice as much food on the world's markets as there is today. But there will also be about twice as many people, and several billions of these people will be living in partially industrialized countries and consuming ten times as much power, water, timber and irreplaceable minerals as they are consuming now. In a word, the food situation will be as bad as it is today, and the raw materials situation will be considerably worse.

To find a solution to the problem of over-organization is hardly less difficult than to find a solution to the problem of natural resources and increasing numbers. On the verbal level and in general terms the answer is perfectly simple. This, it is a political axiom that power follows property. But it is now a historical fact that the means of production are fast becoming the monopolistic property of Big Business and Big Government. Therefore, if you believe in democracy, make arrangements to distribute property as widely as possible.

Or take the right to vote. In principle, it is a great privilege. In practice, as recent history has repeatedly shown, the right to vote, by itself, is no guarantee of liberty. Therefore, if you wish to avoid dictatorship by referendum, break up modern society's merely functional collectives into self-governing, voluntarily co-operating groups, capable of functioning outside the bureaucratic systems of Big Business and Big Government.

Over-population and over-organization have produced the modern metropolis, in which a fully human life of multiple personal relationships has become almost impossible. Therefore, if you wish to avoid the spiritual impoverishment of individuals and whole societies, leave the metropolis and revive the small country community, or alternatively humanize the metropolis by creating within its network of mechanical organization the urban equivalents of small country communities, in which individuals can meet and cooperate as complete persons, not as the mere embodiments of specialized functions.

All this is obvious today and, indeed, was obvious fifty years ago. From Hilaire Belloc to Mr. Mortimer Adler, from the early apostles of co-operative credit unions to the land reformers of modern Italy and Japan, men of good will have for generations been advocating the decentralization of economic power and the widespread distribution of property. And how many ingenious schemes have been propounded for the dispersal of production, for a return to small-scale "village industry." And then there were Dubreuil's elaborate plans for giving a measure of autonomy and initiative to the various departments of a single large industrial organization. There were the Syndicalists, with their blueprints for a stateless society organized as a federation of productive groups under the auspices of the trade unions. In America, Arthur Morgan and Baker Bromwell have set forth the theory and described the practice of a new kind of community living on the village and small-town level.

Professor Skinner of Harvard has set forth a psychologist's view of the problem in his *Walden Two*, a Utopian novel about a self-sustaining and autonomous community, so scientifically organized that nobody is ever led into anti-social temptation and, without resort to coercion or undesirable propaganda, everyone does what he or she ought to do, and everyone is happy and creative. In France, during and after the Second World War, Marcel Barbu and his followers set up a number of self-governing, non-hierarchical communities of production, which were also communities for mutual aid and full human living. And meanwhile, in London, the Peckham Experiment has demonstrated that it is possible, by co-ordinating health services with the wider interests of the group, to create a true community even in a metropolis.

We see, then, that the disease of over-organization has been clearly recognized, that various comprehensive remedies have been prescribed and that experimental treatments of symptoms have been attempted here and there, often with considerable success. And yet, in spite of all this preaching and this exemplary practice, the disease grows steadily worse. We know that it is unsafe to allow power to be concentrated in the hands of a ruling oligarchy; nevertheless power is in fact being concentrated in fewer and fewer hands. We know that, for most people, life in a huge modern city is anonymous, atomic, less than fully human; nevertheless the huge cities grow steadily huger and the pattern of urban-industrial living remains unchanged. We know that, in a very large and complex society, democracy is almost meaningless except in relation to autonomous groups of manageable size; nevertheless more and more of every nation's affairs are managed by the bureaucrats of Big Government and Big Business. It is only too evident that, in practice, the problem of over-organization is almost as hard to solve as the problem of over-population. In both cases we know what ought to be done; but in neither case have we been able, as yet, to act effectively upon our knowledge.

At this point we find ourselves confronted by a very disquieting question: Do we really wish to act upon our knowledge? Does a majority of the population think it worth while to take a good deal of trouble, in order to halt and, if possible, reverse the current drift toward totalitarian control of everything? In the United States—and America is the prophetic image of the rest of the urban-industrial world as it will be a few years from now—recent public opinion polls have revealed that an actual majority of young people in their teens, the voters of tomorrow, have no faith in democratic institutions, see no objection to the censorship of unpopular ideas, do not believe that government of the people by the people is possible and would be perfectly content, if they can continue to live in the style to which the boom has accustomed them, to be ruled, from above, by an oligarchy of assorted experts. That so many of the well fed young television-watchers in the world's most powerful democracy should be so completely indifferent to the idea of self-government, so blankly uninterested in freedom of thought and the right to dissent, is distressing, but not too surprising. "Free as a bird," we say, and envy the winged creatures for their power of unrestricted movement in all the three dimensions. But, alas, we forget the dodo.

Any bird that has learned how to grub up a good living without being compelled to use its wings will soon renounce the privilege of flight and remain forever grounded. Something analogous is true of human beings. If the bread is supplied regularly and copiously three times a day, many of them will be perfectly content to live by bread alone—or at least by bread and circuses alone. "In the end," says the Grand Inquisitor in Dostoevsky's parable, "in the end they will lay their freedom at our feet and say to us, 'make us your slaves, but feed us.'" And when Alyosha Karamazov asks his brother, the teller of the story, if the Grand Inquisitor is speaking ironically, Ivan answers, "Not a bit of it! He claims it as a merit for himself and his Church that they have vanquished freedom and done so to make men happy." Yes, to make men happy; "for nothing," the Inquisitor insists, "has ever been more insupportable for a man or a human society than freedom." Nothing, except the absence of freedom; for when things go badly, and the rations are reduced, the grounded dodos will clamor again for their wings—only to renounce them, yet once more, when times grow better and the dodo-farmers become more lenient and generous. The young people who now think so poorly of democracy may grow up to become fighters for freedom. The cry of "Give me television and hamburgers, but don't bother me with the responsibilities of liberty," may give place, under altered circumstances, to the cry of "Give me liberty or give me death." If such a revolution takes place, it will be due in part to the operation of forces over which even the most powerful rulers have very little control, in part to the incompetence of those rulers, their inability to make effective use of the mind-manipulating instruments with which science and technology have supplied, and will go on supplying, the would-be tyrant. Considering how little they knew and how poorly they were equipped, the Grand Inquisitors of earlier times did remarkably well. But their successors, the well-informed, thoroughly scientific dictators of the future will undoubtedly be able to do a great deal better. The Grand Inquisitor reproaches Christ with having called upon men to be free and tells Him that "we have corrected Thy work and founded it upon miracle, mystery and authority." But miracle, mystery and authority are not enough to guarantee the indefinite survival of a dictatorship. In my fable of *Brave New World,* the dictators had added science to the list and thus were able to enforce their authority by manipulating the bodies of embryos, the reflexes of infants and the minds of children and adults. And, instead of merely talking about miracles and hinting symbolically at mysteries, they were able, by means of drugs, to give their subjects the direct experience of mysteries and miracles—to transform mere faith into ecstatic knowledge. The older dictators fell because they could never supply their subjects with enough bread, enough circuses, enough miracles and mysteries. Nor did they possess a really effective system of mind-manipulation. In the past free-thinkers and revolutionaries were often the products of the most piously orthodox education. This is not surprising. The methods employed by orthodox educators were and still are extremely inefficient. Under a scientific dictator education will really work—with the result that most men and women will grow up to love their servitude and will never dream of revolution. There seems to be no good reason why a thoroughly scientific dictatorship should ever be overthrown.

Meanwhile there is still some freedom left in the world. Many young people, it is true, do not seem to value freedom. But some of us still believe that, without freedom, human beings cannot become fully human and that freedom is therefore supremely valuable. Perhaps the forces that now menace freedom are too strong to be resisted for very long. It is still our duty to do whatever we can to resist them.

P.S.

Insights, Interviews & More . . .

*

About the author

About the book

Read on

About the author

Aldous Huxley
A Life of the Mind

Courtesy of the Granger Collection

POET, PLAYWRIGHT, novelist, short-story writer, travel writer, essayist, critic, philosopher, mystic, and social prophet, Aldous Huxley was one of the most accomplished and influential English literary figures of the mid-twentieth century. In the course of an extraordinary prolific writing career, which began in the early 1920s and continued until his death in 1963, Huxley underwent a remarkable process of self-transformation from a derisive satirist of England's chattering classes to a deeply religious writer preoccupied with the human capacity for spiritual transcendence. Yet in everything Huxley wrote, from the most frivolous to the most profound, there runs the common thread of his search to explain the meaning and possibilities of human life and perception.

Aldous Huxley was born in Surrey, England, in 1894, the son of Leonard Huxley, editor of the prestigious *Cornhill* magazine, and of Julia Arnold, niece of the poet and essayist Matthew Arnold, and sister of Mrs. Humphrey Ward. He was the grandson of T. H. Huxley, the scientist. Thus by "birth and disposition," as one biographer put it, Huxley belonged to England's intellectual aristocracy.

As Sybille Bedford writes in her fascinating biography, *Aldous Huxley* (Alfred A. Knopf / Harper & Row, 1974): "What we know about him as a young child is the usual residue of anecdote and snapshot. During his first years his head was proportionately enormous, so that he could not walk till he was two because he was apt to topple over. 'We put father's hat on him and it fitted.' In another country, at a great distance in time and place, when he lay ill and near his end in southern California, a friend, wanting to distract him, said, 'Aldous, didn't you ever have a nickname when you were small?' and Aldous, who hardly ever talked about his childhood or indeed about himself (possibly because one did not ask) said promptly, 'They called me Ogie. Short for Ogre.'

"The Ogre was a pretty little boy, the photographs . . . show the high forehead, the (then) clear gaze, the tremulous mouth and a sweetness of expression, an alertness beyond that of other angelic little boys looking into a camera. Aldous, his brother Julian tells us, sat quietly a good deal of the time 'contemplating the strangeness of things.'

"'I used to watch him with a pencil,' said his cousin and contemporary Gervas Huxley, 'you see, he was always drawing. . . . My earliest memory of him is sitting—absorbed—to me it was magic, a little boy of my own age drawing so beautifully.'

"He was delicate; he had mischievous moods; he could play. He carried his rag doll about him for company until he was eight. He was fond of grumbling. They gave him a milk mug which bore the inscription: *Oh, isn't the world extremely flat / With nothing whatever to grumble at.*

". . . And Aldous aged six being taken with all the Huxleys to the unveiling of the statue of his grandfather at the Natural History museum by the Prince of Wales, and his mother trying, in urgent whispers, to persuade Julian, then ►

"'They called me Ogie. Short for Ogre.'"

Aldous Huxley ***(continued)***

a young Etonian, to give up his top hat—a very young Etonian and a very new top hat—to Aldous, queasy, overcome, to be sick in."

> "The loss of sight was an 'event,' Huxley later wrote, 'which prevented me from becoming a complete public school English-gentleman.'"

When Huxley was a sixteen-year-old student at Eton, he contracted a disease that left him almost totally blind for two years and seriously impaired his vision for years to come. The loss of sight was an "event," Huxley later wrote, "which prevented me from becoming a complete public school English-gentleman." It also ended his early dreams of becoming a doctor. Yet, in a curious way, though he abandoned science for literature, Huxley's outlook remained essentially scientific. As his brother, the zoologist Julian Huxley, wrote, science and mysticism were overlapping and complementary realms in Aldous Huxley's mind: "The more [science] discovers and the more comprehension it gives us of the mechanisms of existence, the more clearly does the mystery of existence itself stand out."

Huxley took his undergraduate degree in literature at Balliol College, Oxford, in 1916, and spent several years during World War I working in a government office. After teaching briefly at Eton, he launched his career as a professional writer in 1920 by taking a job as a drama critic for the *Westminster Gazette,* and a staff writer for *House and Garden* and *Vogue.* Possessed of seemingly infinite literary energy, he wrote poetry, essays, and fiction in his spare time, publishing his first novel, *Crome Yellow,* in 1921. This bright, sharp, mildly shocking satire of upper-class artists won Huxley an immediate reputation as a dangerous wit. He swiftly composed several more novels in a similar vein, including *Antic Hay* (1923) and *Those Barren Leaves* (1925).

In *Point Counter Point* (1928), considered by many critics his strongest novel, Huxley broke new ground, both stylistically and thematically. In a narrative that jumps abruptly from scene to scene and character to character, Huxley confronts modern man's disillusionment with religion, art, sex, and politics. The character Philip Quarles, a novelist intent on "transform[ing] a detached intellectual skepticism into a way of harmonious all-round living," is the closest Huxley came to painting his own portrait in fiction. *Brave New World* (1932), though less experimental in style than *Point Counter Point*, is more radical in its pessimistic view of human nature. Huxley's antiutopia, with its eerie combination of totalitarian government and ubiquitous feel-good drugs and sex, disturbed many readers of his day; but it has proven to be his most enduring and influential work.

During the 1930s, Huxley turned increasingly toward an exploration of fundamental questions of philosophy, sociology, politics, and ethics. In his 1936 novel *Eyeless in Gaza* he wrote of a man's transformation from cynic to mystic, and as war threatened Europe once again, he allied himself with the pacifist movement and began lecturing widely on peace and internationalism.

" During the 1930s, Huxley turned increasingly toward an exploration of fundamental questions of philosophy, sociology, politics, and ethics. "

For a number of years Huxley lived in Italy, where he formed a close relationship with D. H. Lawrence, whose letters he edited in 1933. In 1937, Huxley and his Belgian-born wife, Maria Nys, and their son, Matthew, left Europe to live in Southern California for the rest of his life. Maria Huxley died of cancer in 1955, and the following year Huxley married the Italian violinist and psychotherapist Laura Archera.

In the 1940s and 1950s, Huxley changed ▸

direction yet again as he became fascinated by the spiritual life, in particular with the possibility of direct communication between people and the divinity. Huxley read widely in the writings of the mystics and assembled an anthology of mystical writing called *The Perennial Philosophy* (1945). Around this time he began experimenting with mind-altering drugs like mescaline and LSD, which he came to believe gave users essentially the same experiences that mystics attained through fasting, prayer, and meditation. *The Doors of Perception* (1954) and *Heaven and Hell* (1956), Huxley's books about the effects of what he termed psychedelic drugs, became essential texts for the counterculture during the 1960s. Yet Huxley's brother Julian cautions against the image of Aldous as a kind of spiritual godfather to hippies: "One of Aldous's major preoccupations was how to achieve self-transcendence while yet remaining a committed social being—how to escape from the prison bars of self and the pressures of here and now into realms of pure goodness and pure enjoyment."

"One of Aldous's major preoccupations was how to achieve self-transcendence while yet remaining a committed social being."

Huxley pursued his quest for "pure goodness and pure enjoyment" right up to the end of his life on November 22, 1963. Today he is remembered as one of the great explorers of twentieth-century literature, a writer who continually reinvented himself as he pushed his way deeper and deeper into the mysteries of human consciousness.

Too Far Ahead of Its Time? The Contemporary Response to *Brave New World* (1932)

CONSIDERING THE STATUS it enjoys as a classic today, reviews for Huxley's *Brave New World* were surprisingly negative. Though a few favorable notices appeared when the book was published in February 1932, the majority of reviewers dismissed the novel as weak in plot and characterization, shallow, mechanical in structure, and monotonous in tone. In dismissing the book, it wasn't that many critics failed to understand what point Huxley was making, but rather that they did not find his point relevant, insightful, alarming, or particularly original. ("A lugubrious and heavy-handed piece of propaganda," pronounced M. C. Dawson in the journal *Books.*) With the rise of Fascism in western Europe and a world shaken by massive economic depression, perhaps the novel hit too close to the bone; or maybe Huxley's harsh and unsettling vision was simply too far ahead of its time.

The reviewer for the British journal *New Statesman and Nation* led the charge: "[T]his squib about the future is a thin little joke, epitomised in the undergraduate jest of civilization dated A.F., and a people who refer reverently to 'our Ford'—not a bad little joke, and what it lacks in richness Mr. Huxley tries to make up by repetition; but we want rather more to a prophecy than Mr. Huxley gives us. . . . The fact is that Mr. Huxley does not really care for the story—the idea alone excites him. There are brilliant, sardonic little ▸

"With the rise of Fascism in western Europe and a world shaken by massive economic depression, perhaps the novel hit too close to the bone."

Too Far Ahead of Its Time? ***(continued)***

splinters of hate aimed at the degradation he has foreseen for our world; there are passages in which he elaborates conjectures and opinions already familiar to readers of his essays. . . . There are not surprises in it; and if he had no surprises to give us, why should Mr. Huxley have bothered to turn this essay in indignation into a novel?" This reviewer concludes that *Brave New World* is inert as a work of art: "Nothing can bring it alive."

Several reviewers expressed discomfort—or outright disgust—at Huxley's preoccupation with sexuality. They were offended at the freewheeling, emotionless promiscuity of Huxley's utopians. As the anonymous reviewer for London's *Times Literary Supplement* wrote, "it is not easy to become interested in the scientifically imagined details of life in this mechanical Utopia. Nor is there compensation in the amount of attention that he gives to the abundant sex life of these denatured human beings."

“ 'It is not easy to become interested in the scientifically imagined details of life in this mechanical Utopia. Nor is there compensation in the amount of attention that he gives to the abundant sex life of these denatured human beings.' ”

Granville Hicks, briefly the literary spokesman for the Communist Party USA, attacked *Brave New World* primarily on political grounds. Huxley's most grievous sin, in Hicks's opinion, was his failure to address the important social issues of the day. "With war in Asia, bankruptcy in Europe, and starvation everywhere, what do you suppose Aldous Huxley is now worrying about? . . . The unpleasantness of life in the utopia that, as he sees it, is just a century or two ahead," Hicks declared sarcastically in *The New Republic*. His partisan assault ended with a nasty salvo aimed at Huxley himself as an exemplar of the privileges and oppressive values of the ruling class: "[He] has money, social position, talent, friends, prestige, and he is effectively insulated from the misery of the masses. Of course he wants something to worry about—even if he has to go a long, long way to find it. . . . Mr. Huxley must have his chance to suffer and be brave."

That was the lowest blow any reviewer delivered.

The positive reviews were, by and large, rather restrained and cautious. "Huxley has made rowdy and impertinent sport of the World State," John Chamberlain wrote in his polite if somewhat mystified review in the *New York Times.* The only critic to see beyond the caustic laughter to the serious, even savage protest at the heart of the book was Edward Cushing, writing in the *Saturday Review of Literature*: "Mr. Huxley is eloquent in his declaration of an artist's faith in man, and it is his eloquence, bitter in attack, noble in defense, that when one has closed his book, one remembers—rather than his cleverness and his wit, which one admires and forgets." This was as enthusiastic as any critic allowed himself to be.

Despite the initial tepid response, *Brave New World* struck an extraordinary chord with the public, and over the subsequent six decades it has been reread and interpreted by generations of readers. After World War II, Huxley added a foreword to the book in which he assessed the radical changes in the world situation since its first publication. He admitted one "vast and obvious failure of foresight"—the absence of any reference to nuclear fission. And he speculated that his utopia, which he had projected six hundred years into the future, was actually approaching far sooner: "Today it seems quite possible that the horror may be upon us within a single century."

“'Today it seems quite possible that the horror may be upon us within a single century.'”

Prophecies Fulfilled
The Contemporary Response to *Brave New World Revisited* (1958)

"'It is rather alarming to find that only twenty-seven years [after writing *Brave New World*] quite a number of those forecasts have already come true, and come true with vengeance.'"

WHEN INTERVIEWED on the television program *Brain Trust* in 1958, Aldous Huxley declared, "It is rather alarming to find that only twenty-seven years [after writing *Brave New World*] quite a number of those forecasts have already come true, and come true with vengeance. . . . Some of them were foreseen, and I think some of them I didn't have the imagination to foresee, but I think there is a whole armory at the disposal of potential dictators at the moment."

It was the height of the Cold War when Huxley was asked to write a series of articles for *Newsday* that discussed how a political dictator might manipulate and control the population by altering its thoughts and behavior. But as he researched the topic, the scope of Huxley's concerns grew, and the articles published as "Tyranny Over the Mind" became a wider-ranging examination of the problem of freedom in an age of over population, over organization, and improved techniques of propaganda. The articles were published in book form as *Brave New World Revisited.*

The *New York Times Book Review* wrote that "Huxley uses his erudite knowledge of human relations to compare our actual world with his prophetic fantasy of 1931. It is a frightening experience, indeed, to discover how much of his satirical prediction of a distant future became reality in so short a time." The *Chicago Sunday Tribune* found *Brave New World Revisited* "a thought-jabbing, terrifying book," while *Time and Tide* (London) warned that it delivered "a message which, enforced by Mr. Huxley's seriousness and clear dialectic on dealing with social problems, we cannot ignore."

When he wrote *Brave New World Revisited,* Huxley was sixty-three years old and afflicted with serious eye problems that might have impeded a lesser intellect. As his bother Julian remarked in his *Memories,* "How Aldous managed to absorb (and still more digest) the colossal amount of facts and ideas which furnished his mind remains a mystery.... With his one good eye, he managed to skim through learned journals, popular articles, and books of every kind. He was apparently able to take them in at a glance, and what is more, to remember their essential content. His intellectual memory was phenomenal, doubtless trained by a tenacious will to surmount the original horror of threatened blindness."

"I am sick and tired of this kind of writing," Huxley confessed after he had finished *Brave New World Revisited,* "but at the same time find it frustratingly difficult to find the right story line for my projected Utopian novel." That novel—*Island*—which Huxley saw as "a kind of reverse *Brave New World,*" was published in 1962, the year before Huxley's death.

"His intellectual memory was phenomenal, doubtless trained by a tenacious will to surmount the original horror of threatened blindness."

A Letter to George Orwell

Taken from *Letters of Aldous Huxley*, edited by Grover Smith, Harper & Row, 1969:

> "My own belief is that the ruling oligarchy will find less arduous and wasteful ways of governing and of satisfying its lust for power, and these ways will resemble those which I described in *Brave New World*."

To George Orwell (E. H. Blair)
Wrightwood. Cal.
21 October, 1949

Dear Mr. Orwell,

It was very kind of you to tell your publishers to send me a copy of your book. It arrived as I was in the midst of a piece of work that required much reading and consulting of references; and since poor sight makes it necessary for me to ration my reading, I had to wait a long time before being able to embark on *Nineteen Eighty-Four*. Agreeing with all that the critics have written of it, I need not to tell you, yet once more, how fine and how profoundly important the book is. May I speak instead of the thing with which the book deals—the ultimate revolution? The first hints of a philosophy of the ultimate revolution—the revolution which lies beyond politics and economics, and which aims at the total subversion of the individual's psychology and physiology—are to be found in the Marquis de Sade, who regarded himself as the continuator, the consummator, of Robespierre and Babeuf. The philosophy of the ruling minority in *Nineteen Eighty-Four* is a sadism which has been carried to its logical conclusion by going beyond sex and denying it. Whether in actual fact the policy of the boot-on-the-face can go on indefinitely seems doubtful. My own belief is that the ruling oligarchy will find less arduous and wasteful ways of governing and of satisfying its lust for power, and these ways will resemble those which I described in *Brave New World*. I have had occasion recently to look into the history of animal magnetism and hypnotism, and have been greatly struck by the way in which, for a hundred and fifty years, the world has refused to take serious cognizance of the discoveries of Mesner, Braid, Esdaile, and the rest. Partly because of the prevailing materialism and partly because of prevailing respectability, nineteenth-century philosophers and men of science were not willing to investigate the odder facts of psychology for practical men, such as politicians, soldiers and policemen, to apply in the field of government. Thanks to the voluntary ignorance of our fathers, the advent of the ultimate revolution was delayed for five or six generations. Another lucky accident was Freud's inability to hypnotize successfully and his consequent disparagement of hypnotism. This delayed the general application of hypnotism to psychiatry for at least forty years. But now psychoanalysis is being combined with hypnosis; and hypnosis has been made easy and indefinitely extensible through the use of barbiturates, which induce a hypnoid and suggestible state in even the most recalcitrant subjects. Within the next generation I believe that the world's rulers will discover that infant conditioning and narco-hypnosis are more efficient, as instruments of government, than clubs and prisons, and that the lust for power can be just as completely satisfied by suggesting people into loving their servitude as by flogging and kicking them into obedience. In other words, I feel that the nightmare of *Nineteen Eighty-Four* is destined to modulate into the nightmare of a world having more resemblance to that which I imagined in *Brave New World*. The change will be brought about as a result of a felt need for increased efficiency. Meanwhile, of course, there may be a large scale biological and atomic war—in which case we shall have nightmares of other and scarcely imaginable kinds.

Thank you once again for the book.

Yours sincerely,
Aldous Huxley

"The lust for power can be just as completely satisfied by suggesting people into loving their servitude as by flogging and kicking them into obedience."

The Complete Aldous Huxley Bibliography

Dates are the year of first publication.

The Burning Wheel	1916
Jonah	1917
The Defeat of Youth and Other Poems	1918
Leda	1920
Limbo: Notes and Essays	1920
Crome Yellow	1921
Mortal Coils: Five Stories	1922
On the Margin	1923
Antic Hay	1923
Little Mexican	1924
Those Barren Leaves	1925
Along the Road: Notes and Essays	1925
Two or Three Graces: Four Stories	1926
Jesting Pilate: An Intellectual Holiday (The Diary of a Journey)	1926
Essays New and Old (U.S. title: *Essays Old and New*)	1926
Proper Studies	1927
Point Counter Point	1928
Do What You Will: Essays	1929
Brief Candles	1930
Vulgarity in Literature and Other Essays: Digressions from a Theme	1930
The World of Light	1931
The Cicadas and Other Poems	1931
Music at Night and Other Essays	1931
Brave New World	1932
Texts and Pretexts: An Anthology of Commentaries	1932
Beyond the Mexique Bay	1934
Eyeless in Gaza	1936
The Olive Tree and Other Essays	1936
What Are You Going to Do About It?: The Case for Constructive Peace	1936
Ends and Means: An Enquiry into the Nature of Ideals and into the Methods Employed for Their Realization	1937
After Many a Summer Dies the Swan	1939
Gray Eminence: A Study in Religion and Politics	1941
The Art of Seeing	1942
Time Must Have a Stop	1944
The Perennial Philosophy	1946
Science, Liberty, and Peace	1946
Ape and Essence	1948
The Gioconda Smile	1948
Themes and Variations	1950
The Devils of Loudun	1952
The Doors of Perception	1954
The Genius and the Goddess	1955
Heaven and Hell	1956
Adonis and the Alphabet and Other Essays(U.S. title: *Tomorrow and Tomorrow and Tomorrow*)	1956
Brave New World Revisited	1958
Island	1962
Literature and Science	1963

Have You Read?

The Doors of Perception and Heaven and Hell

Two classic complete books in which Huxley explores, as only he can, the mind's remote frontiers and the unmapped areas of human consciousness. These two books became essential for the counterculture during the 1960s and influenced a generation's perception of life.

"A challenge is forcibly put, ideas are freshly and prodigally presented."

—*San Francisco Chronicle*

The Perennial Philosophy

An astonishing collection of writings drawn from the world's great religions, edited and commented upon by Huxley with characteristic insight, wit, and passion.

"It is the masterpiece of all anthologies. As Mr. Huxley has proved before, he can find and frame rare beauty in literature, and here, long before Freud, writers are quoted who combine beauty with proud psychology."

—*New York Times*

Have You Read? ***(continued)***

Island

In this, his last novel, Huxley transports us to a Pacific island where, for a hundred and twenty years, an ideal society has flourished. On the island of Pala—as in the *Brave New World*—science has helped to advance the founder's plans. But this time those plans have the goal of freeing each person, not enslaving him. Inevitably this island of bliss attracts the envy and enmity of the surrounding world—not least because of its vast oil reserves. A conspiracy is underway to take over Pala, and events begin to move when an agent of the conspirators, a newspaperman named Faranby, is shipwrecked on the island.

"Island *is a welcome and in many ways unique addition to the select company of books—from Plato to now—that have presented, in imaginary terms, a coherent view of what society is not but might be.*"

—New York Times Book Review

BOOKS BY ALDOUS HUXLEY

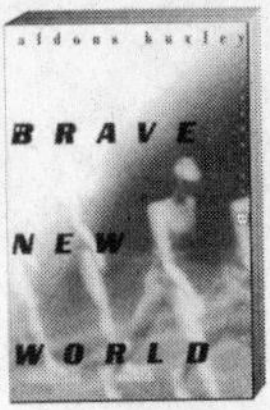

BRAVE NEW WORLD

ISBN 0-06-092987-1 (paperback)

A fantasy of the future that sheds a blazing critical light on the present—considered to be Aldous Huxley's most enduring masterpiece.

BRAVE NEW WORLD REVISITED

ISBN 0-06-095551-1 (paperback)

Brave New World Revisited is a trenchant plea that humankind should educate itself for freedom before it is too late.

BRAVE NEW WORLD & BRAVE NEW WORLD REVISITED

ISBN 0-06-077609-9 (paperback)

The prophetic fantasy *Brave New World* coupled with the non-fiction comparison to the modern-day *Brave New World Revisited.*

THE DOORS OF PERCEPTION AND HEAVEN AND HELL

ISBN 0-06-059518-3 (paperback)

Two classic complete books—*The Doors of Perception* and *Heaven and Hell*—in which Aldous Huxley explores the mind's remote frontiers and the unmapped areas of human consciousness.

ISLAND

ISBN 0-06-008549-5 (paperback)

Huxley transports us to a Pacific island where, for 120 years, an ideal society has flourished. Inevitably, this island of bliss attracts the envy and enmity of the surrounding world.

THE PERENNIAL PHILOSOPHY

ISBN 0-06-057058-X (paperback)

With great wit and stunning intellect, Aldous Huxley examines the spiritual beliefs of various religious traditions and explains them in terms that are personally meaningful.

WHAT EVERY VETERAN SHOULD KNOW

79th EDITION

BOOK PRICE - $25.00 – INCLUDES SHIPPING

This is the 79th Edition of the book "WHAT EVERY VETERAN SHOULD KNOW," a service officer's guide since 1937.

Monthly supplements are available from the publisher, which provide updates to the information contained in this book. A one-year subscription to the supplement service is $35.00.

The material herein covers veterans' benefits, rights, privileges, and services over which the Department of Veterans Affairs has jurisdiction. All references to "VA" pertain to the Department of Veterans Affairs. Revised and new laws passed by the 114th Congress as of December 31, 2014, are incorporated in this text.

This guide was prepared solely for convenient reference purposes, and does not have the effect of law. Although diligent effort has been made to ensure its accuracy, in the event of any conflict between this book and any regulation, the latter is, of course, controlling.

Veterans and the dependents of deceased veterans are advised to contact their local veterans organization service officers, or the nearest Veterans Administration Office, for help in completing any valid claim.

VETERANS INFORMATION SERVICE
P.O. Box 111
East Moline, Illinois 61244-0111
Telephone: (309) 757-7760
Fax: (309) 278-5304
Email: help@vetsinfoservice.com
www.vetsinfoservice.com

WHAT EVERY VETERAN SHOULD KNOW

VETERANS INFORMATION SERVICE
P.O. Box 111
East Moline, Illinois 61244-0111

Phone: (309) 757-7760
Fax: (309) 278-5304
E-mail: help@vetsinfoservice.com
www.vetsinfoservice.com

A NOTE TO THE READER:

Revised and new laws passed by the 114th Congress as of December 31, 2014, are incorporated in the text of this book. Chapter 1 of the book contains a brief summary of some of the important legislative changes affecting veterans' benefits during 2014.

You will find a Table of Contents, listing the main subject headings. For your convenience there is also a complete index in the back of the book, as well as an Edge Index on the back cover.

We hope you enjoy this edition of **WHAT EVERY VETERAN SHOULD KNOW**. Any comments or suggestions for future improvements are welcome.

Library of Congress Cataloging in Serials
ISSN 1532-8112
ISBN 0-9820586-6-7

Publisher:

Veterans Information Service
P.O. Box 111
East Moline, IL 61244-0111

[redacted]

TABLE OF CONTENTS

CHAPTER 1

2015 UPDATES

Following is a brief summary of some of the important legislative changes, as well as VA-policy changes, affecting veterans' benefits during 2014.

VA ANNOUNCES DENTAL INSURANCE AVAILABILITY

The VA announced it's now offering dental insurance to veterans enrolled in VA health care, as well as to some of their eligible family members. The offering is part of a three-year pilot program, and over 8 million veterans and 400,000 civilians are eligible. Eligible individuals include those who receive care under the Civilian Health and Medical Program of the Veterans Affairs Department (CHAMPVA).

Veterans have the opportunity to choose plans offering by either Delta Dental or Met-Life. Delta Dental is the company responsible for the management of the Tricare Retiree Dental Program, while MetLife is the insurer responsible for the Tricare Dental Program for active-duty families.

VA EXPANDS PROVISION OF TBI BENEFITS

The VA has officially put new regulations in place, making it easier for some veterans diagnosed with traumatic brain injury (TBI) to receive additional disability compensation.

The VA announced the implementation of a new regulation that impacts some veterans living with TBI who also have Parkinson's disease, certain types of dementia, depression, unprovoked seizures or certain diseases of the hypothalamus and pituitary glands.

VA INTRODUCES HEALTH ID CARDS

The VA announced the rollout of secure veterans health identification cards. The new cards are designed to have additional security features. The card is called the Veterans

Health Identification Card, which is similar to a traditional health insurance ID card. It displays the veteran's member and plan ID, and demonstrates their enrollment in VA healthcare.

Each VHIC is personalized, showing the emblem of the veteran's branch of service, and it also has Braille and important phone numbers and instructions for emergency care.

VA ELIMINATES INCOME REPORTING REQUIREMENT

The VA announced the removal of the annual income reporting requirement for most veterans enrolled in the VA healthcare system. Beginning in March 2014, the VA began utilizing income information as reported from the IRS and Social Security administration.

SGLI PREMIUM ADJUSTMENT ANNOUNCED

The VA announced an increase in the monthly premium rate of the Servicemembers' Group Life Insurance (SGLI) program, which became effective July 1, 2014.

The increase made the premiums 7 cents per $1,000 of insurance, up from 6.5 cents.

VETERANS ACCESS, CHOICE AND ACCOUNTABILITY ACT OF 2014 SIGNED INTO LAW

The Veterans Access, Choice and Accountability Act of 2014 was created as a means to help veterans avoid long waits for health care, which has been a significant problem at the VA health centers around the country for a number of years. It also aims to make it less difficult to fire senior-level VA officials who are negligent in their work.

Specific provisions include devoting $10 billion to pay private doctors to treat qualifying veterans who can't prompt appointments at VA hospitals and outpatient clinics, as well as $5 billion for hiring more doctors, nurses and other medical professionals. The bill also authorizes $1.3 billion to open 27 new VA outpatient clinics and medical facilities across 18 states and Puerto Rico.

Under the law, the VA secretary has the authority to immediately fire poorly performing senior executives.

The bill also expands a scholarship program for children of veterans killed in the line of duty, to include surviving spouses.

All returning and eligible dependents can qualify for in-state tuition at public colleges and universities.

The bill cuts funding for annual bonuses for VA employees by $40 million.

The full information about the bill is as follows:

Expiring Authorities Act of 2014 (Public Law 113-175), as a bipartisan response to the health care access issues facing VA.

The Choice Act provides new authorities, funding, and other tools to help support and reform VA. The below summary serves as an overview of the Choice Act and is not meant to serve as an exhaustive review of the legislation.

Improvement of Access to Care from Non-VA Providers

VETERANS CHOICE PROGRAM

As directed by the Choice Act, VA will administer the "Veterans Choice Fund" to implement the Veterans Choice Program ("the Program").

The Program will operate for 3 years or until the Fund is exhausted. The Program will provide Veterans who were enrolled as of August 1, 2014 or eligible to enroll as a recently discharged combat Veteran with a Veterans Choice Card, and allow those Veterans who are unable to schedule an appointment within 30 days of their preferred date or the clinically appropriate date, or on the basis of their place of residence to elect to receive care from eligible non-VA health care entities or providers.

This is separate from VA's existing program providing Veterans care outside of the VA system. Eligible non-VA entities or providers must enter into agreements with VA to furnish care, must maintain the same or similar credentials and licenses as VA providers, and must submit to VA a copy of any medical records related to care and services provided under the Program for inclusion in the Veteran's VA electronic medical record.

CLAIMS PROCESSING

VA will establish and implement a system to process and pay claims for are delivered to Veterans by non-VA providers under the Program and other non-VA care authorities.

PROJECT ACCESS RECEIVED CLOSER TO HOME (ARCH)

Project ARCH, is an existing pilot program intended to improve access for eligible Veterans by connecting them to health care services closer to home. Eligibility for the pilot program is based on specific criteria, including driving distance from a VHA health care facility for primary care, acute hospital care, or tertiary care. The pilot program is carried out in 5 specific Veterans Integrated Service Networks. The Choice Act extends this pilot for approximately 2 years.

ENHANCEMENT OF COLLABORATION

VA will work with the Indian Health Service (IHS) to ensure that certain medical facilities operated by an Indian tribe or tribal organization are aware of the opportunity to negotiate reimbursement agreements with VA.

VA will enter into contracts or agreements with certain Native Hawaiian Health Care Systems for reimbursement of direct care services provided to eligible Veterans.

ADDITIONAL EXPANSION OF ACCESS TO CARE

EXTENSION OF ASSISTED LIVING PILOTS

Pursuant to the Choice Act, VA will extend the Assisted Living Pilot Program for Veterans with Traumatic Brain Injury for 3 years, through October 6, 2017. This program assesses the effectiveness of providing assisted living services to eligible Veterans with traumatic brain injuries to "enhance the rehabilitation, quality of life, and community integration of such Veterans."

MOBILE VET CENTERS AND MOBILE MEDICAL CENTERS

VA will improve access to telemedicine and other health care services through standardization and greater use of mobile vet centers and mobile medical centers.

REVIEWING AND EXPANDING CAPACITY AND PROCESSES

INDEPENDENT ASSESSMENTS

To ensure high-quality care, VA will enter into one or more contracts with an independent third party or parties for assessments of the hospital care, medical services, and other health care processes in VA medical facilities. The assessments will be submitted to Congress, the newly established Commission on Care, and posted online.

TECHNOLOGY TASK FORCE

A Technology Task Force will review VA's patient scheduling processes and supporting software, and will do so at no cost to the government. The task force will propose specific actions VA might take to improve our performance in this area and will submit their recommendations to the Secretary and to Congress. VA will implement the recommendations of the task force that the Secretary considers feasible, advisable, and cost effective.

MAJOR FACILITY LEASES

The Choice Act authorizes 27 major medical facility leases in 18 states and Puerto Rico.

PUBLICLY AVAILABLE DATA

Each VA medical facility will post on a Web site the wait-times for scheduling an appointment at VA facilities for primary care, specialty care, and hospital care and medical services based on the general severity of the condition of the Veteran. Whenever the wait-times for scheduling such appointments change, VA will publish the revised wait times.

VA will develop a comprehensive data set that will be made accessible to the public. This data set will include applicable patient safety, quality of care, and outcome measures for VA health care.

VA will ensure that Veterans have increased access to information about their doctors. The "Our Doctors" web site will be updated and made more accessible on www.va.gov. Additionally, each Veteran undergoing a surgical procedure through VA will be provided with information on the credentials of the surgeon performing the procedure.

PRESIDENTIAL COMMISSION ON CARE

An independent Commission on Care ("the Commission") will be established to undertake a comprehensive evaluation and assessment of access to health care at VA. The Commission will be made up of 15 voting members selected by Congress and the President and will submit a report of their findings and recommendations to the Secretary and the President. VA and other Federal agencies will be required to implement each recommendation that the President considers feasible, advisable, and able to implement without further legislation.

HEALTH CARE STAFFING

NEW RESIDENCY POSITIONS

Over a five-year period, the legislation directs the VA to increase its number of Graduate Medical Education residency positions by up to 1,500. An emphasis will be placed on creating residency positions that improve Veterans' access to primary care, mental health, and other specialties the Secretary deems appropriate

VHA STAFFING REQUIREMENTS

The VA Office of Inspector General will identify annually the top five occupations with the largest staffing shortages. An initial report will be provided by February 3, 2015, and an annual report will be provided no later than September 30th of each year. The Secretary will have the authority to recruit and directly appoint qualified personnel to serve in these specific occupations.

Training and Education

The law extends the VA's existing Health Professionals Educational Assistance Program from December 31, 2014, to December 31, 2019. The Choice Act also increases the maximum reimbursement ceiling for the Education Debt Reduction Program from $60,000 to $120,000.

VA is directed to implement a clinic management training program for two years, with continuously updated materials, to provide in-person, standardized education on health care management to appropriate VA employees.

EMPLOYEE PERFORMANCE PLANS

VA will ensure that scheduling and wait-time metrics or goals are not included as factors in employee performance evaluations or when calculating whether to pay performance awards.

VETERANS BENEFITS

VBA Initiatives/ Program Requirements
Veterans Benefits

VA will expand the Marine Gunnery Sergeant John David Fry Scholarship to include the spouses of servicemembers who died in the line of duty.

Programs of education at public colleges and universities may not be approved for Post-9/11 GI Bill and Montgomery GI Bil (MGIB) benefits if they do not charge all recently released veterans and their family members in-state tuition and fees.

The Choice Act directs VA to extend the reduction in the amount of pension provided by VA for veterans covered by Medicaid living in nursing facilities until September 30, 2024. VA will also extend the requirement to collect funding fees for housing loans until this date.

Departmental Personnel Authorities and Related Procedures

EMPLOYEE DISCIPLINARY PROCEDURES

VA will revise human resources policies to include penalties for employees who knowingly falsify or require another employee to falsify data regarding access to care or quality measures.

EMPLOYEE AWARDS AND BONUSES

VA will limit the amount of awards and bonuses paid to VA employees each year for fiscal year 2015 to fiscal year 2024.

REMOVAL OF SENIOR EXECUTIVES

The Choice Act provides new authority for VA to seek removal or transfer Senior Executives based on poor performance or misconduct, with an abbreviated process for an expedited appeal.

VA IMPLEMENTS CHOICE CARD PROGRAM

The most visible outcome of VACAA, the Choice Card, will be available to veterans enrolled in VA health care as of August 1, 2014. Veterans with active duty service in a theater of combat operations within the previous five years are also eligible to receive a Choice Card.

To facilitate a smooth implementation of the new program, the card and a letter explaining eligibility for the program will be sent to beneficiaries in three phases:

1. to veterans who live 40 miles from any VA health care facility;
2. to those who have been waiting for their requested appointment for more than 30 days and;
3. the remaining 8 million veterans are scheduled to receive a card by January 2015.

Receiving the card does not mean a veteran is automatically eligible for the program. The card will include a toll-free number that can be used to determine eligibility. Critically, the VA must give pre-authorization for care. Each episode of care will be authorized for no more than 60 days.

The VA has signed contracts with two private health care companies to help administer the Veterans Choice Program: Health Net and Triwest. These contractors were also selected earlier in 2014 to execute the Patient Centered Community Care (PC3) contracts to help ease the access demand across VA.

CHAPTER 2

DISABILITY COMPENSATIONFOR SERVICE-CONNECTED DISABILITIES

(TITLE 38, CHAPTER 11)

BENEFIT DESCRIPTION

In grateful recognition of their dedication and sacrifice, the United States, through the Veterans Administration has provided its former servicemen and women with compensation and pension programs designed to assist disabled veterans and their dependents. The disability compensation program provides financial assistance to veterans with service-connected disabilities to compensate them for the loss of, or reduction in earning power resulting from comparable injuries and disease in civil life.

Disability compensation payments vary in amount, depending on the impairment of earning capacity suffered by the veteran. The degree is assessed in multiples of 10, from 10 percent to 100 percent, with special statutory rates for such disabilities as blindness and loss of use of limbs.

There was a 1.7% COLA increase that became law in 2014.

The VA shall adopt and apply a schedule of ratings in reductions in earning capacity from specific injuries or combination of injuries. The rating shall be based, as far as practicable, upon the average impairments of earning capacity resulting from such injuries in civil occupations. The Administrator shall from time to time readjust this schedule or ratings in accordance with experience. The rates of compensation payments are not automatically adjusted for inflation, and they can be increased only if Congress passes specific enabling legislation. However, almost without exception, each Congress has acted to grant an increase equal to the consumer price index or the cost-of-living formula that determines the social security old-age increase.

If a veteran is evaluated as having a service-connected disability of 30 percent or more, the veteran is entitled to additional allowances for his or her dependents. In addition, in cases where a veteran has suffered certain severe disabilities, the veteran may be entitled to *special monthly compensation* (SMC), which can provide compensation payments at a rate much greater than the 100 percent rate. Severely disabled veterans in need of regular aid and attendance, or daily health-care services may be eligible for additional compensation.

2014 UPDATE: VA EXPANDS PROVISION OF TBI BENEFITS

The VA has officially put new regulations in place, making it easier for some veterans diagnosed with traumatic brain injury (TBI) to receive additional disability compensation.

The VA announced the implementation of a new regulation that impacts some veterans living with TBI who also have Parkinson's disease, certain types of dementia, depression, unprovoked seizures or certain diseases of the hypothalamus and pituitary glands.

2014 UPDATE: VA ELIMINATES INCOME REPORTING REQUIREMENT

The VA announced the removal of the annual income reporting requirement for most veterans enrolled in the VA healthcare system. Beginning in March 2014, the VA began utilizing income information as reported from the IRS and Social Security administration.

SAME SEX MARRIED COUPLES

The Obama administration announced a decision to extend veteran benefits to same-sex married couples, as a result of the Supreme Court's decision to strike down the *Defense of Marriage Act*. Veterans' spouses are now eligible to collect benefits, regardless of sexual orientation.

WAR TIME DISABILITY COMPENSATION

ELIGIBILITY

Fully Developed Claims: The VA announced that veterans who submit a Fully Developed Claim for a service-connected disability may be eligible to receive retroactive disability benefits of up to one year.

There is no time limit for applying for VA disability compensation. However, veterans are encouraged to apply within one year of release from active duty. If a claim is filed within this period, entitlement may be established retroactively to the date of separation from service. If a claim is filed beyond one year of release from active duty, the effective date of eligibility for benefits will be based upon the date of the claim, not the date of separation.

A veteran may be entitled to VA disability compensation for any medical condition or injury that was incurred in, or aggravated by his or her military service. The veteran must have been discharged or released under conditions other than dishonorable from the period of service in which the injury or disease was incurred or aggravated. No compensation shall be paid if the disability is a result of the person's own willful misconduct or abuse of alcohol or drugs.

There is no time limit for applying for VA disability compensation. However, veterans are encouraged to apply within one year of release from active duty. If a claim is filed within this period, entitlement may be established retroactively to the date of separation from service. If a claim is filed beyond one year of release from active duty, the effective date of eligibility for benefits will be based upon the date of the claim, not the date of separation.

INDIVIDUAL UNEMPLOYABILITY

There is a benefit administered by the U.S. Department of Veterans Affairs (VA) that is payable under certain conditions when a veteran has one or more service connected disabilities rated less than 100% that interfere with his or her ability to secure or retain employment. This benefit is known as Individual Unemployability (I.U.). I.U. must be established on a factual basis.

I.U. establishes entitlement to compensation at the 100% disability rate even though a veteran's combined disabilities are less than a scheduler 100% rating.

To apply for I.U. benefits VA form 21-8940, Application for Increased Compensation Based on Unemployability, must be submitted to the VA with current medical evidence on the extent of the service connected disabilities.

When an application for I.U. benefits is received by the VA, VA must first decide whether the veteran meets the requirements for a scheduler 100% rating before considering I.U.

The scheduler requirements for I.U. benefits are provided in the Code of Federal Regulations (38 CFR 4.16), which states in essence, that total disability ratings for compensation may be assigned when there is one disability rated at 60% or more, or two or more disabilities combined at 70% or more, with at least one of the combined disabilities rated at least 40%.

In addition, for the purpose of one 60% disability, or one 40% disability in the case of combined disabilities, the following will be considered one disability:

- Disabilities of one or both upper or lower extremities, including the bilateral factor if applicable.
- Disabilities resulting from common etiology or a single accident
- Disabilities affecting a single body system, such as, orthopedic, digestive, respiratory, cardiovascular-renal, neuropsychiatric
- Multiple injuries incurred in action
- Multiple disabilities incurred as a Prisoner of War (POW)

When considering I.U., the VA looks at the following evidence:

- Current degree of service connected disability
- Employment status
- Results of VA examination(s)
- Hospital reports and/or outpatient treatment records
- Current physical and mental status
- Nature of employment
- Reason employment was terminated
- Whether disabilities meet scheduler consideration (38 CFR 4.16)
- Whether Extra Scheduler consideration is warranted (38 CFR 3.321(b)(1)

In addition, VA will take in to consideration the veteran's previous type of occupation (such as physical or non-physical) and his or her level of formal education.

Factors that may not be taken in to account when considering I.U. are:

- Age
- Non service connected (NSC) disabilities
- Injuries occurring after military service
- Availability of work

In certain situations where a veteran does not meet the percentage standards under 38 CFR 4.16 for scheduler consideration of I.U but the evidence supports that the veteran is unemployable due to his or her service connected conditions, VA rating boards may submit to the Director of Compensation and Pension Service for an Extra Scheduler consideration.

Once an I.U. rating is granted, VA will pay service connected compensation at the 100% rate.

Receipt of I.U. benefits does not mean that a veteran is never allowed to work again; however, if a veteran receiving I.U. benefits obtains substantially gainful employment, I.U. benefits can be terminated.

VA's definition of substantial gainful employment is basically any amount earned above the annual poverty limit for one person set by the U.S. Census Bureau. In 2012 the poverty limit for one person was $11,170.

Amounts earned below the Census Bureau annual poverty limit are considered marginal employment and do not affect receipt of I.U. benefits.

Each year after the U.S. Census Bureau sets the new poverty limit, VA publishes notice in the Federal Register.

OTHER BENEFITS OR PAYMENTS THAT MAY AFFECT VA DISABILITY COMPENSATION

By law, receipt of certain types of military pay may affect an individual's eligibility for VA Disability Compensation. Following are the categories of pay that may affect eligibility:

VA PENSION BENEFITS

Occasionally, a veteran may be entitled to both VA Compensation benefits, and VA Pension benefits. The VA is prohibited from paying both benefits concurrently. In the event a veteran is entitled to both, he or she must elect to receive one benefit or the other. This election prevails, even if the option paying a lower benefit is chosen, and even if the election reduces the benefits payable to his or her dependents.

SELECTED RESERVE AND NATIONAL GUARD

Since September 11, 2001, numerous members of the Armed Forces Reserves have been called to active duty. Some of these individuals had already filed claims for VA compensation, based on earlier periods of active service. In September 2004, the VA General Counsel issued a precedent opinion that discussed the effect of a return to active service on a pending disability compensation claim.

In general, a veteran's return to active duty does not affect his or her claim for VA benefits, and does not alter either the veteran's right or the VA's duty to develop and adjudicate the claim. If the veteran is temporarily unable to report for a medical examination, or take some other required action because of his or her return to active duty, the VA must defer processing the claim until the veteran can take the required action. The VA cannot deny a claim because a veteran is temporarily unavailable due to a return to active duty.

A veteran is not entitled to receive both active duty pay and VA disability compensation for the same period of time. However, he or she is permitted to elect the higher benefit. If a veteran with a pending claim dies on active duty before the claim is decided, an eligible survivor may be entitled to any accrued benefits payable.

FULLY DEVELOPED CLAIMS

The Fully Developed Claims (FDC) program is an optional new initiative that offers Servicemembers, Veterans, and survivors faster decisions from VA on compensation, pension, and survivor benefit claims.

Veterans, Servicemembers, and survivors simply submit all relevant records in their possession, and those records which are easily obtainable, such as private medical records, at the time they make their claim and certify that they have no further evidence to submit. VA can then review and process the claim more quickly.

By filing an FDC, Veterans, Servicemembers and survivors take charge of their claim by providing all the evidence at once. By then certifying that there is no more evidence, VA can issue a decision faster.

File an FDC without risk. Participation will not affect the attention your claim receives from qualified VA rating staff or the benefits to which you're entitled. If VA determines other records exist and are required to decide a claim, VA will simply remove the claim from the FDC program and process it through the traditional claims process. Once you initiate your FDC, you'll have up to one year to complete it. Should VA approve your claim, you'll be paid back to the day you initiated your claim.

TYPES OF CLAIMS

There are many types of claims for disability compensation. For example, if you're filing a VA claim for the very first time, you have an **original claim**. A **reopened claim** means you have new *and* material evidence and you want VA to reconsider a claim it once denied. There are also **new claims**, **secondary claims**, and **special claims**.

WHO CAN FILE A CLAIM

Veterans may file an FDC for disability compensation for the following reasons:

- An injury, disability, or condition believed to have occurred or been aggravated by military service.
- A condition caused or aggravated by an existing service-related condition.

Servicemembers may use the Benefits Delivery at Discharge (BDD) program ateBenefits.va.gov to submit a Fully Developed Claim before discharge.

- The BDD program is available nationwide to all Servicemembers on full-time active duty, including members of the National Guard, Reserve, and Coast Guard.
- Servicemembers who do not meet the BDD criteria or have 1-59 days remaining in service should submit a Quick Start claim on eBenefits.va.gov.

WHAT'S THE BEST WAY TO FILE AN FDC?

- The best way to file an FDC is electronically at eBenefits.va.gov. Once you log on to your account, VA recommends you appoint an accredited Veterans Service Officer to help you initiate your claim, gather the required medical records and evidence, and submit your claim.
- If you prefer to file your FDC by paper, complete VA Form 21-526EZ and visit your local regional office. While there, you can appoint an accredited Veterans Service Officer to help you prepare and submit your claim. You can also appoint your accredited Veterans Service Officer online at eBenefits.va.gov.

MILITARY RETIRED PAY

Historically, veterans were not permitted to receive ***full*** military retirement pay and VA compensation benefits at the same time. Veterans who were entitled to both had to either elect one of the benefits, or waive the amount of retirement pay which equaled the amount of VA disability compensation to which he or she was entitled. This issue was commonly known as "concurrent receipt".

Because there was often a tax advantage to receive VA disability compensation, which is tax free, rather than military retirement pay, most disabled retirees chose to have a $1 reduction in their retired pay for each $1 of VA disability compensation they received.

Since this type of rule against "concurrent receipt" does not apply to any other group of federal or state retirees, many individuals and service organizations felt this was unfair discrimination against disabled military retirees.

This has been a very hot topic for the last several years, and Congress and the President have taken several steps toward eliminating the bar to concurrent receipt of full military retired pay and full disability compensation.

DETAILS OF CRSC PAYMENTS

- CRSC payments will be in the amount of the VA disability compensation paid for whatever percentage of the member's disability rating is due to combat-related disabilities, as determined by the parent service.
- Retirees must apply to their parent service for CRSC payments.
- There is no phase-in period for CRSC.
- CRSC is not subject to taxation.
- Individuals must apply for CRSC. For detailed information, individuals should contact the following:

ARMY:
DEPARTMENT OF THE ARMY
U.S. Army Physical Disabilities Agency/
Combat Related Special Compensation (CRSC)
200 Stovall Street
Alexandria, VA 22332-0470
(866) 281-3254

NAVY AND MARINE CORPS:
Department of Navy Naval Council of Personnel Boards
Combat-Related Special Compensation Branch
720 Kennon Street S.E., Suite 309
Washington Navy Yard, DC 20374-5023
(877) 366-2772

AIR FORCE:
United States Air Force Personnel Center Disability Division (CRSC)
550 C Street West, Suite 6
Randolph AFB TX 78150-4708
(800) 525-0102

Details Of Concurrent Receipt

For those retirees eligible for concurrent receipt (50% - 100%), there is to be a ten-year phase-out of the disability offset. For 2004, qualifying retirees should have seen their retired pay increase by a flat monthly amount for these ratings:

Disability Rating	Amount Of Monthly Increase
100%	$750
90%	$500
80%	$350
70%	$250
60%	$125
50%	$100

The remaining retired pay offset is then to be phased out over the following nine years:

Year	Remaining Offset To Be Reduced By
2005	10%
2006	20%
2007	30%
2008	40%
2009	50%
2010	60%
2011	70%
2012	80%
2013	90%
2014	100%

By January 2014, disabled retirees with 50% and higher ratings were entitled to full concurrent receipt of military retired pay and VA disability compensation.

Because Concurrent Receipt is the restoration of retired pay, it is thus subject to the same tax provisions as a veteran's retired pay. If an individual's retired pay is taxable, concurrent receipt payments are taxable. If an individual's retired pay is non-taxable, concurrent receipt payments are to be non-taxable.

Concurrent Receipt is automatic. If you qualify you will automatically see an increase in your monthly retirement check.

What If A Retiree Is Eligible For Both The CRSC And Concurrent Receipt Programs?

Retirees eligible for both programs will be able to make an election between the two programs, depending on which one is more advantageous.

Because the CRSC program provides full payment immediately, versus the 10—year phase in for concurrent receipt, the election can be changed each year. (This recognizes that a retiree who is 100% disabled, but only 60% of that is due to combat-related conditions, may find it advantageous to elect full CRSC payments for a few years until the concurrent receipt payment rises to a level that exceeds the CRSC payment. Because CRSC payments are tax-free, and non-disability retired pay is not, this could also figure into a retiree's election decision.

BENEFIT RATES FOR SERVICE-CONNECTED DISABILITY COMPENSATION

VA compensation and pension benefits cost of living allowance (COLA) is paid based on the Social Security Administration (SSA) COLA. By statue, compensation COLA may not be more than the SSA COLA; and pension COLA is equal to the SSA COLA.

This year SSA increased COLA by 1.7%. The new rates are reflected in the following charts:

BASIC RATES OF DISABILITY COMPENSATION –RATES EFFECTIVE DECEMBER 1, 2014:		
Title 38, USC 1114 subsection:	*DISABILITY RATING*	**Monthly Benefit**
(a)	10 percent	$133.77
(b)	20 percent	$263.23
(c)	30 percent	$407.75
(d)	40 percent	$587.36
(e)	50 percent	$836.13
(f)	60 percent	$1,059.09
(g)	70 percent	$1,334.71
(h)	80 percent	$1,551.48
(i)	90 percent	$1,743.48
(j)	100 percent	$2,906.83

DETAILED RATES OF DISABILITY COMPENSATION –RATES EFFECTIVE DECEMBER 1, 2014:

	DISABILITY RATING									
DEPENDENT STATUS	10%	20%	30%	40%	50%	60%	70%	80%	90%	100%
Veteran Alone	133.17	263.23	407.75	587.36	836.13	1059.09	1334.71	1551.48	1743.48	2906.83
Veteran & Spouse	133.17	263.23	455.75	651.38	917.13	1156.09	1447.71	1680.40	1888.48	3068.90
Veteran & Spouse & 1 Child	133.17	263.23	491.75	699.36	976.13	1227.09	1530.71	1775.48	1995.48	3187.60
Veteran & No Spouse & 1 Child	133.17	263.23	439.75	630.36	890.13	1124.09	1409.71	1637.48	1840.48	3015.22

DEPENDENT STATUS	*DISABILITY RATING*									
	10%	20%	30%	40%	50%	60%	70%	80%	90%	100%
Veteran & Spouse & No Children & 1 Parent	133.17	263.23	494.75	730.36	982.13	1234.09	1538.71	1784.48	2005.48	3198.96
Veteran & Spouse & 1 Child & 1 Parent	133.17	263.23	5530.75	751.36	1041.13	1305.09	1621.71	1879.48	2112.48	3317.66
Veteran & Spouse & No Children & 2 Parents	133.17	263.23	533.74	755.36	1047.13	1312.09	1629.71	1888.48	2122.48	3329.02
Veteran & Spouse & 1 Child & 2 Parents	133.17	263.23	560.94	790.29	1088.09	1360.50	1684.70	1951.03	2193.01	3390.10
Veteran & No Spouse & No Children & 1 Parent	133.17	263.23	569.75	803.36	1106.13	1383.09	1712.71	1983.48	2229.48	3447.72
Veteran & No Spouse & 1 Child & 1 Parent	133.17	263.23	478.75	682.36	955.13	1202.09	1500.71	1741.48	1957.48	3145.28
Veteran & No Spouse & No Children & 2 Parents	133.17	263.23	485.75	691.36	966.13	1215.09	1516.71	1759.48	1977.48	3166.95
Veteran & No Spouse & 1 Child & 2 Parents	133.17	263.23	517.75	734.36	1020.13	1280.09	1591.71	1845.48	2074.48	3275.34

ADDITIONAL AMOUNT PAYABLE FOR SPOUSE REQUIRING AID & ATTENDANCE-RATES EFFECTIVE DECEMBER 1, 2014								
Disability Rating	30%	40%	50%	60%	70%	80%	90%	100%
Monthly Benefit	$44.00	29.00	74.00	89.00	104.00	1180.00	133.00	148.65

ADDITIONAL AMOUNT PAYABLE FOR EACH ADDITIONAL CHILD UNDER AGE 18-RATES EFFECTIVE DECEMBER 1, 2014								
Disability Rating	30%	40%	50%	60%	70%	80%	90%	100%
Monthly Benefit	$24.00	32.00	40.00	48.00	56.00	64.00	72.00	80.52

ADDITIONAL AMOUNT PAYABLE FOR EACH ADDITIONAL CHILD OVER AGE 18 ATTENDING SCHOOL-RATES EFFECTIVE DECEMBER 1, 2014								
Disability Rating	30%	40%	50%	60%	70%	80%	90%	100%
Monthly Benefit	$78.00	104.00	130.00	156.00	182.00	208.00	234.00	260.13

Notes:
Rates for Children over age 18 attending school are shown separately in the above chart. All other entries in the above charts reflect rates for children under age 18, or helpless.

All references in the preceding charts to parents refer to parents who have been determined to be dependent by the Secretary of Veterans Affairs.

HIGHER STATUTORY AWARDS FOR CERTAIN MULTIPLE DISABILITIES

TITLE 38, USC 1114 SUBSECTION (K)

If a veteran, as the result of a service-connected disability, has suffered the anatomical loss or loss of use of one or more creative organs, or one foot, or one hand, or both buttocks, or 25 percent or more tissue from a single breast or from both breasts in combination (loss by mastectomy or partial mastectomy or following radiation treatment), or blindness of one eye, having only light perception, or has suffered complete organic aphonia with constant inability to communicate by speech, or deafness of both ears, having absence of air and bone conduction, the rate of compensation shall be **$103.23** per month for each such loss or loss of use.

This additional amount is independent of any other disability compensation provided in subsections (a) through (j) of the above table, or subsection (s) described below; however, in no event may the total amount exceed **$3,622.29** per month.

In the event the veteran has suffered one or more of the disabilities previously specified in this subsection, in addition to the requirement for any of the rates specified in subsections (l) through (n), described below, the rate of compensation shall be increased by **$103.23** per month for each such loss or loss of use, but in no event may exceed **$5081.80** per month.

Title 38, USC 1114 subsection (l)

If the veteran, as the result of a service-connected disability, has suffered the anatomical loss or loss of use of both feet, or of one hand and one foot, or is blind in both eyes, with 5/200 visual acuity or less, or is permanently bedridden or so helpless as to be in need of regular aid and attendance, the monthly compensation shall be **$3,622.29**.

Title 38, USC 1114 subsection (m)

If the veteran, as the result of a service-connected disability, has suffered the anatomical loss or loss of use of both hands, or of both legs at a level, or with complications, preventing natural knee action with prostheses in place, or of one arm and one leg at levels, or with complications, preventing natural elbow and knee action with prostheses in place, or has suffered blindness in both eyes, having only light perception, or has suffered blindness in both eyes, rendering such veteran so helpless as to be in need of regular aid and attendance, the monthly compensation shall be **$4,532.64**.

Title 38, USC 1114 subsection (n)

If the veteran, as the result of a service-connected disability, has suffered the anatomical loss or loss of use of both arms at levels, or with complications, preventing natural elbow action with prostheses in place, has suffered the anatomical loss of both legs so near the hip as to prevent the use of prosthetic appliances, or has suffered the anatomical loss of one arm and one leg so near the shoulder and hip as to prevent the use of prosthetic appliances, or has suffered the anatomical loss of both eyes, or has suffered blindness without light perception in both eyes, the monthly compensation shall be **$5,349.15**.

Title 38, USC 1114 subsection (o)

If the veteran, as the result of a service-connected disability, has suffered disability under conditions which would entitle such veteran to two or more of the rates provided in one or more subsections (l) through (n) of this section, no condition being considered twice in the determination, or if the veteran has suffered bilateral deafness (and the hearing impairment in either one or both ears is service connected) rated at 60% or more disabling, and the veteran has also suffered service-connected total blindness with 5/200 visual acuity or less, or if the veteran has suffered service-connected total deafness in one ear or bilateral deafness (and the hearing impairment in either one or both ears is service connected) rated at 40% or more disabling, and the veteran has also suffered service-connected blindness having only light perception or less, or if the veterans has suffered the anatomical loss of both arms so near the shoulder as to prevent the use of prosthetic appliances, the monthly compensation shall be **$5,522.62**.

Title 38, USC 1114 subsection (p)

In the event a veteran's service-connected disabilities exceed the requirements for any of the rates previously prescribed in this section, the Secretary of Veterans Affairs may allow the next higher rate, or an intermediate rate, but in no event in excess of **$5,522.62**.

In the event a veteran has suffered service-connected blindness with 5/200 visual acuity or less, and (1) has also suffered bilateral deafness (and the hearing impairment in either one or both ears is service connected) rated at no less than 30% disabling, the Secretary of Veterans Affairs shall allow the next higher rate, or (2) has also suffered service-connected total deafness in one ear or service-connected anatomical loss or loss of use of one hand or one foot, the Secretary shall allow the next intermediate rate, but in no event in excess of **$5,522.62**.

In the event a veteran has suffered service-connected blindness, having only light perception or less, and has also suffered bilateral deafness (and the hearing impairment in either one or both ears is service-connected) rated at 10 or 20% disabling, the Secretary shall allow the next intermediate rate, but in no event in excess of **$5,616.50**.

In the event a veteran has suffered the anatomical loss or loss of use, or a combination of anatomical loss and loss of use, of three extremities, the Secretary shall allow the next higher rate or intermediate rate, but in no event in excess of **$5,616.50**.

Any intermediate rate under this subsection shall be established at the arithmetic mean, rounded down to the nearest dollar, between the two rates concerned.

Title 38, USC 1114 subsection (r)

If a veteran is entitled to compensation under (o) of this section, at the maximum rate authorized under (p) of this section, or at the intermediate rate authorized between the rates authorized under subsections (n) and (o) of this section and at the rate authorized under subsection (k) of this section, is in need of regular aid and attendance, then, in addition to such compensation:

- The veteran shall be paid a monthly aid and attendance allowance at the rate of **$2,177.03**; or
- If the veteran, in addition to such need for regular aid and attendance, is in need of a higher level of care, such veteran shall be paid a monthly aid and attendance allowance at the rate of **$3,244.38**, in lieu of the allowance authorized in the previous paragraph. Need for a higher level of care shall be considered to be need for personal health-care services provided on a daily basis in the veteran's home by a person who is licensed to provide such services or who provides such services under the regular supervision of a licensed health-care professional. The existence of the need for such care shall be determined by a physician employed by the VA, or in areas where no such physician is available, by a physician carrying out such function under contract or fee arrangement based on an examination by such physician.

Title 38, USC 1114 subsection (s)

If a veteran has a service-connected disability rated as total, and:

- Has additional service-connected disability or disabilities independently ratable at 60% or more; or
- By reason of such veteran's service-connected disability or disabilities, is permanently housebound, and then the monthly compensation shall be **$3,253.67**.

For the purposes of this subsection, the requirement of "permanently housebound" will be considered to have been met when the veteran is substantially confined to such veteran's house (ward or clinical areas, if institutionalized) or immediate premised due to a service-connected disability or disabilities which it is reasonable certain will remain throughout such veteran's lifetime.

Title 38, USC 1114 subsection (t)

This subsection was repealed by *Public Law 99-576.*

ADDITIONAL COMPENSATION FOR DEPENDENTS (38 USC 1115)

Any veteran entitled to compensation under 38 USC 1114, and whose disability is rated not less than 30%, shall be entitled to additional compensation for dependents in the following monthly amounts:

If and while the veteran is rated totally disabled and:

1.	Has a spouse but no child living:	$162.10
2.	Has a spouse and one child living:	280.77
	(plus for each additional living child under age 18):	80.52
3.	Has no spouse, but one child living:	108.39
	(plus for each additional living child under age 18):	80.52
4.	Has a mother or father, either or both dependent upon him for support - for each parent so dependent:	130.06

5.	For a spouse who is a patient in a nursing home, or who is so helpless or blind as to require the regular aid and attendance of another person:	148.62 for a totally disabled veteran, and proportionate amounts for partially disabled veterans.
6.	For each child who is between the ages of 18-23, and who is pursuing a course of instruction at an approved educational institution:	260.13 for a totally disabled veteran, and proportionate amounts for partially disabled veterans.

Adjustment To Individual VA Awards

There will be no adjustment of VA awards. Special Compensation paid under 10 USC 1413 is provided under chapter 71, title 10, USC, "Computation of Retired Pay." However, it is NOT RETIRED PAY. It is to be paid from funds appropriated for pay and allowances of the recipient member's branch of service. Eligible retirees in receipt of VA disability compensation may receive this special compensation in addition to their VA disability compensation.

Presumptions

Presumption of Sound Condition

Every veteran will be assumed to have been in sound medical condition when examined, accepted, and enrolled for service, except any defects, infirmities, or disorders noted at the time of the examination, acceptance, and enrollment, or if there is clear and unmistakable evidence showing that the injury or disease did exist before acceptance and enrollment, and the injury or disease was not aggravated by such service.

Presumptions of Service-Connection Relating to Certain Chronic Diseases and Disabilities

In the case of any veteran who served for 90 days or more during a period of war, any of the following shall be considered to have been incurred in, or aggravated by such service, notwithstanding there is no record of evidence of such disease during the period of service:

- A chronic disease (detailed below), becoming manifest to a degree of 10% or more within one year from the date of separation from such service.
- A tropical disease (detailed below), and the resultant disorders or disease originating because of therapy, administered in connection with such diseases, or as a preventative thereof, becoming manifest to a degree of 10% or more within one year from the date of separation from such service. Additionally, if it is shown to exist at a time when standard and accepted treatises indicate that the incubation period thereof commenced during active service, it shall be deemed to have incurred during such service.
- Active tuberculosis disease developing a 10% degree of disability or more within 3 years from the date of separation from such service.
- Multiple sclerosis developing a 10% degree of disability or more within seven years from the date of separation from such service.
- Hansen's disease developing a 10% degree of disability or more within three years from the date of separation from such service.

CHRONIC DISEASES:

- Amyotrophic lateral sclerosis (ALS)
- Anemia, primary
- Arteriosclerosis
- Arthritis
- Atrophy, progressive muscular
- Brain hemorrhage
- Brain thrombosis
- Bronchiectasis
- Calculi of the kidney, bladder, or gallbladder
- Cardiovascular-renal disease, including hypertension
- Cirrhosis of the liver
- Coccidiodomycosis
- Diabetes mellitus
- Encephalitis lethargica residuals
- Endocarditis
- Endocrinopathies
- Epilepsies
- Hansen's disease
- Hodgkin's disease
- Leukemia
- Lupus erythematosus, systemic
- Myasthenia gravis
- Myelitis
- Myocarditis
- Nephritis
- Organic diseases of the nervous system
- Osteitis deformans (Paget's disease)
- Osteomalacia

- Palsy, bulbar
- Paralysis agitans
- Psychoses
- Purpura idiopathic, hemorrhagic
- Raynaud's disease
- Sarcoidosis
- Scleroderma
- Sclerosis, amyotrohpic lateral
- Sclerosis, multiple
- Syringomyelia
- Thromboangiitis obilterans (Buerger's disease)
- Tuberculosis, active
- Tumors, malignant, or of the brain or spinal cord or peripheral nerves
- Ulcers, peptil (gastric or duodenal)
- Other chronic diseases the Secretary of Veterans Affairs may add to this list.

TROPICAL DISEASES:

- Amebiasis
- Blackwater fever
- Cholera
- Dracontiasis
- Dysentery
- Filiariasis
- Hansen's disease
- Leishmaniasis, including kala-azar
- Loiasis
- Malaria
- Onchocerciasis
- Oroya fever
- Pinta
- Plague
- Schistosomiasis
- Yaws
- Yellow fever
- Other tropical diseases the Secretary of Veterans Affairs may add to this list.

Presumptions Of Service-Connection Relating To Certain Diseases And Disabilities For Former Prisoners Of War

In the case of any veteran who is a former prisoner of war, and who was detained or interned for not less than thirty days, any of the following which became manifest to a degree of 10% or more after active military, naval or air service, shall be considered to have been incurred in or aggravated by such service, notwithstanding that there is no record of such disease during the period of service:

In the case of any veteran who is a former prisoner of war, and **who was detained or interned for not less than thirty days,** any of the following which became manifest to a degree of 10% or more after active military, naval or air service, shall be considered to have been incurred in or aggravated by such service, notwithstanding that there is no record of such disease during the period of service:

- Avitaminosis
- Beriberi (including beriberi heart disease, which includes Ischemic Heart Disease-coronary artery disease-for former POWs who suffered during captivity from edema-swelling of the legs or feet- also known as "wet" beriberi)
- Chronic dysentery
- Helminthiasis
- Malnutrition (including optic atrophy associated with malnutrition)
- Pellagra
- Any other nutritional deficiency
- Peripheral neuropathy, except where directly related to infectious causes
- Irritable bowel syndrome
- Peptic ulcer disease
- Cirrhosis of the liver (This condition was added as part of *Public Law 108-183*, The *Veterans Benefit Act of 2003*.)
- Atherosclerotic heart disease or hypertensive vascular disease (including hypertensive heart disease) and their complications (including myocardial infarction, congestive heart failure and arrhythmia) These conditions were added as part of Public Law 109-233.
- Stroke and its complications This condition was added as part of *Public Law 109-233*.
- The *Veterans Benefits Improvement Act* added osteoporosis to the list of disabilities presumed to be service-connected (and therefore compensable through VA disability compensation) in the case of veterans who are former prisoners of war, if the Secretary determines that such veteran has post-traumatic stress disorder (PTSD).

In the case of any veteran who is a former prisoner of war, and **who was detained or interned for any period of time,** any of the following which became manifest to a degree of 10% or more after active military, naval or air service, shall be considered to have been incurred in or aggravated by such service, notwithstanding that there is no record of such disease during the period of service:

- Psychosis
- Any of the anxiety states

- Dysthymic disorder (or depressive neurosis)
- Organic residuals of frostbite, if the VA determines the veteran was interned in climatic conditions consistent with the occurrence of frostbite
- Post-traumatic osteoarthritis

Presumptions Relating To Certain Diseases Associated With Exposure To Radiation

VA may pay compensation for radiogenic diseases under two programs specific to radiation-exposed veterans and their survivors:

STATUTORY LIST

- Veterans who participated in nuclear tests by the U.S. or its allies, who served with the U.S. occupation forces in Hiroshima or Nagasaki, Japan, between August 1945 and July 1946, or who were similarly exposed to ionizing radiation while a prisoner of war in Japan, are eligible for compensation for cancers specified in legislation.

- The definition of radiation-risk activities was expanded in March 2002 to include service at Amchitka Island, Alaska, prior to January 1, 1974, if a veteran was exposed while performing duties related to certain underground nuclear tests.

- The new definition also included service at gaseous diffusion plants located in Paducah, Ky., Portsmouth, Ohio and an area known as K25 at Oak Ridge, Tenn.

The types of cancer covered by these laws are:

- All forms of leukemia
- Cancer of the thyroid,
- Cancer of the breast,
- Cancer of the pharynx,
- Cancer of the esophagus,
- Cancer of the stomach,
- Cancer of the small intestine,
- Cancer of the pancreas,
- Cancer of the bile ducts,
- Cancer of the gall bladder,
- Cancer of the salivary gland,
- Cancer of the urinary tract,
- Lymphomas (except Hodgkin's disease),
- Multiple myeloma,
- Primary liver cancer.
- Bone Cancer

- Brain Cancer
- Colon Cancer
- Lung Cancer
- Ovary Cancer

The new rules apply to those veterans who participated in "radiation-risk activities" while on active duty, during active duty for training or inactive duty training as a member of a reserve component.

Regulatory List

Disability compensation claims of veterans who were exposed to radiation in service and who develop a disease within specified time periods not specified in the statutory list are governed by regulation. Under the regulations, various additional factors must be considered in determining service-connection, including amount of radiation exposure, duration of exposure, and elapsed time between exposure and onset of the disease. VA regulations identify all cancers as potentially radiogenic, as well as certain other non-malignant conditions: posterior subcapsular cataracts; non-malignant thyroid nodular disease; parathyroid adenoma; and tumors of the brain and central nervous system.

A final rule that expanded the regulatory list from more than a dozen specific cancers to add "any other cancer" (any malignancy) was published Sept. 24, 1998. The rulemaking began following a 1995 review of the radiogenicity of cancer generally by the Veterans Advisory Committee on Environmental Hazards. It concluded that, on the basis of current scientific knowledge, exposure to ionizing radiation can be a contributing factor in the development of any malignancy. VA also will consider evidence that diseases other than those specified in regulation may be caused by radiation exposure.

Presumptions Of Service-Connection For Diseases Associated With Exposure To Certain Herbicide Agents

A disease specified below, becoming manifest in a veteran, who, during active military, naval, or air service, served in the Republic of Vietnam during the period beginning on January 9, 1962, and ending on May 7, 1975 shall be considered to have been incurred in or aggravated by such service, notwithstanding that there is no record of evidence of such disease during the period of such service.

In 2011, the Department of Veterans Affairs published a final regulation expanding the dates when illnesses caused by herbicide exposure can be presumed to be related to Agent Orange.

Under the final regulation, published in the *Federal Register,* the VA will presume herbicide exposure for any Veteran who **served between April 1, 1968 and August 21,**

1971, in a unit determined by the VA and the Department of Defense to have operated in an area in or near the Korean demilitarized zone in which herbicides were applied.

The diseases referred to above are:

- **Acute and Subacute Peripheral Neuropathy**

  A nervous system condition that causes numbness, tingling, and motor weakness. Under VA's rating regulations, it must be at least 10% disabling within 1 year of exposure to Agent Orange and resolve within 2 years after the date it began.

- **AL Amyloidosis**

  A rare disease caused when an abnormal protein, amyloid, enters tissues or organs.

- **B Cell Leukemias** Cancers which affect B cells, such as hairy cell leukemia.

- **Chloracne (or Similar Acneform Disease)**

  A skin condition that occurs soon after dioxin exposure and looks like common forms of acne seen in teenagers. Under VA's rating regulations, chloracne (or other acneform disease similar to chloracne) must be at least 10% disabling within 1 year of exposure to Agent Orange.

- **Chronic Lymphocytic Leukemia**

  A disease that progresses slowly with increasing production of excessive numbers of white blood cells.

- **Diabetes Mellitus (Type 2)**

  A disease characterized by high blood sugar levels resulting from the body's inability to respond properly to the hormone insulin.

- **Hodgkin's Disease**

  A malignant lymphoma (cancer) characterized by progressive enlargement of the lymph nodes, liver, and spleen, and by progressive anemia.

- **Ischemic Heart Disease**

  A disease characterized by a reduced supply of blood to the heart.

- **Multiple Myeloma**

  A cancer of specific bone marrow cells that is characterized by bone marrow tumors in various bones of the body.

- **Non-Hodgkin's Lymphoma**

  A group of cancers that affect the lymph glands and other lymphatic tissue.

- **Parkinson's Disease**

  A motor system condition with symptoms that include trembling of the limbs and face and impaired balance.

- **Porphyria Cutanea Tarda**

  A disorder characterized by liver dysfunction and by thinning and blistering of the skin in sun-exposed areas. Under VA's rating regulations, it must be at least 10% disabling within 1 year of exposure to Agent Orange.

- **Prostate Cancer**

  Cancer of the prostate; one of the most common cancers among men.

- **Respiratory Cancers**

  Cancers of the lung, larynx, trachea, and bronchus.

- **Soft Tissue Sarcoma (other than Osteosarcoma, Chondrosarcoma, Kaposi's sarcoma, or Mesothelioma)**

  A group of different types of cancers in body tissues such as muscle, fat, blood and lymph vessels, and connective tissues.

- Each additional disease (if any) that the Secretary of the VA determines warrants a presumption of service-connection by reason of having positive association with exposure to an herbicide agent, becomes manifest within the period (if any) prescribed in such regulations in a veteran who, during active military, naval, or air service, served in the Republic of Vietnam during the period beginning on January 9, 1962 and ending on May 7, 1975, and while so serving was exposed to that herbicide agent.

Veterans having a disease referred to above, shall be presumed to have been exposed during such service to an herbicide agent containing dioxin or 2,4-dichlorophenoxyacetic acid, and may be presumed to have been exposed during such service to any other chemical compound in an herbicide agent, unless there is affirmative evidence to establish that the veteran was not exposed to any such agent during that service.

If the Secretary of the VA later determines that a previously established presumption of service-connection for one of the above diseases is no longer warranted, all veterans currently awarded compensation on the basis of the presumption shall continue to be entitled to receive compensation. Additionally, all survivors of any such veterans who were awarded dependency and indemnity compensation shall continue to be entitled to receive dependency and indemnity compensation on that basis.

PRESUMPTIONS OF SERVICE-CONNECTION FOR ILLNESSES ASSOCIATED WITH SERVICE IN THE PERSIAN GULF DURING THE PERSIAN GULF WAR

Like all other veterans, veterans of the Persian Gulf War can receive service-connected compensation for mental and physical disabilities that were incurred during, or aggravated by their service in the armed forces.

Recent legislation also authorized disability compensation for Persian Gulf veterans with chronic, **undiagnosed** illness resulting in a permanent disability that developed after they left the Persian Gulf.

Congress created this legislation after many Persian Gulf War veterans reported they were suffering from multi-symptom disabilities that are poorly understood by the medical profession, and may be classified as "undiagnosed" by one physician, or referred to as "chronic fatigue syndrome" by another physician.

Public Law 107-103, signed by then-President Bush on December 27, 2001, extended the presumptive period for disabilities associated with Persian Gulf War service until December 31, 2011, or such later date as prescribed by VA.

To be entitled to disability compensation due to an undiagnosed illness, the claimant must meet the following requirements:

1. The veteran must qualify as a Persian Gulf War veteran.
   VA considers an individual to be a Persian Gulf War veteran if he or she served on active military, naval, or air service in the Southwest Asia theater of operations during the Persian Gulf War. This includes service in Iraq, Kuwait, Saudi Arabia, the neutral zone between Iraq and Saudi Arabia, Bahrain, Qatar, the United Arab Emirates, Oman, the Gulf of Aden, the Gulf of Oman, the Persian Gulf, the Arabian Sea, the Red Sea, and the airspace above these locations.

   The veteran's period of service must have included service in the designated area after August 2, 1990. Since members of the armed services are still serving in the area of operations, they qualify as Persian Gulf veterans because the end date for the Persian Gulf War has not been set.

2. The veteran must suffer from a "qualifying chronic disability."

   A "qualifying chronic disability" can be any of the following (or combination of the following):

   a. An undiagnosed illnesses;
   b. A medically unexplained chronic multi-symptom illness (such as chronic fatigue syndrome, fibromyalgia, or irritable bowel syndrome) that is defined by a cluster of signs or symptoms;
   c. Any diagnosed illness that the VA Secretary determines warrants a presumption of service connection.

VA considers disabilities to be chronic if they have existed for 6 months or more, or if they have exhibited intermittent episodes of improvement and worsening over a 6-month period. The 6-month period is measured from the earliest date that the signs or symptoms manifested.

3. The "qualifying chronic disability" must have appeared either during active duty in the Southwest Asia Theater of Operations during the Gulf War or it must have manifested to a degree of at least 10 percent during the presumptive period.

The following symptoms may be manifestations of an undiagnosed illness:

- Fatigue
- Skin disorders
- Headaches
- Muscle pain
- Joint pain
- Neurological symptoms
- Neuropsychological symptoms
- Symptoms involving the respiratory system
- Sleep disturbances
- Gastrointestinal symptoms
- Cardiovascular symptoms
- Abnormal weight loss
- Menstrual disorders
- Any poorly defined chronic multi-symptom illness of unknown etiology characterized by 2 or more of the above symptoms.

Rates of compensation depend upon the degree of disability, and follow a payment schedule that is adjusted annually and applies to all veterans. Please refer to the charts detailed earlier in this chapter for the current rates payable.

"PRESUMPTIVE" ILLNESSES IN IRAQ, AFGHANISTAN

In late 2010, VA the VA established new presumptions of service connection for nine specific infectious diseases associated with military service in Southwest Asia beginning on or after the start of the first Gulf War on August 2, 1990, through the conflict in Iraq and on or after September 19, 2001, in Afghanistan.

The nine diseases are:
Brucellosis,
Campylobacter jejuni,
Coxiella burnetii (Q fever),
Malaria,
Mycobacterium tuberculosis,
Nontyphoid Salmonella,
Shigella,
Visceral leishmaniasis and
West Nile virus.

A veteran now only has to show service in Southwest Asia or Afghanistan and that he or she had one of the nine diseases within a certain time after service, and has a current disability as a result of that disease, subject to certain time limits for seven of the diseases

LOU GEHRIG'S DISEASE

AMYOTROPHIC LATERAL SCLEROSIS (ALS)

On December 10, 2001, VA reported that veterans who served in the Gulf during the period from August 2, 1990 through July 31, 1991, and who subsequently developed Lou Gehrig's Disease will be compensated.

Anyone seeking more information should contact the VA Gulf War Helpline at (800) 749-8387.

VA has evidence that veterans who deployed to the Gulf War are nearly twice as likely as their non-deployed counterparts to develop Lou Gehrig's Disease, technically known as amyotrohpic lateral sclerosis, or ALS.

VA has established a national ALS registry to identify veterans with the disease – regardless of when they served – and track their health status. Veterans with ALS who enroll will complete an initial telephone interview covering their health and military service, and will be interviewed twice yearly thereafter.

For more information about VA's ALS registry, call toll free (877) 342-5257.

PRESUMPTIONS REBUTTABLE

If there is affirmative evidence to the contrary, or evidence to establish that an intercurrent injury or disease which is a recognized cause of any of the diseases or disabilities mentioned in the above sections, has been suffered between the date of separation from service and the onset of any such diseases or disabilities, or if the disability is due to the veteran's own willful misconduct, payment of compensation shall not be made.

SPECIAL PROVISIONS RELATING TO CLAIMS BASED UPON EFFECTS OF TOBACCO PRODUCTS

Effective June 10, 1998, a veteran's death or disability will not be considered to have resulted from personal injury suffered, or disease contracted in the line of duty if the injury or disease is attributable to the use of tobacco products by the veteran during the veteran's service.

PEACETIME DISABILITY COMPENSATION

BASIC ENTITLEMENT

A veteran may be entitled to VA disability compensation for any medical condition or injury that was incurred in, or aggravated by his or her military service, during any period other than a period of war. The veteran must have been discharged or released under conditions other than dishonorable from the period of service in which the injury or disease was incurred or aggravated.

No compensation shall be paid if the disability is a result of the person's own willful misconduct or abuse of alcohol or drugs.

PRESUMPTION OF SOUND CONDITION

Every person employed in the active military, naval, or air service during any period other than a period of war, for 6 months or more, will be assumed to have been in sound medical condition when examined, accepted, and enrolled for service, except any defects, infirmities, or disorders noted at the time of the examination, acceptance, and enrollment, or if there is clear and unmistakable evidence showing that the injury or disease did exist before acceptance and enrollment, and the injury or disease was not aggravated by such service.

PRESUMPTIONS RELATING TO CERTAIN DISEASES

If a veteran who served in the active military, naval, or air service after December 31, 1946, during any period other than a period of war, for 6 months or more, contracts any of the following, it shall be considered to have been incurred in, or aggravated by such service, notwithstanding there is no record of evidence of such disease during the period of service:

- A chronic disease, becoming manifest to a degree of 10% or more within one year from the date of separation from such service.
- A tropical disease, and the resultant disorders or disease originating because of therapy, administered in connection with such diseases, or as a preventative thereof, becoming manifest to a degree of 10% or more within one year from

the date of separation from such service. Additionally, if it is shown to exist at a time when standard and accepted treatises indicate that the incubation period thereof commenced during active service, it shall be deemed to have incurred during such service.

- Active tuberculosis disease developing a 10% degree of disability or more within 3 years from the date of separation from such service.
- Multiple sclerosis developing a 10% degree of disability or more within seven years from the date of separation from such service.
- Hansen's disease developing a 10% degree of disability or more within three years from the date of separation from such service.

In the case of any veteran who served for 90 days or more during a period of war, service-connection will not be granted in any case where the disease or disorder is shown by clear and unmistakable evidence to have had its inception before or after active military, naval, or air service.

Presumptions Rebuttable

If there is affirmative evidence to the contrary, or evidence to establish that an intercurrent injury or disease which is a recognized cause of any of the diseases or disabilities mentioned in the above sections, has been suffered between the date of separation from service and the onset of any such diseases or disabilities, or if the disability is due to the veteran's own willful misconduct, payment of compensation shall not be made.

Rates Of Peacetime Disability Compensation

The compensation payable shall be the same as the compensation payable for Wartime Disability Compensation. Please refer to the charts presented earlier in this chapter.

Additional Compensation For Dependents

Any veteran entitled to peacetime disability compensation, and whose disability is rated as 30% or greater, will be entitled to additional monthly compensation for dependents in the same amounts payable for Wartime Disability Compensation. Please refer to the charts presented earlier in this chapter.

GENERAL DISABILITY COMPENSATION PROVISIONS

How To Apply For Disability Compensation Benefits

The Department of Veteran Affairs (VA) has announced the elimination of the need for veterans to complete the Eligibility Verification Report (EVR), annually. According to the VA, this is a way of cutting the red tape for veterans, and working toward eliminating the claims backlog. The VA reports that it will implement a new process to confirm veterans benefits eligibility, and staff members that had previously been responsible for processing the old form will now focus on eliminating the compensation claims backlog.

Previously, beneficiaries had been required to complete an EVR each year in order to ensure the continuation of pension benefits. With the new change in eligibility confirmation, the VA says it will work with the Internal Revenue Service (IRS) and the Social Security Administration (SSA), to confirm eligibility for benefits.

In order to apply for disability compensation benefits from the VA, Form 21-526, Veteran's Application for Compensation or Pension, must be completed and returned to the VA Regional Office serving the veteran's area (refer to Chapter 36 for a listing of regional offices). In addition to the application, the following documents must be submitted:

- Service Medical Records: In order to expedite processing of the claim, if an applicant has his or her service medical records, they should be submitted with the application. If not included with the application, VA will contact the veteran's service department to obtain them.
- Other Medical Records: Any medical records from private doctors or hospitals pertaining to the claim should be submitted along with the application.
- Dependency Documents: Copies of pertinent birth, marriage, death and divorce certificates should be submitted along with the application.
- Military Discharge / DD Form 214-Copy 4-Member Copy: In order to expedite processing of the claim, if an applicant has a copy of his or her DD-214, it should be submitted with the application. If not included with the application, VA will attempt to obtain verification from the veteran's service department.
- Copies of missing DD Forms 214 may be obtained from the National Personnel Records Center - 9700 Page Blvd. - St. Louis, MO - 63132-5100.

If any of the pertinent supporting evidence is not immediately available, the applicant should send in the application anyway. The date VA receives the application is important! If VA approves the claim, benefit payments usually begin from the date the application is received, regardless of when the claim is approved.

ADJUDICATION

Adjudication means a judicial decision made by the Veterans Administration in claims filed within their jurisdiction. There is an Adjudication Division in each regional office, under the direction of an adjudication officer, who is responsible for the preparation of claims.

Upon the receipt of an original application in the Adjudication Division, it will be referred to the Authorization Unit for review and development in accordance with established procedures. All reasonable assistance will be extended a claimant in the prosecution of his or her claim, and all sources from which information may be elicited will be thoroughly developed prior to the submission of the case to the rating board. Every legitimate assistance will be rendered a claimant in obtaining any benefit to which he or she is entitled, and the veteran will be given every opportunity to substantiate his or her claim. Information and advice to claimants will be complete, and will be given in words that the average person can understand.

VA personnel must at all times give to claimants and other properly interested and recognized individuals courteous and satisfactory service which is essential to good public relations. It is incumbent upon the claimant to establish his or her case in accordance with the law. This rule, however, should not be highly technical and rigid in its application. The general policy is to give the claimant every opportunity to substantiate the claim, to extend all reasonable assistance in its prosecution, and to develop all sources from which information may be obtained. Information and advice to claimants will be complete and expressed, so far as possible, in plain language, which can be easily read and understood by persons not familiar with the subject matter.

BENEFITS FOR PERSONS DISABLED BY TREATMENT OR VOCATIONAL REHABILITATION

Compensation shall be awarded for a qualifying additional disability or a qualifying death of a veteran in the same manner as if such additional disability or death were service-connected, provided:

- The disability or death was caused by hospital care, medical or surgical treatment, or examination was furnished under any law administered by the VA, either by a VA employee, or in a VA facility, and the proximate cause of the disability or death was:
- Carelessness, negligence, lack of proper skill, error in judgment, or similar instance of fault on the part of the VA in furnishing the hospital care, medical treatment, surgical treatment, or examination; or
- An event not reasonably foreseeable.
- The disability or death was proximately caused by the provision of training and rehabilitation services by the VA (including a service-provider used by the VA) as part of an approved rehabilitation program.

Effective December 1, 1962, if an individual is awarded a judgment against the United States in a civil action brought pursuant to Section 1346(b) of Title 28, or enters into a settlement or compromise under Section 2672 or 2677 of Title 28 by reason of a disability or death treated pursuant to this section as if it were service-connected, then no benefits shall be paid to such individual for any month beginning after the date such judgment, settlement, or compromise on account of such disability or death becomes final until the aggregate amount of benefits which would be paid out for this subsection equals the total amount included in such judgment, settlement, or compromise.

PERSON HERETOFORE HAVING A COMPENSABLE STATUS

The death and disability benefits outlined in this chapter, shall, notwithstanding the service requirements thereof, be granted to persons heretofore recognized by law as having a compensable status, including persons whose claims are based on war or peacetime service rendered before April 21, 1898

.

AGGRAVATION

A preexisting injury or disease will be considered to have been aggravated by active military, naval, or air service, if there is an increase in disability during such service, unless there is a specific finding that the increase in disability is due to the natural progress of the disease.

CONSIDERATION TO BE ACCORDED TIME, PLACE AND CIRCUMSTANCES OF SERVICE

Consideration shall be given to the places, types, and circumstances of each veteran's service. The VA will consider the veteran's service record, the official history of each organization in which such veteran served, such veteran's medical records, and all pertinent medical and lay evidence. The provisions of *Public Law 98-542 – Section 5 of the Veterans' Dioxin and Radiation Exposure Compensation Standards Act* shall also be applied.

In the case of any veteran who engaged in combat with the enemy in active service with a military, naval, or air organization of the United States during a period of war, campaign, or expedition, the Secretary shall accept as sufficient proof of service-connection of any disease or injury alleged to have been incurred in or aggravated by such service, if consistent with the circumstances, conditions, or hardships of such service. This provision will apply even if there is no official record of such incurrence or aggravation in such service. Every reasonable doubt in such instance will be resolved in favor of the veteran.

Service-connection of such injury or disease may be rebutted only by clear and convincing evidence to the contrary. The reasons for granting or denying service-connection in each case shall be recorded in full.

DISAPPEARANCE

If a veteran who is receiving disability compensation disappears, the VA may pay the compensation otherwise payable to the veteran to such veteran's spouse, children, and parents. Payments made to such spouse, child, or parent shall not exceed the amounts payable to each if the veteran had died from a service-connected disability.

COMBINATION OF CERTAIN RATINGS

The VA shall provide for the combination of ratings and pay compensation at the rates prescribed previously in this chapter to those veterans who served during a period of war and during any other time, who have suffered disability in the line of duty in each period of service.

Combined ratings can be figured out by the following formula:

1. Subtract the highest rating, for the major disability, from 100%
2. Multiply the rating for the next lower disability by the sum remaining after the first subtraction.
3. Add the product to the major rating to arrive at the combined rating for two disabilities.

If there are three rated service-connected disabilities, then, after the combined rating for the two larger ratings has been calculated, subtract such combined rating from 100% and multiply the rating for the third disability times the remainder, and add the resulting product to the combined rating of the first two disabilities to arrive at the combined rating for the three disabilities.

Thus, if a veteran has a 60% disability, a 40% disability, and a 20% disability, the following calculation would be done to arrive at the combined rating of 81%:

1. 100 – 60 = 40
2. 40 X .40 = 16
3. 16 + 60 = 76
4. 100 – 76 = 24
5. 24 X .20 = 4.8 (round up to 5)
6. 76 + 5 = 81%

TAX EXEMPTION

Compensation and pension may not be assigned to anyone, and are exempt from taxation (including income tax). No one can attach, levy, or seize a compensation or pension check either before or after receipt. Property purchased with money received from the government is not protected.

PROTECTION OF SERVICE CONNECTION

Service connection for any disability or death granted under this title which has been in force for ten or more years shall not be severed on or after January 1, 1962, unless it is shown that the original grant of service connection was based on fraud, or it is clearly shown from military records that the person concerned did not have the requisite service or character of discharge. The mentioned period shall be computed from the date determined by the VA as the date on which the status commenced for rating purposes.

PRESERVATION OF RATINGS

Public Law 88-445, approved August 19, 1964, effective the same date, amends Section 110, Title 38, U.S. Code as follows:

The law provides that a disability which has been continuously rated at or above a given percentage for 20 years or longer for the purpose of service connection compensation under laws administered by the VA shall not thereafter be rated at any lesser percentage except upon showing that the rating was based on fraud.

SPECIAL CONSIDERATION FOR CERTAIN CASES OF LOSS OF PAIRED ORGANS OR EXTREMITIES

If a veteran has suffered any of the following, the VA shall assign and pay to the veteran the applicable rate of compensation, as if the combination of disabilities were the result of a service-connected disability:

- Blindness in one eye as a result of a service-connected disability, and blindness in the other eye as a result of a non-service-connected disability not the result of the veteran's own willful misconduct; or
- The loss or loss of use of one kidney as a result of a service-connected disability, and involvement of the other kidney as a result of a non-service connected disability not the result of the veteran's own willful misconduct; or
- Total deafness in one ear as a result of a service-connected disability, and total deafness in the other ear as the result of non-service-connected disability not the result of the veteran's own willful misconduct; or
- The loss or loss of use of one hand or one foot as a result of a service-connected disability and the loss or loss of use of the other hand or foot as a result of non-service-connected disability not the result of the veteran's own willful misconduct; or
- Permanent service-connected disability of one lung, rated 50% or more disabling, in combination with a non-service-connected disability of the other lung that is not the result of the veteran's own willful misconduct.

If a veteran described above receives any money or property of value pursuant to an award in a judicial proceeding based upon, or a settlement or compromise of, any cause of action for damages for the non-service-connected disability, the increase in the rate of compensation otherwise payable shall not be paid for any month following a month in which any such money or property is received until such time as the total of the amount of such increase that would otherwise have been payable equals the total of the amount of any such money received, and the fair market value of any such property received.

PAYMENT OF DISABILITY COMPENSATION IN DISABILITY SEVERANCE CASES

The deduction of disability severance pay from disability compensation, as required by Section 1212(c) of Title 10, shall be made at a monthly rate not in excess of the rate of compensation to which the former member would be entitled based on the degree of such former member's disability, as determined on the initial Department rating.

TRIAL WORK PERIODS AND VOCATIONAL REHABILITATION FOR CERTAIN VETERANS WITH TOTAL DISABILITY RATINGS

The disability rating of a qualified veteran who begins to engage in a substantially gainful occupation after January 31, 1985, may not be reduced on the basis of the veteran having secured and followed a substantially gainful occupation unless the veteran maintains such an occupation for a period of 12 consecutive months.

("Qualified Veteran" means a veteran who has a service-connected disability or disabilities, not rated as total, but who has been awarded a rating of total of disability by reason of inability to secure or follow a substantially gainful occupation as a result of such disability or disabilities.)

Counseling services, placement, and post placement services shall be available to each qualified veteran, whether or not the veteran is participating in a vocational rehabilitation program.

ASBESTOS EXPOSURE

Veterans who were exposed to asbestos while in service and developed a disease related to asbestos exposure may receive service-connected compensation benefits.

If you served in any of the following occupations, you may have been exposed to asbestos: mining, milling, shipyard work, insulation work, demolition of old buildings, carpentry and construction, the manufacturing and installation of products such as flooring, roofing, cement sheet, pipe products, or the servicing of friction products such as clutch facings and brake linings.

Additionally, if you served in Iraq or other countries in that region, you could have been exposed to asbestos when older buildings were damaged and the contaminant was released into the air.

ELIGIBILITY REQUIREMENTS

- You must be a Veteran who was discharged under conditions other than dishonorable
- You must have been exposed to asbestos while in military service
- You must have a disease or disability related to the asbestos exposure that occurred in military service

EVIDENCE REQUIREMENTS

- The evidence must show asbestos exposure while in military service. This may include your military occupation specialty and/or where you were stationed.
- The evidence must show you have a disease or disability related to asbestos and a relationship exists between the exposure to asbestos in military service and the disease/disability.

Note: You must claim a disease or disability. Exposure, in and of itself, is not a condition that is subject to service connection.

Normally, VA will initiate a VA medical examination and request an opinion regarding the relationship of the disease or disability to asbestos exposure that occurred during military service.

CHAPTER 3

MISCELLANEOUS BENEFITS

AUTOMOBILES, ADAPTIVE EQUIPMENT, HOUSING GRANTS, CLOTHING ALLOWANCE *AND MEDAL OF HONOR PENSION*

AUTOMOBILE ASSISTANCE PROGRAM

The VA offers an automobile assistance program for eligible veterans, or eligible members of the Armed Forces serving on active duty who are suffering from a disability as described below, if such disability is the result of an injury incurred or disease contracted in or aggravated in the line of duty in the active military, naval, or air service. Following are highlights of the VA program:

FINANCIAL ASSISTANCE

Qualified veterans may receive a ***one-time*** payment from VA of up to **$20,114.34** to be used toward the purchase of an automobile or other conveyance. The law requires that this amount be adjusted annually by the percentage increase in the Consumer Price Index.

ELIGIBILITY REQUIREMENTS FOR RECEIPT OF ONE-TIME PAYMENT:

Veterans or service members who are entitled to Disability Compensation under Chapter 11 of Title 38 due to one of the following service-connected losses:

Qualified veterans may receive a ***one-time*** payment from VA of up to **$20,114.34** to be used toward the purchase of an automobile or other conveyance.

- The loss or permanent loss of use of one or both feet; or

- The loss or permanent loss of use of one or both hands; or
- The permanent impairment of vision of both eyes of the following status:
- Central visual acuity of 20/200 or less in the better eye, with corrective glasses, or central visual acuity of more than 20/200 if there is a field defect in which the peripheral field has contracted to such an extent that the widest diameter of visual field subtends an angular distance no greater than twenty degrees in the better eye.

ADAPTIVE EQUIPMENT

In addition to the one-time payment described above, VA will also pay for installation of adaptive equipment deemed necessary to insure that the eligible veteran will be able to safely operate the vehicle, and to satisfy the applicable state standards of licensure.

VA will also repair, replace, or reinstall adaptive equipment determined necessary for the operation of a vehicle acquired under this program, or for the operation of a vehicle an eligible veteran may previously or subsequently have acquired.

Eligibility Requirements For Receipt Of Adaptive Equipment:

- The loss or permanent loss of use of one or both feet; or
- The loss or permanent loss of use of one or both hands; or
- The permanent impairment of vision of both eyes of the following status:
- Central visual acuity of 20/200 or less in the better eye, with corrective glasses, or central visual acuity of more than 20/200 if there is a field defect in which the peripheral field has contracted to such an extent that the widest diameter of visual field subtends an angular distance no greater than twenty degrees in the better eye; or
- Ankylosis (immobility) of one or both knees; or
- Ankylosis (immobility) of one or both hips.

Adaptive Equipment Available for Installation

The term adaptive equipment, means generally, any equipment which must be part of or added to a vehicle manufactured for sale to the general public in order to make it safe for use by the claimant, and to assist him or her in meeting the applicable standards of licensure of the proper licensing authority.

Following is a partial list of adaptive equipment available under this program:

- Power steering;
- Power brakes;

- Power window lifts;
- Power seats;
- Special equipment necessary to assist the eligible person into and out of the automobile or other conveyance;
- Air-conditioning equipment, if such equipment is necessary to the health and safety of the veteran and to the safety of others, regardless of whether the automobile or other conveyance is to be operated by the eligible person or is to be operated for such person by another person;
- Any modification of the size of the interior space of the automobile or other conveyance if necessary for the disabled person to enter or operate the vehicle;
- Other equipment, not described above, if determined necessary by the Chief Medical Director or designee in an individual case.

Eligible veterans are not entitled to adaptive equipment for more than 2 vehicles at any one time during any four-year period. (In the event an adapted vehicle is no longer available for use by the eligible veteran due to circumstances beyond his or her control, i.e. loss due to fire, theft, accident, etc., an exception to this four-year provision may be approved.)

SPECIALLY ADAPTED HOUSING GRANTS

There are three types of grants that may be payable:

- Specially Adapted Housing Grants (SAH)
- Special Housing Adaptations Grants (SHA)
- Temporary Residence Adaptation Grants (TRA)

Specially Adapted Housing Grant (SAH)

The VA may approve a grant of not more than 50% of the cost of building, buying, or remodeling adapted homes, or paying indebtedness on homes previously acquired, up to a maximum of **$70,465.**

Public law 110-289 directed that the maximum grant amount will be adjusted annually. The amount will either increase or stay the same each year – it cannot decrease. For Fiscal Year 2015, the aggregate amount of assistance available for the Paraplegic Housing (PH) grant increased from $67,555 to $70,465.

To qualify for this grant, veterans must be entitled to compensation for permanent and total service-connected disability due to:

- Loss or loss of use of both lower extremities, which prevents movement without the aid of braces, crutches, canes, or a wheelchair; or

- Disability which includes:
- Blindness in both eyes, having only light perception; **with**
- Loss or loss of use of one lower extremity; or
- Loss or loss of use of one lower extremity together with:
- Residuals of organic disease or injury; **or**
- The loss or loss of use of one upper extremity, which so affects the functions of balance or propulsion as to preclude locomotion without using braces, canes, crutches, or a wheelchair.
- Loss of, or loss of use, of both upper extremities such as to preclude use of the arms at or above the elbows.
- A severe burn injury (as so determined.)

Eligibility For Active Duty Members

Public Law 108-183, The *Veterans Benefits Act of 2003*, which became law on December 16, 2003, extended eligibility for the $70,465 grant to members of the Armed Forces serving on ***active duty*** who are suffering from a disability as described above, if such disability is the result of an injury incurred or disease contracted in or aggravated in the line of duty in the active military, naval, or air service.

Public Law 110-289, the *Economic and Housing Recovery Act of 2008*, dated July 30, 2008, extended eligibility for active duty servicemembers to the same extent, and made them subject to the same limitations, as veterans.

- An eligible veteran or active duty service member can use his or her benefit up to **three times**, as long as the aggregate amount of assistance does not exceed the maximum amounts allowable.
- This benefit extends to previous grant recipients, however, they cannot obtain a subsequent grant(s) to pay for adaptations made prior to June 15, 2006, or to reduce an existing mortgage principal balance for properties acquired prior to June 15, 2006.

SPECIAL HOUSING ADAPTATION GRANT (SHA)

VA may approve a grant for the actual cost, up to a maximum of **$14,093**, for adaptations to a veteran's residence that are determined by VA to be reasonably necessary. *Public Law 110-289* directed that the maximum grant amount will be adjusted annually, based on a cost-of-construction index. The amount will either increase or stay the same each year- it cannot decrease.

The grant may also be used to assist veterans in acquiring a residence that already has been adapted with special features for the veteran's disability.

To qualify for this grant, veterans must be entitled to compensation for permanent and total service-connected disability due to:

- Blindness in both eyes, with 5/200 visual acuity or less; or
- Anatomical loss or loss of use of both hands.

TEMPORARY RESIDENCE ADAPTATIONS GRANT (TRA)

Eligible veterans and servicemembers who are temporarily residing in a home owned by a family member may also receive a Temporary Residence Adaptation (TRA) grant to help the veteran or servicemember adapt the family member's home to meet his or her special needs. While the SAH and SHA grants require ownership and title to a house, in creating the TRA, Congress recognized the need to allow veterans and active duty members who may not yet own homes to have access to the adaptive housing grant program.

- VA may provide a **TEMPORARY RESIDENCE ADAPTATION GRANT** of up to 30,934 (for those eligible for the $70,465) to assist a veteran in adapting a family member's home to meet the veteran's special needs.

- VA may provide a **TEMPORARY RESIDENCE ADAPTATION GRANT** of up to $5,523 (for those eligible for the $14,093 grant) to assist a veteran in adapting a family member's home to meet the veteran's special needs.

SUPPLEMENTAL FINANCING – LOAN GUARANTY

Veterans who have available loan guaranty entitlement may also obtain a guaranteed loan or possibly a direct loan from VA to supplement the grant to acquire a specially adapted home. Please refer to Chapter 22 of this book for specific information on VA Loan Guaranties.

CLOTHING ALLOWANCE

In 2011, a final regulation was published in the *Federal Register* expanding the eligibility criteria for veterans with multiple prosthetic and orthopedic devices or those who use prescription medications for service-related skin conditions.

The new regulation provides the criteria for more than one annual clothing allowance in situations where distinct garments are affected. Payment for more than one clothing allowance for eligible veterans will begin in 2012. Form 10-8678 is being revised to allow for application for more than one yearly clothing allowance payment.

The VA shall pay a clothing allowance of **$777.29** per year (rate effective December 1, 2014 and payable beginning August 1, 2015) to each veteran who:

As of December 1, 2014, the annual clothing allowance increased to $777.29, per year.

- Because of a service-connected disability, wears or uses a prosthetic or orthopedic appliance (including a wheelchair) which the VA determines tends to wear out or tear the clothing of the veteran; or

- Uses medication prescribed by a physician for a skin condition that is due to a service-connected disability, and which the VA determines causes irreparable damage to the veteran's outer garments.

As of December 1, 2014, the Medal of Honor pension is $1,299.61 per month.

The law further states that VA shall pay, in a lump sum, to each person who is in receipt of the Medal of Honor Pension, an amount equal to the total amount of special pension that the person would have received during the period beginning on the 1st day of the 1st month beginning after the date of the act for which the person was awarded the Medal of Honor, and ending on the last day of the month preceding the month in which the person's special pension commenced.

For each month of a period referred to in the previous paragraph, the amount of special pension payable shall be determined using the rate of special pension that was in effect for such month.

The Secretary of the Department of the Army, the Department of the Navy, the Department of the Air Force, or the Department of Transportation will determine the eligibility of applicants to be entered on the Medal of Honor Roll and will deliver to the Secretary of the Department of Veterans Affairs a certified copy of each certificate issued in which the right of the person named in the certificate to the special pension is set forth. The special pension will be authorized on the basis of such certification.

The special pension will be paid in addition to all other payments under laws of the United States. However, a person awarded more than one Medal of Honor may not receive more than one special pension.

CHAPTER 4

PENSION: NON-SERVICE CONNECTED DISABILITY

BENEFIT DESCRIPTION

Non-Service Connected Disability Pension is a Department of Veterans Affairs benefits program that provides financial support to wartime veterans having limited income. The amount payable under this program depends on the type and amount of income the veteran and family members receive from other sources. Monthly payments are made to bring a veteran's total annual income (including other retirement and Social Security income) to an established support level. (Unreimbursed medical expenses may reduce countable income.)

DEFINITIONS

Indian Wars: means the campaigns, engagements, and expeditions of the United States military forces against Indian tribes or nations, service in which has been recognized heretofore as pensionable service.

World War I: means the period April 6, 1917, through November 11, 1918. In the case of a veteran who served with the United States military forces in Russia, the ending date is April 1, 1920. Service after November 11, 1918 and before July 2, 1921 is considered World War I for compensation or pension purposes, if the veteran served in the active military, naval, or air service after April 5, 1917 and before November 12, 1918.

Civil War Veteran: includes a person who served in the military or naval forces of the Confederate States of America during the Civil War, and the term "active military or naval service" includes active service in those forces.

Period of War: means the Mexican border period, World War I, World War II, the Korean conflict, the Vietnam era, the Persian Gulf War, and the period beginning on the date of any future declaration of war by the Congress and ending on the date prescribed by Presidential proclamation or concurrent resolution of the Congress.

Permanently and Totally Disabled: for the purposes of this chapter, a person shall be considered to be permanently and totally disabled if such person is unemployable as a result of a disability reasonably certain to continue throughout the life of the disabled person, or:

- Suffering from any disability which is sufficient to render it impossible for the average person to follow a substantially gainful occupation, but only if it is reasonably certain that such disability will continue throughout the life of the disabled person; or
- Suffering from any disease or disorder determined by the VA Secretary to be of such a nature or extent as to justify a determination that persons suffering are permanently and totally disabled; or
- Is a patient in a nursing home for long-term care because of disability; or
- Is disabled, as determined by the Social Security Administration (SSA) for purpose of benefits administered by the SSA; or
- Is unemployable, as a result of suffering from any disability which is sufficient to render it impossible for the average person to follow a substantially gainful occupation, but only if it is reasonable certain that such disability will continue throughout the life of the person, or otherwise justifying a determination of permanent and total disability.

Regular Aid and Attendance: for the purposes of this chapter, a person shall be considered to be in need of regular aid and attendance if such person is:

- A patient in a nursing home; or
- Helpless or blind, or so nearly helpless or blind as to need or require the aid and attendance of another person.

Permanently Housebound: for the purposes of this chapter, the requirement of "permanently housebound" will be considered to have been met when the veteran is substantially confined to such veteran's house (ward or clinical areas, if institutionalized) or immediate premises due to a disability or disabilities, which it is reasonably certain will remain throughout such veteran's lifetime.

Annual Income: In determining annual income under this chapter, all payments of any kind or from any source (including salary, retirement or annuity payments, or similar income, which has been waived, irrespective of whether the waiver was made pursuant to statue, contract, or otherwise) shall be included except:

- Donations from public or private relief or welfare organizations;
- Payments under this chapter;

- Amounts equal to amounts paid by a spouse of a veteran for the expenses of such veteran's last illness, and by a surviving spouse or child of a deceased veteran for:
- Such veteran's just debts;
- The expenses of such veteran's last illness; and
- The expenses of such veteran's burial to the extent such expenses are not reimbursed through Chapter 23 of Title 38, United States Code (Burial Benefits);
- Amounts equal to amounts paid:
- By a veteran for the last illness and burial of such veteran's deceased spouse or child; or
- By the spouse of a living veteran or the surviving spouse of a deceased veteran for the last illness and burial of a child of such veteran;
- Reimbursements of any kind for any casualty loss, but the amount excluded under this clause may not exceed the greater of the fair market value or reasonable replacement value of the property involved at the time immediately preceding the loss;
- Profit realized from the disposition of real or personal property other than in the course of a business;
- Amounts in joint accounts in banks and similar institutions acquired by reason of death of other joint owner;
- Amounts equal to amounts paid by a veteran, veteran's spouse, or surviving spouse, or by or on behalf of a veteran's child for unreimbursed medical expenses, to the extent that such amounts exceed 5% of the maximum annual rate of pension (including any amount of increased pension payable on account of family members but not including any amount of pension payable because a person is in need of regular aid and attendance, or because a person is permanently housebound) payable to such veteran surviving spouse, or child.
- In the case of a veteran or surviving spouse pursuing a course of education or vocational rehabilitation or training, amounts equal to amounts paid by such veteran or surviving spouse for such course of education or vocational rehabilitation or training, including:
- Amounts paid for tuition, fees, books, and materials; and
- In the case of such a veteran or surviving spouse in need of regular aid and attendance, unreimbursed amounts paid for unusual transpiration expenses in connection with the pursuit of such course of education or vocational rehabilitation or training, to the extent that such amounts exceed the reasonable expenses which would have been incurred by a nondisabled person using an appropriate means of transportation (public transportation, if reasonably available); and

- In the case of a child, or any current-work income received during the year, to the extent that the total amount of such income does not exceed an amount equal to the sum of:

- The lowest amount of gross income for which an income tax return is required under section 6012(a) of the Internal Revenue Code of 1986, to be filed by an individual who is not married, is not a surviving spouse, and is not a head of household; and

- If the child is pursuing a course of postsecondary education or vocational rehabilitation or training, the amount paid by such child for such course of education or vocational rehabilitation or training, including the amount paid for tuition, fees, books, and materials.

ELIGIBILITY

- Veteran was discharged from service under other than dishonorable conditions; and
- Veteran served 90 days or more of active duty with at least 1 day during a period of war time. However, 38 CFR 3.12a requires that anyone who enlisted after 9/7/80 generally has to serve at least 24 months or the full period for which a person was called or ordered to active duty in order to receive any benefits based on that period of service; and
- Veteran is permanently and totally disabled, or is age 65 or older; and
- Veteran's countable family income is below a yearly limit set by law.

AMOUNT OF VA PAYMENTS

If eligible, VA pays the difference between a recipient's countable family income and the annual income limit set by law (see following charts) for his or her status. This difference is generally paid in 12 equal monthly installments.

****The table on the next page wasn't available from the VA at time of publication, so figures are based on the estimates of Veterans Information Service. If there is a discrepancy, always follow information provided by the VA.**

FAMILY INCOME LIMITS

IMPROVED PENSION ANNUAL RATES-EFFECTIVE DECEMBER 1, 2014	
STATUS OF VETERAN:	**ANNUAL INCOME LIMITATION:**
Permanently & totally disabled veterans:	
Veteran alone	$12,867.00
Veteran with one dependent	16,850.00
Each additional dependent child	2,197.00
Veteran – Aid and Attendance:	
Veteran alone	21,465.00
Veteran with one dependent	25,447.00
Each additional dependent child	2,197.00
Veteran – Housebound:	
Veteran alone	15,723.00
Veteran with one dependent	19,708.00
Each additional dependent child	2,197.00
Two veterans married to one another:	16,850.00
Each additional dependent child	2,197.00
Add for Mexican Border Period or World War I Veterans:	2,321.00
Child Earned Income Exclusion effective 1-1-2014 –	$10,150

MAXIMUM ANNUAL INCOME LIMITATIONS FOR PROTECTED PENSIONS EFFECTIVE DECEMBER 1, 2014

Pensioners entitled to benefits as of December 31, 1978, who do not elect to receive a pension under the Improved Pension Program, may continue to receive pension benefits at the rates they were entitled to receive on December 31, 1978 or June 30, 1960, as long as they remain permanently and totally disabled, do not lose a dependent, and their income does not exceed the income limitation, adjusted annually.

**** The table on the next page wasn't available from the VA at time of publication, so figures are based on the estimates of Veterans Information Service. If there is a discrepancy, always follow information provided by the VA.**

PENSION LAW IN EFFECT ON DECEMBER 31, 1978 (SECTION 306): THE RATE ENTITLED TO ON DECEMBER 31, 1978 MAY BE CONTINUED IF THE RECIPIENT'S IVAP FOR 2014 IS BELOW THE FOLLOWING LIMITS:	
STATUS OF RECIPIENT:	**ANNUAL INCOME LIMITATION:**
Veteran / widow with no dependents	$ 14,634.00
Veteran / widow with one or more dependent	19,671.00
Child (no entitled veteran or surviving spouse)	11,965.00
Veteran with no dependents in receipt of A&A	14,160.00
Veteran with one dependent in receipt of A&A	20,197.00
Surviving spouse's income exclusion	4,671.00

PENSION LAW IN EFFECT ON JUNE 30, 1960 (OLD LAW): THE RATE ENTITLED TO ON JUNE 30, 1960 MAY BE CONTINUED IF THE RECIPIENT'S IVAP FOR 2011 IS BELOW THE FOLLOWING LIMITS:	
STATUS OF RECIPIENT:	**ANNUAL INCOME LIMITATION:**
Veteran / widow with no dependents	$ 12,813.00
Veteran / widow with one or more dependents	18,470.00
Child (no entitled veteran or surviving spouse)	12,813.00

MONTHLY BENEFIT PAYABLE TO ELIGIBLE VETERANS RECEIVING DISABILITY PENSION UNDER LAWS IN EFFECT JUNE 30, 1960 OR DECEMBER 31, 1978	
VETERAN'S ENTITLEMENT:	**RATE PAYABLE:**
Basic Rates	$ 68.28
10 Years or Age 65	81.28
If Entitled To Aid & Attendance	139.82
If Entitled To Housebound	103.23

APPLYING FOR BENEFITS

Veterans can apply for a Disability Pension by completing VA Form 21-526, Veteran's Application for Compensation or Pension. If available, the applicant should attach copies of dependency records (marriage and children's birth certificates) and current medical evidence (doctor and hospital reports). The completed form should be sent to the veteran's VA Regional Office. (Refer to Chapter 36 for a listing of all VA regional offices.) If any of the pertinent supporting evidence is not immediately available, the applicant should send in the application anyway. The date VA receives the application is important! If VA approves the claim, benefit payments usually begin from the date the application is received, regardless of when the claim is approved.

NET WORTH LIMITATION

The VA shall deny or discontinue the payment of pension to a veteran under this chapter when the corpus of the estate of the veteran, or, if the veteran has a spouse, the corpus of the estates of the veteran and of the veteran's spouse is such that under all the circumstances, including consideration of the annual income of the veteran, the veteran's spouse, and the veteran's children, it is reasonable that some part of the corpus of such estates be consumed for the veteran's maintenance.

The VA shall deny or discontinue the payment of increased pension under this chapter on account of a child when the corpus of such child's estate is such that under all the circumstances, including consideration of the veteran's and spouse's income, and the income of the veteran's children, it is reasonable that some part of the corpus of such child's estate be consumed for the child's maintenance. During the period such denial or discontinuance remains in effect, such child shall not be considered as the veteran's child for purposes of this chapter.

COMBINATION OF RATINGS

The VA shall provide that, for the purpose of determining whether or not a veteran is permanently and totally disabled, ratings for service-connected disabilities may be combined with ratings for non-service-connected disabilities.

Where a veteran is found to be entitled to a Non-Service-Connected Disability Pension, and is also entitled to Service-Connected Disability Compensation, the VA shall pay the veteran the greater benefit.

VOCATIONAL TRAINING FOR CERTAIN PENSION RECIPIENTS

In the case of a veteran who is awarded a Non-Service-Connected Disability Pension, the VA shall, based on information on file with the VA, make a preliminary finding whether such veteran, with the assistance of a vocational training program, has a good potential for achieving employment. If such potential is found to exist, the VA shall solicit from the veteran an application for vocational training. If the veteran thereafter applies for such training, the VA shall provide the veteran with an evaluation, which may include a personal interview, to determine whether the achievement of a vocational goal is reasonably feasible.

If the VA, based on the evaluation, determines that the achievement of a vocational goal by a veteran is reasonably feasible, the veteran shall be offered, and may elect to pursue a vocational training program.

If the veteran elects to pursue such a program, the program shall be designed in consultation with the veteran in order to meet the veteran's individual needs, and shall be set forth in an individualized written plan of vocational rehabilitation.

A vocational training program under this section:

- May not exceed 24 months unless, based on a determination by the VA that an extension is necessary in order for the veteran to achieve a vocational goal identified in the written plan formulated for the veteran, the VA grants an extension for a period not to exceed 24 months.
- May not include the provision of any loan or subsistence allowance, or any automobile adaptive equipment.
- May include a program of education at an institution of higher learning, only in a case in which the Secretary of the VA determines that the program involved is predominantly vocational in content.

When a veteran completes a vocational training program, the VA may provide the veteran with counseling, placement and post-placement services for a period not to exceed 18 months.

A veteran may not begin pursuit of a vocational training program under this chapter after the later of:

- December 31, 1995; or
- The end of a reasonable period of time, as determined by the VA, following either the evaluation of the veteran or the award of pension to the veteran.

In the case of a veteran who has been determined to have a permanent and total non-service-connected disability and who, not later than one year after the date the veteran's eligibility for counseling under this chapter expires, secures employment within the scope of a vocational goal identified in the veteran's individualized written plan of vocational rehabilitation (or in a related field which requires reasonably developed skills, and the use of some or all of the training or services furnished the veteran under such plan), the evaluation of the veteran as having a permanent and total disability may not be terminated be reason of the veteran's capacity to engage in such employment until the veteran first maintains such employment for a period of not less than 12 consecutive months.

PROTECTION OF HEALTHCARE ELIGIBILITY

In the case of a veteran whose entitlement to pension is terminated after January 31, 1985, by reason of income from work or training, the veteran shall retain for a period of three years, beginning on the date of such termination, all eligibility for care and services that the veteran would have had if the veteran's entitlement to pension had not been terminated.

DISAPPEARANCE

When a veteran receiving a non-service-connected disability pension from the VA disappears, the VA may pay the pension otherwise payable to such veteran's spouse and children. Payments made to a spouse or child shall not exceed the amount to which each would be entitled if the veteran died of a non-service-connected disability.

CHAPTER 5

SURVIVOR BENEFITS: DEPENDENCY AND INDEMNITY COMPENSATION FOR SERVICE-CONNECTED DEATHS

Dependency and Indemnity Compensation (DIC) payments may be available for:

- Surviving spouses who have not remarried
- Surviving spouses who remarry after attaining age 57
- Unmarried Children under 18;
- Helpless children;
- Children between 18 and 23, if attending a VA-approved school; and
- Low-income parents of deceased servicemembers or veterans.

DEFINITIONS

The following definitions apply only to CHAPTER 6 - DEPENDENCY AND INDEMNITY COMPENSATION FOR SERVICE-CONNECTED DEATHS:

Veteran: in this chapter, the term includes a person who died in the active military, naval, or air service.

Social Security Increase: in this chapter, the term means the percentage by which benefit amounts payable under Title II of the Social Security Act (42 U.S.C. 401 et seq.) are increased for any fiscal year as a result of a determination under section 215(i) of such Act (42 U.S.C. 415(i)).

Permanently Housebound: for the purposes of this chapter, the requirement of "permanently housebound" will be considered to have been met when the individual is substantially confined to such individual's house (ward or clinical areas, if institutionalized) or immediate premises due to a disability or disabilities, which it is reasonably certain will remain throughout such individual's lifetime.

ELIGIBILITY

To receive Dependency and Indemnity Compensation (DIC), an individual must be an eligible survivor of a veteran who died from:

- A disease or injury incurred or aggravated while on active duty or active duty for training; or
- An injury incurred or aggravated in the line of duty while on inactive duty training; or
- A disability compensable by VA.
- The death cannot be a result of the veteran's willful misconduct.

DIC also may be authorized for survivors of veterans who at the time of death, were determined to be totally disabled as a result of military service, even though their service-connected disabilities did not cause their deaths. The survivor qualifies if:

- The veteran was continuously rated totally disabled for a period of 10 or more years immediately preceding death; or
- The veteran was so rated for a period of at least five years from the date of military discharge; or
- The veteran was a former prisoner of war who died after Sept. 30, 1999, and who was continuously rated totally disabled for a period of at least one year immediately preceding death.

To qualify as an eligible survivor, an individual must have proof of the following:

- Proof that he or she was married to the veteran for at least 1 year (Note: If a child was born, there is no time requirement); AND
- Proof that the marriage was VALID; AND
- Proof that he or she lived with the veteran continuously until his/her death or, if separated, the surviving spouse wasn't at fault; AND
- Proof that he or she did not remarry. (Note: The remarriage of the surviving spouse of a veteran shall not bar the furnishing of DIC if the remarriage is terminated by death, divorce, or annulment, unless the VA determines that the divorce or annulment was secured through fraud or collusion.)
- *Public Law 108-183, The Veterans Benefits Act of 2003*, restored DIC eligibility, effective January 1, 2004, for surviving spouses who remarry after age 57. Qualifying spouses who remarried at age 57 or older prior to enactment of this

bill had until December 16, 2004 to apply for reinstatement of these benefits. No retroactive benefits will be paid for any period prior to January 1, 2004.

OR

- The individual is an unmarried child of a deceased veteran; AND
- The individual is under age 18, or between the ages of 18 and 23 and attending school.

Note: Certain helpless adult children and some parents of deceased veterans are entitled to DIC. Call VA at (800) 827-1000 for the eligibility requirements for these survivors.

AMOUNT OF DIC PAYMENTS TO SURVIVING SPOUSES

- Surviving spouses of veterans who died after January 1, 1993, receive a basic monthly rate of **$1,254.19 (effective December 1, 2014)**
- Surviving spouses entitled to DIC based on the veteran's death prior to January 1, 1993, receive the greater of:
    - The basic monthly rate of **$1,254.19.00, or**
    - An amount based on the veteran's pay grade. (See following sections for Pay Grade tables and Determination of Pay Grade.)

There are additional DIC payments for dependent children. (Refer to the following charts.)

ADDITIONAL ALLOWANCES FOR SURVIVING SPOUSES

- Add **$266.32** to the basic monthly rate if, at the time of the veteran's death, the veteran was in receipt of, or entitled to receive compensation for a service-connected disability rated totally disabling (including a rating based on individual unemployability) for a continuous period of at least 8 years immediately preceding death AND the surviving spouse was married to the veteran for those same 8 years.
- Add **$310.71** per child to the basic monthly rate for each dependent child under age 18.
- If the surviving spouse is entitled to Aid & Attendance, add **$310.71** to the basic monthly rate.
- If the surviving spouse is Permanently Housebound, add **$145.55** to the basic monthly rate

**The above figures and below tables weren't available from the VA at time of publication, so figures are based on the estimates of Veterans Information Service. If there is a discrepancy, always follow information provided by the VA.

SURVIVING SPOUSE DIC RATES IF VETERAN'S DEATH WAS PRIOR TO JANUARY 1, 1993-RATES EFFECTIVE DECEMBER 1, 2014			
PAY GRADE	Monthly Rate	Pay Grade	Monthly Rate
E-1*:	$1254.19	W-4**:	$1499.87
E-2*:	$1259.19	O-1**:	$1324.39
E-3* (see footnote #1):	1254.19	O-2**:	$1369.81
E-4*:	$1254.19	O-3**:	$1463.75
E-5*:	$1259.19	O-4:	$1551.48
E-6*:	$1259.19	O-5:	$1707.35
E-7**:	$1297.55	O-6:	$1925.16
E-8**:	$1369.81	O-7:	$2043.20
E-9** (see footnote #2):	$1428.64 or 1516.41	O-8:	$2282.32
W-1**:	$1324.39	O-9:	$2441.29
W-2**:	$1377.03	O-10 (see footnote #3):	$2873.80 or 2677.67
W-3**:	$1417.29		

Footnotes to Table:
* Add $266.32 if veteran rated totally disabled 8 continuous years prior to death, and surviving spouse was married to veteran those same 8 years.
1. A surviving spouse of an Aviation Cadet or other service not covered by this table is paid the DIC rate for enlisted E-3 under 34.
2. $1516.41 is for a veteran who served as Sergeant Major of the Army or Marine Corps, Senior Enlisted Advisor of the Navy, Chief Master Sergeant of the Air Force, or Master Chief Petty Officer of the Coast Guard.
3. $2873.80 is for a veteran who served as Chairman of the Joint Chiefs of Staff, Chief of Staff of the Army or Air Force, Chief of Naval Operations, or Commandant of the Marine Corps.

DETERMINATION OF PAY GRADE

With respect to a veteran who died in the active military, naval, or air service, such veteran's pay grade shall be determined as of the date of such veteran's death, or as of the date of a promotion after death, while in a missing status.

With respect to a veteran who did not die in the active military, naval, or air service, such veteran's pay grade shall be determined as of:

- The time of such veteran's last discharge or release from active duty under conditions other than dishonorable; or
- The time of such veteran's discharge or release from any period of active duty for training or inactive duty training, if such veteran's death results from service-connected disability incurred during such period, and if such veteran was not thereafter discharged or released under conditions other than dishonorable from active duty.

If a veteran has satisfactorily served on active duty for a period of six months or more in a pay grade higher than that specified in the previous paragraphs of this section, and any subsequent discharge or release from active duty was under conditions other than dishonorable, the higher pay grade shall be used if it will result in greater monthly payments to such veteran's surviving spouse under this chapter. The determination as to whether an individual has served satisfactorily for the required period in a higher pay grade shall be made by the Secretary of the department in which such higher pay grade was held.

The pay grade of any person not otherwise described in this section, but who had a compensable status on the date of such person's death under laws administered by the Secretary, shall be determined by the head of the department under which such person performed the services by which such person obtained such status.

DIC PAYMENTS TO CHILDREN

Whenever there is no surviving spouse of a deceased veteran entitled to DIC, DIC shall be paid in equal shares to the children of the deceased veteran at the following monthly rates (effective December 1, 2014):

Number of Children	Total Payable (to be divided in equal shares):
1	$529.55
2	$761.80
3	$994.06
4	$1182.96
5	$1371.87
6	$1560.77

- If DIC is payable monthly to a person as a surviving spouse, and there is a child (of such person's deceased spouse) who has attained the age of 18, and who, while under such age, became permanently incapable of self-support, DIC shall be paid monthly to each such child, concurrently with the payment of DIC to the surviving spouse, in the amount of **$529.55**.

- If DIC is payable monthly to a person as a surviving spouse, and there is a child (of such person's deceased spouse) who has attained the age of 18 and who, while under the age of 23, is pursuing a course of instruction at a VA-approved educational institution, DIC shall be paid monthly to each such child, concurrently with the payment of DIC to the surviving spouse, in the amount of **$263.23.**

DIC PAYMENTS FOR PARENTS

Parents whose child died in-service or from a service-connected disability may be entitled to DIC if they are in financial need. Parents may be biological, step, adopted, or *in loco parentis.*

The monthly payment for parents of deceased veterans depends upon their income. The following 3 charts outline the monthly rates payable, **effective December 1, 2014,** under various conditions.

****The below tables weren't available from the VA at time of publication, so figures are based on the estimates of Veterans Information Service. If there is a discrepancy, always follow information provided by the VA.**

Chart #1 Sole Surviving Parent Unremarried orRemarried Living With Spouse

Income Not Over:	*Monthly Rate:*	*Income Not Over:*	*Monthly Rate:*
$ 800	$ 621	$ 2,500	$ 483
900	613	2,600	475
1,000	605	2,700	467
1,100	597	2,800	459
1,200	588	2,900	451
1,300	581	3,000	437
1,400	573	3,100	434
1,500	564	3,200	426
1,600	556	3,300	418
1,700	548	3,400	410
1,800	540	3,500	402
1,900	532	3,600	394
2,000	524	3,700	385
2,100	516	3,800	377
2,200	507	3,900	369
2,300	499	4,000	361
2,400	491	4,100	353

Income Not Over:	Monthly Rate:	Income Not Over:	Monthly Rate:
$4,200	$345	$6,300	$174
4,300	337	6,400	166
4,400	328	6,500	158
4,500	320	6,600	150
4,600	312	6,700	141
4,700	304	6,800	133
4,800	296	6,900	125
4,900	288	7,000	117
5,000	280	7,100	109
5,100	272	7,200	101
5,200	263	7,300	93
5,300	255	7,400	84
5,400	247	7,500	76
5,500	239	7,600	68
5,600	231	7,700	60
5,700	223	7,800	52
5,800	215	7,900	44
5,900	206		
6,000	198	*If A&A add:*	337
6,100	190	*If living w/ spouse:19,673*	
6,200	182	***If not living w/ spouse: 14,636*	

Chart #2 - One of Two Parents Not Living With Spouse

Income Not Over:	Monthly Rate:	Income Not Over:	Monthly Rate:
$ 800	$ 450	$3,600	$ 226
900	443	3,700	218
1,000	436	3,800	210
1,100	429	3,900	201
1,200	421	4,000	193
1,300	413	4,100	185
1,400	405	4,200	177
1,500	397	4,300	169
1,600	388	4,400	161
1,700	380	4,500	153
1,800	372	4,600	144
1,900	364	4,700	136
2,000	356	4,800	128
2,100	348	4,900	120
2,200	340	5,000	112
2,300	332	5,100	104
2,400	323	5,200	96
2,500	315	5,300	89
2,600	307	5,400	79
2,700	299	5,500	71
2,800	291	5,600	63
2,900	283	5,700	55
3,000	275	5,800	47
3,100	266	5,900	39
3,200	258	6,000	30.51
3,300	250	6,313- 14,391	5
3,400	242		
3,500	234	*If A&A add:*	$337

Chart #3-1 of 2 Parents Living with Spouse or Other Parent

Income Not Over:	*Monthly Rate:*	*Income Not Over:*	*Monthly Rate:*
$1,000	$422	$4,000	$248
1,100	419	4,100	240
1,200	416	4,200	232
1,300	413	4,300	224
1,400	410	4,400	216
1,500	407	4,500	207
1,600	403	4,600	199
1,700	399	4,700	191
1,800	395	4,800	183
1,900	391	4,900	175
2,000	385	5,000	167
2,100	380	5,100	159
2,200	375	5,200	151
2,300	369	5,300	142
2,400	365	5,400	134
2,500	359	5,500	126
2,600	353	5,600	118
2,700	347	5,700	110
2,800	341	5,800	102
2,900	335	5,900	94
3,000	327	6,000	85
3,100	320	6,100	77
3,200	313	6,200	69
3,300	305	6,300	61
3,400	297	6,400	53
3,500	289	6,500	45
3,600	281	6,600	37
3,700	273	6,800	20
3,800	264	6,900	12
3,900	256	*If A&A add:*	337

MISCELLANEOUS INFORMATION REGARDING INCOME LIMITATIONS FOR PARENTS

The VA may require, as a condition of granting or continuing DIC to a parent that such parent, other than one who has attained 72 years of age, and has been paid DIC during 2 consecutive calendar years, file for a calendar year with the VA, a report showing the total income which such parent expects to receive in that year, and the total income which such parent received in the preceding year. The parent or parents shall notify the VA whenever there is a material change in annual income.

In determining income under this section, all payments of any kind, or from any source shall be included except:

- Payments of a death gratuity;
- Donations from public or private relief or welfare organizations;
- Payments under this chapter (DIC), Chapter 11 of *Title 38, United States Code* (Disability Compensation), and *Chapter 15 of Title 38, United States Code* (Non-Service Connected Disability/Death Pension);
- Payments under policies of servicemembers group life insurance, United States Government life insurance, or national service life insurance, and payments of servicemen's indemnity;
- 10% of the amount of payments to an individual under public or private retirement, annuity, endowment, or similar plans or programs;
- Amounts equal to amounts paid by a parent of a deceased veteran for:
- A deceased spouse's just debts;
- The expenses of the spouse's last illness, to the extent such expenses are not reimbursed under Chapter 51 of Title 38 of the United States Code;
- The expenses of the spouse's burial to the extent that such expenses are not reimbursed under Chapter 23 or Chapter 51 of *Title 38 of the United States Code*;
- Reimbursements of any kind for any casualty loss (as defined in regulations which the VA shall prescribe), but the amount excluded under this clause may not exceed the greater of the fair market value or the reasonable replacement value of the property involved at the time immediately preceding the loss;
- Amounts equal to amounts paid by a parent of a deceased veteran for:
- The expenses of the veteran's last illness, and
- expenses of such veteran's burial, to the extent that such expenses are not reimbursed under Chapter 23 of *Title 38 of the United States Code*;
- Profit realized from the disposition of real or personal property other than in the course of a business;
- Payments received for discharge of jury duty or obligatory civic duties;
- Payments of annuities elected under Subchapter I of Chapter 73 of *Title 10*.

Where a fraction of a dollar is involved, annual income shall be fixed at the next lower dollar.

The VA may provide by regulation for the exclusion from income under this section of amounts paid by a parent for unusual medical expenses.

SPECIAL PROVISIONS RELATING TO SURVIVING SPOUSES

No Dependency and Indemnity Compensation shall be paid to the surviving spouse of a veteran dying after December 31, 1956, unless such surviving spouse was married to such veteran:

- Before the expiration of 15 years after the termination of the period of service in which the injury or disease causing the death of the veteran was incurred or aggravated; or
- For one year or more; or
- For any period of time if a child was born of the marriage, or was born to them before the marriage.

APPLYING FOR DEPENDENCY AND INDEMNITY COMPENSATION

Eligible surviving spouses and dependent children can apply for DIC by completing VA Form 21-534, "Application for Dependency and Indemnity Compensation or Death Pension by Surviving Spouse or Child". If available, copies of dependency records (marriage records, divorce records, & children's birth certificates) should be attached to the application. A copy of the veteran's DD Form 214 and a copy of the veteran's death certificate should also be included with the completed application.

Note:
If any of the pertinent supporting evidence is not immediately available, the applicant should send in the application anyway. The date VA receives the application is important! If VA approves the claim, benefit payments usually begin from the date the application is received, regardless of when the claim is approved.

The completed form should be sent to the applicable VA Regional Office (refer to Chapter 36 for a listing of all VA regional offices.)

CHAPTER 6

SURVIVOR BENEFITS: DEATH PENSIONS

A Death Pension is a benefit paid to eligible dependents of deceased wartime veterans.

DEFINITIONS

Veteran: as used in this chapter, includes a person who has completed at least 2 years of honorable active military, naval, or air service, as certified by the appropriate authority, but whose death in such service was not in line of duty.

Indian Wars: means the campaigns, engagements, and expeditions of the United States military forces against Indian tribes or nations, service in which has been recognized heretofore as pensionable service.

World War I: means the period April 6, 1917, through November 11, 1918. In the case of a veteran who served with the United States military forces in Russia, the ending date is April 1, 1920. Service after November 11, 1918 and before July 2, 1921 is considered World War I for compensation or pension purposes, if the veteran served in the active military, naval, or air service after April 5, 1917 and before November 12, 1918.

Civil War Veteran: includes a person who served in the military or naval forces of the Confederate States of America during the Civil War, and the term "active military or naval service" includes active service in those forces.

Period of War: means the Mexican border period, World War I, World War II, the Korean conflict, the Vietnam era, the Persian Gulf War, and the period beginning on the date of any future declaration of war by the Congress and ending on the date prescribed by Presidential proclamation or concurrent resolution of the Congress.

Regular Aid and Attendance: for the purposes of this chapter, a person shall be considered to be in need of regular aid and attendance if such person is:

- A patient in a nursing home; or
- Helpless or blind, or so nearly helpless or blind as to need or require the aid and attendance of another person.

Permanently Housebound: for the purposes of this chapter, the requirement of "permanently housebound" will be considered to have been met when the surviving spouse is substantially confined to such surviving spouse's house (ward or clinical areas, if institutionalized) or immediate premises due to a disability or disabilities, which it is reasonably certain will remain throughout such surviving spouse's lifetime.

ELIGIBILITY REQUIREMENTS

Eligible dependents may qualify for a Death Pension if:

- The deceased veteran was discharged from service under other than dishonorable conditions; **AND**
- He or she served 90 days or more of active duty with at least 1 day during a war, or must have had a service-connected disability justifying discharge for disability. If the veteran died in service but not in the line of duty, pension may be payable if the veteran had completed at least two years of honorable service; **AND**
- The dependent is the surviving spouse (spouse must not have remarried), or the unmarried child of the deceased veteran (children must be under age 18, or under age 23 if attending a VA-approved school); **AND**
- The dependent's countable income is below an annual limit set by law (See below for 2012 annual income limitations.)

(Children who become incapable of self-support because of a disability before age 18 may be eligible for a pension as long as the condition exists, unless the child marries or the child's income exceeds the applicable limit.)

ADDITIONAL REQUIREMENTS

No Death Pension shall be paid under this chapter to a surviving spouse of a veteran unless the spouse was married to the veteran:

Before:

- December 14, 1944, in the case of a surviving spouse of a Mexican Border period or World War I veteran; or
- January 1, 1957 in the case of a surviving spouse of a World War II veteran; or
- February 1, 1965, in the case of a surviving spouse of a Korean conflict veteran; or

- May 8, 1985, in the case of a surviving spouse of a Vietnam era veteran, or
- January 1, 2001, in the case of a surviving spouse of a veteran of the Persian Gulf War;
- For one year or more; or
- For any period of time if a child was born of the marriage, or was born to them before the marriage.

ANNUAL INCOME LIMITATIONS

DEATH PENSION RATE TABLE FOR SURVIVING SPOUSES & CHILDREN-RATES EFFECTIVE DECEMBER 1, 2014	
Maximum Annual Pension Rate (MAPR) Category	Annual Income Must Be Less Than:
Surviving Spouse Alone (No Dependent Child):	$8,629
Surviving Spouse With One Dependent Child:	11,296
Child Alone:	2,198
Housebound Spouse Without Dependents:	10,547
Housebound Spouse With One Dependent:	13,209
Surviving Spouse In Need Of Aid And Attendance (No Dependent Child):	13,794
Surviving Spouse In Need Of Aid And Attendance With One Dependent Child:	16,455
For Each Additional Child:	2,198
Child Earned Income Exclusion Effective 1/1/2014:	10,150

MAXIMUM ANNUAL INCOME LIMITATIONS FOR PROTECTED PENSIONS

EFFECTIVE DECEMBER 1, 2014

Pensioners entitled to benefits as of December 31, 1978, who do not elect to receive a pension under the Improved Pension Program, may continue to receive pension benefits at the rates they were entitled to receive on December 31, 1978 or June 30, 1960, as long as they remain permanently and totally disabled, do not lose a dependent, and their income does not exceed the income limitation, adjusted annually.

PENSION LAW IN EFFECT ON DECEMBER 31, 1978 (SECTION 306):

THE RATE ENTITLED TO ON DECEMBER 31, 1978 MAY BE CONTINUED IF THE RECIPIENT'S-IVAP FOR 2014 IS BELOW THE FOLLOWING LIMITS:

STATUS OF RECIPIENT:		ANNUAL INCOME LIMITATION:
Surviving spouse with no dependents	$	14,635
Surviving spouse with one or more dependents		19,672
Child (no entitled veteran or surviving spouse)		11,965

PENSION LAW IN EFFECT ON JUNE 30, 1960 (OLD LAW):

THE RATE ENTITLED TO ON JUNE 30, 1960 MAY BE CONTINUED IF THE RECIPIENT'S IVAP FOR 2011 IS BELOW THE FOLLOWING LIMITS:

STATUS OF RECIPIENT:		ANNUAL INCOME LIMITATION:
Surviving spouse with no dependents		12,814
Surviving spouse with one or more dependents		18,470
Child only (no entitled veteran or surviving spouse)		12,814

Note: Some income is not counted toward the yearly limit (for example, welfare benefits, some wages earned by dependent children, and Supplemental Security Income).

In determining the annual income of a surviving spouse, if there is a child of the veteran in the custody of the surviving spouse, that portion of the annual income of the child that is reasonably available to or for the surviving spouse shall be considered to be income of the surviving spouse, unless in the judgment of the VA, to do so would work a hardship on the surviving spouse.

****The above tables weren't available from the VA at time of publication, so figures are based on the estimates of Veterans Information Service. If there is a discrepancy, always follow information provided by the VA.**

NET WORTH LIMITATION

The VA shall deny or discontinue payment of pension to a surviving spouse when the corpus of the estate of the surviving spouse is such that under all the circumstances, including consideration of the income of the surviving spouse and the income of any child from whom the surviving spouse is receiving increased pension, it is reasonable that some part of the corpus of such estate be consumed for the surviving spouse's maintenance.

The VA shall deny or discontinue the payment of increased pension on account of a child when the corpus of such child's estate is such that under all the circumstances, including consideration of the income of the surviving spouse and such child and the income of any other child for whom the surviving spouse is receiving increased pension, it is reasonable that some part of the corpus of the child's estate be consumed for the child's maintenance. During the period such denial or discontinuance remains in effect, such child shall not be considered as the surviving spouse's child for purposes of this chapter.

The VA shall deny or discontinue payment of pension to a child when the corpus of the state of the child is such that under all the circumstances, including consideration of the income of the child, the income of any person with whom such child is residing who is legally responsible for such child's support, and the corpus of the estate of such person, it is reasonable that some part of the corpus of such estate be consumed for the child's maintenance.

APPLYING FOR DEATH PENSION BENEFITS

> ***Special Note:*** *If any of the pertinent supporting evidence is not immediately available, the applicant should send in the application anyway. The date VA receives the application is important! If VA approves the claim, benefit payments usually begin from the date the application is received, regardless of when the claim is approved*

Eligible surviving spouses and dependent children can apply for Death Pension benefits by completing VA Form 21-534, "Application for Dependency and Indemnity Compensation or Death Pension by Surviving Spouse or Child". If available, copies of dependency records (marriage & children's birth certificates) should be attached to the application. A copy of the veteran's DD Form 214 and a copy of the veteran's death certificate should also be included with the completed application.

The completed forms should be sent to the applicable VA Regional Office. (Refer to Chapter 36 for a listing of all VA regional offices.)

CHAPTER 7

SURVIVOR BENEFITS: MISCELLANEOUS BENEFITS FOR SURVIVING SPOUSES AND CHILDREN

SURVIVOR BENEFIT PLAN (SBP)

The Survivor Benefit Plan (SBP) was established by Congress effective September 21, 1972 (*Public Law 92-425*) to provide a monthly income to survivors of retired military personnel upon the member's death when retired pay stops. Survivors of members who die while on active duty, and survivors of members recalled to active duty from retirement who die while on active duty may also be protected by the SBP.

The SBP is free for active duty service members with 20 years of qualifying service. The SBP for retirees is paid for by premium payments from a retiree's paycheck. There is a tax break for the retiree in that the amount of the SBP premium is not included in the taxable portion of his or her retired pay.

> *The SBP annuity is protected from inflation, so in 2014 the premiums and annuity payments were adjusted to reflect the 1.7% COLA increase.*

At retirement, full basic SBP for spouse and children will take effect *automatically* if you make no other valid election. You may not reduce or decline spouse coverage without your spouse's written consent. This means you will have to have your spouse's input in the decision and his or her signature is required. You may choose coverage for a former spouse or, if you have no spouse or children, you may be able to cover an "insurable interest" (such as, a business partner or parent).

If you elect to participate in the SBP you will be required to pay a monthly premium. SBP Premiums and benefits are based on the "base amount" or benefit level that you elect.

Your base amount can be any amount from full coverage down to as little as $300 a month. Full coverage is based on your full retired pay meaning your spouse will receive **55%** of your retirement pay. If you select lesser coverage then your spouse will receive 55% percent of your elected "base amount."

Note: A surviving spouse's SBP annuity is reduced when they reach age 62 and become eligible for Social Security. This is called the Social Security offset. In the past the offset reduced the SBP annuity to 35 percent of the base amount. The offset created a need for members to purchase a Supplemental Survivor Benefit Plan (SSBP) policy. Fortunately the *National Defense Authorization Act of 2005* established a phase out of the offset by 2008, thus eliminating the need for the SSBP. Details of the *National Defense Authorization Act of 2005* are described below.

PHASED-IN INCREASE IN BASIC ANNUITY

One major provision of the Ronald W. Reagan FY2005 *National Defense Authorization Act* included an increase in the minimum SBP annuity for survivors age 62 and older from 35% to 55% over a 3-year period.

The FY 2005 *Defense Authorization Act* included provisions to eliminate the social security offset under SBP by increasing the annuities paid to survivors of military retirees who are 62 or older from 35 percent of retired pay to the percentages indicated below:

- For months after September 2005 and before April 2006: 40%
- For months after March 2006 and before April 2007: 45%
- For months after March 2007 and before April 2008: 50%
- For months after March 2008: 55%

Note: *Public Law 108-183, The Veterans Benefits Act of 2003* provided that, for surviving spouses who remarry after attaining age 57, Dependency and Indemnity Compensation (DIC) be paid with no reduction of certain other Federal benefits to which a surviving spouse might be entitled. This provision, in essence eliminates the requirement for DIC to offset military SBP annuities, as was required under prior law. In other words, concurrent receipt of DIC and SBP without an offset of either is now allowed for surviving spouses who remarry after attaining age 57.

SPECIAL SURVIVOR INDEMNITY ALLOWANCE (SSIA)

Section 644 of the *National Defense Authorization Act (NDAA) for Fiscal Year 2008* created the Special Survivor Indemnity Allowance (SSIA). This allowance is payable to all Survivor Benefit Plan (SBP) annuitants whose annuity has been offset for receipt of Dependency and Indemnity Compensation (DIC) from the Department of Veterans Affairs (DVA). This allowance becomes payable for the month of October 2008 in the monthly amount of $50. This amount will be increased as per the following schedule:

October 2008	**$50**
October 2009	**$60**
October 2010	**$70**
October 2011	**$80**
October 2012	**$90**
October 2013	**$100**

The payment remains at $100 from October 2013, until March 1, 2016, when this allowance is currently scheduled to terminate.

This allowance is taxable. Your DIC payment address will be used for your SSIA payment. If you are currently receiving your DIC payment from the DVA at your home address, your SSIA payment will also be sent there. If your DIC payment is paid via electronic funds transfer (EFT) by the DVA, your DIC electronic payment address will be used for the SSIA payment.

Questions concerning this allowance may be directed to the Cleveland Center at 1-800-321-1080, between 7 a.m. and 7:30 p.m., Eastern Time, Monday through Friday, or write to Defense Finance and Accounting Service, U.S. Military Annuitant Pay, P.O. Box 7131, London, KY 40742-7131.

SURVIVOR BENEFIT PLAN – MINIMUM INCOME ANNUITY

Effective December 1, 2014, the SBP-MIW annuity limitation is $8,629.

Eligible surviving spouses of military retirees who did not participate in the plan, and who died prior to September 21, 1973 are eligible for SBP-MIW (Survivor Benefit Plan - Minimum Income Annuity). To be eligible the surviving spouse must not be remarried, must be eligible for VA death pension, and must have income for VA purposes, excluding any SBP annuity, of less than the MIW-SBP annuity limitation. Effective December 1, 2014, the SBP-MIW annuity limitation is $8,629.

BENEFITS FOR CHILDREN OF WOMEN VIETNAM VETERANS BORN WITH CERTAIN BIRTH DEFECTS

Section 401 of *P.L. 106-416*, which became law on November 1, 2000 directed the Secretary of VA to identify birth defects of children of female Vietnam veterans that: (1) are associated with service during the Vietnam era; and (2) result in the permanent physical or mental disability of such children. The law excludes from such defects familial or birth-related defects or injuries. The law further directs the Secretary to provide to such children necessary health care to address the defect and any associated disability. It authorizes the Secretary to provide vocational training to such a child if the achievement of a vocational goal is reasonably feasible.

The law also directs the Secretary to pay a monthly allowance to such a child, the amount to be determined through a schedule rating the various defects and disabilities and their degrees. The receipt of such allowance shall not infringe upon the right to receive any other benefit to which the individual is entitled. Such allowance shall not be considered income for purposes of other veterans' benefits for which income limitations exist. In the case of an eligible child whose only covered birth defect is spina bifida, a monetary allowance shall be paid under these provisions only. An eligible individual shall be provided only one program of vocational training.

The monthly allowance is set at four levels, depending upon the degree of disability suffered by the child.

CHILDREN OF WOMEN VIETNAM VETERANS BORN WITH CERTAIN BIRTH DEFECTS (P.L 106-419)-RATES EFFECTIVE 12-01-2014	
Disability Level	**Monthly Allowance**
Level I	$145.00
Level II	$314.00
Level III	$1072.00
Level IV	$1827.00

CHAPTER 8

BURIAL AND MEMORIAL BENEFITS

DIGNIFIED BURIAL OF UNCLAIMED VETERANS ACT

On December 30, 2012 the Dignified Burial of Unclaimed Veterans Act of 2012 was sent the President for signature into law. The new law will contain the following provisions:

Cemetery Matters: The bill authorizes the Secretary of Veterans Affairs (VA) to furnish a casket or urn for a deceased veteran with no known living kin.

Veterans Freedom of Conscience Protection: Under the bill, in cases where family or the next of kin of a deceased veteran can be identified, the bill requires the VA to ensure that the expressed wishes of the next of kin are met with regards to memorial service, funeral or interment at a national cemetery.

Improved Communication Between Department of Veterans Affairs And Medical Examiners and Funeral Directors: The bill requires the VA to obtain information from the relevant medical examiner, funeral director, service group or other entity regarding the steps taken to determine if the deceased has no next of kin.

Identification and Burial of Unclaimed or Abandoned Human Remains: The VA will be required to cooperate with veterans service organizations to assist entities in possession of unclaimed or abandoned remains of veterans, with the department authorized to determine whether such remains are eligible for burial in a national cemetery.

Restoration, Operation and Maintenance of Clark Veterans Cemetery by American Battle Monuments Commission: The bill authorizes the appropriation of $5 million for site preparation and construction at the Clark Veterans Cemetery located in the Philippines. The bill directs the American Battle Monuments Commission to restore and operate the cemetery once a cooperative agreement is reached with the government of the Philippines.

REIMBURSEMENT OF BURIAL EXPENSES

The Veterans Benefits Administration administers a burial benefits program designed to assist claimants in meeting the funeral and burial costs of a deceased veteran. The type and amount of benefits payable depends on the veteran's individual service record and cause of death.

SERVICE-CONNECTED DEATH

If a veteran's death is service-connected, the VA will pay a burial allowance of up to $2,000 (*for deaths on or after 9-11-2001 - prior to 9-11-2001, the burial allowance was $1,500*). If the veteran is buried in a VA national cemetery, some or all of the cost of moving the deceased to the national cemetery nearest the veteran's home may also be reimbursed. There is no time limit for applying for a service-connected burial allowance. The person who bore the veteran's burial expense may claim reimbursement from any VA regional office.

NON-SERVICE CONNECTED DEATH

If a veteran's death is not service-connected, there are two types of payments the VA may make:

BURIAL AND FUNERAL EXPENSE ALLOWANCE

For deaths on or after October 1, 2011, VA will pay up to $700 toward burial and funeral expenses (***if hospitalized by VA at time of death***), or $300 toward burial and funeral expenses (***if not hospitalized by VA at time of death***), and a $700.00 plot-interment allowance (if not buried in a national cemetery).

For deaths on or after December 1, 2001, but before October 1, 2011, VA will pay up to $300 toward burial and funeral expenses and a $300 plot-interment allowance. The plot interment allowance is $150 for deaths prior to December 1, 2001. If the death happened while the veteran was in a VA hospital or under VA contracted nursing home care, some or all of the costs for transporting the Veteran's remains may be reimbursed.

An annual increase in burial and plot allowances, for deaths occurring after October 1, 2011, begins in fiscal year 2013 based on the Consumer Price Index for the preceding 12-month period.

You may be eligible for a VA burial allowance if:

You paid for a Veteran's burial or funeral, *AND*

You have not been reimbursed by another government agency or some other source, such as the deceased veteran's employer, *AND*

The Veteran was discharged under conditions other than dishonorable.

IN ADDITION, AT LEAST ONE OF THE FOLLOWING CONDITIONS MUST BE MET:

- The veteran was in receipt of VA pension or compensation at the time of death; or
- The veteran was, at the time of death, receiving military retired pay in lieu of compensation; or
- The veteran, at the time of death, had an original or reopened claim pending, and had been found entitled to compensation or pension from a date prior to the date of death; or
- The veteran's death occurred in a VA facility; or
- The veteran died while traveling, under proper authorization and at VA expense, to or from a specified place for the purpose of examination, treatment, or care; or
- The veteran died on or after October 9, 1996, while a patient at an approved State nursing home or while residing in a VA-approved State nursing home, is transferred to a non-VA facility for acute medical care, and then dies at that location. (Contact a VA regional office for a complete listing of approved State nursing homes.); or
- The veteran's remains are being held by a State or political subdivision of a State, there is no next of kin or other person claiming the body and the veteran's estate does not have enough resources to cover the cost of the funeral and burial, and the veteran served during wartime or was released from active service for a disability incurred or aggravated in the line of duty.

PAYMENT MAY BE MADE TO:

- The creditor who provided services or furnished merchandise in connection with burial, funeral, transportation, plot or interment; or
- The person or persons whose personal funds were used to pay such expenses; or
- The representative of the estate of the deceased veteran or claimant when the estate funds were used to pay the expenses or the veteran or claimant prepaid them.

PLOT ALLOWANCE

If a veteran is not buried in a cemetery that is under U.S. government jurisdiction, the VA may also pay a plot allowance of $700 (for deaths on or after 12/1/2001 - prior to 12/1/2001, the plot allowance was $150), provided that the veteran was discharged under conditions other than dishonorable; and:

- The veteran was discharged from active duty because of a disability incurred or aggravated in the line of duty; or

- The veteran was receiving VA pension or compensation at the time of death, or would have been entitled to receive VA pension or compensation, but for receipt of military retirement or disability pay; or
- The veteran died in a VA facility.

The plot allowance may be paid to the state if a veteran is buried without charge for the cost of a plot or interment in a state-owned cemetery reserved solely for veteran burials. Burial expenses paid by the deceased veteran's employer or a state agency will not be reimbursed.

Reimbursement of Transportation Costs

The costs of transporting a veteran's body to the place of burial may be authorized if a veteran's death occurs while:

- In route for a VA authorized examination, treatment or care; or
- The veteran is properly hospitalized at an approved medical center domiciliary; or
- The veteran is in a nursing home under the direct jurisdiction of the VA; or if the veteran's death occurred on or after October 9, 1996, while a patient at an approved State nursing home; or
- The costs of transporting the veteran's body to the place of burial may also be authorized if the veteran is buried in a national cemetery, and died of a service-connected condition. If burial is not in the national cemetery nearest the veteran's last place of residence, the total reimbursement will not be more than the amount which would have been payable for burial in the nearest national cemetery.

Filing Claim for Reimbursement of Expenses

Reimbursement of burial expenses may be applied for by submitting VA Form 21-530, "Application for Burial Allowance." A certified copy of the death certificate, proof of the veteran's military service (Form DD-214), and itemized bills of the funeral and burial expenses must be submitted by the person(s) filing the claim(s).

The itemized bills must clearly show the name of the veteran for whom services were performed, the nature and cost of the service rendered, all credits, and the name(s) of the person or persons by whom payment in whole or in part was made.

The itemized bills must clearly show the name of the veteran for whom services were performed, the nature and cost of the service rendered, all credits, and the name(s) of the person or persons by whom payment in whole or in part was made.

If the undertaker's bill is not paid, he is entitled to file claim for reimbursement.

If more than one person is entitled to reimbursement, each claimant must submit a separate VA Form 21-530 containing the signature of the person who authorized services or the responsible official. Any burial allowance awarded will be apportioned according to the proportionate share paid by each, unless a waiver is executed in favor of one of such person by the other person or persons. However, in no case will there be allowed the person in whose favor payment is waived a sum greater than that which was paid by him/her toward the burial, funeral, and transportation expenses. If two or more persons have paid such expenses from their personal funds, and one or more of such persons dies before filing claim, no consideration will be given to the amount paid by the deceased person(s).

If applying for reimbursement of transportation expenses, a statement of account identifying the charges for transporting the body is required.

Unpaid Balance Due Persons who Performed Services

If there is an unpaid balance due the person who performed burial, funeral, and transportation services, such claim as a creditor for the statutory burial allowance will be given priority over any claim for reimbursement based on use of personal funds, unless there is executed by such creditor a waiver in favor of the person or persons whose personal funds were used in making the partial payment of the account.

No reimbursement may be made to a State, County, or other governmental subdivision.

Veteran's Estate

The representative of a deceased person's estate may file a claim for reimbursement, if estate funds were used to pay the expenses of the veteran's burial, funeral, and transportation. Accordingly, if otherwise in order, reimbursement may be made to the estate, regardless of whether such person pre-deceased the veteran or was deceased at the time the expenses were incurred or paid, or burial of the veteran actually occurred.

DEATH OF ACTIVE DUTY PERSONNEL

The VA does not pay a burial or plot interment allowance if a veteran dies while on active military duty. However, such veteran is entitled to certain benefits from the military. Information should be obtained from the branch of the armed forces in which the person served at time of death.

BURIAL OF UNCLAIMED BODIES

Dignified Burial of Unclaimed Veterans Act of 2012

The bill authorizes the Secretary of Veterans Affairs (VA) to furnish a casket or urn for a deceased veteran with no known living kin.

Under the bill, in cases where family or the next of kin of a deceased veteran can be identified, the bill requires the VA to ensure that the expressed wishes of the next of kin are met with regards to memorial service, funeral or interment at a national cemetery.

The bill requires the VA to obtain information from the relevant medical examiner, funeral director, service group or other entity regarding the steps taken to determine if the deceased has no next of kin.

VA will be required to cooperate with veterans service organizations to assist entities in possession of unclaimed or abandoned remains of veterans, with the department authorized to determine whether such remains are eligible for burial in a national cemetery.

If the body of an eligible deceased veteran is unclaimed by relatives or friends, the Director of any regional VA office or any VA medical center is authorized to arrange for burial in either a national cemetery or in a cemetery or section of a cemetery, owned by a state, a state agency, or political subdivision of a state, and used solely for the interment of persons eligible for burial in a national cemetery.

If an organization provides a burial or furnishes a burial plot as a humanitarian measure, and not pursuant to a legal obligation, it may be reimbursed for its actual cost. Reimbursement to such organization cannot exceed the maximum benefits payable based on the veteran's eligibility.

CORRECTION OF DISCHARGE TO HONORABLE CONDITIONS

Public Law 88-3 (H.R. 212) provides that where burial allowance was not payable at the time of a veteran's death because of the nature of his discharge from service, but after death his discharge is corrected by competent authority so as to reflect a discharge under conditions other than dishonorable, claim may be filed within two years from the date of correction of the discharge.

LEGAL EXECUTION

The execution of a veteran as a lawful punishment for a crime does not of itself preclude a payment of the statutory burial allowances.

STATE BURIAL ALLOWANCE

There are some burial allowances allowed by states or counties for the burial of needy veterans, and in some instances, of their dependents. Check with the veteran's state or county of residence for specific information.

ASSISTANCE TO CLAIMANTS

It is incumbent upon the claimant to establish his case in accordance with the law. This rule, however, will not be highly technical or rigid in its application. The general policy of the VA is to give the claimant every opportunity to substantiate his claim, to extend all reasonable assistance in its prosecution, and develop all sources from which information may be obtained. Assistance may also be secured from post, state, and national service officers or veterans' organizations.

MISCELLANEOUS

If the deceased veteran is entitled to payment in full of burial expenses by the Employees' Compensation Commission, Workman's Compensation, or employer, the Veterans Administration will make no payment.

APPEAL

An appeal may be made within one year from the date of denial of a claim. The appeal must be sent to the regional VA office that denied the claim. (For specific information regarding Appeals Procedures, refer to Chapter 36 of this book.)

BURIAL FLAGS

The VA shall furnish a United States flag, at no cost, for burial or memorial purposes in connection with the death of an eligible veteran who served honorably in the U.S. Armed Forces.

Public Law 105-261, added eligibility for former member of the Selected Reserve who:

- Completed at least one enlistment as a member of the Selected Reserve or, in the case of an officer, completed the period of initial obligated service as a member of the Selected Reserve; or
- Was discharged before completion of the person's initial enlistment as a member of the Selected Reserve or, in the case of an officer, period of initial obligated service as a member of the Selected Reserve, for a disability incurred or aggravated in line of duty; or
- Who died while a member of the Selected Reserve.

Burial flags may not be furnished on behalf of deceased veterans who committed capital crimes.

After the burial of the veteran, the flag shall be given to his next of kin. If no claim is made for the flag by the next of kin, it may be given, upon request, to a close friend or associate of the deceased veteran. If a flag is given to a close friend or associate of the deceased veteran, no flag shall be given to any other person on account of the death of such veteran.

When burial is in a national, state or post cemetery, a burial flag will automatically be provided. When burial is in a private cemetery, an American flag may be obtained by a service officer, an undertaker or other interested person from the nearest Veterans Administration office or most U.S. Post Offices. VA Form 2008, "Application for United States Flag for Burial Purposes", must be completed and submitted along with a copy of the veteran's discharge papers. Generally, the funeral director will help the next of kin with this process.

The proper way to display the flag depends upon whether the casket is open or closed. VA Form 2008 provides the proper method for displaying and folding the flag. The burial flag is not suitable for outside display, because of its size and fabric.

After burial of a veteran, the flag should be folded in military style and presented to the next of kin at the cemetery. Local veteran organizations, when presenting the flag, usually say something like this:

"In the name of the United States government and name of veterans organization, (such as A.L., D.A.V., V.F.W., and American Veterans of World War II, etc.) we present you this flag, in loving memory of our departed comrade."

Presenting of the flag is sometimes a difficult task when there is a disagreement in the family. However, the Veterans Administration gives the following order of preference to be followed:

1. Widow or widower (even if separated but not divorced)
2. Children according to age (minor child may be issued flag on application signed by guardian)
3. Father, including adopted, step and foster father
4. Mother, including adopted, step and foster mother
5. Brothers or sisters, including brothers and sisters of half blood.
6. Uncles or aunts
7. Nephews or nieces
8. Cousins, grandparents, etc. (but not in-laws)

If two relatives have equal rights, the flag will be presented to the elder one.

Following a veteran's burial, the United States flag received by the next of kin may be donated to the VA, for use on national holidays at VA national cemeteries. If the next of kin chooses to make such a donation, it should be given or mailed to the Director of any national cemetery selected by the donor with a written request that the flag be flown at that location. If the flag is brought into a Veterans Service Division, it will be accepted and forwarded to the cemetery chosen by the donor. A Certificate of Appreciation is presented to the donor for providing their loved ones' burial flag to a national cemetery.

Please note that VA cannot provide flag holders for placement on private headstones or markers. These flag holders may be purchased from private manufacturing companies.

The law allows the VA to issue one flag for a veteran's funeral. The VA cannot replace it if it is lost, destroyed, or stolen. However, if this occurs, a local veteran's organization or other community group may be able to assist you in obtaining another flag.

HEADSTONES AND MARKERS IN PRIVATE CEMETERIES

2012 Update: New Form Available for Ordering Grave Marker Medallion In 2012 the VA introduced a new form, **VA Form 40-1330M**, which is now used as the sole form for families to order a grave marker medallion. Prior to the change, families of the deceased used a form to order the medallion that was the same as the form used to order a government headstone or grave marker. The medallion is given instead of a traditional government headstone or marker, specifically for veterans whose death occurred on or after November 1, 1990. The medallion is intended for use for those veterans whose grave is located in a private cemetery, and marked with a privately purchased headstone or marker.

The VA is required to furnish an appropriate headstone or marker for the graves of eligible veterans buried in private cemeteries, whose deaths occur on or after December 27, 2001, regardless of whether the grave is already marked with a non-government marker. Headstones or markers may not be furnished on behalf of deceased veterans who committed capital crimes.

For all deaths occurring prior to September 11, 2001, the VA may provide a headstone or marker only for graves that are not marked with a private headstone.

Spouses and dependents buried in a private cemetery are not eligible for a Government-provided headstone or marker.

Flat markers in granite, marble, and bronze; and upright headstones in granite and marble are available. The style chosen must be consistent with existing monuments at the place of burial. Niche markers are also available to mark columbaria used for cremated remains.

Government-furnished headstones and markers must be inscribed with the name of the deceased, branch of service, and the year of birth and death, in this order. Headstones and markers also may be inscribed with other items, including an authorized emblem of belief and, space permitting, additional text including military grade, rate or rank, war service such as "World War II", complete dates of birth and death, military awards, military organizations, and civilian or veteran affiliations. To apply, and to obtain specific information on available styles, contact the cemetery where the headstone or marker is to be placed.

When burial occurs in a private cemetery, an application for a government-furnished headstone or marker must be made to VA. The government will ship the headstone or marker free of charge, but will not pay for its placement. To apply, complete VA Form 40-1330M (**application form updated in 2012**), and forward it along with a *copy* of the veteran's military discharge documents (do not send original discharge documents, as they will not be returned) to:

Director
Memorial Programs Service (403)
Department of Veterans Affairs
810 Vermont Avenue, NW
Washington, DC 20420-0001

BRONZE MEDALLIONS

VA made available a new medallion to be affixed to an existing privately purchased headstone or marker to signify the deceased's status as a veteran.

If requested, the medallion will be furnished in lieu of a traditional government headstone or marker for veterans that died on or after November 1, 1990, and whose grave is marked with a privately purchased headstone or marker.

The medallion is currently available in three sizes, 5 inches, 3 inches, and 1 ½ inches. Each medallion will be inscribed with the word VETERAN across the top and the Branch of Service at the bottom. Appropriate affixing adhesive, instructions and hardware will be provided with the medallion.

Important: This benefit is only applicable if the grave is marked with a privately purchased headstone or marker. In these instances, eligible veterans are entitled to either a traditional government-furnished headstone or marker, or the new medallion, but not both.

ELIGIBILITY RULES FOR A GOVERNMENT HEADSTONE OR MARKER IN A PRIVATE CEMETERY

1. **Veterans and Members of the Armed Forces (Army, Navy, Air Force, Marine Corps, Coast Guard):**

    a. Any veterans or members of The Armed Forces who dies while on active duty.

    b. Any veteran who was discharged under conditions other than dishonorable. With certain exceptions, service beginning after September 7, 1980, as an enlisted person, and service after October 16, 1981, as an officer, must be for a minimum of 24 months or the full period for which the person was called to active duty. (Examples include those serving less than 24 months in the Gulf War or Reservists that were federalized by Presidential Act.) Undesirable, bad conduct, and any other type of discharge other than honorable may or may not qualify the individual for veterans benefits, depending upon a determination made by a VA Regional Office. Cases presenting multiple discharges of varying character are also referred for adjudication to a VA Regional Office.

2. **Members of Reserve Components and Reserve Officers' Training Corps:**

a. Reservists and National Guard members who, at time of death, were entitled to retired pay under Chapter 1223, Title 10, United States Code, or would have been entitled, but for being under the age of 60.

b. Members of reserve components who die while hospitalized or undergoing treatment at the expense of the United States for injury or disease contracted or incurred under honorable conditions while performing active duty for training or inactive duty training, or undergoing such hospitalization or treatment.

c. Members of the Reserve Officers' Training Corps of the Army, Navy, or Air Force who die under honorable conditions while attending an authorized training camp or on an authorized cruise, while performing authorized travel to or from that camp or cruise, or while hospitalized or undergoing treatment at the expense of the United States for injury or disease contracted or incurred under honorable conditions while engaged in one of those activities.

d. Members of reserve components who, during a period of active duty for training, were disabled or died from a disease or injury incurred or aggravated in the line of duty or, during a period of inactive duty training, were disabled or died from an injury incurred or aggravated in the line of duty.

3. **Commissioned Officers, National Oceanic and Atmospheric Administration:**

a. A commissioned Officer of the National Oceanic and Atmospheric Administration (formerly titled the Coast and Geodetic Survey and the Environmental Science Services Administration) with full-time duty on or after July 29, 1945.

b. A commissioned Officer who served before July 29, 1945, and:

i. Was assigned to an area of immediate military hazard while in time of war, or of a Presidentially declared national emergency as determined by the Secretary of Defense; or

ii. Served in the Philippine Islands on December 7, 1941, and continuously in such islands thereafter; or

iii. Transferred to the Department of the Army or the Department of the Navy under the provisions of the Act of May 22, 1917.

4. **Public Health Service:**

a. A Commissioned Officer of the Regular or Reserve Corps of the Public Health Service who served on full-time duty on or after July 29, 1945. If the service of the particular Public Health Service Officer falls within the meaning of active duty for training, as defined in section 101(22), title 38, United States Code, he or she must have been disabled or died from a disease or injury incurred or aggravated in the line of duty.

b. A Commissioned Officer of the Regular or Reserve Corps of the Public Health Service who performed full-time duty prior to July 29, 1945:

   i. In time of war;

   ii. On detail for duty with the Army, Navy, Air Force, Marine Corps, or Coast Guard; or,

   iii. While the Service was part of the military forces of the United States pursuant to Executive Order of the President.

c. A Commissioned Officer serving on inactive duty training as defined in section 101(23), title 38, United States Code, whose death resulted from an injury incurred or aggravated in the line of duty.

5. World War II Merchant Mariners

a. United States Merchant Mariners with oceangoing service during the period of armed conflict, December 7, 1941, to December 31, 1946. Prior to the enactment of *Public Law 105-368*, United States Merchant Mariners with oceangoing service during the period of armed conflict of December 7, 1941, to August 15, 1945, were eligible. With enactment of *Public Law 105-368*, the service period is extended to December 31, 1946, for those dying on or after November 11, 1998. A DD-214 documenting this service may be obtained by submitting an application to Commandant (G-MVP-6), United States Coast Guard, 2100 2nd Street, SW, Washington, DC 20593. Notwithstanding, the Mariner's death must have occurred after the enactment of *Public Law 105-368* and the interment not violate the applicable restrictions while meeting the requirements held therein.

b. United States Merchant Mariners who served on blockships in support of Operation Mulberry during World War II.

PERSONS NOT ELIGIBLE FOR A HEADSTONE OR MARKER

1. Disqualifying Characters of Discharge

A person whose only separation from the Armed Forces was under dishonorable conditions or whose character of service results in a bar to veterans benefits.

2. **Discharge from Draft**

   A person who was ordered to report to an induction station, but was not actually inducted into military service.

3. **Person Found Guilty of a Capital Crime**

   Eligibility for a headstone or marker is prohibited if a person is convicted of a federal capital crime and sentenced to death or life imprisonment, or is convicted of a state capital crime, and sentenced to death or life imprisonment without parole. Federal officials are authorized to deny requests for headstones or markers to persons who are shown by clear and convincing evidence to have committed a Federal or State capital crime but were not convicted of such crime because of flight to avoid prosecution or by death prior to trial.

4. **Subversive Activities**
   Any person convicted of subversive activities after September 1, 1959, shall have no right to burial in a national cemetery from and after the date of commission of such offense, based on periods of active military service commencing before the date of the commission of such offense, nor shall another person be entitled to burial on account of such an individual. Eligibility will be reinstated if the President of the United States grants a pardon.

5. **Active or Inactive Duty for Training**

   A person whose only service is active duty for training or inactive duty training in the National Guard or Reserve Component, unless the individual meets the following criteria.

   a. Reservists and National Guard members who, at time of death, were entitled to retired pay under Chapter 1223, title 10, United States Code, or would have been entitled, but for being under the age of 60. Specific categories of individuals eligible for retired pay are delineated in section 12731 of Chapter 1223, title 10, United States Code.

   b. Members of reserve components who die while hospitalized or undergoing treatment at the expense of the United States for injury or disease contracted or incurred under honorable conditions while performing active duty for training or inactive duty training, or undergoing such hospitalization or treatment.

   c. Members of the Reserve Officers' Training Corps of the Army, Navy, or Air Force who die under honorable conditions while attending an authorized training camp or on an authorized cruise, while performing authorized travel to or from that camp or cruise, or while hospitalized or undergoing treatment at the expense of the United States for injury or disease contracted or incurred under honorable conditions while engaged in one of those activities.

d. Members of reserve components who, during a period of active duty for training, were disabled or died from a disease or injury incurred or aggravated in line of duty or, during a period of inactive duty training, were disabled or died from an injury incurred or aggravated in line of duty.

6. **Other Groups**
Members of groups whose service has been determined by the Secretary of the Air Force under the provisions of Public Law 95-202 as not warranting entitlement to benefits administered by the Secretary of Veterans Affairs.

BURIAL IN NATIONAL CEMETERIES

In 2012 the VA announced plans to move forward with plan to provide burial options for veterans who live in rural areas, where no national, state or tribal cemeteries are available. The plan is part of the Rural Initiative Plan, in which the VA will work to build small National Veterans Burial Grounds that will be located inside existing rurally-located public or private cemeteries. These burial grounds will also be located where the un-served veteran population is 25,000 or less, within a 75-mile radius.

The VA announced plans to open eight National Veteran Burial Grounds. A National Veterans Burial Ground will consist of a small area of three to five acres, located within an existing public or private cemetery that will be managed by the VA. The VA will provide a full range of burial options and be responsible for the maintenance and operation of the burial lots. These sections will be held to the national shrine standards that are in place at VA national cemeteries.

The National Cemetery Administration honors Veterans with a final resting place and lasting memorials that commemorate their service to our nation.

Veterans and service members who meet the eligibility requirements and their eligible dependents may be buried in one of the VA's national cemeteries. The National Cemetery Administration currently includes 122 national cemeteries. The Department of the Army administers 2 national cemeteries, and the Department of the Interior administers 14 national cemeteries. There are also numerous state cemeteries for veterans throughout the U.S. For a listing of all national cemeteries as well as state veterans cemeteries refer to the listing at the end of this chapter.

Effective under *Public Law 112-154*, reservations for more than one space at Arlington National Cemetery will no longer be accepted, and reservations will not be honored until the time of death, unless there is a case of extraordinary circumstances.

HONORING AMERICA'S VETERANS AND CARING FOR CAMP LEJEUNE FAMILIES ACT OF 2012

BECAME PUBLIC LAW 112-154 ON AUGUST 5, 2012

This law, signed into effect by President Obama, provided sweeping legislation for veterans, including limitations on protestors at military funerals. The law prohibits protestors at military funerals from protesting two hours before or after a military funeral, and the must hold their protests at least 300 feet from the site of the funeral.

RESPECT FOR AMERICA'S FALLEN HEROES ACT

BECAME *PUBLIC LAW 109-228* ON MAY 29, 2006

On May 29, 2006, then-President Bush signed the *Respect For America's Fallen Heroes Act* into law. This law does the following:

- Prohibits a demonstration on the property of a cemetery under the control of the National Cemetery Administration or on the property of Arlington National Cemetery unless the demonstration has been approved by the cemetery superintendent or the director of the property on which the cemetery is located.

> The Respect for America's Fallen Heroes Act prohibits certain demonstrations at cemeteries under the control of the National Cemetery Administration and at Arlington National Cemetery.

- Prohibits, with respect to the above cemeteries, a demonstration during the period beginning 60 minutes before and ending 60 minutes after a funeral, memorial service, or ceremony is held, which:
  - Takes place within 150 feet of a road, pathway, or other route of ingress to or egress from such cemetery property; or
  - Is within 300 feet of such cemetery and impedes access to or egress from such cemetery.

- The term "Demonstration" includes the following:
  - Any picketing or similar conduct.
  - Any oration, speech, use of sound amplification equipment or device, or similar conduct that is not part of a funeral, memorial service, or ceremony.
  - The display of any placard, banner, flag, or similar device, unless the display is part of a funeral, memorial service, or ceremony.
  - The distribution of any handbill, pamphlet, leaflet, or other written or printed matter other than what is distributed as part of a funeral, memorial service, or ceremony.

- Amends the federal criminal code to provide criminal penalties for violations of such prohibitions.

- Express the sense of Congress that each state should enact similar legislation to restrict demonstrations near any military funeral.

ELIGIBILITY

The VA national cemetery directors have the primary responsibility for verifying eligibility for burial in VA national cemeteries. A dependent's eligibility for burial is based upon the eligibility of the veteran. To establish a veteran's eligibility, a copy of the official military discharge document bearing an official seal or a DD 214 is usually sufficient. The document must show that release from service was under conditions other than dishonorable. A determination of eligibility is usually made in response to a request for burial in a VA national cemetery.

The cemeteries administered by the National Cemetery Administration and the Department of the Interior use the eligibility requirements that follow. The Department of the Interior can be contacted at:

U.S. Department of the Interior
National Park Service
1849 C Street, N.W.
Washington, D.C. 20240
(202) 208-4621

The Department of the Army should be contacted directly for inquiries concerning eligibility for interment in either of the two cemeteries under its jurisdiction (call (703) 695-3250).

Eligibility requirements for burial in state veterans cemeteries are the same, or similar, to the eligibility requirements that follow. However, some states also have residency and other more restrictive requirements. Please contact the specific state cemetery for its eligibility requirements.

The following veterans and members of the Armed Forces (Army, Navy, Air Force, Marine Corps, Coast Guard) are eligible for burial in a VA national cemetery:

VETERANS AND MEMBERS OF THE ARMED FORCES

- Any member of the Armed Forces of the U.S. who dies on active duty.

- Any citizen of the U.S. who, during any war in which the U.S. has been engaged, served in the Armed Forces of any U.S. ally during that war, whose last active service was terminated honorably by death or otherwise, and who was a citizen of the U.S. at the time of entry into such service and at the time of death.

- Any veteran discharged under conditions other than dishonorable, and who has completed the required period of service. With certain exceptions, service beginning after September 7, 1980, as an enlisted person, and service after October 16, 1981, as an officer, must be for a minimum of 24 months or the full period for which the person was called to active duty.

MEMBERS OF RESERVE COMPONENTS AND RESERVE OFFICERS' TRAINING CORPS

- Reservists and National Guard members with 20 years of qualifying service, who are entitled to retired pay, or would be entitled, if at least 60 years of age.
- Members of reserve components who die under honorable conditions while hospitalized or undergoing treatment at the expense of the U.S. for injury or disease contracted or incurred under honorable conditions, while performing active duty for training, or inactive duty training, or undergoing such hospitalization or treatment.
- Members of the Reserve Officers' Training Corps of the Army, Navy, or Air Force who die under honorable conditions while attending an authorized training camp or cruise, or while traveling to or from that camp or cruise, or while hospitalized or undergoing treatment at the expense of the U.S. for injury or disease contracted or incurred under honorable conditions while engaged in one of those activities.
- Members of reserve components who, during a period of active duty for training, were disabled or died from a disease or injury incurred or aggravated in the line of duty, or, during a period of inactive duty training, were disabled or died from an injury incurred or aggravated in the line of duty.

COMMISSIONED OFFICERS, NATIONAL OCEANIC AND ATMOSPHERIC ADMINISTRATION

- A Commissioned Officer of the National Oceanic and Atmospheric Administration with full-time duty on or after July 29, 1945.
- A Commissioned Officer of the National Oceanic and Atmospheric Administration who served before July 29, 1945, and:
- Was assigned to an area of immediate hazard described in the Act of December 3, 1942 (56 Stat. 1038; 33 U.S.C. 855a), as amended;
- Served in the Philippine Islands on December 7, 1941, and continuously in such islands thereafter.

PUBLIC HEALTH SERVICE

- A Commissioned Officer of the Regular or Reserve Corps of the Public Health Service who served on full-time duty on or after July 29, 1945. If the service of such Officer falls within the meaning of active duty for training, he must have been disabled or died from a disease or injury incurred or aggravated in the line of duty.

- A Commissioned Officer of the Regular or Reserve Corps of the Public Health Service who performed full-time duty prior to July 29, 1945:
    a. In time of war; or
    b. On detail for duty with the Army, Navy, Air Force, Marine Corps, or Coast Guard; or
    c. While the service was part of the military forces of the U.S. pursuant to Executive Order of the President.

- A Commissioned Officer of the Regular or Reserve Corps of the Public Health Service serving on inactive duty training as defined in Section 101 (23), title 39, U.S. Code, whose death resulted from an injury incurred or aggravated in the line of duty.

World War II Merchant Mariners

- U.S. Merchant Mariners with oceangoing service during the period of armed conflict, December 7, 1941 to December 31, 1946. Prior to the enactment of Public Law 105-368, United States Merchant Mariners with oceangoing service during the period of armed conflict of December 7, 1941, to August 15, 1945, were eligible. With enactment of Public Law 105-368, the service period is extended to December 31, 1946, for those dying on or after November 11, 1998.
- U.S. Merchant Mariners who served on blockships in support of Operation Mulberry during WWII.

The Philippine Armed Forces

- Any Philippine veteran who was a citizen of the United States or an alien lawfully admitted for permanent residence in the United States at the time of their death; and resided in the United States at the time of their death; and:
- Was a person who served before July 1, 1946, in the organized military forces of the Government of the Commonwealth of the Philippines, while such forces were in the service of the Armed Forces of the United States pursuant to the military order of the President dated July 26, 1941, including organized guerilla forces under commanders appointed, designated, or subsequently recognized by the Commander in Chief, Southwest Pacific Area, or other competent authority in the Army of the United States who dies on or after November 1, 2000; or
- Was a person who enlisted between October 6, 1945, and June 30, 1947, with the Armed Forces of the United States with the consent of the Philippine government, pursuant to Section 14 of the Armed Forces Voluntary Recruitment Act of 1945, and who died on or after December 16, 2003.

Spouses and Dependents

- The spouse or surviving spouse of an eligible veteran is eligible for interment in a national cemetery even if that veteran is not buried or memorialized in a national cemetery. In addition, the spouse or surviving spouse of a member of the Armed Forces of the United States whose remains are unavailable for burial is also eligible for burial.

- The surviving spouse of an eligible veteran who had a subsequent remarriage to a non-veteran and whose death occurred on or after January 1, 2000, is eligible for burial in a national cemetery, based on his or her marriage to the eligible veteran.
- The minor children of an eligible veteran. For the purpose of burial in a national cemetery, a minor child is a child who is unmarried and:
- Under 21 years of age; or
- Under 23 years of age and pursuing a full-time course of instruction at an approved educational institution.
- An unmarried adult child of an eligible veteran if the child became permanently physically or mentally disabled and incapable of self-support before reaching 21 years of age, or before reaching 23 years of age if pursuing a full-time course of instruction at an approved educational institution.
- Any other persons or classes of persons as designated by the Secretary of Veterans Affairs or the Secretary of the Air Force.
- The *Veterans' Benefits Act of 2010* contains a provision which allows a parent whose child gave their life in service to our country to be buried in a national cemetery with that child when their veteran child has no living spouse or children.

THE FOLLOWING ARE NOT ELIGIBLE FOR BURIAL IN A VA NATIONAL CEMETERY:

- A former spouse of an eligible individual whose marriage to that individual has been terminated by annulment or divorce, if not otherwise eligible.
- Family members other than those specifically described above.
- A person whose only separation from the Armed Forces was under dishonorable conditions, or whose character of service results in a bar to veterans benefits.
- A person ordered to report to an induction station, but not actually inducted into military service.
- Any person found guilty of a capital crime. Interment or memorialization in a VA cemetery or in Arlington National Cemetery is prohibited if a person is convicted of a federal capital crime and sentenced to death or life imprisonment, or is convicted of a state capital crime, and sentenced to death or life imprisonment without parole. Federal officials are authorized to deny burial in veterans' cemeteries to persons who are shown by clear and convincing evidence to have committed a federal or state capital crime but were not convicted of such crime because of flight to avoid prosecution or by death prior to trial. The Secretary is authorized to provide aid to states for the

establishment, expansion and/or improvement of veterans cemeteries on the condition that the state is willing to prohibit interment or memorialization in such cemeteries of individuals convicted of federal or state capital crimes, or found by clear and convincing evidence to have committed such crimes, without having been convicted of the crimes due to flight to avoid prosecution or death prior to trial.

- Any person convicted of subversive activities after September 1, 1959, shall have no right to burial in a national cemetery from and after the date of commission of such offense, based on periods of active military service commencing before the date of the commission of such offense, nor shall another person be entitled to burial on account of such an individual. Eligibility will be reinstated if the President of the United States grants a pardon.

REQUESTS FOR GRAVESITES IN NATIONAL CEMETERIES

Under Public Law 112-154 the Secretary of the Army will be responsible for decisions regarding organizations wishing to place monuments honoring the service of a group or individual at Arlington. This became law in 2012.

An eligible veteran or family member may be buried in the VA national cemetery of his choice, provided space is available. A veteran may not reserve a gravesite in his name prior to his death. However, any reservations made under previous programs will be honored. The funeral director or loved one making the burial arrangements must apply for a gravesite at the time of death. No special forms are required when requesting burial in a VA national cemetery. The person making burial arrangement should contact the national cemetery in which burial is desired at the time of need.

If possible, the following information concerning the deceased should be provided when the cemetery is first contacted:

- Full name and military rank;
- Branch of service;
- Social security number;
- VA claim number, if applicable;
- Date and place of birth;
- Date and place of death;
- Date of retirement or last separation from active duty; and
- Copy of any military separation documents (such as DD-214)

When a death occurs and eligibility for interment in a national cemetery is determined, grave space is assigned by the cemetery director in the name of the veteran or family member.

One gravesite is permitted for the interment of all eligible family members, unless soil conditions or the number of family decedents necessitate more than one grave.

There is no charge for burial in a national cemetery.

The availability of grave space varies among each National Cemetery. In many cases, if a national cemetery does not have space for a full-casket burial, it may still inter cremated remains. Full-casket gravesites occasionally become available in such cemeteries due to disinterment or cancellation of prior reservations. The cemetery director can answer such questions at the time of need.

Most national cemeteries do not typically conduct burials on weekends. However, weekend callers trying to make burial arrangements for the following week will be provided with the phone number of one of three strategically located VA cemetery offices that remains open during weekends.

BURIAL AT SEA

The National Cemetery Administration cannot provide burial at sea. For information, contact the United States Navy Mortuary Affairs office toll-free at 866-787-0081.

FURNISHING AND PLACEMENT OF HEADSTONES AND MARKERS

In addition to the gravesite, burial in a VA national cemetery also includes furnishing and placement of the headstone or marker, opening and closing of the grave, and perpetual care. Many national cemeteries also have columbaria or gravesites for cremated remains. (Some state veterans' cemeteries may charge a nominal fee for placing a government-provided headstone or marker.)

SPECIAL NOTES:

- For persons with 20-years service in the National Guard or Reserves, entitlement to retired pay must be subsequent to November 1, 1990 in order to qualify for a government-provided headstone or marker. A copy of the Reserve Retirement Eligibility Benefits Letter must accompany the application. Active duty service while in the National Guard or Reserves also establishes eligibility.
- Service prior to World War I requires detailed documentation to prove eligibility such as muster rolls, extracts from State files, military or State organizations where served, pension or land warrants, etc.

Flat bronze, granite, or marble grave markers and upright marble or granite headstones are available to mark graves in the style consistent with existing monuments in the national cemetery. Niche markers are also available for identifying cremated remains in columbaria. The following is a brief description of each type:

- Upright Marble and Upright Granite: 42 inches long, 13 inches wide, 4 inches thick, approximately 230 pounds.
- Flat Bronze: 24 inches long, 12 inches wide, ¾ inch rise, approximately 18 pounds. Anchor bolts, nuts and washers for fastening to base are supplied with marker. The government does not provide the base.
- Flat Granite and Flat Marble: 24 inches long, 12 inches wide, 4 inches thick, approximately 130 pounds.
- Bronze Niche: 8 ½ inches long, 5 ½ inches wide, 7/16 inch rise, approximately 3 pounds. Mounting bolts and washers are supplied with marker.
- There are also two special styles of upright marble headstones and flat markers available - one for those who served with the Union Forces during the Civil War or the Spanish-American War; and one for those who served with the Confederate Forces during the Civil War.

INSCRIPTIONS

Headstones and markers are inscribed with the name of the deceased, branch of service, year of birth, and year of death.

The word "Korea" may be included on government headstones and markers for the graves of those members and former members of the United States Armed Forces who served within the areas of military operations in the Korean Theater between June 27, 1950 and July 27, 1954; and for headstones and markers for active duty decedents who lost their lives in Korea or adjacent waters as a result of hostile action subsequent to the 1953 Armistice.

The word "Vietnam" may be included on government headstones and markers for the graves of those members and former members of the United States Armed Forces who died in Vietnam or whose death was attributable to service in Vietnam, and on the headstones and markers of all decedents who were on active duty on or after August 5, 1964.

The words "Lebanon" or "Grenada" may be included on government headstones and markers for those killed as a result of those military actions.

The words "Panama" and "Persian Gulf" may be included on government headstones and markers for those killed as a result of those military actions.

If desired, the following inscriptions can also be made (space permitting):

- Military grade
- Military rank
- Military rate
- Identification of war service

- Months and days of birth and death
- An authorized emblem of religious belief (see following list of available emblems)
- Military awards (documentation of award must be provided)
- Military organizations
- Civilian or veteran affiliations

With the VA's approval, terms of endearment that meet acceptable standards of good taste may also be added. Most optional inscriptions are placed as the last lines of the inscription. No other graphics are permitted on government-provided headstones and markers, and inscriptions will be in English text only. Civilian titles such as "Doctor or Reverend" are not permitted on the name line of government-provided headstones and markers.

Available Emblems of Belief for Placement on Government Headstones and Markers:

- Christian Cross
- Buddhist (Wheel of Righteousness)
- Hebrew (Star of David)
- Presbyterian Cross
- Russian Orthodox Cross
- Lutheran Cross
- Episcopal Cross
- Unitarian Church (Flaming Chalice)
- United Methodist Church
- Aaronic Order Church
- Mormon (Angel Moroni)
- Native American Church of North America
- Serbian Orthodox
- Greek Cross
- Bahai (9 Pointed Star)
- Atheist
- Muslim (Crescent and Star)

- Hindu
- Konko-Kyo Faith
- Community of Christ
- Sufism Reoriented
- Tenrikyo Church
- Seicho-No-Ie
- Church of World Messianity (Izunome)
- United Church of Religious Science
- Christian Reformed Church
- United Moravian Church
- Eckankar
- Christian Church
- United Church of Christ
- Christian & Missionary Alliance
- Humanist Emblem Of Spirit
- Presbyterian Church (USA)
- Izumo Taishakyo Mission Of Hawaii
- Soka Gakkai International - USA
- Sikh (Khanda)
- Christian Scientist (Cross and Crown)
- Muslim (Islamic 5 Pointed Star)

ORDERING A HEADSTONE OR MARKER

For burial of a veteran in a national, state veteran, or military post cemetery, the cemetery will order the headstone or marker, and can give loved ones information on style, inscription, and shipment. Shipment and placement of the headstone or marker is provided at no cost.

When burial is in a private cemetery, VA Form 40-1330, "Application for Standard Government Headstone or Marker" must be submitted by the next of kin or a representative, such as funeral director, cemetery official or veterans' counselor, along with the veteran's military discharge documents, to request a Government-provided headstone or marker. Do not send original documents, as they will not be returned.

HEADSTONES AND MARKERS FOR SPOUSES AND CHILDREN

The VA will issue a headstone or marker for an eligible spouse or child buried in a national, state veteran or military post cemetery. However, the VA cannot issue a headstone or marker for a spouse or child buried in a private cemetery.

The VA will issue a headstone or marker for an eligible spouse or child buried in a national, state veteran or military post cemetery. However, the VA cannot issue a headstone or marker for a spouse or child buried in a private cemetery.

The applicant can, however, request to reserve inscription space below the veteran's inscription, so that the non-veteran's commemorative information can be inscribed locally, at private expense, when the non-veteran is buried. The applicant may also choose to have his/her name and date of birth added at Government expense, when the headstone or marker is ordered. The date of death may then be added, at private expense, at the time of his/her death.

COMMEMORATION OF UNIDENTIFIED REMAINS

Many national cemeteries have areas suitable to commemorate veterans whose remains were not recovered or identified, were buried at sea, or are otherwise unavailable for interment. In such instances, the VA will provide a memorial headstone or marker to be placed in that section of the cemetery. The words *"In Memory of"* must precede the authorized inscription.

CHECKING ORDER STATUS

To check the status of a previously ordered headstone or marker for placement in a private cemetery, applicants may call the VA's Applicant Assistance Line at (800) 697-6947. The line is open weekdays, from 8:00 A.M. to 5:00 P.M., Eastern Standard Time.

REPLACEMENT OF HEADSTONES AND MARKERS

> *For guidance on obtaining a replacement headstone or marker, call (800) 697-6947.*

The government will replace a previously furnished headstone or marker if it: becomes badly damaged, is vandalized, is stolen, becomes badly deteriorated, the inscription becomes illegible, is different from that ordered by the applicant, becomes damaged in transit, or the inscription is incorrect.

Government headstones or markers in private cemeteries damaged by cemetery personnel will not be replaced at government expense.

If a marble or granite headstone or marker is permanently removed from a grave, it must be destroyed. Bronze markers must be returned to the contractor.

MILITARY HONORS

The rendering of Military Funeral Honors is a way to show the nation's deep gratitude to those who have faithfully defended our country in times of war and peace. It is the final demonstration a grateful nation can provide to the veterans' families.

The following service members are eligible for Military Funeral Honors:

- Military members on active duty or in the Selected Reserve at time of death;
- Former military members who served on active duty and departed under conditions other than dishonorable;
- Former military members who completed at least one term of enlistment or period of initial obligated service in the Selected Reserve, and departed under conditions other than dishonorable;
- Former military members discharged from the Selected Reserve due to a disability incurred or aggravated in the line of duty.

All eligible veterans receive basic Military Funeral Honors, if requested by the deceased veteran's family. As provided by law, an honor guard detail for the burial of an eligible veteran shall consist of not less than two members of the Armed Forces. One member of the detail shall be a representative of the parent Service of the deceased veteran. The honor detail will, at a minimum, perform a ceremony that includes the folding and presenting of the American flag to the next of kin, and the playing of Taps. Taps will be played by a bugler, if available, or by electronic recording.

The ceremonial bugle consists of a small cone-shaped device inserted deep into the bell of a bugle that plays an exceptionally high-quality rendition of Taps that is virtually indistinguishable from a live bugler.

The ceremonial bugle will be offered to families as an alternative to the pre-recorded Taps played on a stereo, but will not be used as a substitute for a live bugler when one is available. Live buglers will continue to play at veterans' funerals whenever available.

Funeral Directors have the responsibility of assisting loved ones in requesting military honors. A toll-free telephone number has been established for funeral directors requesting military honors.

The Department of Defense (DOD) has provided registered funeral home directors with a military funeral honors kit and information on how to contact the appropriate military organization to perform the honors ceremony.
Questions about the Military Funeral Honors program should be sent to:

Department of Defense
Directorate for Public Inquiry and Analysis
Room 3A750, The Pentagon
Washington, DC 20301-1400

PREPARATIONS WHICH CAN BE MADE PRIOR TO DEATH

It is suggested that veterans and their families prepare in advance by discussing cemetery options, collecting the veteran's military information (including discharge papers), and by contacting the cemetery where the veteran wishes to be buried. If burial will be in a private cemetery and a government headstone or marker will be requested, VA Form 40-1330 can be completed in advance and placed with the veteran's military discharge papers for use at the time of need.

BURIAL LOCATION ASSISTANCE

The VA National Cemetery Administration can provide limited burial location assistance to family members and close friends of descendants thought to be buried in a VA national cemetery.

The National Cemetery Administration will research its records to determine if the decedent is buried in one of VA's national cemeteries. A request can include a maximum of ten specific names to locate.

The National Cemetery Administration does not have information on persons buried in cemeteries other than its national cemeteries. Its records do not contain any personal, military or family information – only information regarding whether or not an individual is buried in a VA national cemetery, and if so, where, can be provided.

The "Gravesite Locator" tool is available online at the VA's website.

If the online tool is not available or helpful, you may submit a written request. No form is required to request this information, and no fee is charged. The following information should be provided:

- Full name, including any alternate spellings, of descendent;
- Date and place of birth;
- Date and place of death;
- State from which the individual entered active duty;
- Military service branch;
- Mailing address and phone number of individual requesting the information.

Allow approximately 4 weeks for a reply.

Requests should be sent to:

U.S. Department of Veterans Affairs
National Cemetery Administration (41C1)
Burial Location Request
810 Vermont Avenue, N.W.
Washington, D.C. 20420

U.S. MILITARY CEMETERIES AND MONUMENTS OVERSEAS

The *American Battle Monuments Commission (ABMC)* a small, independent agency of the U.S. government's executive branch, maintains 24 American military cemeteries, and 27 memorials, monuments, or markers. (The VA is not responsible for maintaining cemeteries and monuments honoring deceased veterans buried on foreign soil.)

ABMC SERVICES

The ABMC can provide interested parties with:

- Name, location, and information on cemeteries and memorials.
- Plot, row and grave number or memorialization location of Honored War Dead.
- Best in-country routes and modes of travel to cemeteries or memorials.
- Information on accommodations near cemeteries or memorials.
- Escort service for relatives to grave and memorial sites within the cemeteries.
- Letters authorizing fee-free passports for members of the immediate family traveling overseas to visit a grave or memorialization site.
- Black and white photographs of headstones and Tablets of the Missing on which the names of dead or missing are engraved.
- Arrangements for floral decorations placed at graves and memorialization sites.

- An Honor Roll Certificate containing data on a Korean War casualty suitable for framing.
- Polaroid color photographs of donated floral decorations in place.
-

THE ANDREWS PROJECT

The commission also provides friends and relatives of those interred in its cemeteries or memorialized on its Tablets of the Missing with color lithographs of the cemetery or memorial on which is mounted a photograph of the headstone or commemorative inscription. The Andrews Project, named in honor of its sponsor, the late Congressman George W. Andrews, is ABMC's most popular service.

For further information, contact the ABMC at:

American Battle Monuments Commission
Arlington Court House Plaza II
2300 Clarendon Blvd., Suite 500
Arlington, VA 22201
(703) 696-6897

PASSPORTS TO VISIT OVERSEAS CEMETERIES

Family members who wish to visit overseas graves and memorial sites of World War I and World War II veterans are eligible for "no-fee" passports. Family members eligible for the "no-fee" passports include surviving spouses, parents, children, sisters, brothers and guardians of the deceased veteran buried or commemorated in American military cemeteries on foreign soil. For further information contact the American Battle Monuments Commission at the address and phone number indicated in the previous section.

PRESIDENTIAL MEMORIAL CERTIFICATES

Under *Public Law 112-154*, servicemembers who die on active-duty are eligible for Presidential Memorial Certificates

A Presidential Memorial Certificate is an engraved paper certificate that has been signed by the current president, honoring the memory of any honorably discharged deceased veteran.

Presidential Memorial Certificates may be distributed to a deceased veteran's next of kin and loved ones. More than one certificate can be provided per family, and there is no time limit for applying for the certificate.

Presidential Memorial Certificates may not be furnished on behalf of deceased veterans who committed capital crimes.

Requests for a Presidential Memorial Certificate can be made in person at any VA regional office, by faxing the request and all supporting documents (copy of discharge and death certificate) to (202) 565-8054, or by U.S. Mail.

There is no form to use when requesting a certificate. A copy of the veteran's discharge documents and a return mailing address should be included with any request. Written requests should be sent to:

Presidential Memorial Certificates (41A1C)
Department of Veterans Affairs
5109 Russell Road
Quantico, VA 22134-3903

LISTS OF NATIONAL CEMETERIES

Some national cemeteries can bury only cremated remains or casketed remains of eligible family members of those already buried. Contact the cemetery director for information on the availability of space

DEPARTMENT OF VETERANS AFFAIRS NATIONAL CEMETERIES

ALABAMA

Alabama National Cemetery
3133 Highway 119
Montevallo, AL 35115
(866) 547-5078

Fort Mitchell National Cemetery
553 Highway 165
Seale, AL 36875
(334) 855-4731

Mobile National Cemetery
1202 Virginia Street
Mobile, AL 36604
For information please contact:
Barrancas National Cemetery
(850) 453-4846

ALASKA

Fort Richardson National Cemetery
Building #997, Davis Highway
P. O. Box 5-498
Fort Richardson, AK 99505
(907) 384-7075

Sitka National Cemetery
803 Sawmill Creek Road
Sitka, AK 99835
For information please contact:
Fort Richardson National Cemetery
(907) 384-7075

ARIZONA

National Memorial Cemetery of Arizona
23029 North Cave Creek Road
Phoenix, AZ 85024
(480) 513-3600

Prescott National Cemetery
500 Highway 89 North
Prescott, AZ 86301
For information please contact National Memorial Cemetery of Arizona (480) 513-3600

ARKANSAS

Fayetteville National Cemetery
700 Government Avenue

Fayetteville, AR 72701
(479) 444-5051

Fort Smith National Cemetery
522 Garland Avenue
Fort Smith, AR 72901
(479) 783-5345

Little Rock National Cemetery
(Currently closed to new burials-updated 2013. De facto place for burials is currently State Veterans Cemetery.
2523 Confederate Boulevard
Little Rock, AR 72206
(501) 324-6401

State Veterans Cemetery
1501 West Maryland Ave
North Little Rock, AR 72120
(501) 992-0310

CALIFORNIA

Fort Rosecrans National Cemetery
P. O. Box 6237 Point Loma
San Diego, CA 92106
(619) 553-2084

Golden Gate National Cemetery
1300 Sneath Lane
San Bruno, CA 94066
(650) 761-7737

Los Angeles National Cemetery
950 South Sepulveda Boulevard
Los Angeles, CA 90049
(310) 268-4675

Riverside National Cemetery
22495 Van Buren Boulevard
Riverside, CA 92518
(909) 653-8417

Sacramento Valley National Cemetery
5810 Midway Road
Dixon, CA 95620
(707) 693-2460

San Francisco National Cemetery
P. O. Box 29012
Presidio of San Francisco
San Francisco, CA 94129
For information please contact Golden Gate National Cemetery (650) 761-1646

San Joaquin Valley National Cemetery
32053 West McCabe Road
Gustine, CA 95322
(209) 854-1040

COLORADO

Fort Logan National Cemetery
3698 South Sheridan Boulevard
Denver, CO 80235
(303) 761-0117

Fort Lyon National Cemetery
VA Medical Center
Fort Lyon, CO 81038
For information please contact Fort Logan National Cemetery
(303) 761-0117

FLORIDA

Barrancas National Cemetery
Naval Air Station
80 Hovey Road
Pensacola, FL 32508-1099
(850) 453-4108

Bay Pines National Cemetery
P. O. Box 477
Bay Pines, FL 33504-0477
(727) 398-9426

Florida National Cemetery
6502 SW 102nd Avenue
Bushnell, FL 33513
(352) 793-7740 or 1074
Jacksonville National Cemetery
4083 Lannie Road
Jacksonville, FL 32218-1247
(904) 358-3510

Sarasota National Cemetery
9810 State Hwy 72
Sarasota, FL 34241
(941) 861-9840

South Florida National Cemetery
6501 S. State Road 7
Lake Worth, FL 33467
Phone: (561) 649-6489

St. Augustine National Cemetery
104 Marine Street
St. Augustine, FL 32084
For information please contact
Florida National Cemetery
(352) 793-7740

GEORGIA

Georgia National Cemetery
2025 Mount Carmel Church Lane
Canton, GA 30114
(866) 236-8159

Marietta National Cemetery
500 Washington Avenue
Marietta, GA 30060
(866) 236-8159

HAWAII

National Memorial Cemetery of the Pacific
2177 Puowaina Drive
Honolulu, HI 96813-1729
(808) 523-3720

ILLINOIS

Abraham Lincoln National Cemetery
27034 South Diagonal Road
Elwood, IL 60421
(815) 423-9958

Alton National Cemetery
600 Pearl Street
Alton, IL 62003
For information please contact
Jefferson Barracks National Cemetery
(314) 260-8691

Camp Butler National Cemetery
5063 Camp Butler Road; RR #1
Springfield, IL 62707
(217) 492-4070

Danville National Cemetery
1900 East Main Street
Danville, IL 61832
(217) 554-4550

Mound City National Cemetery
P. O. Box 128
Mound City, IL 62963
For information please contact
Jefferson Barracks National Cemetery
(314) 260-8691

Quincy National Cemetery
36th and Maine Street
Quincy, IL 62301
For information please contact
Rock Island National Cemetery
(309) 782-2094

Rock Island National Cemetery
Rock Island Arsenal
P. O. Box 737
Moline, IL 61265
Rock Island, IL 61299-7090
(309) 782-2094

INDIANA

Crown Hill National Cemetery
700 West 38th Street
Indianapolis, IN 46208
For information please contact
Marion National Cemetery
(765) 674-0284

Marion National Cemetery
VA Medical Center
1700 East 38th Street
Marion, IN 46952
(765) 674-0284

New Albany National Cemetery
1943 Ekin Avenue
New Albany, IN 47150
For information please contact
Zachary Taylor National Cemetery
(812) 948-5234

IOWA

Keokuk National Cemetery
1701 J Street
Keokuk, IA 52632
For information please contact
Rock Island National Cemetery
(309) 782-2094

KANSAS

Fort Leavenworth Natl Cemetery
Fort Leavenworth, KS 66027
For information please contact
Leavenworth National Cemetery
(913) 758-4105

Fort Scott National Cemetery
P. O. Box 917
Fort Scott, KS 66701
(620) 223-2840

Leavenworth National Cemetery
P. O. Box 1694
Leavenworth, KS 66048
(913) 758-4105

KENTUCKY

Camp Nelson National Cemetery
6980 Danville Road
Nicholasville, KY 40356
(859) 885-5727

Cave Hill National Cemetery
701 Baxter Avenue
Louisville, KY 40204
For information please contact
Zachary Taylor National Cemetery
(502) 893-3852

Danville National Cemetery
277 North First Street
Danville, KY 40442
For information please contact
Camp Nelson National Cemetery
(859) 885-5727
Lebanon National Cemetery
20 Highway 208
Lebanon, KY 40033
(502) 893-3852

Lexington National Cemetery
833 West Main Street
Lexington, KY 40508
For information please contact
Camp Nelson National Cemetery
(859) 885-5727

Mill Springs National Cemetery
Nancy, KY 42544
For information please contact
Camp Nelson National Cemetery
(859) 885-5727

Zachary Taylor National Cemetery
4701 Brownsboro Road
Louisville, KY 40207
(502) 893-3852

LOUISIANA

Alexandria National Cemetery
209 East Shamrock Street
Pineville, LA 71360
For information please contact
Natchez National Cemetery
(318) 449-1793

Baton Rouge National Cemetery
220 North 19th Street
Baton Rouge, LA 70806
For information please contact
Port Hudson National Cemetery
(225) 654-3767
Port Hudson National Cemetery
20978 Port Hickey Road
Zachary, LA 70791
(225) 654-3767

MAINE

Togus National Cemetery
VA Medical and Regional Office Center
Togus, ME 04330
For information please contact Massachusetts National Cemetery
(508) 563-7113

MARYLAND

Annapolis National Cemetery
800 West Street
Annapolis, MD 21401
For information please contact Baltimore National Cemetery
(410) 644-9696

Baltimore National Cemetery
5501 Frederick Avenue
Baltimore, MD 21228
(410) 644-9696

Loudon Park National Cemetery
3445 Frederick Avenue
Baltimore, MD 21228
For information please contact Baltimore National Cemetery
(410) 644-9696

MASSACHUSETTS

Massachusetts National Cemetery
Bourne, MA 02532
(508) 563-7113

MICHIGAN

Fort Custer National Cemetery
15501 Dickman Road
Augusta, MI 49012
(269) 731-4164

GREAT LAKES NATIONAL CEMETERY
4200 Belford Road
Holly, MI 48842
(866) 348-8603

MINNESOTA

Fort Snelling National Cemetery
7601 34th Avenue, South
Minneapolis, MN 55450-1199
(612) 726-1127

MISSISSIPPI

Biloxi National Cemetery
P. O. Box 4968
Biloxi, MS 39535-4968
(601) 388-6668

Corinth National Cemetery
1551 Horton Street
Corinth, MS 38834
For information please contact Memphis National Cemetery
(901) 386-8311

Natchez National Cemetery
41 Cemetery Road
Natchez, MS 39120
(601) 445-4981

MISSOURI

Jefferson Barracks National Cemetery
2900 Sheridan Road
St. Louis, MO 63125
(314) 260-8691

Jefferson City National Cemetery
1024 East McCarty Street
Jefferson City, MO 65101
For information please contact Jefferson Barracks National Cemetery
(314) 260-8691

Springfield National Cemetery
1702 East Seminole Street
Springfield, MO 65804
(417) 881-9499

NEBRASKA

Fort McPherson National Cemetery
HCO1, Box 67
Maxwell, NE 69151
(308) 582-4433

NEW JERSEY

Beverly National Cemetery
R.D. #1, Bridgeboro Road
Beverly, NJ 08010
(609) 877-5460

Finn's Point National Cemetery
RFD # 3, Fort Mott Road, Box 542
Salem, NJ 08079
For information please contact
Beverly National Cemetery
(609) 877-5460

NEW MEXICO

Fort Bayard National Cemetery
P. O. Box 189
Fort Bayard, NM 88036
For information please contact
Fort Bliss National Cemetery
(915) 564-0201
Santa Fe National Cemetery
501 North Guadalupe Street
Santa Fe, NM 87501
(505) 988-6400

NEW YORK

Bath National Cemetery
VA Medical Center
Bath, NY 14810
(607) 664-4853

Calverton National Cemetery
210 Princeton Boulevard
Calverton, NY 11933-1031
(631) 727-5410 or 5770

Cypress Hills National Cemetery
625 Jamaica Avenue
Brooklyn, NY 11208
For information please contact
Long Island National Cemetery
(631) 454-4949

Long Island National Cemetery
2040 Wellwood Avenue
Farmingdale, NY 11735-1211
(631) 454-4949

Saratoga National Cemetery
200 Duell Road
Schuylerville, NY 12871-1721
(518) 581-9128

Woodlawn National Cemetery
1825 Davis Street
Elmira, NY 14901
(607) 732-5411

NORTH CAROLINA

New Bern National Cemetery
1711 National Avenue
New Bern, NC 28560
(252) 637-2912

Raleigh National Cemetery
501 Rock Quarry Road
Raleigh, NC 27610
(252) 637-2912

Salisbury National Cemetery
202 Government Road
Salisbury, NC 28144
(704) 636-2661

Wilmington National Cemetery
2011 Market Street
Wilmington, NC 28403
For information please contact New Bern National Cemetery
(252) 637-2912

OHIO

Dayton National Cemetery
VA Medical Center
4100 West Third Street
Dayton, OH 45428-1008
(937) 262-2115

Ohio Western Reserve National Cemetery
P.O. Box 8
10175 Rawiga Road
Rittman, OH 44270
(330) 335-3069

OKLAHOMA

Fort Gibson National Cemetery
1423 Cemetery Road
Fort Gibson, OK 74434
(918) 478-2334

Fort Sill National Cemetery
24665 N-S Road 260
Elgin, OK 73538
(580) 492-3200

OREGON

Eagle Point National Cemetery
2763 Riley Road
Eagle Point, OR 97524
(541) 826-2511

Roseburg National Cemetery
VA Medical Center
Roseburg, OR 97470
(541) 826-2511

Willamette National Cemetery
11800 S.E. Mt. Scott Boulevard
Portland, OR 97266-6937
(503) 273-5250

PENNSYLVANIA

Indiantown Gap National Cemetery
R. R. #2, P. O. Box 484
Annville, PA 17003-9618
(717) 865-5254
National Cemetery of the Alleghenies
1158 Morgan Road
Bridgeville, PA 15017
(724) 746-4363

Philadelphia National Cemetery
Haines Street and Limekiln Pike
Philadelphia, PA 19138
For information please contact
Beverly National Cemetery
(609) 877-5460

PUERTO RICO

Puerto Rico National Cemetery
Avenue Cementario Nacional #50
Bayamon, PR 00960
(787) 798-8400

SOUTH CAROLINA
Beaufort National Cemetery
601 Boundary Street
Beaufort, SC 29902
(843) 524-3925
Florence National Cemetery
803 East National Cemetery Road
Florence, SC 29501
(843) 669-8783

Fort Jackson National Cemetery
4170 Percival Rd
Columbia, SC 29229
(866) 577-5248

SOUTH DAKOTA

Black Hills National Cemetery
P. O. Box 640
Sturgis, SD 57785
(605) 347-3830
Fort Meade National Cemetery
Old Stone Road
Sturgis, SD 57785
For information please contact
Black Hills National Cemetery
(605) 347-3830

Hot Springs National Cemetery
VA Medical Center
Hot Springs, SD 57747
For information please contact
Black Hills National Cemetery
(605) 347-3830

TENNESSEE

Chattanooga National Cemetery
1200 Bailey Avenue
Chattanooga, TN 37404
(423) 855-6590

Knoxville National Cemetery
939 Tyson Street, N.W.
Knoxville, TN 37917
(423) 855-6590

Memphis National Cemetery
3568 Townes Avenue
Memphis, TN 38122
(901) 386-8311

Mountain Home National Cemetery
P. O. Box 8
Mountain Home, TN 37684
(423) 979-3535

Nashville National Cemetery
1420 Gallatin Road, South
Madison, TN 37115-4619
(615) 860-0086

TEXAS

Dallas-Fort Worth
National Cemetery
2191 Mountain Creek Parkway
Dallas, TX 75211
(214) 467-3374

Fort Bliss National Cemetery
5200 Fred Wilson Road
P. O. Box 6342
Fort Bliss, TX 79906
(915) 564-0201

Fort Sam Houston National
Cemetery
1520 Harry Wurzbach Road
San Antonio, TX 78209
(210) 820-3891

Houston National Cemetery
10410 Veterans Memorial Drive
Houston, TX 77038
(281) 447-8686

Kerrville National Cemetery
VA Medical Center
3600 Memorial Boulevard
Kerrville, TX 78028
For information please contact
Fort Sam Houston National
Cemetery
(210) 820-3891

San Antonio National Cemetery
517 Paso Hondo Street
San Antonio, TX 78202
For information please contact
Fort Sam Houston National
Cemetery
(210) 820-3891

VIRGINIA

Alexandria National Cemetery
1450 Wilkes Street
Alexandria, VA 22314
For information please contact
Quantico National Cemetery
(703) 221-2183
Balls Bluff National Cemetery
Route 7
Leesburg, VA 22075
For information please contact
Culpeper National Cemetery
(540) 825-0027

City Point National Cemetery
10th Avenue and Davis Street
Hopewell, VA 23860
For information please contact
Fort Harrison National Cemetery
(804) 795-2031

Cold Harbor National Cemetery
Route 156 North
Mechanicsville, VA 23111
For information please contact
Fort Harrison National Cemetery
(804) 795-2031

Culpeper National Cemetery
305 U.S. Avenue
Culpeper, VA 22701
(540) 825-0027

Danville National Cemetery
721 Lee Street
Danville, VA 24541
For information please contact
Salisbury National Cemetery
(704) 636-2661

Fort Harrison National Cemetery
8620 Varina Road
Richmond, VA 23231
(804) 795-2031

Glendale National Cemetery
8301 Willis Church Road
Richmond, VA 23231
For information please contact
Fort Harrison National Cemetery
(804) 795-2031

Hampton National Cemetery
Cemetery Road at Marshall Avenue
Hampton, VA 23667
(757) 723-7104

Hampton National Cemetery
VA Medical Center
Emancipation Drive
Hampton, VA 23667
(757) 723-7104

Quantico National Cemetery
P. O. Box 10
18424 Joplin Road (Route 619)
Triangle, VA 22172
(703) 221-2183 (local)

Richmond National Cemetery
1701 Williamsburg Road
Richmond, VA 23231
For information please contact
Fort Harrison National Cemetery
(804) 795-2031

Seven Pines National Cemetery
400 East Williamsburg Road
Sandston, VA 23150
For information please contact
Fort Harrison National Cemetery
(804) 795-2031

Staunton National Cemetery
901 Richmond Avenue
Staunton, VA 24401
(540) 825-0027

Winchester National Cemetery
401 National Avenue
Winchester, VA 22601
For information please contact
Culpeper National Cemetery
(540) 825-0027

WASHINGTON

Tahoma National Cemetery
18600 Southeast 240th Street
Kent, WA 98042-4868
(425) 413-9614

WEST VIRGINIA

Grafton National Cemetery
431 Walnut Street
Grafton, WV 26354
For information please contact
West Virginia National Cemetery
(304) 265-2044
West Virginia National Cemetery
Route 2, Box 127
Grafton, WV 26354
(304) 265-2044

WISCONSIN

Wood National Cemetery
5000 W National Ave,
Bldg 1301
Milwaukee, WI 53295-4000
(414) 382-5300

DEPARTMENT OF THE INTERIOR NATIONAL CEMETERIES

DISTRICT OF COLUMBIA

Battleground National Cemetery
C/O Superintendent, Rock Creek Park
3545 Williamsburg Lane, NW
Washington, DC 20008
(202) 282-1063

GEORGIA

Andersonville National Historic Site
Route 1, Box 800
Andersonville, GA 31711
(912) 924-0343

LOUISIANA

Chalmette National Cemetery
C/O Jean Lafitte National
Historical Park and Preserve
365 Canal Street, Suite 2400
New Orleans, LA 70130
(504) 589-3882
(504) 589-4430

MARYLAND

Antietam National Battlefield
Box 158
301) 432-5124
Sharpsburg, MD 21782-0158
(301) 432-5124

MISSISSIPPI

Vicksburg National Military Park
3201 Clay Street
Vicksburg, MS 39180
(601) 636-0583

MONTANA

Little Bighorn Battle
National Monument
Custer National Cemetery
P. O. Box 39
Crow Agency, MT 59022
(406) 638-2621

PENNSYLVANIA

Gettysburg National Military Park
97 Taneytown Road
Gettysburg, PA 17325-2804
(717) 334-1124

TENNESSEE

Andrew Johnson National
Historic Site
P. O. Box 1088
Greeneville, TN 37744
(423) 638-3551
Fort Donelson National Battlefield
P. O. Box 434
Dover, TN 37058
(615) 232-5348

Shiloh National Military Park
Route 1, Box 9
Shiloh, TN 38376-9704
(901) 689-5275

Stones River National Battlefield
3501 Old Nashville Highway
Murfreesboro, TN 37129
(615) 893-9501

VIRGINIA

Fredericksburg and Spotsylvania
County Battlefields Memorial
National Military Park
120 Chatham Lane
Fredericksburg, VA 22405
(540) 371-0802

Poplar Grove National Cemetery
Petersburg National Battlefield
1539 Hickory Hill Road
Petersburg, VA 23803
(804) 732-3531

Yorktown Battlefield Cemetery
Colonial National Historical Park
P. O. Box 210
Yorktown, VA 23690
(757) 898-3400

DEPARTMENT OF THE ARMY NATIONAL CEMETERIES

United States Soldiers' & Airmen's
Home National Cemetery
21 Harewood Road, NW
Washington, DC 20011
(202) 829-1829

Arlington National Cemetery
Interment Services Branch
Arlington, VA 22211
(703) 695-3250 or 3255

STATE VETERANS CEMETERIES

ARIZONA

Southern Arizona Veterans Memorial
1300 Buffalo Soldier Trail
Sierra Vista, AZ 85635
(520) 458-7144

ARKANSAS

Arkansas Veterans Cemetery
1501 W Maryland Avenue
North Little Rock, AR 72120
(501) 683-2259

CALIFORNIA

Veterans Memorial Grove Cemetery
Veterans Home of California
Yountville, CA 94599
(707) 944-4600

Northern California Veterans Cemetery
P.O. Box 76
11800 Gas Point Road
Igo, CA 96047
(866) 777-4533

COLORADO

Colorado State Veterans Cemetery At Homelake
3749 Sherman Avenue
Monte Vista, CO 81144
(719) 852-5118

Veterans Memorial Cemetery Of Western Colorado
2830 D Road
Grand Junction, CO 81505
(970) 263-8986

CONNECTICUT

Colonel Raymond F. Gates
Memorial Cemetery
Veterans Home and Hospital
287 West Street
Rocky Hill, CT 06067
(860) 721-5838
Spring Grove Veterans Cemetery
Darien, CT
C/O Veterans Home and Hospital
287 West Street
Rocky Hill, CT 06067
(860) 721-5838

Middletown Veterans Cemetery
C/O Veterans Home and Hospital
287 West Street
Rocky Hill, CT 06067
(860) 721-5838

DELAWARE

Delaware Veterans Memorial
Cemetery
2465 Chesapeake City Road
Bear, DE 19701
(302) 834-8046

Delaware Veterans Memorial
Cemetery-Sussex County
RD 5 Box 100
Millsboro, DE 19966
(302) 934-5653

GEORGIA

Georgia Veterans Memorial Cemetery
2617 Vinson Highway
Milledgeville, Georgia 31061
(478) 445-3363

Georgia Veterans Memorial Cemetery
8819 U.S. Highway 301
Glennville, Georgia 30427
(912)-654-5398

HAWAII

Director, Office of Veterans
Services
459 Patterson Road
E-Wing, Room 1-A103
Honolulu, HI 96189
(808) 433-0420

Hawaii State Veterans Cemetery
45-349 Kamehameha Highway
Kaneohe, HI 96744
(808) 233-3630

East Hawaii Veterans
Cemetery - No. I
County of Hawaii
25 Aupuni Street
Hilo, HI 96720
(Island of Hawaii)
(808) 961-8311

East Hawaii Veterans
Cemetery - No. II
County of Hawaii
25 Aupuni Street
Hilo, HI 96720
(Island of Hawaii)
(808) 961-8311

Kauai Veterans Cemetery
County of Kauai Public Works
3021 Umi Street
Lihue, HI 96766
(Island of Kauai)
(808) 241-6670

Maui Veterans Cemetery
1295 Makawao Avenue, Box 117
Makawao, HI 96768
(Island of Maui)
(808) 572-7272

Hoolehua Veterans Cemetery
(Molokai)
P. O. Box 526
Kauna Kakai, HI 96748
(Island of Molokai)
(808) 553-3204

West Hawaii State
Veterans Cemetery
(Currently under construction – located on the Island of Hawaii near town of Kona)
(808) 961-8311

Lanai Veterans Cemetery
(Currently under construction – located on the Island of Lanai)
(808) 565-6979

IDAHO

Idaho Veterans Cemetery
10101 North Horseshoe Bend Road
Boise, ID 83714
(208) 334-4796

ILLINOIS

Sunset Cemetery
Illinois Veterans Home
1707 North 12th Street
Quincy, IL 62301
(217) 222-8641

INDIANA

Indiana State Soldiers Home Cemetery
3851 North River Road
West Lafayette, IN 47906-3765
(765) 463-1502

Indiana Veterans Memorial Cemetery
1415 North Gate Road
Madison, IN 47250
(812) 273-9220

IOWA

Iowa Veterans Home and Cemetery
13th & Summit Streets
Marshalltown, IA 50158
(641) 753-4309

Iowa Veterans Cemetery
34024 Veterans Memorial Drive
Adel, Iowa 50003-3300
(515) 996-9048

KANSAS

Kansas Veterans Cemetery
At Fort Dodge
714 Sheridan, Unit #66
Fort Dodge, KS 67801
(620) 338-8775
Kansas Veterans Cemetery
At Wakeeney
P.O. Box 185
4035 13th Street
Wakeeney, KS 67672
(785) 743-5685

Kansas Veterans Cemetery
At Winfield
1208 North College
Winfield, KS 67156
(620) 229-2287

KENTUCKY

Kentucky Veterans Cemetery-Central
1111 Louisville Road
Frankfort, Kentucky
(502) 564-9281
Kentucky Veterans Cemetery-North
205 Eibeck Lane
P.O. Box 467
Williamstown, Kentucky 41097
(859)-823-0720

Kentucky Veteran's Cemetery-West
5817 Fort Campbell Boulevard
Hopkinsville, Kentucky 42240
(270) 707-9653

LOUISIANA

Northwest Louisiana Veterans Cemetery
7970 Mike Clark Road
Keithville, Louisiana 71047
(318) 925-0612

MAINE

Maine Veterans Memorial Cemetery (Closed)
Civic Center Drive
Augusta, Maine

Maine Veterans Memorial Cemetery--Mt. Vernon Rd.
163 Mt. Vernon Road
Augusta, ME 04330
(207) 287-3481

Northern Maine Veterans Cemetery-Caribou
37 Lombard Road
Caribou, ME 04736
(207)-492-1173

MARYLAND

Maryland State
Veterans Cemeteries
Federal Building-31 Hopkins Plaza
Baltimore, MD 21201
(410) 962-4700

Cheltenham Veterans Cemetery
11301 Crain Highway
P. O. Box 10
Cheltenham, MD 20623
(301) 372-6398

Crownsville Veterans Cemetery
1080 Sunrise Beach Road
Crownsville, MD 21032
(410) 987-6320 or
(301) 962-4700

Eastern Shore Veterans Cemetery
6827 East New Market
Ellwood Road
Hurlock, MD 21643
(410) 943-3420

Garrison Forest Veterans Cemetery
11501 Garrison Forest Road
Owings Mills, MD 21117
(410) 363-6090
Rocky Gap Veterans Cemetery
14205 Pleasant Valley Road, NE
Flintstone, MD 21530
(301) 777-2185

MASSACHUSETTS

Massachusetts State Veterans
Cemetery (Agawam & Winchendon)
1390 Main Street
Agawam, MA 01001
(413) 821-9500

Winchendon Veterans Cemetery
111 Glenallen Street
Winchendon, MA 01475
(978) 297-9501

MICHIGAN

Grand Rapids Home for Veterans
Cemetery
3000 Monroe, NW
Grand Rapids, MI 49505
(616) 364-5400

MINNESOTA

MN State Veterans Cemetery
15550 HWY 15
Little Falls, MN 56345
(320) 616-2527

MISSOURI

St. James Missouri Veterans Home
Cemetery
620 North Jefferson
St. James, MO 65559
(573) 265-3271

Missouri Veterans Cemetery -
Higgensville, MO
20109 Bus. Hwy. 13
Higgensville, MO 64037
(660) 584-5252

Missouri Veterans Cemetery –
Springfield. MO
5201 South Southwood Road
Springfield, MO 65804
(417) 823-3944

Missouri State Veterans Cemetery –
Bloomfield
17357 Stars and Strips Way
Bloomfield, Missouri 63825
(573) 568-3871
Missouri State Veterans Cemetery -
Jacksonville
1479 County Road 1675
Jacksonville, Missouri 65260
(660) 295-4237

MONTANA

State Veterans Cemetery
Fort William H. Harrison
Box 5715
Helena, MT 59604
(406) 324-3740

State Veterans Cemetery
Miles City
Highway 59
Miles City, MT 59301
(406) 324-3740

Montana Veterans Home Cemetery
P. O. Box 250
Columbia Falls, MT 59912
(406) 892-3256

NEBRASKA

Nebraska Veterans
Home Cemetery
Burkett Station
Grand Island, NE 68803
(308) 385-6252, Ext. 230

NEVADA

Commissioner of Veterans Affairs
1201 Terminal Way, Room 108
Reno, NV 89520
(775) 688-1155

Northern Nevada Veterans
Memorial Cemetery
14 Veterans Way
Fernley, NV 89408
(775) 575-4441

Southern Nevada Veterans
Memorial Cemetery
1900 Buchanan Boulevard
Boulder City, NV 89005
(702) 486-5920

NEW HAMPSHIRE

NH State Veterans Cemetery
110 Daniel Webster Hwy, Route 3
Boscawen, NH 03303
(603) 796-2026

NEW JERSEY

Brigadier General William C. Doyle
Veterans Memorial Cemetery
350 Provenceline Road, Route #2
Wrightstown, NJ 08562
(609) 758-7250

New Jersey Memorial Home
Cemetery (Closed)
524 N.W. Boulevard
Vineland, NJ 08360
(609) 696-6350

NORTH CAROLINA

Western Carolina State Veterans
Cemetery
962 Old Highway 70, West
Black Mountain, NC 28711
(828) 669-0684

Coastal Carolina State Veterans
Cemetery
P. O. Box 1486
Jacksonville, NC 28541
(910) 347-4550 or 3570

Sandhills State Veterans Cemetery
P. O. Box 39
400 Murchison Road
Spring Lake, NC 28390
(910) 436-5630 or 5635

NORTH DAKOTA

North Dakota Veterans Cemetery
1825 46th Street
Mandan, ND 58554
(701) 667-1418

OHIO

Ohio Veterans Home Cemetery
3416 Columbus Avenue
Sandusky, OH 44870
(419) 625-2454, Ext. 200

Oklahoma

Oklahoma Veterans Cemetery
Military Department (OKFAC)
3501 Military Circle N.E.
Oklahoma City, OK 73111-4398
(405) 228-5334

Pennsylvania

Pennsylvania Soldiers and
Sailors Home Cemetery
P. O. Box 6239
560 East Third Street
Erie, PA 16512-6239
(814) 871-4531

Rhode Island

Rhode Island Veterans Cemetery
301 South County Trail
Exeter, RI 02822-9712
(401) 268-3088

South Carolina

M.J. "Dolly" Cooper Veterans Cemetery
140 Inway Drive
Anderson, SC 29621
(864) 332-8022

South Dakota

SD Veterans Home Cemetery
2500 Minnekahta Avenue
Hot Springs, SD 57747
(605) 745-5127

Tennessee

East Tennessee State
Veterans Cemetery
5901 Lyons View Pike
Knoxville, TN 37919
(865) 594-6776

Middle Tennessee
Veterans Cemetery
7931 McCrory Lane
Nashville, TN 37221
(615) 532-2238

West Tennessee
Veterans Cemetery
4000 Forest Hill/Irene Road
Memphis, TN 38125
(901) 543-7005

Texas

Central Texas State Veterans Cemetery
11463 South Highway 195
Killeen, Texas 76542
(512) 463-5977

Rio Grande Valley
State Veterans Cemetery
2520 South Inspiration Road
Mission, TX 78572
(956) 583-7227

Utah

Utah State Veterans Cemetery
Utah Parks and Recreation
17111 South Camp Williams Road
Bluffdale, UT 84065
(801) 254-9036

Vermont

Vermont Veterans Home War
Memorial Cemetery
325 North Street
Bennington, VT 05201
(802) 442-6353

Vermont Veterans Memorial
Cemetery
120 State Street
Montpelier, VT 05602-4401
(802) 828-3379

VIRGINIA

Virginia Veterans Cemetery
10300 Pridesville Road
Amelia, VA 23002
(804) 561-1475
Albert G. Horton, Jr. Memorial Veterans Cemetery
5310 Milner's Road
Suffolk, Virginia 23434
(757) 334-4731

WASHINGTON

Washington Soldiers Home Colony and Cemetery
1301 Orting-Kapowsin Highway
Orting, WA 98360
(360) 893-4500

Washington Veterans Home Cemetery
P. O. Box 698
Retsil, WA 98378
(360) 895-4700

WISCONSIN

Northern Wisconsin Veterans Memorial Cemetery
N4063 Wildcat Road QQ
Spooner, WI 54801
(715) 635-5360

Wisconsin Veterans Memorial Cemetery
Wisconsin Veterans Home
N2665 Highway QQ
King, WI 54946
(715) 258-5586

Southern Wisconsin Veterans Memorial Cemetery
21731 Spring Street
Union Grove, WI 53182
(262) 878-5660

WYOMING

Oregon Trail Veterans Cemetery
89 Cemetery Road, Box 669
Evansville, WY 82636
(307) 235-6673

TERRITORIES

Guam Veterans Cemetery
490 Chalan Palayso
Agatna Heights, Guam 96910
(671) 475-4225

SAIPAN

CNMI Veterans Cemetery
Military/Veterans Affairs
P.O. Box 503416
Saipan, MP 96950
(670) 664-2650

NOTE:
All state cemeteries (except Nevada, Pennsylvania, Wyoming and Utah) restrict burials to state residents.

CHAPTER 9

HEALTHCARE BENEFITS

Individuals are encouraged to contact the nearest VA benefits or healthcare facility to obtain the latest information regarding healthcare benefits. Legislation often changes the specific regulations regarding healthcare and nursing home care.

2014 UPDATE: VA INTRODUCES HEALTH ID CARDS

The VA announced the rollout of secure veterans health identification cards. The new cards are designed to have additional security features. The card is called the Veterans Health Identification Card, which is similar to a traditional health insurance ID card. It displays the veteran's member and plan ID, and demonstrates their enrollment in VA healthcare.

VA IMPLEMENTS CHOICE CARD PROGRAM

The most visible outcome of VACAA, the Choice Card, will be available to veterans enrolled in VA health care as of August 1, 2014. Veterans with active duty service in a theater of combat operations within the previous five years are also eligible to receive a Choice Card.

To facilitate a smooth implementation of the new program, the card and a letter explaining eligibility for the program will be sent to beneficiaries in three phases:

1. to veterans who live 40 miles from any VA health care facility;
2. to those who have been waiting for their requested appointment for more than 30 days and;
3. the remaining 8 million veterans are scheduled to receive a card by January 2015.

Receiving the card does not mean a veteran is automatically eligible for the program. The card will include a toll-free number that can be used to determine eligibility. Critically, the VA must give pre-authorization for care. Each episode of care will be authorized for no more than 60 days.

VETERAN HEALTH REGISTRIES

Certain veterans can participate in a VA health registry and receive free medical examinations, including laboratory and other diagnostic tests, when determined necessary by an examining clinician.

GULF WAR REGISTRY:

For veterans who served in the Gulf War and Operation Iraqi Freedom

DEPLETED URANIUM REGISTRIES:

VA maintains two registries for veterans possibly exposed to depleted uranium. The first is for veterans who served in the Gulf War, including Operation Iraqi Freedom. The second is for veterans who served elsewhere, including Bosnia and Afghanistan.

AGENT ORANGE REGISTRY:

For veterans possible exposed to dioxin or other toxic substances in herbicides used during the Vietnam War, while serving in Korea in 1968 or 1969, or as a result of testing, transporting, or spraying herbicides for military purposes.

IONIZING RADIATION REGISTRY:

For veterans possibly exposed to atomic radiation during the following activities:

- Atmospheric detonation of a nuclear device;
- Occupation of Hiroshima or Nagasaki from August 6, 1945 through July 1, 1946;
- Internment as a prisoner of war in Japan during WW II
- Serving in official military duties at the gaseous diffusion plants at Paducah, KY; Portsmouth, OH; or the K-25 area at Oak Ridge, TN for at least 250 days before February 1, 1992, or in Longshot, Milrow or Cannikin underground nuclear tests at Amchitka Island, Alaska, before January 1, 1974; or
- Treatment with nasopharyngeal (NP) radium during military service.]

ELIGIBILITY

The primary factor in determining a veteran's eligibility to receive VA health care benefits is "veteran status." "Veteran status" is established by active duty service in the military, naval, or air service and a discharge or release from active military service under other than dishonorable conditions.

The veteran's length of service may also matter. It depends on when he or she served. There is no length of service requirement for:

- Former enlisted persons who started active duty before September 8, 1980; or

- Former officers who first entered active duty before October 17, 1981.

All other veterans must have 24 months of continuous active duty military service or meet one of the exceptions described below.

EXCEPTIONS TO THE 24-MONTH ACTIVE DUTY RULE

The 24 continuous months of active duty service requirement does not apply to:

- Reservists who were called to Active Duty and who completed the term for which they were called, and who were granted an "other than dishonorable" discharge; or
- National Guard members who were called to Active Duty by federal executive order, and who completed the term for which they were called, and who were granted an "other than dishonorable" discharge; or
- Veterans requesting a benefit for, or in connection with, a service-connected condition or disability; or
- Veterans who were discharged or released from active duty under section 1171 or 1173 of title 10; or
- Veterans who were discharged or released from active duty for a disability incurred or aggravated in line of duty; or
- Veterans who have been determined by VA to have compensable service-connected conditions; or
- Veterans requesting treatment for and/or counseling of sexual trauma that occurred while on active military service, for treatment of conditions related to ionizing radiation or for head or neck cancer related to nose or throat radium treatment while in the military.

ENROLLMENT

In February 2012 the VA announced the creation of a new enrollment application for servicemembers. The online application for VA health benefits, VA "Form 1010EZ" became available for servicemembers returning from deployment, and is used to enroll servicemembers in the VA healthcare system.

In order to qualify for VA healthcare, a veteran must first become enrolled. Veterans must answer a few questions, and are then are then assigned by VA to one of the priority groups discussed later in this chapter.

All veterans seeking VA healthcare are required to be enrolled unless they are in one of the following categories:

- VA rated the individual as having a service-connected disability of 50% or more;

- It has been less than one year since the veteran was discharged from military service for a disability that the military determined was incurred or aggravated in the line of duty, and has not yet been rated by VA;
- Veteran is seeking care from VA for a service-connected disability only.

As part of the enrollment process, a veteran may select any VA health care facility to serve as his or her primary treatment facility.

There are three ways a veteran can apply to enroll in healthcare benefits. The first is to obtain the enrollment form, "10-10EZ" from their local VA Medical Center or Clinic, in person. The second way is telephone; by calling (877) 222-VETS (8387) Monday through Friday between 8:00 a.m. and 8:00 p.m. Eastern Time. The third way to apply is online, through the VA's website.

The healthcare benefits enrollment form can also be accessed online at the following web address:

https://www.1010ez.med.va.gov/sec/vha/1010ez/

The application will be processed and forwarded to the VA Health Eligibility Center in Atlanta, GA. The Health Eligibility Center will notify the veteran of his or her status.

Once enrolled, most veterans will remain enrolled from year to year without further action on their part. However, certain veterans are required to provide income information to determine their priority level. These veterans will be mailed a "VA Form 10-10 EZ" for completion for re-enrollment on an annual basis, or they can renew their benefits by visiting the VA's website.

A veteran may choose not to be re-enrolled, or changes in VA funding may reduce the number of priority groups VA can enroll in a given fiscal year. If VA cannot renew enrollment for another year, the veteran will be notified in writing before their enrollment period expires.

PRIORITY GROUPS

The number of veterans who can be enrolled in the health care program is determined by the amount of money Congress gives VA each year. Since funds are limited, VA set up priority groups to make sure that certain groups of veterans are able to be enrolled before others.

Once a veteran applies for enrollment, his or her eligibility will be verified. Based on the individual's specific eligibility status, he or she will be assigned a priority group.

The priority groups range from 1-8 with 1 being the highest priority for enrollment. Some veterans may have to agree to pay copay to be placed in certain priority groups.

A veteran may be eligible for more than one Enrollment Priority Group. In that case, VA will always place him or her in the highest priority group that he or she is eligible for. Under the Medical Benefits Package, the same services are generally available to all enrolled veterans.

Once a veteran applies for enrollment, his or her eligibility will be verified. Based on the individual's specific eligibility status, he or she will be assigned a priority group.

The priority groups are complicated and some reference financial thresholds.

Priority Group 1

- Veterans with service-connected disabilities rated 50% or more disabling; or
- Veterans determined by VA to be unemployable due to service-connected conditions.

Priority Group 2

- Veterans with service-connected disabilities rated 30% or 40% disabling.

Priority Group 3

- Veterans who are former POWs;
- Veterans whose discharge was for a disability that was incurred or aggravated in the line of duty;
- Veterans with service-connected disabilities rated 10% or 20% disabling;
- Veterans who are Purple Heart recipients (unless eligible for a higher Priority Group);
- Veterans who are Medal of Honor Recipients;
- Veterans awarded special eligibility classification under Title 38, U.S.C., Section 1151, "benefits for individuals disabled by treatment or vocational rehabilitation".

Priority Group 4

- Veterans who are receiving aid and attendance or housebound benefits from VA;
- Veterans who have been determined by VA to be catastrophically disabled.

Priority Group 5

- Nonservice-connected veterans and service-connected veterans rated 0% disabled whose annual income and net worth are below the established dollar threshold. (Veterans in this priority group must provide VA with information on their annual income and net worth in order to determine whether they are below the "means test" threshold; or agree to co-payment requirements. The threshold is adjusted annually, and announced in January. In making the assessment, the veteran's household income is considered.);

- Veterans receiving VA pension benefits;
- Veterans eligible for Medicaid benefits.

Priority Group 6

- Veterans with 0% service-connected conditions, but receiving VA compensation benefits
- Veterans exposed to ionizing radiation during atmospheric testing or during the occupation of Hiroshima and Nagasaki
- Project 112/SHAD participants
- Veterans who served in the Republic of Vietnam between January 9, 1962 and May 7, 1975
- Veterans who served in the Southwest Asia theater of operations from August 2, 1990 through November 11, 1998
- Veterans who served in a theater of combat operations after November 11, 1998 as follows:
- Veterans discharged from active duty on or after January 28, 2003, for five years post discharge

Priority Group 7

- Veterans with incomes below the geographic means test (GMT) income thresholds and who agree to pay the applicable copayment

Priority Group 8

- Veterans with gross household incomes above the VA national income threshold and the geographically-adjusted income threshold for their resident location and who agrees to pay copays
- Veterans eligibility for enrollment: Noncompensable 0% service-connected and:
- Subpriority a: Enrolled as of January 16, 2003, and who have remained enrolled since that date and/or placed in this subpriority due to changed eligibility status
- Subpriority b: Enrolled on or after June 15, 2009 whose income exceeds the current VA National Income Thresholds or VA National Geographic Income thresholds by 10% or less
- Veterans eligibility for enrollment: Non-service-connected and:

- Subpriority c: Enrolled as of January 16, 2003, and who remained enrolled since that date and or/placed in this subpriority due to changed eligibility status
- Subpriority d: Enrolled on or after June 15, 2009 and whose income exceeds the current VA National Income Thresholds or VA National Geographic Income thresholds by 10% or less
- Veterans not eligible for enrollment: veterans not meeting the criteria below:
- Subpriority e: Noncompensable 0% service-connected
- Subpriority f: Non-service-connected

SPECIAL ACCESS TO CARE

Service Disabled Veterans: Veterans who are 50 percent or more disabled from service-connected conditions, unemployable due to service-connected conditions, or receiving care for a service-connected disability receive priority in scheduling of hospital or outpatient medical appointments.

MEANS TEST

Most veterans who do not receive a VA disability or pension payment or have a VA special eligibility, such as a recently discharged combat veteran must complete "VA form 10-10EZ." These veterans must provide information on their prior income year total gross household income and net worth to determine eligibility status, and copay responsibility for VA health care and/or prescription medication. Total gross household income includes income of the veteran, spouse and dependent children.

TRAVEL BENEFITS

Once enrolled in the VA health system, health care benefits become completely portable throughout the entire VA system. Enrolled veterans who are traveling or who spend time away from their primary treatment facility may obtain care at any VA health care facility across the country, without having to reapply.

EXISTING HEALTHCARE COVERAGE

Since VA health care depends primarily on annual congressional appropriations, veterans are allowed to keep their current healthcare coverage and are encouraged to do so. Veterans with private insurance or other coverage such as DoD, Medicare, or Medicaid may find these coverages to be a supplement to their VA enrollment. The use of other available healthcare coverage does not affect a veteran's enrollment status. VA does not charge the veteran for insurance company co-payments and deductibles.

When applying for medical care, all veterans will be asked to provide information pertaining to health insurance coverage, including policies held by spouses. VA is obligated to submit claims to insurance carriers for the recovery of costs for medical care provided to nonservice-connected veterans and service-connected veterans for nonservice-connected conditions.

Copayment Requirements

2013 Update: The VA announced a new program aimed at increasing access to healthcare closer to home for American Indian and Alaska native veterans. The program is a partnership between the VA and Indian Health Services. As a result of the program, the VA will be able to reimburse the Indian Health Services for direct care services provided to eligible veterans. Under the agreement, VA copayments don't apply to eligible American Indian and Alaska Native Veterans.

As of May 7, 2012, the VA announced veterans would no longer be charged a co-payment upon receiving care in their home via telehealth conferencing.

While some veterans qualify for cost-free health care services based on a compensable service-connected condition or other qualifying factor, most veterans are required to complete an annual financial assessment or Means Test to determine if they qualify for cost-free services.

Veterans whose income and net worth exceed the established Means Test threshold, as well as those who choose not to complete the financial assessment must agree to pay required copayments to become eligible for VA health care services.

Along with their enrollment confirmation and priority group assignment, enrollees will receive information regarding their copayment requirements, if applicable.

Veterans may qualify for cost-free health care and/or medications based on:

- Receiving a Purple Heart Medal, or
- Former Prisoner of War Status, or
- In receipt of Medal of Honor (may take copay test to determine prescription copay status)
- 50% or more compensable service-connected disabilities (0-40% compensable service-connected may take copay test to determine prescription copay status), or
- Low income, or
- Other qualifying factors including treatment related to their military service experience. (Some veterans are not charged a copay for health care or medications furnished for treatment of conditions related to their military service experience. This includes exposure to Agent Orange, Ionizing Radiation, Environmental Contaminants during the Gulf War, Project 112/SHAD, Nose and Throat Radium treatment, or Sexual Trauma while in the military, or care of combat-related conditions for 2 years following discharge from active duty.

Copayment Rates – Current as of January 2014

OUTPATIENT SERVICES	
Basic Services – Services provided by a primary care clinician	$15/visit
Specialty Care Services – services provided by a clinical specialist such as surgeon, radiologist, audiologist, optometrist, cardiologist, and specialty tests such as magnetic resonance imagery (MRI), computerized axial tomography (CAT) scan, and nuclear medicine studies	$50 /visit
Footnotes for outpatient services: • Copayment amount is limited to a single charge per visit regardless of the number of health care providers seen in a single day. The copayment amount is based on the highest level of service received. • There is no copayment requirement for preventive services such as screenings and immunizations.)	
MEDICATIONS	
Veterans in Priority Groups 2-6, for each 30-day supply of medication for treatment of nonservice-connected conditions	$8/prescription
(The total amount paid annually by veterans in Priority Groups 2 through 6 is limited to $960.)	
Effective July 1, 2010, Veterans in Priority Groups 7-8, , for each 30-day supply of medication for treatment of nonservice-connected conditions	$9/prescription
(Veterans in Priority Groups 7-8 do not qualify for medication copay annual cap.)	
Veterans in Priority Group 1 do not pay for medications.	
INPATIENT SERVICES	
Inpatient copayment for the first 90 days of care during a 365-day period	$1,132
Inpatient copayment for each additional 90 days of care during a 365 day period	$566
Per Diem Charge Daily Charge	$2/day $10/day
Footnote for inpatient services: Lower income veterans who live in high-cost areas may qualify for a reduction of inpatient copay charges.	
Long-Term Care	
Nursing Home Care / Inpatient Respite Care / Geriatric Evaluation	Maximum of $97/day Adult
Day Health Care / Outpatient Geriatric Evaluation / Outpatient Respite Care	Maximum of $15/day
Domiciliary Care	Maximum of $5/day
Footnote for inpatient services: Copays for Long-Term Care services start on the 22nd day of care during any 12-month period—there is no copay requirement for the first 21 days. Actual copay charges will vary from veteran to veteran depending upon financial information submitted on VA Form 10-10EZ.	

HARDSHIP DETERMINATION

A Hardship Determination is a process by which a veteran may request to be placed in a different priority group based on a change in his or her financial situation from the previous year. Circumstances that may warrant hardship consideration would be the loss of employment, business bankruptcy, or out-of-pocket medical expenses.

INFORMATION FOR VETERANS ABOUT MEDICARE PRESCRIPTION DRUG BENEFITS

Beginning January 1, 2006, Medicare prescription drug coverage (Medicare Part D) became available to everyone with Medicare Part A or B coverage. The Medicare prescription drug coverage is wholly voluntary on the part of the participant. Each individual must decide whether to participate based on his or her own circumstances.

HOW THIS AFFECTS VETERANS:

- Each veteran must decide whether to enroll in a Medicare Part D plan based on his or her own situation.
- An individual's VA prescription drug coverage will not change based on his or her decision to participate in Medicare Part D.
- VA prescription drug coverage is considered by Medicare to be at least as good as Medicare Part D coverage. (Therefore, it is considered to be **creditable coverage**. Refer to following section for more information regarding creditable coverage.)
- If an individual's spouse is covered by Medicare, he or she must decide whether to enroll in a Medicare Part D plan regardless of the veteran's decision to participate.

CREDITABLE COVERAGE

Most entities that currently provide prescription drug coverage to Medicare beneficiaries, including VA, must disclose whether the entity's coverage is "creditable prescription drug coverage."

- Enrollment in the VA health care system is creditable coverage. This means that VA prescription drug coverage is at least as good as the Medicare Part D coverage.
- Because they have creditable coverage, veterans enrolled in the VA health care program who chose not to enroll in a Medicare Part D plan before May 15, 2006 will not have to pay a higher premium on a permanent basis ("late enrollment penalty") if they enroll in a Medicare drug plan during a later enrollment period.
- However, if an individual un-enrolls in VA health care or if he or she loses his or her enrollment status through no fault of his/her own (such as an enrollment decision by VA that would further restrict access to certain Priority

Groups), he or she may be subject to the late enrollment penalty unless he or she enrolls in a Medicare Part D plan within 62 days of losing VA coverage.

- If a veteran becomes a patient or inmate in an institution of another government agency (for example, a state veterans home, a state institution, a jail, or a corrections facility), he or she may not have creditable coverage from VA while in that institution. For further information, individuals should contact the institution where the veteran resides, the VA Health Benefits Service Center at (877) 222-VETS, or the local VA medical facility.

COVERED SERVICES – STANDARD BENEFITS

VA's medical benefits package provides the following health care services to all enrolled veterans:

Preventive Care Services

- Immunizations
- Physical Examinations (including eye and hearing examinations)
- Health Care Assessments
- Screening Tests
- Health Education Programs

Ambulatory (Outpatient) Diagnostic and Treatment Services

- Emergency outpatient care in VA facilities
- Medical
- Surgical (including reconstructive/plastic surgery as a result of disease or trauma)
- Chiropractic Care
- Bereavement Counseling
- Mental Health
- Substance Abuse

Hospital (Inpatient) Diagnostic and Treatment

- Emergency inpatient care in VA facilities
- Medical
- Surgical (including reconstructive/plastic surgery as a result of disease or trauma)

- Mental Health
- Substance Abuse

MEDICATIONS AND SUPPLIES (WHEN PRESCRIBED BY A VA PHYSICIAN)

LIMITED BENEFITS

The following is a partial listing of acute care services which may have limitations and special eligibility criteria:

- Ambulance Services
- Dental Care (refer to Chapter 11 of this book for additional details.)
- Durable Medical Equipment
- Eyeglasses (see footnote below)
- Hearing Aids (see footnote below)
- Home Health Care
- Homeless Programs
- Maternity and Parturition Services—usually provided in non-VA contracted hospitals at VA expense, care is limited to the mother (costs associated with the care of newborn are not covered)
- Non-VA Health Care Services
- Orthopedic, Prosthetic, and Rehabilitative Devices
- Rehabilitative Services
- Readjustment Counseling
- Sexual Trauma Counseling

Footnote: To qualify for hearing aids or eyeglasses, the individual must have a VA service-connected disability rating of 10% or more. An individual may also qualify if he or she is a former prisoner of war, Purple Heart recipient, require this benefit for treatment of a 0% service-connected condition, or are receiving increased pension based on the need for regular aid and attendance or being permanently housebound.

GENERAL EXCLUSIONS

The following is a partial listing of general exclusions:

- Abortions and abortion counseling

- Cosmetic surgery except where determined by VA to be medically necessary for reconstructive or psychiatric care
- Gender alteration
- Health club or spa membership, even for rehabilitation
- In-vitro fertilization
- Drugs, biological, and medical devices not approved by the Food and Drug Administration unless part of formal clinical trial under an approved research program or when prescribed under a compassionate use exemption.
- Medical care for a veteran who is either a patient or inmate in an institution of another government agency if that agency has a duty to provide the care or services.
- Services not ordered and provided by licensed/accredited professional staff
- Special private duty nursing

NON-VA EMERGENCY CARE

The VA announced in February 2012 that there would be a change in the regulations for how emergency care is provided to veterans in non-VA facilities. The new regulation extends the authority of the VA to pay for emergency care that is provided to eligible veterans at non-VA healthcare facilities, until it is possible for the veteran to be safely transferred to a VA facility.

Veterans are eligible for emergency care at non-VA facilities only if:

- It is determined that VA health care facilities were not feasibly available; that a delay in medical attention would have endangered his or her life or health; and the veteran is personally liable for the cost of services; AND
- The care is for a service-connected condition; OR
- If enrolled, the veteran has been provided care by a VA clinician or provider within the past 24 months.

TRAVEL BENEFITS

Veterans may qualify for beneficiary travel payments if they fall into one of the following categories:

- Have a service-connected rating of 30 percent or more;
- Are traveling for treatment of a service-connected condition;
- Receive a VA pension;

- Are traveling for a scheduled compensation or pension examination;
- Income does not exceed the maximum annual VA pension rate;
- If the medical condition requires an ambulance or a specially equipped van, the individual is unable to defray the cost, and the travel is pre-authorized.

CHAPTER 10

NURSING HOME AND LONG-TERM CARE BENEFITS

STANDARD BENEFITS

The following long-term care services are available to all enrolled veterans:

- Geriatric Evaluation

  A geriatric evaluation is the comprehensive assessment of a veteran's ability to care for him/herself, his/her physical health, and social environment, which leads to a plan of care. The plan could include treatment, rehabilitation, health promotion, and social services. These evaluations are performed by inpatient Geriatric Evaluation and Management (GEM) Units, GEM clinics, geriatric primary care clinics, and other outpatient settings.

- Adult Day Health Care

  The adult day health care (ADHC) program is a therapeutic day care program, providing medical and rehabilitation services to disabled veterans in a combined setting.

- Respite Care

  Respite care provides supportive care to veterans on a short-term basis to give the caregiver a planned period of relief from the physical and emotional demands associated with providing care. Respite care can be provided in the home or other noninstitutional settings.

- Home Care

  Skilled home care is provided by VA and contract agencies to veterans that are homebound with chronic diseases and includes nursing, physical/occupational therapy, and social services.

- Hospice/Palliative Care

  Hospice/palliative care programs offer pain management, symptom control, and other medical services to terminally ill veterans or veterans in the late stages of the chronic disease process. Services also include respite care as well as bereavement counseling to family members.

FINANCIAL ASSESSMENT FOR LONG-TERM CARE SERVICES

For veterans who are not automatically exempt from making copayments for long-term care services, a separate financial assessment must be completed to determine whether they qualify for cost-free services or to what extent they are required to make long term care copayments. For those veterans who do not qualify for cost-free services, the financial assessment for long term care services is used to determine the copayment requirement. Unlike copayments for other VA health care services, which are based on fixed charges for all, long-term care copayment charges are individually adjusted based on each veteran's financial status.

LIMITED BENEFITS

NURSING HOME CARE

While some veterans qualify for indefinite nursing home care services, other veterans may qualify for a limited period of time. Among those that automatically qualify for indefinite nursing home care are veterans whose service-connected condition is clinically determined to require nursing home care and veterans with a service-connected rating of 70% or more. Other veterans—with priority given to those with service-connected conditions—may be provided short-term nursing home care if space and resources are available.

The Department of Veterans Affairs (VA) provides both short-term and long-term care in nursing homes to veterans who aren't sick enough to be in the hospital but are too disabled or elderly to take care of themselves. Priority is given to veterans with service-connected disabilities.

PRIORITY GROUPS

The VA is required to provide nursing home care to any veteran who:

- needs nursing home care because of a service-connected disability
- has a combined disability rating of 70% or more, or
- has a disability rating of at least 60% and is:
    - deemed unemployable, or
    - has been rated permanently and totally disabled.

- Other veterans in need of nursing care will be provided services if resources are available after the above groups are taken care of.

Types of Nursing Care Available

Community Living Centers. Some VA Medical Centers have Community Living Centers (these used to be called Nursing Home Care Units or VA Nursing Homes). These centers are typically located within the VA Medical Center itself or in a separate building.

Contract Nursing Home Care. Nursing home care in public or private nursing homes is also available to some veterans. Stays in these nursing homes can be limited, however, for veterans with ratings less than 70% and for veterans who do not need care due to a service-connected disability.

State Veterans Homes. State Veterans Homes are nursing homes run by the state and approved by the VA. Sometimes the VA will pay for part of the care a veteran gets at a state veterans' home.

ELIGIBILITY FOR COMMUNITY LIVING CENTERS (CLCS)

To receive care in a Community Living Center/VA nursing home, a veteran must:

- be enrolled in the VA Health Care System
- be psychiatrically and medically stable
- provide documentation specifying whether short or long-term care is needed, an estimation of how long the stay will be, and when discharge will occur, and
- show priority for a stay in a CLC.

However, meeting the above criteria does not automatically ensure admission. CLCs make decisions about whether to admit a veteran based on the following factors:

- availability services in the CLC
- what sort of care the veteran needs, and
- whether the CLC can competently provide the type of care the veteran needs.

Co-Pays

Veterans required to make co-pays are typically those:

- without a service-connected disability rated at least 10%, and
- whose income is higher than the VA's maximum annual pension rate.

How to Apply for CLC Care

Typically a veteran's physician will submit the application requesting care in a CLC. Veterans who are not exempt from co-pays must complete VA Form 10-10EC, Application for Extended Care Services.

Eligibility for Contract Nursing Home Care

Any veteran who needs Contract Nursing Home Care for a service-connected disability or is receiving VA home health care after discharge from a VA hospital is eligible for direct admission. To be admitted, all that is required is for a VA physician or authorized private physician to determine that nursing home care is needed. Veterans rated 70% or more service-connected should also be eligible.

Other veterans are eligible to be transferred into Contract Nursing Home Care (also called a Community Nursing Home) if the VA determines the care is needed and:

- the veteran is in a VA hospital, nursing home, domiciliary, or has been receiving VA outpatient care, or
- an active member of the Armed Forces who was in a DOD hospital, needs nursing care, and will be an eligible veteran upon discharge.

Time Limits for Contract Nursing Home Care

Veterans who are not in the priority groups are technically limited to six months of care, but this may be reduced to 30 to 60 days if resources are limited. Veterans in the priority groups are technically entitled to unlimited free care, but again may receive shorter stays due to a lack of funding and resources to accommodate them.

Many veterans can extend their stay by relying on payments from Medicare and Medicaid.

How to Apply for Contract Nursing Home Care

Typically application will be made by a veterans' doctor, social worker or nurse, using VA Form 10-0415, Geriatrics and Extended Care (GEC) Referral.

Eligibility for State Veterans Homes

In some cases, the VA will help pay for a veteran's care at a State Veterans Home. The payments the VA will make are called per diem aid. A home must meet the VA standards for nursing home care to receive per diem aid. In addition, the VA will not pay more than half the cost of the veteran's care.

State homes provide hospital care, nursing home care, domiciliary care, and sometimes adult day care. To receive per diem aid, veterans must meet VA eligibility requirements for the type of care they will receive.

States usually have their own eligibility requirements, in addition to the VA's requirements, such as residency requirements. The veterans home will apply for VA aid for a veteran's care by submitting VA Form 10-10EZ, Application for Medical Benefits.

The VA will pay per diem aid for a veteran's care indefinitely.

Reduction in VA Pension

A veteran who begins to receive nursing home care will have his or her monthly pension payment reduced to $90 if:

- the veteran has no dependents
- the veteran is living in a Medicaid-approved nursing facility, and
- the nursing home care is paid for by Medicaid.

Domiciliary Care

Domiciliary care provides rehabilitative and long-term, health maintenance care for veterans who require some medical care, but who do not require all the services provided in nursing homes. Domiciliary care emphasizes rehabilitation and return to the community. VA may provide domiciliary care to veterans whose annual income does not exceed the maximum annual rate of VA pension or to veterans who have no adequate means of support.

SERVICES AND AIDS FOR BLIND VETERANS

Veterans with corrected central vision of 20/200 or less in both eyes, or field loss to 20 degrees or less in both eyes are considered to be blind.

Blind veterans may be eligible for many of the benefits detailed throughout this book, including, but not limited to: Disability Compensation, Health Insurance, Adaptive Equipment, and Training & Rehabilitation. In addition to these benefits, there are a number of miscellaneous benefits due veterans of all wars who were blinded as the result of their war service. Many individual states offer special programs and benefits for the blind.

Services are available at all VA medical facilities through Visual Impairment Services Team (VIST) coordinators.

The VIST Coordinator is a case manager who has major responsibility for the coordination of all services for legally blind veterans and their families. Duties include providing and/or arranging for appropriate treatment, identifying new cases of blindness, providing professional counseling, resolving problems, arranging annual healthcare reviews, and conducting education programs relating to blindness.

Blind veterans may be eligible for services at a VA medical center, or for admission to a VA blind rehabilitation center or clinic. In addition, blind veterans entitled to receive disability compensation may receive VA aids for the blind, which may include:

- A total health and benefits review by a VA Visual Impairment Services team;
- Adjustment to blindness training;
- Home Improvements and Structural Alterations to homes (HISA Program);
- Specially adapted housing and adaptations;

- Low-vision aids and training in their use;
- Electronic and mechanical aids for the blind, including adaptive computers and computer-assisted devices;
- Guide dogs, including the expense of training the veteran to use the dog, and the cost of the dog's medical care;
- Talking books, tapes, and Braille literature, provided from the Library of Congress.

GUIDE DOGS / SERVICE DOGS

As previously mentioned, VA may provide guide dogs to blind veterans. Additionally, *Public Law 107-135* (signed by then-President Bush January 23, 2002) states that VA may provide:

- Service dogs trained for the aid of the hearing impaired to veterans who are hearing impaired, and are enrolled under Section 1705 of Title 38; and
- Service dogs trained for the aid of persons with spinal cord injury or dysfunction or other chronic impairment that substantially limits mobility to veterans with such injury, dysfunction, or impairment who are enrolled under section 1705 of Title 38.

VA may also pay travel and incidental expenses for the veteran to travel to and from the veteran's home while becoming adjusted to the dog.

The VA operates nine blind rehabilitation centers in the United States and Puerto Rico. Rehabilitation centers offer comprehensive programs to guide individuals through a process that eventually leads to maximum adjustment to the disability, reorganization of the person's life, and return to a contributing place in the family and community. To achieve these goals, the rehabilitation centers offer a variety of skill courses to veterans, which are designed to help achieve a realistic level of independence. Services offered at rehabilitation centers include:

- Orientation and mobility;
- Living skills;
- Communication skills;
- Activities of daily living;
- Independent daily living program;
- Manual skills;
- Visual skills;
- Computer Access Training Section;
- Physical conditioning;
- Recreation;

- Adjustment to blindness;
- Group meetings.

The VA also employs Blind Rehabilitation Outpatient Specialists (BROS) in several areas, including:

- Albuquerque, NM
- Ann Arbor, MI
- Bay Pines / St. Petersburg, FL
- Baltimore, MD
- Boston, MA
- Cleveland, OH
- Dallas, TX
- Gainesville, FL
- Los Angeles, CA
- Phoenix, AZ
- Portland, OR
- San Antonio, TX
- San Juan, PR
- Seattle, WA
- West Haven, CT

Blind Rehabilitation Outpatient Specialists are multi-skilled, experienced, blind instructors who teach skills in the veteran's home environment, and/or local VA facility.

HOME IMPROVEMENTS AND STRUCTURAL ALTERATIONS (HISA)

The HISA program provides funding for disabled veterans to make home improvements necessary for the continuation of treatment or for disability access to the home, essential lavatory and sanitary facilities.

Disabled veterans may be eligible for HISA when it is determined medically necessary or appropriate for the effective and economical treatment of the service-connected disability.

Veterans who are rated 50% or higher are not required to prove their service-connected disability is the reason for their HISA request, although veterans rated less than 50% must demonstrate their disability is the cause of the HISA improvements.

Lifetime home improvement benefits may not exceed $6,800 (U.S.). Any costs that exceed $6,800 (U.S.) will be the veteran's responsibility. This amount is provided to veterans with a service-connected condition or a non-service-connected condition of a veteran rated 50 percent or more service-connected. Home improvement benefits of up to $2,000 may be provided to all other veterans registered in the VA healthcare system.

To apply, veterans must submit the following documentation:

- A letter from describing the physical disability and a description of the request home improvement and/or structural alteration;
- A statement from the attending physician or therapist. This statement should describe the physical condition/disability, why the home modification(s) are medically necessary or appropriate for the effective and economical treatment of the service-connected disabling condition;
- A drawing of the work to be undertaken. This drawing can be hand sketched. It should include the height, width and length dimensions. It does not have to be a formal blueprint or architectural drawing;
- A completed, signed home ownership or a rental lease form with a letter from the landlord agreeing with the modifications if required;
- A completed and signed "VA Form 10-0103", Veterans Application for Assistance;
- Documentation verifying that the provider/contractor is licensed/bonded;
- An itemized cost estimate of the proposed improvement and/or structural alteration from the provider/contractor.

Preauthorization must be obtained before beginning any alterations, otherwise, HISA benefits will be denied.

CHAPTER 11

DENTAL BENEFITS

VA OUTPATIENT DENTAL BENEFITS

Outpatient dental benefits are provided by the Department of Veterans Affairs according to law. In some instances, the dental care may be extensive, while in other cases treatment may be limited.

VA OFFERS DENTAL PROGRAM

VA is partnering with Delta Dental and MetLife to allow eligible Veterans, plus family members receiving care under the Civilian Health and Medical Program (CHAMPVA), to purchase affordable dental insurance beginning Nov. 15, VA officials announced.

More than 8 million veterans who are enrolled in VA health care can choose to purchase one of the offered dental plans. This three year pilot has been designed for veterans with no dental coverage, or those individuals who already eligible for VA dental care and would like to purchase additional coverage.

Participation in the program doesn't impact eligibility for entitlement of other VA dental programs, services and treatment.

There are no eligibility limitations based on service-connected disability rating or enrollment priority assignment. Coverage for this new dental program began January 1, 2014.

Also eligible for the benefits are the nearly 400,000 spouses and dependent children who are reimbursed for most medical expenses under the CHAMPVA program.

ELIGIBILITY

Veterans are eligible for outpatient dental treatment if they are determined by VA to meet one of the following criteria:

- Those having a service-connected compensable dental disability or condition are eligible for any needed dental care.
- Those who were prisoners of war are eligible for any needed dental care. *Public Law 108-170*, which became law December 6, 2003, eliminated the requirement that a prisoner of war have been detained or interned for a period of 90 days or more.
- Those who have a service-connected disability rated 100% disabling, or are unemployable and paid at the 100% rate due to service-connected conditions are eligible for any needed dental care.
- Please note that veterans paid at the 100% rate based on a temporary rating, such as extended hospitalization for a service-connected disability, convalescence or pre-stabilization are not eligible for comprehensive outpatient dental services based on this temporary rating.
- Those who are participating in a VA rehabilitation program are eligible for dental care necessary to complete their program.
- Apply for dental care within 180 days of discharge or release (under conditions other than dishonorable) from a period of active duty of 90 days or more during the Persian Gulf War era
- Those having a service-connected noncompensable dental condition or disability resulting from combat wounds or service trauma are eligible for repeat care for the service-connected condition(s).
- Those having a dental condition clinically determined by VA to be currently aggravating a service-connected medical condition are eligible for dental care to resolve the problem.
- Those with nonservice-connected dental conditions or disabilities for which treatment was begun while in a VA medical center, when it is clinically determined to be necessary to complete such dental treatment on an outpatient basis.
- Those receiving outpatient care or scheduled for inpatient care may receive dental care if the dental condition is clinically determined to be complicating a medical condition currently under treatment
- Certain veterans enrolled in a VA Homeless Program for 60 consecutive days or more may receive certain medically necessary outpatient dental services.

ENHANCED TRICARE RETIREE DENTAL PROGRAM

The TRICARE Retiree Dental Program (TRDP) was established February 1, 1998. It provides dental care for Uniformed Service retirees, unremarried surviving spouses, and certain other family members. Enrollment in TRDP is voluntary. The TRDP is funded solely by enrollees, and receives **no** government subsidy.

The basic Tricare Retiree Dental Program (TRDP) is available only to those who were enrolled in the TDRP program prior to September 1, 2000, and who chose to remain enrolled in the basic program.

Effective September 1, 2000, the Enhanced Tricare Retiree Dental Program took effect, and new enrollments in the basic program were discontinued.

The TRICARE Retiree Dental Program is administered by the Federal Services division of Delta Dental Plan of California. The TRICARE Retiree Dental Program is designed to provide Uniformed Services retirees and their families with optimum dental coverage at an affordable cost.

Changes Include:

• Annual maximum increased to $1,300 from $1,200

• Lifetime orthodontic maximum increased to $1,750 from $1,500

• Annual Accident coverage maximum increased to $1,200 from $1,000

• Option to substitute a periodontal maintenance (specialized cleaning for one of the two yearly dental cleanings

• Most enrollees will see a lower monthly premium

ELIGIBILITY REQUIREMENTS:

Eligibility requirements for enrollment in the TRDP are set forth by the federal government in the law that established the program. Applicants may be required to submit additional information if it is needed by Delta to verify eligibility. To enroll in the enhanced program, an individual must be one of the following:

- A member of the Uniformed Services who is entitled to Uniformed Services retired pay, even if you are 65 or older;
- A current spouse of an enrolled member;
- A member of the retired Reserve/Guard, including a "gray-area" reservist, who is entitled to retired pay but does not actually begin receiving it until age 60;
- A child of an enrolled member, up to age 21 (to age 23 if a full-time student, or older if disabled before losing eligibility);
- An unremarried surviving spouse or eligible child of a deceased member who died on retired status or while on active duty;
- A Congressional Medal of Honor recipient and eligible family members, or an unremarried surviving spouse/eligible family members of a deceased recipient;
- A current spouse and/or eligible child of a non-enrolled member with documented proof the member is:
    - Eligible to receive ongoing, comprehensive dental care from the Department of Veterans Affairs;
    - Enrolled in a dental plan through employment and the plan is not available to family members; or
    - Unable to obtain benefits through the TRDP due to a current and enduring medical or dental condition.

Those who are not eligible for this program are:

- Former spouses of eligible members;
- Remarried surviving spouses of deceased members;
- Family members of non-enrolled retirees who do not meet one of the three special circumstances noted above.

PREMIUMS

Premium rates for the enhanced TRICARE Retiree Dental Program vary depending on the retiree's location.

COVERAGE

This chart provides an overview of coverage under the enhanced TRICARE Retiree Dental Program for patients who visit a participating network dentist.

Benefits available during the first 12 months of enrollment:	***Delta Pays:**
Diagnostic services	100%
Preventive services	100%
Basic Restorative services	80%
Endodontics	60%
Periodontics	60%
Oral Surgery	60%
Emergency	80%
Dental Accident Coverage	100%

Additional services available after 12 months of continuous enrollment:	
Cast Crowns, Onlays & Bridges	50%
Partial/Full Dentures	50%
Dental Implants	50%
Orthodontics	50%

Deductibles & Maximums	
Annual Deductible	$50
Annual Maximum	$1200
Orthodontic Maximum	$1500
Dental Accident Maximum	$1000
Benefit Year: May 1- April 30	

*The percentage paid by Delta is based on the allowed amount for each procedure. Out-of-pocket costs may be higher if care is received from a non-participating provider.

NATIONAL GUARD AND RESERVE PERSONNEL

National Guard and Reserve personnel who elect to enroll in the TRICARE Retiree Dental Program (TRDP) within 120 days after retirement are now eligible to skip the 12-month waiting period normally required for certain TRDP benefits.

Effective February 1, 2005, officials authorized a waiver from requiring retired National Guard/Reserve men and women who meet the criteria to be enrolled in the TRDP for 12 months prior to gaining the maximum allowed benefits for cast crowns, cast restorations, bridges, dentures and orthodontics for both adults and children.

Additionally, this waiver can be applied retroactively to February 1, 2004 for any Guard and Reserve enrollees who can document their enrollment in the TRDP within 120 days after their retirement effective date.

All new enrollees seeking to obtain the waiver should submit a copy of their retirement orders together with their application.

CONTACT INFORMATION

Covered benefits are subject to certain limitations. For more information on all covered services and detailed information on benefit levels, limitations, exclusions, program policies and payments for non-participating providers, please contact:

Delta Dental of California
Federal Services
P.O. Box 537008
Sacramento, CA 95853-7008
(888) 838-8737

BASIC TRICARE RETIREE DENTAL PROGRAM

The basic program is available only to those who were enrolled in the TRDP *prior to September 1, 2000*, when the enhanced program took effect, and who wish to remain enrolled in the basic program rather than upgrade their enrollment to the enhanced program.

Retirees who are enrolled in the basic program and have questions about their coverage should contact:

Delta Dental of California
Federal Services
P.O. Box 537008
Sacramento, CA 95853-7008
(888) 838-8737

TRICARE SELECTED RESERVE DENTAL PROGRAM BENEFITS

Individuals with at least one year of service commitment remaining who are serving in the Army Reserve, Naval Reserve, Air Force Reserve, Marine Corps Reserve, Coast Guard Reserve, Army National Guard or Air National Guard, may be eligible to enroll in the Tricare Selected Reserve Dental Program (TSRDP).

The Department of Defense works in conjunction with Humana Military Healthcare Services to offer and administer the TRICARE Selected Reserve Dental Program.

Coverage remains available as long as an individual maintains his or her Reserve status, and is shown as eligible on the DEERS record.

The information provided in this section is intended only as a brief overview. Humana Military Healthcare Services has a staff of trained Beneficiary Services Representatives who are available to answer your questions. They can be reached at (800) 86

CHAPTER 12

CHAMPVA

Although similar, CHAMPVA and TRICARE are completely separate programs, with totally different beneficiary populations. While the benefits provided are similar, the programs are administered separately, with significant differences in claim filing procedures and preauthorization requirements.

Under CHAMPVA, VA shares the cost of covered healthcare services and supplies with eligible beneficiaries.

Under CHAMPVA, VA shares the cost of covered healthcare services and supplies with eligible beneficiaries.

The administration of CHAMPVA is centralized to the Health Administration Center in Denver, Colorado.

ELIGIBILITY REQUIREMENTS

To be eligible for CHAMPVA, you cannot be eligible for TRICARE/CHAMPUS and you must be in one of these categories:

- The spouse or child of a veteran who has been rated permanently and totally disabled for a service-connected disability by a VA regional office; or
- The surviving spouse or child of a veteran who died from a VA-rated service connected disability; or
- The surviving spouse or child of a veteran who was at the time death rated permanently and totally disabled from a service connected disability; or

- The surviving spouse or child of a military member who died in the line of duty, not due to misconduct (in most of these cases, these family members are eligible for TRICARE, not CHAMPVA).

Update: An eligible CHAMPVA sponsor may be entitled to receive medical care through the VA health care system based on his or her own veteran status. Additionally, as the result of a recent policy change, if the eligible CHAMPVA sponsor is the spouse of another eligible CHAMPVA sponsor, both may now be eligible for CHAMPVA benefits. In each instance where the eligible spouse requires medical attention, he or she may choose the VA health care system or coverage under CHAMPVA for his/her health care needs. If you have been previously denied CHAMPVA benefits and you believe you would now be qualified, please call (800) 733-8387.

BENEFITS

In general, CHAMPVA covers most healthcare services and supplies that are medically and psychologically necessary. Upon confirmation of eligibility, applicants will receive program material that specifically addresses covered and non-covered services and supplies.

CHAMPVA GENERAL EXCLUSIONS

- Services determined by VA to be medically unnecessary;
- Care as part of a grant, study, or research program;
- Care considered experimental or investigational;
- Care for persons eligible for benefits under other government agency programs, except Medicaid and State Victims of Crime Compensation programs;
- Care for which the beneficiary is not obligated to pay, such as services obtained at a health fair;
- Care provided outside the scope of the provider's license or certification;
- Custodial, domiciliary, or rest cures;
- Dental care (except treatment related to certain covered medical conditions);
- Medications that do not require a prescription (except insulin);
- Personal comfort and convenience items;
- Services rendered by providers suspended or sanctioned by other Federal entities.

RETENTION OF CHAMPVA FOR SURVIVING SPOUSES REMARRYING AFTER AGE 55

Eligibility for CHAMPVA ends at midnight on the date of your remarriage if you remarry prior to age 55. However, *Public Law 107-330* (signed by then-President Bush on December 6, 2002) contained a provision stating that:

> *"For marriages occurring on or after February 4, 2003, the remarriage after age 55 of the surviving spouse of a veteran shall not bar the furnishing of benefits under CHAMPVA to such person as the surviving spouse of the veteran".*

The law also contained a provision allowing those widows who remarried prior to February 4, 2003, and were over the age of 55 and lost their CHAMPVA benefits, to apply to have their medical benefits reinstated. However, such widows had to apply for reinstatement of benefits by February 4, 2004. (The deadline was later extended to December 16, 2004.)

Termination of Remarriage: If a widow(er) of a qualifying sponsor remarries, and the remarriage is later terminated by death, divorce, or annulment he or she may reestablish CHAMPVA eligibility. The beginning date of re-eligibility is the first day of the month after termination of the remarriage or December 1, 1999, whichever date is later. To reestablish CHAMPVA eligibility, copies of the marriage certificate and death, divorce, or annulment documents (as appropriate) must be provided.

APPLYING FOR CHAMPVA AND FILING CLAIMS

Generally, applicants can expect to receive written notification from the Health Administration Center within 45 days from the mailing of the application.

Prospective applicants should contact the Health Administration Center at (800) 733-8387.

Applications may also be requested by FAX at (303) 331-7804.

To check the status of your claim online, visit the following website: http://www.va.gov/hac/forbeneficiaries/champva/champva.asp

For general questions, information on payments, or to reprocess a denied claim, please send your request to:

VA Health Administration Center
CHAMPVA
PO Box 469063
Denver CO 80246-9063

For submitting new health care claims only, please use:

VA Health Administration Center
CHAMPVA Claims
PO Box 469064
Denver CO 80246-9064

To streamline the process, applicants are encouraged to complete the *Application for CHAMPVA Benefits, (VA 10D)* in its entirety and to attach all required documents. As further explained on the application, required documents include a copy of each applicant's Medicare card (if Medicare eligible) and a school certification for all applicant children between the ages of 18 and 23.

CHAMPVA AS SECONDARY PAYER

CHAMPVA is intended to serve as a safety net in the event other coverage is not available—rather than being the primary carrier. While families with other health insurance are not disqualified from CHAMPVA benefits, CHAMPVA's safety net protection only kicks in after the application of all other policies—including benefits available from the enrollment in a health maintenance organization (HMO).

Exceptions to CHAMPVA's secondary payer status are supplemental CHAMPVA policies, Medicaid, and State Victims Compensation Programs—CHAMPVA assumes primary payer in these cases.

Beneficiaries enrolled in an HMO cannot elect to waive the HMO benefits without forfeiting their CHAMPVA benefits. CHAMPVA benefits, however, do apply to covered services that are not covered by the HMO.

HEALTHCARE SERVICES AT VA FACILITIES

Under the CHAMPVA In-house Treatment Initiative (CITI for short), CHAMPVA beneficiaries may receive cost-free healthcare services at participating VA facilities.

Although some VA facilities are not CITI participants due to the volume of veterans they are responsible for serving, most are. **The CITI program is not available to beneficiaries with Medicare or with an HMO insurance plan**

MEDICARE IMPACT

CHAMPVA is always the secondary payer to Medicare.

If a person is eligible for CHAMPVA, under age 65 and enrolled in both Medicare Parts A & B, SSA documentation of enrollment in both Parts A&B is required.

CHAMPVA is always the secondary payer to Medicare.

For benefits to be extended past age 65, the individual must meet the following conditions:

- If he or she turned 65 before June 5, 2001, and only has Medicare Part A, he or she will be eligible for CHAMPVA without having to have Medicare Part B coverage.
- If he or she turned 65 on/or before June 5, 2001, and has Medicare Parts A and B, he or she must keep both Parts to be eligible.
- If he or she turned 65 on or after June 5, 2001, he or she must be enrolled in Medicare Parts A and B to be eligible.

CHAPTER 13

TRICARE AND TRICARE FOR LIFE

TRICARE is the Department of Defense's worldwide health care program for active duty and retired uniformed services members and their families. TRICARE offers several health plan options to meet your specific needs.

- TRICARE For Life
- TRICARE Global Remote Overseas
- TRICARE Prime
- TRICARE Prime Overseas
- TRICARE Prime Remote
- TRICARE Reserve Select
- TRICARE Standard and Extra
- TRICARE Standard Overseas
- U.S. Family Health Plan
- TRICARE Young Adult

TRICARE FOR LIFE

TRICARE For Life (TFL) is TRICARE's Medicare-wraparound coverage available to *all* Medicare-eligible TRICARE beneficiaries, regardless of age, provided they have Medicare Parts A and B.

While Medicare is your primary insurance, TRICARE acts as your secondary payer minimizing your out-of-pocket expenses. TRICARE benefits include covering Medicare's coinsurance and deductible.

KEY FEATURES OF TRICARE FOR LIFE INCLUDE:

- Minimal **out-of-pocket costs** (aside from Medicare part B premium).
- No enrollment fees for TFL. But, you must purchase Medicare Part B and pay monthly premiums to be eligible for TFL.
- Coordination of benefits between Medicare and TRICARE

- TRICARE is the secondary payer for all services covered by both TRICARE and Medicare.
- TRICARE is the primary payer for those services covered only by TRICARE. Additional steps may be required in order to coordinate benefits if you have other health insurance in addition to TRICARE and Medicare.
- Freedom to manage your own health care
- No assigned primary care manager.
- Visit any Medicare provider.
- Receive care at a military treatment facility on a space-available basis.
- No claims to file (in most cases).
- Your provider files your claim with Medicare
- Medicare processes the claims
- Medicare forwards it electronically to TRICARE.
- TRICARE pays similarly to TRICARE Standard in those overseas locations where Medicare is not available.

ELIGIBILITY

TFL is available to all Medicare-eligible TRICARE beneficiaries, regardless of age, including retired members of the National Guard and Reserve who are in receipt of retired pay, family members, widows and widowers and certain former spouses. Dependent parents and parents-in-law are not eligible for TFL.

Note: *If you're under age 65, have Medicare Part B, and live in a TRICARE Prime service area, you have the option to enroll in **TRICARE Prime**; TRICARE waives your TRICARE Prime enrollment fee.*

You should confirm that your Medicare status is current in the **Defense Enrollment Eligibility Reporting System** (DEERS). Your uniformed services ID card and your Medicare card, which must reflect enrollment in Medicare Part B, are evidence of your TFL eligibility.

TRICARE GLOBAL REMOTE OVERSEAS

TRICARE Global Remote Overseas (TGRO) is a TRICARE Prime option offered in designated remote overseas locations for active duty service members and their families. TRICARE has partnered with International SOS to identify the best local providers and facilities and develop a network of licensed, qualified physicians in remote overseas areas. The TGRO contractor's careful selection of providers is the first step in ensuring quality care.

Only physicians who are licensed and who have graduated from an accredited medical school are included in the core network. To access a list of TGRO providers please visit the TGRO Provider Directory. The TGRO network is updated daily.

KEY FEATURES OF TGRO INCLUDE:

- Enrollment is required, but there are no enrollment fees.
- Fewer out-of-pocket costs than TRICARE Standard Overseas.
- You receive most care from your primary care manager (PCM).
- Your PCM or TGRO Call Center refers you to specialists when necessary and will tell you when you need to go to another city, country or the U.S. for quality care.
- No claims to file (in most cases).

ELIGIBILITY

In general, TGRO is available to the following beneficiaries:

- Permanently-assigned active duty service members living in designated remote locations.
- Command-sponsored active duty family members living with their active duty sponsors in designated remote locations
- Activated National Guard and Reserve members living in designated remote locations when their orders are for more than 30 consecutive days.
- Command-sponsored family members of activated National Guard and Reserve living with their sponsors in designated remote locations

TRICARE PRIME

TRICARE Prime is a managed care option offering the most affordable and comprehensive coverage. TRICARE Prime is available in Prime Service Areas in each TRICARE Region. To find out if you live in a Prime Service Area, contact your regional contractor. If you don't, you may be eligible for TRICARE Prime Remote, or you may use TRICARE Standard and Extra.

KEY FEATURES INCLUDE:

- Enrollment is required.
- Fewer out-of-pocket costs than other TRICARE options.
- Enhanced vision and preventive coverage.
- Priority access for care at military treatment facilities.
- Receive most care from an assigned primary care manager (PCM).
- Your PCM refers you to specialists when necessary.
- No claims to file (in most cases).
- Easy to transfer enrollment when you move.
- Time and distance access standards for care, including wait times for urgent, routine and specialty care.

ELIGIBILITY

You may enroll in TRICARE Prime as long as you are not entitled to Medicare based on age (65). (At age 65, you become eligible for **TRICARE For Life** as long as you have

Medicare Parts A and B). The following beneficiaries who live in a Prime Service area may enroll in TRICARE Prime:

- Active duty service members* and their families.
- Retired service members and their families.
- Surviving family members (widowed spouses, children)
- Eligible former spouses.
- Activated National Guard/Reserve members* and their families.
- Retired National Guard and Reserve members and their families (upon reaching age 60)
- Medal of Honor recipients and their families.

*Active duty service members and activated National Guard/Reserve members must enroll in one of the TRICARE Prime options (includes TRICARE Prime, TRICARE Prime Remote, TRICARE Prime Overseas and TRICARE Global Remote Overseas)

TRICARE PRIME OVERSEAS

TRICARE Prime Overseas is a managed care plan for active duty service members and their eligible family members residing together in overseas locations in which TRICARE Prime Overseas is available. Retirees and retiree family members are not eligible for TRICARE Prime Overseas.

KEY FEATURES OF TRICARE PRIME OVERSEAS INCLUDE:

- Enrollment required, but no enrollment fees.
- Fewer out-of-pocket costs than TRICARE Standard Overseas.
- Enhanced coverage for vision and clinical preventive services.
- You receive most care from your primary care manager (PCM).
- Your PCM refers you to specialists when necessary.
- No claims to file (in most cases).
- Easy to transfers from one overseas area to another or back to the United States.
- Time and distance access standards for care, including wait times for urgent, routine and specialty care.
- Point of service option available (in certain circumstances) to receive care without requesting a referral from your PCM (resulting in higher out-of-pocket costs)

ELIGIBILITY

In general, TRICARE Prime Overseas is available to the following beneficiaries:

- Active duty service members residing in overseas areas in which Prime is offered.
- Active duty family members who:
    - Accompany their sponsor;

- Are command-sponsored on their permanent change of station orders or relocate on service sponsored/funded orders;
- Are eligible in the Defense Enrollment Eligibility Reporting System; and
- Enroll through the nearest TRICARE Service Center.

TRICARE PRIME REMOTE

TRICARE Prime Remote (TPR) is a managed care option similar to TRICARE Prime for active duty service members and their eligible family members while they are assigned to remote duty stations in the United States.

Remote locations are those that are 50 miles or an hour drive time from a military treatment facility and the ZIP code areas are pre-determined.

Note: TRICARE Global Remote Overseas is a similar program available in remote locations outside of the United States

KEY FEATURES OF TRICARE PRIME REMOTE INCLUDE:

- Enrollment required to participate
- Active duty service members must enroll
- Active duty family members have the option to enroll or use TRICARE Standard and Extra
- Flexible enrollment options:
  - Online via the Beneficiary Web Enrollment Web Site
  - Submit a *TRICARE Prime Enrollment and PCM Change Form* through the mail
  - Receive most care from an assigned network primary care manager (PCM) who will provide referrals for specialty care.
  - If a network PCM is not available, care is received from any TRICARE-authorized provider.
- Fewer out-of-pocket costs.
- Eligible for travel reimbursement if referred for medically necessary care far from home.
- Enhanced coverage for vision and clinical preventive services.
- Time and distance access standards for care.
- No claims to file (in most cases).
- Easy to transfer enrollment when moving to another location in your TRICARE region or to a new TRICARE region.

TRICARE RESERVE SELECT

TRICARE Reserve Select (TRS) is a premium-based health plan that qualified National Guard and Reserve members may purchase. TRS, which requires a monthly premium, offers coverage similar to TRICARE Standard and Extra.

KEY FEATURES OF TRS INCLUDE:

- Available worldwide to most Selected Reserve members (and families) when not on active duty orders or covered under the Transitional Assistance Management Program.
- Must qualify for and purchase TRS to participate.
- Must pay monthly premiums. Failure to pay monthly premiums on time may result in disenrollment and an enrollment lockout.
- Freedom to manage your own health care; no assigned primary care manager.
- Visit any TRICARE-authorized provider or qualified host nation provider (if located overseas).
- Pay fewer out-of-pocket costs when choosing a provider in the TRICARE network.
- Network providers not available overseas.
- No referrals are required, but some care may require prior authorization.
- May have to pay for services when they are received and then seek reimbursement.
- May have to submit health care claims.
- May receive care in a military treatment facility (MTF) on a space-available basis only.
- Offers comprehensive health care coverage including TRICARE's prescription drug coverage.

TRICARE STANDARD AND EXTRA

TRICARE Standard is a fee-for-service option. When you use TRICARE Standard, you have more choice in providers as you can seek care from any TRICARE-authorized provider (network or non-network), but you'll pay higher out-of-pocket costs.

To reduce your out-of-pocket costs, use the TRICARE Extra option by seeking care TRICARE network providers. Using TRICARE Extra is like using a Preferred Provider Option (PPO).

KEY FEATURES INCLUDE:

- Freedom to choose any TRICARE-authorized provider.
- Referrals not required, but some care may require prior authorization.
- Highest out-of-pocket costs.
- You may have to submit health care claims.
- Save time and money with the TRICARE Extra option:
    - Visit a TRICARE network provider.
    - Pay fewer out-of-pocket costs.
    - Network providers will file claims for you.
    - Receive care in a military treatment facility on a space-available basis only.
- TRICARE Standard is available worldwide, but Extra option is not available overseas.

- Enrollment NOT required

Eligibility

In general, the following are eligible for TRICARE Standard and Extra:

- Active duty family members.
- Retirees and their family members
- Surviving family members (widowed spouses, children)
- Eligible former spouses
- Family members of activated National Guard or Reserve members
- Retired National Guard and Reserve members and their families (upon reaching age 60)
- Medal of Honor recipients and their families

TRICARE STANDARD OVERSEAS

TRICARE Standard Overseas is a fee-for-service option. TRICARE Standard Overseas gives you more choices in the providers you can see for care, but costs you more in out-of-pocket costs. TRICARE Extra is not available in overseas locations.

Key features of TRICARE Standard Overseas includes:

- Higher out-of-pocket costs than TRICARE Prime Overseas.
- Freedom to choose from any qualified host nation provider.
- Referrals not required, but some care may require prior authorization.
- You may have to pay for services when they are received and then seek reimbursement.
- You may have to submit health care claims.
- There is no assigned primary care manager.
- No enrollment process, which means no enrollment forms to fill out and no annual enrollment fees for retirees and others.
- Receive care in a military treatment facility on a space-available basis only.

Eligibility

In general, TRICARE Standard Overseas is available to the following beneficiaries:

- Active duty family members living overseas with their sponsors and those who have relocated with service sponsored/funded orders.
- Non-command sponsored active duty family members who reside overseas.
- Retirees and their family members who reside overseas.
- Survivors who reside overseas.
- Eligible former spouses who reside overseas.
- National Guard or Reserve family members who are living overseas while their sponsor is on active duty for more than 30 consecutive days.

U.S. FAMILY HEALTH PLAN

The US Family Health Plan is an additional TRICARE Prime option available through networks of community-based, not-for-profit health care systems in six areas of the United States. You must be enrolled in the Defense Eligibility Reporting System (DEERS) and reside in the one of the designated US Family Health Plan service areas.

KEY FEATURES OF THE US FAMILY HEALTH PLAN INCLUDE:

- The only TRICARE Prime program that offers benefits to beneficiaries age 65 and over, regardless of whether or not you participate in Medicare Part B. (See "Should I get Medicare Part B" below.)
- Few out-of-pocket costs (similar to TRICARE Prime).
- You do not access Medicare providers, military treatment facilities (MTFs) or TRICARE network providers, but instead receive your care from a primary care physician that you select from a network of private physicians affiliated with one of the not-for-profit health care systems offering the plan. Your primary care physician assists you in getting appointments with specialists in the area and coordinates your care.
- You will benefit from the same level of prescription coverage as that available under the TRICARE program and at the same costs. However, you may only use your US Family Health Plan's list of retail or on-site pharmacies and the US Family Health Plan mail order service instead of TRICARE retail, mail-order or MTF pharmacies.
- If you move or un-enroll from the US Family Health Plan, you may choose any TRICARE program that you are eligible for and that is available in your area.
- Each US Family Health Plan site offers enhanced benefits and services such as discounts for eyeglasses, hearing aids and dental care. These enhancements will vary by US Family Health Plan site.
- There are no claims to file when plan-approved providers are used.
- Enrollment is required. You may enroll at anytime throughout the year and enrollment is automatically renewed each year unless you take action to un-enroll. Enrollment fees, if applicable, may transfer to another US Family Health Plan location or to TRICARE Prime.
- You are encouraged to enroll in the US Family Health Plan as a complete family unit, but you may enroll on an individual basis. When you enroll in the US Family Health Plan, you are committing to the plan for one year unless moving out of the area or un-enrolling for another qualified reason.

ELIGIBILITY

Eligible beneficiaries include:

- Active duty family members.
- Retirees and their eligible family members.
- Survivors.
- Former spouses.

- Medal of Honor recipients and their families.
- Family members of activated National Guard or Reserve Members.

Should I Get Medicare Part B?

You do not need to have Medicare Part B to enroll in the US Family Health Plan. However, if you do not enroll in Medicare Part B when first eligible, and subsequently choose to do so, you will pay (in addition to the normal Medicare Part B monthly premium) an annual 10% penalty for each year you were eligible to enroll in Medicare Part B and did not.

In addition, you will only be able to in Medicare Part B enroll during the general enrollment period, January 1-March 31, of each year, and your Part B benefits will not be effective until July 1 of that year. You are encouraged to enroll in Medicare Part B when first eligible.

If you are entitled to Medicare Part A and decide to un-enroll from the US Family Health Plan, you will then be able to use the TRICARE For Life benefit, but only if you also are enrolled in Medicare Part B. Additionally, if you subscribe to Medicare Part B, you pay only copayments for prescription drugs and your annual enrollment fee is waived. Medicare Part B also adds coverage for End Stage Renal Disease, a condition that usually involves kidney failure. Medicare Part B is not required for the US Family Health Plan, but you should carefully consider whether or not it is in your best interest to enroll.

TRICARE YOUNG ADULT

TRICARE Young Adult is a premium-based health care plan that qualified dependents may purchase. TRICARE Young Adult provides medical and pharmacy benefits, but dental coverage is not included. The plan allows dependent adult children to purchase TRICARE coverage after eligibility for "regular" TRICARE coverage ends at age 21 (or age 23 if enrolled in a full course of study at an approved institution of higher learning). There are two options to select from at enrollment; Prime and Standard.

Eligibility

You may be eligible if you are:

- An adult child of an eligible sponsor. Eligible sponsors include:
    - Active duty servicemembers
    - Retired servicemembers
    - Activated Guard/Reserve members
    - Non-activated Guard/Reserve members using TRICARE Reserve Select
    - Retired Guard/Reserve members using TRICARE Retried Reserve
- Unmarried
- At least age 21, but not yet age 26
    - (If you are enrolled in a full course of study at an approved institution of higher learning and your sponsor provides 50 percent

of your financial support, your eligibility may not begin until age 23 or upon graduation, whichever comes first.)

- Not eligible to enroll in an employer-sponsored health plan based on your own employment
- Not otherwise eligible for TRICARE program coverage

Key Features of TRICARE Young Adult Prime Coverage

- In the United States, the Prime Option is available only in Prime Service Areas to children of active duty and retired service members

- If you live in an area where the US Family Health Plan is offered, you may enroll in the US Family Health Plan for your prime option

- If your sponsor is on active duty you may also select the Prime Option when you live with your sponsor:
  - In remote U.S. Zip Codes if your sponsor is enrolled in TRICARE Prime remote and;
  - Anywhere overseas if you are command-sponsored

- If your sponsor is using TRICARE Reserve Select or TRICARE Retired Reserve, the Prime Option is not available to you

- With the Prime Option, you will have an assigned primary care manager (PCM), either at a military treatment facility (MTF) or in the TRICARE network, who will provide the majority of your care

- Your PCM will refer you to a specialist for care when he or she is unable to provide that care. Your PCM will also coordinate with your regional contractor for authorization, to find a specialist in the network, and will file claims on your behalf.

- Other benefits include enhanced vision and preventative services, and travel reimbursement for some specialty care

- Children of active duty servicemembers pay no out-of-pocket costs for any type of care as long as care is received from PCM or with a referral.

Key Features of TRICARE Young Adult Standard Option

- All dependent children who qualify for TRICARE Young Adult may select the Standard Option

- You may visit any TRICARE-authorized provider, network or non-network. Care at military treatment facilities is available on a space-available basis only. You do not need a referral for any type of care but some services may require prior authorization.

- The type of provider determines how much you'll pay out-of-pocket. If you're visiting a network provider you'll pay less out-of-pocket and the provider will file claims for you.
-

TRANSITIONAL ASSISTANCE MANAGEMENT PROGRAM

The Transitional Assistance Management Program (TAMP) provides 180 days of transitional health care benefits upon separation from active duty service. Service members who meet the criteria below are eligible for TRICARE benefits for themselves and their family members.

- A member who is involuntarily separated from active duty.
- A member of a reserve component who is separated from active duty to which called or ordered in support of a contingency operation if the active duty is for a period of more than 30 days.
- A member who is separated from active duty for which the member is involuntarily retained under Section 12305 (also referred to as "stop loss") of Title 10, U.S.C., in support of a contingency operation.
- A member who is separated from active duty served pursuant to a voluntary agreement of the member to remain on active duty for a period of less than one year in support of a contingency operation.

For those who qualify, the 180-day TAMP period begins upon the sponsor's separation. During TAMP, sponsors and family members are eligible to use one of the following health plan options:

TRICARE Prime (enrollment required)

TRICARE Standard and Extra

TRICARE Prime Overseas (enrollment required)

TRICARE Standard Overseas

CONTINUED HEALTH CARE BENEFIT PROGRAM (CHCBP)

The Continued Health Care Benefit Program (CHCBP) is a premium-based health care program administered by Humana Military Health Care Services, Inc. (Humana Military). CHCBP offers temporary transitional health coverage (18-36 months) after TRICARE eligibility ends. If you qualify, you can purchase CHCBP within 60 days of loss of eligibility for either regular TRICARE or Transitional Assistance Management Program (TAMP) coverage.

CHCBP acts as a bridge between military health benefits and your new civilian health plan. CHCBP benefits are comparable to TRICARE Standard with the same benefits, providers and program rules. The main difference is that you pay premiums to participate.

WHO IS ELIGIBLE?

Under certain circumstances, the following beneficiaries may be eligible:

- Former active duty service members released from active duty (under other than adverse conditions) and their eligible family members. Coverage is limited to 18 months.
- Un-remarried former spouses who were eligible for TRICARE on the day before the date of the final decree of divorce, dissolution or annulment. Coverage is usually limited to 36 months however some un-remarried former spouses may continue coverage beyond 36 months if they meet certain criteria. Contact Humana Military for details.
- Children who cease to meet the requirements to be an eligible family member and were eligible for TRICARE on the day before ceasing to meet those requirements. Coverage is limited to 36 months.
- Certain unmarried children by adoption or legal custody. Coverage is limited to 36 months.

For more information about CHCBP, call (800) 444-5445. Contact your regional contractor or a Beneficiary Counseling and Assistance Coordinator (BCAC) to discuss your eligibility for this program.

EXTENDED CARE HEALTH OPTION

The TRICARE Extended Care Health Option (ECHO) provides financial assistance to eligible beneficiaries who qualify based on specific mental or physical disabilities and offers an integrated set of services and supplies not available through the basic TRICARE program. TRICARE ECHO doesn't replace basic TRICARE programs; it supplements the benefits of the TRICARE program option that eligible beneficiaries use.

ECHO benefits are only available to qualified active duty family members (including family members of activated National Guard or Reserve members). Active duty family members must qualify for ECHO through ECHO case managers in each TRICARE region.

ELIGIBILITY

The TRICARE Extended Care Health Option (ECHO) is available ***only to active duty family members*** who have a qualifying condition.

Qualifying conditions include:

- Moderate or severe mental retardation
- A serious physical disability
- An extraordinary physical or psychological condition of such complexity that the beneficiary is homebound
- A diagnosis of a neuromuscular developmental condition or other condition in an infant or toddler that is expected to precede a diagnosis of moderate or severe mental retardation or a serious physical disability
- Multiple disabilities, which may qualify if there are two or more disabilities affecting separate body systems

If you or your provider believes a qualifying condition exists, talk to a case manager or with your regional contractor or TRICARE Area Office (if stationed overseas) to determine eligibility for TRICARE ECHO benefits.

To begin using TRICARE ECHO, qualifying family members must be enrolled in the *Exceptional Family Member Program* and must be registered for TRICARE ECHO with their regional contractor or TRICARE Area Office. There is no enrollment fee for TRICARE ECHO.

PRE-ACTIVATION BENEFIT FOR NATIONAL GUARD AND RESERVE

National Guard and Reserve members who are issued delayed-effective-date active duty orders for more than 30 days in support of a contingency operation may qualify for "early eligibility for TRICARE" beginning on the later of:

(a) the date their orders were issued; or
(b) 90 days before they report to active duty.

National Guard and Reserve members who qualify for the pre-activation benefit are covered as "active duty service members" and receive active duty medical and dental benefits.

Additionally, when National Guard or Reserve members qualify for pre-activation benefits, family members who are registered in the Defense Enrollment Eligibility Reporting System are also covered under TRICARE up to 90 days before the sponsor's active duty service begins. Family members become covered by TRICARE as "active duty family members during the pre-activation period and while the sponsor is activated.

The member's Service personnel office will tell members if they are eligible for pre-activation benefits when they receive their delayed-effective-date active duty orders.

PHARMACY BENEFITS

TRICARE prescription drug coverage is available to all TRICARE-eligible beneficiaries who are enrolled in the Defense Enrollment Eligibility Reporting System (DEERS). Prescription drug coverage is the same regardless of which health plan option you are using and it is available worldwide.

Eligible beneficiaries include:

- Active duty service members and their families
- Activated National Guard and Reserve Members and their families (on Title 10 or Title 32 [federal] orders)
- Retired service members and their families

- Retired National Guard and Reserve Members and their families (age 60 and above and receiving retired pay)
- Survivors, widows/widowers and certain former spouses
- Medal of Honor recipients and their families
- Beneficiaries enrolled in TRICARE Reserve Select or the Continued Health Care Benefit Program
- Other beneficiaries listed in DEERS as eligible for TRICARE, including foreign force members and their families.

CHIROPRACTIC CARE

In 2001, the *National Defense Authorization Act* established the Chiropractic Health Care Program. The program is currently available to active duty service members (including activated National Guard and Reserve members) at designated military treatment facilities (MTFs) throughout the United States.

ELIGIBILITY

- Active duty service members and activated National Guard or Reserve members must obtain chiropractic care at a designated MTF and must receive a referral from their primary care manager (PCM).
- Family members, retirees and their family members, un-remarried former spouses and survivors **are not eligible** for this program. They may be referred to non-chiropractic health care services in the Military Health System (e.g., physical therapy or orthopedics) or may seek chiropractic care in the local community at their own expense.

ACCESS TO CHIROPRACTIC CARE

During the course of treatment, the service member's PCM will determine if specialty care (traditional or chiropractic care) is required. If chiropractic care is considered an option, the service member will undergo a screening process to rule out any medical conditions that would prohibit chiropractic care. If appropriate, the PCM will refer the service member to a chiropractic provider for treatment.

While receiving chiropractic care, the service member will continue to see his or her PCM and the duration/frequency of the chiropractic services will be determined by the PCM and follow the usual referral process.

Chiropractic care received outside of the designated locations is not covered under the Chiropractic Health Care Program.

TRICARE CATASTROPHIC CAP

The TRICARE catastrophic cap limits the amount of out-of-pocket expenses a family will have to pay for TRICARE-covered medical services. The cap applies to the allowable charges for covered services—annual deductibles, Prime enrollment fees, pharmacy co-pays, and other cost shares based on TRICARE-allowable charges. Out-of-pocket expenses paid under the TRICARE Prime point-of-service (POS) option (deductibles and cost-shares) are not applied to the annual enrollment year catastrophic cap. Additionally, any POS charges incurred after the catastrophic cap has been met are the beneficiary's financial responsibility.

The catastrophic cap amount depends on an individual's profile, and should be obtained from TRICARE directly.

TRICARE REGIONS

NORTH

TRICARE's North region includes Connecticut, Delaware, the District of Columbia, Illinois, Indiana, Kentucky, Maine, Maryland, Massachusetts, Michigan, New Hampshire, New Jersey, New York, North Carolina, Ohio, Pennsylvania, Rhode Island, Vermont, Virginia, West Virginia, and Wisconsin (and some zip code areas in Iowa, Missouri, and Tennessee). Health Net Federal Services, Inc. is the new regional contractor providing health care services and network-provider support in the TRICARE North region.

Health Net's customer service representatives are available Monday – Friday, 8 a.m. to 7 p.m. in all North region time zones, at (877) TRICARE (877-874-2273).

SOUTH

TRICARE's South region includes Alabama, Arkansas, Florida, Georgia, Louisiana, Mississippi Oklahoma, South Carolina, and Tennessee (excluding 35 Tennessee zip codes in the Fort Campbell, KY area), and Texas (excluding, only, the extreme southwestern El Paso-area). Humana-Military is the regional contractor providing health care services and network provider support in the TRICARE South region.

Humana's customer service representatives are available Monday – Friday, 8 a.m. to 6 p.m. in all South region time zones, at (800) 444-5445.

WEST

TRICARE's West region includes Alaska, Arizona, California, Colorado, Hawaii, Idaho, Iowa (except 82 Iowa zip codes that are in the Rock Island, Illinois area), Kansas, Minnesota, Missouri (except the St. Louis area), Montana, Nebraska, Nevada, New Mexico, North Dakota, Oregon, South Dakota, Texas (the southwestern corner, including El Paso, only) Utah, Washington, and Wyoming. TriWest Healthcare Alliance is the regional contractor providing health care services and network-provider support in the TRICARE West region.

TriWest's customer service representatives are available Monday – Friday, 8 a.m. to 6 p.m. in the West Region time zone in which you reside, at (888) TRIWEST (888-874-9378).

EUROPE AREA

The TRICARE Europe area is managed by the TAO Europe located at Sembach Air Base in Germany, and includes Europe, Africa and the Middle East.

Customer service representatives can be reached at (888) 777-8343.

Latin America and Canada Area

The TRICARE Latin America and Canada (TLAC) area is managed by the TAO TLAC located at Fort Gordon, Georgia and includes Central and South America, the Caribbean Basin, Canada, Puerto Rico and the Virgin Islands.

Customer service representatives can be reached at (888) 777-8343.

Pacific Area

The TRICARE Pacific area is managed by the TAO Pacific located at Camp Lester in Okinawa, Japan, and includes Guam, Japan, Korea, Asia, New Zealand, India and Western Pacific remote countries.

Customer service representatives can be reached at (888) 777-8343.

AFFORDABLE CARE ACT

The Affordable Care Act, also known as the health care law, was created to expand access to coverage, control health care costs and improve health care quality and care coordination. The health care law does not change VA health benefits or Veterans' out-of-pocket costs.

Three things you should know:

- VA wants all Veterans to receive health care that improves their health and well-being.
- If you are enrolled in VA health care, you don't need to take additional steps to meet the health care law coverage standards. The health care law does not change VA health benefits or Veterans' out-of-pocket costs.
- If you are not enrolled in VA health care, you can apply at any time.

Veterans Enrolled in VA Health Care

Veterans enrolled in VA health care programs have health coverage that meets the new health care law's standard. You do not have to take any additional steps to have health coverage.

Veterans Not Enrolled in VA Health Care

Veterans not currently enrolled in VA health care program can apply for enrollment at any time.

Family Members

VA offers health care benefits for certain family members of Veterans through programs such as the Civilian Health and Medical Program of the Department of Veterans Affairs (CHAMPVA) and the Spina Bifida program. Your family members who are not enrolled in a VA health care program should use the Marketplace to get coverage.

CHAPTER 14

VA'S FIDUCIARY PROGRAM

BENEFIT DESCRIPTION

VA's Fiduciary Program was established to protect Veterans and other beneficiaries who, due to injury, disease, or due to age, are unable to manage their financial affairs. VA will only determine an individual to be unable to manage his or her financial affairs after receipt of medical documentation or if a court of competent jurisdiction has already made the determination.

Upon determining a beneficiary is unable to manage his or her financial affairs, VA will appoint a fiduciary. The fiduciary, normally chosen by the beneficiary, must undergo an investigation of their suitability to serve. This investigation includes a criminal background check, review of credit report, personal interview, and recommendations of character references. Only after a complete investigation is a fiduciary appointed to manage a beneficiaries VA benefits. The fiduciary is responsible to the beneficiary and oversees financial management of VA benefit payments. Generally, family members or friends serve as fiduciaries for beneficiaries; however, when friends and family are not able to serve, VA looks for qualified individuals or organizations to serve as a fiduciary.

WHAT IS THE FIDUCIARY PROGRAM?

The purpose of the Department of Veterans Affairs (VA) Fiduciary Program is to protect Veterans and beneficiaries who are unable to manage their VA benefits through the appointment and oversight of a fiduciary.

If you have been determined unable to manage your VA benefits, the VA will conduct a field examination to appoint a fiduciary to assist you.

THE VA FIELD EXAMINATION

A VA field examination will be scheduled for the purpose of appointing a fiduciary to assist you in managing your VA benefits. During the field examination, please have the following information available for review by the field examiner:

Photo identification.

The source and amount of all monthly bills, recurring expenses (annual, bi-annual, quarterly, etc.), and income.

A list of all assets, to include bank accounts, owned property, stocks, bonds, life insurance, burial plans, etc.

A list of all current medications.

Name, phone number, and address of your primary care doctor.

Name, phone number, and address of your next of kin.

SELECTION PROCESS

During the selection process, the VA will first seek to qualify the individual you desire to serve as your fiduciary.

The fiduciary selection is based on an assessment of the qualifications of the proposed fiduciary. When seeking a fiduciary the following individuals may be considered:

- A spouse or family member
- Court-appointed fiduciaries
- Another interested party, or
- A professional fiduciary

An assessment of the qualifications of a proposed fiduciary includes, but is not limited to:

- The willingness to serve and abide by all agreements
- An interview with a VA representative
- Credit report review
- An inquiry into the criminal background, and
- Interviews with character witnesses

WHAT ARE MY RIGHTS?

The determination that you are unable to manage your VA benefits does not affect your non-VA finances, or your right to vote or contract.

You have the right to appeal VA's decision finding that you are unable to manage your VA benefits. You also have the right to appeal VA's selection of the fiduciary. If you disagree with the VA on either of these matters you may:

- appeal to the Board of Veterans' Appeals (Board) by telling us you disagree with our decision and want the Board to review it, or
- give us evidence we do not already have that may lead us to change our decision.

FIDUCIARY

HOW TO APPLY

To become a fiduciary for a family member or friend, submit a request with the beneficiary's name and VA file number, and your name and contact information to the VA regional office nearest you.

To become a professional fiduciary, submit your resume with cover letter to the following e-mail address: VA_Fiduciary@va.gov. Include your name, the name of your organization (if applicable), mailing address, and e-mail address with your request.

SELECTION PROCESS

The fiduciary selection is based on an assessment of the qualifications of the proposed fiduciary. When seeking a fiduciary the following individuals may be considered:

- A spouse or family member
- Court-appointed fiduciaries
- Another interested party, or
- A professional fiduciary

CHAPTER 15

VOCATIONAL REHABILITATION AND EMPLOYMENT SERVICES FOR VETERANS WITH SERVICE-CONNECTED DISABILITIES

OVERVIEW

2013 UPDATE: IMPROVING JOB OPPORTUNITIES FOR VETS ACT OF 2013

THE LAW CONTAINS THE FOLLOWING PROVISIONS:

Directs the Secretary of Veterans Affairs (VA), for a certain four-year period, to require training establishments applying for state approval of on-the-job training programs to certify that the wages to be paid an eligible veteran or person upon entrance into training will be increased in regular periodic increments until, by the last full month of the training period, they will be at least 75% (currently 85%) of the wages paid for the job for which such eligible veteran or person is being trained.

Requires the Secretary to enter into agreements with the heads of other federal departments and agencies to operate similar on-the-job training programs to train eligible veterans or persons to perform skills necessary for employment by the department or agency operating the program.

Extends from November 30 through December 31, 2016, the requirement of a reduced pension ($90 per month) for veterans (with neither spouse nor child) or surviving spouses (with no child) covered by Medicaid plans under title XIX of the Social Security Act for services furnished by nursing facilities.

Vocational Rehabilitation and Employment VetSuccess is a program which helps eligible disabled veterans get and keep lasting, suitable jobs. It also helps seriously disabled veterans achieve independence in daily living. A VA veteran who is eligible for an evaluation under Chapter 31 must first apply for services and receive an appointment with a Vocational Rehabilitation Counselor (VRC). The VRC will work with the veteran to determine if an employment handicap exists as a result of his or her service connected disability. If an employment handicap is established and the veteran is found entitled to services. The VRC and the veteran will continue counseling to select a track of services and jointly develop a plan to address the veteran's rehabilitation and employment needs.

The rehabilitation plan will specify an employment or independent living goal, identify intermediate goals, and outline services and resources that VA will provide to assist the veteran to achieve his / her goals. The VRC and the veteran will work together to implement the plan to assist the veteran to achieve his or her employment and / or independent living goals.

For a veteran found not to be entitled to services, the VRC will help him or her locate other resources to address any rehabilitation and employment needs identified during the evaluation. Referral to other resources may include state vocational rehabilitation programs; Department of Labor employment programs for disabled veterans; state, federal or local agencies providing services for employment or small business development; internet-based resources for rehabilitation and employment; and information about applying for financial aid.

The program offers a number of services to help each eligible disabled veteran reach his or her rehabilitation goal. These services include:

- Vocational and personal counseling;
- Evaluation of abilities, skill and interests;
- Assistance finding and keeping a suitable job, including special employer incentives;
- If needed, education and training such as certificate, two, or four year college programs;
- Financial aid;
- If needed, training such as on-the-job and non-paid work experiences;
- Supportive rehabilitation services and additional counseling;
- Medical and dental treatment, if needed;
- Education and training benefits for dependent children with the birth defect spina bifida, caused by a veteran-parent's service in the Vietnam theater.
- Vocational and educational guidance and counseling to certain veteran's dependents eligible for one of VA's educational benefit programs.

ELIGIBILITY

Usually, a veteran must first be awarded a monthly VA Disability Compensation payment. In some cases, veterans may be eligible if they are not getting VA compensation (for example, if they are awaiting discharge from the service because of a disability, OR they are entitled to VA compensation but have decided not to reduce their military retirement or disability pay).

Eligibility is also based on meeting the following conditions:

- The veteran served on or after September 16, 1940; and
- The veteran's discharge or release from active duty was under was under other than dishonorable conditions; and
- The veteran's service-connected disabilities are rated at least 20% disabling by VA (**NOTE:** Effective October 1, 1993, a veteran may be eligible for Vocational Rehabilitation if he or she is rated 10% disabled, and has a serious employment handicap.); and
- The veteran needs Vocational Rehabilitation to overcome an employment handicap; and
- It has been less than 12 years since VA notified the veteran of his or her eligibility. (A veteran may have longer than 12 years to use this benefit if certain conditions prevented him or her from training.)

AMOUNT OF VA PAYMENTS

If a veteran needs training, VA will pay his or her training costs, such as:

- Tuition and fees;
- Books;
- Supplies;
- Equipment; and
- Special services (such as prosthetic devices, lip-reading training, or signing for the deaf), if needed

While a veteran is in training, VA will also pay him or her a monthly benefit to help with living expenses, called a subsistence allowance. Details are provided in the next section of this chapter.

SUBSISTENCE ALLOWANCE (CHAPTER 31)

In some cases, a veteran requires additional education or training in order to become employable. A Subsistence Allowance may then be paid each month, and is based on the rate of attendance (full-time or part-time) and the number of dependents. The charts on the following page reflect the rates as of October 1, 2013.

The following Subsistence Allowance rates are paid for training in an Institution of Higher Learning:

Number Of Dependents	Full Time	Three Quarter Time	One Half Time
No Dependents	$594.47	$446.67	$298.88
One Dependent	$737.39	$553.85	$370.30
Two Dependents	$868.96	$649.68	$435.27
Each Additional Dependent	$63.34	$48.71	$32.50

Subsistence Allowance is paid for full time training only, in the following training programs:
Nonpay or nominal pay on-job training in a federal, state, local, or federally recognized Indian tribe agency; training in the home; vocational course in a rehabilitation facility or sheltered workshop; institutional non-farm cooperative.

Number Of Dependents	Full Time
No Dependents	$594.47
One Dependent	$737.39
Two Dependents	$868.34
Each Additional Dependent	$63.34

The following rates are paid for Work Experience programs:
Nonpay or nominal pay work experience in a federal, state, local or federally recognized Indian tribe agency.

Number Of Dependents	Full Time	Three Quarter Time	One Half Time
No Dependents	$594.47	$446.67	$298.88
One Dependent	$737.39	$553.85	$370.30
Two Dependents	$868.96	$649.68	$435.27
Each Additional Dependent	$63.34	$48.71	$32.50

Subsistence Allowance is paid for full time training only in the following training programs:
Farm cooperative, apprenticeship, or other on-job training.

Number of Dependents	Full Time
No Dependents	$519.77
One Dependent	$628.55
Two Dependents	$724.41
Each Additional Dependent	$47.12

Subsistence Allowance is paid at the following rates for combined training programs:
Combination of Institutional and On-Job Training (Full Time Rate Only).

Number Of Dependents	Institutional Greater than one half	On-The-Job Greater than one half
No Dependents	$594.47	$519.77
One Dependent	$737.39	$628.55
Two Dependents	$868.96	$724.41
Additional Dependents	$63.34	$42.12

Subsistence Allowance is paid at the following rates for Non-farm Cooperative Training:
Non-farm Cooperative Institutional Training and Non-farm Cooperative On-Job Training - Full Time Rate Only.

Number Of Dependents	FT Non-farm Coop/Institutional	FT Non-farm Coop/On-The-Job
No Dependents	$594.47	$519.77
One Dependent	$737.39	$628.55
Two Dependents	$868.96	$724.41
Each Additional Dependent	$63.34	$47.12

Subsistence Allowance is paid at the following rates for Independent Living programs:
A subsistence allowance is paid each month during the period of enrollment in a rehabilitation facility when a veteran is pursuing an approved Independent Living Program plan. Subsistence allowance paid during a period of Independent Living Services is based on rate of pursuit and number of dependents.

Number Of Dependents	Full Time	Three Quarter Time	One Half Time
No Dependents	$594.74	$446.67	$298.88
One Dependent	$737.39	$553.85	$370.30
Two Dependents	$868.96	$649.68	$435.27
Each Additional Dependent	$63.34	$48.71	$32.50

Subsistence Allowance is paid at the following rates for Extended Evaluation programs:
A subsistence allowance is paid each month during the period of enrollment in a rehabilitation facility when a veteran requires this service for the purpose of extended evaluation. Subsistence allowance during a period of extended evaluation is paid based on the rate of attendance and the number of dependents.

Number of Dependents	Full Time	Three Quarter Time	One Half Time	One Quarter Time
No Dependents	$594.47	$446.67	$298.88	$149.41
One Dependent	$737.39	$553.85	$370.30	$185.17
Two Dependents	$868.96	$649.68	$435.27	$217.64
Each Additional Dependent	$63.34	$48.71	$32.50	$16.21

PROGRAM FOR UNEMPLOYABLE VETERANS

Veterans awarded 100% disability compensation based upon unemployability may still request an evaluation, and, if found eligible, may participate in a vocational rehabilitation program and receive help in getting a job. A veteran who secures employment under the special program will continue to receive 100% disability compensation until the veteran has worked continuously for at least 12 months.

ELECTION OF ALTERNATE SUBSISTENCE ALLOWANCE UNDER *PUBLIC LAW 111-377*

This option is included for your use in comparing subsistence allowance rates that may be available to certain Veterans participating in the Chapter 31 program.

The VA is authorized to allow a Veteran, entitled to both a Chapter 31 subsistence allowance and *Post 9/11 GI Bill* Chapter 33 educational assistance, to elect to receive a payment in an alternate amount instead of the regular Chapter 31 subsistence allowance.

The alternate payment will be based on the military basic allowance for housing (BAH) for an E-5 with dependents residing in the zip code of the training facility. Training in foreign institutions and training that is solely on-line or in-home will be based on the national average BAH.

The Department of Defense (DoD) sets BAH rates each calendar year. BAH for full-time may be calculated at the DoD website:

- https://www.defensetravel.dod.mil/site/bahCalc.cfm
    - Enter **year** ("2011"), **zip code** of the training facility (school, employer for OJT programs, or agency approved for work experience programs), and "**E-5**"
    - Click "calculate"
    - Use rate for E-5 with dependents

PARALYMPIC VETERANS BENEFIT

Some veterans in training for the U.S. Paralympics may qualify for a monthly subsistence allowance from VA. The allowance is pegged to the subsistence allowance for participants in a full time institutional program under chapter 31 of title 38 of the U.S. Code. According to the new rule, the VA will pay the allowance to a veteran with a service-connected or non-service-connected disability if the veteran is invited by the U.S. Paralympics to compete for a slot on the U.S. Paralympic team or is residing at the U.S. Paralympic training center for training or competition. Applications for the allowance must be submitted through the U.S. Paralympics. Through the program, VA will pay a monthly allowance to a veteran with a service-connected or non-service-connected disability if the veteran meets the minimum military standard or higher (e.g., Emerging, Talent Pool, National Team) in his or her respective sport at a recognized competition. Besides making the military standard, an athlete must also be nationally or internationally classified by his or her respective sport federation as eligible for Paralympic competition within six or 12 months of a qualifying performance.

Athletes must also have established training and competition plans and are responsible for turning in monthly and quarterly reports in order to continue receiving a monthly assistance allowance. The allowance base for an athlete approved for monetary assistance ranges from $566.97 up to $1,084.00 per month, depending on the number of dependents.

VOCATIONAL TRAINING FOR CHILDREN WITH SPINA BIFIDA

To qualify for entitlement to a vocational training program an applicant must be a child:

- To whom VA has awarded a monthly allowance for spina bifida; and
- For whom VA has determined that achievement of a vocational goal is reasonably feasible.

A vocational training program may not begin before a child's 18th birthday, or the date of completion of secondary schooling, whichever comes first.

Depending on the need, a child may be provided up to 24 months of full-time training.

VOCATIONAL TRAINING FOR CHILDREN OF FEMALE VIETNAM VETERANS BORN WITH CERTAIN BIRTH DEFECTS

Section 401 of *P.L. 106-416*, which became law on November 1, 2000 directed the Secretary of VA to identify birth defects of children of female Vietnam veterans that: (1) are associated with service during the Vietnam era; and (2) result in the permanent physical or mental disability of such children. The law excludes from such defects familial or birth-related defects or injuries. The law further directs the Secretary to provide to such children a monthly monetary allowance, as well as necessary health care to address the defect and any associated disability. It authorizes the Secretary to provide vocational training to such a child if the achievement of a vocational goal is reasonably feasible.

INDEPENDENT LIVING SERVICES

These services can help an individual with disabilities so severe that he or she cannot work. These services can lessen the individual's need to rely on others by giving him or her the skills needed to live as independently as possible at home and in the community.

Independent living services include:

- Extended evaluation of the individual's independent living needs;
- Training in activities of daily living;
- Case management;
- Personal adjustment counseling;
- Assistive technology;
- Training to improve the individual's chances of reaching a vocational goal.

APPLYING FOR BENEFITS

Interested veterans can apply by filling out "VA Form 28-1900", "Disabled Veterans Application for Vocational Rehabilitation", and mailing it to the VA regional office serving his or her area. (For a complete list of VA Regional Offices, refer to Chapter 36 of this book.)

CHAPTER 16

VET CENTERS

Vet Centers serve veterans and their families by providing a continuum of quality care that adds value for veterans, families, and communities. Care includes:

- Professional readjustment counseling;
- Professional counseling for posttraumatic stress disorder;
- Marital and family counseling;
- Substance abuse information and referral;
- Community education;
- Outreach to special populations, including disenfranchised and unserved veterans;
- The brokering of services with community agencies;
- Provides a key access link between the veteran and other services in the U.S. Department of Veterans Affairs;
- Promotion of wellness activities with veterans to help them reach quality health and life goals, and diminish the need for more intensive healthcare.

ELIGIBILITY

Vet Centers serve the following veterans:

WAR ZONE VETERANS- ALL ERAS, INCLUDING:

- **Vietnam War** – February 28, 1961 to May 7, 1975
- Vietnam Era Veterans Not In The War Zone – August 5, 1964 to May 7, 1975

- **Korean War** – June 27, 1950 to July 27, 1954 (eligible for the Korean Service Medal)
- **World War II** – There are 3 eligible categories:

  1. European-African-Middle Eastern Campaign Medal – December 7, 1941 to November 8, 1945
  2. Asiatic-Pacific Campaign Medal – December 7, 1941 to March 2, 1946
  3. American Campaign Medal – December 7, 1941 to March 2, 1946

- **Lebanon** – August 25, 1982 to February 26, 1984
- **Grenada** – October 23, 1983 to November 21, 1983
- **Panama** – December 20, 1989 to January 31, 1990
- **Persian Gulf** – August 2, 1990 to a date to be set by law or Presidential Proclamation
- **Somalia** – September 17, 1992 to a date to be set by law or Presidential Proclamation
- **Operation Joint Endeavor, Operation Joint Guard, & Operation Joint Forge** - Vet Center eligibility has been extended to veterans who participated in one or more of the three successive operations in the former Yugoslavia (Bosnia-Herzegovina and Croatia, aboard U.S. Naval vessels operating in the Adriatic Sea, or air spaces above those areas).
- **Global War on Terrorism** – Veterans who serve or have served in military expeditions to combat terrorism on or after September 11, 2001 and before a terminal date yet to be established.

SEXUAL TRAUMA AND HARASSMENT COUNSELING

Veterans of both sexes, all eras. Vet Center services include individual readjustment counseling, referral for benefits assistance, group readjustment counseling, liaison with community agencies, marital and family counseling, substance abuse information and referral, job counseling and placement, sexual trauma counseling, and community education.

At the VA, Veterans can receive free, confidential treatment for mental and physical health conditions related to MST. You may be able to receive this MST-related care even if you are not eligible for other VA services. To receive these services, you do not need a VA service-connected disability rating, to have reported the incident when it happened, or have other documentation that it occurred.

Knowing that MST survivors may have special concerns, every VA healthcare facility has an MST Coordinator who can answer any questions you might have about VA's MST services. VA has a range of services available to meet Veterans where they are at in their recovery:

- Every VA healthcare facility has providers knowledgeable about treatment for problems related MST. Many have specialized outpatient mental health services focusing on sexual trauma. Vet Centers also have specially trained sexual trauma counselors.
- VA has almost two dozen programs nationwide that offer specialized MST treatment in a residential or inpatient settings. These programs are for Veterans who need more intense treatment and support.
- Because some Veterans do not feel comfortable in mixed-gender treatment settings, some facilities have separate programs for men and women. All residential and inpatient MST programs have separate sleeping areas for men and women.

BEREAVEMENT COUNSELING

The Department of Veteran Affairs (VA) offers bereavement counseling to parents, spouses and children of Armed Forces personnel who died in the service of their country. Also eligible are family members of reservists and National Guardsmen who die while on duty.

VET CENTER LOCATIONS

ALABAMA

Birmingham Vet Center
1500 5th Avenue South
Birmingham, AL 35205
(205) 731-0550

Mobile Vet Center
2577 Government Boulevard
Mobile, AL 36606
(251) 478-5906

Montgomery Vet Center Outstation
Colonial Park, Bldg. 600, #603
Montgomery, AL 35233
(334) 396-1986

ALASKA

Anchorage Vet Center
4201 Tudor Centre Dr, Suite 115
Anchorage, AK 99508
(907) 563-6966

Fairbanks Vet Center
542 4th Avenue
Suite 100
Fairbanks, AK 99701
(907) 456-4238

Kenai Vet Center
Building F, Suite 4
Red Diamond Center
43335 K-Beach Road
Kenai, AK 99669
(907) 260-7640

Wasilla Vet Center
851 East Westpoint Ave, Suite 109
Wasilla, AK 99654
(907) 376-4318

ARIZONA

Chinle Vet Center Outstation
P.O. Box 1934
Chinle, AZ 86503
(928) 674-3682

Hopi Vet Center Outstation 2
P.O. Box 267
Keams Canyon, AZ 86034
(928) 738-5166

Phoenix East Valley Vet Center
1303 South Longmore, Suite 5
Mesa, AZ 85202
(480) 610-6727

Phoenix Vet Center
77 East Weldon Avenue, Suite 100
Phoenix, AZ 85012-2075
(602) 640-2981

Prescott Vet Center
161 South Granite Street
Prescott, AZ 86303
(928) 778-3469

Tucson Vet Center
3055 North 1st Avenue
Tucson, AZ 85719
(520) 882-0333

ARKANSAS

North Little Rock Vet Center
201 West Broadway
Suite A
Little Rock, AR 72114
(501) 324-6395

Veterans Health Care System of the Ozarks
1100 North College Avenue
Fayetteville, AR 72703
(479) 443-4301

CALIFORNIA

4B Pacific Western Regional Office
420 Executive Court North, Suite G
Fairfield, CA 94534
(707) 646-2988

Chico Vet Center
280 Cohasset Road
Chico, CA 95926
(530) 899-8549

Concord Vet Center
1899 Clayton Rd, Suite 140
Concord, CA 94520
(925) 680-4526

Corona Vet Center
800 Magnolia Avenue, Suite 110
Corona, CA 92879-8202
(909) 734-0525

East Los Angeles Vet Center
5400 E Olympic Blvd, #140
East Los Angeles, CA 90022
(323) 728-9966

Eureka Vet Center
2830 G Street, Suite A
Eureka, CA 95501
(707) 444-8271

Fresno Vet Center
3636 North 1st St, Suite 112
Fresno, CA 93726
(559) 487-5660

Los Angeles Vet Center
1045 W. Redondo Beach Blvd.,
Suite 150
Gardena, CA 90247
(310)-767-1221

Modesto Vet Center
1219 N. Carpenter Rd., Suite 12
Modesto, CA 95351
(209) 569-0713

Oakland Vet Center
1504 Franklin St, Suite 200
Oakland, CA 94612
(510) 763-3904

Redwood City Vet Center
2946 Broadway Street
Redwood City, CA 94062
(650) 299-0672

Rohnert Park Vet Center
6225 State Farm Drive
Suite 101
Rohnert Park, CA 94928
(707) 586-3295

Sacramento Vet Center
1111 Howe Avenue
Suite 390
Sacramento, CA 95825
(916) 566-7430

San Bernardino Vet Center
155 West Hospitality Lane
Suite #140
San Bernardino, CA 92408
(909) 890-0797

San Diego Vet Center
2900 6th Avenue
San Diego, CA 92103
(619) 294-2040

San Francisco Vet Center
505 Polk Street
San Francisco, CA 94102
(415) 441-5051

San Jose Vet Center
278 North 2nd Street
San Jose, CA 95112
(408) 993-0729

San Marcos Vet Center
One Civic Center Dr., Suite 140
San Marcos, CA 92069
(760) 744-6914

Santa Cruz County Vet Center
1350 41st Ave, Suite 102
Capitola, CA 95010
(831)-464-4575

Sepulveda Vet Center
9737 Hascle Street
Sepulveda, CA 91343
(818) 892-9227

Ventura Vet Center
790 E. Santa Clara St., Suite 100
Ventura, CA 93001
(805)-585-1860

West Los Angeles Vet Center
5730 Uplander Way, Suite 100
Culver City, CA 90230
(310) 641-0326

COLORADO

Boulder Vet Center
2336 Canyon Blvd, Suite 130
Boulder, CO 80302
(303) 440-7306

Colorado Springs Vet Center
416 East Colorado Avenue
Colorado Springs, CO 80903
(719) 471-9992
4A Western Mountain
Regional Office
789 Sherman Street, Suite 570
Denver, CO 80203
(303) 393-2897

Denver Vet Center
7465 E Academy Boulevard

Denver, CO 80220
(303) 326-0645

Ft. Collins Vet Center Outstation
1100 Poudre River Dr. (Lower)
Ft. Collins, CO 80524
(970) 221-5176

Grand Junction Vet Center
2472 F. Road Unit 16
Grand Junction, CO 81505
(970) 245-4156

Pueblo Vet Center Outstation
509 E. 13th St.
Pueblo, CO 81001
(719) 546-6666

CONNECTICUT

New Haven Vet Center
141 Captain Thomas Boulevard
New Haven, CT 06516
(203) 932-9899

Norwich Vet Center
5 Cliff Street
Norwich, CT 06360
(860) 887-1755

Wethersfield Vet Center
30 Jordan Lane
Wethersfield, CT 06109
(860) 563-2320

DELAWARE

Wilmington Vet Center
1601 Kirkwood Highway
Wilmington, DE 19805
(302) 994-1660

DISTRICT OF COLUMBIA

Washington, D.C. Vet Center
1250 Taylor Street, NW
Washington, DC 20011
(202) 726-5212

FLORIDA

Bay Pines Vet Center
789 Sherman Street, Suite 570
Denver, CO 80203
(303) 393-2897

Fort Lauderdale Vet Center
713 NE 3rd Avenue
Fort Lauderdale, FL 33304
(954) 356-7926

Ft. Myers Outstation Vet Center
3691 Evans
Ft. Myers, FL 33901
(239) 938-1100

Gainesville Vet Center
105 NW 75th Street, Suite #2
Gainesville, FL 32607
(352) 331-1408

Jacksonville Vet Center
300 East State Street
Jacksonville, FL 32202
(904) 232-3621

Key Largo Vet Center Outstation
105662 Overseas Hwy.
Key Largo, FL 33037
(305) 451-0164
Melbourne Vet Center
2098 Sarno Road
Melbourne, FL 32935
(321) 254-3410

Miami Vet Center
2700 SW 3rd Avenue
Suite 1A
Miami, FL 33129
(305) 859-8387

Orlando Vet Center
5575 S Semoran Blvd
Suite 36
Orlando, FL 32822
(407) 857-2800

Palm Beach Vet Center
2311 10th Avenue, North #13
Palm Beach, FL 33461
(561) 585-0441

Pensacola Vet Center
4501 Twin Oaks Drive
Pensacola, FL 32506
(850) 456-5886

Sarasota Vet Center
4801 Swift Road
Sarasota, FL 34231
(941) 927-8285

St. Petersburg Vet Center
2880 1st Avenue, N.
St. Petersburg, FL 33713
(727) 893-3791

Tallahassee Vet Center
548 Bradford Road
Tallahassee, FL 32303
(850) 942-8810

Tampa Vet Center
8900N Armenia Ave, #312
Tampa, FL 33604
(813) 228-2621

GEORGIA

Atlanta Vet Center
1440 Dutch Valley Place
Suite G, Box 29
Atlanta, GA 30324
(404) 347-7264

Macon Vet Center
750 Riverside Drive
Macon, GA 31201
(478) 477-3813

North Atlanta Vet Center
930 River Centre Plaza
Lawrenceville, GA 30043
(770) 963-1809

Savannah Vet Center
8110A White Bluff Road
Savannah, GA 31406
(912) 652-4097

GUAM

Agana Vet Center
222 Chalan Santo Papa Street
Reflection Center, Suite 102
Agana, Guam 96910
(671) 472-7160

Guam Vet Center
222 Chalan Santo Papa Reflection Ctr.
Ste 201
Hagatna, GU 96910
(671) 472-7160

HAWAII

Hilo Vet Center
120 Keawe Street
Suite 201
Hilo, HI 96720
(808) 969-3833

Honolulu Vet Center
1680 Kapiolani Boulevard
Suite F3
Honolulu, HI 96814
(808) 973-8387

Kailua-Kona Vet Center
Pottery Terrace, Fern Building
75-5995 Kuakini Highway, #415
Kailua-Kona, HI 96470
(808) 329-0574
Lihue Vet Center
3-3367 Kuhlo Highway
Suite 101
Lihue, HI 96766
(808) 246-1163

Wailuku Vet Center
35 Lunalilo
Suite 101
Wailuku, HI 96793
(808) 242-8557

IDAHO

Boise Vet Center
5440 Franklin Road, Suite 100
Boise, ID 83705
(208) 342-3612

Pocatello Vet Center
1800 Garrett Way
Pocatello, ID 83201
(208) 232-0316

ILLINOIS

Chicago Vet Center
2038 West 95th Street
Suite 200
Chicago, IL 60643
(773) 881-9900

Chicago Heights Vet Center
1600 Halsted Street
Chicago Heights, IL 60411
(708) 754-0340

East St. Louis Vet Center
1265 North 89th Street, Suite 5
East St. Louis, IL 62203
(618) 397-6602

Evanston Vet Center
565 Howard Street
Evanston, IL 60202
(847) 332-1019

Moline Vet Center
1529 46th Avenue, #6
Moline, IL 61265
(309) 762-6954

Oak Park Vet Center
155 S Oak Park Blvd
Oak Park, IL 60302
(708) 383-3225

Peoria Vet Center
3310 North Prospect Street
Peoria, IL 61603
(309) 688-2170

Rockford Vet Center Outstation
4960 E. State St. #3
Rockford, IL 61108
(815)-395-1276

Springfield Vet Center
624 South 4th Street
Springfield, IL 62703
(217) 492-4955

INDIANA

Evansville Vet Center
311 North Weinbach Avenue
Evansville, IN 47711
(812) 473-5993

Fort Wayne Vet Center
528 West Berry Street
Fort Wayne, IN 46802
(260) 460-1456

Gary Vet Center
6505 Broadway Ave.
Merrillville, IN 46410
219-736-5633

Indianapolis Vet Center
3833 Meridian, Suite 120
Indianapolis, IN 46208
(317) 927-6440

IOWA

Cedar Rapids Vet Center
1642 42nd Street, N.E.
Cedar Rapids, IA 52402
(319) 378-0016

Des Moines Vet Center
2600 Martin Luther King Jr. Parkway
Des Moines, IA 50310
(515) 284-4929

Sioux City Vet Center
1551 Indian Hills Drive
Sioux City, IA 51104
(712) 255-3808

KANSAS

Manhattan Vet Center
205 South 4th Street, Suite B
Manhattan, KS 66502
Phone: (785) 587-8257

Wichita Vet Center
413 South Pattie
Wichita, KS 67211
(316) 265-3260

KENTUCKY

Lexington Vet Center
301 East Vine Street, Suite C
Lexington, KY 40507
(859) 253-0717

Louisville Vet Center
1347 South 3rd Street
Louisville, KY 40208
(502) 634-1916

LOUISIANA

Baton Rouge Vet Center
5207 Essen Lane, Suite 2
Baton Rouge, LA 70809
(225) 757-0042

New Orleans Vet Center
2200 Veterans Blvd, Suite 114
Kenner, LA 70062
(504) 464-4743

Shreveport Vet Center
2800 Youree Drive
Building 1, Suite 105
Shreveport, LA 71104
(318) 861-1776

MAINE

Bangor Vet Center
352 Harlow Street
Bangor, ME 04401
(207) 947-3391

Caribou Vet Center
York Street Complex
Caribou, ME 04736
(207) 496-3900

Lewiston Vet Center
Parkway Complex
29 Westminster Street
Lewiston, ME 04240
(207) 783-0068

Portland Vet Center
475 Stevens Avenue
Portland, ME 04103
(207) 780-3584

Sanford Vet Center
628 Main Street
Springvale, ME 04083
(207) 490-1513

MARYLAND

Baltimore Vet Center
1777 Reisterstown Road
Suite 199
Baltimore, MD 21208
(410) 764-9400

Cambridge Vet Center
5510 West Shore Drive
Cambridge, MD 21613
(410) 228-6305

Elkton Vet Center
103 Chesapeake Blvd, Suite A
Elkton, MD 21921
(410) 394-4485

Harford County Vet Center Outstation
223 W. Bel Air Avenue
Aberdeen, MD 21001
(410)-272-6771
Silver Spring Vet Center
1015 Spring St, Suite 101
Silver Spring, MD 20910
(301) 589-1073

Towson Vet Center
305 W. Chesapeake Ave
Suite 300
Towson, MD 21204
(410) 828-6619

MASSACHUSETTS

Boston Vet Center
665 Beacon Street
Boston, MA 02215
(617) 424-0665

Brockton Vet Center
1041-L Pearl Street
Brockton, MA 02401
(508) 580-2730

Hyannis Vet Center
474 West Main Street
Hyannis, MA 02601
(508) 778-0124

Lowell Vet Center
73 East Merrimack Street
Lowell, MA 01852
(978) 453-1151

New Bedford Vet Center
468 North Street
New Bedford, MA 02740
(508) 999-6920

Springfield Vet Center
1985 Main Street
Northgate Plaza
Springfield, MA 01103
(413) 737-5167

Worcester Vet Center
597 Lincoln Street
Worcester, MA 01605
(508) 856-7428

MICHIGAN

Dearborn Vet Center
2881 Monroe Street
Suite 100
Deerborn, MI 48124
(313) 277-1428

Detroit Vet Center
4161 Cass Avenue
Detroit, MI 48201
(313) 831-6509

Escanaba Vet Center
3500 Ludington Street
Suite # 110
Escanaba , MI 49829
(906) 233-0244

Grand Rapids Vet Center
1940 Eastern SE
Grand Rapids, MI 48507
(616) 243-0385

Michigan Upper Peninsula Vet Center
2600 College Ave.
Escanaba, MI 49829
(906) 789-9732

MINNESOTA

Duluth Vet Center
405 East Superior Street
Duluth, MN 55802
(218) 722-8654

St. Paul Vet Center
2480 University Avenue
St. Paul, MN 55114
(651) 644-4022

MISSISSIPPI

Biloxi Vet Center
288 Veterans Avenue
Biloxi, MS 39531
(228) 388-9938

Jackson Vet Center
1755 Lelia Dr.
Suite 104
(601) 965-5727

MISSOURI

Kansas City Vet Center
3931 Main Street
Kansas City, MO 64111
(816) 753-1866

St. Louis Vet Center
2345 Pine Street
St. Louis, MO 63103
(314) 231-1260

MONTANA

Billings Vet Center
1234 Avenue C
Billings, MT 59102
(406) 657-6071

Missoula Vet Center
500 North Higgins Avenue
Missoula, MT 59802
(406) 721-4918

NEBRASKA

Lincoln Vet Center
920 L Street
Lincoln, NE 68508
(402) 476-9736

Omaha Vet Center
2428 Cuming Street
Omaha, NE 68131
(402) 346-6735

NEVADA

Las Vegas Vet Center
1040 East Sahara Avenue
Suite 102
Las Vegas, NV 89104
(702) 388-6368

Reno Vet Center
1155 West 4th Street
Suite 101
Reno, NV 89503
(775) 323-1294

NEW HAMPSHIRE

Berlin Vet Center
515 Main Street
Gorham, NH 03581
(603) 752-2571

Manchester Vet Center
103 Liberty Street
Manchester, NH 03104
(603) 668-7060

NEW JERSEY

Jersey City Vet Center
115 Christopher Columbus Drive
Room 200
Jersey City, NJ 07302
(201) 748-4467
Newark Vet Center
45 Academy Street
Suite 303
Newark, NJ 07102
(973) 645-5954

Trenton Vet Center
171 Jersey St., Building 36
Trenton, NJ 08611
(609) 989-2260

Ventnor Vet Center
6601 Ventnor Avenue, Suite 105
Ventnor, NJ 08406
(609) 487-8387

NEW MEXICO

Albuquerque Vet Center
1600 Mountain Road, NW
Albuquerque, NM 87104
(505) 346-6562

Farmington Vet Center
4251 East Main, Suite B
Farmington, NM 87402
(505) 327-9684

Las Cruces Vet Center
230 S. Water Street
Las Cruces, NM 88001
(575) 523-9826

Santa Fe Vet Center
2209 Brothers Road, Suite 110
Santa Fe, NM 87505
(505) 988-6562

NEW YORK

Albany Vet Center
875 Central Avenue
Albany, NY 12206
(518) 438-2505
Babylon Vet Center
116 West Main Street
Babylon, NY 11702
(631) 661-3930

Binghamton Vet Center
53 Chenango Street
Binghamtom, NY 13901
(866) 716-8213

Bronx Vet Center
226 East Fordham Road
Room 220
Bronx, NY 10458
(718) 367-3500

Brooklyn Vet Center
25 Chapel Street, Suite 604
Brooklyn, NY 11201
(718) 330-2825

Buffalo Vet Center
564 Franklin Street
Buffalo, NY 14202
(716) 882-0505

Harlem Vet Center
55 West 125th Street
New York, NY 10027
(212) 426-2200

Manhattan Vet Center
32 Broadway, 2nd Floor
Suite 200
New York, NY 10004
(212) 742-9591

Middletown Vet Center
726 East Main Street, Suite 203
Middletown, NY 10940
(845) 342-9917

Rochester Vet Center
1867 Mount Hope Avenue
Rochester, NY 14620
(585) 232-5040

Staten Island Vet Center
150 Richmond Terrace
Staten Island, NY 10301
(718) 816-4499

Syracuse Vet Center
716 East Washington Street
Syracuse, NY 13210
(315) 478-7127

Watertown Vet Center
210 Court Street
Watertown, NY 13601
(866) 610-0358

White Plains Vet Center
300 Hamilton Avenue
White Plains, NY 10601
(914) 682-6250

Woodhaven Vet Center
75-10B 91st Avenue
Woodhaven, NY 11421
(718) 296-2871

NORTH CAROLINA

Charlotte Vet Center
223 South Brevard Street
Suite 103
Charlotte, NC 28202
(704) 333-6107

Fayetteville Vet Center
4140 Ramsey St., Suite 110
Fayetteville, NC 28311
(910) 488-6252

Greensboro Vet Center
2009 South Elm-Eugene Street
Greensboro, NC 27406
(336) 333-5366

Greenville Vet Center
150 Arlington Blvd., Suite B
Greenville, NC 27858
(252) 355-7920

Raleigh Vet Center
1649 Old Louisburg Road
Raleigh, NC 27604
(919) 856-4616

NORTH DAKOTA

Bismarck Vet Center
1684 Capital Way
Bismarck, ND 58501
(701) 244-9751

Fargo Vet Center
3310 Fiechtner Drive, Suite 100
Fargo. MD 58103
(701) 237-0942

Minot Vet Center
2041 3rd Street, N.W.
Minot, ND 58701
(701) 852-0177

OHIO

Cincinnati Vet Center
801-B West 8th Street
Cincinnati, OH 45203
(513) 763-3500

Cleveland Heights Center
2022 Lee Road
Cleveland Heights, OH 44118
(216) 932-8471

Columbus Vet Center
30 Spruce Street
Columbus, OH 43215
(614) 257-5550

Dayton Vet Center
6th Floor, East Medical Plaza
627 Edwin
Dayton, OH 45408
(937) 461-9150
McCafferty Outstation Vet Center
4242 Lorain Avenue, Suite 201
Cleveland, OH 44113
(216) 939-0784

Parma Vet Center
5700 Pearl Rd., Suite 102
Parma, OH 44129
(440) 845-5023

Toledo Vet Center
1565 S. Byrne Road, Suite 104
Toledo, OH 43614
(419) 213-7533

OKLAHOMA

Oklahoma City Vet Center
3033 North Walnut, Suite 101W
Oklahoma City, OK 73105
(405) 270-5184

Tulsa Vet Center
1408 South Harvard
Tulsa, OK 74112
(918) 748-5105

OREGON

Eugene Vet Center
1255 Pearl Street
Eugene, OR 97403
(541) 465-6918

Grants Pass Vet Center
211 S.E. 10th Street
Grants Pass, OR 97526
(541) 479-6912

Portland Vet Center
8383 N.E. Sandy Blvd, Suite 110
Portland, OR 97220
(503) 273-5370

Salem Vet Center
617 Chemeketa St., N.E.
Salem, OR 97301
(503) 362-9911

PENNSYLVANIA

DuBois Vet Center
100 Meadow Lane
Suite 8
DuBois, PA 15801
(814) 372-2095

Erie Vet Center
1001 State Street
Suites 1 & 2
Erie, PA 16501
(814) 453-7955

Harrisburg Vet Center
1500 N 2nd Street, Suite 2
Harrisburg, PA 17102
(717) 782-3954

McKeesport Vet Center
2001 Lincoln Way
McKeesport, PA 15131
(412) 678-7704

Philadelphia Vet Center
801 Arch Street, Suite 102
Philadelphia, PA 19107
(215) 627-0238

Philadelphia Vet Center
101 East Olney Avenue
Philadelphia, PA 19120
(215) 924-4670

Pittsburgh Vet Center
2500 Baldwick Road
Pittsburgh, PA 15205
(412) 920-1765

Scranton Vet Center
1002 Pittston Avenue
Scranton, PA 18505
(570) 344-2676

Williamsport Vet Center
805 Penn Street
Williamsport, PA 17701
(570) 327-5281

PUERTO RICO

Arecibo Vet Center
52 Gonzalo Marin Street
Arecibo, Puerto Rico 00612-4702
(787) 879-4510
Ponce Vet Center
35 Mayor Street
Ponce, Puerto Rico 00730
(787) 841-3260

San Juan Vet Center
Condominio Medical Center Plaza
Suite LC8A and LC9
Rio Piedras, Puerto Rico 00921
(787) 749-4409

RHODE ISLAND

Warwick Vet Center
2038 Warwick Avenue
Warwick, RI 02889
(401) 739-0167

SOUTH CAROLINA

Columbia Vet Center
1513 Pickens Street
Columbia, SC 29201
(803) 765-9944

Greenville Vet Center
14 Lavinia Avenue
Greenville, SC 29601
(864) 271-2711

North Charleston Vet Center
5603A Rivers Avenue
North Charleston, SC 29406
(843) 747-8387

SOUTH DAKOTA

Pine Ridge Vet Center Outstation
P.O. Box 910, 105 E. Hwy 18
Martin, SD 57747
(605) 685-1300

Rapid City Vet Center
621 Sixth Street, Suite 101
Rapid City, SD 57701
(605) 348-0077

Sioux Falls Vet Center
601 S. Cliff Ave., Suite C
Sioux Falls, SD 57104
(605) 330-4552

TENNESSEE

Chattanooga Vet Center
951 Eastgate Loop Road
Building 5700, Suite 300
Chattanooga, TN 37411
(423) 855-6570

Johnson City Vet Center
1615A West Market Street
Johnson City, TN 37604
(423) 928-8387

Knoxville Vet Center
2817 East Magnolia Avenue
Knoxville, TN 37914
(865) 545-4680

Memphis Vet Center
1835 Union, Suite 100
Memphis, TN 38104
(901) 544-0173

Nashville Vet Center
1420 Donelson Pike Suite A-5
Nashville, TN 37217
(615) 366-1220

TEXAS

Amarillo Vet Center
3414 Olsen Blvd., Suite E
Amarillo, TX 79109
(806) 354-9779

Austin Vet Center
1110 W William Cannon Dr
Suite 301
Austin, TX 78745
(512) 416-1314

Corpus Christi Vet Center
4646 Corona, Suite 250
Corpus Christi, TX 78411
(361) 854-9961

Dallas Vet Center
5232 Forest Lane, Suite 111
Dallas, TX 75244
(214) 361-5896

El Paso Vet Center
1155 Westmoreland
Suite 121
El Paso, TX 79925
(915) 772-0013

Fort Worth Vet Center
1305 West Magnolia, Suite B
Forth Worth, TX 76104
(817) 921-9095
Houston Vet Center
503 Westheimer
Houston, TX 77006
(713) 523-0884

Houston Vet Center
701 N. Post Oak Rd., Suite 102
Houston, TX 77024
(713) 682-2288

Killeen Heights Vet Center
302 Millers Crossing, Suite #4
Harker Heights, TX 76548
(254) 953-7100

Laredo Vet Center
6020 McPherson Road, #1A
Laredo, TX 78041
(956) 723-4680

Lubbock Vet Center
3208 34th Street
Lubbock, TX 79410
(806) 792-9782

McAllen Vet Center
801 Nolana Loop, Suite 115
McAllen, TX 78504
(956) 631-2147

Midland Vet Center
3404 W. Illinois, Suite 1
Midland, TX 79703
(432) 697-8222

San Antonio Vet Center
231 West Cypress Street
San Antonio, TX 78212
(210) 472-4025

UTAH

Provo Vet Center
750 North 200 West
Suite 105
Provo, UT 84601
(801) 377-1117

Salt Lake City Vet Center
1354 East 3300 South
Salt Lake City, UT 84106
(801) 584-1294

VERMONT

South Burlington Vet Center
359 Dorset Street
South Burlington, VT 05403
(802) 862-1806

White River Junction Vet Center
222 Holiday Drive
Gilman Office Center Building #2
White River Junction, VT 05001
(802) 295-2908

VIRGINIA

Alexandria Vet Center
8796 Sacramento Drive
Suites D & E
Alexandria, VA 22309
(703) 360-8633

Norfolk Vet Center
2200 Colonial Avenue, Suite 3
Norfolk, VA 23517
(757) 623-7584

Richmond Vet Center
4202 Fitzhugh Avenue
Richmond, VA 23230
(804) 353-8958

Roanoke Vet Center
350 Albemarle Avenue, S.W.
Roanoke, VA 24016
(540) 342-9726

VIRGIN ISLANDS

St. Croix Vet Center
The Village Mall
Rural Route 2
Box 10553, Kingshill
St. Croix, Virgin Islands 00850
(340) 778-5553

St. Thomas Vet Center
9800 Buccaneer Mall, Suite 8
St. Thomas, Virgin Islands 00802
(340) 774-6674

WASHINGTON

Bellingham Vet Center
3800 Byron Avenue, Suite 124
Bellingham, WA 98229
(360) 733-9226

Everett Vet Center
3311 Wetmore Avenue
Everett, WA 98201
(425)252-9701

Seattle Vet Center
2030 9th Avenue, Suite 210
Seattle, WA 98121
(206) 553-2706

Spokane Vet Center
100 North Mullan Road, Suite 102
Spokane, WA 99206
(509) 444-8387

Tacoma Vet Center
4916 Center Street, Suite E
Tacoma, WA 98409
(253) 565-7038

Yakima Valley Vet Center
1111 North 1st Street
Suite 1
Yakima, WA 98901
(509) 457-2736

WEST VIRGINIA

Beckley Vet Center
101 Ellison Avenue
Beckley, WV 25801
(304) 252-8220
Charleston Vet Center
521 Central Avenue
Charleston, WV 25302
(304) 343-3825

Huntington Vet Center
3135 16th Street Road
Suite 11
Huntington, WV 25701
(304) 523-8387

Logan Vet Center Outstation
21 Main Street West
Henlawson, WV 25624
(304) 752-4453

Martinsburg Vet Center
900 Winchester Avenue
Martinsburg, WV 25401
(304) 263-6776
Morgantown Vet Center
1083 Greenbag Road
Morgantown, WV 26508
(304) 291-4303

Parkersburg Vet Center Outstation
2311 Ohio Avenue, Suite D
Pakersburg, WV 26101
(304) 485-1599

Princeton Vet Center
905 Mercer Street
Princeton, WV 24740
(304) 425-5653

Wheeling Vet Center
1206 Chapline Street
Wheeling, WV 26003
(304) 232-0587

Wisconsin

Madison Vet Center
147 South Butler Street
Madison, WI 53703
(608) 264-5342

Milwaukee Vet Center
5401 North 76th Street
Milwaukee, WI 53218
(414) 536-1301

Wyoming

Casper Vet Center
111 South Jefferson
Casper, WY 82601
(307) 261-5355

Cheyenne Vet Center
2424 Pioneer Avenue, Suite 103
Cheyenne, WY 82001
(307) 778-7370

CHAPTER 17

EDUCATION BENEFITS OVERVIEW

The Veterans' Administration administers ten educational assistance programs, each with different eligibility criteria. Typically, a veteran's eligibility is based on his or her dates of active duty. Generally, only the VA can determine an applicant's eligibility. Specific information regarding educational benefits can be obtained from the Education Service of the VA (888) GI-BILL-1 or any VA regional office.

> *MGIB, REAP, & MGIB-SR are discussed in the following three chapters. This chapter discusses the remaining seven educational assistance programs.*

An individual can be eligible for more than one of the available education benefits. If so, he or she must elect which benefit to receive. Payments for more than one benefit at a time may not be made.

The VA strongly encourages individuals who qualify for more than one type of education benefit to discuss their education plans with a Veterans Benefits Counselor so that all options can be explored, and maximum benefits can be paid.

VETERANS EDUCATIONAL ASSISTANCE PROGRAM (VEAP) – CHAPTER 32

The Post-Vietnam Veterans' Educational Assistance Program is also known as VEAP or Chapter 32.

VEAP provides education and training opportunities to eligible persons who contributed to the program while on active duty. If an individual did not contribute, or received a refund of contributions, he or she is not eligible for VEAP benefits. The initial contribution must have been made by March 31, 1987. The maximum contribution by any individual participant is $2,700. A participating member's contributions are matched on a $2 for $1 basis by the Government.

Beginning August 1, 2011, break (or interval pay) became no longer be payable under VEAP except during periods your school is closed as a result of an Executive Order of the President or an emergency (such as a natural disaster or strike). For example, if your Fall term ends on December 15th and your Spring term begins January 10th, your January housing allowance will cover 15 days in December and your February housing allowance will cover 21 days in January.

VEAP ELIGIBILITY

To qualify for VEAP benefits, individuals must have:

- Entered active duty for the first time between January 1, 1977 and June 30, 1985; and
- Enrolled in and contributed to VEAP before April 1, 1987; and
- Served for a continuous period of 181 days or more (Individuals may be eligible if discharged from a shorter period of active duty for a service-connected disability.); and
- Been discharged or released from service under conditions other than dishonorable; and
- Completed 24 continuous months of active duty if enlisted for the first time after September 7, 1980, or entered active duty as an officer or enlistee after October 16, 1981. (Individuals meet this requirement if they completed a shorter period of active duty to which the service department called or ordered the individual.)

Benefits are generally payable for 10 years following a veteran's release from active duty.

Individuals may be eligible for VEAP benefits if they did not complete 24 continuous months of active duty if they:

- Received VA disability compensation or military disability retirement; or
- Served a period of at least 24 continuous months of active duty before October 17, 1981; or
- Were discharged or released for early out, hardship, or service-connected disability.

Individuals may be eligible for VEAP benefits while still on active duty if they:

- Entered active duty for the first time after December 31, 1976, and before July 1, 1985; and
- Enrolled in and contributed to VEAP before April 1, 1987, and have at least three months of contributions available (For an elementary or high school program, at least one month of contributions must be available.); and

- Served for a continuous period of 181 days or more; and
- Completed their first active duty commitment.

The following types of active duty do not establish eligibility:

- Time assigned by the military to a civilian institution for the same course provided to civilians;
- Time served as a cadet or midshipman at a service academy;
- Time spent on active duty for training in the National Guard or Reserve.

NOTE: Individuals are not eligible for VEAP if they are eligible for the Montgomery GI Bill-Active Duty based on prior eligibility for Vietnam Era Veterans' Educational Assistance.

APPROVED COURSES

VEAP benefits may be received for a wide variety of training, including:

- Training for a high school diploma or the equivalent
- Undergraduate or graduate degrees from a college or university
- Cooperative training programs
- Accredited independent study programs leading to standard college degrees
- Courses leading to certificates or diplomas from business, technical or vocational schools
- Vocational flight training (Individuals must have a private pilot's license and meet the medical requirements for a desired license before beginning training, and throughout the flight training program)
- Apprenticeship or job training programs offered by a company or union
- Correspondence courses
- VA may approve programs offered by institutions outside of the United States, when they are pursued at educational institutions of higher learning, and lead to a college degree. Individuals must receive VA approval prior to attending or enrolling in any foreign programs.
- Effective March 1, 2001, benefits may be payable for licensing or certification tests. The tests are those needed to enter, maintain, or advance into employment in a civilian vocation or profession. The eligible veteran or family member may receive payment of the fee charged for the test or $2,000, whichever is less. The tests must be approved for VA benefits.

If an individual is seeking a college degree, the school must admit him or her to a degree program by the start of the third term.

Restrictions on Training

- Bartending and personality development courses
- Non-accredited independent study courses
- Any course given by radio
- Self-improvement courses such as reading, speaking, woodworking, basic seamanship, and English as a second language
- Any course which is avocational or recreational in character
- Farm cooperative courses
- Audited courses
- Courses not leading to an educational, professional, or vocational objective
- Courses an individual has previously taken and successfully completed
- Courses taken by a Federal government employee under the Government Employees' Training Act
- Courses paid for in whole or in part by the Armed Forces while on active duty
- Courses taken while in receipt of benefits for the same program from the Office of Workers' Compensation Programs

The VA must reduce benefits for individuals in Federal, State or local prisons after being convicted of a felony.

An individual may not receive benefits for a program at a proprietary school if he or she is an owner or official of the school.

Part-Time Training

Individuals unable to attend school full-time should consider going part-time. Benefit rates and entitlement charges are less than the full-time rates. For example, if a student receives full-time benefits for 12 months, the entitlement charge is 12 months. However, if the student receives ½ time benefits for 12 months, the charge is 6 months. VA will pay for less than ½ time training if the student is not receiving Tuition Assistance for those courses.

Remedial, Deficiency and Refresher Training

Remedial and deficiency courses are intended to assist a student in overcoming a deficiency in a particular area of study. In order for such courses to be approved, the courses must be deemed necessary for pursuit of a program of education.

Refresher training is for technological advances that occurred in a field of employment. The advance must have occurred while the student was on active duty, or after release.

There is an entitlement charge for these courses.

Tutorial Assistance

Students may receive a special allowance for individual tutoring if they entered school at one-half time or more. To qualify, the student must have a deficiency in a subject. The school must certify the tutor's qualifications, and the hours of tutoring. Eligible students may receive a maximum monthly payment of $100.00. The maximum total benefit payable is $1,200.00.

There is no entitlement charge for the first $600.00 of tutorial assistance.

To apply for tutorial assistance, students must submit "VA Form 22-1990t", Application and Enrollment Certification for Individualized Tutorial Assistance. The form should be given to the certifying official in the office handling VA paperwork at the school for completion.

MONTHS OF BENEFITS / ENTITLEMENT CHARGED

Individuals are charged one full day of entitlement for each day of full-time benefits paid.

Eligible members may be entitled to receive up to 36 months of VEAP benefits. Usually, the number of monthly payments for full-time training is the same as the number of months an individual contributed to VEAP.

Benefits are generally payable for 10 years following a veteran's release from active duty.

Individuals qualifying for more than one VA education program may receive a maximum of 48 months of benefits. For example, if a student used 30 months of Dependents' Educational Assistance, and is eligible for chapter 1606 benefits, he or she could have a maximum of 18 months of entitlement remaining.

Individuals are charged one full day of entitlement for each day of full-time benefits paid.

For correspondence and flight training, one month of entitlement is charged each time VA pays one month of benefits. For cooperative programs, one month of entitlement is used for each month of benefits paid.

For apprenticeship and job training programs, the entitlement charge changes every 6 months. During the first 6 months, the charge is 75% of full time. For the second 6 months, the charge is 55% of full time. For the remainder of the program, the charge is 35% of full time.

RATES OF EDUCATIONAL ASSISTANCE PAY

The total dollar amount of VEAP benefits is:

- An individual's total contributions, plus
- Matching funds equal to 2 times the individual's contributions, plus

- Any additional contributions or kickers made by the Department of Defense

The amount of money an individual receives each month depends on the type of training and the training time.

INSTITUTIONAL TRAINING:

The monthly benefit payment will vary depending on the amount and number of contributions. Divide the total contributions by the number of months contributed, and this equals the full-time institutional rate.

Example:

Step 1:
$1,800 individual contributions
+3,600 matching funds (2 times individual contribution)
+ -0- kicker

$5,400 TOTAL ENTITLEMENT

Step 2:
$5,400 divided by 36 months of contributions = $150 monthly full-time institutional rate

(No amount in excess of an individual's total entitlement can be paid.)

CORRESPONDENCE TRAINING

An individual can be reimbursed for the entire established charges paid for a correspondence course. However, no amount in excess of an individual's total entitlement can be paid.

FLIGHT TRAINING

Individuals taking flight training will receive 60% of the approved charges for the course, including solo hours. (VA does not pay for solo hours before October 1, 1992.) No amount in excess of an individual's total entitlement can be paid.

APPRENTICESHIP OR JOB TRAINING

The monthly benefit amount is:

- 75% of the full-time rate for the first 6 months of training;
- 55% of the full-time rate for the second 6 months of training;
- 35% of the full-time rate for the rest of the training.

Monthly payments are reduced if an individual works less than 120 hours a month.

COOPERATIVE TRAINING

Individuals may receive payment at 80% of the rate to which he or she is entitled for institutional training.

ELIGIBILITY PERIODS

Benefits end 10 years from the date of the individual's last discharge or release from active duty.

VA can extend the 10-year period by the amount of time a service member was prevented from training during the period due to a disability or being held by a foreign government or power.

VA may extend the 10-year period if the individual reenters active duty for 90 days or more after becoming eligible. The extension ends 10 years from the date of discharge or release from the later period. Periods of active duty of less than 90 days can qualify for extensions only if discharge or release was due to:

Benefits end 10 years from the date of the individual's last discharge or release from active duty.

- A service-connected disability; or
- A medical condition existing before active duty; or
- Hardship; or
- A reduction in force.

If a discharge is upgraded by the military, the 10-year period begins on the date of the upgrade.

MISCELLANEOUS INFORMATION

- Any change in educational, professional or vocational objectives is considered a "change of program." The law permits one change of program without prior VA approval, provided an individual's attendance, conduct and progress in the last program were satisfactory. Additional "changes of program" require prior VA approval. VA will not charge a change of program if the individual enrolls in a new program after successful completion of the immediately preceding program.
- Once an individual starts receiving benefits, he must maintain satisfactory attendance, conduct and progress. The VA may stop benefits if an individual does not meet the standards set by the school. VA may later resume benefits

if the individual reenters the same program at the same school, and the school approves the reentry, and certifies it to VA.

- If the individual does not reenter the same program at the same school, VA may resume benefits if the cause of unsatisfactory attendance, conduct or progress has been removed; and the program that the student intends to pursue is suitable to his or her abilities, aptitudes and interests.

APPLICATION FOR BENEFITS

When the individual finds a school, program, company, apprenticeship or job-training program, there are two important steps that must be followed:

1. Make sure the program is approved for VA training. Contact the local VA regional office if there are any questions.
2. Compete "VA Form 22-1990", "Application for Education Benefits." The completed form should be sent to the VA regional office with jurisdiction over the State where training will occur. (See the following section for Areas of VA jurisdiction.) Individuals not on active duty should send copy 4 of Form DD-214 along with the completed "VA Form 22-1990."

Following receipt of an application, VA will review it and advise if anything else is needed.

If an individual has started training, the application and Notice of Basic Eligibility should be taken to the school, employer or union. The certifying official should complete "VA Form 22-1999," Enrollment Certification, and send all the forms to VA.

TRAINING FOR UNEMPLOYED VETERANS

The VA announced in May 2012, that veterans who are unemployed and between the ages of 35 and 60 are eligible to apply for new education benefits, that will cover the cost of certain education programs for up to one year. The program is a joint effort between the VA and the Department of Labor. The program, called the Veterans Retraining Assistance Program (VRAP), is part of the *Veterans Opportunity to Work (VOW) to Hire Heroes Act of 2012*. The program offers veterans who qualify, up to twelve months of assistance that is equal to the full-time Montgomery GI Bill-Active Duty rate, which is currently set at $1,473 per month. Veterans became eligible to apply for VRAP on a first-come, first-serve basis on May 15, 2012. Assistance from this benefit is set to end March 31, 2014.

The following are the qualifications required to be eligible for the new program:

- Must be between the ages of 35 and 60, unemployed on the day of application, and not dishonorably discharged; and

Start education or training after July 1, 2012, in a VA-approved program of education offered by a community college or technical school leading to an associate's degree, non-college degree or a certificate for a high-demand occupation as defined by the DoL; and

Not be eligible for any other VA education benefit program (e.g. Post-9/11 GI Bill, Montgomery GI Bill, or Vocational Rehabilitation and Employment); and

Not be enrolled in a federal or state job training program within the last 180 days; and

Not receive VA compensation at the 100% rate due to Individual Unemployability (IU)

AREAS OF VA JURISDICTION

Eastern VA
Regional Office
PO Box 4616
Buffalo, NY
14240-4616

Connecticut
Delaware
District of Columbia
Maine
Maryland
Massachusetts
New Hampshire
New Jersey
New York
Ohio
Pennsylvania
Rhode Island
Vermont
Virginia
West Virginia
Foreign Schools

Southern VA
Regional Office
PO Box 100022
Decatur, GA 30031-7022

Alabama
Florida
Georgia
Mississippi
North Carolina
Puerto Rico
South Carolina
U.S. Virgin Islands

Western VA
Regional Office
PO Box 8888
Muskogee, OK
74402-8888

Alaska
Arizona
Arkansas
California
Hawaii
Idaho
Louisiana
New Mexico
Nevada
Oklahoma
Oregon
Philippines
Texas
Utah
Washington
American Samoa
Guam
Midway
Wake Island
Any of the islands in the Federated States of the Marshall Islands, the Republic of Micronesia, or the Republic of Palau

Central VA
Regional Office
PO Box 66830
St. Louis, MO
63166-6830

Colorado
Illinois
Indiana
Iowa
Kansas
Kentucky
Michigan
Minnesota
Missouri
Montana
Nebraska
North Dakota
South Dakota
Tennessee
Wisconsin
Wyoming

Once a completed verification form has been submitted, the student should receive a check within 2 weeks. If a check is not received by then, the VA should immediately be contacted so that appropriate action can be taken.

PROCEDURES FOR RECEIPT OF MONTHLY PAYMENTS

After selecting a school and submitting an application to VA, the school official must complete an enrollment certification, and submit it to the appropriate VA regional office. If a student meets the basic eligibility requirements for benefits, and the program or course is approved, VA will process the enrollment based on certified training time.

If a student is enrolled in a degree program at a college or university, he or she will receive payment after the first of each month for the training during the preceding month. If a student is enrolled in a certificate or diploma program at a business, technical, or vocational school, he or she will not receive payment until they have verified their attendance. Students will receive a "Student Verification of Enrollment Form 22-8979" each month, and must complete and return it to the appropriate VA regional office. After processing, VA will release a check.

If an individual is in an apprenticeship or job-training program, he or she will receive a form to report the hours worked each month. The form must be signed and given to the certifying official for the company or union. The certifying official must complete the form and send it to the appropriate VA regional office. After processing, VA will release a check.

If an individual is taking a correspondence course, he or she will receive a form each quarter, on which the student must show the number of lessons completed that quarter. The completed form should be sent to the school for certification of the number of lessons serviced during the quarter. The school will send the form to the appropriate VA regional office. After processing, VA will release a check. Payments are based on the number of lessons serviced by the school.

VA will send flight schools a supply of blank monthly certification of flight training forms. The school must complete the form by entering the number of hours, the hourly rate, and the total charges for flight training received during the month. The student should review and sign the completed form, and send it to the appropriate VA regional office. After processing, VA will release a check.

NOTE: It is against the law for schools to cash VA checks under a Power of Attorney Agreement.

TIMELY RECEIPT OF VERIFICATION FORMS AND CHECKS

Once a completed verification form has been submitted, the student should receive a check within 2 weeks. If a check is not received by then, the VA should immediately be contacted so that appropriate action can be taken.

Students taking courses leading to a degree at a college or university should receive their checks for each month by the fifth of the next month. If it is not received by then, the VA should be immediately contacted so that appropriate action can be taken.

Students taking courses leading to a certificate or diploma from a business, technical, or vocational school should receive their verification forms for each month by the fifth of the following month. If it is not received by then, the VA should be immediately contacted so that another form can be issued.

ADVANCE PAYMENTS

An advance payment for the initial month, or partial month and the following month may be made, if:

- The school agrees to handle advance payments; and
- Training is one-half time or more; and
- A request is made by the individual in writing; and
- The VA receives the enrollment certification at least 30 days prior to the start of classes.

Advance payments are made out to the individual, and sent to the applicable school for delivery to the individual registration. VA cannot issue a check more than 30 days before classes start. Before requesting an advance payment, students should verify with the school certifying official that the school has agreed to process advance payments.

Requests for advance payments must be on "VA Form 22-1999," Enrollment Certification, or a sheet of paper attached to the enrollment certification.

Once a student receives an advance payment at registration, the school must certify to VA that the student received the check. If a student reduces enrollment, or withdraws from all courses during the period covered by an advance payment, he or she must repay the overpayment to VA.

If an individual believes that the amount of a VA check is incorrect, the VA should be contacted before the check is cashed.

DIRECT DEPOSIT

Payments can be sent directly to a student's savings or checking account through Direct Deposit (Electronic Funds Transfer). To sign up for direct deposit by phone, students must call (877) 838-2778.

STUDENT RESPONSIBILITIES

To ensure timely receipt of correct payments, students should be sure to promptly notify the VA of:

- Any change in enrollment
- Any change in address

In addition, students should use reasonable judgment when accepting and cashing a check. All letters from VA about monthly rates and effective dates should be read carefully. If a student thinks the amount of a VA check is wrong, VA should be contacted *before* cashing the check. Any incorrect checks should be returned to VA.

If a student cashes a check for the wrong amount, he or she will be liable for repayment of any resulting overpayment.

Recovery of Overpayments

VA must take prompt and aggressive action to recover overpayments. Students have the right to request a waiver of the overpayment, or verification that the amount is correct. If an overpayment is not repaid or waived, VA may add interest and collection fees to the debt. VA may also take one or more of the following actions to collect the debt:

- Withhold future benefits to apply to the debt;
- Refer the debt to a private collection agency;
- Recover the debt from any Federal income tax refund;
- Recover the debt from the salary (if student is a Federal employee);
- File a lawsuit in Federal court to collect the debt;
- Withhold approval of a VA home loan guarantee.

An individual's reserve component will act to collect penalties caused by unsatisfactory participation in the reserve.

Changes in Enrollment

If a student withdraws from one or more courses after the end of the school's drop period, VA will reduce or stop benefits on the date of reduction or withdrawal. Unless the student can show that the change was due to *mitigating circumstances*, the student may have to repay **all** benefits for the course.

VA defines *mitigating circumstances* as "unavoidable and unexpected events that directly interfere with the pursuit of a course, and which are beyond the student's control.

Examples of reasons VA may accept include:

- Extended illness;
- Severe illness or death in immediate family;
- Unscheduled changes in employment; and

- Lack of child care.

Examples of reasons VA may not accept include:

- Withdrawal to avoid a failing grade;
- Dislike of the instructor; and
- Too many courses attempted.

VA may ask the student to furnish evidence to support the reason for change, such as physician or employer written statements.

The first time a student withdraws from up to 6 credit hours, VA will "excuse" the withdrawal, and pay benefits for the period attended.

If a student receives a grade that does not count toward graduation, all benefits for the course may have to be repaid.

If a student receives a non-punitive grade, the school will notify VA, and VA may reduce or stop benefits. The student may not have to repay the benefits if he or she can show that the grades were due to mitigating circumstances.

WORK-STUDY PROGRAMS

Students may be eligible for an additional allowance under a work-study program that allows students to perform work for VA in return for an hourly wage. Students may perform outreach services under VA supervision, prepare and process VA paperwork, work at a VA medical facility or National Cemetery, or perform other approved activities.

Students must attend school at the three-quarter of full-time rate.

VA will select students for the work-study program based on different factors. Such factors include:

- Disability of the student;
- Ability of the student to complete the work-study contract before the end of his or her eligibility for education benefits;
- Job availability within normal commuting distance to the student.

VA will give the highest priority to a veteran who has a service-connected disability or disabilities rated by VA at 30% or more

The number of applicants selected will depend on the availability of VA-related work at the school or at VA facilities in the area.

Students may work during or between periods of enrollment, and can arrange with VA to work any number of hours during his or her enrollment. However, the maximum number of hours a student may work is 25 times the number of weeks in the enrollment period.

Students will earn an hourly wage equal to the Federal or State minimum wage, whichever is greater. If a student works at a college or university, the school *may* pay the difference between the amount VA pays and the amount the school normally pays other work-study students doing the same job.

Students interested in taking part in a work-study program must complete VA Form 228691, "Application for Work-Study Allowance." Completed forms should be sent to the nearest VA regional office.

EDUCATIONAL COUNSELING

VA can provide services to help eligible individuals understand their educational and vocational strengths and weaknesses and to plan:

- An educational or training goal, and the means by which the goal can be reached; or
- An employment goal for which an individual qualifies on the basis of present training or experience.

VA can also help plan an effective job search.

Counseling is available for:

- Service members eligible for VA educational assistance; or
- Service members on active duty and within 180 days of discharge; or
- Veterans with discharges that are not dishonorable, who are within one year from date of discharge.

VOCATIONAL REHABILITATION

Vocational rehabilitation helps disabled veterans become independent in daily living. Veterans may also receive assistance in selecting, preparing for, and securing employment that is compatible with their interests, talents, skills, physical capabilities, and goals.

Veterans may qualify for Training and Rehabilitation under Chapter 31 of Title 38, United States Code, if:

- The veteran has a service-connected disability or disabilities rated by VA at 20% or more; and
- The veteran received a discharge from active duty that was not dishonorable; and
- The veteran has an employment handicap.

Vocational rehabilitation helps disabled veterans become independent in daily living. Veterans may also receive assistance in selecting, preparing for, and securing employment that is compatible with their interests, talents, skills, physical capabilities, and goals.

Veterans may also qualify with a service-connected disability or disabilities rated by VA at 10%, and:

- The veteran has a serious employment handicap; or
- The veteran first applied for vocational rehabilitation benefits before November 1, 1990, reapplied after that date, and has an employment handicap.

To apply for vocational rehabilitation, VA form 28-1900, Disabled Veterans Application for Vocational Rehabilitation, must be completed and sent to the nearest VA regional office.

For detailed information on vocational rehabilitation, refer to Chapter 14 of this book.

REFUND OF VEAP BENEFITS

If a service member does not wish to use his or her VEAP benefits, he or she must apply to the nearest VA regional office for a refund of his or her contributions.

APPEAL OF VA DECISION

VA decisions on education benefits may be appealed within one year of the date an individual receives notice of a VA decision.

For detailed information on filing an appeal, please refer to Chapter 35 of this book.

EDUCATIONAL AND ASSISTANCE TEST PROGRAM (SECTION 901)

This program was included as part of the "Department of Defense Authorization Act of 1981". The test program is funded by the Department of Defense, and administered by the VA. "Section 901" has been used to identify the program since its inception. However, the title "chapter 107" may also be used.

Section 901 is a noncontributory program in which an eligible participant, or in some cases his or her dependent(s), may receive an educational assistance and subsistence allowance while training at an accredited institution.

Basic eligibility to section 901 benefits was limited to a small group of servicepersons who enlisted between September 30, 1980 and October 1, 1981, met strict guidelines and were selected by the Department of Defense. The Waco Regional Office processes all section 901 payments.

Beginning August 1, 2011, break (or interval pay) was no longer be payable under the Educational Assistance Test Program except during periods your school is closed as a result of an Executive Order of the President or an emergency (such as a natural disaster or strike). For example, if your Fall term ends on December 15th and your Spring term begins January 10th, your January housing allowance will cover 15 days in December and your February housing allowance will cover 21 days in January.

EDUCATIONAL ASSISTANCE PILOT PROGRAM (SECTION 903)

Section 903 is a modified Chapter 32 (VEAP) program, in which the Service Department makes the individual's monthly contributions. Eligibility was limited to a small group of participants, selected by the service department, who enlisted between November 30, 1980 and October 1, 1981. Individuals must have been selected for the pilot program.

SURVIVORS' AND DEPENDENTS EDUCATIONAL ASSISTANCE PROGRAM (DEA) – CHAPTER 35

The Survivors' and Dependents Educational Assistance Program (DEA) was enacted by Congress to provide education and training opportunities to eligible dependents of certain veterans. The program offers up to 45 months of education benefits.

ELIGIBILITY REQUIREMENTS

To qualify, one must be the son, daughter or spouse of:

- A veteran who died, or is permanently and totally disabled as the result of a service-connected disability, which arose out of active service in the Armed Forces.
- A veteran who died from any cause while such service-connected disability was in existence.
- A service member who is missing in action or captured in the line of duty by a hostile force.

- A service member who is being forcibly detained or interned in the line of duty by a foreign power.
- A service member who is hospitalized or receiving outpatient treatment for a service connected permanent and total disability and is likely to be discharged for that disability. This change is effective December 23, 2006.

ELIGIBILITY PERIOD: SON OR DAUGHTER

As a son or daughter (including stepchild or adopted child), as long as the individual has entitlement left, he or she may generally receive benefits under this program from age 18 to 26 (8 years).

However, in certain instances, benefits may begin before age 18 and continue after age 26. In some instances, the individual may choose among possible beginning dates.

EFFECT OF ACTIVE DUTY ON ELIGIBILITY

Following are the effects of active duty on an individual's period of eligibility. (See also **Effect of Active Duty on Entitlement.**)

- Individuals may not receive DEA benefits while on active duty in the Armed Forces.
- To receive DEA benefits after military service, discharge must not be under dishonorable conditions.
- The eligibility period can generally extend for eight years from the date of the individual's first unconditional release from active duty, if his or her service was between ages 18 and 26. But this extension can't go beyond the individual's 31st birthday.
- If, on or after September 11, 2001, an individual is called to active duty under title 10, or if he or she was involuntarily ordered to full-time National Guard duty under section 502 (f) of title 32 (State authority), in most cases VA can extend the eligibility period for DEA by the number of months and days spent on active duty plus four months. This extension may go beyond the 31st birthday, depending on the facts in the claim.

OTHER EXTENSIONS OF THE ELIGIBILITY PERIOD

CIRCUMSTANCES BEYOND AN INDIVIDUAL'S CONTROL

If evidence is provided that training had to stop because of conditions beyond an individual's control, in some cases VA can extend eligibility for the period he or she had to stop training.

Circumstances that may be considered beyond control (if verified by evidence) include:

- Service in an official missionary capacity;
- Immediate family or financial obligations that require the individual to stop training, for example, to take employment;

- Unavoidable conditions of employment that require the individual to stop training;
- The individual's illness or death; or illness in his or her immediate family.

IN TRAINING WHEN ELIGIBILITY ENDS

If an individual is enrolled in training when eligibility ends, in most cases VA can extend his or her eligibility to the end of the semester or quarter, or to the end of twelve weeks if the course isn't operated on a semester or quarter basis.

MARRIAGE

As a son or daughter, marriage doesn't affect the period of eligibility.

ELIGIBILITY PERIOD: SPOUSE

If a spouse is eligible because the veteran has a permanent and total service-connected disability, benefits generally end 10 years from one of the following dates:

- Effective date of the veteran's permanent and total disability evaluation;
- Date VA notifies the veteran of the permanent and total disability evaluation;
- Beginning date chosen by the spouse, between the date the spouse become eligible and the date VA notifies the veteran of the permanent and total disability evaluation.
- If the VA rated the veteran permanently and totally disabled with an effective date of 3 years from discharge a spouse will remain eligible for 20 years from the effective date of the rating. This change is effective October 10, 2008 and no benefits may be paid for any training taken prior to that date.

SERVICE MEMBER HELD CAPTIVE OR MISSING

If a spouse is eligible because the veteran or service member is being held or is missing, as:

A prisoner of war;
Missing in action; or
Forcibly held by a foreign government or power;

His or her 10-year period of eligibility begins on the 91st day after the date the service member was listed as a captive or missing.

If the veteran or service member is released from captivity, or is determined to be alive and no longer missing, the spouse's period of eligibility ends on that date. If the spouse is enrolled in training on that date, his or her eligibility may be extended to the end of the term or course.

VETERAN DIED ON ACTIVE DUTY

If a spouse is eligible because the veteran died on active duty, his or her eligibility period is 20 years from the date of death.

EFFECT OF ACTIVE DUTY ON ELIGIBILITY

Following are the effects of active duty on the eligibility period:

- Individuals may not receive DEA benefits while on active duty in the Armed Forces.
- To receive DEA benefits after military service, his or her discharge must not be under dishonorable conditions.
- If, on or after September 11, 2001, the individual was called to active duty under title 10, or involuntarily ordered to full-time National Guard duty under section 502 (f) of title 32 (State authority), in most cases VA can extend the eligibility period for DEA by the number of months and days spent on active duty plus four months.

EFFECT OF DIVORCE ON ELIGIBILITY

If marriage to the veteran ends in divorce, the spouse's eligibility for DEA benefits ends on that date. But if he or she is in training, and the divorce occurs through no fault of him or her, VA can extend the eligibility as explained in the next section under ***While in Training.***

EXTENSIONS OF ELIGIBILITY PERIOD

DISABILITY

VA may be able to extend the 10-year eligibility period by the amount of time the spouse was prevented from training during that period because of a disability he or she incurred.

WHILE IN TRAINING

If the spouse is enrolled in training when his or her eligibility ends, in most cases VA can extend eligibility to the end of the semester or quarter, or to the end of twelve weeks if the course isn't operated on a semester or quarter basis.

EFFECT OF REMARRIAGE

Before age 57:

- If a surviving spouse remarries before age 57, his or her eligibility ends on the date of remarriage.

- If an individual remarried after November 30, 1999, and the remarriage ends, VA may reinstate eligibility to DEA. The remarriage must be ended by death, divorce, or because the individual stopped living with his or her spouse and stopped holding him or herself out to the public as the person's spouse.
- If a surviving spouse remarried after October 31, 1990, but before November 30, 1999, VA can't reinstate eligibility, even if remarriage ends.

After age 57:

- If a surviving spouse remarries on or after January 1, 2004, and is 57 or older, he or she can still be eligible for DEA benefits.
- (If the surviving spouse remarried after age 57 and before December 16, 2003, ***he or she must have applied in writing before December 16, 2004,*** for eligibility to be reinstated.)

Note: Remarrying after age 57 doesn't extend the 10-year period of eligibility that was established before remarriage.

Example: A surviving spouse established eligibility for a 10-year period ending on November 15, 2005, which is 10 years from the date of the veteran's death. She remarried in April 2004 at age 58. She will keep her eligibility for DEA through November 15, 2005.

MONTHS OF BENEFITS PAYABLE

The following applies to sons and daughters (including stepchildren and adopted children), spouses and surviving spouses.

Individuals may be entitled to receive up to 45 months of DEA benefits. They may receive a maximum of 48 months of benefits combined if they are eligible under more than one VA education program.

Individuals are charged one full day for each day of full-time benefits paid. Entitlement is charged in months and days. Each month is counted as 30 days. If he or she trains part-time, VA adjusts the entitlement charge according to the training time

EFFECT OF ACTIVE DUTY ON AVAILABLE MONTHS OF BENEFITS

- If an individual is called up to active duty under title 10 (federal authority) while he or she is receiving benefits, and has to drop out of school without receiving credit, VA will restore (give back) the months of benefits used for that period of training.
- If called up under title 32 (State authority), VA can't restore the months of benefits used.

PENSION, COMPENSATION, AND DIC PROGRAMS

A son or daughter who is eligible for Chapter 35 benefits, as well as pension, compensation, or Dependency & Indemnity Compensation (DIC) based on school attendance, must elect which benefit to receive. An election of Chapter 35 benefits is a bar to further payment of pension, compensation, or DIC after the age of 18.

NOTE: If a program will last longer than 45 months, the son or daughter may find it to his or her advantage to defer Chapter 35 benefits. He or she could continue to receive pension, compensation, or DIC benefits which are payable as a result of school attendance. *The VA strongly encourages individuals who qualify for more than one type of education benefit to discuss their education plans with a Veterans Benefits Counselor so that all options can be explored, and maximum benefits can be paid.*

APPROVED COURSES

A State agency or VA must approve each program offered by a school or company.

Individuals may receive benefits for a wide variety of training, including:

- Undergraduate degrees from a college or university
- Graduate degrees from a college or university
- Cooperative training programs
- Accredited independent study programs leading to a college degree
- Courses leading to a certificate or diploma from business, technical, or vocational schools
- Apprenticeship or job training program offered by a company or union
- Correspondence courses (spouses only)
- Farm cooperative courses
- Secondary school programs for individuals who are not high school graduates
- Secondary school deficiency or remedial courses to qualify for admission to an educational institution
- Effective November 1, 2000, persons eligible for DEA became able to receive benefits for VA-approved preparation courses for college and graduate school entrance exams. (The law also allows children to pursue these courses before age 18.)
- Effective March 1, 2001, benefits became payable for licensing or certification tests. The tests are those needed to enter, maintain, or advance into employment in a civilian vocation or profession. The eligible veteran or family member may receive payment of the fee charged for the test or $2,000, whichever is less. The tests must be approved for VA benefits. Contact the VA for a complete list of approved certification tests.

VA may approve programs offered by institutions outside of the United States, when they are pursued at educational institutions of higher learning, and lead to a college degree. Individuals must receive VA approval prior to attending or enrolling in any foreign programs.

An eligible son or daughter who is handicapped by a physical or mental disability that prevents pursuit of an educational program may receive Special Restorative Training. This may involve speech and voice correction, language retraining, lip reading, auditory training, Braille reading and writing, etc.

A State agency or VA must approve each program offered by a school or company.

An eligible spouse or son or daughter over age 14 who is handicapped by a physical or mental disability that prevents pursuit of an educational program may receive Specialized Vocational Training. This includes specialized courses, alone or in combination with other courses, leading to a vocational objective that is suitable for the person and required by reason of physical or mental handicap.

If an individual is seeking a college degree, the school must admit the individual to a degree program by the start of the individual's third term.

Restrictions on Training

Benefits are not payable for the following courses:

- Non-accredited independent study courses
- Bartending and personality development courses
- Correspondence courses (if you are a dependent or surviving child)
- Any course given by radio
- Vocational flight training
- Self-improvement courses such as reading, speaking, woodworking, basic seamanship, and English as a 2nd language
- Any course which is avocational or recreational in character
- Audited courses
- Courses not leading to an educational, professional, or vocational objective
- Courses previously taken and successfully completed
- Courses taken by a Federal government employee under the Government Employee's Training Act
- Courses taken while in receipt of benefits for the same program from the Office of Workers' Compensation Programs

VA must reduce benefits for individuals in Federal, State, or local prisons after being convicted of a felony.

An individual may not receive benefits for a program at a proprietary school if her or she is an owner or official of the school.

An individual may not receive benefits under this program while serving on active duty in the Armed Forces.

Part-Time Training

Individuals unable to attend school full-time should consider going part-time. Benefit rates and entitlement charges are less than the full-time rates. For example, if a student receives full-time benefits for 12 months, the entitlement charge is 12 months. However, if the student receives ½ time benefits for 12 months, the charge is 6 months. VA will pay for less than ½ time training if the student is not receiving Tuition Assistance for those courses.

Remedial, Deficiency and Refresher Training

Remedial and deficiency courses are intended to assist a student in overcoming a deficiency in a particular area of study.

Refresher training is available only at the elementary or secondary level. It is for reviewing or updating material previously covered in a course satisfactorily completed.

There is no entitlement charge for these courses for the first 5 months of training.

Tutorial Assistance

Students may receive a special allowance for individual tutoring performed after September 30, 1992, if they entered school at one-half time or more. To qualify, the student must have a deficiency in a subject. The school must certify the tutor's qualifications, and the hours of tutoring. Eligible students may receive a maximum monthly payment of $100.00. The maximum total benefit payable is $1,200.00.

There is no entitlement charge for the first $600.00 of tutorial assistance.

To apply for tutorial assistance, students must submit VA Form 22-1990t, Application and Enrollment Certification for Individualized Tutorial Assistance. The form should be given to the certifying official in the office handling VA paperwork at the school for completion.

You may receive up to 45 months of education benefits. Effective Oct. 1, 2013, some DEA beneficiaries may be eligible for up to 81 months of GI Bill benefits if they use the Survivors and Dependents Educational Assistance program in conjunction with an entitlement from other VA education programs.

RATES OF EDUCATIONAL ASSISTANCE

The following basic monthly rates are effective October 1, 2014:

BASIC MONTHLY RATES SURVIVORS' AND DEPENDENTS EDUCATIONAL ASSISTANCE PROGRAM (DEA)					
Type of Training	Full-Time	Three-Quarter Time	One-Half Time	Less than ½ Time, But More Than ¼ Time	One-Quarter Time
Institutional	$1018.00	$763.00	$506.00	Tuition & Fees, not to exceed $506.00	Tuition & Fees, not to exceed $254.50
Farm Cooperative Training	$819.00	$615.00	$408.00		
Correspondence Training	Entitlement charged at the rate of one month for each $1003.00 paid.				
Apprenticeship On-The-Job Training -	First six months: $743.00 Second six months: $557.00 Third six months: $367.00 Remainder of program: $186.00				
Special Restorative Training:	$1018.00				
Accelerated Charges: Cost of Tuition & Fees in Excess of:	$315.00				
Entitlement Reduced 1 Day For Each	$33.93 (1/30th of Full-Time Rate)				

CHANGE OF PROGRAM

Any change in educational, professional or vocational objectives is considered a "*change of program.*" VA will not charge a change of program when a student enrolls in a new program, provided he or she successfully completed the immediately preceding program.

SPOUSE, WIDOW OR WIDOWER OF VETERAN

A spouse, widow, or widower of a veteran may make one change of program without prior VA approval if attendance, conduct, and progress in the last program were satisfactory. VA may approve additional changes if the proposed programs are suitable to the student's abilities, aptitudes, and interests.

Child of Veteran

VA may approve a change of program for sons or daughters if it finds that the new program is suitable to the student's abilities, aptitudes, and interests.

ATTENDANCE, CONDUCT AND PROGRESS

Once an individual starts receiving benefits, he must maintain satisfactory attendance, conduct and progress. The VA may stop benefits if an individual does not meet the standards set by the school. VA may later resume benefits if the individual reenters the same program at the same school, and the school approves the reentry, and certifies it to VA.

If the individual does not reenter the same program at the same school, VA may resume benefits if the cause of unsatisfactory attendance, conduct or progress has been removed; and the program that the student intends to pursue is suitable to his or her abilities, aptitudes and interests.

APPLICATION FOR BENEFITS

When the individual finds a school, company or apprenticeship, there are two important steps that must be followed:

1. Make sure the program is approved for VA training. Contact the local VA regional office if there are any questions.
2. Complete VA Form 22-5490, "Application for Survivors' and Dependents' Educational Assistance." The completed form should be sent to the VA regional office with jurisdiction over the State where training will occur. Sons or daughters under legal age must have the application signed by a parent or guardian. Sons or daughters of age can apply alone.

Following receipt of an application, VA will review it and advise if anything else is needed.

If an individual has started training, the application and Notice of Basic Eligibility should be taken to the school, employer or union. The certifying official should complete VA Form 22-1999, "Enrollment Certification," and send all the forms to VA.

PROCEDURES FOR RECEIPT OF MONTHLY PAYMENTS

After selecting a school and submitting an application to VA, the school official must complete an enrollment certification, and submit it to the appropriate VA regional office. If a student meets the basic eligibility requirements for benefits, and the program or course is approved, VA will process the enrollment based on certified training time.

If a student is enrolled in a degree program at a college or university, he or she will receive payment after the first of each month for the training during the preceding month. If a student is enrolled in a certificate or diploma program at a business, technical, or vocational school, he or she will not receive payment until they have verified their attendance. Students will receive a "Student Verification of Enrollment Form 22-8979" each month, and must complete and return it to the appropriate VA regional office. After processing, VA will release a check.

If an individual is in an apprenticeship or job-training program, he or she will receive a form to report the hours worked each month. The form must be signed and given to the certifying official for the company or union. The certifying official must complete the form and send it to the appropriate VA regional office. After processing, VA will release a check.

If an individual is taking a correspondence course, he or she will receive a form each quarter, on which the student must show the number of lessons completed that quarter. The completed form should be sent to the school for certification of the number of lessons serviced during the quarter. The school will send the form to the appropriate VA regional office. After processing, VA will release a check. Payments are based on the number of lessons serviced by the school.

NOTE: It is against the law for schools to cash VA checks under a Power of Attorney Agreement.

TIMELY RECEIPT OF VERIFICATION FORMS AND CHECKS

Students taking courses leading to a degree at a college or university should receive their checks for each month by the fifth of the next month. If it is not received by then, the VA should be immediately contacted so that appropriate action can be taken.

Requests for advance payments must be on VA Form 22-1999, Enrollment Certification, or a sheet of paper attached to the enrollment certification.

Students taking courses leading to a certificate or diploma from a business, technical, or vocational school should receive their verification forms for each month by the fifth of the following month. If it is not received by then, the VA should be immediately contacted so that another form can be issued.

One a completed verification form has been submitted, the student should receive a check within 2 weeks. If a check is not received by then, the VA should immediately be contacted so that appropriate action can be taken.

ADVANCE PAYMENTS

An advance payment for the initial month, or partial month and the following month may be made, if:

- The school agrees to handle advance payments; and
- Training is one-half time or more; and

- A request is made by the individual in writing; and
- The VA receives the enrollment certification at least 30 days prior to the start of classes.

Advance payments are made out to the individual, and sent to the applicable school for delivery to the individual registration. VA cannot issue a check more than 30 days before classes start. Before requesting an advance payment, students should verify with the school certifying official that the school has agreed to process advance payments.

Requests for advance payments must be on VA Form 22-1999, "Enrollment Certification," or a sheet of paper attached to the enrollment certification.

Once a student receives an advance payment at registration, the school must certify to VA that the student received the check. If a student reduces enrollment, or withdraws from all courses during the period covered by an advance payment, he or she must repay the overpayment to VA.

If an individual believes that the amount of a VA check is incorrect, the VA should be contacted before the check is cashed.

Direct Deposit

Payments can be sent directly to a student's savings or checking account through Direct Deposit (Electronic Funds Transfer). To sign up for direct deposit by phone, students must call (877) 838-2778.

Student Responsibilities

To ensure timely receipt of correct payments, students should be sure to promptly notify the VA of:

- Any change in enrollment;
- Any change in address;
- Any change in marital status (separation from the veteran, divorce from the veteran, or remarriage following the death of the veteran).

In addition, students should use reasonable judgment when accepting and cashing a check. All letters from VA about monthly rates and effective dates should be read carefully. If a student thinks the amount of a VA check is wrong,

VA should be contacted **before** cashing the check. Any incorrect checks should be returned to VA.

If a student cashes a check for the wrong amount, he or she will be liable for repayment of any resulting overpayment.

Recovery of Overpayments

VA must take prompt and aggressive action to recover overpayments. Students have the right to request a waiver of the overpayment, or verification that the amount is correct. If an overpayment is not repaid or waived, VA may add interest and collection fees to the debt. VA may also take one or more of the following actions to collect the debt:

- Withhold future benefits to apply to the debt;
- Refer the debt to a private collection agency;
- Recover the debt from any Federal income tax refund;
- Recover the debt from the salary (if student is a Federal employee);
- File a lawsuit in Federal court to collect the debt;
- Withhold approval of a VA home loan guarantee.

CHANGES IN ENROLLMENT

If a student withdraws from one or more courses after the end of the school's drop period, VA will reduce or stop benefits on the date of reduction or withdrawal. Unless the student can show that the change was due to *mitigating circumstances*, the student may have to repay **all** benefits for the course.

VA defines *mitigating circumstances* as "unavoidable and unexpected events that directly interfere with the pursuit of a course, and which are beyond the student's control.

Examples of reasons VA may accept include:

- Extended illness;
- Severe illness or death in immediate family;
- Unscheduled changes in employment; and
- Lack of child care.

Examples of reasons VA may not accept include:

- Withdrawal to avoid a failing grade;
- Dislike of the instructor; and
- Too many courses attempted.

(VA may ask the student to furnish evidence to support the reason for change, such as physician or employer written statements.)

The first time a student withdraws from up to 6 credit hours, VA will "excuse" the withdrawal, and pay benefits for the period attended.

If a student receives a grade that does not count toward graduation, all benefits for the course may have to be repaid.

If a student receives a non-punitive grade, the school will notify VA, and VA may reduce or stop benefits. The student may not have to repay the benefits if he or she can show that the grades were due to mitigating circumstances.

WORK-STUDY PROGRAMS

Students may be eligible for an additional allowance under a work-study program that allows students to perform work for VA in return for an hourly wage. Students may perform outreach services under VA supervision, prepare and process VA paperwork, work at a VA medical facility or National Cemetery, or perform other approved activities.

Students must attend school at the three-quarter of full-time rate.

VA will select students for the work-study program based on different factors. Such factors include:

- Disability of the student;
- Ability of the student to complete the work-study contract before the end of his or her eligibility for education benefits;
- Job availability within normal commuting distance to the student;
- VA will give the highest priority to a veteran who has a service-connected disability or disabilities rated by VA at 30% or more.

The number of applicants selected will depend on the availability of VA-related work at the school or at VA facilities in the area.

Students may work during or between periods of enrollment, and can arrange with VA to work any number of hours during his or her enrollment. However, the maximum number of hours a student may work is 25 times the number of weeks in the enrollment period.

Students will earn an hourly wage equal to the Federal or State minimum wage, whichever is greater. If a student works at a college or university, the school **may** pay the difference between the amount VA pays and the amount the school normally pays other work-study students doing the same job.

Students interested in taking part in a work-study program must complete VA Form 22,8691, "Application for Work-Study Allowance." Completed forms should be sent to the nearest VA regional office.

EDUCATIONAL COUNSELING

Upon request, VA will provide counseling services, including testing, to help qualified individuals:

- Select an educational, vocational, or professional objective;
- Develop a plan to achieve the above objective;
- Overcome any personal or academic problems that may interfere with the successful achievement of the stated objective.

Qualified VA personnel are available to provide counseling services free of charge to qualified individuals. Individuals must pay the cost of any travel to and from the place at which VA provides counseling.

VA requires and provides counseling for each disabled child who needs special services to pursue a program of education and for certain other eligible children.

VA requires and provides counseling for disabled spouses and those who need specialized programs of vocational training as a result of the handicapping effects of their disabilities.

Individuals should contact the nearest VA regional office to make counseling appointments.

APPEAL OF VA DECISION

VA decisions on education benefits may be appealed within one year of the date an individual receives notice of a VA decision.

For detailed information on filing an appeal, please refer to Chapter 35 of this book.

RESTORED ENTITLEMENT PROGRAM FOR SURVIVORS (REPS)

The *Restored Entitlement Program for Survivors* (REPS) is authorized by Section 156 of *Public Law 97-377*. This program restores social security benefits that were reduced or terminated *by Public Law 97-35*, the *Omnibus Budget Reconciliation Act of 1981*. This act eliminated the "parent with child in care" benefit when a surviving spouse's last child in care attained age 16. REPS restores the benefit until the youngest child in care attains 18, unless entitled to another Social Security benefit of equal or greater value.

The REPS program is funded by the Department of Defense, based on Social Security rules, and administered by the VA.

REPS benefits are payable to certain spouses and children of veterans who died while on active duty before August 13, 1981, or died from disabilities incurred in active duty before August 13, 1981. If a surviving spouse remarries, his or her benefits are terminated. If the child in care leaves the parent's custody, marries or dies, REPS entitlement ends. REPS benefits are reduced by $1 for each $2 of earned income over the exempt amount for Social Security (announced by Social Security Administration at the beginning of each calendar year).

REPS benefits are payable to unmarried children between the ages of 18 and 22 who are full-time students at approved schools beyond the high school level. Benefits are awarded

on a school year basis. Each year verification must be received before any additional benefits can be awarded. If the child marries or reduces to less than full-time attendance, benefits will be discontinued. If the child has earned income or wages, REPS benefits are reduced.
REPS benefits are not payable based on service in the commissioned corps of the National Oceanic and Atmospheric Administration, or the Public Health Service.

To apply for REPS benefits, VA Form 21-8924, "Application of Surviving Spouse or Child for REPS Benefits" must be completed and sent to the local VA regional VA office for basic eligibility determination.

Once completed, the application will be forwarded to the St. Louis office for processing. A *Student Beneficiary Report* is mailed to each student receiving REPS benefits each March. The report confirms enrollment, and allows students to report any earnings.

For specific information, contact the nearest regional VA office.

OMNIBUS DIPLOMATIC SECURITY AND ANTITERRORISM ACT

Public Law 99-399, The *Omnibus Diplomatic Security and Antiterrorism Act of 91986* (the Antiterrorism Act) became effective January 21, 1981. This program is designed to provide educational assistance for persons held as captives, and their dependents.

Under this Act, VA may provide education benefits to:

- Former captives who were employees of the United States Government. Individuals providing personal services to the United States similar to that provided by civil service employees may also be eligible. This includes foreign nationals and resident aliens of the United States.
- Former captives taken during hostile action resulting from their relationship with the United States.
- Family members of individuals in captivity or individuals who die while in captivity.

VA will provide educational benefits to persons eligible under the *Antiterrorism Act* that are identical to those provided to eligible persons under Chapter 35 of title 38, U.S. Code (Survivors' and Dependents' Educational Assistance Program).

All inquiries regarding this Act should be directed to the nearest VA regional office.

CHAPTER 18

EDUCATION BENEFITS - MONTGOMERY G.I. BILL

(MGIB), CHAPTER 30

ELIGIBILITY REQUIREMENTS

The Montgomery G.I. Bill (MGIB) establishes education benefits for four categories of individuals, based on active duty service. The benefits available under each category may vary depending on individual situations and lengths of active duty service. The eligibility requirements for each category are described below. However, the following two requirements must be met by all individuals, no matter which category his or her eligibility falls under:

1. **Character Of Discharge:**

   To use MGIB after an individual is separated from active duty, an individual's discharge must be fully honorable. Discharges "under honorable conditions" and "general" discharges don't establish eligibility for MGIB

2. **Completed High School:**

   To use MGIB as an active duty member, or after separation from active duty, an individual must obtain a high school diploma or equivalency certificate before applying for benefits.

Completing 12 hours toward a college degree before applying for benefits also meets this requirement. This is a change in eligibility rules that became effective November 1, 2000. If an individual wasn't previously eligible because he or she did not meet the high school requirement, the change provides a second chance.

In addition to the above requirements, individuals must meet requirements from one of the four following categories. (Individuals who entered active duty before July 1, 1985 may only qualify under Categories 2, 3, or 4.)

CATEGORY I

- The veteran must have entered active duty for the first time on or after July 1, 1985.
- The veteran must have enrolled in MGIB (didn't decline MGIB in writing upon entry into active duty).

Exception: If an individual declined MGIB in writing, he or she may not change this decision at a later date unless:

- The individual qualifies under Category 3; or
- The individual withdrew his or her election not to participate during the "open period" for withdrawal (December 1, 1988 through June 30, 1989).
- Individuals who graduated from a service academy and received a commission are not eligible.
- Individuals who became commissioned upon completing an ROTC scholarship program are not eligible, unless one of the following exceptions applies:
- The individual received a commission after becoming eligible for MGIB.
- The individual received a commission after September 30, 1996, and received less than $3,400 during any one year of his or her ROTC program.
- Individuals who received loan repayment from the military for their education are not eligible. (Note: Individuals who received loan repayment for one period of active duty, may still be eligible based on another period of active duty, as long as they did not decline MGIB when they first entered active duty.
- To use MGIB while on active duty, an individual must serve two continuous years of active duty.
- To use MGIB after separation from active duty, the individual must have served 3 continuous years of active duty, unless discharged early for one of the following reasons:
- Convenience of the government (veteran must have served 30 months if he had a 3-year obligation)
- Service-connected disability

- Hardship
- A medical condition the individual had before service
- A condition that interfered with performance of duty
- Certain reductions in force (RIF)

Exception: To use MGIB after separation from active duty, the individual may only need 2 years of active duty if:

- He or she first enlisted for 2 years of active duty; or
- The individual has an obligation to serve 4 years in the Selected Reserve (the 2 X 4 program). The individual must enter the Selected Reserve within one year of release from active duty; or
- The individual was separated early for one of the following reasons:
- Convenience of the government (veteran must have served 20 months if he had a 2-year obligation)
- Service-connected disability
- Hardship
- A medical condition the individual had before service
- A condition that interfered with performance of duty
- Certain reductions in force (RIF)

SERVICE IN THE NATIONAL GUARD OR RESERVE

Service in the National Guard or reserve is qualifying as active duty for MGIB benefits only under the following conditions:

1. Full-time National Guard or Reserve service authorized under title 10, U.S. Code (Active Guard/Reserve, or AGR) is considered active duty for purposes of qualifying for VA education benefits, unless the service is active duty for training.
2. Full-time National Guard service under title 32, U.S. Code (State authority) is considered active duty for purposes of qualifying for VA education benefits, provided the service was first performed after November 29, 1989 (with no previous active duty); and is for the purpose of organizing, administering, recruiting, instructing, or training the National Guard. Duty for the purpose of performing operations (such as drug interdiction, for example) is not considered active duty for MGIB benefits.

CATEGORY II

- The veteran had remaining entitlement under the Vietnam Era Veterans' Educational Assistance Program (chapter 34 of Title 38, U.S. Code) on December 31, 1989; and

- The veteran served on active duty for any number of days during the period October 19, 1984 to June 30, 1985, and then continued on active duty without a break from July 1, 1985 through:
- June 30, 1988, or
- June 30, 1987, and then served four years in the Selected Reserve after release from active duty. The individual must have entered the Selected Reserve within one year of his or her release from active duty.

- The individual wasn't on active duty on October 19, 1984, but reentered active duty after that date, and served three continuous years on active duty on or after July 1, 1985, or two years on active duty followed by four years in the Selected Reserve on or after July 1, 1985. (This option became effective December 27, 2001.)
- Individuals who graduated from a service academy and received a commission after December 31, 1976 are not eligible.
- Individuals who received a commission after September 30, 1996 upon completing an ROTC scholarship program are not eligible, unless one of the following exceptions applies:
- The individual received a commission after becoming eligible for MGIB.
- The individual completed ROTC without a full scholarship.
- The individual received a commission after September 30, 1996, and received less than $3,400 during any one year of his or her ROTC program.

CATEGORY III

A veteran may qualify if:

- The veteran was on active duty on September 30, 1990, and was involuntarily separated after February 2, 1991; or
- The veteran was involuntarily separated on or after November 30, 1993.
- Effective October 23, 1992, the law was expanded to allow the same opportunity to elect MGIB benefits before separation to members voluntarily separated under either the Voluntary Separation Incentive (VSI) or Special Separation Benefit (SSB) program.
- If the member was eligible for the Post Vietnam Era Veterans' Educational Assistance Program (VEAP), he must elect to receive MGIB benefits, and apply for a refund of contributions to Chapter 32.
- The member must have had his military pay reduced by $1,200 before discharge.

Members qualifying under Category III based on a voluntary or involuntary separation are not eligible for MGIB benefits until the day following discharge.

(If a veteran eligible under Category 3 had a chapter 32 *kicker,* VA will pay the basic chapter 30 rate and an additional amount based upon the amount of the remaining kicker.)

CATEGORY IV

Individuals may qualify under Category IV if they were on active duty on October 9, 1996, and were VEAP participants with money in the VEAP fund. These individuals must have elected MGIB, and paid $1,200 by October 9, 1997.

Individuals may also be eligible if they served on full time active duty in the National Guard between June 10, 1985 and November 29, 1989, and elected to have their National Guard service count toward establishing eligibility for MGIB benefits by July 9, 1997.

Effective November 1, 2000, VEAP participants, whether they had contributions in their accounts or not, could become eligible for MGIB if they:

- Made an irrevocable election to receive MGIB; and
- Were VEAP participants on or before October 9, 1996; and
- Continuously served on active duty from October 9, 1996 through April 1, 2000; and
- Made a payment of $2,700. The payment will be made by reducing their basic pay before their discharge from service. If $2,700 is not collected before discharge from pay reductions, veterans must make payments to the military service in the amount needed to bring the total to $2,700. DoD can also collect the additional amount by reducing retired or retainer pay.

  (NOTE: This payment, unlike earlier contributions to VEAP is *not refundable.)* The payment does not go into the VEAP account, it is deposited into the Treasury of the United States as miscellaneous receipts; and
- Met other VEAP eligibility requirements.
- VEAP participants must have made this election on or before October 31, 2001.

TRANSFERABILITY OF GI BILL TO DEPENDENTS

Eligible soldiers may now transfer up to 18 months of their GI Bill to spouses or children.

This pilot program is authorized under Title 38, U.S. Code, Chapter 30 (amended by *PL 107-107*), the Montgomery GI Bill (MGIB).

ELIGIBILITY REQUIREMENTS

Participants must ensure they meet the following eligibility requirements and take the following actions to participate in the program:

- MGIB-era Soldiers who are eligible for MGIB must have enrolled in the MGIB upon initial entry to active duty and paid the $1,200 for MGIB enrollment. (Not eligible are Vietnam Ear-Rollover, VEAP conversion, and Involuntary Separation.)
- Completed at least 6 years of service in the Armed Forces at the time of reenlistment.
- Reenlist for a period of at least 4 years and complete DD Form 2366-2 with their servicing Army Retention Career Counselor.
- Qualify for a MOS Specific Selective Reenlistment Bonus (SRB) and entitled to a Zone B or Zone C bonus at the time of reenlistment.

The following individuals may receive transfer of entitlement:

- The spouse of the individual making the transfer;
- One or more of the children of the individual making the transfer; or
- A combination of the individuals referred above.

A dependent to whom the entitlement is transferred may not begin using the entitlement until:

Spouse:
The Soldier has completed at least six years of service in the Armed Forces.

Child:
The Soldier has completed at least 10 years of service in the Armed Forces, and either:

- The completion by the child of the requirement of a secondary school diploma (or equivalency certificate); or
- The attainment by the child of 18 years of age.

DISCHARGES AND SEPARATIONS

As previously mentioned, if the veteran is separated from active duty, the character of discharge must specifically be listed as "Honorable." "Under Honorable Conditions," or a "General" discharge do not establish eligibility. A discharge for one of the following reasons may result in a reduction of the required length of active duty to qualify for benefits under the MGIB:

- Convenience of the Government; or
- Disability; or
- Hardship; or
- Medical conditions existing before entry into Service; or
- Force reductions; or
- Medical condition which is not a disability due to misconduct, but which prevents satisfactory performance of duty.

CERTAIN TYPES OF ACTIVE DUTY WHICH DO NOT ESTABLISH ELIGIBILITY

The following types of active duty do not establish eligibility for MGIB benefits:

- Time assigned by the military to a civilian institution to take the same course provided to civilians.
- Time served as a cadet or a midshipman at a service academy.
- Time spent on active duty for training in the National Guard or Reserve.

Please note: Time assigned by the military to a civilian institution, and time served at a service academy does not break the continuity of active duty required to establish eligibility for MGIB benefits. Active duty for training does count toward the four years in the Selected Reserve under the 2 by 4 program.

APPROVED COURSES

This program provides veterans up to 36 months of education benefits. The benefits may be used for:

- Undergraduate or graduate degrees from a college or university;
- Cooperative training programs;
- Accredited independent study programs leading to standard college degrees;
- Courses leading to certificates or diplomas from business, technical or vocational schools;
- Vocational flight training (from September 30, 1990 only – Individuals must have a private pilot's license and meet the medical requirements for a desired license before beginning training, and throughout the flight training program);
- Apprenticeship / job training programs offered by a company or union;

- Correspondence courses;
- VA may approve programs offered by institutions outside of the United States, when they are pursued at educational institutions of higher learning, and lead to an associate or higher degree, or the equivalent. Individuals must receive VA approval prior to attending or enrolling in any foreign programs;

RESTRICTIONS ON TRAINING

- Bartending and personality development courses;
- Non-accredited independent study courses;
- Any course given by radio;
- Self-improvement courses such as reading, speaking, woodworking, basic seamanship, and English as a second language;
- Any course which is avocational or recreational in character;
- Farm cooperative courses;
- Audited courses;
- Courses not leading to an educational, professional, or vocational objective;
- Courses an individual has previously completed;
- Courses taken by a Federal government employee under the Government Employees' Training Act;
- Courses paid for in whole or in part by the Armed Forces while on active duty;
- Courses taken while in receipt of benefits for the same program from the Office of Workers' Compensation Programs.

The VA must reduce benefits for individuals in Federal, State or local prisons after being convicted of a felony.

An individual may not receive benefits for a program at a proprietary school if he or she is an owner or official of the school.

Benefits are generally payable for 10 years following a veteran's release from active duty.

PART-TIME TRAINING

Individuals unable to attend school full-time should consider going part-time. Benefit rates and entitlement charges are pro-rated as follows:

- Individuals who are on active duty or training at less than one-half time, will receive the lesser of:
  - The monthly rate based on tuition and fees for the course(s); or
  - The maximum monthly rate based on training time.
- Individuals training at less than one-half time will receive payment in one sum for the whole enrollment period.
-

REMEDIAL, DEFICIENCY AND REFRESHER TRAINING

Remedial and deficiency courses are intended to assist a student in overcoming a deficiency in a particular area of study. In order for such courses to be approved, the courses must be deemed necessary for pursuit of a program of education.

Refresher training is for technological advances that occurred in a field of employment. The advance must have occurred while the student was on active duty, or after release.

There is an entitlement charge for these courses.

TUTORIAL ASSISTANCE

Students may receive a special allowance for individual tutoring, if attending school at one-half time or more. To qualify, the student must have a deficiency in a subject. The school must certify the tutor's qualifications, and the hours of tutoring. Eligible students may receive a maximum monthly payment of $100.00. The maximum total benefit payable is $1,200.00.

There is no entitlement charge for the first $600.00 of tutorial assistance.

To apply for tutorial assistance, students must submit VA Form 22-1990t, "Application and Enrollment Certification for Individualized Tutorial Assistance." The form should be given to the certifying official in the office handling VA paperwork at the school for completion.

MONTHS OF BENEFITS / ENTITLEMENT CHARGED

Individuals who complete their full period of enlistment may receive up to 36 months of MGIB benefits.

Individuals are considered to have completed their full enlistment period if they are discharged for the convenience of the government after completing 20 months of an enlistment of less than three years; or 30 months of an enlistment of three years or more.

Individuals will earn only one month of entitlement for each month of active duty after June 39, 1985, if they are discharged for other specific reasons (i.e. service-connected disability, reduction in force, hardship, etc.) before completing the enlistment period.

Individuals will earn one month of entitlement for each four months in the Selected Reserve after June 30, 1985.

Individuals qualifying for more than one VA education program may receive a maximum of 48 months of benefits. For example, if a student used 30 months of Dependents' Educational Assistance, and is eligible for chapter 1606 benefits, he or she could have a maximum of 18 months of entitlement remaining.

Individuals are charged one full day of entitlement for each day of full-time benefits paid. For correspondence and flight training, individuals use one month of entitlement each time the VA pays the equivalent of one month of full-time benefits. Individuals pursuing a cooperative program use one month for each month of benefits paid.

For apprenticeship and job-training programs, the entitlement charge during the first 6 months is 75% of full-time. For the second six months, the charge is 55% of full-time. For the rest of the program, the charge is 35% of full-time.

VA can extend entitlement to the end of a term, quarter, or semester if the ending date of an individual's entitlement falls within such period. If a school does not operate on a term basis, entitlement can be extended for 12 weeks.

RATES OF EDUCATIONAL ASSISTANCE AFTER SEPARATION FROM ACTIVE DUTY

The basic monthly rates increase October 1 every year with the Consumer Price Index (CPI) increase. While in training, students receive a letter with the current rates when the increase goes into effect each year. The rates may increase at other times by an act of Congress.

BASIC MONTHLY RATES FOR COLLEGE AND VOCATIONAL SCHOOL

For approved programs in college and vocational or technical schools, basic payments are monthly and the rates are based on training time. When students train at less than half time, they will be paid tuition and fees. But if tuition and fees amount to more than would be paid at the half-time rate (or the quarter-time rate if training at quarter-time or less), payments will be limited to the half time (or the quarter-time rate).

For on-the-job training (OJT) and apprenticeship programs, rates are monthly and based on the length of time in the program. MGIB rates decrease as the student's wages increase according to an approved wage schedule.

RATES FOR OTHER TYPES OF TRAINING

For correspondence courses, students receive 55% of the approved charges for the course.

For flight training, students receive 60% of the approved charges for the course.
For reimbursement of tests for licenses or certifications, students receive 100% of the charges up to a maximum of $2,000 per test.

RATES OF EDUCATIONAL ASSISTANCE WHILE ON ACTIVE DUTY

If a service member goes to school while on active duty, he or she may have two options for using MGIB benefits. The may be eligible to receive:

- "Regular" MGIB; or
- Tuition Assistance plus MGIB, or Tuition Assistance "Top-Up"

USING "REGULAR" MGIB ON ACTIVE DUTY

If a service member uses "regular" MGIB while on active duty, VA can pay whichever is less:

- The monthly rate based on tuition and fees for your course(s); or
- The maximum monthly MGIB rate (basic rate plus any increases he or she may qualify for).

The basic monthly rates increase October 1 every year with the Consumer Price Index (CPI) increase. While in training, students receive a letter with the current rates when the increase goes into effect each year. The rates may increase at other times by an act of Congress.

USING TUITION ASSISTANCE "TOP-UP"

If a student is on active duty, he or she may be eligible to receive Tuition Assistance (TA) from his or her branch of service. If the student has been on active duty for two years, he or she may also be eligible to use MGIB to supplement, or "top up," the TA. Top-up covers the remaining percentage of costs approved for TA that TA alone doesn't' cover—***up to specified limits***. For example, if a student's service authorizes 75% of costs, top-up can pay the remaining 25% of costs approved for TA.

DETAILED RATES OF EDUCATIONAL ASSISTANCE

THE RATES, EFFECTIVE OCTOBER 1, 2014, ARE DETAILED IN THE FOLLOWING CHARTS.

BASIC MONTHLY RATES EFFECTIVE OCTOBER 1, 2014

MONTGOMERY G.I. BILL - ACTIVE DUTY (MGIB), CHAPTER 30

Type of Training	Full-Time	Three-Quarter Time	One-Half Time	Less than ½ Time, But More Than ¼ Time	One-Quarter Time
Institutional	$1717.00	1287.75	858.50	Tuition & Fees, not to exceed $858.50	429.25
Cooperative Training	$1717.00 (Full-Time Only)				
Correspondence Training	Entitlement charged at the rate of one month for each $1648.00 paid				
Apprenticeship On-The-Job Training -	First six months: $1287.75 Second six months: $944.35 Remainder of program: $600.95				
Flight Training	Entitlement charged at the rate of one month for each $1717.00 paid				

BASIC MONTHLY RATES EFFECTIVE OCTOBER 1, 2014 FOR PERSONS WHOSE INITIAL ACTIVE DUTY OBLIGATION WAS LESS THAN THREE YEARS, AND WHO SERVED LESS THAN THREE YEARS (EXCLUDING 2 X 4 PARTICIPANTS)					
Type of Training	Full-Time	Three-Quarter Time	One-Half Time	Less than ½ Time, But More Than ¼ Time	One-Quarter Time
Institutional	$1395.00	$1046.25	$697.50	Tuition & Fees, not to exceed $697.50	$348.75
Cooperative Training	$1395.00 (Full-Time Only)				
Correspondence Training	Entitlement charged at the rate of one month for each $1395.00 paid				
Apprenticeship On-The-Job Training -	First six months: $1287.75 Second six months: $944.35 Remainder of program: $600.95				
Flight Training	Entitlement charged at the rate of one month for each $1717.00 paid				

BASIC INSTITUTIONAL RATES EFFECTIVE OCTOBER 1, 2014 FOR PERSONS WITH REMAINING ENTITLEMENT UNDER CHAPTER 34 OF TITLE 38, U.S.C.				
Time	No Dependents	One Dependent	Two Dependents	Each Add'l Dependent
Full	$1905.00	$1941.00	$1972.00	$16.00
Three-Quarter	$1429.25	$1455.75	$1479.25	$12.00
One-Half	$952.50	$970.50	$986.00	$8.50
Less Than 1/2, But More Than 1/4	Tuition and fees, not to exceed the rate of $952.50			
One-Quarter	Tuition and fees, not to exceed the rate of $476.25			
Cooperative	$1905.00	$1941.00	$1972.00	$16.00

BASIC JOB TRAINING RATES EFFECTIVE OCTOBER 1, 2014 FOR PERSONS WITH REMAINING ENTITLEMENT UNDER CHAPTER 34 OF TITLE 38, U.S.C. APPRENTICESHIP AND ON-THE-JOB TRAINING				
Time	No Dependents	One Dependent	Two Dependents	EACH ADD'L DEPENDENT
First six months	$1390.75	1402.88	1413.75	$5.25
Second six months	1003.73	1010.08	1017.78	$3.85
Third six months	624.75	630.88	635.60	2.45
Remainder	612.85	618.63	623.88	$2.45

SPECIAL NOTES:

- Cooperative Training is full time only.
- Individuals taking correspondence courses will receive 55% of the approved charges for the course.
- Individuals taking flight training will receive 60% of the approved charges for the course, including solo hours.

INCREASED ABOVE BASIC RATES

Individuals may qualify for the following increases above their basic monthly rates. These increases don't apply to correspondence courses, the test for a license or certification, or flight training.

COLLEGE FUND

Certain branches of service may offer the College Fund. The College Fund money, or "kicker," is an additional amount of money that increases the basic MGIB monthly benefit and is included in the VA payment.
Important: Students can't receive College Fund money without receiving MGIB. A common misunderstanding is that the College Fund is a separate benefit from MGIB. The College Fund is an add-on to the MGIB benefit.

VEAP "KICKER."

VA pays an additional amount, commonly known as a "kicker," if directed by the Department of Defense (DoD). If an individual is eligible under Category 3 or Category 4 and has a VEAP kicker, he or she can receive the amount of the VEAP kicker contributed by the service department divided by the total months of MGIB eligibility.

ACCELERATED PAYMENTS FOR EDUCATION LEADING TO EMPLOYMENT IN HIGH TECHNOLOGY

One of the provisions contained in the *Veterans Education and Benefits Expansion Act of 2001* (*Public Law 107-103*) called for accelerated payments for education leading to employment in high technology, effective October 1, 2002. Following are questions and answers provided by the VA regarding this provision.

WHAT IS AN ACCELERATED PAYMENT?

An accelerated payment is a lump sum payment of 60% of tuition and fees for certain high cost, high tech programs. If a participant does not have sufficient entitlement to cover 60% of tuition and fees, he or she will receive pay based on the actual remaining entitlement.

VA will make accelerated payments for one term, quarter, or semester at a time. However, if the program is not offered on a term, quarter or semester basis, the accelerated payment is paid for the entire program. To qualify, a participant must be enrolled in a high tech program and must certify that he or she intends to seek employment in a high tech industry as defined by VA. Accelerated payment is paid instead of Montgomery GI Bill benefits that would otherwise have been received.

WHO QUALIFIES FOR ACCELERATED PAYMENTS?

Only individuals eligible for the Montgomery GI Bill - Active Duty (Chapter 30) qualify for accelerated payments.

HOW HIGH DO THE TUITION AND FEES HAVE TO BE?

To receive accelerated payment, the tuition and fees must be more than double the Montgomery GI Bill benefits that a participant would otherwise receive for that term. For example, if the full-time rate is $732 and a participant is enrolled in a 4-month semester, the tuition and fees must be over $5,856 (4 months x $732=$2,928; $5,856=2 x $2,928) before he or she could receive an accelerated payment.

If a participant receives $900 in monthly benefits, the tuition and fees must be over $7,200 (4 months x $900=$3,600; $7,200= 2 x $3,600).

If a participant receives $1,050 in monthly benefits, the tuition and fees must be over $8,400 (4 months x $1,050 = $4,200; 2 x $4,200 = $8,400).

WHAT PROGRAMS QUALIFY FOR ACCELERATED PAYMENT?

Both degree and non-degree programs qualify. A participant must be enrolled in a program in one of the following categories:

- Life science or physical science (but not social science);
- Engineering (all fields);
- Mathematics;
- Engineering and science technology;
- Computer specialties; and·
- Engineering, science, and computer management

WHAT INDUSTRIES QUALIFY FOR ACCELERATED PAYMENTS?

A participant must intend to seek employment in one of the following industries:

- Biotechnology;
- Life Science Technologies;
- Opto-electronics;
- Computers and telecommunications;
- Electronics;
- Computer-integrated manufacturing;
- Material Design;
- Aerospace;
- Weapons;
- Nuclear technology

HOW DOES A PARTICIPANT APPLY FOR ACCELERATED PAYMENTS?

The individual must ask the school to include his or her request for accelerated payment to VA when it sends the enrollment information to VA for processing. The individual's request must include his or her certification of intent to seek employment in a high technology industry.

HOW IS THE EDUCATION ENTITLEMENT CHARGED?

VA will divide the accelerated payment by the amount of the individual's full-time monthly rate (including kickers and additional contributions) and will reduce the entitlement by the resulting number of months and days.

Example: Jill received an accelerated payment of $3,600. Her full-time rate is $900. VA will charge her entitlement as follows: $3,600/$900 = 4 months.

WHEN CAN ACCELERATED PAYMENTS BE MADE?

Accelerated payments may only be made for terms or other enrollment periods that begin on or after October 1, 2002.

CAN SCHOOL RELATED EXPENSES (SUCH AS BOOKS, SUPPLIES, AND LIVING EXPENSES) BE COUNTED AS TUITION AND FEES FOR ACCELERATED PAYMENTS?

No. Only the school's tuition and fees can be considered for accelerated payment.

CAN AN INDIVIDUAL RECEIVE ACCELERATED PAYMENTS FOR SHORT, NON-DEGREE COURSE?

Yes, as long as they are approved for VA benefits. Short, expensive, IT courses offered by businesses typically are <u>not</u> approved for VA benefits.

CAN AN INDIVIDUAL RECEIVE ACCELERATED PAYMENTS FOR NON-TECHNICAL COURSES (SUCH AS ENGLISH, HISTORY, ETC.) WHEN TAKING THOSE COURSES AS PART OF A HIGH TECHNOLOGY PROGRAM?

Yes. However, the degree or certificate must require the completion of these other non-technical courses.

IS IT POSSIBLE TO RECEIVE AN ACCELERATED PAYMENT CHECK BEFORE A SCHOOL TERM BEGINS?

No. VA needs to verify that the individual has enrolled before sending out the large payment. VA will pay the student as soon after the start of the term as possible. Individuals will receive payment faster if they receive direct deposit.

DOES A STUDENT HAVE TO VERIFY ENROLLMENT EACH MONTH IF HE OR SHE RECEIVES AN ACCELERATED PAYMENT?

No. After the individual completes his or her enrollment, VA will ask the student to verify that he or she have received the accelerated payment. VA will also ask the individual to indicate how he or she used the accelerated payment (such as toward tuition, fees and books and supplies). VA is asking the latter question for statistical purposes only because the law requires them to collect this information. A student's answer will have no bearing on his or her entitlement to the accelerated payment. The student must respond to these questions within 60 days from the end of the enrollment period or VA will create an overpayment equal to the accelerated payment. As with any course, the student must notify VA of any change in his or her enrollment. The student's school must report any changes as well.

IS THERE ANY FINANCIAL RISK WITH ACCELERATED PAYMENT?

Yes. If a student receives a grade, which does not count toward graduation requirements, he or she may have to repay all or part of the accelerated payment, depending on the circumstances. This could be a large amount of money.

DO THE ACCELERATED PAYMENTS HAVE TO BE PAID BACK IF THE INDIVIDUAL FAILS TO FIND EMPLOYMENT IN A HIGH TECHNOLOGY INDUSTRY?

No. The fact that he or she intended to find employment in a high technology industry is sufficient.

LIST OF APPROVED HIGH TECHNOLOGY PROGRAMS

1.09 Animal Sciences
01.0901 Animal Sciences, General
01.0902 Agricultural Animal Breeding
01.0903 Animal Health
01.0904 Animal Nutrition
01.0905 Dairy Science
01.0906 Livestock Management
01.0907 Poultry Science

01.10 Food Science and Technology
01.1001 Food Science
01.1002 Food Technology and Processing
01.1099 Food Science and Technology
01.1101 Plant Sciences General
01.1102 Agronomy and Crop Science
01.1103 Horticultural Science
01.1104 Agricultural and Horticultural Plant Breeding
01.1105 Plant Protection and Integrated Pest Management
01.1106 Range Science Management

01.12 Soil Sciences
01.1201 Soil Science and Agronomy General
01.1202 Soil Chemistry and Physics
01.1203 Soil Microbiology
01.1299 Soil Sciences

03.01 Natural Resources Conservation and Research
03.0104 Environmental Science

03.03 Fishing and Fisheries Sciences and Management

03.05 Forestry
03.0501 Forestry, General
03.0502 Forest Sciences and Biology
03.0506 Forest Management/Forest Resources Management
03.0508 Urban Forestry
03.0509 Wood Science and Wood Products/Pulp and Paper Technology
03.0510 Forest Resources Production and Management
03.0511 Forest Technology/Technician

03.06 Wildlife and Wildlands Science and Management

09.07 Radio, Television, and Digital Communication
09.0702 Digital Communication and Media/Multimedia

11.0101 Computer and Information Sciences, General
11.0102 Artificial Intelligence and Robotics
11.0103 Information Technology
11.0199 Computer and Information Sciences

11.02 Computer Programming
11.0201 Computer Programming/Programmer General
11.0202 Computer Programming Specific Applications

11.03 Data Processing
11.0301 Data Process and Data Processing Technology/Technician

11.04 Information Science/Studies

11.05 Computer Systems Analysis

11.07 Computer Science

11.08 Computer Software and Media Application
11.0801 Web Page, Digital/Multimedia and Information Resources Design
11.0802 Data Modeling/Warehousing and Database Administration
11.0803 Computer Graphics
11.0899 Computer Software and Media Applications, Other.

11.09 Computer System Networking and Telecommunications

11.10 Computer/Information Technology Administration and Management
11.1001 System Administration/Administrator
11.1002 System, Networking and LAN/WAN Management/Manager
11.1003 Computer and Information Systems Security
11.1004 Web/Multimedia Management and Webmaster

***14. Engineering.**
Instructional program that prepare individuals to apply mathematical and scientific principles to the solution of practical problems.
***15. Engineering Technologies/Technicians.**
Instructional programs that prepare individuals to apply basic engineering principles and technical skills in support of engineering and related projects.

***26. Biological and Biomedical Sciences.**
Instructional programs that focus on the biological sciences and the non-clinical biomedical sciences, and that prepare individuals for research and professional careers as biologist and biomedical scientist.

***27. Mathematics and Statistics.**
Instructional programs that focus on the systematic study of logical symbolic language and its applications.

***29. Military Technologies.**
A program that prepares individuals to undertake advanced and specialized leadership and technical responsibilities for the armed services and related national security organizations. Includes instruction in such areas as weapons systems and technology, communications, intelligence, management, logistics and strategy.

30.01 Biological and Physical Sciences

30.06 System Science and Theory

30.08 Mathematics and Computer Science

30.10 Biopsychology

30.11 Gerontology

30.16 Accounting and Computer Science

30.17 Behavioral Sciences

30.18 Natural Sciences

30.19 Nutrition Sciences

30.24 Neuroscience

30.25 Cognitive Science

***40. Physical Sciences.**
Instructional programs that focus on the scientific study of inanimate objects, processes of matter and energy, and associated phenomena.

***41. Science Technologies/Technicians.**
Instructional programs that prepare individuals to apply scientific principles and technical skills in support of scientific research and development.

42.11 Physiological Psychology/Psychobiology

42.19 Psychometrics and Quantitative Psychology

42. 24 Psychopharmacology
42.26 Forensic Psychology

***51.14 Medical Clinical Sciences/Graduate Medical Studies**
51.1401 Medical Scientist (MS, PhD)

NOTE: "*" means all programs are considered high technology programs within that discipline.

ELIGIBILITY PERIODS

Benefits generally end 10 years from the date of an individual's last discharge or release from active duty. The VA may extend the 10-year period by the amount of time an individual is prevented from training due to a disability, or the individual is being held by a foreign government or power.

The VA may extend the 10-year period if an individual reenters active duty for 90 days or more after becoming eligible. The extension ends 10 years from the date of discharge or release from the later period. Periods of active duty of less than 90 days may qualify for extensions, only if the discharge or release was for:

- A service-connected disability; or
- A medical condition existing before active duty; or
- Hardship; or
- A reduction in force.

If an individual's discharge is upgraded by the military, the 10-year period begins on the date of the upgrade.

Special Note For Individuals Eligible Under The 2 By 4 Program

If an individual is eligible based upon two years of active duty followed by four years in the Selected Reserve, the individual may have 10 years from release from active duty, or 10 years from the completion of the four-year Selected Reserve obligation to use benefits, whichever is later.

MISCELLANEOUS INFORMATION

- Any change in educational, professional or vocational objectives is considered a "change of program." The law permits one change of program without prior VA approval, provided an individual's attendance, conduct and progress in the last program were satisfactory. Additional "changes of program" require prior VA approval. VA will not charge a change of program if the individual enrolls in a new program after successful completion of the immediately preceding program.
- Once an individual starts receiving benefits, he must maintain satisfactory attendance, conduct and progress. The VA may stop benefits if an individual does not meet the standards set by the school. VA may later resume benefits if the individual reenters the same program at the same school, and the school approves the reentry, and certifies it to VA.
- If the individual does not reenter the same program at the same school, VA may resume benefits if the cause of unsatisfactory attendance, conduct or progress has been removed; and the program that the student intends to pursue is suitable to his or her abilities, aptitudes and interests.

APPLICATION FOR BENEFITS

VA Form 22-1990, "Application for Education Benefits" must be completed. The form may be obtained from individual schools, from any VA regional office, or by calling (888) GIBILL-1.

The completed form should be sent to the VA regional office with jurisdiction over the state in which the individual will train.

If an individual is not on active duty, copy 4 of DD Form 214 ("Certificate of Release or Discharge from Active Duty"), must also be sent to the VA. If an individual is on active duty, enrollment must be approved by the Base Education Services Officer, and service must be verified by the Commanding Officer.

If training has already started, the school, employer, or union should complete VA Form 22-1999 ("Enrollment Certification") and submit it along with the application.

PROCEDURES FOR RECEIPT OF MONTHLY PAYMENTS

Students will receive a Student Verification of Enrollment Form 22-8979 each month, and must complete and return it to the appropriate VA regional office. After processing, VA will release a check.

After selecting a school and submitting an application to VA, the school official must complete an enrollment certification, and submit it to the appropriate VA regional office. If a student meets the basic eligibility requirements for benefits, and the program or course is approved, VA will process the enrollment based on certified training time.

If a student is enrolled in a degree program at a college or university, or a certificate or diploma program at a business, technical, or vocational school, they will not receive payment until they have verified their attendance. Students will receive a "Student Verification of Enrollment Form 22-8979" each month, and must complete and return it to the appropriate VA regional office. After processing, VA will release a check.

If an individual is in an apprenticeship or job-training program, he or she will receive a form to report the hours worked each month. The form must be signed and given to the certifying official for the company or union. The certifying official must complete the form and send it to the appropriate VA regional office. After processing, VA will release a check.

If an individual is taking a correspondence course, he or she will receive a form each quarter, on which the student must show the number of lessons completed that quarter. The completed form should be sent to the school for certification of the number of lessons serviced during the quarter. The school will send the form to the appropriate VA regional office. After processing, VA will release a check. Payments are based on the number of lessons serviced by the school.

VA will send flight schools a supply of blank monthly certification of flight training forms. The school must complete the form by entering the number of hours, the hourly rate, and the total charges for flight training received during the month. The student should review and sign the completed form, and send it to the appropriate VA regional office. After processing, VA will release a check.

NOTE: It is against the law for schools to cash VA checks under a Power of Attorney Agreement.

TIMELY RECEIPT OF VERIFICATION FORMS AND CHECKS

Students should receive their verification forms for each month by the fifth of the following month. If it is not received by then, the VA should be immediately contacted so that another form can be issued.

One a completed verification form has been submitted, the student should receive a check within 2 weeks. If a check is not received by then, the VA should immediately be contacted so that appropriate action can be taken.

ADVANCE PAYMENTS

An advance payment for the initial month, or partial month and the following month may be made, if:

1. The school agrees to handle advance payments; and
2. Training is one-half time or more; and
3. A request is made by the individual in writing; and
4. The VA receives the enrollment certification at least 30 days prior to the start of classes.

Advance payments are made out to the individual, and sent to the applicable school for delivery to the individual registration. VA cannot issue a check more than 30 days before classes start. Before requesting an advance payment, students should verify with the school certifying official that the school has agreed to process advance payments.

Requests for advance payments must be on VA Form 22-1999, "Enrollment Certification," or a sheet of paper attached to the enrollment certification.

Once a student receives an advance payment at registration, the school must certify to VA that the student received the check. If a student reduces enrollment, or withdraws from all courses during the period covered by an advance payment, he or she must repay the overpayment to VA.

If an individual believes that the amount of a VA check is incorrect, the VA should be contacted before the check is cashed.

DIRECT DEPOSIT

Chapter 30 payments can be sent directly to a student's savings or checking account through Direct Deposit (Electronic Funds Transfer). To sign up for direct deposit by phone, students must call (877) 838-2778.

STUDENT RESPONSIBILITIES

To ensure timely receipt of correct payments, students should be sure to promptly notify the VA of:

- Any change in enrollment;
- Any change in address;
- Any change in selected reserve status;
- Any changes affecting a student's dependents (if a student is receiving an allowance which includes an additional amount for dependents).

In addition, students should use reasonable judgment when accepting and cashing a check. All letters from VA about monthly rates and effective dates should be read carefully. If a student thinks the amount of a VA check is wrong, VA should be contacted **before** cashing the check. Any incorrect checks should be returned to VA.

If a student cashes a check for the wrong amount, he or she will be liable for repayment of any resulting overpayment.

RECOVERY OF OVERPAYMENTS

VA must take prompt and aggressive action to recover overpayments. Students have the right to request a waiver of the overpayment, or verification that the amount is correct. If an overpayment is not repaid or waived, VA may add interest and collection fees to the debt. VA may also take one or more of the following actions to collect the debt:

- Withhold future benefits to apply to the debt;
- Refer the debt to a private collection agency;
- Recover the debt from any Federal income tax refund;
- Recover the debt from the salary (if student is a Federal employee);
- File a lawsuit in Federal court to collect the debt;
- Withhold approval of a VA home loan guarantee.

CHANGES IN ENROLLMENT

If a student withdraws from one or more courses after the end of the school's drop period, VA will reduce or stop benefits on the date of reduction or withdrawal. Unless the student can show that the change was due to *mitigating circumstances*, the student may have to repay **all** benefits for the course.

VA defines *mitigating circumstances* as "unavoidable and unexpected events that directly interfere with the pursuit of a course, and which are beyond the student's control.

Examples of reasons VA may accept include:

- Extended illness;
- Severe illness or death in immediate family;
- Unscheduled changes in employment; and
- Lack of child care.

Examples of reasons VA may not accept include:

- Withdrawal to avoid a failing grade;
- Dislike of the instructor; and
- Too many courses attempted.

(VA may ask the student to furnish evidence to support the reason for change, such as physician or employer written statements.)

The first time a student withdraws from up to 6 credit hours, VA will "excuse" the withdrawal, and pay benefits for the period attended.

If a student receives a grade that does not count toward graduation, all benefits for the course may have to be repaid. Affected students should check the school's grading policy with the office handling VA paperwork.

If a student receives a non-punitive grade, the school will notify VA, and VA may reduce or stop benefits. The student may not have to repay the benefits if he or she can show that the grades were due to mitigating circumstances.

WORK-STUDY PROGRAMS

Students may be eligible for an additional allowance under a work-study program that allows students to perform work for VA in return for an hourly wage. Students may perform outreach services under VA supervision, prepare and process VA paperwork, work at a VA medical facility or National Cemetery, or perform other approved activities.

Students must attend school at the three-quarter of full-time rate.

VA will select students for the work study program based on different factors. Such factors include:

- Disability of the student;
- Ability of the student to complete the work-study contract before the end of his or her eligibility for education benefits;
- Job availability within normal commuting distance to the student;
- VA will give the highest priority to a veteran who has a service-connected disability or disabilities rated by VA at 30% or more.

The number of applicants selected will depend on the availability of VA-related work at the school or at VA facilities in the area.

Students may work during or between periods of enrollment, and can arrange with VA to work any number of hours during his or her enrollment. However, the maximum number of hours a student may work is 25 times the number of weeks in the enrollment period.

Students will earn an hourly wage equal to the Federal or State minimum wage, whichever is greater. If a student works at a college or university, the school **may** pay the difference between the amount VA pays and the amount the school normally pays other work-study students doing the same job.

Students may elect to be paid in advance for 40% of the number of hours in the work-study agreement, or for 50 hours, whichever is less. After completion of the hours covered by the first payment, VA will pay the student after completion of each 50 hours of service.

Students interested in taking part in a work-study program must complete VA Form 22-8691, "Application for Work-Study Allowance." Completed forms should be sent to the nearest VA regional office.

EDUCATIONAL COUNSELING

VA can provide services to help eligible individuals understand their educational and vocational strengths and weaknesses and to plan:

- An educational or training goal, and the means by which the goal can be reached; or
- An employment goal for which an individual qualifies on the basis of present training or experience.

VA can also help plan an effective job search.

Counseling is available for:

- Service members who are on active duty, and are within 180 days of discharge, and are stationed in the United States; or
- Veterans with discharges that are not dishonorable, who are within one year from date of discharge.

VOCATIONAL REHABILITATION

Veterans may qualify for Training and Rehabilitation under Chapter 31 of Title 38, United States Code, if:

- The veteran has a service-connected disability or disabilities rated by VA at 20% or more; and
- The veteran received a discharge from active duty that was not dishonorable; and
- The veteran has an employment handicap.

Veterans may also qualify with a service-connected disability or disabilities rated by VA at 10%, and:

- The veteran has a serious employment handicap; or
- The veteran first applied for vocational rehabilitation benefits before November 1, 1990, reapplied after that date, and has an employment handicap.

Vocational rehabilitation helps disabled veterans become independent in daily living. Veterans may also receive assistance in selecting, preparing for, and securing employment that is compatible with their interests, talents, skills, physical capabilities, and goals.

To apply for vocational rehabilitation, VA for 28-1900, "Disabled Veterans Application for Vocational Rehabilitation," must be completed and sent to the nearest VA regional office.

For detailed information on vocational rehabilitation refer to Chapter 14 of this book.

APPEAL OF VA DECISION

VA decisions on education benefits may be appealed within one year of the date an individual receives notice of a VA decision.

For detailed information on filing an appeal, please refer to Chapter 35 of this book.

CHAPTER 19

EDUCATION BENEFITS: **POST-9/11 G.I. BILL, CHAPTER 33**

The Post-9/11 GI Bill (or so-called *GI Bill for the 21st century*) is a new education benefit program for individuals who served on active duty on or after September 11, 2001. It boasts the most comprehensive education benefits package since the original GI Bill was signed into law in 1944.

The new bill goes well beyond helping to pay for tuition; many veterans who served after September 11, 2001, will get full tuition and fees, a new monthly housing stipend, and a $1,000 a year stipend for books and supplies. The new bill also gives Reserve and Guard members who have been activated for more than 90 days since 9/11 access to the same GI Bill benefits.

Post-9/11 GI Bill benefits are payable for training pursued on or after August 1, 2009. No payments can be made under this program for training pursued before this date.

VETERANS EDUCATIONAL ASSISTANCE IMPROVEMENTS ACT OF 2010

Effective August 1, 2009, but not payable until October 1, 2011:

Certain National Guard members mobilized on Title 32 orders on-or-after September 11, 2001 are now eligible for the Post-9/11 GI Bill and any qualifying Title 32 mobilization may be used to increase his or her percentage of eligibility.

Limits active duty members to the net cost for tuition and fees prorated based on the eligibility tiers (40%-100%) previously established for Veterans. (Same limitations apply to transferee spouses of active duty servicemembers.)

The Post-9/11 GI Bill will now pay all public school in-state tuition and fees; this includes graduate training, etc.

MGIB-AD & MGIB-SR College fund payments will now be paid on a monthly basis instead of a lump-sum at the beginning of the term.

Reimbursement is now available for multiple Licensing and Certification Tests.

Reimbursement is now available for fees paid to take national examinations used for admission to an institution of higher learning (e.g. SAT, LSAT, ACT, GMAT, etc).

Vocational Rehabilitation participants may now elect the higher housing allowance offered by the *Post-9/11 GI Bill* if otherwise eligible for the Post-9/11 GI Bill.

If training at greater than ½ time the housing allowance is now prorated according to the training time the individual is enrolled (rounded to the nearest tenth). So, if a student's full housing allowance is $1000, and he or she is attending ¾ time - the housing allowance would be $800 (80% of $1000).

Break or interval pay is no longer payable under any VA education benefit program unless under an Executive Order of the President or due to an emergency situation such as a natural disaster or strike. Entitlement which previously would have been used for break pay will be available for use during a future enrollment.

This means that if the semester ends December 15, the housing allowance is paid for the first 15 days of December only. Benefits will begin again when the new semester begins (e.g. January 15), and the student will be paid for the remaining days of that month and term.

Students using other VA education programs are included in this change. Monthly benefits will be prorated in the same manner.

NOAA and PHS personnel are now eligible to transfer their entitlement to eligible dependents

If a student is training at greater than ½ time, his or her housing allowance is now prorated according to the training time he or she is enrolled. For example, if full housing allowance for is $1000, and the student is attending ¾ time - the housing allowance would be $750 (¾ of $1000)

Housing allowance is now payable to students enrolled solely in distance learning. The housing allowance is ½ the national average BAH for an E-5 with dependents (the rate would be $673.50 for 2011).

Non-college degree programs, on-the-job training, and flight training programs are now covered under the Post-9/11 GI Bill.

The book stipend is now payable to active duty members.

ELIGIBILITY

If an individual has served a total of at least 90 consecutive days on active duty in the Armed Forces since September 11, 2001, he or she is eligible. However, the amount of benefits received under this program is determined by the actual amount of accumulated post 9/11 service the individual has.

An individual may be eligible if he or she has served at least 90 aggregate days on active duty after September 10, 2001, and is still on active duty, or was honorably:

- Discharged from the active duty; or
- Released from active duty and placed on the retired list or temporary disability retired list; or
- Released from active duty and transferred to the Fleet Reserve or Fleet Marine Corps Reserve; or
- Released from the active duty for further service in a reserve component of the Armed Forces.

Individuals may also be eligible if they were honorably discharged from active duty for a service-connected disability, and served 30 continuous days after September 10, 2001.

Some periods of active duty service are excluded. Periods of service under the following do not count toward qualification for the *Post 9/11 GI Bill*:
NOAA, PHS, or Active Guard Reserve;
ROTC under 10 U.S.C. 2107(b);
Service academy contract period;

- Service terminated due to defective enlistment agreement;
- Service used for loan repayment; and
- Selected reserve service used to establish eligibility under the *Montgomery GI Bill* (MGIB chapter 30), MGIB for Selected Reserve (MGIB-SR Chapter 1606), or the Reserve Education Assistance Program (REAP chapter 1607).

Under the MGIB, officers who received their commission through a service academy, or an ROTC scholarship were ineligible. There are no such restrictions under the new program. Any officer, who was previously ineligible, will be eligible for the new program, assuming they have at least 90 days of post 9/11 active duty service.

Similarly, military members who previously declined the MGIB are eligible for the new program.

If, on August 1, 2009, a servicemember was eligible for MGIB-SR or REAP, and he or she qualifies for the *Post-9/11 GI Bill*, he or she must make an irrevocable election to receive benefits under the *Post-9/11 GI Bill*. The individual then loses any right to future MGIB-SR or REAP benefits.

BENEFIT AMOUNT PAYABLE

The new rates depend on the length of post 9/11 active duty service, the state of residence, and the number of courses taken. Like the MGIB, the *Post-9/11 GI Bill* pays 36 months of full time education benefits. So, if an individual goes to school full-time, he or she will receive the full benefit rates for 36 months. If he or she goes to school 1/2 time, he or she will receive half of the monthly entitlement for 72 months, etc.

Based on the length of active duty service, eligible participants are entitled to receive a percentage of the following:

- Cost of tuition and fees, not to exceed the most expensive in-state undergraduate tuition at a public institution of higher education (paid directly to the school);
- Monthly housing allowance equal to the basic allowance for housing payable to a military E-5 with dependents, in the same zip code as the primary school (paid directly to the servicemember or veteran);
- Yearly books and supplies stipend of up to $1,000 per year (paid directly to the servicemember or veteran); and
- A one-time payment of $500 paid to certain individuals relocating from highly rural areas.

(The housing allowance and books and supplies stipend are not payable to individuals on active duty. The housing allowance is not payable to those pursuing training at half time or less or to individuals enrolled solely in distance learning programs.)

The following chart outlines the breakdown of benefits based on amount of service:

Member Serves	Percentage of Maximum Benefit Payable
At least 36 months	100%
At least 30 continuous days on active duty and must be discharged due to service-connected disability	100%
At least 30 months, but less than 36 months	90%
At least 24 months, but less than 30 months	80%
At least 18 months, but less than 24 months	70%
At least 12 months, but less than 18 months	60%
At least 06 months, but less than 12 months	50%
At least 90 days, but less than 06 months	40%

2014-2015 MAXIMUM IN-STATE TUITION & FEES

Post-9/11 GI Bill (Chapter 33) Payment Rates For 2014 Academic Year (August 1, 2014 - July 31, 2015)
The Post-9/11 GI Bill program is comprised of multiple payments. All payments and maximum amounts listed on this page are applicable to individuals eligible for the full benefit (100% eligibility tier). If you are not eligible for the full benefit, the payment and maximum amounts listed will be prorated based on your eligibility percentage.

MAXIMUM TUITION & FEE REIMBURSEMENT PER ACADEMIC YEAR

Public School: All Tuition & Fee Payments for an in-State Student

Private or Foreign School: Up to $20,235.02 per academic year National Maximum

CONTRIBUTIONS

Unlike the MGIB and VEAP, the new MGIB does not require the servicemember to elect or decline, nor make monthly contributions. Unfortunately, if someone has already contributed to the GI Bill, he or she won't get their money back, unless they use all of their new GI Bill entitlements. If they do, the $1,200 contribution to the MGIB (or a proportional amount, if they used any of their MGIB entitlement) will be added to his or her final new GI Bill education payment. If an individual is currently paying into the MGIB, he or she can stop now, and still be eligible for the new program.

COVERED EXPENSES

The plan covers any approved programs offered by a school in the United States that is authorized to grant an associate (or higher) degree.

The plan may also pay for tutorial assistance, or up to $2,000 for the reimbursement of one licensing or certification test.

If a servicemember transferred to the *Post-9/11 GI Bill* from MGIB-Active Duty, MGIB-SR, or REAP, he or she may also receive Post-9/11 benefits for flight training, apprenticeship, or on-the-job training programs, and correspondence courses.

COLLEGE FUNDS

If the member is eligible for a "kicker," such as the Army or Navy College Fund, or a Reserve "Kicker," he or she will still receive the extra monthly benefit under the new GI bill. This monthly amount will be paid to the member, not to the university.

COLLEGE LOAN REPAYMENT

Individuals, who were previously ineligible for the MGIB because they elected the College Loan Repayment Program (CLRP), are eligible for the new GI Bill, but only active duty service performed after their initial active duty service obligation counts toward the new benefits. In other words, if they were initially enlisted for five years and received the CLRP, they would have to reenlist or extend their enlistment in order to take advantage of the new GI Bill.

TRANSFERRING BENEFITS TO DEPENDENTS

While the Post-9/11 GI Bill offers a very generous post-service education benefit, a special provision of the program allows career service members the opportunity to share their education benefits with immediate family members.

Allowing career service members to transfer their GI Bill benefits to family members has long been one of the most requested items among military family readiness and advocacy groups.

ELIGIBLE INDIVIDUALS

Any member of the Armed Forces (active duty or Selected Reserve, officer or enlisted) on or after August 1, 2009, who is eligible for the Post-9/11 GI Bill, and:

Has at least 6 years of service in the Armed Forces on the date of election and agrees to serve 4 additional years in the Armed Forces from the date of election.
Has at least 10 years of service in the Armed Forces (active duty and/or selected reserve) on the date of election, is precluded by either standard policy (service or DoD) or statute from committing to 4 additional years, and agrees to serve for the maximum amount of time allowed by such policy or statute, or

Is (or becomes) retirement eligible during the period from August 1, 2009, through August 1, 2013. A service member is considered to be retirement eligible if he or she has completed 20 years of active duty or 20 qualifying years of reserve service.

For those individuals eligible for retirement on August 1, 2009, no additional service is required.

For those individuals who have an approved retirement date after August 1, 2009, and before July 1, 2010, no additional service is required.

For those individuals eligible for retirement after August 1, 2009, and before August 1, 2010, 1 year of additional service after approval of transfer is required.

For those individuals eligible for retirement on or after August 1, 2010, and before August 1, 2011, 2 years of additional service after approval of transfer are required.

For those individuals eligible for retirement on or after August 1, 2011, and before August 1, 2012, 3 years of additional service after approval of transfer required.

ELIGIBLE FAMILY MEMBERS

An individual approved to transfer an entitlement to educational assistance under this section may transfer the individual's entitlement to:

- The individual's spouse.
- One or more of the individual's children.
- Any combination of spouse and child.

A family member must be enrolled in the Defense Eligibility Enrollment Reporting System (DEERS) and be eligible for benefits, at the time of transfer to receive transferred educational benefits.

A child's subsequent marriage will not affect his or her eligibility to receive the educational benefit; however, after an individual has designated a child as a transferee under this section, the individual retains the right to revoke or modify the transfer at any time.

A subsequent divorce will not affect the transferee's eligibility to receive educational benefits; however, after an individual has designated a spouse as a transferee under this section, the eligible individual retains the right to revoke or modify the transfer at any time.

NATURE OF TRANSFER

An eligible Service member may transfer up to the total months of unused Post-9/11 GI Bill benefits, or the entire 36 months if the member has used none.

Family member use of transferred educational benefits is subject to the following:

SPOUSE:

- May start to use the benefit immediately.
- May use the benefit while the member remains in the Armed Forces or after separation from active duty.
- Is not eligible for the monthly stipend or books and supplies stipend while the member is serving on active duty.
- Can use the benefit for up to 15 years after the service member's last separation from active duty.

CHILD:

- May start to use the benefit only after the individual making the transfer has completed at least 10 years of service in the Armed Forces.

- May use the benefit while the eligible individual remains in the Armed Forces or after separation from active duty.

- May not use the benefit until he/she has attained a secondary school diploma (or equivalency certificate), or reached 18 years of age.

- Is entitled to the monthly stipend and books and supplies stipend even though the eligible individual is on active duty.

- Is not subject to the 15-year delimiting date, but may not use the benefit after reaching 26 years of age.

VEAP & THE POST 9/11 BENEFIT

If someone is eligible for both VEAP and the Post-9/11 GI Bill he or she may un-enroll from VEAP and receive a refund of contributions, or leave the remaining contributions in the VEAP account and remain eligible for both benefit programs.

NOTE: Students may not receive benefits under more than one program at the same time.

EXPIRATION DATE

Eligibility for the new GI Bill expires 15 years from the last period of active duty of at least 90 consecutive days. If released for a service-connected disability after at least 30 days of continuous service, eligibility ends 15 years from when the member is released for the service-connected disability.

YELLOW RIBBON PROGRAM

The Post-9/11 GI Bill pays up to the highest public in-state undergraduate tuition. Tuition and fees may exceed that amount for individuals attending a private institution, graduate school or attending in a non-resident status.

The Yellow Ribbon Program is a provision of the *Post-9/11 Veterans Education Assistance Act of 2008*. Its purpose is to address enrollment at institutions that cost more than the Post-9/11 GI Bill's tuition benefit cap.

This program allows institutions of higher learning (degree granting institutions) in the United States to voluntarily enter into an agreement with VA to fund tuition expenses that exceed the highest public in-state undergraduate tuition rate. The institution can waive up to 50% of those expenses and VA will match the same amount as the institution. To be eligible, the student must be:

A veteran receiving benefits at the 100% benefit rate payable;

A transfer-of-entitlement eligible dependent child; or

A transfer-of-entitlement eligible spouse of a veteran.

The Institution of Higher Learning (IHL) must agree to:

Provide contributions to eligible individuals who apply for the Yellow Ribbon Program on a first-come first-served basis, regardless of the rate at which the individual is pursuing training in any given academic year;

Provide contributions during the current academic year and all subsequent academic years in which the student maintains satisfactory progress, conduct, and attendance;
Make contributions toward the program on behalf of the individual in the form of a waiver;

Choose the percentage that will be waived and waive the same percentage (up to 50%) of established charges that exceed the in-State maximum for each student eligible;
State the maximum number of individuals for whom contributions will be made in any given academic year.

WORK-STUDY PROGRAM

Veterans and eligible transfer-of-entitlement recipients who train at the three-quarter rate of pursuit or higher may be eligible for a work study program in which they work for VA and receive hourly wages. Students under the work-study program must be supervised by a VA employee and all duties performed must relate to VA. The types of work allowable include:

- VA paperwork processing at schools or other training facilities.
- Assistance with patient care at VA hospitals or domiciliary care facilities.
- Work at national or state veterans' cemeteries.
- Other VA-approved activities.

CHAPTER 20

EDUCATION BENEFITS: **RESERVE EDUCATIONAL ASSISTANCE PROGRAM (REAP)**—CHAPTER 1607

H.R. 4200 created a new education benefit called the **Reserve Educational Assistance Program (REAP)** or Chapter 1607. This new program makes certain individuals who were activated after September 11, 2001 either eligible for education benefits or eligible for increased benefits.

PURPOSE

Chapter 1607 provides educational assistance to members of the reserve components called or ordered to active duty in response to a war or national emergency (contingency operations) as declared by the President or Congress.

Note: "Contingency operations" as defined in title 10 U.S. Code means "military operations that are designated by the Secretary of Defense as an operation in which members of the armed forces are or may become involved in military actions, operations or hostilities against an enemy of the United States or against opposing military force; or results in the call or order to, or retention on active duty of members of the uniformed services...."

ELIGIBILITY

The Secretaries of each military service, Department of Defense, and Department of Homeland Security (Coast Guard) will determine eligibility.

The law requires DoD to give individuals written notification of eligibility for REAP.

- Unlike the MGIB-Active Duty, service members do not have to pay anything to participate in Chapter 1607.

- A member of a reserve component who serves on active duty on or after September 11, 2001 under title 10 U.S. Code for a contingency operation and who serves at least 90 consecutive days or more is eligible for chapter 1607.

- National Guard members also are eligible if their active duty is under section 502(f), title 32 U.S.C. and they serve for 90 consecutive days when authorized by the President or Secretary of Defense for a national emergency and is supported by federal funds. Individuals are eligible as soon as they reach the 90-day point whether or not they are currently on active duty. DoD will fully identify contingency operations that qualify for benefits under chapter 1607.

- Disabled members who are injured or have an illness or disease incurred or aggravated in the line of duty and are released from active duty before completing 90 consecutive days are also eligible.

Note: Members released early for disability incurred or aggravated in the line of duty may receive Chapter 1607 benefits at the 40% rate. The member is entitled to Chapter 1607 benefits for 10 years from the date of eligibility.)

PAYMENT RATES

The benefit amount payable under Chapter 1607 is a percentage of the MGIB (Chapter 30) 3-year rate, based on the number of continuous days served on active duty.

Time Reserve Member Serves on Active Duty	Percentage of Ch 30 (3-Year Rate)
90 days but less than one year	40%
One year but less than two years	60%
Two years or more	80%

The following basic monthly rates are effective October 1, 2014:

INSTITUTIONAL TRAINING			
Training Time	Consecutive service of 90 days but less than one year	Consecutive service of 1 year or more	Consecutive service of 2 years or more
Full Time	$686.80	1030.20	1373.60
¾ Time	515.10	772.65	1030.20
½ Time	343.40	515.10	686.80
Less than ½ time, but more than ¼ time	343.40 (tuition & fees only)	515.10 (tuition & fees only)	686.80 (tuition & fees only)
¼ time or less	171.70 (tuition & fees only)	257.55 (tuition & fees only)	343.40 (tuition & fees only)

CORRESPONDENCE TRAINING	
40% Level	22% of the approved cost of course
60% Level	33% of the approved cost of course
80% Level	44% of the approved cost of course

FLIGHT TRAINING	
40% Level	24% of the approved cost of course
60% Level	36% of the approved cost of course
80% Level	48% of the approved cost of course

APPRENTICESHIP AND ON-THE-JOB TRAINING-RATES EFFECTIVE OCTOBER 1, 2014			
Training Period	Consecutive service of 90 days, but less than one year	Consecutive service of 1 year or more	Consecutive service of 2 years or more
First six months of training	$515.10	772.65	1030.20
Second six months of training	377.47	566.61	755.48
Remaining pursuit of training	240.38	360.57	480.76

COOPERATIVE TRAINING			
Training Time	Service of 90 days, but less than one year	Service of 1 year or more	Service of 2 years or more
Monthly Rate	$688.80	$1030.20	$1373.60

Note: Some reservists may contribute up to an additional $600 to the GI Bill to receive increased monthly benefits. For an additional $600 contribution, they may receive up to $5400 in additional GI Bill benefits

APPLYING FOR BENEFITS

VA Regional Processing Offices in Atlanta, St. Louis, Buffalo, and Muskogee will accept applications and supporting documents for Chapter 1607 claims. VA will take action on your claim at this time.

INDIVIDUALS WHO HAVE NEVER SUBMITTED AN EDUCATION CLAIM TO VA:

Submit an ***Application for VA Education Benefits (VA Form 22-1990)*** and submit any available documents such as Discharge from Military Service (DD Form 214), copies of orders to active duty and anything else available as evidence of qualifying service.

Annotate "Chapter 1607" prominently on all correspondence and documents.

INDIVIDUALS WHO HAVE PREVIOUSLY FILED A CLAIM FOR EDUCATION BENEFITS:

A new application form is not required. However, individuals should submit any available documents such as Discharge from Military Service (DD Form 214), copies of orders to active duty and anything else available as evidence of qualifying service to help establish eligibility for this program. Individuals should also submit a **"Request For Change of Program or Place of Training" (VA form 22-1995)** which should be annotated "1607."

Annotate "Chapter 1607" prominently on all correspondence and documents.

EARLIEST ELIGIBILITY DATE

Chapter 1607 benefits may be paid before the date of enactment the law, which was October 28, 2004. Chapter 1607 benefits are **potentially** payable from December 9, 2001 (90 days after September 11, 2001) for persons who were serving on a contingency operation on September 11, 2001 and who were in school on December 9, 2001.

MONTHS OF BENEFITS PAYABLE

Individuals may receive 36 months of full time entitlement at his or her given rate. A Chapter 1607 participant may not use more than 48 months of entitlement under any combination of VA Educational programs. For example, if he or she has already used 20 months of Chapter 1606, he or she will only receive 28 months of Chapter 1607

.

BENEFIT ENDING DATE

Individuals may use benefits under Chapter 1607 as long as they remain within their component. Benefits must be terminated if an individual leaves the Reserves or participates in a ROTC program under Title 10 Section 2107.

Note: There is no fixed delimiting period (ending date) for persons eligible under chapter 1607, as there is for all of the other VA education programs so long as an individual does not leave his or her Reserve component. There is one exception: If an individual is separated from the Ready Reserve for a disability which was not the result of his or her own willful misconduct, he or she is entitled to chapter 1607 benefits for 10-years after the date of entitlement.

RECEIPT OF OTHER VA EDUCATION BENEFITS

Individuals must make an irrevocable election choosing which program they want their military service to count towards. Individuals also cannot receive assistance under more than one VA Education program at one time.

If an individual is eligible for a Chapter 1606 kicker, he or she can still be paid that kicker while receiving Chapter 1607.

APPROVED COURSES

The following programs are available:

- College or University Degree Programs
- Vocational Programs
- Independent Study or Distance Learning Programs
- Correspondence Courses
- Flight Training
- On-the-Job Training and Apprenticeship Programs
- Tuition Assistance Top-Up Program
- Entrepreneurship Courses

NOTE: VA does not approve schools or programs for benefits. Each individual state approves schools and courses. To find out if your school or program is approved for VA Educational Benefits under REAP, contact your school's VA Certifying Official, or call VA at (888) 442-4551.

CHAPTER 20

EDUCATION BENEFITS - MONTGOMERY G.I. BILL – SELECTED RESERVE (MGIB-SR), CHAPTER 1606

The Montgomery GI Bill-Selected Reserve Program is for members of the Selected Reserve, including the Army Reserve, Navy Reserve, Air Force Reserve, Marine Corps Reserve, Coast Guard Reserve, Army National Guard and Air National Guard. While the reserve components decide who is eligible for the program, VA makes the payments for the program. Chapter 1606 is the first educational program that does not require service in the *active* Armed Forces in order to qualify.

ELIGIBILITY REQUIREMENTS

- Member must have signed a 6-year obligation to serve in the Selected Reserve after June 30, 1985. (Officers must have agreed to serve 6 years in addition to his or her original obligation.) For some types of training, it is necessary to have a 6-year commitment that began after September 30, 1990. Call (888) GIBILL-1 for more information;
- Member must have completed his or her Initial Active Duty for Training (IADT);
- Member must maintain Selected Reserve Status - Serve in a drilling Selected Reserve unit and remain in good standing;
- Member must meet the requirement to receive a high school diploma or equivalency certificate before completing IADT. Member must remain in good standing while serving in an active Selected Reserve Unit;

- Effective November 1, 2000, veterans and reservists can apply for MGIB-SR benefits any time after receiving their high school diploma or equivalency certificate. It no longer has to be received prior to the end of the individual's first period of active duty.

If an individual enters active duty in the Selected Reserve (AGR, TAR, FTS) after November 29, 1989, he or she must have been eligible *before* November 29, 1989 in order to remain eligible.

ELIGIBILITY RESTRICTIONS

MGIB – AD:
An individual can't be eligible for MGIB – SR if he or she elected to have his or her service in the Selected Reserve credited toward establishing eligibility under the Montgomery GI Bill – Active Duty

ROTC (Reserve Officers' Training Corps) scholarship under section 2107 of title 10, U.S. Code:
An individual can't be eligible for MGIB – SR if he or she is receiving financial assistance through the Senior ROTC program under this section of the law.

Note: However, an individual may still be eligible for MGIB – SR if he or she receives financial assistance under ***Section 2107a*** of title 10, U.S. Code. This financial assistance program is for specially selected members of the Army Reserve and National Guard only. Individuals should check with their ROTC advisor for more information.

Note: There's no restriction on service academy graduates receiving MGIB – SR. Service academy graduates who received a commission aren't eligible under MGIB – AD.

If an individual enters Active Guard and Reserve (AGR) status, his or her eligibility for MGIB – SR will be suspended. He or she may be eligible for MGIB – AD. The individual may resume MGIB – SR eligibility after AGR status ends.

APPROVED COURSES

Individuals may receive benefits for a wide variety of training, including:

- Undergraduate degrees from a college or university;
- Beginning November 30, 1993, graduate degrees from a college or university;
- Accredited independent study programs leading to standard college degrees;
- Technical courses for a certificate at a college or university.

Individuals with 6-year commitments beginning after September 30, 1990 may take the following types of training:

- Courses leading to a certificate or diploma from business, technical, or vocational schools;
- Cooperative training;
- Apprenticeship or job training programs offered by companies;
- Correspondence training;
- Independent study programs;
- Flight training (Individuals must have a private pilot's license, and must meet the medical requirements for the desired license program before beginning training, and throughout the flight training program.)

VA may approve programs offered by institutions outside of the United States, when they are pursued at educational institutions of higher learning, and lead to a college degree. Individuals must receive VA approval prior to attending or enrolling in any foreign programs.

Eligibility for this program is determined by the Selected Reserve components. Payments for the program are made by the VA.

A state agency or VA must approve each program offered by a school or company.

If an individual is seeking a college degree, the school must admit the individual to a degree program by the start of the individual's third term.

RESTRICTIONS ON TRAINING

Benefits are not payable for the following courses:

- Courses paid by the military Tuition Assistance program, if student is enrolled at less than ½ time;
- Courses taken while student is receiving a Reserve Officers' Training Corps scholarship;
- Non-accredited independent study courses;
- Bartending and personality development courses;
- Any course given by radio;
- Self-improvement courses such as reading, speaking, woodworking, basic seamanship, and English as a 2nd language;
- Any course which is avocational or recreational in character;
- Farm-cooperative courses;
- Audited courses;

- Courses not leading to an educational, professional, or vocational objective;
- Courses previously taken and successfully completed;
- Courses taken by a Federal government employee under the *Government Employee's Training Act*;
- Courses taken while in receipt of benefits for the same program from the Office of Workers' Compensation Programs.

VA must reduce benefits for individuals in Federal, State, or local prisons after being convicted of a felony.
An individual may not receive benefits for a program at a proprietary school if he or she is an owner or official of the school.

PART-TIME TRAINING

Individuals unable to attend school full-time should consider going part-time. Benefit rates and entitlement charges are less than the full-time rates. For example, if a student receives full-time benefits for 12 months, the entitlement charge is 12 months. However, if the student receives ½ time benefits for 12 months, the charge is 6 months. VA will pay for less than ½ time training if the student is not receiving Tuition Assistance for those courses.

REMEDIAL, DEFICIENCY AND REFRESHER TRAINING

Remedial and deficiency courses are intended to assist a student in overcoming a deficiency in a particular area of study. Individuals may qualify for benefits for remedial, deficiency, and refresher courses if they have a 6-year commitment that began after September 30, 1990. In order for such courses to be approved, the courses must be deemed necessary for pursuit of a program of education.

Refresher training is for technological advances that occurred in a field of employment. The advance must have occurred while the student was on active duty, or after release.

There is an entitlement charge for these courses.

TUTORIAL ASSISTANCE

Students may receive a special allowance for individual tutoring performed after September 30, 1992, if they entered school at one-half time or more. To qualify, the student must have a deficiency in a subject. The school must certify the tutor's qualifications, and the hours of tutoring. Eligible students may receive a maximum monthly payment of $100.00. The maximum total benefit payable is $1,200.00.

There is no entitlement charge for the first $600.00 of tutorial assistance.

To apply for tutorial assistance, students must submit VA Form 22-1990t, "Application and Enrollment Certification for Individualized Tutorial Assistance." The form should be given to the certifying official in the office handling VA paperwork at the school for completion.

MONTHS OF BENEFITS / ENTITLEMENT CHARGED

Eligible members may be entitled to receive up to 36 months of education benefits. Benefit entitlement ends 10 years from the date the member becomes eligible for the program, or on the day the member leaves the Selected Reserve. (If a member's Reserve or National Guard unit was deactivated during the period October 1, 1991 through September 30, 1999, or if the member was involuntarily separated from service during this same period, eligibility for MGIB-SR benefits is retained for the full 10-year eligibility period. Eligibility for MGIB-SR benefits is also retained if a member is discharged due to a disability that was not caused by misconduct. Eligibility periods may be extended if a member is ordered to active duty.)

Individuals qualifying for more than one VA education program may receive a maximum of 48 months of benefits. For example, if a student used 30 months of Dependents' Educational Assistance, and is eligible for chapter 1606 benefits, he or she could have a maximum of 18 months of entitlement remaining.

Individuals are charged one full day of entitlement for each day of full-time benefits paid. For correspondence and flight training, one month of entitlement is charged each time VA pays one month of benefits. For cooperative programs, one month of entitlement is used for each month of benefits paid.

For apprenticeship and job training programs, the entitlement charge changes every 6 months. During the first 6 months, the charge is 75% of full time. For the second 6 months, the charge is 55% of full time. For the remainder of the program, the charge is 35% of full time.

RATES OF EDUCATIONAL ASSISTANCE PAY

The following basic monthly rates are effective October 1, 2014:

BASIC MONTHLY RATES MONTGOMERY G.I. BILL – SELECTED RESERVE (MGIB-SR), CHAPTER 1606				
Type of Training	**Full-Time**	**Three-Quarter Time**	**One-Half Time**	**Less than ½ Time**
Institutional	$367.00	$274.00	$182.00	$91.75
Cooperative Training	$367.00 (Full-Time Only)			
Correspondence Training	Entitlement charged at the rate of one month for each $367.00 paid *(Payment for correspondence courses is made at 55% of the approved charges for the course.)*			
Apprenticeship On-The-Job Training -	First six months: $275.25 Second six months: $201.85 Remainder of program: $128.45			
Flight Training	Entitlement charged at the rate of one month for each $367.00 paid *(Payment for flight training is made at 60% of the approved charges for the course, including solo hours.)*			

ELIGIBILITY PERIODS

Under previous law, benefits typically ended upon separation from the Reserves. Section 530 of the *National Defense Authorization Act of 2008* **increased the time period that a reservist may use SRMGIB benefits to ten years after separation from the Reserves**, as long as the member's discharge characterization is honorable. **This revision is backdated to October 28, 2004.**

For individuals who separated from the Selected Reserve prior to 10/28/2004, generally benefits end the day of separation. For individuals who stayed in the Selected Reserve, generally benefits ended 14 years from the date the individual became eligible for the program.

Exceptions: If an individual stayed in the Selected Reserve, VA could generally extend the 14-year period if:

- The individual couldn't train due to a disability caused by Selected Reserve service; or
- The individual was activated for service in the Persian Gulf Era (which hasn't ended for purposes of VA education benefits); or
- The individual's eligibility expired during a period of his or her enrollment in training.

MISCELLANEOUS INFORMATION

- Any change in educational, professional or vocational objectives is considered a "change of program." The law permits one change of program without prior VA approval, provided an individual's attendance, conduct and progress in the last program were satisfactory. Additional "changes of program" require prior VA approval. VA will not charge a change of program if the individual enrolls in a new program after successful completion of the immediately preceding program.
- Once an individual starts receiving benefits, he must maintain satisfactory attendance, conduct and progress. The VA may stop benefits if an individual does not meet the standards set by the school. VA may later resume benefits if the individual reenters the same program at the same school, and the school approves the reentry, and certifies it to VA.
- If the individual does not reenter the same program at the same school, VA may resume benefits if the cause of unsatisfactory attendance, conduct or progress has been removed; and the program that the student intends to pursue is suitable to his or her abilities, aptitudes and interests.
- Effective November 1, 2000, VA education benefits can be paid (with some exceptions) for school breaks, if the breaks do not exceed 8 weeks; and the terms before and after the breaks are not shorter than the break. Prior to November 1 2000, VA education benefits could be paid only if the breaks did not exceed a calendar month.

APPLICATION FOR BENEFITS

When an individual becomes eligible for the program, his or her unit will provide the individual with a "Notice of Basic Eligibility, DD Form 2384," or DD Form 2384-1 (for persons who establish eligibility on or after October 1, 1990). The unit will also code the eligibility into the Department of Defense personnel system.

When the individual finds a school, program, company, apprenticeship or job-training program, there are two important steps that must be followed:

- Make sure the program is approved for VA training. Contact the local VA regional office if there are any questions.
- Complete VA Form 22-1990, "Application for Education Benefits." The completed form should be sent to the VA regional office with jurisdiction over the state where training will occur.

Following receipt of an application, VA will review it and advise if anything else is needed. If an individual has started training, the application of "Basic Eligibility" should be taken to the school, employer or union. The certifying official should complete VA Form 22-1999, "Enrollment Certification," and send all the forms to VA.

PROCEDURES FOR RECEIPT OF MONTHLY PAYMENTS

After selecting a school and submitting an application to VA, the school official must complete an enrollment certification, and submit it to the appropriate VA regional office. If a student meets the basic eligibility requirements for benefits, and the program or course is approved, VA will process the enrollment based on certified training time.

VA will accept the Notice of Basic Eligibility to pay benefits for 120 days after an individual's eligibility date. If the eligibility date is more than 120 days before the training program starts, VA will not approve the claim unless the Department of Defense personnel system shows that the individual is eligible. Only a student's reserve component can update the DoD personnel system. VA cannot change an individual's eligibility record.

When VA approves a claim, it will issue a letter with the details of the benefits payable. The first payment should be received within a few days of receipt of the letter.

If a student is enrolled in a degree program at a college or university, he or she will receive payment after the first of each month for the training during the preceding month. If a student is enrolled in a certificate or diploma program at a business, technical, or vocational school, he or she will not receive payment until they have verified their attendance. Students will receive a "Student Verification of Enrollment Form 22-8979" each month, and must complete and return it to the appropriate VA regional office. After processing, VA will release a check.

If an individual is in an apprenticeship or job-training program, he or she will receive a form to report the hours worked each month. The form must be signed and given to the certifying official for the company or union. The certifying official must complete the form and send it to the appropriate VA regional office. After processing, VA will release a check.

If an individual is taking a correspondence course, he or she will receive a form each quarter, on which the student must show the number of lessons completed that quarter. The completed form should be sent to the school for certification of the number of lessons serviced during the quarter. The school will send the form to the appropriate VA regional office. After processing, VA will release a check. Payments are based on the number of lessons serviced by the school.

VA will send flight schools a supply of blank monthly certification of flight training forms. The school must complete the form by entering the number of hours, the hourly rate, and the total charges for flight training received during the month. The student should review and sign the completed form, and send it to the appropriate VA regional office. After processing, VA will release a check.

NOTE: It is against the law for schools to cash VA checks under a Power of Attorney Agreement.

TIMELY RECEIPT OF VERIFICATION FORMS AND CHECKS

Students taking courses leading to a degree at a college or university should receive their checks for each month by the fifth of the next month. If it is not received by then, the VA should be immediately contacted so that appropriate action can be taken.

Students taking courses leading to a certificate or diploma from a business, technical, or vocational school should receive their verification forms for each month by the fifth of the following month. If it is not received by then, the VA should be immediately contacted so that another form can be issued.

One a completed verification form has been submitted, the student should receive a check within 2 weeks. If a check is not received by then, the VA should immediately be contacted so that appropriate action can be taken.

ADVANCE PAYMENTS

An advance payment for the initial month, or partial month and the following month may be made, if:

- The school agrees to handle advance payments; and
- Training is one-half time or more; and
- A request is made by the individual in writing; and
- The VA receives the enrollment certification at least 30 days prior to the start of classes.

Advance payments are made out to the individual, and sent to the applicable school for delivery to the individual registration. VA cannot issue a check more than 30 days before classes start. Before requesting an advance payment, students should verify with the school certifying official that the school has agreed to process advance payments.

Requests for advance payments must be on VA Form 22-1999, Enrollment Certification, or a sheet of paper attached to the enrollment certification.

Once a student receives an advance payment at registration, the school must certify to VA that the student received the check. If a student reduces enrollment, or withdraws from all courses during the period covered by an advance payment, he or she must repay the overpayment to VA.

If an individual believes that the amount of a VA check is incorrect, the VA should be contacted before the check is cashed.

DIRECT DEPOSIT

Payments can be sent directly to a student's savings or checking account through Direct Deposit (Electronic Funds Transfer). To sign up for direct deposit by phone, students must call (877) 838-2778.

STUDENT RESPONSIBILITIES

To ensure timely receipt of correct payments, students should be sure to promptly notify the VA of:

- Any change in enrollment;
- Any change in address;
- Any change in selected reserve status (If an individual changes units or components, both the old and new units must report the change to VA through the components' eligibility data systems.)

In addition, students should use reasonable judgment when accepting and cashing a check. All letters from VA about monthly rates and effective dates should be read carefully. If a student thinks the amount of a VA check is wrong, VA should be contacted **before** cashing the check. Any incorrect checks should be returned to VA.

If a student cashes a check for the wrong amount, he or she will be liable for repayment of any resulting overpayment.

If an individual does not participate satisfactorily in the Selected Reserve, his or her eligibility ends. His or her component can require that a penalty be paid, based on a portion of payments received.

RECOVERY OF OVERPAYMENTS

VA must take prompt and aggressive action to recover overpayments. Students have the right to request a waiver of the overpayment, or verification that the amount is correct. If an overpayment is not repaid or waived, VA may add interest and collection fees to the debt. VA may also take one or more of the following actions to collect the debt:

- Withhold future benefits to apply to the debt;
- Refer the debt to a private collection agency;
- Recover the debt from any Federal income tax refund;
- Recover the debt from the salary (if student is a Federal employee);
- File a lawsuit in Federal court to collect the debt;
- Withhold approval of a VA home loan guarantee.

An individual's reserve component will act to collect penalties caused by unsatisfactory participation in the reserve.

CHANGES IN ENROLLMENT

If a student withdraws from one or more courses after the end of the school's drop period, VA will reduce or stop benefits on the date of reduction or withdrawal. Unless the student can show that the change was due to *mitigating circumstances*, the student may have to repay **all** benefits for the course.

VA defines *mitigating circumstances* as "unavoidable and unexpected events that directly interfere with the pursuit of a course, and which are beyond the student's control.

Examples of reasons VA may accept include:

- Extended illness;
- Severe illness or death in immediate family;
- Unscheduled changes in employment; and
- Lack of child care.

Examples of reasons VA may not accept include:

- Withdrawal to avoid a failing grade;
- Dislike of the instructor; and
- Too many courses attempted.

(VA may ask the student to furnish evidence to support the reason for change, such as physician or employer written statements.)

The first time a student withdraws from up to 6 credit hours, VA will "excuse" the withdrawal, and pay benefits for the period attended.

If a student receives a grade that does not count toward graduation, all benefits for the course may have to be repaid.

If a student receives a non-punitive grade, the school will notify VA, and VA may reduce or stop benefits. The student may not have to repay the benefits if he or she can show that the grades were due to mitigating circumstances.

WORK-STUDY PROGRAMS

Students may be eligible for an additional allowance under a work-study program that allows students to perform work for VA in return for an hourly wage. Students may perform outreach services under VA supervision, prepare and process VA paperwork, work at a VA medical facility or National Cemetery, or perform other approved activities.

Students must attend school at the three-quarter of full-time rate.

VA will select students for the work-study program based on different factors. Such factors include:

- Disability of the student;

- Ability of the student to complete the work-study contract before the end of his or her eligibility for education benefits;
- Job availability within normal commuting distance to the student;
- VA will give the highest priority to a veteran who has a service-connected disability or disabilities rated by VA at 30% or more.

The number of applicants selected will depend on the availability of VA-related work at the school or at VA facilities in the area.

Students may work during or between periods of enrollment, and can arrange with VA to work any number of hours during his or her enrollment. However, the maximum number of hours a student may work is 25 times the number of weeks in the enrollment period.

Students will earn an hourly wage equal to the Federal or State minimum wage, whichever is greater. If a student works at a college or university, the school **may** pay the difference between the amount VA pays and the amount the school normally pays other work-study students doing the same job.

Students interested in taking part in a work-study program must complete VA Form 22-8691, Application for Work-Study Allowance. Completed forms should be sent to the nearest VA regional office.

EDUCATIONAL COUNSELING

VA can provide services to help eligible individuals understand their educational and vocational strengths and weaknesses and to plan:

- An educational or training goal, and the means by which the goal can be reached; or
- An employment goal for which an individual qualifies on the basis of present training or experience.

VA can also help plan an effective job search.

Counseling is available for:

- Service members eligible for VA educational assistance; and
- Service members on active duty and within 180 days of discharge; or
- Veterans with discharges that are not dishonorable, who are within one year from date of discharge.

VOCATIONAL REHABILITATION

Veterans may qualify for Training and Rehabilitation under Chapter 31 of Title 38, United States Code, if:

- The veteran has a service-connected disability or disabilities rated by VA at 20% or more; and
- The veteran received a discharge from active duty that was not dishonorable; and
- The veteran has an employment handicap.

Veterans may also qualify with a service-connected disability or disabilities rated by VA at 10%, and:

- The veteran has a serious employment handicap; or
- The veteran first applied for vocational rehabilitation benefits before November 1, 1990, reapplied after that date, and has an employment handicap.

Vocational rehabilitation helps disabled veterans become independent in daily living. Veterans may also receive assistance in selecting, preparing for, and securing employment that is compatible with their interests, talents, skills, physical capabilities, and goals.

To apply for vocational rehabilitation, VA for 28-1900, Disabled Veterans Application for Vocational Rehabilitation, must be completed and sent to the nearest VA regional office.

APPEAL OF VA DECISION

VA decisions on education benefits may be appealed within one year of the date an individual receives notice of a VA decision. Examples of *VA decisions* include:

- Training time,
- Change of program,
- School or course approval.

If a service member disagrees with a decision about his or her basic eligibility, he or she must contact the unit, National Guard Education Officer, or Army Reserve Education Services Officer. VA does not have authority under the law to reverse eligibility determinations. If the eligibility status is corrected, VA will pay benefits for periods during which the individual was eligible.

CHAPTER 21

LIFE INSURANCE

VA insurance programs were developed to provide insurance benefits for veterans and servicemembers who may not be able to get insurance from private companies because of a service connected disability or because of the extra risks involved in military service.

VA has responsibility for veterans' and servicemembers' life insurance programs. Listed below are the eight life insurance programs managed by VA. The first four programs listed are closed to new issues. The last four are still issuing new policies.

2014 Update: SGLI PREMIUM ADJUSTMENT ANNOUNCED

The VA announced an increase in the monthly premium rate of the Servicemembers' Group Life Insurance (SGLI) program, which became effective July 1, 2014.

The increase made the premiums 7 cents per $1,000 of insurance, up from 6.5 cents.

DIVIDENDS PAID TO USGLI POLICYHOLDERS

Dividends are paid on all but a few USGLI policies.

Reserves set aside in the trust funds continue to earn interest each year in excess of what is needed to pay future claims allowing VA to pay dividends.

DISABILITY PROVISIONS

USGLI policies (except Special Endowment at Age 96) contain a provision that matures the policy upon the insured's total permanent disability. Under this provision:

- Proceeds are payable in installments of $5.75 monthly per $1,000 of insurance, as long as the insured remains totally and permanently disabled, with 240 payments guaranteed.
- If the insured dies before all guaranteed installments have been paid, the balance is payable to his or her named beneficiary.
- No additional premium is charged.
- There is no limit as to the age at which a disability may occur.

FILING A DEATH CLAIM

To file a death claim, the beneficiary should complete "VA Form 29-4125, Claim for One Sum Payment" The completed form should be mailed or faxed, along with a death certificate to:

Department of Veterans Affairs
Regional Office and Insurance Center
PO Box 7208
Philadelphia, PA 19101
Fax: (215) 381-3561

If the beneficiary desires monthly payments instead of one lump sum, additional information is needed. The beneficiary should call the Insurance Center at (800) 669-8477 for instructions.

CUSTOMER SERVICE

Any questions regarding USGLI should be directed to the VA Life Insurance Program at (800) 669-8477.

NATIONAL SERVICE LIFE INSURANCE

(1940-1951) POLICY PREFIX - V, H, N OR AN

The National Service Life Insurance program (NSLI) was established on October 8, 1940 to meet the insurance needs of World War II military personnel and veterans. Like USGLI coverage, insured individuals could keep their NSLI coverage after discharge from service.

Any questions regarding NSLI should be directed to the VA Life Insurance Program at (800) 669-8477.

Over 22 million policies were issued under the NSLI program. The majority of policies VA administers directly are NSLI policies. This program remained open until April 25, 1951, when two new programs were established for Korean War servicemembers and veterans.

The NSLI program provides for:

- A maximum amount of $10,000 insurance coverage. (However, this limit does not include paid-up additional insurance which can be purchased with the annual dividends.);
- Individual policies issued to each policyholder;
- Certain contractual rights whereby a policyholder can bring a suit against VA in a US District Court. Administrative decisions of the Board of Veterans Appeals can be appealed to the Court of Veterans Appeals.

PREMIUM RATES "CAPPED" FOR TERM POLICIES

NSLI "V" term policies can be renewed indefinitely. At the older ages, premium rates increase significantly to cover the higher death rates at those ages.

In 1984, the VA "capped" premium rates at the age 70 rate. This means that a term policyholder's premium will never increase over the age 70 -premium rate.

Effective September 11, 2000, "capped" NSLI term policies receive a termination dividend if a policy lapses, or if the policyholder voluntarily cancels their policy. The termination dividend will be used to purchase paid-up additional whole life insurance.

DIVIDENDS PAID TO NSLI POLICYHOLDERS

After the reserve level requirements are determined by the Insurance Actuarial Staff, any surplus funds are returned to policyholders as a dividend.

DISABILITY PROVISIONS

All NSLI policies provide for

- A waiver of premiums at no extra cost if the insured becomes totally disabled for six months or longer prior to age 65.
- An optional "Total Disability Income Provision" covering disability before age 65, providing a monthly income of up to $100 per month, as long as total disability continues.

"H" INSURANCE

"H" policies were issued between August 1, 1946, and December 31, 1949, to veterans with service-incurred disabilities.

On November 11, 1998, the President signed into law the *Veterans Programs Enhancement Act of 1998* (*Public Law 105-368*), which contained provisions affecting VA benefits. Included in the legislation was the merger of "H" policies into the regular NSLI "V" policies. Under the new law:

- All "H" policies were to be converted to "V" policies by January 1999.
- Converted policies now have the same premium rates and policy provisions as "V" policies.
- "H" policyholders now receive dividends.

FILING A DEATH CLAIM

To file a death claim, the beneficiary should complete "VA Form 29-4125, Claim for One Sum Payment." The completed form should be mailed or faxed, along with a death certificate to:

Department of Veterans Affairs
Regional Office and Insurance Center
PO Box 7208
Philadelphia, PA 19101
Fax: (215) 381-3561

If the beneficiary desires monthly payments instead of one lump sum, additional information is needed. The beneficiary should call the Insurance Center at (800) 669-8477 for instructions.

CUSTOMER SERVICE

Any questions regarding NSLI should be directed to the VA Life Insurance Program at (800) 669-8477.SERVICEMEN'S INDEMNITY INSURANCE

(1951-1956)

In 1951, NSLI was replaced by Servicemen's Indemnity Insurance, which automatically covered active duty servicemembers for $10,000 at no cost to the individual. Servicemembers remained covered for 120 days after their discharge.

VETERANS' SPECIAL LIFE INSURANCE – VSLI (1951-1956) POLICY PREFIX – RS OR W

> *The Veterans' Special Life Insurance program was closed to new issues at the end of 1956.*

Discharged servicemembers who had Servicemen's Indemnity Insurance could replace their coverage with Veterans' Special Life Insurance (VSLI). VSLI was established in 1951 to meet the insurance needs of veterans who served during the Korean Conflict, and the post Korean period through January 1, 1957. The VSLI program allowed these newly discharged servicemembers to apply for $10,000 of contract term insurance. Application had to be made during the 120-day period during which they remained covered by Servicemen's Indemnity Insurance. (The $10,000 policy limit does not include *paid-up additional insurance*, which can be purchased with the annual dividends.)

In the early 1950's, commercial life insurance companies began to view the government's life insurance programs for veterans as competition for their business and began lobbying Congress to remove the government from the life insurance business. As a result, the Veterans' Special Life Insurance program was closed to new issues at the end of 1956.

FEATURES OF "RS" AND "W" POLICIES:

There are two types of VSLI policies:

"RS" - FIVE-YEAR LEVEL PREMIUM TERM POLICIES:

- These were the original policies available in this program.
- "RS" policies could remain in force as 5 Year Level Premium Term beyond the age of 50.
- To provide financial relief from the high premium rates at advanced ages, "RS" term premiums were capped at the age 70-renewal rate effective May 1, 1989. This meant that the annual premium for these policies would not exceed $69.73 per $1,000 of coverage.

Effective September 11, 2000, "capped" VSLI term policies receive a termination dividend if a policy lapses, or if the policyholder voluntarily cancels their policy. The termination dividend will be used to purchase paid-up additional whole life insurance.

"W" - FIVE-YEAR LEVEL PREMIUM TERM POLICIES:

- A 1959 legislative change permitted "RS" policyholders to convert to permanent plans or to exchange their policies for a special lower premium term policy. These newer policies are identified by the prefix "W."

- To avoid "W" term policyholders from keeping their policies into advanced ages (when premiums are very high), these policies had to be converted to permanent plans before age 50, or coverage ceased. There are no longer any "W" term policyholders eligible for this conversion.

Disability Provisions

All VSLI policies provide for:

- A waiver of premiums at no extra cost based on the insured's total disability lasting six months or longer and starting before age 65.
- An optional Total Disability Income Provision covering disability before age 65, providing a monthly income of $10 per $1,000 of insurance, is available at an extra cost.

Filing a Death Claim

To file a death claim, the beneficiary should complete "VA Form 29-4125, Claim for One Sum Payment."

The completed form should be mailed or faxed, along with a death certificate to:

Department of Veterans Affairs
Regional Office and Insurance Center
PO Box 7208
Philadelphia, PA 19101
Fax: (215) 381-3561

If the beneficiary desires monthly payments instead of one lump sum, additional information is needed. The beneficiary should call the Insurance Center at (800) 669-8477 for instructions.

Customer Service

Any questions regarding VSLI should be directed to the VA Life Insurance Program at (800) 669-8477.

SERVICE-DISABLED VETERANS INSURANCE-S-DVI (1951-PRESENT) (POLICY PREFIX - RH OR ARH)

The only new insurance issued between 1957 and 1965 to either servicemembers or veterans was Service-Disabled Veterans Insurance. This insurance was (and still is) available to veterans with a service-connected disability.

S-DVI, also called "RH Insurance" is available in a variety of permanent plans, as well as term insurance. Policies are issued for a maximum face amount of $10,000.

S-DVI is open to veterans separated from the service on or after April 25, 1951, who receive a service-connected disability rating of 0% or greater. New policies are still being issued under this program.

To apply for Supplemental S-DVI, you must file "VA Form 29-0188, Application for Supplemental Service-Disabled Veterans (RH) Life Insurance" or send a letter requesting this insurance over your signature. You must apply for the coverage within one year from notice of the grant of waiver of premiums.

Eligibility For S-DVI Insurance ("RH")

Veterans are eligible to apply for S-DVI if they meet the following four criteria:

- They have received a rating for a service-connected disability (even if only 0%).
- They were released from active duty under any other condition than dishonorable on or after April 25, 1951.
- They are in good health except for any service-related condition.
- They apply for the insurance within two years from the date service-connection is established.

Eligibility For Supplemental S-DVI ("Supplemental RH")

Under the *Veterans Benefits Act of 2010*, and effective October 1, 2011, the amount of supplemental coverage to S-DVI policyholders increased from $20,000 to $30,000.

Premiums may not be waived on this supplemental coverage.

S-DVI policyholders are eligible for this supplemental coverage if:

- They are eligible for a waiver of premiums.
- They apply for the coverage within one year from notice of the grant of waiver.
- Are under age 65.

GRATUITOUS S-DVI ("ARH")

Congress enacted legislation in 1959 to protect veterans who become incompetent from a service-connected disability while eligible to apply for S-DVI, but who die before an application is filed. "ARH" insurance is:

- Issued posthumously;
- Payable to a preferred class of the veteran's relatives;
- Payable in a lump sum only.

Premiums For S-DVI Insurance

The premiums charged for this coverage are:

- Based on the rates a healthy individual would have been charged when the program began in 1951.
- Insufficient to pay all of the claims because the program insures many veterans with severe disabilities.
- Waived for totally disabled veterans (27% of S-DVI policyholders).
- Supplemented on an annual basis by Congressional appropriations.

Effective November 1, 2000, the VA "capped" premium rates at the age 70 rate. This means that a term policyholder's premium will never increase over the age 70 -premium rate.

There are no reserves or surplus funds in this program. Therefore, dividends are *not* paid.

Disability Provisions

S-DVI policies (except supplemental coverage) provide for the following disability benefits:

- A waiver of premiums at no extra premium based on the insured's total disability lasting six months or longer and starting before age 65;
- A total disability premium waiver in cases where the disability commenced prior to the effective date of the policy, providing the disability is service-connected.

The optional Total Disability Income Provision is not available under this program.

Filing A Death Claim

To file a death claim, the beneficiary should complete "VA Form 29-4125, Claim for One Sum Payment." The completed form should be mailed or faxed, along with a death certificate to:

Department of Veterans Affairs
Regional Office and Insurance Center
PO Box 7208
Philadelphia, PA 19101
Fax: (215) 381-3561

If the beneficiary desires monthly payments instead of one lump sum, additional information is needed. The beneficiary should call the Insurance Center at (800) 669-8477 for instructions.

CUSTOMER SERVICE

Any questions regarding USGLI should be directed to the VA Life Insurance Program at (800) 669-8477.

VETERANS' REOPENED INSURANCE - VRI (1965-1966) POLICY PREFIX - J, JR, OR JS

Beginning May 1, 1965, veterans who had been eligible to obtain insurance between October 8, 1940 and January l, 1957, could once again apply for government life insurance. They had one year to apply for this "reopened" insurance, which was available *only* to disabled veterans. Approximately 228,000 VRI policies were issued. No term insurance policies were issued in this program.

The maximum face amount of a policy is $10,000. However, this limit does not include *paid-up additional insurance*, which can be purchased with the dividends that are paid annually on these policies.

PREMIUM RATES

Premium rates for this insurance depend on the nature and severity of the disability.

DISABILITY PROVISIONS

VRI policies provide for:

- A waiver of premium at no extra premium based on the insured's total disability lasting six months or longer, and starting prior to age 65.
- An optional total disability income benefit covering disability occurring before age 65 for "J" policyholders. (This is **not** available on policies prefixed by "JR" or "JS".) Payments are made at the rate of $10 monthly per $1,000 of coverage, as long as the insured remains totally disabled.

DIVIDENDS PAID TO VRI POLICYHOLDERS

The VRI program began paying dividends in 1980 in order to more equitably distribute the surplus earnings of the program.

FILING A DEATH CLAIM

To file a death claim, the beneficiary should complete "VA Form 29-4125, Claim for One Sum Payment." The completed form should be mailed or faxed, along with a death certificate to:

Department of Veterans Affairs
Regional Office and Insurance Center
PO Box 7208
Philadelphia, PA 19101
Fax: (215) 381-3561

If the beneficiary desires monthly payments instead of one lump sum, additional information is needed. The beneficiary should call the Insurance Center at (800) 669-8477 for instructions.

CUSTOMER SERVICE

Any questions regarding VRI should be directed to the VA Life Insurance Program at (800) 669-8477.

SERVICEMEMBERS' GROUP LIFE INSURANCE - SGLI (1965-PRESENT)

SGLI is supervised by the Department of Veterans Affairs and is administered by the Office of Servicemembers' Group Life Insurance (OSGLI) under terms of a group insurance contract.

Effective December 1, 2005, a new program of insurance was created under SGLI, called Traumatic Servicemembers' Group Life Insurance (TSGLI). This coverage provides servicemembers protection against loss due to traumatic injuries and is designed to provide financial assistance to members so their loved ones can be with them during their recovery from their injuries. The coverage ranges from $25,000 to $100,000 depending on the nature of the injury.

(See following section for further information regarding Traumatic Injury Coverage.)

ELIGIBILITY FOR SGLI

Full-time coverage is available for:

- Commissioned, warrant and enlisted members of the Army, Navy, Air Force, Marine Corps and Coast Guard;
- Commissioned members of the National Oceanic and Atmospheric Administration and the Public Health Service;

- Cadets or midshipmen of the four United States Service Academies;
- Ready Reservists scheduled to perform at least 12 periods of inactive training per year.
- Members of the Individual Ready Reserves who volunteer for assignment to a mobilization category.
- Part-time coverage is available for eligible members of the Reserves who do not qualify for full-time coverage.

Coverage Amounts

- Effective September 1, 2005 coverage in the SGLI Program increased from $250,000 to $400,000. Coverage must be elected in $50,000 increments.
- A special death gratuity of $150,000 was approved for survivors of servicemembers who:
- Died from October 7, 2001 to September 1, 2005, and
- Died while on active duty.

SGLI coverage is:

- Automatic at the time of entry into a period of active duty or reserve status.
- Available in $50,000 increments up to the maximum of $400,000 of insurance.

Members may decline coverage or may elect reduced coverage by contacting their personnel officer and completing "Form 8286, SGLI Election and Certificate." If such a member later wishes to obtain or increase coverage, proof of good health will be required.

NOTE: *Reservists called to active duty, are* ***automatically*** *insured for $400,000 regardless of whether or not they had previously declined coverage, or elected a lesser amount of coverage while on reserve duty.*

Coverage Periods

Full-time SGLI coverage for members on active duty or active duty for training and members of the Ready Reserve will terminate:

The 120th day after separation or release from duty, or separation or release from assignment to a unit or position of the Ready Reserve;

For members who are totally disabled on the date of separation or release, at the end of the last day of one year following separation or release or at the end of the day on which the insured ceases to be totally disabled, whichever is earlier, but in no event earlier than

120 days following separation or release from such duty; **(NOTE: Refer to important updated information following #4, below.)**

At the end of the 31st day of a continuous period of:

Absence without leave;
Confinement by military authorities under a court-martial sentence involving total forfeiture of pay and allowances; or
Confinement by civilian authorities under sentence adjudged by a civilian court.
*Note: Any insurance terminated as the result of the absence or confinement, together with any beneficiary designation in effect at the time the insurance was terminated, will be automatically restored as of the date the member returns to duty with pay.

The last day of the month in which the member files with the uniformed service, written notice of an election not to be insured.

SGLI Disability Extension Increased to Two Years

On June 15, 2006, the President signed P.L. 109- 233, the *Veterans' Housing Opportunity & Benefits Improvement Act of 2006*. The law extends the period of Servicemembers' Group Life Insurance (SGLI) coverage for totally disabled veterans following separation from active duty or active duty for training to the earlier of:

- The date on which the insured ceases to be totally disabled; or
- The date that is two years after separation or release,

The law makes identical changes with respect to certain reserve assignments in which the individual performs active duty or volunteers for assignment to a mobilization category.

The SGLI Disability Extension is available to you if you are totally disabled at time of discharge. To be considered totally disabled, you must have a disability that prevents you from being gainfully employed OR have one of the following conditions, regardless of your employment status:

- Permanent loss of use of both hands
- Permanent loss of use of both feet
- Permanent loss of use of both eyes
- Permanent loss of use of one hand and one foot
- Permanent loss of use of one foot and one eye
- Permanent loss of use of one hand and one eye
- Total loss of hearing in both ears
- Organic loss of speech (lost ability to express oneself, both by voice and whisper, through normal organs for speech - being able to speak with an artificial appliance is disregarded in determination of total disability)

Part-time coverage terminates as follows:

Part-time coverage is in effect only on the days of active duty or active duty for training, and the hours of inactive duty training, including period of travel to and from duty. A temporary termination of coverage occurs at the end of each such period of duty, including travel time, and coverage is resumed at the commencement of the next period of covered duty or travel.

When part-time coverage is extended for 120 days as the result of a disability, the extended coverage terminates at the end of the 120th day following the Reservist active or inactive period during which the disability was incurred or aggravated.
Unless extended for 120 days because of disability as referred to above, eligibility for part-time coverage terminates at the end of the last day of the member's obligation to perform such duty.

If a member files with the uniformed service a written notice of an election not to be insured, coverage terminates on the last day of the period of active duty or active duty for training, or at the end of the period of inactive duty training, including travel time while returning from such duty during which the election is filed. If the election is filed with a member's uniformed service other than during a period of active duty, active duty for training, or inactive duty the coverage is terminated immediately.

BENEFICIARY SELECTION

Any beneficiary can be named. If none is selected, the insurance is distributed, by law, in the following order:

- Spouse; or
- Children; or
- Parents; or
- Executor of estate; or
- Other next of kin.

An insured should designate a beneficiary by completing "Form SGVL 8286, Servicemembers' Group Life Insurance Election and Certificate." The completed form should be submit to the individual's uniformed service.

OPTIONS FOR PAYMENT OF POLICY PROCEEDS

SGLI proceeds can be paid in a lump sum ***or*** over a 36-month period.

Alliance Account

If the proceeds are to be paid in a lump sum then beneficiaries of SGLI and VGLI will receive the payment of their insurance proceeds via an "*Alliance Account*". Rather than the traditional single check for the full amount of insurance proceeds, the beneficiary receives a checkbook for an interest bearing account from which the beneficiary can write a check for any amount from $250 up to the full amount of the proceeds. The Alliance Account:

- Earns interest at a competitive rate;
- Is guaranteed by Prudential;
- Gives the beneficiary time to make important financial decisions while their funds are secure and earning interest ;
- Gives them instant access to their money at all times.

ACCELERATED BENEFITS

On November 11, 1998, the President signed legislation authorizing the payment of "Accelerated Benefits" in the SGLI and VGLI programs subject to the following:

- Terminally ill insureds will have access of up to 50% of the face amount of their coverage during their lifetime.
- This money will be available in increments of $5,000.
- An insured must have a medical prognosis of life expectancy of 9 months or less.

INSURANCE OPTIONS AFTER SEPARATION FROM SERVICE

When released from active duty or the Reserve, members with full-time SGLI coverage can convert their coverage to Veterans Group Life Insurance ***or*** to an individual commercial life insurance policy with any one of 99 participating commercial insurance companies.

FILING DEATH CLAIMS

A beneficiary may file a claim for VGLI proceeds by submitting *Form SGLV 8283, Claim For Death Benefits*, to:

Office of Servicemembers' Group Life Insurance
213 Washington Avenue
Newark, NJ 07102-2999

TAXATION

SGLI proceeds that are payable at the death of the insured are excluded from gross income for tax purposes. (The value of the proceeds, however, may be included in determining the value of an estate, and that estate may ultimately be subject to tax.)

If SGLI proceeds are paid to a beneficiary in 36 equal installments, the interest portion included in these installments is also exempt from taxation. In addition, delayed settlement interest (interest accrued from the date of the insured's death to the date of settlement) is also exempt from taxation.

A beneficiary is not required to report to the Internal Revenue Service any installment interest or delayed settlement interest received in addition to the proceeds.

CUSTOMER SERVICE

Any questions regarding SGLI should be directed to the office of Servicemembers' Group Life Insurance (OSGLI) at (800) 419-1473.

TRAUMATIC INJURY PROTECTION UNDER SERVICEMEMBERS' GROUP LIFE INSURANCE (TSGLI)

TSGLI is a program that provides automatic traumatic injury coverage to all servicemembers covered under the Servicemembers' Group Life Insurance (SGLI) program. Every member who has SGLI also has TSGLI effective December 1, 2005. This coverage applies to active duty members, reservists, funeral honors duty and one-day muster duty. The premium for TSGLI is a flat rate of $1 per month for most service members. This benefit is also provided retroactively for members who incur severe losses as a result of traumatic injury between October 7, 2001 and December 1, 2005 if the loss was the direct result of injuries incurred in Operations Enduring Freedom or Iraqi Freedom. For the purposes of TSGLI only, "incurred in Operation Enduring Freedom or Operation Iraqi Freedom" means that the member must have been deployed outside the United States on orders in support of OEF or OIF or serving in a geographic location that qualified the service member for the Combat Zone Tax Exclusion under the Internal Revenue Service Code.

VA has amended its regulations to add certain genitourinary injuries to the Schedule of Covered Losses under the Servicemembers' Group Life Insurance Traumatic Injury Protection Program, or TSGLI.

The service member is the beneficiary of TSGLI. The member cannot name someone other than himself or herself as the TSGLI beneficiary. If the member is incompetent, the benefit will be paid to his or her guardian or attorney-in-fact. If the service member is deceased, the TSGLI payment will be made to the beneficiary or beneficiaries of the member's basic SGLI.

TSGLI coverage will pay a benefit of between $25,000 and $100,000 depending on the loss directly resulting from the traumatic injury.

In 2011 the VA announced that servicemembers with severe injuries to the genitourinary organs are now eligible for Servicemembers' Group Life Insurance Traumatic Injury Protection (TSGLI). The first payments for eligible veterans and servicemembers began December 1, 2011. Eligibility is retroactive to injuries received on or after October 7, 2001.

EXPANSION OF COVERED LOSSES

1) Loss of Sight
Loss of Sight lasting 120 days or more is considered as "permanent", qualifying the service member for the same payment rate as for permanent loss of sight ($100,000 for both eyes, $50,000 for one eye).

2) Uniplegia
Uniplegia (complete and total paralysis of one limb) has been added to the schedule of losses with payment at $50,000.

3) Amputation of the Hand
The definition of amputation of the hand has been expanded to include loss of four fingers (on the same hand) or loss of thumb, with payment remaining at $50,000 for one affected hand and $100,000 for both hands.

4) Amputation of the Foot
The definition of amputation of the foot has been expanded to include loss of all toes, with the payment remaining at $50,000 for one affected foot and $100,000 for both feet.

5) Loss of Four Toes
A new category has been created for loss of four toes (on the same foot and not including the big toe) with payment at $25,000 for one affected foot and $50,000 for both feet.

6) Loss of Big Toe
A new category has been created for the loss of the big toe, with payment at $25,000 for one affected foot and $50,000 for both feet.

7) Limb Salvage
Coverage has been expanded to include limb salvage (multiple surgeries intended to save a limb rather than amputate) with payment equivalent to amputation.
8) Burns
The burn standard, currently 3rd degree (full thickness) burns to at least 30% of face or body, has been expanded to include 2nd degree (partial thickness) burns to at least 20% of the face or body.

9) Hospitalization as a Proxy for ADL Loss
Continuous 15-day inpatient hospital care is deemed a proxy for the first ADL eligibility period for OTI (Other Traumatic Injury) and TBI (Traumatic Brain Injury) claims.

10) Facial Reconstruction
Facial Reconstruction, required as a result of traumatic avulsion of the face or jaw that causes discontinuity defects, has been added to the schedule of losses, with payment levels of $25,000 to $75,000, depending upon the severity of the injury.

11.) Losses to the Genitourinary System
Effective beginning in 2011, the VA amended its regulations to add certain genitourinary system injuries to the Schedule of Covered Losses. These are injuries that occur to the genitals or urinary system. Payments range from $25,000 to $50,000 and are retroactive to October 7, 2001. The new losses added to the TSGLI Schedule of Covered Losses include the following:

- Anatomical loss of penis
- Permanent loss of use of the penis
- Anatomical loss of one or both of the testicles
- Permanent loss of use of both testicles
- Anatomical loss of the vulva, uterus or vaginal canal
- Permanent loss of use of the vulva or vaginal canal
- Anatomical loss of one or both ovaries
- Permanent loss of use of both ovaries
- Total and permanent loss of urinary system function

SCHEDULE OF LOSSES

For losses listed in Part I, multiple injuries resulting from a single traumatic event may be combined with each other and treated as one loss for purposes of a single payment (except where noted otherwise), however, the total payment amount MAY NOT exceed $100,000.

For losses listed in Part II, payment amounts MAY NOT be combined with payment amounts in Part I - only the higher amount will be paid. The total payment amount MAY NOT exceed $100,000 for multiple injuries resulting from a single traumatic event.

PART I

	Loss	Payment Amount
1.	**Sight:** Total and permanent loss of sight OR loss of sight that has lasted 120 days • For each eye	$50,000
2.	**Hearing:** Total and permanent loss of hearing • For one ear • For both ears	$25,000 $100,000
3.	**Speech:** Total and permanent loss of speech	$50,000
4.	**Quadriplegia:** complete paralysis of all four limbs	$100,000

5.	**Hemiplegia:** complete paralysis of the upper and lower limbs on one side of the body	$100,000
6.	**Paraplegia:** complete paralysis of both lower limbs	$100,000
7.	**Uniplegia:** complete paralysis of one limb* **Note: Payment for uniplegia of arm cannot be combined with loss 9, 10 or 14 for the same arm. Payment for uniplegia of leg cannot be combined with loss 11, 12, 13 or 15 for the same leg.*	$50,000
8.	**Burns:** 2nd degree or worse burns to at least 20% of the body including the face OR, at least 20% of the face	$100,000
9.	**Amputation of hand:** Amputation at or above the wrist • For each hand* **Note: Payment for loss 9 cannot be combined with payment for loss 10 for the same hand.*	$50,000
10.	**Amputation of 4 fingers on 1 hand OR thumb alone:** Amputation at or above the metacarpophalangeal joint • For each hand	$50,000
11.	**Amputation of foot:** Amputation at or above the ankle • For each foot* **Note: Payment for loss 11 cannot be combined with payments for losses 12 or 13 for the same foot.*	$50,000
12.	**Amputation of all toes including the big toe on 1 foot:** Amputation at or above the metatarsophalangeal joint • For each foot **Note: Payment for loss 12 cannot be combined with payments for loss 13 for the same foot.*	$50,000
13.	**Amputation of big toe only, OR other 4 toes on 1 foot:** Amputation at or above the metatarsophalangeal joint • For each foot	$25,000
14.	**Limb salvage of arm:** Salvage of arm in place of amputation • For each arm* **Note: Payment for loss 14 cannot be combined with payments for losses 9 or 10 for the same arm.*	$50,000
15.	**Limb salvage of leg:** Salvage of leg in place of amputation • For each leg* **Note: Payment for loss 15 cannot be combined with payments for losses 11, 12 or 13 for the same leg.*	$50,000

16.	**Facial Reconstruction** – reconstructive surgery to correct traumatic avulsions of the face or jaw that cause discontinuity defects.	
	• **Jaw** – surgery to correct discontinuity loss of the upper or lower jaw	$75,000
	• **Nose** – surgery to correct discontinuity loss of 50% or more of the cartilaginous nose	$50,000
	• **Lips** – surgery to correct discontinuity loss of 50% or more of the upper or lower lip ○ For one lip ○ For both lips	 $50,000 $75,000
	• **Eyes** – surgery to correct discontinuity loss of 30% or more of the periorbita For each eye	$25,000
	• **Facial Tissue** – surgery to correct discontinuity loss of the tissue in 50% or more of any of the following facial subunits: forehead, temple, zygomatic, mandibular, infraorbital or chin. For each facial subunit	$25,000
	Note 1: Injuries listed under facial reconstruction may be combined with each other, but the maximum benefit for facial reconstruction may not exceed $75,000. *Note 2: Any injury or combination of injuries under facial reconstruction may also be combined with other injuries listed in Part I and treated as one loss, provided that all injuries are the result of a single traumatic event. However, the total payment amount may not exceed $100,000.*	
17.	**Coma from traumatic injury AND/OR Traumatic Brain Injury resulting in inability to perform at least 2 Activities of Daily Living (ADL)** • at 15th consecutive day of coma or ADL loss • at 30th consecutive day of coma or ADL loss • at 60th consecutive day of coma or ADL loss • at 90th consecutive day of coma or ADL loss	 $25,000 an additional $25,000 an additional $25,000 an additional $25,000
18.	**Hospitalization due to traumatic brain injury** • at 15th consecutive day of hospitalization *Note 1: Payment for hospitalization replaces the first payment period in loss 17.*	$25,000

	Note 2: Duration of hospitalization includes dates on which member is transported from the injury site to a facility described in § 9.20(e)(6)(xiii), admitted to the facility, transferred between facilities, and discharged from the facility.	
19.	**Genitourinary Losses**	
	Anatomical loss of the penis Anatomical loss of the penis is defined as amputation of the glans penis or any portion of the shaft of the penis above the glans penis (i.e. closer to the body) or damage to the glans penis or shaft of the penis that requires reconstructive surgery.	50,000
	Permanent loss of use of the penis Permanent loss of use of the penis is defined as damage to the glans penis or shaft of the penis that results in complete loss of the ability to perform sexual intercourse that is reasonably certain to continue throughout the lifetime of the member.	50,000
	Anatomical loss of one testicle Anatomical loss of the testicle(s) is defined as the amputation of, or damage to, one or both testicles that requires testicular salvage, reconstructive surgery, or both.	25,000
	Anatomical loss of both testicles See above – Same definition as anatomical loss of one testicle	50,000
	Permanent loss of use of both testicles Permanent loss of use of both testicles is defined as damage to both testicles resulting in the need for hormonal replacement therapy that is medically required and reasonably certain to continue throughout the lifetime of the member.	50,000
	Anatomical loss of the vulva, uterus, or vaginal canal Anatomical loss of the vulva, uterus, or vaginal canal is defined as the complete or partial amputation of the vulva, uterus, or vaginal canal or damage to the vulva, uterus, or vaginal canal that requires reconstructive surgery.	50,000
	Permanent loss of use of the vulva or vaginal canal Permanent loss of use of the vulva or vaginal canal is defined as damage to the vulva or vaginal canal that results in complete loss of the ability to perform sexual intercourse that is reasonably certain to continue throughout the lifetime of the member.	50,000

	Anatomical loss of one ovary Anatomical loss of the ovary(ies) is defined as the amputation of one or both ovaries or damage to one or both ovaries that requires ovarian salvage, reconstructive surgery, or both.	25,000
	Anatomical loss of both ovaries See above – Same definition as anatomical loss of one ovary.	50,000
	Permanent loss of use of both ovaries Permanent loss of use of both ovaries is defined as damage to both ovaries resulting in the need for hormonal replacement therapy that is medically required and reasonably certain to continue throughout the lifetime of the member.	50,000
	Total and permanent loss of urinary system function Total and permanent loss of urinary system function is defined as damage to the urethra, ureter(s), both kidneys, bladder, or urethral sphincter muscle(s) that requires urinary diversion and/or hemodialysis, either of which is reasonably certain to continue throughout the lifetime of the member.	50,000
	Note 1: Losses due to genitourinary injuries may be combined with each other, but the maximum benefit for genitourinary losses may not exceed $50,000. Note 2: Any genitourinary loss may be combined with other (TSGLI) injuries listed in § 9.20(f)(1) through (18) and treated as one loss, provided that all losses are the result of a single traumatic event. However, the total payment may not exceed $100,000.	

PART II

	Loss	Payment Amount
20.	**Traumatic injury resulting in inability to perform at least 2 Activities of Daily Living (ADL)** • at 30th consecutive day of ADL loss • at 60th consecutive day of ADL loss • at 90th consecutive day of ADL loss	$25,000 an additional $25,000 an additional $25,000

	• at 120th consecutive day of ADL loss	an additional $25,000
21.	**Hospitalization due to traumatic injury** • at 15th consecutive day of hospitalization *Note 1: Payment for hospitalization replaces the first payment period in loss 19. Note 2: Duration of hospitalization includes dates on which member is transported from the injury site to a facility described in § 9.20(e)(6)(xiii), admitted to the facility, transferred between facilities, and discharged from the facility.*	$25,000

SERVICEMEMBERS' GROUP LIFE INSURANCE FAMILY COVERAGE

The *Veterans' Opportunities Act of 2001* extended life insurance coverage to spouses and children of members insured under the SGLI program, effective November 1, 2001.

AMOUNT OF COVERAGE

Eligible individuals may purchase up to $100,000 of SGLI coverage for a spouse, in increments of $10,000. However, individuals may not purchase more SGLI coverage for a spouse than he or she has for him/herself.

Each dependent child of every active duty servicemember or reservist who is insured under SGLI is automatically insured for $10,000.

ELIGIBILITY

Family coverage is available for the spouses and children of:

- Active duty servicemembers; and
- Members of the Ready Reserve of a uniformed service.

Note: *Family coverage is available only for members insured under the SGLI program. Family coverage is not available for those insured under the VGLI program.*

PREMIUMS

SGLI coverage for children is free. For monthly premiums for spouses, individuals should call (800) 419-1473.

DEPENDENT CHILD COVERAGE EXTENDED TO INCLUDE STILLBORN CHILDREN

Public law 110-389 expanded the Servicemembers' Group life Insurance (SGLI) program to include a member's "stillborn child" as an insurable dependent. SGLI dependent coverage provides for a $10,000 payment to the insured service member upon the death of the member's dependent child. The law was enacted October 10, 2008, and on November 18, 2009, regulations implementing section 402 of the *Veterans' Benefits Improvement Act of 2008*, were published in the Federal Register, and immediately went into effect. This change applies only for stillbirths on or after October 10, 2008, the effective date of PL 110-389

DECLINING COVERAGE

If an individual does not want insurance coverage for a spouse, or wants a reduced amount of coverage, he or she must complete "form SGLV-82861, Family Coverage Election", and submit it to his or her personnel officer.

TERMINATION OF COVERAGE

Coverage for a spouse ends 120 days after any of the following events:

- The date elected in writing to terminate a spouse's coverage;
- The date elected in writing to terminate the service member's own coverage;
- The date of the service member's death;
- The date the service member's coverage terminates;
- The date of divorce.

A spouse can covert his or her coverage to a policy with a commercial company within 120 days following one of the events listed above. He or she should contact the Office of Servicemembers' Group Life Insurance at (800) 419-1473.

Coverage for a service member's children ends 120 days after any of the following events:

- The date elected in writing to terminate the service member's own coverage;
- The date the service member separates from service;
- The date of the service member's death;

- The date the child is no longer the service member's dependent.
- No conversion options are available to children.

Payment of Proceeds

The service member is paid the proceeds due to the death of a spouse or child. If the service member were to die before payment could be made, the proceeds of a spouse or child claim would be paid to the member's beneficiary, as designated by the member.

VETERANS' GROUP LIFE INSURANCE – VGLI (1974-PRESENT)

VMLI is issued to those severely disabled veterans and servicemembers who have received grants for specially adapted housing from VA. These grants are issued to veterans and servicemembers whose movement or vision is substantially impaired because of their disabilities.

Policyholders have three options for their VMLI coverage. They may decline the increase and retain their pre-October level of VMLI coverage and premium, accept the maximum amount of VMLI coverage for which they are eligible, or select a different amount of VMLI coverage. Coverage may not exceed the maximum allowed by law, or their mortgage balance, whichever is less.

VGLI, like SGLI, is supervised by the Department of Veterans Affairs, but is administered by the Office of Servicemembers' Group Life Insurance (OSGLI). VGLI provides for the conversion of Servicemembers' Group Life Insurance to a five-year renewable term policy of insurance protection after a service member's separation from service.

Effective April 11, 2011, VGLI insureds who are under age 60 and have less than $400,000 in coverage can purchase up to $25,000 of additional coverage on each five-year anniversary of their coverage, up to the maximum $400,000. No medical underwriting is required for the additional coverage.

Eligibility For VGLI

Full-time coverage is available for the following members:

- Full-time SGLI insureds that are released from active duty or the Reserves, or;
- Ready Reservists who have part-time SGLI coverage, and who, while performing active duty or inactive duty for training for a period of less than 31 days, incur a disability or aggravate a preexisting disability that makes them uninsurable at standard premium rates, or;

- Members of the Individual Ready Reserve (IRR) and Inactive National Guard (ING), or;
- A member of the Public Health Service (PHS) or Inactive Reserve Corps (IRC), or;
- A member who had part-time SGLI and who, while performing duty (or traveling directly to or from duty), suffered an injury or disability which renders him/her uninsurable at standard premium rates.

Coverage Amounts

VGLI is issued in multiples of $10,000 up to a maximum of $400,000, but not for more than the amount of SGLI coverage the member had in force at the time of separation from active duty or the reserves.

VGLI Renewal

Members may renew their VGLI coverage under the following conditions:

- Members who have separated from service may renew their VGLI coverage for life in 5-year term periods.
- Members of the IRR or ING may renew their VGLI for additional 5-year term periods, as long as they remain in the IRR or ING.
- Rather than renew, a member also has the right at any time to **convert** VGLI to an individual commercial life insurance policy with any one of 99 participating commercial insurance companies.

Increasing VGLI Coverage

- You can increase your VGLI coverage by up to $25,000 on the five-year anniversary date of your coverage policy if you meet all of the following criteria:
- You have an active VGLI policy.
- You currently have less than $400,000 of VGLI.
- You will be under age 60 on your next policy anniversary date.
- You must request the increase during the 120-day period prior to the 5-year anniversary of your policy
- For more information on increasing your VGLI coverage, contact the Office of Servicemembers' Group Life Insurance online at osgli.osgli@prudential.com or by calling 1-800-419-1473.

How To Apply For VGLI

VGLI applications are mailed to eligible members, generally within 60 days after separation, and again shortly before the end of the 16-month application period. Applications are mailed to the address shown on the member's DD-Form 214 or equivalent separation orders. ***It is the member's responsibility, however, to apply within the time limits, even if they do not receive an application in the mail.***

Applications should be mailed to:

Office Of Servicemembers' Group Life Insurance
P.O. Box 5000
Millville, New Jersey 08332-9928.

Time Limits To Apply For VGLI

To be eligible, a member must apply for VGLI within the following time limits:

- Ordinarily, a member must submit an application to the OSGLI with the required premium within 120 days following separation from service.
- If a member is totally disabled at the time of separation from active duty and is granted extended free SGLI coverage, he or she may apply for VGLI anytime during the one-year period of extension.
- Individuals who are assigned to the IRR and ING have 120 days after assignment to apply, without evidence of good health, and one year after that with evidence of good health.
- If an application or the initial premium has not been submitted within the time limits above, VGLI may still be granted if an application, the initial premium and **evidence of insurability** (good health) are submitted to OSGLI within 1 year and 120 days following termination of SGLI. **Applications will not be accepted after one year and 120 days.**
- An application for an incompetent member may be made by a guardian, committee, conservator or curator. In the absence of a court appointed representative, the application may be submitted by a family member or anyone acting on the member's behalf.

VGLI Premiums Rates

VGLI premium rates are determined by age group and amount of insurance. To lessen the high cost of term insurance at the older ages, a Decreasing Term Option is available, starting at age group 60 to 64. Under this option an insured pays a level premium for life, while the insurance amount declines by 25% for three subsequent five-year renewals. At that point, coverage remains level at 25% of the original insurance amount.

Payment Of Premiums

Once the VGLI application is approved, the OSGLI will send the insured a certificate and a supply of monthly premium payment coupons.

Premiums may be paid:

- Monthly;
- Quarterly;
- Semiannually;
- Annually;
- By monthly allotment from military retirement pay;
- By monthly deduction from VA compensation payments.

If the insured does not pay the premium when it is due, or within a grace period of 60 days, the VGLI coverage will lapse. If VGLI lapsed due to failure to pay the premiums on time, the insured will receive a notification of the lapse and a reinstatement form. The insured may apply to reinstate coverage at any time within 5 years of the date of the unpaid premium. If the insured applies for reinstatement within 6 months from the date of lapse, the individual only needs to provide evidence that he or she is in the same state of health on the date of reinstatement as on the date of lapse. Otherwise, the individual may need to provide proof of good health.

Beneficiary Selection

Any beneficiary can be named. If none is selected, the insurance is distributed, by law, in the following order:

- Spouse, or
- Children, or
- Parents, or
- Executor of estate, or
- Other next of kin.

To name a beneficiary, the insured must submit "Form SGLV 8712, Beneficiary Designation-Veterans' Group Life Insurance." The completed form should be sent to:

Office of Servicemembers' Group Life Insurance
213 Washington Avenue
Newark, NJ 07102-2999

When an insured converts SGLI to VGLI following separation from service, a new beneficiary designation form must be completed. If a new form is not filed, the SGLI beneficiary designation will be considered the VGLI designation for up to 60 days after the effective date of the VGLI. If a new beneficiary is not designated after this 60-day period, the proceeds would be paid "By Law" under the order of precedence in the law.

ALLIANCE ACCOUNT

VGLI proceeds can be paid in a lump sum or over a 36-month period.
If the proceeds are to be paid in a lump sum then beneficiaries of SGLI and VGLI will receive the payment of their insurance proceeds via an "Alliance Account".

Rather than the traditional single check for the full amount of insurance proceeds, the beneficiary receives a checkbook for an interest bearing account from which the beneficiary can write a check for any amount from $250 up to the full amount of the proceeds. The Alliance Account:

- Earns interest at a competitive rate;
- Is guaranteed by Prudential;
- Gives the beneficiary time to make important financial decisions while their funds are secure and earning interest;
- Gives them instant access to their money at all times.

ACCELERATED BENEFITS

On November 11, 1998, the President signed legislation authorizing the payment of "Accelerated Benefits" in the SGLI and VGLI programs subject to the following:

- Terminally ill insureds will have access of up to 50 percent of the face amount of their coverage during their lifetime.
- This money will be available in increments of $5,000.
- An insured must have a medical prognosis of life expectancy of 9 months or less.

FILING DEATH CLAIMS

A beneficiary may file a claim for VGLI proceeds by submitting "Form SGLV 8283," Claim For Death Benefits, to:

Office of Servicemembers' Group Life Insurance
213 Washington Avenue
Newark, NJ 07102-2999

TAXATION

VGLI proceeds are exempt from taxation. Any installment interest or delayed settlement interest that a beneficiary receives in addition to the proceed is also exempt from taxation, and does not need to be reported to the IRS.

Customer Service

Any questions regarding VGLI should be directed to the office of Servicemembers' Group Life Insurance (OSGLI) at (800) 419-1473.

VETERANS' MORTGAGE LIFE INSURANCE – VMLI (1971-PRESENT)

The Veterans' Mortgage Life Insurance (VMLI) program began in 1971, and is designed to provide financial protection to cover eligible veterans' home mortgages in the event of death. VMLI is issued to those severely disabled veterans, under age 70, who have received grants for Specially Adapted Housing from VA. (Refer to Chapter 4 of this book for information regarding Specially Adapted Housing.) **Veterans must apply for VMLI before their 70th birthday.**

> *Effective January 1, 2012, the maximum amount of VMLI coverage was increased to $200,000.*
>
> *Any veteran whose mortgage balance was over $150,000 at the time they obtained VMLI coverage is eligible for the increase.*

The *Veterans Benefits Act of 2010* increased the maximum amount of VMLI coverage from $90,000 to $150,000, which became effective October 1, 2011. On January 1, 2012, the amount increased from $150,000 to 200,000, under the same law. The insurance is payable if the veteran dies before the mortgage is paid off. VA will pay the amount of money still owed on the mortgage up to $200,000.

The insurance is payable only to the mortgage lender. The day-to-day operations of the program are handled by the Philadelphia VAROIC.

Coverage Amounts

VMLI coverage decreases as the insured's mortgage falls below $90,000. This reduced coverage cannot be reinstated. However, if the home is sold and a new home is purchased the veteran becomes eligible once again for the maximum amount of coverage.

Payment Of VMLI Proceeds

Certain conditions apply to the payment of VMLI benefits:

- The insurance is payable at the death of the veteran only to the mortgage holder.
- If the title of the property is shared with anyone other than the veteran's spouse, the insurance coverage is only for the percentage of the title that is in the veteran's name.

- No insurance is payable if the mortgage is paid off before the death of the insured or if it was paid off by other mortgage insurance before the VMLI payment is made.

The insurance will be canceled for any of the following conditions:

- The mortgage is paid in full.
- Termination of the veteran's ownership of the property securing the loan.
- The request of the veteran.
- Failure of the veteran to submit timely statements or other required information.

PREMIUMS

Premiums are determined by the insurance age of the veteran, the outstanding balance of the mortgage at the time of application, and the remaining length of time the mortgage has to run. Veterans who desire insurance will be advised of the correct premium when it is determined.

Premiums ***must*** be paid by deduction from the veteran's monthly compensation or pension payments, if the veteran is receiving such payments. If such payments are not being received the veteran may make direct payments, on a monthly, quarterly, semiannual, or annual basis, to the VA Insurance Center in Philadelphia, Pennsylvania.

DIVIDEND OPTIONS

If a policyholder is eligible for a dividend, he or she may choose from several dividend options that are available:

- **Cash**, paid to policyholder by US Treasury check.
- **Credit**, held in account for the insured with interest. Can be used to prevent policy lapse. Will be refunded upon the insured's request, or will be included in the award to the beneficiary(ies) at the time of the insured's death.
- **Paid-Up Additions (PUA'S)**, used as a net single premium to purchase additional paid-up insurance. Available only on "V," "RS," "W," "J," "JR," and "JS" policies. PUA's will be whole life insurance if the basic insurance is an endowment policy.
- **Deposit**, held in account for insured with interest. Available only on permanent plan policies. Considered part of the policy's cash value for the purpose of purchasing reduced paid-up insurance, or if the policy lapses, extended insurance (except for "K" or "JS" policies). Will be refunded upon the insured's request. Will be included in the award to the beneficiary(ies) at the time of the insured's death.
- **Premium**, applied to pay premiums in advance.

- **Indebtedness**, applied toward a loan or lien on a policy.
- **Net Cash**, used to pay an annual premium with any remainder paid to the policyholder under the cash option.
- **Net PUA**, used to pan an annual premium with any remainder used to purchase paid-up additional insurance.
- **Net Loan-Lien**, used to pay an annual premium with any remainder used to reduce an outstanding loan or lien.

To change the method in which dividends are paid, individuals should speak with an Insurance Specialist at (800) 669-8477

MISCELLANEOUS INFORMATION ABOUT GOVERNMENT LIFE INSURANCE POLICIES

Power of Attorney is not acceptable for executing a change of beneficiary for government life insurance, even if certain state statutes allow it. Only a court appointed guardian that is recognized by state statutes can execute a beneficiary designation. If the state statute does not give the guardian broad powers to authorize a beneficiary change, a specific court order is needed to effectuate a change.

Assignment of government life insurance is not allowed, for any reason, nor can ownership of a policy be transferred. Only the insured can exercise the rights and privileges inherent in the ownership of the policy.

Policy Loans are available on permanent plans of insurance. The policyholder can take up to 94% of the reserve value of the policy, less any indebtedness. The policy cannot be lapsed, and premiums must be paid or waived at least one year before a policy has a loan value. Changes in interest rates are made on October 1 of each year, if warranted. Rate changes are tied to the "ten year constant maturities", U.S. Treasury securities index.

A policyholder can apply for a loan by filing *VA Form 29-1546, Application for Policy Loan.* The completed form can be faxed to (215) 381-3580, or mailed to:

Department of Veterans Affairs
Regional Office and Insurance Center
PO Box 7327
Philadelphia, PA 19101

An Annual Insurance Policy Statement is mailed to the insured on the policy anniversary date of each policy. The statement provides the insured with information about his or her VA insurance. The statement should be reviewed for accuracy each year, and the VA should be contacted immediately if there are any discrepancies.

CHAPTER 22

HOME LOAN GUARANTIES

GENERAL INFORMATION

The purpose of the VA loan guaranty program is to help veterans and active duty personnel finance the purchase of homes with competitive loan terms and interest rates. The VA does not actually lend the money to veterans. VA guaranteed loans are made by private lenders, such as banks, savings & loans, or mortgage companies. The VA guaranty means the lender is protected against loss if the veteran fails to repay the loan.

The VA Loan Guaranty Service is the organization within the VA that has the responsibility of administering the home loan program.

In 2011 the VA announced that those veterans who qualify and submit to a short sale or deed in-lieu of foreclosure may be eligible to receive $1,500 in relocation assistance. The VA has instructed mortgage lenders to provide the funds in order to help borrowers cover the cost of moving or other expenses incurred during the process.

In 2012 Under *Public Law 112-154*, veterans in specially adapted housing or those in receipt of VA home loans, which have property hindered or destroyed by a natural disaster, became eligible to receive VA assistance. The law also extended the VA's authority to extend the guarantee of timely payment of principal and interest of mortgage loans. The VA's authority was also extended with regard to the collection of loan fees and adjustment of maximum home loan guarantee amounts.

VA GUARANTEED LOANS OFFER THE FOLLOWING IMPORTANT FEATURES:

- Equal opportunity for all qualified veterans to obtain a VA guaranteed loan.
- No down payment (unless required by the lender or the purchase price is more than the reasonable value of the property).
- Buyer is informed of reasonable value.
- Buyer's interest rate is negotiable.

- Buyer has the ability to finance the VA funding fee (plus reduced funding fees with a down payment of at least 5%, and exemption for veterans receiving VA compensation).
- Closing costs are comparable with other financing types (and may be lower).
- No mortgage insurance premiums are necessary.
- An assumable mortgage may be available.
- Buyer has the right to prepay without penalty.

VA GUARANTEED LOANS DO NOT DO THE FOLLOWING:

- Guarantee that a home is free of defects
- VA only guarantees the loan. It is the veteran's responsibility to assure that he or she is satisfied with the property being purchased. Veterans should seek expert advice as necessary, before legally committing to a purchase agreement.
- If a veteran has a home built, VA cannot compel the builder to correct construction defects, although VA does have the authority to suspend a builder from further participation in the VA home loan program.
- VA cannot guarantee the veteran is making a good investment.
- VA cannot provide a veteran with legal service.

USES FOR VA LOAN GUARANTIES

VA loan guaranties can be used for the following:

> *Veterans must certify that they plan to live in the home they are buying or building in order to qualify for a VA loan guaranty.*

- To purchase, construct, or improve a home.
- To purchase and improve a home concurrently.
- To purchase a residential condominium or townhouse unit in a VA approved project. (If one veteran is purchasing the property, the total number of separate units cannot be more than 4.)
- To purchase a manufactured home or a manufactured home and manufactured home lot.
- To purchase and improve a manufactured home lot on which to place a manufactured home which the veteran already owns and occupies.
- To refinance an existing home loan.
- To refinance an existing VA loan to reduce the interest rate, and make energy-efficient improvements.

- To refinance an existing manufactured home loan in order to acquire a lot.
- To improve a home by installing a solar heating and/or cooling system, or other energy efficient improvements.

Veterans must certify that they plan to live in the home they are buying or building in order to qualify for a VA loan guaranty.

VA loan guaranties are available only for property located in the United States, its territories, or possessions (Puerto Rico, Guam, Virgin Islands, American Samoa, and Northern Mariana Islands).

VA loan guaranties are not available for farm loans, unless there is a home on the property, which will be personally occupied by the veteran. Non-realty loans for the purchase of equipment, livestock, machinery, etc. are not made. Other loan programs for farm financing may be available through the Farmers Home Administration, which gives preference to veteran applicants. (Interested veterans should refer to the local telephone directory for the phone number of a local office.)

Although business loans are not available through VA, the Small Business Administration (SBA) has a number of programs designed to help foster and encourage small business enterprises, including financial and management assistance. Each SBA office has a veteran's affairs officer available to speak with. (Interested veterans should refer to the local telephone directory for the phone number of a local SBA office, or call (800) 827-5722.)

ELIGIBILITY REQUIREMENTS

Individuals may qualify for VA home loan guaranties if their service falls within any of the following categories:

WORLD WAR II ELIGIBILITY REQUIREMENTS:

- Active duty on or after September 16, 1940 and prior to July 26, 1947; and
- Discharge or separation under other than dishonorable conditions; and
- At least 90 days of total service, unless discharged earlier for a service-connected disability.
- Unremarried widows of above-described eligible individuals who died as a result of service.
- Widows of above-described eligible individuals who died as a result of service **who remarried after age 57**.

POST WORLD WAR II ELIGIBILITY REQUIREMENTS:

- Active duty on or after July 26, 1947 and prior to June 27, 1950; and
- Discharge or separation under other than dishonorable conditions; and

- At least 181 days continuous service, unless discharged earlier for a service-connected disability.
- Unremarried widows of above-described eligible individuals who died as a result of service.
- Widows of above-described eligible individuals who died as a result of service **who remarried after age 57**.

KOREAN CONFLICT ELIGIBILITY REQUIREMENTS:

- Active duty on or after June 27, 1950 and prior to February 1, 1955; and
- Discharge or separation under other than dishonorable conditions; and
- At least 90 days of total service, unless discharged earlier for a service-connected disability.
- Unremarried widows of above-described eligible individuals who died as a result of service.
- Widows of above-described eligible individuals who died as a result of service who remarried after age 57.

POST-KOREAN CONFLICT ELIGIBILITY REQUIREMENTS:

- Active duty on or after February 1, 1955 and prior to August 5, 1964; and
- Discharge or separation under other than dishonorable conditions; and
- At least 181 days continuous service, unless discharged earlier for a service-connected disability.
- Unremarried widows of above-described eligible individuals who died as a result of service.
- Widows of above-described eligible individuals who died as a result of service **who remarried after age 57**. (This provision is effective January 1, 2004.)

VIETNAM ELIGIBILITY REQUIREMENTS:

- Active duty on or after August 5, 1964, and prior to May 8, 1975. (For those serving in the Republic of Vietnam, the beginning date is February 28, 1961.); and
- Discharge or separation under other than dishonorable conditions; and
- At least 90 days of total service, unless discharged earlier for a service-connected disability.
- Unremarried widows of above-described eligible individuals who died as a result of service.
- Widows of above-described eligible individuals who died as a result of service **who remarried after age 57**.

Post-Vietnam Eligibility Requirements for Veterans With Enlisted Service Between May 8, 1975 and September 7, 1980 (if enlisted) or October 16, 1981 (if officer):

- At least 181 days of continuous service, all of which occurred on or after May 8, 1975, unless discharged earlier for a service-connected disability; and
- Discharge or separation under other than dishonorable conditions.
- Unremarried widows of above-described eligible individuals who died as a result of service.
- Widows of above-described eligible individuals who died as a result of service **who remarried after age 57**.

Post-Vietnam Eligibility Requirements for Veterans Separated from Enlisted Service Between September 7, 1980 (October 17, 1981 for Officers) and August 1, 1990:

- At least 24 months of continuous active duty, or the full period (at least 181 days) for which individual was called or ordered to active duty, and discharged or separated under other than dishonorable conditions; or
- At least 181 days of continuous active duty, and discharged due to:
- a hardship; or
- a service-connected, compensable disability; or
- a medical condition which preexisted service, and has not been determined to be service-connected; or
- the convenience of the government as a result of a reduction in force; or
- a physical or mental condition not characterized as a disability, and not the result of misconduct, but which did interfere with the performance of duty.
- Early discharge for a service-connected disability.
- Unremarried widows of above-described eligible persons who died as the result of service.
- Widows of above-described eligible individuals who died as a result of service **who remarried after age 57**.

Persian Gulf War Eligibility Requirements:

- At least 24 months of continuous active duty on or after August 2, 1990, or the full period for which the individual was called or ordered to active duty, and discharged or separated under other than dishonorable conditions; or
- At least 90 days of continuous active duty, and discharged due to:

- A hardship; or
- A service-connected, compensable disability; or
- A medical condition which preexisted service, and has not been determined to be service-connected; or
- The convenience of the government as a result of a reduction in force; or
- A physical or mental condition not characterized as a disability, and not the result of misconduct, but which did interfere with the performance of duty.
- Early discharge for a service-connected disability.
- Unremarried widows of above-described eligible individuals who died as the result of service.
- Widows of above-described eligible individuals who died as a result of service **who remarried after age 57**.

When law or Presidential Proclamation ends the Persian Gulf War, a minimum of 181 days of continuous active duty will be required for those who did not serve during wartime.

Members of the Reserve and National Guard are eligible if activated after August 1, 1990, served at least 90 days, and discharged or separated under other than dishonorable conditions.)

Active Duty Personnel Eligibility Requirements:

Individuals who are now on regular duty (not active duty for training) are eligible after having served 181 days (90 days during the Gulf War), unless discharged or separated from a previous qualifying period of active duty service.

Eligibility Requirements for Members of the Selected Reserve:

- At least 6 years in the Reserves or National Guard, or discharged earlier due to a service-connected disability; and
- Discharged or separated under other than dishonorable conditions; or
- Placed on the retired list; or
- Transferred to an element of the Ready Reserve other than the Selected Reserve; or
- Continue to serve in the Selected Reserve.
- Unremarried widows of above-described eligible persons who died as the result of service.
- Widows of above-described eligible individuals who died as a result of service who remarried after age 57.

ELIGIBILITY REQUIREMENTS FOR OTHER TYPES OF SERVICE:

- Certain U.S. citizens who served in the armed forces of a U.S. ally in World War II.
- Members of organizations with recognized contributions to the U.S. during World War II. (Questions about this type of service eligibility can be answered at any VA regional office.)
- Spouses of American servicemen who are listed as missing-in-action, or prisoners-of-war for a total of 90 days or more.

CERTIFICATE OF ELIGIBILITY

The Certificate of Eligibility is the medium by which VA certifies eligibility for A VA loan guaranty.

Individuals may request a Certificate of Eligibility by completing "VA Form 26-1880 Request for a Certificate of Eligibility for VA Home Loan Benefits." The completed form should be submitted to a VA Eligibility Center along with acceptable proof of service.

Veterans separated after January 1, 1950 should submit DD Form 214, Certificate of Release or Discharge from active Duty.

Veterans separated after October 1, 1979 should submit copy 4 of DD Form 214.

Since there is no uniform document similar to the DD Form 214 for proof of service in the Selected Reserve a number of different forms may be accepted as documentation of service in the Selected Reserve:

- For those who served in the Army or Air National Guard and were discharged after at least 6 years of such service, NGB Form 22 may be sufficient.
- Those who served in the Army, Navy, Air Force, Marine Corps or Coast Guard Reserves may need to rely on a variety of forms that document at least 6 years of participation in paid training periods, or have paid active duty for training.
- Often it will be necessary to submit a combination of documents, such as an Honorable Discharge certificate together with a Retirement Points Statement. It is the reservist's responsibility to obtain and submit documentation of 6 years of honorable service.

In addition, if an individual is now on active duty, and has not been previously discharged from active duty service, he or she must submit a statement of service that includes the name of the issuing authority (base or command), and is signed by or at the direction of an appropriate official. The statement must identify the individual, include the social security number, provide the date of entry on active duty and the duration of any lost time.

The Certificate of Eligibility should be presented to the lender when completing the loan application. (However, if an individual does not have a Certificate, the lender may have the forms necessary to apply for the Certificate of Eligibility.)

PROCEDURES FOR OBTAINING LOANS

- Find a real estate professional to work with.
- Locate a lending institution that participates in the VA program. You may want to get "pre-qualified" at this point - that is, find out how big a loan you can afford. Lenders set their own interest rates, discount points, and closing points.
- Obtain your Certificate of Eligibility. The lender can probably get you a certificate online. Or, you can apply online yourself. To get your Certificate of Eligibility (COE) online, please go to the eBenefits portal at this link. If you need any assistance please call the eBenefits Help Desk at 1-800-983-0937. Their hours are Monday-Friday, 8am to 8pm EST.
- You find a home you want to buy:
  - When you negotiate, make sure the purchase and sales agreement contains a "VA option clause"
  - You may also want the agreement to allow you to "escape" from the contract without penalty if you can't get a VA loan.
- You formally apply to the lender for a VA-backed loan. The lender will complete a loan application and gather the needed documents such as pay stubs and bank statements.
- The lender orders a VA appraisal and begins to "process" all the credit and income information.
- The lending institution reviews the appraisal and all the documentation of credit, income, and assets. The lender then decides whether the loan should be granted.
- Finally, the closing takes place and the property is transferred. The lender chooses a title company, an attorney, or one of their own representatives to conduct the closing. This person will coordinate the date and time.

If a lender cannot be located, the local VA regional office can provide a list of lenders active in the VA program.

A VA loan guaranty does not guarantee approval of a loan. The veteran must still meet the financial institution's income and credit requirements. If a loan is approved, the VA guarantees the loan when it's closed.

VA ELIGIBILITY CENTERS

Regional Loan Center	Jurisdiction	Mailing Address	Telephone Number
Atlanta	Georgia North Carolina South Carolina Tennessee	Department of Veterans Affairs VA Regional Loan Center 1700 Clairmont Rd. Decatur, GA 30033-4032 (Mail: P.O. Box 100023, Decatur, GA 30031-7023)	(888) 768-2132
Cleveland	Connecticut Delaware Indiana Maine Massachusetts Michigan New Hampshire New Jersey New York Ohio Pennsylvania Rhode Island Vermont	Department of Veterans Affairs VA Regional Loan Center 1240 East Ninth Street Cleveland, OH 44199	(800) 729-5772
Denver	Alaska Colorado Idaho Montana Oregon Utah Washington Wyoming	Department of Veterans Affairs VA Regional Loan Center 155 Van Gordon Street Lakewood, CO 80228 (Mail: Box 25126, Denver, CO 80225)	(888) 349-7541
Honolulu	Hawaii Guam American Samoa Commonwealth of the Northern Marianas	Department of Veterans Affairs VA Regional Loan Center Loan Guaranty Division (26) 459 Patteson Rd. Honolulu, HI 96819 *Although not an RLC, this office is a fully functioning Loan Guaranty operation for Hawaii.	(888) 433-0481

Houston	Arkansas Louisiana Oklahoma Texas	Department of Veterans Affairs VA Regional Loan Center 6900 Almeda Road Houston, TX 77030-4200	(888) 232-2571
Phoenix	Arizona California New Mexico Nevada	Department of Veterans Affairs VA Regional Loan Center 3333 N. Central Avenue Phoenix, AZ 85012-2402	(888) 869-0194
Roanoke	District of Columbia Kentucky Maryland Virginia West Virginia	Department of Veterans Affairs VA Regional Loan Center 210 Franklin Road, SW Roanoke, VA 24011	(800) 933-5499
St. Paul	Illinois Iowa Kansas Minnesota Missouri Nebraska North Dakota South Dakota Wisconsin	Department of Veterans Affairs VA Regional Loan Center 1 Federal Drive, Ft. Snelling St. Paul, MN 55111-4050	(800) 827-0611
St. Petersburg	Alabama Florida Mississippi Puerto Rico U.S. Virgin Islands	Department of Veterans Affairs VA Regional Loan Center 9500 Bay Pines Blvd. St. Petersburg, FL 33708 (Mail: P.O. Box 1437, St. Petersburg, FL 33731)	(888) 611-5916

GUARANTY OR ENTITLEMENT AMOUNT

The Honoring America's Veterans and Caring for Camp Lejeune Families Act of 2012 was signed into law and includes a number of changes to the Department of Veterans Affairs' (VA) Loan Guaranty program, including reverting back to the previous method of calculating maximum guaranty.

This resulted in some loan limits increasing. While VA does not have a maximum loan amount, county "limits" must be used to calculate VA's maximum guaranty amount for a particular county. These limits apply to all loans closed August 6, 2012 through December 31, 2012.

Should the loan limit for a county decrease in 2013, VA will guarantee a loan using the previous higher limit if there is proof of a pre-approval based on a sales contract or URLA executed on or before December 31, 2012.

The maximum guaranty amount (available for loans over $144,000) is 25 percent of the 2012 VA Limit shown below. Therefore, a veteran with full entitlement available may borrow up to the 2012 VA Limit shown below and VA will guarantee 25 percent of the loan amount. If a veteran has previously used entitlement that has not been restored, the maximum guaranty amount available to that veteran must be reduced accordingly. Lenders should check their own.

HYBRID ADJUSTABLE RATE MORTGAGES (ARM)

An Adjustable Rate Mortgage is means the interest rate changes with changes in the market. The first-year rate, which is also referred to as a teaser rate, is generally a couple of percentage points below the market rate. The "cap" is the upper limit of the interest rate. If a teaser rate is 4%, and there is a five-point cap, then the highest that an interest rate could go would be 9%. The amount that the interest rate can rise each year is usually limited to one or two percentage points per year, but the frequency at which the rate adjusts can vary. If interest rates go up, an ARM will adjust accordingly.

DOWN PAYMENTS

The VA does not require a down payment be made, provided that:

- The loan is not for a manufactured home or lot (a 5% down payment is required for manufactured home or lot loans); and
- The purchase price or cost does not exceed the reasonable value of the property, as determined by VA; and
- The loan does not have graduated payment features. (Because with a graduated payment mortgage, the loan balance will be increasing during the first years of the loan, a down payment is required to keep the loan balance from going over the reasonable value or the purchase price.)

Even though the VA may not require a down payment, the lender may require one.

CLOSING COSTS AND FEES

The VA regulates the closing costs that a veteran may be charged in connection with closing a VA loan. The closing costs and origination fees must be paid in cash, and cannot be included in the loan itself, except in the case of refinancing loans.

Although some additional costs are unique to certain localities, the closing costs generally include:

- VA appraisal
- Credit report
- Survey
- Title evidence
- Recording fees
- A 1% loan origination fee
- Discount points

A veteran is charged the customary fees for title search, credit report, appraisal and transfer fees, etc., the same as any other borrower, but he is not required to pay commission or brokerage fees for obtaining the loan. In home loans, the lender may also charge a reasonable flat charge, called a funding fee, to cover the costs of originating the loan.

FUNDING FEES

A VA funding fee is payable at the time of loan closing. This fee may be included in the loan and paid from the loan proceeds. The funding fee does not have to be paid by veterans receiving VA compensation for service-connected disabilities, or who but for the receipt of retirement pay, would be entitled to receive compensation for service-connected disabilities, or surviving spouses of veterans who died in service or from a service-connected disability.

The funding fee rates are as follows:

Loan Purpose	Percent Of Loan For Veterans	Percent Of Loan For Reservists
Purchase or construction loan with down payment of less than 5%; or Refinancing loan; or Home improvement loan	2.15%	2.4%
Purchase or construction loan with down payment between 5% and 10%	1.5	1.75
Purchase or construction loan with down payment of 10% or more	1.25	1.5
Manufactured home loan	1.0	1.0
Interest rate reduction loan	0.5	0.5
Assumption of VA guaranteed loan	0.5	0.5
Second or subsequent use without a down payment	3.3	3.3

FLOOD INSURANCE

If the dwelling is in an area identified by the Department of Housing and Urban Development as having special flood hazards, and the sale of flood insurance under the national program is available, such insurance is required on loans made since March 1, 1974. The amount of insurance must be equal to the outstanding loan balance, or the maximum limit of coverage available, whichever is less.

INTEREST RATES

The interest rate on VA loans varies due to changes in the prevailing rates in the mortgage market. One a loan is made, the interest rate set in the note remains the same for the life of the loan. However, if interest rates decrease, a veteran may apply for a new VA loan to refinance the previous loan at a lower interest rate.

REPAYMENT PERIOD

The maximum repayment period for VA home loans is 30 years and 32 days. However, the exact amortization period depends upon the contract between the lender and the borrower.

The VA will guarantee loans with the following repayment terms:

- Traditional Fixed Payment Mortgage
- Equal monthly payments for the life of the loan
- Graduated Payment Mortgage - GPM
    - Smaller than normal monthly payments for the first few years - usually 5 years, which gradually increase each year, and then level off after the end of the "graduation period" to larger than normal payments for the remaining term of the loan. The reduction in the monthly payment in the early years of the loan is accomplished by delaying a portion of the interest due on the loan each month, and by adding that interest to the principal balance.
- Buydown
    - The builder of a new home or seller of an existing home may "buy down" the veteran's mortgage payments by making a large lump sum payment up front at closing that will be used to supplement the monthly payments for a certain period, usually 1 to 3 years.
- Growing Equity Mortgage (GEM)
    - Provides for a gradual annual increase in monthly payments, with all of the increase applied to the principal balance, resulting in early payoff of the loan.

PREPAYMENT OF LOAN

A veteran or serviceman may pay off his entire loan at any time without penalty or fee, or make advance payments equal to one monthly installment or $100, whichever is the lesser amount. Individuals should check with the mortgage holder for the proper procedure.

LOAN DEFAULTS

If a veteran fails to make payments as agreed, the lender may foreclose on the property. If the lender takes a loss, the VA must pay the guaranty to the lender, and the individual must repay this amount to the VA. If the loan closed on or after January 1, 1990, the veteran will owe the VA in the event of default, only if there was fraud, misrepresentation, or bad faith on the veteran's part.

The US Department of Veterans Affairs urges all Veterans who are encountering problems making their mortgage payments to speak with their loan servicers as soon as possible to explore options to avoid foreclosure.

Depending on a Veteran's specific situation, servicers may offer any of the following options to avoid foreclosure:

• Repayment Plan: The borrower makes regular installment each month plus part of the missed installments.

• Special Forbearance: The servicer agrees not to initiate foreclosure to allow time for borrowers to repay the missed installments. An example would be when a borrower is waiting for a tax refund.

• Loan Modification: Provides the borrower a fresh start by adding the delinquency to the loan balance and establishing a new payment schedule.

• Additional time to arrange a private sale: The servicer agrees to delay foreclosure to allow a sale to close if the loan will be paid off.

• Short Sale: When the servicer agrees to allow a borrower to sell his/her home for a lesser amount than what is currently required to payoff the loan.

• Deed-in-Lieu of Foreclosure: The borrower voluntarily agrees to deed the property to the servicer instead of going through a lengthy foreclosure process.

RELEASE OF LIABILITY

Any veteran who sells or has sold a home purchased with a VA loan guaranty may request release from liability to the VA. (If the VA loan closed prior to March 1, 1988, the application forms for a release of liability must be requested from the VA office that guaranteed the loan. If the VA loan closed on or after March 1, 1988, then the application forms must be requested from the lender to whom the payments are made.) The loan must be current, the purchaser must assume full liability for the loan, and the purchaser must sign an Assumption of Liability Agreement. The VA must approve the purchaser from a credit standpoint.

For loans closed on or after March 1, 1988, release of liability is not automatic. To approve the assumer and grant the veteran release from liability, the lender or VA must be notified, and release of liability must be requested.

If the loan was closed prior to March 1, 1988, the purchaser may assume the loan without approval from VA or the lender. However, the veteran is encouraged to request a release of liability from VA, regardless of the loan's closing date. If a veteran does not obtain a release of liability, and VA suffers a loss on account of a default by the assumer, or some future assumer, a debt may be established against the veteran. Also, strenuous collection efforts will be made against the veteran if a debt is established.

The release of a veteran from liability to the VA does not change the fact that the VA continues to be liable on the guaranty.

RESTORATION OF ENTITLEMENT

Veterans who have used all or part of their entitlement may restore their entitlement amount to purchase another home, provided:

- The property has been sold, and the loan has been paid in full; or
- A qualified veteran buyer has agreed to assume the outstanding balance on the loan, and agreed to substitute his entitlement for the same amount of entitlement the original veteran owner used to get the loan. (The veteran buyer must also meet the occupancy, income, and credit requirements of the VA and the lender.)
- If the veteran has repaid the VA loan in full, but has not disposed of the property securing that loan, the entitlement may be restored ONE TIME ONLY.

Restoration of entitlement does not occur automatically. The veteran must apply for restoration by completing "Form 26, 1880." Completed forms may be returned to any VA regional office or center (A copy of the HUD-1, Closing Statement, or other appropriate evidence of payment in full should also be submitted with the completed Form 26, 1880.) Application forms for substitution of entitlement can be requested from the VA office that guaranteed the loan.

If the requirements for restoration of entitlement cannot be met, veterans who had a VA loan before may still have remaining entitlement to use for another VA loan. The current amount of entitlement available to eligible veterans has been increased over time by changes in the law.

For example, in 1974 the maximum guaranty entitlement was $12,500. Today the maximum guaranty entitlement is $36,000 (for most loans under $144,000). So, if a veteran used the $12,500 guaranty in 1974, even if that loan is not paid off, the veteran could use the $23,500 difference between the $12,500 entitlement originally used and the current maximum of $36,000 to buy another home with a VA loan guaranty.

DIRECT HOME LOANS

VA direct home loans are only available to:

- Native American veterans who plan to buy, build, or improve a home on Native American trust land; or
- Certain eligible veterans who have a permanent and total service-connected disability, for specially adapted homes.

NATIVE AMERICAN VETERANS LIVING ON TRUST LANDS

A VA direct loan can be used to purchase, construct, or improve a home on Native American trust land. These loans may also be used to simultaneously purchase and improve a home, or to refinance another VA direct loan made under this program in order to lower the interest rate. VA direct loans are generally limited to the cost of the home or $80,000, whichever is less.

To qualify for a VA direct loan, the tribal organization or other appropriate Native American group must be participating in the VA direct loan program. The tribal organization must have signed a *Memorandum of Understanding* with the Secretary of Veterans Affairs that includes the conditions governing its participation in the program.

Veterans should contact their regional VA office for specific information regarding direct home loans.

RESALE OF REPOSSESSED VA HOMES

The VA sells homes that it acquires after foreclosure of a VA guaranteed loan. These homes are available to veterans and non-veterans.
The properties are available for sale to the general public through the services of private sector real estate brokers. The VA cannot deal directly with purchasers. Real estate brokers receive the keys to the properties and assist prospective purchasers in finding, viewing, and offering to purchase them.

Participating brokers receive instructional material regarding the sales program, and are familiar with VA sales procedures. VA pays the sales commission.
Offers to purchase VA acquired properties must be submitted on VA forms. Offers cannot be submitted on offer forms generally used in the real estate industry.

VA financing is available for most, but not all, property sales. The down payment requirements are usually very reasonable, the interest rate is established by VA based on market conditions. Any prospective purchaser who requests VA financing to purchase a VA-owned property must have sufficient income to meet the loan payments, maintain the property, and pay all other obligation. The purchaser must have acceptable credit, and must also have enough funds remaining for family support.

Anyone interested should consult a local real estate agent to find out about VA-acquired properties listed for sale in the area.

HUD / FHA LOANS

Veterans are not eligible for VA financing based on service in World War I, Active Duty for Training in the Reserves, or Active Duty for Training in the National Guard (unless "activated" under the authority of Title 10, U.S. Code). However, these veterans may qualify for a HUD / FHA veteran's loan.

The VA's only role in the HUD / FHA program is to determine the eligibility of the veteran, and issue a *Certificate of Veteran Status*, if qualified. Under this program, financing is available for veterans at terms slightly more favorable than those available to non-veterans.

A veteran may request a "Certificate of Veteran Status" by completing "VA form 26-8261a." The completed form and required attachments should be submitted to the veteran's regional VA office for a determination of eligibility.

SERVICEMEMBERS CIVIL RELIEF ACT (SCRA)

The Servicemembers Civil Relief Act expanded and improved the former Soldiers' and Sailors' Civil Relief Act (SSCRA). It is designed to provide a wide range of protections for people entering the military, being called to active duty, and deployed servicemembers. The goal of the SCRA is to postpone or suspend particular civil obligations, in order for the servicemember to devote full attention to service duties. It is also designed to relieve stress on family members of deployed servicemembers. Among these obligations a servicemember may be exempt from are mortgage payments.

The new law expands the current law in place to protect servicemembers and their families from eviction from housing while the servicemember is on active duty.

Based on provisions of a recent SCRA Foreclosure Settlement completed by the Federal government, five major servicers (Bank of America, JPMorgan Chase, Ally (GMAC), CitiMortgage, and Wells Fargo) must provide the following relief to service members and veterans:

- Conduct a review of every servicemember foreclosure since 2006 and provide any who were wrongly foreclosed with compensation equal to a minimum of lost equity, plus interest and $116,785;
- Refund money lost because they were wrongfully denied the opportunity to reduce their interest rates to the 6% cap;
- Provide relief for service members who are forced to sell their homes for less than the amount they owe on their mortgage due to a Permanent Change in Station;
- Extend certain foreclosure protections afforded under the Servicemember Civil Relief Act to service members serving in harm's way.

CHAPTER 23

OVERSEAS BENEFITS

MEDICAL BENEFITS

The Foreign Medical Program (FMP) is a healthcare benefits program for U.S. veterans with VA-rated service-connected conditions who are residing or traveling abroad (except Canada and the Philippines). Services provided in Canada and the Philippines are under separate jurisdictions, as indicated later in this chapter.

In 2011 the VA announced a new program to provide comprehensive compensation and pension (C&P) examinations for veterans living overseas.

Under the FMP, VA assumes payment responsibility for *certain necessary medical services associated with the treatment of* ***service-connected conditions***.

The Foreign Medical Program Office in Denver, Colorado has jurisdiction over all foreign provided services, with the exception of medical services received in Canada and the Philippines. It is responsible for all aspects of the program, including application processing, verification of eligibility, authorization of benefits, and payments of claims.

In September 2011, the VA announced the creation of a new program to provide comprehensive compensation and pension (C&P) examinations to U.S. veterans living overseas. The program includes providing a medical assessment to evaluate veterans' current disabilities that may be related to their military service.

If VA has previously determined a veteran has a service-connected medical condition, the examination helps determine the current severity of the condition, which could affect the amount of VA disability compensation payable or entitlement to additional benefits. During this time, the VA also conducted its first C&P examinations using telehealth technology, which is designed to ease the burden of travel for U.S. veterans living overseas. The VA plans to provide these services in various locations in Europe and Asia.

Individuals who are traveling to or reside in one of the following countries should use the following number to contact the FMP Office in Denver, Colorado: (877) 345-8179
Germany

Panama
Australia
Italy
England
UK
Japan
Spain.

For individuals who are in Mexico or Costa Rica, first dial the U.S.A code and then (877) 345-8179. The number also works from the United States.

Generally, as long as the service is medically necessary for the treatment of a VA rated service-connected condition, it will be covered by the FMP. Additionally, the services must be accepted by VA and / or the U.S. Medical community (such as the American Medical Association and the U.S. Food and Drug Administration.)

EXCLUSIONS TO MEDICAL BENEFITS

The following services are not covered by the Foreign Medical Program:

- Procedures, treatments, drugs, or devices that are experimental or investigational;
- Family planning services and sterilization;
- Infertility services;
- Plastic surgery primarily for cosmetic purposes;
- Procedures, services, and supplies related to sex transformations;
- Non-acute institutional care such as long-term inpatient psychiatric care and nursing home care;
- Day care and day hospitalization;
- Non-medical home care (aid and attendance);
- Abortions
- Travel, meals, and lodging (including transportation costs to return to the United States)

PROSTHESIS

If an individual residing in a foreign country requires a prosthesis for a VA rated service-connected condition, and the cost of the prosthetic appliance is less than $300 (U.S. currency), the individual may purchase the prosthetic appliance from a local healthcare provider, and send the invoice to the FMP Office for reimbursement, or the healthcare provider may bill the VA.

If the cost of the prosthetic appliance exceeds $300 (U.S. currency), the individual must obtain preauthorization for the VA Foreign Medical Program Office (see address below).

APPLICATION PROCESS – REGISTRATION

Although pre-registration for eligible veterans is not necessary, veterans who are permanently relocating to a country under the FMP's jurisdiction are encouraged to notify the FMP once a permanent foreign address is established. At that time, FMP will provide detailed program material, such as benefit coverage, benefit limitations, selecting healthcare providers, and claim filing instructions.

Veterans who are simply traveling, and are not planning a permanent relocation do not need to notify the FMP of their travel plans. Program materials are available, however, upon request.

The FMP can be contacted at:

VA Health Administration Center
Foreign Medical Program (FMP)
P.O. Box 65021
Denver, CO 80206-9021
Phone: (303) 331-7590
Fax: (303) 331-7803

MEDICAL SERVICES IN CANADA

The VA Medical and Regional Office Center in White River Junction, Vermont, is responsible for determining eligibility of U.S. veterans for reimbursement of medical treatment while traveling or residing in Canada. The local offices of Veterans' Affairs-Canada assists veterans in obtaining authorizations for treatment, arranging for treatment (if necessary), and providing information about the medical treatment program.

The same exclusions listed earlier in this chapter also apply to medical services in Canada, and VA assumes payment responsibility only for *certain necessary medical services associated with the treatment of* ***service-connected conditions.***

To receive reimbursed medical treatment, an authorization must be obtained from the White River Junction office **prior to treatment** (unless an emergency situation exists).

When required by the VA to support a claim for disability benefits, Veterans' Affairs-Canada will make arrangement for disability examinations for veterans residing in Canada. In some instances, arrangements will be made locally in Canada. In other instances, arrangements will be made at bordering VA medical facilities.

Information on how to obtain medical services in Canada, including procedures for filing claims, can be obtained by contacting the following office:

VAM & RO Center (136FC)
North Hartland Road
White River Junction, VT 05009-0001
Fax: (802) 296-5174

Or

Veterans Affairs-Canada
Foreign Countries Operations
Room 1055
264 Wellington Street
Ottawa, Ontario, Canada K1A 0P4
(613) 943-7461

MEDICAL SERVICES IN THE PHILLIPINES

The Republic of the Philippines is the only foreign country in which the VA operates a regional office and outpatient clinic.

The same exclusions listed earlier in this chapter also apply to medical services in the Philippines, and VA assumes payment responsibility only for *certain necessary medical services associated with the treatment of* ***service-connected conditions.***

To receive reimbursed medical treatment, an authorization must be obtained **prior to treatment** (unless an emergency situation exists).

Information on how to obtain medical services in the Philippines, including procedures for filing claims, can be obtained by contacting the following office:

U.S. Department of Veterans Affairs
Manila Regional Office & Outpatient Clinic
1501 Roxas Boulevard
1302 Pasay City, Philippines
TEL: 011-632-318-8387

Virtually all VA monetary benefits, including compensation, pension, educational assistance, and burial allowances, are payable regardless of an individual's place of residence.

However, there are some program limitations in foreign jurisdictions, including:

- Home-loan guaranties are available only in the United States and selected territories and possessions.
- Educational benefits are limited to approved degree-granting programs in institutions of higher learning

Information and assistance are available to U.S. veterans worldwide at American embassies and consulates. In Canada, the local offices of Veterans Affairs-Canada provide information and assistance. Individuals may call toll-free within Canada, (888) 996-2242.

In the Philippines, service is available at the VA Regional Office and Outpatient Clinic in Manila:

VA Regional Office
1131 Roxas Boulevard
Manila, Philippines
011-632-521-7521

DIRECT DEPOSIT

The conventional method of direct deposit is not available outside of the U.S. However, there are foreign banks with branches in the United States, through which direct deposit can be established. Once the funds are received in the U.S. branch through electronic funds transfer, the U.S. branch transfers the money to the foreign branch.

While this process may take a few days longer than direct deposit within the United States, it is still quicker than having checks mailed overseas through the Department of State or International Priority Airmail.

CHAPTER 24

AGENT ORANGE, MUSTARD GAS, RADIATION AND PROJECT 112 / SHAD

AGENT ORANGE

Agent Orange was an herbicide used in Vietnam to defoliate trees and remove cover for the enemy. Agent Orange and other herbicides used in Vietnam were tested or stored elsewhere, including some military bases in the United States. The name "Agent Orange" came from the orange identifying stripe used on the 55-gallon drums in which it was stored.

The U.S. military herbicide program in South Vietnam took place between 1961 and 1975. Herbicides were sprayed in all 4 military zones of Vietnam. More than 19 million gallons of various herbicide combinations were used. Agent Orange was the combination of herbicides the U.S. military used most often.

Heavily sprayed areas included:

- Inland forests near the demarcation zone;
- Inland forests at the junction of the borders of Cambodia, Laos, and South Vietnam;
- Inland forests north and northwest of Saigon;
- Mangrove forests on the southernmost peninsula of Vietnam;
- Mangrove forests along major shipping channels southeast of Saigon.

VA has offered special access to health services and studies since 1978, when it initiated a medical surveillance program for Vietnam veterans with health concerns. By 1981, VA offered priority medical care to Vietnam veterans with any health problems, which may have resulted from Agent Orange exposure. That program continues today.

TOLL-FREE AGENT ORANGE HELPLINE

The toll-free telephone number for the helpline is (800) 749-8387.

Callers can speak directly to VA representatives Monday through Friday from 8:00 a.m. to 4:00 p.m., Central Standard Time, or access a 24-hour automated system.

ELIGIBILITY FOR VETERANS' DISABILITY COMPENSATION

Veterans may be eligible for disability compensation if they have a service-related disability and were discharged under conditions other than dishonorable.

These Veterans are eligible for the Agent Orange Registry health exam:

VIETNAM

Veterans who served in Vietnam between 1962 and 1975, regardless of length of time.

Veterans who served aboard smaller river patrol and swift boats that operated on the inland waterways of Vietnam (also known as "Brown Water Veterans")

KOREA

Veterans who served in a unit in or near the Korean Demilitarized Zone (DMZ) anytime between April 1, 1968 and August 31, 1971.

THAILAND

U.S. Air Force Veterans who served on Royal Thai Air Force (RTAF) bases near U-Tapao, Ubon, Nakhon Phanom, Udorn, Takhli, Korat, and Don Muang, near the air base perimeter anytime between February 28, 1961 and May 7, 1975.

U.S. Army Veterans who provided perimeter security on RTAF bases in Thailand anytime between February 28, 1961 and May 7, 1975.

U.S. Army Veterans who were stationed on some small Army installations in Thailand anytime between February 28, 1961 and May 7, 1975. However, the Amy Veteran must have been a member of a military police (MP) unit or was assigned a military occupational specialty whose duty placed him or her at or near the base perimeter.

OTHER POTENTIAL AGENT ORANGE EXPOSURES

Veterans who may have been exposed to herbicides during a military operation or as a result of testing, transporting, or spraying herbicides for military purposes. Learn about herbicide tests and storage outside Vietnam.

IN-VIETNAM EXPOSURE TO AGENT ORANGE:

Veterans who served on land in Vietnam, went ashore when a ship docked to the shore of Vietnam, or served on the inland waterways of Vietnam anytime between January 9, 1962 and May 7, 1975 (including brief visits), and who have a disease that VA recognizes as associated with Agent Orange exposure are presumed to have been exposed to Agent Orange.

This includes:

> ***"Brown Water Veterans"*** who served aboard river patrol and swift boats that operated on inland waterways anytime between January 9, 1962 and May 7, 1975; and
>
> ***"Blue Water Veterans"*** who went ashore when a ship docked to the shore of Vietnam or served aboard ships that operated on the inland waterways of Vietnam anytime between January 9, 1962 and May 7, 1975.

VA ISSUES LIST OF SHIPS WITH AGENT ORANGE EXPOSURE

In 2010, the Department of Veterans Affairs Compensation and Pension (C&P) Service initiated a program to collect data on Vietnam naval operations for the purpose of providing regional offices with information to assist with development of claims based on herbicide exposure from Navy Veterans.

To date, the Department of Veterans Affairs (VA) has received verification from various sources showing that a number of offshore "blue water naval vessels" conducted operations on the inland "brown water" rivers and delta areas of Vietnam. The VA also has identified certain vessel types that operated primarily or exclusively on the inland waterways.

Veterans whose military records show they were on the ships or boats with the following designations or ships that were part of the Mobile Rivervine Force or Inshore Fire Support (ISF) Division 93 mean the veteran qualifies for presumption of Agent Orange exposure:

LCM (Landing Craft, Mechanized)
LCU (Landing Craft, Utility)
LCVP (Landing Craft, Vehicle, Personnel)
LST (Landing Ship, Tank)
PBR (Patrol Boat, River)

PCF (Patrol Craft, Fast or Swift Boat)
PG (Patrol Gunboat)
WAK (Cargo Vessel)
WHEC (High Endurance Cutter)
WLB (Buoy Tender)
WPB (Patrol Boat)
YFU (Harbor Utility Craft)

If a veteran's vessel is not included in the Mobile Rivervine Force or the Inshore Fire Support (ISF) Division 93, the veteran should check the following alphabetized list of ships that qualify for Agent Orange presumption (updated January 2012):

Ship Name	Activities in Vietnam
Ajax (AR-6)	Anchored in Vung Tau area for repair duties with evidence of shore-based repairs during June 1968, September to October 1969, April to May 1970, and August to November 1971
Alamo (LSD-33)	Conducted numerous troop, supply, and equipment landings with smaller boats at Da Nang and elsewhere between 1965 and 1972 with evidence that crewmembers went ashore for beach parties
Aludra (AF-55)	Conducted in-port replenishments at Cam Ranh Bay, Vung Tau and An Thoi during March 1969 and docked to pier at Da Nang April 17-18, 1969
Antelope (PG-86)	Operated primarily or exclusively on Vietnam's inland waterways
Asheville (PG-84)	Operated primarily or exclusively on Vietnam's inland waterways
Askari (ARL-30)	Operated primarily or exclusively on Vietnam's inland waterways
Ault (DD-689)	Operated on Mekong River Delta and Soirap River May 26, 1967
Barracks Barge (APL-26)	Operated primarily or exclusively on Vietnam's inland waterways
Barracks Barge (APL-30)	Operated primarily or exclusively on Vietnam's inland waterways
Barry (DD-933)	Operated on Saigon River during December 1965
Basilone (DD-824)	Operated on Saigon River, May 24-25, 1966
Bayfield (APA-33)	Conducted troop on loading and "mike boat" landings at Da Nang, Chu Lai, Baie de My Han, and Cua Viet River from July through October 1965 and February through May 1967
Belle Grove (LSD-2)	Operated primarily or exclusively on Vietnam's inland waterways
Benewah (APB-35)	Operated primarily or exclusively on Vietnam's inland waterways
Benner (DD-807)	Operated on inland Ganh Rai Bay and Rung Sat Special Zone during June 26-July 1, 1968
Bexar (APA-237)	Operated primarily or exclusively on Vietnam's inland waterways
Bigelow (DD-942)	Docked to pier at Da Nang for one hour on April 19, 1967
Black (DD-666)	Operated on Saigon River July 13-19, 1966
Blue (DD-744)	Anchored in Da Nang Harbor on April 21, 1968, with crew members going ashore for a picnic
Bolster (ARS-38)	Crew operated on land to extract USS Clark County (LST-601) from beach after grounding at Duc Pho from November 18 to December 1, 1967
Boxer (LPH-4)	Docked to pier at Cam Ranh Bay on September 9, 1965
Braine (DD-630)	Docked to pier at Da Nang on November 27, 1966
Brownson (DD-868)	Operated on Song Nha Be and Ganh Rai Bay areas of Mekong River Delta during February 1967
Brule (AKL-28)	Operated primarily or exclusively on Vietnam's inland waterways
Buck (DD-761)	Operated on Mekong River delta and Saigon River during October 1966
Cabildo (LSD-16)	Delivered equipment to Nha Be via the Long Tau River during June 1968 Conducted numerous troop, supply, and equipment landings at Da Nang, Cam Ranh Bay, and Vung Tau from July 1965 to November 1968

Ship Name	Activities in Vietnam
Card (ACV-11)	Mined, sunk, and salvaged in Saigon River Harbor during May 1964
Canberra (CAG-2)	Operated on Saigon River from March 31 through April 1, 1966, on Cua Viet River during December 15, 1966 and on Mekong Delta Ham Luong River during January 15, 1967
Canon (PG-90)	Operated primarily or exclusively on Vietnam's inland waterways
Carronade (IFS 1)	Operated primarily or exclusively on Vietnam's inland waterways
Carter Hall (LSD-3) (Landing Ship Dock)	Conducted troop-landing operations with "mike boats" at Da Nang, Dong Ha on Cua Viet River, and Nha Be on Saigon River, as well as three-month duty as "boat repair ship" at Da Nang, from July 1965 through November 1968
Castor (AKS-1) (General Stores Ship)	Docked to pier at Da Nang on October 7, 1966
Catamount (LSD-17)	Operated on Song Nah Be River during April 1969
Cavalier (APA-37)	Conducted troop landings at Chu Lai and served as Da Nang station ship, with crew members going ashore, from March-August 1966
Charles S. Sperry (DD-697)	Docked at Da Nang during January 1966
Chicago (CG-11)	Deck logs show a utility boat went ashore for one hour with eight crew members aboard while anchored in Da Nang Harbor on May 22, 1969
Chevalier (DD-805)	Operated on Saigon River during June 15-21, 1966 and on Vung Ganh Rai area of Mekong River delta during January 25, 1968
Clarion River (LSMR 409)	Operated primarily or exclusively on Vietnam's inland waterways
Cleveland (LPD-7)	Operated on Cua Viet River and at Dong Ha, as well as Hue River, with "mike boats" from November 1967 through 1968 and on the Saigon River during September 1969
Cohoes (AN-78)	Operated primarily or exclusively on Vietnam's inland waterways
Colleton (APB-36)	Operated primarily or exclusively on Vietnam's inland waterways
Colonial (LSD-18) (Landing Ship Dock)	Traveled on Saigon River to Nha Be on June 22 and September 25-30, 1969
Comstock (LSD-19)	Operated primarily or exclusively on Vietnam's inland waterways
Conway (DD-507)	Operated on Saigon River during early August 1966
Conflict (MSO-426) (Minesweeper-Ocean)	Operated on Saigon River April 1, 1966 and Song Huong River (Perfume River) May 14, 1966 and docked to piers at Cam Ranh Bay on September 30, October 7, 27, 28, and 31, 1971
Core (ACV-13)	Traveled on Saigon River to delivered aircraft to Saigon during June 1965
Crockett (PG-88)	Operated primarily or exclusively on Vietnam's inland waterways
Current (ARS-22) (Salvage Ship)	Conducted salvage operations on Saigon River during July 1964 and April 1967 and inland waterway of Qui Nhon Bay/Harbor during May 1967 and August 1971
Currituck (AV-7)	Traveled up Saigon River to Saigon during early 1964; operated in Mekong River delta during June 1965; anchored at Cam Ranh Bay for month-long periods during 1966 and 1967 to repair and tend to Navy sea planes, with the likelihood that crew members went ashore on liberty leave
Dahlgren (DLG-12) (Guided Missile Cruiser)	Sent motorized whaleboat and captain's gig ashore while anchored in Da Nang Harbor on June 4, 1967
Damato (DD-871)	Operated on Saigon River from December 12-13, 1967
Davidson (DE-1045) (Destroyer Escort)	Operated on Vung Ganh Rai and Rung Sat Special Zone of Mekong River Delta from September 16 to October 5, 1967 Sent motorized whaleboat ashore while anchored off coast of Tan My on September 20, 1972
De Haven (DD-727)	Operated on Saigon River during early March 1967
Dennis J. Buckley (DD-808)	Operated on Mekong River Delta, Saigon River and Ganh Rai Bay from December 19, 1966 to January 16, 1967
Denver (LPD-9)	Docked to pier at Da Nang to load troops and vehicles on March 24 and June 1, 1971
Dubuque (LPD-8)	Docked at Da Nang on March 15, 1970

Ship Name	Activities in Vietnam
Duluth (LPD-6) (Amphibious Transport Dock)	Docked to pier at Da Nang during December 1968 and March, April, and October 1971
Duncan (DDR-874)	Operated on Saigon River during September and October 1965
Du Pont (DD-941)	Operated on Mekong River Delta during October 1968
Durham (LKA-114) (Amphibious Cargo Ship)	Docked to piers at Da Nang during March 20-21, July 20-21, August 18-19, and September 7, 1970
Dyess (DD-880)	Operated on Saigon River and Rung Sat Special Zone from June 19-July 1, 1966
Eldorado (AGC-11) (Amphibious Force Flagship)	Sent crewmembers ashore for beach party at Cam Ranh Bay during July 1970
Elkhorn (AOG-7)	Operated primarily or exclusively on Vietnam's inland waterways
Epperson (DD-719)	Docked to Da Nang Pier on October 4, 1970
Epping Forest (MCS-7)	Conducted "goodwill" tours at Cam Ranh Bay and Nha Trang with crewmembers going ashore and Vietnamese coming aboard during September-October 1964, and mine sweep of Cua Viet River using smaller vessels from main ship during May 1968
Esteem (MSO-438)	Crewmembers painted a Vietnamese orphanage while docked at inland waterway Qui Nhon Bay/Harbor during December 1967
Estes (AGC-12)	Anchored in mouth of Mekong River during January 1967 Conducted troop and supply beach landings during March and July-August 1965, at Chu Lai, Da Nang, and Qui Nhon and conducted small boat landings and a beach picnic at Vung Tau during April 1968
Eversole (DD-789)	Sent motorized whaleboat ashore to Chu Lai from offshore anchorage to transfer two crewmembers on July 25, 1972
Finch (DER-328)	Crewmembers painted a Vietnamese orphanage while docked at inland waterway Qui Nhon Bay/Harbor during December 1967
Fiske (DD-842)	Operated on Mekong River, June 16-21, 1966
Floyd B. Parks (DD-884)	Operated on Saigon River and Ganh Rai Bay during February and March 1968
Force (MSO-445)	Docked to pier at Cam Ranh Bay March 13-15, 1972 and at Vung Tau April 25-May 3, 1972
Fortify (MSO-446)	Traveled up the Saigon River to Saigon September 19-22, 1964
Francis River (LSMR 525)	Operated primarily or exclusively on Vietnam's inland waterways
Gallop (PG-85)	Operated primarily or exclusively on Vietnam's inland waterways
Geiger (T-AP-197)	Docked at Qui Nhon November 23-26, 1965
General R M Blatchford (AP-153) (Transport Ship)	Landed elements of 1st Infantry Division at Vung Tau by small boats during October 1965
Genessee (AOG-8)	Operated primarily or exclusively on Vietnam's inland waterways
George Clymer APA-27) (Amphibious Attack Transport)	Conducted troop and supply "mike boat" beach landings during July 1965 and March to July, 1966, at Da Nang and Chu Lai. Navigated Saigon River to Saigon Port during January 1963.
George K. Mackenzie (DD-836)	Operated in Ganh Rai Bay area north of Vung Tau during February 1969
Graffias (AF-29) (Stores Ship)	Docked to pier at Da Nang for resupply on February 20 and November 25, 1967, and conducted other in-port replenishments at An Thoi and Vung Tau during 1967
Grapple (ARS-7) (Salvage Ship)	Conducted numerous repair and salvaging operations while moored to piers in Da Nang, Chu Lai, Cam Ranh Bay, and Tan My from November 1970 through April 1971 and August 1972 through January 1973
Grasp (ARS-24)	Conducted salvaging operations on Song Cua Dia River and other inland waters from February through April 1969

Ship Name	Activities in Vietnam
Gunston Hall (LSD-5)	Delivered equipment to Saigon via Saigon River during March 1968 Conducted numerous troop, supply, and equipment landings at Da Nang, Chu Lai, etc. during 1966 and from March 1968 to February 1970
Gurke (DD-783)	Operated on Ganh Rai Bay, Saigon River, and Mekong River during October 1966
Hamner (DD-718)	Operated on Song Lon Tao and Long Song Tao Rivers, August 15 to September 1, 1966
Hanson (DD-832)	Anchored in Saigon River on September 13, 1966
Harbor Tug 84 (YTB-84)	Operated primarily or exclusively on Vietnam's inland waterways
Harbor Tug 85 (YTB-85)	Operated primarily or exclusively on Vietnam's inland waterways
Hector (AR-7)	Anchored in Vung Tau Harbor repairing other vessels from July 20 to August 16, 1970, with deck logs stating that crew members went ashore on liberty leave
Henrico (APA-45)	Conducted numerous troop landings at Da Nang, Chu Lai, and Hue from March through May 1965 and from August 1966 through March 1967
Henry B. Wilson (DDG-7)	Docked at Da Nang pier on April 2, 1967
Herbert J Thomas (DD-833)	Operated in Mekong River Delta during December 1966
Hermitage (LSD-34)	Conducted numerous troop landings in Da Nang area from June through October 1967 and docked to Da Nang pier June 2-3, 1967
Higbee (DD-806)	Operated on Vung Ganh Rai area of Mekong River Delta from March 1-12, 1969
Holder (DD-819)	Operated on Vung Ganh Rai and Saigon River August 5, 1966
Hugh Purvis (DD-709)	Operated on the inland waters of Qui Nhon Bay during January 1969
Indra (ARL-37)	Operated primarily or exclusively on Vietnam's inland waterways
Ingersoll (DD-652)	Operated on Saigon River October 24-25, 1965
Ingraham (DD-694)	Operated 10 miles up Saigon River on November 12, 1965
Inflict (MSO-456)	Traveled up the Saigon River to Saigon from September 19-22, 1964
Isle Royale (AD-29) (Destroyer Tender-Repair Ship)	Salvaged the beached USS Mahnomen County (LST-912) at Chu Lai during January 1967 with crewmembers going ashore for stripping operations
Jamestown (AGTR-3)	Conducted numerous month-long deployments along the Vietnam coast collecting data, with photographic evidence that crewmembers went ashore, between January 1966 and September 1969
John R. Craig (DD-885)	Anchored off Nha Trang during summer 1968 with crewmembers going ashore for beach party
John W. Thomason (DD-760)	Operated on Nga Be River during 1969
Joseph Strauss (DDG-16)	Operated on Mekong River Delta March 4, 1966 and Ganh Rai Bay during November 7 and December 7, 1968
Kishwaukee (AOG-9)	Operated primarily or exclusively on Vietnam's inland waterways
Krishna (ARL-38)	Operated primarily or exclusively on Vietnam's inland waterways
Kula Gulf (CVE-108)	Used as helicopter and troop transport docked at Cam Ranh Bay, November 13-16, 1965
Lang (DE-1060)	Docked to pier #4 in Da Nang Harbor for 38 minutes on January 5, 1972, and sent whaleboat to and from shore with "briefing personnel" on January 8, 1973
Leary (DD-879)	Operated on Baie de Ganh Rai of the Mekong River Delta on October 9, 1967
Lenawee (APA-195)	Conducted troop and supply landings at Da Nang and Chu Lai from April 1965 to December 1966
Leonard F. Mason (DD-852)	Operated on Vung Ganh Rai Bay and channels during August 1969
Lloyd Thomas (DD-764)	Operated on Ganh Rai Bay and Saigon River area during December 28, 1970
Loftberg (DD-759)	Operated on Song Nha Be River from February 18-21 and April 14-15, 1969 and on Song Cua Dai River from April 10-12, 1969

Ship Name	Activities in Vietnam
Long Beach (CGN-9) (Guided Missile Cruiser, Nuclear)	While anchored in Da Nang Harbor, deck logs show that utility boats went ashore with passengers on May 5, 1968 and the Captains Gig went ashore on September 4, 1969
Lowe (DE-325)	Anchored in Saigon Harbor during April 1966
Loyalty (MSO-457)	Traveled up the Saigon River to Saigon September 19-22, 1964, and docked to a pier at Cam Ranh Bay on April 9 and 25, 1971
Lucid (MSO-458)	Docked to pier at Da Nang for off-loading and on loading equipment during May 1967
Lyman K. Swenson (DD-729)	Traveled up Saigon River for a 4-day visit to Saigon in May 1964
Mahan (DLG-11)	Visited Saigon via Saigon River October 24-28, 1962 and sent a "group of personnel" ashore at Da Nang for a short tour of Monkey Mountain on October 6, 1968
Mahopac (ATA-196)	Moored in Saigon during October 6-9, 1965, and operated on Mekong River from October 30-November 3, 1966
Mansfield (DD-728)	Operated on Saigon River August 8-19, 1967 and December 21-24, 1969
Marathon (PG-89)	Operated primarily or exclusively on Vietnam's inland waterways
Mark (AKL-12)	Operated primarily or exclusively on Vietnam's inland waterways
Mars (AFS-1) (Combat Stores Ship)	Operated on Mekong River July 8, 1966 Conducted numerous on shore supply replenishments at Da Nang, Cam Ranh Bay, Vung Tau, and An Thoi from May 1965 to November 1972 with evidence of crewmembers going ashore
Mathews (AKA-96)	On loaded supplies at Da Nang and delivered them up to the Cua Viet River to Dong Ha with "mike boats" from August through December 1967
Maury (AGS-16)	Conducted surveys of Mekong River Delta and other coastal area and rivers from November 1965-1969
McKean (DD-784)	Operated on Mekong and Saigon River Deltas during March 14-15, 1967
Mercer (APB-39)	Operated primarily or exclusively on Vietnam's inland waterways
Merrick (AKA-97) (Attack Cargo Ship)	Participated in Operation Jackstay amphibious landings while on inland Saigon River Delta during March 1966 Conducted troop and cargo beach landing with small boats at Hue, Chu Lai, Saigon River Delta, and Da Nang from July 1965 through November 1968
Montrose (APA-212)	Operated on Song Hue River December 1965, operated on Long Tau River during March 1967, and operated on Cua Viet River and at Dong Ha during May 1967
Morton (DD-948)	Operated on Vung Ganh Rai and Saigon River during April 1966 and February 1969
Mullinnix (DD-944)	Operated on Vung Ganh Rai and Saigon River from August 5-6, 1966
Myles C. Fox (DD-829)	Anchored off Qui Nhon and Nha Trang with crew members going ashore from February 5-20, 1967
Navarro (APA-215)	Conducted troop on and off loading operations from May 1965 to February 1968 at Da Nang, Chu Lai, and Quang Ngai Province
Newell (DER-322)	Docked at Port of Nha Trang from December 22-24, 1965
Newman K. Perry (DD-883)	Operated on Mekong River Delta and Saigon River from November 23-28, 1966
New Orleans (LPH-11)	Docked to pier at Da Nang on March 12, 1970
Niagara Falls (AFS-3)	Unloaded supplies on Saigon River and Cam Ranh Bay, April 22-25, 1968 Conducted on shore supply replenishments with helicopters and small boats at Da Nang, Cam Ranh Bay, Vung Tau, and An Thoi from April 1968 to March 1973
Nicholas (DD-449) (Destroyer)	Operated on Mekong River Delta during January 1967 and Ganh Rai Bay and Mekong River Delta during August 1968
Norris (DD-859)	Conducted operations on inland Song Nga Bay during November-December 1966
Noxubee (AOG-56)	Operated primarily or exclusively on Vietnam's inland waterways

Ship Name	Activities in Vietnam
Nueces (APB-40)	Operated primarily or exclusively on Vietnam's inland waterways
Oak Hill (LSD-7)	Served as station and repair ship in Da Nang Harbor with evidence of crewmembers going ashore from January through March 1966
O'Bannon (DD-450)	Operated on Saigon River during May 22-24, 1966
Okanogan (APA-220)	Operated primarily or exclusively on Vietnam's inland waterways
Okinawa (LPH-3) (Landing Platform Helicopter)	Docked to pier at Cam Ranh Bay to offload aircraft during May 1971
Oklahoma City (CLG-5)	Docked in Saigon during 21-24 July 1964
Orleck (DD-886)	Operated on Mekong River Delta during July 1969
Oxford (AGTR-1)	Conducted numerous month-long deployments along the Vietnam coast collecting data, with likelihood that crew members went ashore, between 1965 and 1969
Ozbourn (DD-846)	Conducted fire support missions on Saigon River October-November 1965 and August-October 1966
Patapsco (AOG-1)	Operated primarily or exclusively on Vietnam's inland waterways
Paul Revere (APA-248)	Assisted with salvage of the USS Card (ACV-11) in Saigon Harbor on Saigon River during May 1964 Conducted small boat troop landings at Qui Nhon, Quang Ngai Province, and elsewhere from August 1965 through April 1966 and August through November 1967.
Perkins (DD-877)	Operated on Saigon River during June 1969
Picking (DD-685)	Operated on Saigon River during November 16, 1965
Pictor (AF-54)	Delivered supplies by small boat to Dong Ha on Cua Viet River during September 1967 and docked to the pier at Da Nang during 1969
Pine Island (AV-12)	Anchored at Da Nang during August 1964, and Cam Ranh Bay for month-long periods during 1965 and 1966, to repair and tend to Navy sea planes, with the likelihood that crew members went ashore on liberty leave
Point Defiance (LSD-31)	Operated on Saigon River during March 1967 and conducted several operations on Saigon River to Saigon Port during October and November 1968 Conducted numerous troop and supply landings with small boats at Da Nang, Qui Nhon, Van Tuong, and Kien Hoa from May 1965 through October 1972.
Ponchatoula (AO-148)	Operated on Mekong River Delta during July 1971
Preston (DD-795)	Operated on Mekong River Delta, Ganh Rai Bay and Saigon River from September 28-29 and December 27-29, 1965, and on Mekong River Delta June 3, 1967
Prichett (DD-561)	Operated on Mekong River Delta and Saigon River during August 1969
Prime (MSO-466)	Docked to pier at Da Nang on February 16, 1967
Providence (CLG-6)	Operated on Saigon River 3 days during January 1964 and on Cua Viet River during August 1972
Ready (PG-87)	Operated primarily or exclusively on Vietnam's inland waterways
Reclaimer (ARS-42)	Operated in Saigon Harbor to salvage USS Card (ACV-11) from sinking in Saigon River during May 1964 and in Rung Sat Special Zone of Mekong River delta salvaging ships during early 1966.
Repose (AH-16) (Hospital Ship)	Operated continuously on close coastal waters from 1966-1970, with the likelihood that crew members went ashore on liberty leave
Richard B. Anderson (DD-786)	Docked to pier at Da Nang on August 29, 1972
Richard E. Kraus (DD-849)	Operated on coastal inlet north of Da Nang from June 2-5, 1966, protecting Marine holding a bridge
Richard S Edwards (DD-950)	Operated on Mekong River Delta in Province of Kien Hoa during February 28 and March 1, 1969

Ship Name	Activities in Vietnam
Rowan (DD-782)	Operated on Song Tra Khuc River and inland waterway Qui Nhon Bay from April through July 1965
Rupertus (DD-851)	Operated on Saigon River during May 1969
Safeguard (ARS-25)	Operated on Ganh Rai Bay and Mekong River Delta during December 8, 1965
Saint Paul (CA-73) (Cruiser)	While anchored in Da Nang Harbor on May 9, 1969 and May 25, 1970, deck logs show limited small boat operations to shore
Salisbury Sound (AV-13)	Traveled up Saigon River to Saigon during June 1964, and anchored at Cam Ranh Bay for month-long periods during 1966, to repair and tend to Navy sea planes, with the likelihood that crew members went ashore on liberty leave
Samuel Gompers (AD-37)	Multiple dockings to piers at Da Nang during April 1972
Satyr (ARL-23)	Operated primarily or exclusively on Vietnam's inland waterways
Sanctuary (AH-17)	Operated continuously on close coastal waters from 1967-1971, with the likelihood that crew members went ashore on liberty leave
Serrano (AGS-24)	Conducted mapping surveys of Mekong River Delta and other coastal and river areas from 1966 through 1969
Shelton (DD-790)	Operated on Saigon River during January 16, 1966
Skagit (AKA-105)	Conducted troop and cargo beach "mike boat" landings at Da Nang, Chu Lai, and Quang Ngai from November 1965 to November 1967
Southerland (DD-743)	Operated on Song Nga Bay and Saigon River July 1966
Sphinx (ARL-24)	Operated primarily or exclusively on Vietnam's inland waterways
Sproston (DD-577)	Operated on Mekong River Delta and Ganh Rai Bay during January 1966
Steinaker (DD-863)	Anchored off Phan Thiet July 25- August 3, 1968 with crewmembers going ashore to visit Junk Base
Strong (DD-758)	Operated in Mekong River Delta and Rung Sat Special Zone during April 1968
Talladega (APA-208)	Operated on Saigon River during October 1967
Tanner (AGS-15)	Conducted surveys of Mekong River Delta and other coastal areas and rivers from October 1966 through 1968
Taussig (DD-746)	Operated on Soirap River in Mekong River Delta during June 15-26, 1966
Tawakoni (ATF-114)	Operated in Saigon Harbor to salvage USS Card (ACV-11) from sinking in Saigon River during May 1964
Tillamook (ATA-192)	Operated on Long Tau branch of Saigon River during January 1966
Thomaston (LSD-28)	Conducted dredge lift on Saigon River during November 1964 Conducted numerous troop and supply landings with small boats at Da Nang, Cam Ranh Bay, Song Co Chien River area, and Cua Viet River area from 1965 to 1972 (**Note:** No Agent Orange exposure for 1975 operations)
Tolovana (AO-64) (Fleet Oiler)	Sent crew ashore for beach party at Phu Quoc during May 1971
Tombigbee (AOG-11)	Operated primarily or exclusively on Vietnam's inland waterways
Tortuga (LSD-26)	Operated primarily or exclusively on Vietnam's inland waterways
Towers (DDG-9)	Operated on Saigon River and Rung Sat Special Zone during July 1966
Tulare (AKA/LKA-112)	Conducted troop and cargo "mike boat" beach landings at Da Nang, Chu Lai, Cam Ranh Bay and Vung Tau from 1966 to 1972
Tutuila (ARG-4)	Operated primarily or exclusively on Vietnam's inland waterways
Union (AKA/LKA-106)	Anchored in mouth of the Hue River while conducting operations during April 1965 and conducted troop and cargo "mike boat" beach landings at Da Nang and Cam Ranh Bay from 1965 to 1969
Ute (ATF-76) (Fleet Ocean Tug)	Conducted numerous salvaging operations on beached vessels from April 1966 through April 1971 with crewmembers going ashore and all attended beach party at Cam Ranh Bay on April 12, 1969

Ship Name	Activities in Vietnam
Valley Forge (LPH-8) (Landing Platform Helicopter)	Operated as helicopter and troop transport with helicopters and smaller vessels transporting troops on and off shore from September 1964 to September 1969
Vancouver (LPD-2)	Conducted numerous amphibious troop beach landings with smaller "mike boats" in the areas of Da Nang, Cam Ranh Bay, Cua Viet River, and Mekong River Delta, from August 1966 through 1971
Vega (AF-59)	Conducted resupply operation in the Mekong River delta area on September 13, 1966, on loaded supplies at An Thoi, Vung Tau, Cam Ranh Bay, and Da Nang during June 1969, and delivered supplies to Da Nang, Cam Ranh Bay, Con Son, An Thoi, and Hon Choi during November to December 1970
Walke (DD-723)	Operated on Mekong River Delta at Vung Ganh Rei September 2, 1969
Warbler (MSC-206) (Minesweeper-Coastal)	Docked to pier at Cam Ranh Bay July 22-25, 1964 and June 18 and July 6, 1970
Warrington (DD-843)	Operated on Mekong River Delta, Rung Sat Special Zone, north of Vung Ganh Rai Bay during March 1967
Washburn (AKA/LKA-108)	Conducted numerous small boat beach landings at Da Nang, Thon My Thuy, Hue on Perfume River, and Dong Ha on Cua Viet River from 1965 to 1969
Weiss (APD/LPR-135)	Conducted troop-landing operations with Marine and SEAL units at various locations in the Mekong River Delta, Rung Sat Special Zone, and Saigon River and routinely surveyed river mouths and canal entrances for amphibious landings from November 1965 through February 1969
Whetstone (LSD-27)	On loaded and delivered troops to D Nang, Hue, Phu Bai, Dong Ha with beach landings and "mike boats" and served as long-term "boat havens" for repairs of smaller vessels at Da Nang and Qui Nhon during 1965, 1966, 1968 and 1969
Whippoorwill (MSC-207)	Docked to pier at Cam Ranh Bay during July 22-25, 1964
White Plains (AFS-4)	Conducted on shore supply replenishments with helicopters and small boats at Da Nang, Cam Ranh Bay, Vung Tau, and An Thoi from January 1969 to March 1973
White River (LSMR 536)	Operated primarily or exclusively on Vietnam's inland waterways
Wiltsie (DD-716)	Operated on Saigon River during July 1966 While operating in close coastal waters during September 1970, two officers and five sailors were sent ashore by helicopter for one night
Winnemucca (YTB-785)	Operated primarily or exclusively on Vietnam's inland waterways

OUTSIDE-VIETNAM EXPOSURE TO HERBICIDES:

Veterans who did not serve inside Vietnam and were exposed elsewhere to Agent Orange or other herbicides may be eligible for service-connection on a "direct" basis. These veterans must show that their diseases are related to their military service in order to qualify for disability compensation.

Additionally, these veterans must show that they were exposed to Agent Orange or other herbicides during military service. This includes:

- Blue Water Veterans who served on ships off the shore of Vietnam that did not dock to the shore of Vietnam or operate on the inland waterways of Vietnam;
- Blue Water Veterans claiming non-Hodgkin's lymphoma as a disability may be granted service connection without showing inland waterway service or that they went ashore when their ships docked to the shore of Vietnam. This is

because VA also recognizes non-Hodgkin's lymphoma as associated with service in Vietnam or the waters offshore of Vietnam during the Vietnam Era.

- Veterans who served in the Korea demilitarized zone in 1968 to 1969;
- In 2011 the VA published a final regulation in the Federal Register stating that the VA will presume herbicide exposure for any veteran who served between April 1, 1968 and August 31, 1971 in or around the Korea demilitarized zone.
- Veterans who served on or near the perimeters of military bases in Thailand during the Vietnam era;
- Veterans who served where herbicides were tested or stored outside of Vietnam.

DETERMINATION OF SERVICE-CONNECTED DISEASES

Veterans who served in Vietnam anytime between January 9, 1962 and May 7, 1975, and who have a disease that VA recognizes as associated with Agent Orange exposure are presumed to have been exposed to Agent Orange. These veterans do not need to show that they were exposed to Agent Orange in order to get disability compensation.

The diseases referred to above are:

- **Acute and Subacute Peripheral Neuropathy:** A nervous system condition that causes numbness, tingling, and motor weakness. Under VA's rating regulations, it must be at least 10% disabling within 1 year of exposure to Agent Orange and resolve within 2 years after the date it began. ****In 2012, the VA recommended that the terms "acute" and "subacute" be replaced with "early onset" and that the requirements that symptoms resolve within two years be eliminated.**
- **AL Amyloidosis:** A rare disease caused when an abnormal protein, amyloid, enters tissues or organs.
- **Chronic B Cell Leukemias:** Cancers which affect B cells, such as hairy cell leukemia.
- **Chloracne (or Similar Acneform Disease):** A skin condition that occurs soon after dioxin exposure and looks like common forms of acne seen in teenagers. Under VA's rating regulations, chloracne (or other acneform disease similar to chloracne) must be at least 10% disabling within 1 year of exposure to Agent Orange.
- **Diabetes Mellitus (Type 2):** A disease characterized by high blood sugar levels resulting from the body's inability to respond properly to the hormone insulin.
- **Hodgkin's Disease:** A malignant lymphoma (cancer) characterized by progressive enlargement of the lymph nodes, liver, and spleen, and by progressive anemia.

- **Ischemic Heart Disease:** A disease characterized by a reduced supply of blood to the heart.
- **Multiple Myeloma:** A cancer of specific bone marrow cells that is characterized by bone marrow tumors in various bones of the body.
- **Non-Hodgkin's Lymphoma:** A group of cancers that affect the lymph glands and other lymphatic tissue.
- **Parkinson's Disease:** A motor system condition with symptoms that include trembling of the limbs and face and impaired balance.
- **Porphyria Cutanea Tarda:** A disorder characterized by liver dysfunction and by thinning and blistering of the skin in sun-exposed areas. Under VA's rating regulations, it must be at least 10% disabling within 1 year of exposure to Agent Orange.
- **Prostate Cancer:** Cancer of the prostate; one of the most common cancers among men.
- **Respiratory Cancers:** Cancers of the lung, larynx, trachea, and bronchus.
- **Soft Tissue Sarcoma (other than Osteosarcoma, Chondrosarcoma, Kaposi's sarcoma, or Mesothelioma):** A group of different types of cancers in body tissues such as muscle, fat, blood and lymph vessels, and connective tissues.
- Each additional disease (if any) that the Secretary of the VA determines warrants a presumption of service-connection by reason of having positive association with exposure to an herbicide agent, becomes manifest within the period (if any) prescribed in such regulations in a veteran who, during active military, naval, or air service, served in the Republic of Vietnam during the period beginning on January 9, 1962 and ending on May 7, 1975, and while so serving was exposed to that herbicide agent.

Veterans having a disease referred to above, shall be presumed to have been exposed during such service to an herbicide agent containing dioxin or 2,4-dichlorophenoxyacetic acid, and may be presumed to have been exposed during such service to any other chemical compound in an herbicide agent, unless there is affirmative evidence to establish that the veteran was not exposed to any such agent during that service.

If the Secretary of the VA later determines that a previously established presumption of service-connection for one of the above diseases is no longer warranted, all veterans currently awarded compensation on the basis of the presumption shall continue to be entitled to receive compensation. Additionally, all survivors of any such veterans who were awarded dependency and indemnity compensation shall continue to be entitled to receive dependency and indemnity compensation on that basis.

AGENT ORANGE REGISTRY

VA developed the Agent Orange Registry Examination Program in 1978 to identify Vietnam veterans concerned about Agent Orange exposure. VA maintains a computerized registry of data from these examinations. Registrants receive periodic updates on Agent Orange studies and VA policy.

There is no cost for eligible veterans. Veterans receive a comprehensive examination, including exposure and medical histories, laboratory tests, and physical exams.

The Agent Orange Registry Exam is not a claim for VA benefits, nor is it required to receive VA benefits.

MUSTARD GAS EXPOSURE AND LONG-TERM HEALTH EFFECTS

In 1991, the Department of Veterans Affairs (VA) relaxed requirements for evaluating mustard gas-related compensation claims because of the confidentiality of some of the World War II testing and a lack of military medical records and follow-up. At that time, a review of studies of the effects of mustard gas exposure led VA to publish regulations authorizing service-connection and disability compensation payments to veterans who were exposed to significant levels of mustard gas and who suffer from chronic forms of certain diseases.

An estimated 4,000 servicemen participated in tests using significant concentrations of mustard gas either in chambers or field exercises in contaminated areas during World War II. This secret testing was conducted in order to develop better protective clothing, masks and skin ointments. There is no central roster of World War II participants in either the laboratory or field tests. The Army conducted tests on Army personnel in the laboratory and in the field. The test sites included:

- Edgewood Arsenal, Maryland;
- Camp Sibert, Alabama;
- Bushnell, Florida;
- Dugway Proving Ground, Utah; and
- San Jose Island, Panama Canal Zone

Military personnel from the U.S. Navy Training Center, Bainbridge, Maryland., also were sent to the Naval Research Lab in Washington, D.C., to participate in tests. Gas testing facilities also were located at Great Lakes Naval Training Center in Illinois and Camp Lejeune, North Carolina.

VETERANS WHO MAY BE ELIGIBLE FOR COMPENSATION

VA policies generally authorize service-connection and compensation payments to veterans who were exposed to mustard gas and/or Lewisite and who suffer from a number of diseases or conditions, including:

- Full-body exposure to nitrogen or sulfur mustard together with the subsequent development of chronic conjunctivitis, keratitis, corneal opacities, scar formation, or the following cancers: nasopharyngeal; laryngeal; lung (except mesothelioma); or squamous cell carcinoma of the skin;
- Full-body exposure to nitrogen or sulfur mustard -- or exposure to Lewisite -- and the subsequent development of a chronic form of laryngitis, bronchitis, emphysema, asthma or chronic obstructive pulmonary disease;
- Full-body exposure to nitrogen mustard with the subsequent development of acute nonlymphocytic leukemia.

Service-connection is not allowed if the claimed condition is due to the veteran's own willful misconduct or if there is affirmative evidence that establishes some other nonservice-related condition or event as the cause of the claimed disability.

Veterans who were exposed to significant amounts of mustard gas and have health problems that may be compensable (or their survivors) may contact the nearest VA regional office at (800) 827-1000 for more information about benefits.

VA PROGRAMS FOR VETERANS EXPOSED TO RADIATION

VA provides special priority for enrollment for health-care services to any veteran exposed to ionizing radiation in connection with:

- Onsite participation in a test involving the atmospheric detonation of a nuclear device (without regard to whether the nation conducting the test was the United States or another nation).
- The American occupation of Hiroshima and Nagasaki, Japan, during the period beginning August 6, 1945, and ending July 1, 1946.
- Internment as a prisoner of war in Japan (or service on active duty in Japan immediately following such internment) during World War II which (as determined by the Secretary of the VA) resulted in an opportunity for exposure to ionizing radiation comparable to that of veterans described above.
- The definition of radiation-risk activities was expanded in March 2002 to include service at Amchitka Island, Alaska, prior to January 1, 1974, if a veteran

was exposed while performing duties related to certain underground nuclear tests.

- The new definition also includes service at gaseous diffusion plants located in Paducah, Ky., Portsmouth, Ohio and an area known as K25 at Oak Ridge, Tenn.

In addition, these veterans are eligible to participate in the VA ionizing radiation registry examination program. VA also pays compensation to veterans and their survivors if the veteran is determined to have a disability due to radiation exposure while in service.

RADIATION STATISTICS

Some 195,000 service members have been identified as participants in the post-World War II occupation of Hiroshima and Nagasaki, Japan. In addition, approximately 210,000 mostly military members are confirmed as participants in U.S. atmospheric nuclear tests between 1945 and 1962 in the United States and the Pacific and Atlantic oceans prior to the 1963 Limited Test Ban Treaty. The Defense Threat Reduction Agency's Nuclear Test Personnel Review program since 1978 has maintained a database of participants in atmospheric nuclear test activities. About one-fourth of the participants received no measurable dose of ionizing radiation, with fewer than one per cent of the nuclear test participants identified as having a dose of 5 rem or higher. (The current federal guideline for U.S. workplace exposure is 5 rem per year.)

DETERMINATION OF SERVICE-CONNECTED DISEASES

VA may pay compensation for radiogenic diseases under two programs specific to radiation-exposed veterans and their survivors:

STATUTORY LIST

Veterans who participated in nuclear tests by the U.S. or its allies, who served with the U.S. occupation forces in Hiroshima or Nagasaki, Japan, between August 1945 and July 1946, or who were similarly exposed to ionizing radiation while a prisoner of war in Japan, are eligible for compensation for cancers specified in legislation.

The types of cancer covered by these laws are:

- All forms of leukemia;
- Cancer of the thyroid,
- Cancer of the breast,
- Cancer of the pharynx,
- Cancer of the esophagus,
- Cancer of the stomach,
- Cancer of the small intestine,

- Cancer of the pancreas,
- Cancer of the bile ducts,
- Cancer of the gall bladder,
- Cancer of the salivary gland
- Cancer of the urinary tract;
- Lymphomas (except Hodgkin's disease);
- Multiple myeloma;
- Primary liver cancer.
- Bone Cancer
- Brain Cancer
- Colon Cancer
- Lung Cancer
- Ovary Cancer

In 2011, the VA expanded the definition of non-Hodgkin's lymphoma to include

- Chronic lymphocytic leukemia;
- Small-cell lymphocytic lymphoma

The new rules apply to those veterans who participated in "radiation-risk activities" while on active duty, during active duty for training or inactive duty training as a member of a reserve component.

REGULATORY LIST

Disability compensation claims of veterans who were exposed to radiation in service and who develop a disease within specified time periods not specified in the statutory list are governed by regulation. Under the regulations, various additional factors must be considered in determining service-connection, including amount of radiation exposure, duration of exposure, and elapsed time between exposure and onset of the disease. VA regulations identify all cancers as potentially radiogenic, as well as certain other non-malignant conditions: posterior subcapsular cataracts; non-malignant thyroid nodular disease; parathyroid adenoma; and tumors of the brain and central nervous system.

A final rule that expanded the regulatory list from more than a dozen specific cancers to add "any other cancer" (any malignancy) was published Sept. 24, 1998. The rulemaking began following a 1995 review of the radiogenicity of cancer generally by the Veterans Advisory Committee on Environmental Hazards. It concluded that, on the basis of current scientific knowledge, exposure to ionizing radiation can be a contributing factor in the development of any malignancy. VA also will consider evidence that diseases other those specified in regulation may be caused by radiation exposure.

RATES OF DISABILITY COMPENSATION

Rates of compensation depend upon the degree of disability and follow a payment schedule that is adjusted annually and applies to all veterans. Please refer to the charts in Chapter 2 of this book.

IONIZING RADIATION REGISTRY PROGRAM

In addition to special eligibility to enroll for VA healthcare for radiation-related conditions, atomic veterans are eligible to participate in VA's Ionizing Radiation Registry examination. Under the Ionizing Radiation Registry program, VA will perform a complete physical examination, including all necessary tests, for each veteran who requests it if the veteran was exposed to ionizing radiation while participating in the nuclear weapons testing program, or if he or she served with the U.S. occupation forces in Hiroshima or Nagasaki. Veterans need not be enrolled for general VA care to be eligible for the Ionizing Radiation Registry.

PROJECT 112 / PROJECT SHAD VETERANS

Veterans who believe their health may have been affected by these tests should contact the SHAD helpline at (800) 749-8387.

Project SHAD, an acronym for Shipboard Hazard and Defense, was part of a larger effort called Project 112, which was a comprehensive program initiated in 1962 by the Department of Defense (DoD) to protect and defend against potential chemical and biological warfare threats.

Project SHAD encompassed a series of tests by DoD to determine the vulnerability of U.S. warships to attacks with chemical and biological warfare agents, and the potential risk to American forces posed by these agents.

Project 112 tests involved similar tests conducted on land rather than aboard ships.

Project SHAD involved service members from the Navy and Army and may have involved a small number of personnel from the Marine Corps and Air Force. Service members were not test subjects, but rather were involved in conducting the tests. Animals were used in some, but not most, tests.

DoD continues to release declassified reports about sea- and land- based tests of chemical and biological materials known collectively as "Project 112." The Department of Veterans Affairs (VA) is working with DoD to obtain information as to the nature and availability of the tests, who participated, duration and agents used. To date, there is no clear evidence of specific, long-term health problems associated with a veteran's participation in Project SHAD, but the VA is conducting a follow-up study to a 2007 Institute of Medicine Study. The results of the follow-up study are expected to be released in 2014.

Veterans who believe their health may have been affected by these tests should contact the SHAD helpline at (800) 749-8387

Public Law 108-170, the Veterans Health Care, Capital Asset, and Business Improvement Act of 2003, enacted December 6, 2003, provides for veterans who participated in Project 112/SHAD to be enrolled in priority enrollment category 6 and as such, to be eligible for VA health care at no cost for any illness possibly related to their participation in that project.

Following is a table provided by the DoD regarding specific ships, tests, and current information available.

(FS = FACT SHEET PR = PERSONNEL ROSTER)

#	*Test Name*	Date	Location	Agent/Stimulant	Investigation Status	Information at VA
1	63-1 Eager Belle I [SHAD]	Jan - Mar 1963	Pacific Ocean	BG	Fact Sheet Released 1/31/2002	FS, PR
	Eager Belle II [SHAD]	Jan, Mar, Jun 1963	Pacific Ocean	BG	Fact Sheet Released 1/31/2002	FS, PR
2	63-2 Autumn Gold [SHAD]	May 1963	Pacific Ocean	BG	Fact Sheet Released 9/13/2001	FS, PR
3	63-3 Whistle Down	Dec 1962 - Feb 1963	Ft. Greely, AK	GB, VX	Fact Sheet Released 10/09/2002	FS
4	63-4 Big Jack A	Feb - Mar 1963	Ft. Sherman, Panama Canal Zone	BG, FP	Fact Sheet Released 10/31/2002	FS
	Big Jack B	Feb - Mar 1963	Ft. Sherman, Panama Canal Zone	TOF	Fact Sheet Released 10/31/2002	FS
5	64-1 Errand Boy [SHAD]	September 1963	Oahu, HI	BG	Fact Sheet Released 6/30/2003	FS, PR
6	64-2 Flower Drum I [SHAD]	Feb - Apr 1964 Aug - Sep 1964	Pacific Ocean	GB, SO_2, MAA	Fact Sheet Released 5/23/2002	FS, PR
	Flower Drum II [SHAD]	Nov - Dec 1964	Pacific Ocean	VX, P32, Bis	Fact Sheet Released 5/23/2002	FS
7	64-3 Little Mo [SHAD]	NA	NA	NA	Test Cancelled	NA
8	64-4 [Red Beva] Shady Grove [SHAD]	Jan - Apr 1965	Pacific Ocean	BG, OU, UL	Fact Sheet Released 9/13/2001	FS, PR
9	64-5 Night Train	Nov 1963 - Jan 1964	Ft. Greely, AK	BG, FP	Fact Sheet Released 10/09/2002	FS
10	64-6 Yellow Leaf	Feb 1964, Apr - May 1966	Ft. Sherman, Panama Canal Zone, Island of Hawaii	BG, Tiara	Fact Sheet Released 10/31/2002	FS
11	64-7 Big Thunder	NA	NA	NA	Test Cancelled	NA
12	64-8 Tall Timber	Apr - Jun 1966	Island of Hawaii	BZ	Fact Sheet Released 10/09/2002	FS
13	64-9 Big Piney	NA	NA	NA	Test Cancelled	NA

#	Test Name	Date	Location	Agent/Stimulant	Investigation Status	Information at VA
14	64-10 [65-18] Black Label	NA	NA	NA	Test Deferred/Renumbered	NA
15	64-11 [65-19] Laurel Grove	NA	NA	NA	Test Deferred/Renumbered	NA
16	65-1 Copper Head [SHAD]	Jan - Feb 1965	Atlantic Ocean off Newfoundland, Canada	BG, FP, Beta-propiolactone	Fact Sheet Released 9/13/2001	FS, PR
17	65-2 Chain Saw	NA	NA	NA	Test Cancelled	NA
18	65-3 West Side I	Jan - Feb 1965	Ft. Greely, AK	BG, FP	Fact Sheet Released 10/09/2002	FS
19	65-4 Magic Sword [SHAD]	May 1965	Baker Island	mosquitoes (Aedes aegypti)	Fact Sheet Released 10/09/2002	FS, PR
20	65-5 Iron Clad [SHAD]	NA	NA	NA	Test Cancelled	NA
21	65-6 Big Tom [SHAD]	May - Jun 1965	Pacific Ocean, off Oahu, HI & surrounding water & airspace	BG, FP	Updated Fact Sheet Released 6/30/2003	FS, PR
22	65-7 Great Sole [SHAD]	NA	NA	NA	Test Cancelled	NA
23	65-8 Lone Wolf [SHAD]	NA	NA	NA	Test Cancelled	NA
24	65-9 Silver Star	NA	NA	NA	Test Cancelled	NA
25	65-10 Little Egypt	NA	NA	NA	Test Cancelled	NA
26	65-11 [Bear River] Sun Down	Feb, Apr 1966	Ft. Greely, AK	GB, MAA, Tiara	Fact Sheet Released 10/09/2002	FS
27	65-12 Devil Hole I	Summer 1965	Ft. Greely, AK	GB, FP	Fact Sheet Released 10/09/2002	FS
28	65-13 High Low [SHAD]	Jan - Feb 1966	Pacific Ocean off San Diego, CA	MAA	Corrected Fact Sheet Released 12/31/2002	FS
29	65-14 Elk Hunt I	Jul - Aug 1964	Ft. Greely, AK	VX	Fact Sheet Released 10/09/2002	FS, PR
	Elk Hunt II	Jun - Jul 1965 Oct - Dec 1965	Ft. Greely, AK & Edgewood Arsenal, MD, & Canada	VX	Fact Sheet Released 10/09/2002	FS, PR
30	65-15 Little Corporal	NA	NA	NA	Test Cancelled	NA
31	65-16 Pine Ridge	May - Jun 1966	Island of Hawaii	GB, BZ	Fact Sheet Released 10/09/2002	FS
32	65-17 Fearless Johnny [SHAD]	Aug - Sep 1965	Pacific Ocean southwest of Oahu, HI	VX, Diethylphthlate	Fact Sheet Released 5/23/2002	FS, PR
33	65-18 [64-10] Black Label	NA	NA	NA	Test Cancelled	NA
34	65-19 [64-11] Laurel Grove	NA	NA	NA	Test Cancelled	NA
35	66-1 Devil Hole II	Jul - Aug 1966	Ft. Greely, AK	VX	Fact Sheet Released 10/09/2002	FS

#	Test Name	Date	Location	Agent/Stimulant	Investigation Status	Information at VA
36	66-2 Red Oak I	Apr - May 1967	Island of Hawaii, Ft. Sherman, Panama Canal Zone	GB	Fact Sheet Released 10/31/2002	FS
37	66-3 Swamp Oak I	Mar - Apr 1966	Ft. Greely, AK	GB	Fact Sheet Released 10/09/2002	FS
38	66-4 Green Mist	Mar - Apr 1967	Island of Hawaii	GB, MAA	Fact Sheet Released 10/09/2002	FS
39	66-5 Purple Sage [SHAD]	Jan - Feb 1966	Pacific Ocean off San Diego, CA	MAA	Fact Sheet Released 5/23/2002	FS, PR
40	66-6 Scarlet Sage [SHAD]	Feb - Mar 1966	Pacific Ocean off San Diego, CA	BG	Fact Sheet Released 1/31/2002	FS, PR
41	66-7 Clay Pigeon I	NA	NA	NA	Test Cancelled	NA
42	66-8 West Side II	Jan - Mar 1965	Southwestern Canada	BG, FP	Fact Sheet Released 10/09/2002	FS
43	66-9 Magic Sword II [SHAD]	NA	NA	NA	Test Cancelled	NA
44	66-10 Pin Point	1966	Unspecified	CS	Fact Sheet Released 10/31/2002	FS
45	66-11 Ebony Sun [SHAD]	NA	NA	NA	Test Cancelled	NA
46	66-12 [Bald Eagle I] Bold Captain [SHAD]	NA	NA	NA	Test Cancelled	NA
47	66-13 Half Note [SHAD]	Aug - Sep 1966	Pacific Ocean, off Hawaii	BG, E.coli, FP SM, calcaflour	Updated Fact Sheet Released 6/30/2003	FS, PR
48	66-14 Sandy Point [SHAD]	NA	NA	NA	Test Cancelled	NA
49	67-1 [68-15] Red Oak II	NA	NA	NA	Test Deferred/Renumbered	NA
50	67-2 Dew Point	Jun - Jul 1967	Ft. Greely, AK	GB	Fact Sheet Released 10/09/2002	FS
51	67-3 [68-11] [69-13] Tiny Doll	NA	NA	NA	Test Deferred/Renumbered	NA
52	67-4 Blue Note [SHAD]	NA	NA	NA	Test Cancelled	NA
53	67-5 Work Horse [SHAD]	NA	NA	NA	Test Cancelled	NA
54	67-6 Blue Tango	Jan - Feb 1967	Hawaii	BG, E.coli, SM	Fact Sheet Released 6/30/2003	FS, PR
55	67-7 [Coincidence] Red Cloud	Nov 1966 - Feb 1967	Ft. Greely, AK	BG, E.coli, SM, TT, ZZ	Fact Sheet Released 10/09/2002	FS
56	67-8 [Autobiography] Watch Dog	Summer 1967	Ft. Greely, AK	BG, E.coli, SM, TT, ZZ	Fact Sheet Released 10/09/2002	FS
57	67-9 [Key Fruit] Gray Fox [SHAD]	NA	NA	NA	Test Cancelled	NA
58	67-10 [Meddled] Night Fire [SHAD]	NA	NA	NA	Test Cancelled	NA

#	Test Name	Date	Location	Agent/Stimulant	Investigation Status	Information at VA
59	67-11 [Expunge] Slow Waltz [SHAD]	NA	NA	NA	Test Cancelled	NA
60	67-12 [68-72] [69-30] [69-70] [69-73] [Expulsion] Sharp Nail [SHAD]	NA	NA	NA	Test Deferred/Renumbered	NA
61	67-13 Steel Point	NA	NA	NA	Test Cancelled	NA
62	68-10 [68-2] Sharp Ravine	NA	NA	NA	Test Cancelled	NA
63	68-11 [67-3] [69-13] Tiny Doll	NA	NA	NA	Test Deferred/Renumbered	NA
64	68-12 [68-1] Narrow Trail	NA	NA	NA	Test Cancelled	NA
65	68-13 [68-4] Rapid Tan	Jul - Aug 1967 May - Jun 1968 Aug - Sep 1968	Phase I & III - Porton Down, England, Phase II - Ralston, Canada	GA, GB, GD, VX	Fact Sheet Released 10/09/2002	FS
66	68-14 [68-3] Channel Crab	NA	NA	NA	Test Cancelled	NA
67	68-15 [67-1] Red Oak II	NA	NA	NA	Test Cancelled	NA
68	68-30 [68-5] [69-74] Prairie Carpet	NA	NA	NA	Test Deferred/Renumbered	NA
69	68-31 [68-6] [69-33] Exit Line	NA	NA	NA	Test Deferred/Renumbered	NA
70	68-33 [68-7] Wicked Slice	NA	NA	NA	Test Cancelled	NA
71	68-50 [68-11] Speckled Start [SHAD]	Sep - Oct 1968	Eniwetok Atoll, Marshall Islands	BG, PG2, uranine dye	Fact Sheet Released 5/23/2002	FS, PR
72	68-51 [68-9] Strange Fruit	NA	NA	NA	Test Cancelled	NA
73	68-52 Cliff Rose	Sep 27, 1967 - Jan 18, 1968	Ft Stewart Georgia and Panama Canal Zone	CS	Fact Sheet Released 12/9/2002*	FS
74	68-53	Apr - Dec 1969	DPG, UT	CS	Fact Sheet Released 10/09/2002	FS
75	68-70 [68-12] Shining Pond	NA	NA	NA	Test Cancelled	NA
76	68-71 [68-13] Folded Arrow [SHAD]	Apr – May 1968	Oahu, HI and surrounding waters	BG	Fact Sheet Released 6/30/2003	FS, PR
77	68-72 [67-12] [69-70] Sharp Nail	NA	NA	NA	Test Deferred/Renumbered	NA
78	68-73 [68-8] [69-73] Leaning Shoe	NA	NA	NA	Test Deferred/Renumbered	NA
79	[68-10] Maple Board	NA	NA	NA	Test Cancelled	NA

#	*Test Name*	Date	Location	Agent/Stimulant	Investigation Status	Information at VA
80	69-10 [SHAD]	May 1969	Vieques, PR	TOF	Fact Sheet Released 10/09/2002	FS, PR
81	69-12	Spring 1969	Edgewood Arsenal, MD	GB, GD, GA, VX	Test Suspended Fact Sheet Released 10/09/2002	FS
82	69-13 [67-3] [68-11] Tiny Doll	NA	NA	NA	Test Cancelled	NA
83	69-14	Jul - Nov 1971	DPG, UT	DEHP	Fact Sheet Released 10/09/2002	FS
84	69-15 [SHAD]	NA	NA	NA	Test Cancelled	NA
85	69-16	NA	NA	NA	Test Cancelled	NA
86	69-30	NA	NA	NA	Test Cancelled	NA
87	69-31 [SHAD]	Aug - Sep 1968	Pacific Ocean off San Diego, CA	BG, MAA	Fact Sheet Released 10/09/2002	FS, PR
88	69-32 [SHAD]	Apr - Jun 1969	Pacific Ocean, southwest of Hawaii	BG, E.coli, SM, Calcaflour	Fact Sheet Released 5/23/2002	FS, PR
89	69-33 [68-6] [68-31] Exit Line [SHAD]	NA	NA	NA	Test Cancelled	NA
90	69-34	NA	NA	NA	Test Cancelled	NA
91	69-35	NA	NA	NA	Test Cancelled	NA
92	69-36 [SHAD]	NA	NA	NA	Test Cancelled	NA
93	69-37	NA	NA	NA	Test Cancelled	NA
94	69-70 [67-12] [68-72] Sharp Nail	NA	NA	NA	Test Cancelled	NA
95	69-71	NA	NA	NA	Test Cancelled	NA
96	69-72 [SHAD]	NA	NA	NA	Test Cancelled	NA
97	69-73 [68-73] [68-8] Leaning Shoe	NA	NA	NA	Test Cancelled	NA
98	69-74 [68-5] [68-30] Prairie Carpet	NA	NA	NA	Test Cancelled	NA
99	69-75	Oct - Dec 1968	Yeehaw Junction, FL	TX	Fact Sheet Released 10/09/2002	FS
100	70-A	NA	NA	NA	Test Cancelled	NA
101	70-B	NA	NA	NA	Test Cancelled	NA
102	70-C (SHAD)	Oct 1972, Feb - Mar 1973	Pacific Ocean, from San Diego CA to Babloa, Panama	NA	Fact Sheet Released 6/30/2003	FS
103	70-D	NA	NA	NA	Test Cancelled	NA
104	70-10	NA	NA	NA	Test Deferred	NA
105	70-11 Ph I, Subtest 3	June 1972 - Nov 1973	Dugway PG, UT	Bis, TOP, FP	Fact Sheet Released 6/30/2003	FS
	70-11 Ph I, Subtest 4	May 1974	Dugway PG, UT	Bis	Fact Sheet Released 6/30/2003	FS
106	70-12	NA	NA	NA	Test Cancelled	NA
107	70-30	NA	NA	NA	Test Deferred	NA

#	*Test Name*	Date	Location	Agent/Stimulant	Investigation Status	Information at VA
108	70-31	NA	NA	NA	Test Cancelled	NA
109	70-50	NA	NA	NA	Test Cancelled	NA
110	70-70 [SHAD]	NA	NA	NA	Test Cancelled	NA
111	70-71 [SHAD]	NA	NA	NA	Test Cancelled	NA
112	70-72	NA	NA	NA	Test Cancelled	NA
113	70-73	Jul - Dec 1970	DPG, UT	BG, FP	Fact Sheet Released 10/09/2002	FS
114	70-74	Au 1972 - Jan 1973	Dugway PG, UT	BG, SM	Fact Sheet Released 6/30/2003	FS
115	71-10	NA	NA	NA	Test Cancelled	NA
116	71-11	NA	NA	NA	Test Cancelled	NA
117	71-12	NA	NA	NA	Test Cancelled	NA
118	71-13	NA	NA	NA	Test Cancelled	NA
119	71-30	NA	NA	NA	Test Cancelled	NA
120	71-31	NA	NA	NA	Test Cancelled	NA
121	71-32	NA	NA	NA	Test Cancelled	NA
122	71-33	NA	NA	NA	Test Cancelled	NA
123	71-34	NA	NA	NA	Test Cancelled	NA
124	71-35	NA	NA	NA	Test Cancelled	NA
125	71-70	NA	NA	NA	Test Cancelled	NA
126	71-75	NA	NA	NA	Test Cancelled	NA
127	72-30 [SHAD]	NA	NA	NA	Test Cancelled	NA
128	72-70 [SHAD]	NA	NA	NA	Test Cancelled	NA
129	73-10	NA	NA	NA	Test Cancelled	NA
130	73-11	NA	NA	NA	Test Cancelled	NA
131	73-12	NA	NA	NA	Test Cancelled	NA
132	73-30	Jan - Feb 1973	Dugway PG, UT	BG, SM, P	Fact Sheet Released 6/30/2003	FS
133	74-10 PH I	Sep - Oct 1973	Dugway PG, UT	DMMP, Bis, Trichloropro pane	Fact Sheet Released 6/30/2003	FS
	74-10 PH II	Apr - May 1974	Dugway PG, Ut	DMMP	Fact Sheet Released 6/30/2003	FS
134	74-030	NA	NA	NA	Test Cancelled	NA

CHAPTER 25

SPINA BIFIDA PROGRAM

VA provides monetary benefits, vocational training, rehabilitation, and certain healthcare benefits to children of Vietnam veterans and certain veterans who served in Korea near the demilitarized zone for disabilities resulting from spina bifida.

Spina bifida is the most frequently occurring permanently disabling birth defect. It affects approximately one of every 1,000 newborns in the United States. Neural tube defects (NTD) are birth defects that involve incomplete development of the brain, spinal cord, and/or protective coverings for these organs. Spina bifida, the most common NTD, results from the failure of the spine to close properly during the first month of pregnancy. (Anencephaly and encephalocele are less common types of NTDs). In severe cases, the spinal cord protrudes through the back of and may be covered by skin or a thin membrane.

Some Vietnam veterans, and certain other veterans have children with spina bifida. While Vietnam veterans and their mates are now moving out of the age category usually associated with childbirth, it is anticipated that some future births will occur and that some of these children may have birth defects, including spina bifida. Some research efforts have suggested that there may be a relationship between exposure by Vietnam veterans to Agent Orange and/or other herbicides used in Vietnam and the subsequent development of spina bifida in some of their children

For the purpose of the Spina Bifida Program, the term ***Vietnam Veteran*** means an individual who performed active military, naval, or air service in the Republic of Vietnam during the period beginning on January 9, 1962, and ending May 7, 1975, without regard to the characterization of the individual's service. Service in the Republic of Vietnam includes service in the waters offshore and service in other locations if the conditions of service involved duty or visitation in the Republic of Vietnam.

Please note, the Spina Bifida Program does not include spina bifida occulta.

Children who have spina bifida and meet the following requirements may be eligible for VA benefits, including healthcare, compensation and vocational training:

- Are biological children of Veterans who served:
- In Vietnam during the period from January 9, 1962 through May 7, 1975, or
    - In or near the Korean demilitarized zone between September 1, 1967 and August 31, 1971 and were exposed to herbicides. Veterans who served in a unit in or near the Korean demilitarized zone anytime between April 1, 1968 and August 31, 1971 are presumed to have been exposed to herbicides.
    - Were conceived after the date on which the Veteran first entered Vietnam or the Korean demilitarized zone during the qualifying service period

The term "herbicide agent" means a chemical in a herbicide used in support of United States and military operations in or near the Korean demilitarized zone, during the period beginning on September 1, 1967, and ending on August 31, 1971.

TOLL-FREE SPINA BIFIDA HOT LINE

In June 2001, VA opened a hot line for Vietnam veterans with questions about health care benefits for their children who have spina bifida.

The number for the hot line is (888) 820-1756.

Callers can speak to a benefits advisor Monday through Friday, from 10:00 a.m. to 1:30 p.m., and from 2:30 p.m. to 4:30 p.m., Eastern time. An after-hours phone message will allow callers to leave their names and telephone numbers for a return call the next business day.

The hot line is managed by VA's Health Administration Center in Denver, Colorado.

MONETARY BENEFITS

VA shall pay a monthly allowance based upon the level of disability to or for a child who is suffering from spina bifida, and who is a child of a Vietnam veteran. Receipt of this allowance shall not affect the right of the child, or the right of any individual based on the child's relationship to that individual, to receive any other benefit to which the child, or that individual, may be entitled under any law administered by VA. If a child suffering from spina bifida is the natural child of two Vietnam veterans, he or she is entitled to only one monthly allowance.

The monthly allowance is set at three levels, depending upon the degree of disability suffered by the child. VA shall determine the level of disability suffered by the child in accordance with the following criteria:

LEVEL I

- The child is able to walk without braces or other external support (although gait may be impaired); and
- Has no sensory or motor impairment of upper extremities; and
- Has an IQ of 90 or higher; and
- Is continent of urine and feces.

LEVEL II

Provided that none of the child's disabilities are severe enough to be evaluated at Level III, and the child is:

- Ambulatory, but only with braces or other external support; or
- Has sensory or motor impairment of upper extremities, but is able to grasp pen, feed self, and perform self care; or
- Has an IQ of at least 70 but less than 90; or
- Requires drugs or intermittent catheterization or other mechanical means to maintain proper urinary bladder function, or mechanisms for proper bowel function.

LEVEL III

- The child is unable to ambulate; or
- Has sensory or motor impairment of upper extremities severe enough to prevent grasping a pen, feeding self, and performing self care; or
- Has an IQ of 69 or less; or
- Has complete urinary or fecal incontinence.

SPINA BIFIDA BENEFIT RATE TABLE (EFFECTIVE 12-01-2014)

Disability Level	***Monthly Allowance***
Level I	$314.00
Level II	$1072.00
Level III	$1,827.00

VOCATIONAL TRAINING FOR CHILDREN WITH SPINA BIFIDA

To qualify for entitlement to a vocational training program an applicant must be a child:

- To whom VA has awarded a monthly allowance for spina bifida and;
- For whom VA has determined that achievement of a vocational goal is reasonably feasible.

A vocational training program may not begin before a child's 18th birthday, or the date of completion of secondary schooling, whichever comes first. Depending on the need, a child may be provided up to 24 months of full-time training.

HEALTHCARE BENEFITS

In addition to monetary allowances, vocational training and rehabilitation, the Department of Veterans Affairs (VA) also provides VA-financed healthcare benefits to Vietnam veterans' birth children diagnosed with spina bifida. For the purpose of this program, spina bifida is defined as all forms or manifestations of spina bifida (except spina bifida occulta), including complications or associated medical conditions related to spina bifida according to the scientific literature.

Healthcare benefits available under this program are limited to those necessary for the treatment of spina bifida and related medical conditions. Beneficiaries should be aware that this program is not a comprehensive healthcare plan and does not cover care that is unrelated to spina bifida.

Administration of the program is centralized to VA's Health Administration Center (HAC) in Denver, Colorado. HAC is responsible for all aspects of the spina bifida healthcare program, including the authorization of benefits and the subsequent processing and payment of claims. All inquiries regarding healthcare benefits should be made directly to HAC.

Healthcare benefits may be claimed for services and supplies starting on the effective date specified in the VA regional office award letter.

Beneficiaries in receipt of a VA regional office spina bifida award will receive an identification card from the Health Administration Center.

There are no beneficiary co-payments or deductibles. VA is the exclusive payer for services provided to beneficiaries under this program, and billing should be sent directly to the Health Administration Center. The determined allowable amount for payment is considered payment in full, and the provider may not bill the beneficiary for the difference between the billed amount and the VA-determined allowed amount.

COVERED BENEFITS

This program provides comprehensive health care for covered services and supplies that are considered medically necessary and appropriate.

General Exclusions

- Care as part of a grant study or research program
- Care considered experimental or investigational
- Care that is not medically necessary or appropriate
- Drugs not approved by the FDA for commercial marketing
- Services provided outside the scope of the provider's license or certification
- Services rendered by providers suspended or sanctioned by a federal agency
- Services, procedures or supplies for which the beneficiary has no legal obligation to pay, such as services obtained at a health fair
- Treatment for spina bifida occulta

Preauthorization Requirements

Although most health care services and supplies do not require approval in advance (preauthorization), some do.

Preauthorization is NOT required for routine health care services and supplies.

Preauthorization IS required for:

Attendants
Dental services
Durable medical equipment (DME) with a total rental or purchase price in excess of $2,000
Mental health services
Hospice care
Substance abuse treatment
Training of family members
Transplantation services
Travel (other than mileage for privately owned automobiles for local travel)

Note: When in doubt, contact the HAC.

Selecting Healthcare Providers

Beneficiaries may select the provider of their choice, as long as the provider is an approved health care provider. The provider must be approved by the Centers for Medicare and Medicaid Services (CMS), Department of Defense TRICARE program, CHAMPVA, JCAHO or may be a health care provider approved for providing services pursuant to a state license or certificate. A provider is not required to contract with the HAC; the HAC does not maintain a list of providers.

CLAIMS

Claims are to be mailed directly to VA's Health Administration Center at the following address.

VA Health Administration Center
PO Box 469065
Denver CO 80246-9065

As a safeguard against claims getting lost in the mail, beneficiaries should keep copies of all claim documents submitted.

FILING DEADLINES

Claims must be filed with the Health Administration Center no later than:

- One year after the date of service; or
- In the case of inpatient care, one year after the date of discharge; or
- In the case of a VA regional office award for retroactive eligibility, 180 days following beneficiary notification of the award.

PAYMENTS

Approved healthcare providers will be paid 100% of the VA-determined allowable charge for covered services. VA payment for covered services constitutes payment in full. Federal regulations prohibit providers from seeking any additional monies from beneficiaries and third party payers such as private insurers, for services paid by VA.

Note: If the beneficiary pays for care and subsequently files a claim for reimbursement, VA payment to the beneficiary will be limited to the VA-allowed amount. For this reason, beneficiaries are advised not to pay their providers-but instead, have the providers bill HAC directly.

OTHER HEALTH INSURANCE

While VA assumes full responsibility for the cost of services related to the treatment of spina bifida and associated conditions, third-party insurers including Medicare and Medicaid, assume payment responsibility for services unrelated to the VA-covered conditions.

EXPLANATION OF BENEFITS

Upon completion of claim processing, an EOB will be mailed to the beneficiary. If a provider files the claim, an EOB will be mailed to them also. The EOB is a summarization of the action taken on the claim and contains, at a minimum, the following information.

- Beneficiary name;
- Description of services and/or supplies provided;
- Dates of service or supplies provided;
- Amount billed;
- VA-allowed amount;
- To whom payment, if any, was made;
- Reasons for denial (if applicable).

RECONSIDERATION OF CLAIMS / APPEALS

If a healthcare provider, beneficiary or beneficiary's representative disagrees with a claim determination, including the VA-allowed amount, a request for reconsideration of the disputed determination may be made. To do so, the request must:

- Be in writing;
- Be accompanied by a copy of the EOB in question; and
- State the specific issue that is being disputed, why the VA determination is considered to be in error, and include any new and relevant information not previously considered.

To meet the filing deadline, requests for reconsideration are to be mailed to the following address within one year of the date of the initial EOB:

VA Health Administration Center
Reconsideration/Appeals
PO Box 460948
Denver CO 80246-0948

Upon complete review of the request and all the relevant documentation and evidence, a written determination will be mailed to the claimant.

CHAPTER 26

BENEFITS FOR POST-TRAUMATIC STRESS DISORDER AND SEXUAL TRAUMA

POST-TRAUMATIC STRESS DISORDER (PTSD)

PTSD is a condition resulting from exposure to direct or indirect threat of death, serious injury, or a physical threat. The events that can cause PTSD are called "stressors" and may include:

- Combat or war exposure;
- Sexual or physical abuse;
- Terrorist attacks;
- Serious accidents, such as a car wreck;
- Natural disasters such as a fire, tornado, hurricane, flood, or earthquake.

> **Experts think PTSD occurs:**
>
> *In about 11-20% of Veterans of the Iraq and Afghanistan wars (Operations Iraqi and Enduring Freedom), or in 11-20 Veterans out of 100.*
>
> *In as many as 10% of Gulf War (Desert Storm) Veterans, or in 10 Veterans out of 100.*
>
> *In about 30% of Vietnam Veterans, or about 30 out of 100 Vietnam Veterans.*

Symptoms of PTSD can include recurrent thoughts of the traumatic event, reduced involvement in work or outside interests, emotional numbing, hyper-alertness, anxiety and irritability. The disorder can be more severe and longer lasting when the stress is human initiated action (example: war, rape, terrorism).

There are many types of treatment for PTSD, including counseling and medicines known as SSRIs.

DISABILITY COMPENSATION

PTSD can be a service-connected disability.

The process of applying for a VA disability for PTSD can take several months, and can be both complicated and quite stressful. The Veterans Service Organizations provide Service Officers at no cost to help veterans and family members pursue VA disability claims.

Service Officers are familiar with every step in the application and interview process, and can provide both technical guidance and moral support. In addition, some Service Officers particularly specialize in assisting veterans with PTSD disability claims. Even if a veteran has not been a member of a specific Veterans Service Organization, the veteran still can request the assistance of a Service Officer working for that organization. In order to get representation by a qualified and helpful Service Officer, you can directly contact the local office of any Veterans Service Organization -- or ask for recommendations from other veterans who have applied for VA disability, or from a PTSD specialist at a VA PTSD clinic or a Vet Center.

Once the VA has awarded service connection for PTSD, it will then review the most current clinical evidence of record to determine how the severity of your symptoms impairs your social and industrial (ability to work) capacity.

The VA has a schedule of rating disabilities, located in title 38 C.F.R., Part 4. The VA has established "Diagnostic Codes" (DC) for various medical and psychiatric disorders, which include a description of the severity of related symptoms and a corresponding disability percentage (called a "rating" or "evaluation").

Although there are different DCs for covered psychiatric disorders, the VA evaluates the level of disability due to psychiatric disorders under the same criteria, regardless of the actual diagnosis. 38 C.F.R. §4.130, DC 9411, governs PTSD ratings. This regulation provides graduated ratings of 0%, 10%, 30%, 50%, 70% or 100%. A 0% rating is noncompensable this means that you have service-connected PTSD, however, there is little or no impairment as a result. VA compensation payments begin at 10% and increase at each rating level.

GENERAL RATING FORMULA FOR MENTAL DISORDERS:

Disability Rating	Description of Disability
100%	Total occupational and social impairment, due to such symptoms as: gross impairment in thought process or communication; persistent delusions or hallucinations; grossly inappropriate behavior; persistent danger of hurting self or others; intermittent inability to perform activities of daily living (including maintenance of minimal personal hygiene); disorientation to time or place; memory loss for names of close relatives, own occupation, or own name
70%	Occupational and social impairment, with deficiencies in most areas, such as work, school, family relations, judgment, thinking, or mood, due to such symptoms as: suicidal ideation; obsessional rituals which interfere with routine activities; speech intermittently illogical, obscure, or irrelevant; near-continuous panic or depression affecting the ability to function independently, appropriately and effectively; impaired impulse control (such as unprovoked irritability with periods of violence); spatial disorientation; neglect of personal appearance and hygiene; difficulty in adapting to stressful circumstances (including work or a work-like setting); inability to establish and maintain effective relationships
50%	Occupational and social impairment with reduced reliability and productivity due to such symptoms as: flattened affect; circumstantial, circumlocutory, or stereotyped speech; panic attacks more than once a week; difficulty in understanding complex commands; impairment of short- and long-term memory (e.g., retention of only highly learned material, forgetting to complete tasks); impaired judgment; impaired abstract thinking; disturbances of motivation and mood; difficulty in establishing and maintaining Effective work and social relationships

30%	Occupational and social impairment with occasional decrease in work efficiency and intermittent periods of inability to perform occupational tasks (although generally functioning satisfactorily, with routine behavior, self-care, and conversation normal), due to such symptoms as: depressed mood, anxiety, suspiciousness, panic attacks (weekly or less often), chronic sleep impairment, mild memory loss (such as forgetting names, directions, recent events)
10%	Occupational and social impairment due to mild or transient symptoms which decrease work efficiency and ability to perform occupational tasks only during periods of significant stress, or; symptoms controlled by continuous medication
0%	A mental condition has been formally diagnosed, but symptoms are not severe enough either to interfere with occupational and social functioning or to require continuous medication

VA SIMPLIFIES ACCESS TO HEALTH CARE AND BENEFITS FOR VETERANS WITH PTSD

In July 2010, VA simplified the process for a veteran to claim service connection for PTSD. VA reduced the evidence needed if the trauma claimed by a veteran is related to "fear of hostile military or terrorist activity," and is consistent with the places, types, and circumstances of the veteran's service.

Previously, unless the veteran was a combat veteran, claims adjudicators were required to undertake extensive record development to corroborate whether a veteran actually experienced the claimed in-service stressor.
The new rule will apply to claims:

- Received by VA on or after July 13, 2010;
- Received before July 13, 2010 but not yet decided by a VA regional office;
- Appealed to the Board of Veterans' Appeals on or after July 13, 2010;
- Appealed to the Board before July 13, 2010, but not yet decided by the Board; and

- Pending before VA on or after July 13, 2010, because the Court of Appeals for Veterans Claims vacated a Board decision and remanded for re-adjudication.

VA MEDICAL CENTER PROGRAMS

While PTSD treatment is available through all of VA's 171 medical centers, a VA network of 124 facilities offers specialized inpatient and outpatient treatment. One notable program consists of PTSD clinical teams that provide outpatient treatment but also work closely with other VA treatment programs, including Vet Centers, to coordinate services and provide information on PTSD throughout the medical center and the community.

In addition to 83 PTSD clinical teams, VA operates 22 specialized inpatient units around the country, plus 13 brief-treatment units, 11 residential rehabilitation programs, and four PTSD day hospitals. There also are four outpatient Women's Stress Disorder and Treatment Teams and eight outpatient-based PTSD Teams Substance Use Disorder demonstration projects. A special focus in the program expansions has included underserved and minority populations, such as African Americans, Hispanics and Native Americans. A specialized PTSD inpatient treatment unit serves women veterans at the Palo Alto, Calif., VA Medical Center's Menlo Park Division.

Each PTSD program offers education, evaluation, and treatment. Program services include:

- One-to-one mental health assessment and testing
- Medicines
- One-to-one psychotherapy and also family therapy
- Group therapy (covers topics such as anger and stress, combat support, partners, or groups for Veterans of specific conflicts

The VA provides treatments shown by research to be effective in treating Veterans. To learn about these treatments and the VA provider training programs, see our fact sheets: Cognitive Processing Therapy and Prolonged Exposure.

Services are conducted by mental health care workers. For more information about types of mental health care workers, see our fact sheet Finding and Choosing a Therapist.

NATIONAL PTSD CENTER

In 1989, VA established the National Center for Post-Traumatic Stress Disorder -- a center for clinical research, training and information on PTSD. The center initially consisted of five divisions with distinct, but complementary responsibilities:

- Behavioral Science;
- Clinical Neurosciences;

- Education;
- Evaluation; and
- Executive and Resource Center Divisions.

Growing recognition of the dimensions of PTSD has brought new programs, such as the Women's Health Sciences Division, located at the Boston VA Medical Center, and the Pacific Islands Division in Honolulu.

MOBILE APPS

The VA announced the development of mobile applications (apps) to provide self-help, education and support. The VA also has treatment companion apps, for use with a health care provider, to make treatment easier. There are apps for iOS and Android devices.

PTSD is a serious mental health condition that often needs professional evaluation and treatment. These apps are not intended to replace needed professional care.

In 2012 the Department of Veterans' Affairs and the Department of Defense announced a new smart phone application designed to help veterans manage PTSD. The app, entitled the PTSD Coach, is aimed at helping to enhance the care of veterans already receiving treatment for PTSD, but can also be helpful for those who want to learn more about PTSD or are considering seeking help for their symptoms. The PTSD Coach allows users to track symptoms, connect with local support services, locate information about PTSD and learn individualized strategies for managing symptoms. The PTSD Coach is free, and can be downloaded at the iTunes store.

HELP FOR FAMILIES

In 2011, the Department of Veterans' Affairs launched a new telephone service to assist family members and friends of veterans to encourage them to seek healthcare for readjustment and mental health issues. The telephone service is called Coaching Into Care and is available by calling **(888) 823-7458.**

MILITARY SEXUAL TRAUMA (MST)

Both women and men can experience sexual harassment or sexual assault during their military service. VA refers to these experiences as military sexual trauma, or MST. Like other types of trauma, MST can negatively impact a person's mental and physical health, even many years later. Some problems associated with MST include:

- Disturbing memories or nightmares;
- Difficulty feeling safe;
- Feelings of depression or numbness;

- Problems with alcohol or other drugs;
- Feeling isolated from other people;
- Problems with anger or irritability;
- Problems with sleep;
- Physical health problems.

VA defines sexual trauma as any lingering physical, emotional, or psychological symptoms resulting from a physical assault of a sexual nature, or battery of a sexual nature. Examples of this are:

- Rape;
- Physical assault;
- Domestic Battering; and
- Stalking.

Treatment for MST

People can recover from trauma. To help veterans do this, VA provides free, confidential counseling and treatment for mental and physical health conditions related to experiences of MST. You do not need to be service-connected and may be able to receive this benefit even if you are not eligible for other VA care. You do not need to have reported the incidents when they happened or have other documentation that they occurred.

Every VA facility has a designated MST Coordinator who serves as a contact person for MST-related issues. This person is your advocate and can help you find and access VA services and programs, state and federal benefits, and community resources.

Every VA facility has providers knowledgeable about treatment for the aftereffects of MST. Many have specialized outpatient mental health services focusing on sexual trauma. Vet Centers also have specially trained sexual trauma counselors.

Nationwide, there are programs that offer specialized sexual trauma treatment in residential or inpatient settings. These are programs for Veterans who need more intense treatment and support.

To accommodate veterans who do not feel comfortable in mixed-gender treatment settings, some facilities throughout VA have separate programs for men and women. All residential and inpatient MST programs have separate sleeping areas for men and women.

COMPENSATION FOR DISABILITIES

Disability Compensation is a monthly payment to a veteran disabled by an injury or a disease incurred or aggravated on active service. The veteran must have been discharged under other than dishonorable conditions to be eligible. The individual must currently be suffering from disabling symptoms to receive compensation. Refer to Chapter 3 of this book for information regarding Disability Compensation.

CHAPTER 27

BENEFITS FOR FORMER PRISONERS OF WAR (POWS)

Over 16,000 POWs are receiving disability compensation for service-connected injuries, diseases or illnesses.

Former American POWs are eligible for special veterans' benefits from the VA, including medical care in VA hospitals and disability compensation for injuries and disease presumed to be caused by internment. Studies have shown that the physical deprivation and psychological stress endured as a captive have life-long effects on subsequent health, social adjustment, and vocational adjustment.

Former prisoners of war (POW) are veterans who, while on active duty in the military, air, or naval service, were forcibly detained or interned in the line of duty by an enemy government or its agents or a hostile force. Periods of war include: World War II, the Korean War, the Vietnam War, and the Persian Gulf War (service after August 2, 1990).

Veterans who, while on active duty during peacetime, were forcibly detained or interned by a foreign government or its agents or a hostile force are also considered former POWs, if the circumstances of the internment were comparable to wartime internment (for example: Iran, Somalia or Kosovo).

A POW Coordinator has been designated at each VA regional office. The POW Coordinator can furnish former POWs with information about the benefits and services available to them.

HEALTHCARE

Former POWs are recognized as a special category of veterans, and will be placed on one of the top three Priority Groups established for VA healthcare by Congress. Those who have a service-connected disability are eligible for VA health care. This includes hospital, nursing home, and outpatient treatment. Former POWs who do not have a service-connected disability are eligible for VA hospital and nursing home care, regardless of the veterans' ability to provide payment. They are also eligible for outpatient care on a priority basis. Public Law 108-170, which became law December 6, 2003, eliminated prescription drug co-payments for former POWs.

Veterans who were POWs may receive complete dental care.

Former POWs are eligible for any prosthetic item, including eyeglasses and hearing aids. A VA physician must order the prosthetic items, when medically indicated, for eligible veterans.

Veterans may enroll in VA healthcare by completing VA Form 10-10, "Application for Medical Benefits."

DISABILITY COMPENSATION

Veterans are encouraged to apply for VA Disability Compensation for any disabilities related to service, whether they were a POW or not. Some disabilities are *presumptive*, which means that if a veteran is diagnosed with certain conditions, and the veteran was a POW for at least 30 days (certain conditions do not include the 30-day requirement), the VA presumes the captivity caused the disability.

PRESUMPTIONS OF SERVICE-CONNECTION RELATING TO CERTAIN DISEASES AND DISABILITIES FOR FORMER PRISONERS OF WAR

Public Law 108-183, The *Veterans Benefits Act of 2003*, eliminated the requirement that a veteran was a POW for at least 30 days for certain conditions. Therefore, there are now two categories of presumptive conditions – those that include the 30-day requirement, and those that do not.

In the case of any veteran who is a former prisoner of war, and **who was detained or interned for thirty days or more,** any of the following which became manifest to a degree of 10% or more after active military, naval or air service, shall be considered to have been incurred in or aggravated by such service, notwithstanding that there is no record of such disease during the period of service:

- Avitaminosis
- Beriberi
- Including beriberi heart disease, which includes Ischemic Heart Disease-coronary artery disease-for former POWs who suffered during captivity from edema-swelling of the legs or feet- also known as "wet" beriberi
- Chronic dysentery
- Helminthiasis

- Malnutrition (including optic atrophy associated with malnutrition)
- Pellagra
- Any other nutritional deficiency
- Peripheral neuropathy, except where directly related to infectious causes
- Irritable bowel syndrome
- Peptic ulcer disease
- Cirrhosis of the liver
- Osteoporosis, on or after September 28, 2009

In the case of any veteran who is a former prisoner of war, and **who was detained or interned for any period of time,** any of the following which became manifest to a degree of 10% or more after active military, naval or air service, shall be considered to have been incurred in or aggravated by such service, notwithstanding that there is no record of such disease during the period of service:

- Psychosis
- Dysthymic disorder, or depressive neurosis
- Post-traumatic osteoarthritis
- Any of the Anxiety States
- Cold Injury
- Stroke and complications
- Heart Disease and complications
- Osteoporosis, on or after October 10, 2008, when Post Traumatic Stress Disorder is diagnosed

Former POWs should file a claim by completing "VA Form 21-526, Application for Compensation or Pension." The VA also offers a POW protocol exam. This is a one-time exam available to all former POWs, and is conducted at a VA medical facility to help determine if any presumptive disabilities exist.

SURVIVORS OF POWS

There are benefits for survivors of POWs. The major benefit is Dependency and Indemnity Compensation (DIC) which is a monthly benefit payable to the surviving spouse (and the former POW's children and parents in some cases) when the former POW:

- Was a service member who died on active duty; or
- Died from service-related disabilities; or

- Died on or before September 30, 1999 and was continuously rated totally disabled for a service connected condition (including individual unemployability) for at least 10 years immediately preceding death; or

- Died after September 30, 1999, and was continuously rated totally disabled for a service-connected condition (including individual unemployability) for at least 1 year immediately preceding death.

DIC is terminated for a surviving spouse who remarries, but can be resumed if the remarriage ends in death, divorce, or annulment. However, a surviving spouse who remarries on or after attaining age 57, and on or after December 16, 2003, can continue to receive DIC.

PRISONER OF WAR MEDAL

A Prisoner of War Medal is available to any member of the U.S. Armed Forces taken prisoner during any armed conflict dating from World War I.

CHAPTER 28

BENEFITS FOR SPECIAL VETERANS GROUPS

BENEFITS FOR FILIPINO VETERANS

Citizens of the Republic of the Philippines who serve today in the U.S. Armed Forces are eligible for VA benefits under the same criteria as other U.S. military veterans but there are differences in available VA benefits for Filipino veterans who served in recognized units of the Philippine Armed Forces. These differences are particularly true for those Filipino veterans that served in World War II.

The Philippine Islands gained their independence from the United States in 1946 after a transition period, interrupted by World War II. During World War II, Filipinos served in a variety of units, some coming under direct U.S. military control, others having no ties to the U.S. military, and still others falling somewhere in the middle. Federal law, international treaties and court cases have taken up the question of which VA benefits should be given to various groups of World War II Filipino veterans.

FOUR CATEGORIES

For purposes of VA benefits and services, the service of members of the Philippine armed forces can be categorized as service in one of four groups:

REGULAR PHILIPPINE SCOUTS (ALSO CALLED OLD PHILIPPINE SCOUTS)

These veterans were members of a small, regular component of the U.S. Army that was considered to be in regular active service. Originally formed in 1901, long before any formal plan for Philippine independence, the Regular Philippine Scouts were part of the U.S. Army throughout their existence.

Special Philippine Scouts (also called New Philippine Scouts)

These individuals were Philippine citizens who served with the U.S. Armed Forces with the consent of the Philippine government, and served between October 6, 1945 and June 30, 1947, inclusive.

Commonwealth Army of the Philippines (also called the Philippine Commonwealth Army)

These individuals were called into the service of the United States Armed Forces of the Far East (USAFFE), its members serving between July 26, 1941 and June 30, 1946, inclusive.

Recognized Guerillas

People in this group served as guerrillas in USAFFE in resistance units recognized by, and cooperating with U.S. forces between April 20, 1942, through June 30, 1946, inclusive.

ELIGIBILITY FOR VA BENEFITS

Regular Philippine Scouts

Regular Philippine Scouts who served with U.S. forces before October 6, 1945, are entitled to all VA benefits, under the same criteria as veterans of the U.S. Armed Forces.

Monetary benefits are payable in Dollars, at the full rate authorized, and their dependents and survivors are entitled to benefits under the eligibility rules common to the survivors of all U.S. veterans.

Special Philippine Scouts (New Philippine Scouts)

These veterans and eligible dependents are entitled to:

- Disability Compensation;
- Clothing Allowance;
- Dependency & Indemnity Compensation (DIC);
- Health care benefits in the U.S. on the same basis as U.S. veterans, provided they reside in the United States, and are citizens or lawfully admitted for permanent residence;
- Burial benefits, at the full-dollar rate, if the veterans were lawfully living in the United States on the date of death, and were U. S. citizens or lawfully admitted

permanent resident aliens. Eligibility applies to death on or after December 16, 2003, based on legislation enacted in 2003.

Note: Monetary benefits are payable at a rate of $.50 of each Dollar authorized. (Commissioned officers are paid at the full rate authorized.) However, those veterans who live in the United States receive full-dollar rate compensation payments if they are either U.S. citizens or lawfully admitted permanent resident aliens.

Benefit Programs Not Available:

- Non-service connected pension benefits for veterans and dependents;
- Death pension;
- Hospital care and outpatient treatment for service-connected or non-service-connected conditions, if the care is provided outside of the U.S., or at facilities outside of the U.S. over which the VA has no jurisdiction, or has not contracted;
- Dental care;
- VA loans such as home loan guarantees;
- Specially adapted homes;
- Automobile or other conveyances;
- Service-disabled veterans insurance (RH);
- Gravemarker or headstone;
- Burial flag;
- Burial in a national cemetery.

COMMONWEALTH ARMY (PHILIPPINE COMMONWEALTH ARMY):

These veterans and eligible dependents are entitled to:

- Disability Compensation;
- Clothing Allowance;
- Dependency & Indemnity Compensation (DIC);
- Health care benefits in the U.S. on the same basis as U.S. veterans, provided they reside in the United States, and are citizens or lawfully admitted for permanent residence;
- Burial benefits, at the full-dollar rate, if the veterans were lawfully living in the United States on the date of death, and were U. S. citizens or lawfully admitted

permanent resident aliens. Eligibility applies to death on or after November 1, 2000, based on legislation enacted in 2000;

- Burial in national cemeteries (for deaths on or after November 1, 2000);
- Headstones and markers (for deaths on or after November 1, 2000);
- Burial Flag (for deaths on or after November 1, 2000).

Note: Monetary benefits are payable at a rate of $.50 of each Dollar authorized. (Commissioned officers are paid at the full rate authorized.) However, those veterans who live in the United States receive full-dollar rate compensation payments if they are either U.S. citizens or lawfully admitted permanent resident aliens.

BENEFIT PROGRAMS NOT AVAILABLE:

- Non-service connected pension benefits for veterans and dependents;
- Death pension;
- Dental care;
- VA loans such as home loan guarantees;
- Specially adapted homes;
- Automobile or other conveyances;
- Service-disabled veterans insurance (RH).

RECOGNIZED GUERILLAS

These veterans and eligible dependents are entitled to:

- Disability Compensation;
- Clothing Allowance;
- Dependency & Indemnity Compensation (DIC);
- Health care benefits in the U.S. on the same basis as U.S. veterans, provided they reside in the United States, and are citizens or lawfully admitted for permanent residence;
- Burial benefits, at the full-dollar rate, if the veterans were lawfully living in the United States on the date of death, and were U. S. citizens or lawfully admitted permanent resident aliens. Eligibility applies to death on or after November 1, 2000, based on legislation enacted in 2000;
- Burial in national cemeteries (for deaths on or after November 1, 2000);
- Headstones and markers (for deaths on or after November 1, 2000);

- Burial Flag (for deaths on or after November 1, 2000).

Note: Monetary benefits are payable at a rate of $.50 of each Dollar authorized. (Commissioned officers are paid at the full rate authorized.) However, those veterans who live in the United States receive full-dollar rate compensation payments if they are either U.S. citizens or lawfully admitted permanent resident aliens.

Benefit Programs Not Available:

- Non-service connected pension benefits for veterans and dependents;
- Death pension;
- Dental care;
- VA loans such as home loan guarantees;
- Specially adapted homes;
- Automobile or other conveyances;
- Service-disabled veterans insurance (RH).

Type of Service	Compensation	Pension	Clothing Allowance
Armed Forces of the U.S.	Yes	Yes	Yes
Regular Philippine Scouts and Insular Force of the U.S. Navy	Yes	Yes	Yes
Special Philippine Scouts	Yes Full rate payments for U.S. residents; half rate payments for non-U.S. residents	No	Yes
Commonwealth Army of the Philippines	Yes Full rate payments for U.S. residents; half rate payments for non-U.S. residents	No	Yes-Half Rate
Guerilla	Yes Full rate payments for U.S. residents; half rate payments for non-U.S. residents	No	Yes-Half Rate

HEALTHCARE BENEFITS

VA provides hospital, nursing home, and outpatient medical care to certain Filipino veterans in the same manner such care is provided to U.S. veterans. Regular Philippine Scouts are eligible for health care benefits based on their status as U.S. veterans. Commonwealth Army, Special Philippine Scouts, and Guerilla veterans are eligible for health care benefits in the U.S. on the same basis as U.S. veterans if they reside in the U.S. and are citizens or are lawfully admitted for permanent residence.

BENEFITS FOR ALLIED VETERANS AND CERTAIN NON-MILITARY GROUPS

ALLIED VETERANS

VA is authorized to provide medical care to certain veterans of nations allied or associated with the United States during World War I or World War II. Such treatment is available at any VA Medical Center if authorized and reimbursed by the foreign government. Necessary paperwork is obtained through the veteran's country in order to receive services for service connected conditions only.

Allied beneficiaries must meet the following eligibility requirements in order to receive VA health care benefits:

The government of the requesting nation must:

- Have a reciprocal agreement with VA;
- Submit proper authorization for services to be provided; and
- Provide a written agreement to reimburse for services provided; and
- The beneficiary must be living in the U.S.
-

MERCHANT MARINE SEAMEN

The Department of Defense announced January 19, 1988, that certain Merchant Marine seamen qualify as veterans.

Merchant seamen who engaged in active, ocean-going service from December 7, 1941 to August 15, 1945 are eligible to apply for a certificate of release or discharge from the DoD. This certificate will then entitle the holder to apply for VA benefits currently available to World War II veterans. This also includes Civil Service crewmembers aboard U.S. Army Transport Service and Naval Transportation vessels in ocean-going service or foreign waters.

Generally, these veterans and their survivors are eligible to apply for the same benefits that are available to other World War II veterans. These benefits include:

- Medical care;
- Disability compensation;
- Disability pension;
- DIC;
- Dental treatment;
- GI Insurance;
- Vocational rehabilitation;

- VA-guaranteed home loans;
- Burial benefits (see following Special Note Regarding Burial Benefits).

These veterans are not eligible for VA-administered education programs, although in certain limited circumstances they may establish eligibility for vocational rehabilitation.

Special Note Regarding Burial Benefits:

The *Veterans Programs Enhancement Act of 1998*, extended the ending qualifying date from August 15, 1945 to December 31, 1946 for eligibility for

- Burial flags;
- Headstones and markers;
- Internment in national cemeteries;
- Burial allowance for certain indigent wartime veterans;
- Markers in memorial areas of national cemeteries;
- Markers in memorial areas of Arlington National Cemetery; and
- Plot allowance payable to a State for burial in certain "state owned" cemeteries or cemetery sections.

Depending on the type of merchant marine service, certification of "qualified service" must come from the Department of Transportation or the Department of Defense. In general, benefits may be provided only for deaths occurring after November 11, 1998. However, in the case of an initial burial or columbarium placement in a national cemetery after November 11, 1998, benefits incident to burial and the provision of a headstone or marker are authorized regardless of the date of death.

Applying for Certificate of Release (Obtaining Veteran Status or Extension of Veteran Status)

Interested mariners or survivors should complete the following steps and mail to the proper address:

1. Compete Form DD2168 (available from all VA regional offices). Supply as much information as possible.
2. Include photocopies of discharges, identification, and any other supporting documents.
3. Survivors need to include a certified death certificate. (The Coast Guard will issue documents for a person listed as an official casualty list without a death certificate.)

4. Send to:
   USCG-National Maritime Center
   (NMC-421)
   Attn: WWII
   100 Forbes Dr.
   Martinsburg, WV 25404
   (888) 427-5662

OTHER NON-MILITARY GROUPS

Through the years, a number of non-military groups have provided military-related service to the United States. Many of these groups have been formally recognized by the Department of Defense, and granted VA benefits. A discharge by a Secretary of Defense is needed to apply for these benefits.

Service in the following groups has been certified as active military service for benefits purposes:

- Women's Air Force Service Pilots (WASPs);
- Signal Corps Female Telephone Operators Unit of World I;
- Engineer Field Clerks;
- Women's Army Auxiliary Corps (WAAC);
- Quartermaster Corps female clerical employees serving with the American Expeditionary Forces in World War I;
- Civilian employees of Pacific naval air bases who actively participated in defense of Wake Island during World War II;
- Reconstruction aides and dietitians in World War I;
- Male civilian ferry pilots;
- Wake Island defenders from Guam;
- Civilian personnel assigned to OSS secret intelligence;
- Guam Combat Patrol;
- Quartermaster Corps members of the Keswick crew on Corregidor during World War II;
- U.S. civilians who participated in the defense of Bataan;
- U.S. merchant seamen who served on blockships in support of Operation Mulberry in the World War II invasion of Normandy;
- American merchant marines in oceangoing service during WW II;
- Civilian Navy IFF radar technicians who served in combat areas of the Pacific during World War II;

- U.S. civilians of the American Field Service who served overseas in World War I;
- U.S. civilians of the American Field Service who served overseas under U.S. armies and U.S. army groups in World War II;
- U.S. civilian employees of American Airlines who served overseas in a contract with the Air Transport Command between Dec. 14, 1941, and Aug. 14, 1945;
- Civilian crewmen of U.S. Coast and Geodetic Survey vessels who served in areas of immediate military hazard while conducting cooperative operations with and for the U.S. Armed Forces between Dec. 7, 1941, and Aug. 15, 1945;
- Members of the American Volunteer Group (Flying Tigers) serving between Dec. 7, 1941, and July 18, 1942;
- U.S. civilian flight crew and aviation ground support employees of United Air Lines who served overseas in a contract with Air Transport Command between Dec. 14, 1941, and Aug. 14, 1945;
- U.S. civilian flight crew and aviation ground support employees of Transcontinental and Western Air, Inc. (TWA), who served overseas in a contract with the Air Transport Command between Dec. 14, 1941, and Aug. 14, 1945;
- U.S. civilian flight crew and aviation ground support employees of Consolidated Vultee Aircraft Corp. (Consairway Division) who served overseas in a contract with Air Transport Command between Dec. 14, 1941, and Aug. 14, 1945;
- U.S. civilian flight crew and aviation ground support employees of Pan American World Airways and its subsidiaries and affiliates, who served overseas in a contract with the Air Transport Command and Naval Air Transport Service between Dec. 14, 1941, and Aug. 14, 1945;
- Honorably discharged members of the American Volunteer Guard, Eritrea Service Command, between June 21, 1942, and March 31, 1943;
- U.S. civilian flight crew and aviation ground support employees of Northwest Airlines who served overseas under the airline's contract with Air Transport Command from Dec. 14, 1941, through Aug. 14, 1945;
- U.S. civilian female employees of the U.S. Army Nurse Corps who served in the defense of Bataan and Corregidor during the period January 2, 1942 to February 3, 1945;
- U.S. Flight crew and aviation ground support employees of Northeast Airlines Atlantic Division, who served overseas as a result of Northeast Airlines' contract with the Air Transport Command during the period December 7, 1941 through August 14, 1945;
- U.S. civilian flight crew and aviation ground support employees of Braniff Airways, who served overseas in the North Atlantic or under the jurisdiction of the North Atlantic Wing, Air Transport Command, as a result of a contract

with the Air Transport Command during the period February 26, 1942 through August 14, 1945.

- Chamorro and Carolina former native police who received military training in the Donnal area of central Saipan and were placed under command of Lt. Casino of the 6th Provisional Military Police Battalion to accompany U.S. Marines on active, combat patrol from Aug. 19, 1945, to Sept. 2, 1945.
- Three scouts/guides, Miguel Tenorio, Penedicto Taisacan, and Cristino Dela Cruz, who assisted the United States Marines in the offensive operations against the Japanese on the Northern Mariana Islands from June 19, 1944, through Sept. 2, 1945.
- The operational Analysis Group of the Office of Scientific Re- search and Development, Office of Emergency Management, which served overseas with the U.S. Army Air Corps from Dec. 7, 1941, through Aug. 15, 1945.
- Service as a member of the Alaska Territorial Guard during World War II or any individual who was honorably discharged under section 8147 of the Department of Defense Appropriations Act of 2001.

CHAPTER 29

NATURALIZATION PREFERENCE

Veterans who served prior to September 11, 2001, are eligible to file for naturalization based on their U.S. military service. An applicant who served three years in the U.S. military and is a lawful permanent resident is excused from any specific period of required residence, period of residence in any specific place, or physical presence within the United States if the application for naturalization is filed while the applicant is still serving in the military or within six months of honorable discharge. Applicants who file for naturalization more than six months after termination of three years of U.S. military service may count any periods of honorable service as residence and physical presence in the United States.

> *Qualifying members of the armed forces who have served at any time during a specified period of hostility may immediately apply for naturalization using the current application – Form N-400 – "Application for Naturalization."*

Aliens and non-citizen nationals with honorable service in the U.S. armed forces during specified periods of hostilities may be naturalized without having to comply with the general requirements for naturalization. This is the only section of the Immigration and Nationality Act, as amended, which allows persons who have not been lawfully admitted for permanent residence to file an application for naturalization.

Any person who has served honorably during qualifying time may file an application at any time in his or her life if, at the time of enlistment, reenlistment, extension of enlistment or induction, such person shall have been in the United States, the Canal Zone, American Samoa or Swain's Island, or, on or after November 18, 1997, aboard a public vessel owned or operated by the United States for non-commercial service, whether or not lawful admittance to the United States for permanent residence has been granted. Certain applicants who have served in the U.S. Armed Forces are eligible to file for naturalization based on current or prior U.S. military service. Such applicants should file the N-400 Military Naturalization Packet.

CHAPTER 30

HOMELESS VETERANS

Approximately one-third of the adult homeless population living on the streets or in shelters has served their country in the armed services. Many other veterans are considered at risk because of poverty, lack of support from family and friends and precarious living conditions in overcrowded or substandard housing.

In 2012 as part of Public Law 112-154, there were a number of changes in homeless and housing programs for veterans. These include:

Authorization of grant funds for the construction of transitional housing for homeless veterans. It also ensures the matching of funds from private and public sources for transitional housing.

Extension of funding for programs designed to assist homeless veterans, including homeless veterans reintegration programs and support services for low-income veteran families.

Public Law 112-154 increases case management and coordination of care for homeless veterans through state and local agencies.

VA has many benefits and services to assist homeless veterans, including:

HOMELESS PROVIDERS GRANT AND PER DIEM PROGRAM

VA's Homeless Providers Grant and Per Diem Program is offered annually (as funding permits) by the Department of Veterans Affairs Health Care for Homeless Veterans (HCHV) Programs to fund community agencies providing services to homeless veterans. The purpose is to promote the development and provision of supportive housing and/or supportive services with the goal of helping homeless veterans achieve residential stability, increase their skill levels and/or income, and obtain greater self-determination.

HOTLINE FOR HOMELESS VETERANS

In March 2010, VA announced a new hotline for homeless veterans:
(877) 4AID VET

Well trained expert responders will staff the hotline 24 hours a day, seven days a week. Responders can provide emergency support and resources to homeless veterans, as well as family members, community agencies and non-VA providers.

LOAN GUARANTEE PROGRAM FOR HOMELESS VETERANS MULTIFAMILY HOUSING

This initiative authorizes VA to guarantee no more than 15 loans with an aggregate value of $100 million within 5 years for construction, renovation of existing property, and refinancing of existing loans, facility furnishing or working capital. No more than 5 loans could be guaranteed under this program prior to November 11, 2001. The amount financed is a maximum of 90% of project costs. Legislation allows the Secretary to issue a loan guarantee for large-scale self-sustaining multifamily loans. Eligible transitional project are those that: 1) Provide supportive services including job counseling; 2) Require veteran to seek and maintain employment; 3) Require veteran to pay reasonable rent; 4) Require sobriety as a condition of occupancy; and, 5) Serves other veterans in need of housing on a space available basis.

STAND DOWNS

Stand Downs are one part of the Department of Veterans Affairs' efforts to provide services to homeless veterans. Stand Downs are typically one to three day events providing services to homeless veterans such as food, shelter, clothing, health screenings, VA and Social Security benefits counseling, and referrals to a variety of other necessary services, such as housing, employment and substance abuse treatment. Stand Downs are collaborative events, coordinated between local VAs, other government agencies, and community agencies who serve the homeless.

For additional information on Stand Down dates and locations, please contact the Homeless Veterans Programs Office at (202) 273-5764.

COMPENSATED WORK THERAPY/TRANSITIONAL RESIDENCE (CWT/TR) PROGRAM

In VA's Compensated Work Therapy/Transitional Residence (CWT/TR) Program, disadvantaged, at-risk, and homeless veterans live in CWT/TR community-based supervised group homes while working for pay in VA's Compensated Work Therapy Program (also known as Veterans Industries). Veterans in the CWT/TR program work about 33 hours per week, with approximate earnings of $732 per month, and pay an average of $186 per month toward maintenance and up-keep of the residence. The average length of stay is about 174 days. VA contracts with private industry and the public sector for work done by these veterans, who learn new job skills, relearn successful work habits, and regain a sense of self-esteem and self-worth.

CHALENG

The Community Homelessness Assessment, Local Education, and Networking Groups (CHALENG) for veterans is a nationwide initiative in which VA medical center and regional office directors work with other federal, state, and local agencies and nonprofit organizations to assess the needs of homeless veterans, develop action plans to meet identified needs, and develop directories that contain local community resources to be used by homeless veterans.

More than 10,000 representatives from non-VA organizations have participated in Project CHALENG initiatives, which include holding conferences at VA medical centers to raise awareness of the needs of homeless veterans, creating new partnerships in the fight against homelessness, and developing new strategies for future action.

For more information, please contact CHALENG at (404) 327-4033.

DCHV

The Domiciliary Care for Homeless Veterans (DCHV) Program provides biopsychosocial treatment and rehabilitation to homeless veterans. The program provides residential treatment to approximately 5,000 homeless veterans with health problems each year and the average length of stay in the program is 4 months. The domiciliaries conduct outreach and referral; vocational counseling and rehabilitation; and post-discharge community support.

DROP-IN CENTERS

These programs provide a daytime sanctuary where homeless veterans can clean up, wash their clothes, and participate in a variety of therapeutic and rehabilitative activities. Linkages with longer-term assistance are also available.

HUD-VASH

This joint Supported Housing Program with the Department of Housing and Urban Development provides permanent housing and ongoing treatment services to the harder-to-serve homeless mentally ill veterans and those suffering from substance abuse disorders. HUD's Section 8 Voucher Program has designated 1,780 vouchers worth $44.5 million for homeless chronically mentally ill veterans. VA staff at 35 sites provide outreach, clinical care and ongoing case management services. Rigorous evaluation of this program indicates that this approach significantly reduces days of homelessness for veterans plagued by serious mental illness and substance abuse disorders.

SUPPORTED HOUSING

Like the HUD-VASH program identified above, staff in VA's Supported Housing Program provides ongoing case management services to homeless veterans. Emphasis is placed on helping veterans find permanent housing and providing clinical support needed to keep veterans in permanent housing. Staff in these programs operates without benefit of the specially dedicated Section 8 housing vouchers available in the HUD-VASH program but are often successful in locating transitional or permanent housing through local means, especially by collaborating with Veterans Service Organizations.

COMPREHENSIVE HOMELESS CENTERS

VA's Comprehensive Homeless Centers (CHCs) place the full range of VA homeless efforts in a single medical center's catchment area and coordinate administration within a centralized framework. With extensive collaboration among non-VA service providers, VA's CHCs in Anchorage, AK; Brooklyn, NY; Cleveland, OH; Dallas, TX; Little Rock, AR; Pittsburgh, PA; San Francisco, CA; and West Los Angeles, CA, provide a comprehensive continuum of care that reaches out to homeless veterans and helps them escape homelessness.

VBA-VHA SPECIAL OUTREACH AND BENEFITS ASSISTANCE

VHA has provided specialized funding to support twelve Veterans Benefits Counselors as members of HCMI and Homeless Domiciliary Programs as authorized by *Public Law 102-590*. These specially funded staff provides dedicated outreach, benefits counseling, referral, and additional assistance to eligible veterans applying for VA benefits. This specially funded initiative complements VBA's ongoing efforts to target homeless veterans for special attention. To reach more homeless veterans, designated homeless veterans coordinators at VBA's 58 regional offices annually make over 4,700 visits to homeless facilities and over 9,000 contacts with non-VA agencies working with the homeless and provide over 24,000 homeless veterans with benefits counseling and referrals to other VA programs. These special outreach efforts are assumed as part of ongoing duties and responsibilities. VBA has also instituted new procedures to reduce the processing times for homeless veterans' benefits claims.

VBA'S ACQUIRED PROPERTY SALES FOR HOMELESS PROVIDERS

This program makes all the properties VA obtains through foreclosures on VA-insured mortgages available for sale to homeless provider organizations at a discount of 20 to 50 percent, depending on time of the market.

VA EXCESS PROPERTY FOR HOMELESS VETERANS INITIATIVE

This initiative provides for the distribution of federal excess personal property, such as hats, parkas, footwear, socks, sleeping bags, and other items to homeless veterans and homeless veteran programs. A Compensated Work Therapy Program employing formerly homeless veterans has been established at the Medical Center in Lyons, NJ to receive, warehouse, and ship these goods to VA homeless programs across the country.

SUPPORTIVE SERVICES FOR VETERAN FAMILIES (SSVF)

In July 2011, the VA announced the award of $60 million in grants to serve homeless and at-risk veterans and their families as part of the Supportive Services for Veteran Families (SSVF) program. The SSVF program awards grants to private non-profits and consumer cooperatives that provide a range of services to eligible low-income veteran families.

VA has been authorized to offer community-based grants through the Supportive Services for Veteran Families (SSVF) Program, which will provide supportive services to very low-income Veteran families in or transitioning to permanent housing. Funds are granted to private non-profit organizations and consumer cooperatives who will assist very low-income veteran families by providing a range of supportive services designed to promote housing stability.

Through the SSVF Program, VA aims to improve very low-income Veteran families' housing stability. Grantees (private non-profit organizations and consumer cooperatives) will provide eligible Veteran families with outreach, case management, and assistance in obtaining VA and other benefits, which may include:

- Health care services
- Daily living services
- Personal financial planning services
- Transportation services
- Fiduciary and payee services
- Legal services
- Child care services
- Housing counseling services

In addition, grantees may also provide time-limited payments to third parties (e.g., landlords, utility companies, moving companies, and licensed child care providers) if these payments help Veterans' families stay in or acquire permanent housing on a sustainable basis.

HEALTHCARE FOR HOMELESS VETERANS PROGRAM (HCHV)

HCHV programs now serve as the hub for a myriad of housing and other services which provide VA a way to outreach and assist homeless Veterans by offering them entry to VA care.

Outreach is the core of the HCHV program. The central goal is to reduce homelessness among Veterans by conducting outreach to those who are the most vulnerable and are not currently receiving services and engaging them in treatment and rehabilitative programs.

Contract Residential Treatment Program ensures that Veterans with serious mental health diagnoses can be placed in community-based programs which provide quality housing and services.

PROGRAM MONITORING AND EVALUATION

VA has built program monitoring and evaluation into all of its homeless veterans' treatment initiatives and it serves as an integral component of each program. Designed, implemented, and maintained by the Northeast Program Evaluation Center (NEPEC) at VAMC West Haven, CT, these evaluation efforts provide important information about the veterans served and the therapeutic value and cost effectiveness of the specialized programs. Information from these evaluations also helps program managers determine new directions to pursue in order to expand and improve services to homeless veterans.

CHAPTER 31

BENEFITS FOR FEMALE VETERANS

Females veterans are entitled to the same benefits that are available to male veterans (see below list), and the VA has also designed a number of programs aimed specifically at female veterans, including healthcare benefits and programs.

Women are the fastest growing group within the veteran population. In the last 10 years, the number of female veterans using VA care has doubled.

2013 Update: The VA announced the launch of a new hotline specifically for female veterans, which launched in April 2013. The hotline, 1-855-VA-WOMEN, is used to provide female veterans with a variety of information about health benefits, and other topics that are critical.

Female veterans are entitled to all of the benefits available to male veterans, including:

- Disability Compensation For Service-Related Disabilities;
- Disability Pension For Non-Service Related Disabilities;
- Education Assistance Programs;
- Work-Study Allowance;
- Vocational Rehabilitation And Counseling;
- Insurance;
- Home Loan Benefits;
- Medical Inpatient And Outpatient Care;
- Substance Abuse Treatment And Counseling;
- Sexual Trauma And Assault Counseling;
- Nursing Home Care;

- Burial Benefits;
- Burial In A VA National Cemetery;
- Employment Assistance;
- Survivors' Benefit Programs.

HEALTHCARE FOR FEMALE VETERANS

In the spring of 2012 the VA announced a new partnership with the American Heart Association to combat heart disease in female veterans. The program, entitled "Go Red for Women," is working to actively address the issues associated with heart disease in women, including smoking, poor diet and obesity, all of which are risk factors. Heart disease has been identified as the leading cause of death among women, and a third of female veterans suffer from high cholesterol or high blood pressure.

Women Veterans Health Care works to make certain that all eligible women Veterans requesting VA care are assured of:

- Comprehensive primary care by a proficient and interested primary care provider
- Privacy, safety, dignity, and sensitivity to gender-specific needs
- The right care in the right place and time
- State-of-the-art health care equipment and technology
- High-quality preventive and clinical care, equal to that provided to male Veterans

SERVICES PROVIDED TO WOMEN VETERANS INCLUDE:

- Primary Care
    - General care includes health evaluation and counseling, disease prevention, nutrition counseling, weight control, smoking cessation, and substance abuse counseling and treatment as well as gender-specific primary care, e.g., cervical cancer screens (Pap smears), breast cancer screens (mammograms), birth control, preconception counseling, Human Papillomavirus (HPV) vaccine, menopausal support (hormone replacement therapy).
- Mental health includes evaluation and assistance for issues such as depression, mood, and anxiety disorders; intimate partner and domestic violence; sexual trauma; elder abuse or neglect; parenting and anger management; marital, caregiver, or family-related stress; and post-deployment adjustment or post-traumatic stress disorder (PTSD).

- Military Sexual Trauma (MST). Women—and men as well—may experience repeated sexual harassment or sexual assault during their military service. Special services are available to women who have experienced MST. VA provides free, confidential counseling and treatment for mental and physical health conditions related to MST.

- Specialty Care

    - Management and screening of chronic conditions includes heart disease, diabetes, cancer, glandular disorders, osteoporosis, and fibromyalgia as well as sexually transmitted diseases such as HIV/AIDS and hepatitis.

    - Reproductive health care includes maternity care, infertility evaluation and limited treatment; sexual problems, tubal ligation, urinary incontinence, and others. VA is prohibited by legislative authority from providing either in-vitro fertilization or abortion services.

    - Rehabilitation, homebound, and long-term care. VA referrals are given to those in need of rehabilitation therapies such as physical therapy, occupational therapy, speech-language therapy, exercise therapy, recreational therapy, and vocational therapy. Homebound and long-term care services are available as well, limited to those meeting specific requirements

The VA has placed a strategic priority on six pillars, which are designed to give women veterans the best possible health care services. These include:

- **Comprehensive Primary Care**: Women Veterans Health Care works closely with Primary Care Services to redesign the way primary care is delivered, which tailors it to the specific needs of women.

- **Women's Health Education**: Women Veterans Health Care has partnered with the VA Employee Education Services to create mini-residencies in women's health, which will allow providers to be more educated in the advanced topics regarding women's health.

- **Reproductive Health**: Women Veterans Health Care is working to implement safe prescribing measures for female veterans of childbearing age. Other efforts include improving follow-up of abnormal mammograms, tracking the timeliness of breast cancer treatment, and ensuring the care women receive from non-VA, maternity and emergency department care.

- **Communication and Partnerships**: Women Veterans Health Care is working to develop a VA-wide communication plan to enhance the language, practice and culture of the VA to be more inclusive of female veterans.

- **Women's Health Research**: Women Veterans Health Care has partnered with the Women's Health Evaluation Initiative based in Palo Alto, CA to develop a series of Sourcebooks with key descriptive information about women Veterans including demographics, population growth over time, diagnoses, utilization and cost of care.

- **Special Women Veteran Populations**: WVHSHG is working to ensure that the needs of all women Veterans are addressed, including those populations that require special attention.
  - Rural and homebound veterans can benefit from emerging technology that will deliver care remotely through "e-clinics", mobile clinics, and home-based care services.
  - Women veterans with mental illnesses can benefit through integration of mental health services within primary care, so that necessary treatment is provided in a comprehensive and coordinated way. Women Veterans Health Care is also working to enhance the availability of woman-safe inpatient psychiatric acute units.
  - Aging women veterans can benefit from the latest advances in medical science and technology to identify and address cardiovascular disease as well as advances in treatments for diabetes, osteoporosis, and menopause.

Referrals are made for services that VA is unable to provide. Women Veterans' Program Managers are available in a private setting at all VA facilities to assist women veterans seeking treatment and benefits.

VA has also established a division within the National Center for Post-Traumatic Stress Disorder, the Women's Health Science Division. The center is based at the Boston VA Medical Center, and conducts clinical research addressing trauma-related problems of female veterans. Veterans may contact the Center at:

VA Medical Center
Women's Health Sciences Division
150 South Huntington Avenue
Boston, MA 02130
(617) 232-9500

WOMEN VETERANS COMPREHENSIVE HEATH CENTERS

Eight Women Veterans Comprehensive Health Centers have been established to develop and enhance programs focusing on the gender-specific healthcare needs of female veterans. The locations are as follows:

Boston VA Medical Center
Boston, Massachusetts
(617) 232-9500, extension 4276
Chicago Area Network
(Hines, Lakeside, North Chicago, and West Side VA Medical Centers)
(312) 569-6168

Durham VA Medical Center
Durham, North Carolina
(919) 286-0411

Minneapolis VA Medical Center
Minneapolis, Minnesota
(612) 725-2030

Southeast Pennsylvania Network
(Coatesville, Lebanon, Philadelphia and Wilmington VA Medical Centers)
(215) 823-44496

San Francisco VA Medical Center
San Francisco, California
(415) 221-4810, extension 2174
Sepulveda / West Los Angeles VA Medical Centers
Sepulveda, California and Los Angeles, California
(415) 221-4810

Tampa VA Medical Center
Tampa, Florida
(813) 972-2000, extension 3678

STATE WOMEN VETERANS COORDINATORS

In addition to the Department of Veterans Affairs' Women Veterans Coordinators that are located at local regional offices and medical centers, there may be an Office of State Veterans Affairs, or a State Commission for Veterans Coordinator available within the State government veterans program. These State offices are part of the veteran-advocate community and their staff may assist female veterans in accessing State and Federal entitlements. For specific information on availability in your state, contact your local VA office.

CHAPTER 32

BENEFITS FOR GULF WAR VETERANS

The first Gulf War, an offensive led by U.S. and coalition troops in January 1991, followed the August 1990 Iraqi invasion of Kuwait. The war was over on February 28, 1991, and an official cease-fire was signed in April 1991. The last U.S. troops who participated in the ground war returned home on June 13, 1991. In all, about 697,000 U.S. troops had been deployed to the Gulf region during the conflict.

Operation Iraqi Freedom, a military campaign which began on March 20, 2003, and Operation New Dawn, named for the reduced role of U.S. troops in Iraq, have created a new group of Gulf War veterans.

With variation in exposures and veterans' concerns ranging from oil well fire smoke to possible contamination from Iraqi chemical/biological agents, VA has initiated wide-ranging research projects evaluating illnesses as well as environmental risk factors.

VA operates a toll-free hotline at (800) 749-8387 to inform veterans of available programs.

The Department of Veterans Affairs (VA) offers Gulf War veterans physical examinations and special eligibility for follow-up care, and it operates a toll-free hotline at (800) 749-8387 to inform these veterans of the program and their benefits. Operators are trained to help veterans with general questions about medical care and other benefits. It also provides recorded messages that enable callers to obtain information 24 hours a day. Beginning in 2012, it was announced Veterans of the Persian Gulf War, with an undiagnosed illness, will have an additional five years to qualify for benefits from the VA. These changes also affect veterans of the Southwest Asia conflict. The change will apply to those veterans who may be eligible to claim VA disability compensation, as well as the ability of survivors to qualify for Dependency and Indemnity Compensation. Under previous VA guidelines, any undiagnosed illness used to establish eligibility for VA benefits had to be apparent by December 31, 2011. The new change in rules will push this date to December 31, 2016.

GULF WAR SERVICE

Gulf War service is active duty in any of the following areas in Southwest Asia during the Gulf War, which began in 1990 and continues to the present:

- Iraq
- Kuwait
- Saudi Arabia
- The neutral zone (between Iraq and Saudi Arabia)
- Bahrain
- Qatar
- The United Arab Emirates
- Oman
- Gulf of Aden
- Gulf of Oman
- Waters of the Persian Gulf, the Arabian Sea, and the Red Sea
- The airspace above these locations

PERSIAN GULF REGISTRY PROGRAM

A free, complete physical examination with basic lab studies is offered to every Gulf War veteran, whether or not the veteran is ill. Veterans do not have to be enrolled in VA healthcare to participate in registry examinations. Results of the examinations, which include review of the veteran's military service and exposure history, are entered into special, computerized registries. The registries enable VA to update veterans on research findings or new compensation policies through periodic newsletters. The registries could also suggest areas to be explored in future scientific research. Registry participants are advised of the results of their examinations in personal consultations and by letters.

SPECIAL ACCESS TO FOLLOW-UP CARE

VA has designated a physician at every VA medical center to coordinate the special registry examination program and to receive updated educational materials and information as experience is gained nationally. Where an illness possibly related to military service in the Southwest Asia Theater of operations during the Gulf War is detected during the examination, follow-up care is provided on a higher-eligibility basis than most non-service-connected care.

STANDARDIZED EXAM PROTOCOLS

VA has expanded its special registry examination protocol as more experience has been gained with the health of Gulf veterans. The protocol elicits information about symptoms and exposures, calls the clinician's attention to diseases common to the Gulf region, and directs baseline laboratory studies including chest X-ray (if one has not been done recently), blood count, urinalysis, and a set of blood chemistry and enzyme analyses that detect the "biochemical fingerprints" of certain diseases. In addition to this core laboratory work for every veteran undergoing the Gulf War program exam, physicians order additional tests and specialty consults as they would normally in following a diagnostic trail -- as symptoms dictate. If a diagnosis is not apparent, facilities follow the "comprehensive clinical evaluation protocol." The protocol suggests 22 additional baseline tests and additional specialty consultations, outlining dozens of further diagnostic procedures to be considered, depending on symptoms.

GULF WAR ILLNESS

Gulf War veterans have reported a variety of medically unexplained symptoms, such as fatigue, headache, joint pains, sleep disturbances and memory problems since serving in the Gulf. VA has recognized certain health problems as associated with Gulf War service or military service.

VA has recognized that certain health problems for Gulf War Veterans are associated with Gulf War service or military service. These Veterans may be eligible for disability compensation and health care for these illnesses. Surviving spouses, children and dependent parents of Gulf War Veterans who died as the result of illnesses associated with Gulf War service may be eligible for survivors' benefits.

For the purposes of these benefits, Gulf War Veterans are Veterans who served on active duty in the Southwest Asia theater of operations any time during the first Gulf War starting August 2, 1990 through the current conflict in Iraq. This includes Veterans who served in Operation Iraqi Freedom (2003-2010) and Operation New Dawn (2010 and continuing).

Illnesses that are associated with Gulf War service include:

- **Medically Unexplained Chronic Multi-symptom Illnesses**

  Gulf War Veterans have reported a variety of medically unexplained symptoms, such as fatigue, headache, joint pains, sleep disturbances and memory problems since serving in the Gulf. VA presumes certain medically unexplained symptoms existing for six months or more are associated with military service in the Gulf. The illnesses must have appeared during active duty in the Southwest Asia theater of operations or by December 31, 2016, and be at least 10 percent disabling.

  Illnesses include medically unexplained multi-symptom illnesses that have existed for six months or more, such as:

  - Chronic fatigue syndrome
  - Fibromyalgia
  - Functional gastrointestinal disorders, a group of conditions marked by chronic or recurrent symptoms related to any part of the gastrointestinal tract. Functional condition refers to an abnormal function of an organ, without a structural alteration in the tissues. Examples include irritable bowel syndrome (IBS),

functional dyspepsia, and functional abdominal pain syndrome. VA's final rule specifying that functional gastrointestinal disorders are covered as presumptive illnesses took effect on August 15, 2011.

- Undiagnosed illnesses with symptoms that may include but are not limited to: abnormal weight loss, cardiovascular symptoms, fatigues, gastrointestinal symptoms, headache, joint pain, menstrual disorders, muscle pain, neurologic symptoms, neuropsychological symptoms, skin conditions, upper and lower respiratory system symptoms, and sleep disturbances

- **Infectious Diseases**

In late 2010, VA established new presumptions of service connection for nine specific infectious diseases associated with military service in Southwest Asia during the first Gulf War starting August 2, 1990, through the conflict in Iraq and on or after September 19, 2001, in Afghanistan. Veterans must have the diseases within the time frames shown below and have a current disability as a result of that disease in order to receive disability compensation:

- Brucellosis
- Campylobacter jejuni
- Coxiella burnetii (Q fever)
- Malaria
- Mycobacterium tuberculosis
- Nontyphoid Salmonella
- Shigella
- Visceral leishmaniasis
- West Nile virus

A veteran now only has to show service in Southwest Asia or Afghanistan and that he or she had one of the nine diseases within a certain time after service, and has a current disability as a result of that disease, subject to certain time limits for seven of the diseases.

- **Amyotrophic Lateral Sclerosis (ALS)**

VA does not presume that amyotrophic lateral sclerosis (ALS) is associated with hazardous exposures during the Gulf War. However, VA has recognized ALS diagnosed in Veterans with 90 days or more of continuously active service in the military was caused by their military service.

OBTAINING COPIES OF HOSPITAL RECORDS

A program is in place to help Gulf War veterans obtain copies of their in-patient hospital records from hospitals established during the Persian Gulf War.

Although these records were always located in the National Personnel Records Center in St. Louis, MO, they were stored only by the name of the hospital and the date of treatment.

An electronic database has been created to cross-reference patient names and social security numbers with their theater hospitals and admission dates.

Veterans may call (800) 497-6261 to find out if their inpatient record has been added to the database, and to obtain the paperwork necessary to request a copy.

CHAPTER 33

SERVICEMEMBERS' CIVIL RELIEF ACT

Congress and state legislatures have long recognized that military service can often place an economic and legal burden on servicemembers. The *Soldiers' and Sailors' Civil Relief Act of 1918* was passed in order to protect the rights of service members while serving on active duty.

Service members were protected from such things as repossession of property, bankruptcy, foreclosure or other such actions while serving in the military. This Act remained in effect until shortly after World War I when it expired. The *Soldiers' and Sailors' Civil Relief Act of 1940* (SSCRA) was passed in order to protect the rights of the millions of service members activated for World War II. The SSCRA has remained in effect until the present day and has been amended many times since 1940 to keep pace with the changing military.

In December 2003, Congress passed legislation renaming SSCRA as the *Servicemembers' Civil Relief Act* (SCRA). The SCRA updates and strengthens the civil protections enacted during World War II.

The SCRA is designed to protect active duty military members, reservists who are in active federal service, and National Guardsmen who are in active federal service. Some of the benefits under the SCRA extend to dependents of active duty military members as well.

Public Law 107-330 extended protections under the SSCRA to members of the National Guard who are called to active service authorized by the President or the Secretary of Defense, or a state governor for a period of more than 30 consecutive days, for purposes of responding to a national emergency declared by the President, and supported by Federal funds.

The SCRA can provide many forms of relief to military members. Below are some of the most common forms of relief.

PROTECTION FROM EVICTION

If a military member is leasing a house or apartment and his or her rent is below a certain amount, the SCRA can protect the individual from being evicted for a period of time, usually three months. The dwelling place must be occupied by either the active duty member or his or her dependents and the rent on the premises cannot exceed $2,975.54 a month (rate as of 2011). This rent ceiling will be adjusted annually for consumer price index (CPI) changes. Additionally, the military member must show that military service materially affects his or her ability to pay rent. If a landlord continues to try to evict the military member or does actually evict the member, he or she is subject to criminal sanctions such as fines or even imprisonment.

TERMINATION OF PRE-SERVICE RESIDENTIAL LEASES

The SCRA also allows military members who are just entering active duty service to lawfully terminate a lease without repercussions. To do this, the service member needs to show that the lease was entered into prior to the commencement of active duty service, that the lease was signed by or on behalf of the service member, and that the service member is currently in military service or was called to active-duty service for a period of 180 days or more. Proper written notice with a copy of orders must be provided to the landlord.

TERMINATION OF RESIDENTIAL LEASES DURING MILITARY SERVICE

The SCRA allows military members who receive permanent change of station (PCS) orders or are deployed for a period of 90 days or more to terminate a lease by providing written notice to the landlord along with a copy of the military orders. The termination of a lease that provides for monthly payment of rent will occur 30 days after the first date on which the next rental payment is due and payable after the landlord receives proper written notice.

MORTGAGES

The SCRA can also provide military members temporary relief from paying their mortgage. To obtain relief, a military member must show that their mortgage was entered into prior to beginning active duty, that the property was owned prior to entry into military service, that the property is still owned by the military member, and that military service materially affects the member's ability to pay the mortgage.

Mortgage foreclosures or lien actions initiated during your military service or within nine months after the end of your military service must be stayed upon your request. This applies only to obligations that you have undertaken before entering active duty. A court may instead "adjust the obligations in a way that preserves the interests of all parties."

Note that the nine-month period reverts to 90 days as of January 1, 2013, unless further extended.

No sale, foreclosure, or seizure of property for a breach of a pre-service mortgage-type obligation is valid if made during or within 9 months after the period of active duty, unless pursuant to a valid court order. This provides the service member tremendous protections from foreclosure in the many states that permit foreclosures to proceed without involvement of the courts. Service members who miss any mortgage payments should immediately see a legal assistance attorney.

MAXIMUM RATE OF INTEREST

Under the SCRA, a military member can cap the interest rate at 6% for all obligations entered into before beginning active duty if the military service materially affects his or her ability to meet the obligations. This can include interest rates on credit cards, mortgages, and even some student loans (except for Federal guaranteed student loans), to name a few. To qualify for the interest rate cap the military member has to show that he or she is now on active duty, that the obligation or debt was incurred prior to entry on active duty, and that military service materially affects the members' ability to pay. To begin the process, the military member needs to send a letter along with a copy of current military orders to the lender requesting relief under the SCRA. The interest rate cap lasts for the duration of active duty service. The interest rate cap will apply from the first date of active-duty service. The military member must provide written notice to the creditor and a copy of military orders not later than 180 days after the servicemember's termination or release from military service.

TERMINATION OF AUTOMOBILE LEASES DURING MILITARY SERVICE

The SCRA allows military members to terminate pre-service automobile leases if they are called up for military service of 180 days or longer. Members who sign automobile leases while on active-duty may be able to terminate an automobile lease if they are given orders for a permanent change of station outside the continental United States or to deploy with a military unit for a period of 180 days or longer.

STAY OF PROCEEDINGS

If a military member is served with a complaint indicating that they are being sued for some reason, they can obtain a "stay" or postponement of those proceedings if the military service materially affects their ability to proceed in the case. A stay can be used to stop the action altogether, or to hold up some phase of it. According to the SCRA, military members can request a "stay" during any stage of the proceedings. However, the burden is on the military member to show that their military service has materially affected their ability to appear in court. In general, individuals can request a stay of the proceedings for a reasonable period of time (30-60 days). For example, if they are being sued for divorce, they can put off the hearing for some period of time, but it is unlikely that a court will allow the proceedings to be put off indefinitely. The stay can be granted in administrative proceedings.

DEFAULT JUDGMENTS

A default judgment is entered against a party who has failed to defend against a claim that has been brought by another party. To obtain a default judgment, a plaintiff must file an affidavit (written declaration of fact) stating that the defendant is not in the military service and has not requested a stay. If someone is sued while on active duty, and fails to respond, and as a result a default judgment is obtained against them, they can reopen the default judgment by taking several steps. First, they must show that the judgment was entered during their military service or within 30 days after they've left the service. Second, they must write to the court requesting that the default judgment be reopened while they are still on active duty or within 90 days of leaving the service. Third, they must not have made any kind of appearance in court, through filing an answer or otherwise, prior to the default judgment being entered. Finally, they must indicate that their military service prejudiced their ability to defend their case and show that they had a valid defense to the action against them.

INSURANCE

Under SCRA, the U.S. Department of Veterans Affairs (VA) will protect, from default for nonpayment of premiums, up to **$250,000** of life insurance for servicemembers called to active duty. (This amount was previously $10,000.) The protection provided by this legislation applies during the insured's period of military service and for a period of two years thereafter. The following are conditions for eligibility for protection:

- The policy must be whole life, endowment, universal life or term insurance.
- The policy must have been in force on a premium-paying basis for at least six months at the time the servicemember applies for benefits.
- Benefits from the policy cannot be limited, reduced or excluded because of military service.
- Policies for which an additional amount of premium is charged due to military service are not eligible for protection under SCRA.

The servicemember must apply for protection of their life insurance by filing "*VA* Form 29-380 "Application For Protection Of Commercial Life Insurance Policy" with his/her insurance company and forwarding a copy of the application to VA.

BENEFITS OF SCRA LIFE INSURANCE PROTECTION

Once the servicemember has applied for protection of their life insurance policy and VA determines that the policy is eligible for protection under SCRA:

- The servicemember is still responsible for making premium payments. However, the policy will not lapse, terminate, or be forfeited because of the servicemember's failure to make premium payments or to pay any indebtedness or interest due during their period of military service or for a period of two years thereafter.
- The rights of the servicemember to change their beneficiary designation or select an optional settlement for a beneficiary are not affected by the provisions of this Act.

Limitations Of SCRA Life Insurance Protection

Once the servicemember has applied for protection of their life insurance policy and VA determines that the policy is eligible for protection under SCRA:

- Premium payments are deferred only, not waived. *During this period, the government does not pay the premiums on the policy but simply guarantees that the premiums will be paid at the end of the servicemember's period of active duty.*
- A servicemember cannot receive dividends, take out a loan, or surrender the policy for cash without the approval of VA. (Dividends or other monetary benefits shall be added to the value of the policy and will be used as a credit when final settlement is made with the insurer.)

- If the policy matures as a result of the insured's death, or any other means, during the protected period, the insurance company will deduct any unpaid premiums and interest due from the settlement amount.

Termination Of Period Under SCRA

The servicemember has up to two years after their military service terminates to repay the unpaid premiums and interest to the insurer. If the amount owed is not paid before the end of the two years, then:

- The insurer treats the unpaid premiums as a loan against the policy.
- The government will pay the insurer the difference between the amount due and the cash surrender value (if the cash surrender value of the policy is less than the amount owed.)
- The amount the United States government pays to the insurance company under the SCRA Act becomes a debt due the government by the insured.
- If the policy matures as a result of the insured's death, or any other means, during the protected period, the insurance company will deduct any unpaid premiums and interest due from the settlement amount.

TAXATION

A service member's state of legal residence may tax military pay and personal property. A member does not lose residence solely because of a transfer to another state pursuant to military orders.

For example, if an Illinois resident who is a member of Illinois Army National Guard is activated to federal military service and sent to California for duty, that person remains an Illinois resident while in California. The service member is not subject to California's authority to tax his/her military income. However, if the service member has a part-time civilian job in California, California will tax his/her non-military income earned in the state.

The Servicemembers Civil Relief Act also contains a provision preventing servicemembers from a form of double taxation that can occur when they have a spouse who works and is taxed in a state other than the state in which they maintain their permanent legal residence. The law prevents states from using the income earned by a servicemember in determining the spouse's tax rate when they do not maintain their permanent legal residence in that state.

Public Law 111-98, which became law on November 11, 2009, provides that when a service member leaves his or her home state in accord with military or naval orders, the service member's spouse may retain residency in his or her home state for voting and tax purposes, after relocating from that state to accompany the service member.

RIGHT TO VOTE

In addition to the protections involving debt payments and civil litigation, the act guarantees service members the right to vote in the state of their home of record and protects them from paying taxes in two different states.

CAUTION

The SSCRA does not wipe out any of an individual's obligations. Rather, it temporarily suspends the right of creditors to use a court to compel an individual to pay, only if the court finds that the inability to pay is due to military service. The obligation to honor existing debts remains, and some day the individual must "pay up."

It is important to remember that the SSCRA affords no relief to persons in the Service against the collection of debts or other obligations contracted or assumed by them **after** entering such Service.

The Relief Act is highly technical. The above summary is intended only to give a general overview of the protection available. The specific nature of all the relief provided under the law is a matter about which an individual may need to contact an attorney. The Act is designed to deal fairly with military personnel and their creditors. While relief is very often available, individuals are expected and required to show good faith in repayment of all debts.

VETERANS BENEFITS ACT OF 2010

- Amends the *Servicemembers Civil Relief Act* (SCRA) to prohibit lessors from charging early termination fees with respect to residential, business, agricultural, or motor vehicle leases entered into by servicemembers who subsequently enter military service or receive orders for a permanent change of station or deployment in support of a military operation.

- Allows a servicemember to terminate a contract for cellular or home telephone service at any time after receiving military orders to deploy for at least 90 days to a location that does not support the contract. Requires the return of any advance payments made by a deploying servicemember under such a contract.

- Allows the Attorney General to bring a civil suit against any violator of the SCRA. Also gives servicemembers a "private right of action" to file their own lawsuits against those who violate their legal rights.

CHAPTER 34

APPEALS

Veterans and other claimants for VA benefits have the right to appeal decisions made by a VA regional office or medical center.

If a claimant wishes to appeal a VA decision, the appeal is first reviewed by the BOARD OF VETERANS APPEALS. If, after review by the Board of Veterans' Appeals, the claimant is still dissatisfied, he or she may appeal to the UNITED STATES COURT OF VETERANS APPEALS. Both entities, along with specific guidelines for the filing of appeals, are discussed in the remainder of this chapter.

BOARD OF VETERANS APPEALS

The Board of Veterans Appeals was established by law to decide appeals for benefits under laws administered by the Veterans Administration. The Board of Veterans' Appeals (BVA) is a part of the Department of Veterans Affairs, located in Washington, D.C. Decisions are made by the members of a section of the Board, appointed with the approval of the president. The Board members are attorneys experienced in veterans' law and in reviewing benefit claims. It is the mission of the Board to decide appeals with sympathetic understanding and as promptly as possible, in order to grant all benefits to which veterans and their dependents and beneficiaries are entitled. Decisions are based on a veteran's entire record.

GENERAL INFORMATION

Anyone who has filed a claim for benefits with VA and has received a determination from a local VA office is eligible to appeal to the Board of Veterans' Appeals. Some decisions, such as eligibility for medical treatment, issued by VA medical centers can also be appealed to the BVA. An appeal can be made based on a complete denial of a claim, or based on the level of benefit granted. For example, if a veteran files a claim for disability, and the local VA office awards a 10% disability, but the veteran feels he or she is more than 10% disabled, the veteran can appeal that determination to the Board of Veterans' Appeals.

Decisions concerning the need for medical care or the type of medical treatment needed (such as a physician's decision to prescribe or not to prescribe a particular drug, or whether to order a specific type of treatment) are not within the BVA's jurisdiction.

- On December 22, 2006 then-President Bush signed *Public Law 109-461*, the *Veterans' Benefits, Healthcare, and Information Technology Act of 2006*. The law allows veterans to hire an agent or attorney to represent them after a Notice of Disagreement has been filed. (A Notice of Disagreement is the written statement submitted by the veteran stating he or she disagrees with the claim decision made by the VA regional office.) Veterans will still have the option of utilizing the representation services provided without charge by many veterans' organizations, but in addition they will have the option of hiring an attorney if they so choose. Until now, the United States Code has not allowed a veteran to hire an attorney until the veteran has received a final Board of Veterans' Appeals (BVA) decision – a process that often takes years from a veterans' initial application.

HOW TO FILE AN APPEAL AND IMPORTANT TIME LIMITS

> You must send your NOD within one year of the date your local VA office mailed you its original decision denying your claim.

No special form is required to begin the appeal process. All that is initially needed is a written statement that the veteran disagrees with a claim decision. This initial statement is known as the "Notice of Disagreement" (NOD). The NOD must include why the veteran disagrees with a regional office decision. For example, perhaps the veteran feels that the office making the decision overlooked or misunderstood some evidence, or misinterpreted the law.

The Notice of Disagreement should be filed at the VA regional office where the veteran's claims file is kept. Normally, this is the same VA regional office or medical facility that issued the decision being appealed. However, if a veteran moves after a filing a claim, his or her claims file is transferred to the appropriate VA regional office, and that is where the NOD should be sent.

After the local VA office reviews a Notice of Disagreement, it is possible that the local office will agree with the NOD, and will change its original decision. However, if the local VA office does not change its decision, it will prepare and mail the veteran a *Statement of the Case*, which includes a VA Form 9 -Substantive Appeal, which the veteran must complete and return. The Statement of Case will summarize the evidence and applicable laws and regulations, and provide a discussion of the reasons for arriving at the decision.

Within 60 days of the date the local VA office issue the Statement of Case, the veteran must submit a completed VA Form 9-Substantive Appeal. Please note that if the one-year period from the date the VA regional office or medical center mailed its original decision is later than this 60-day period, the veteran has until that later one-year date to file the VA Form 9-Substantive Appeal.

Completion of the VA Form 9-Substantive Appeal is very important. The form should include a clear statement of the benefit being sought, as well as any mistakes the veteran feels VA made when issuing its decision. VA Form 9-Substantive Appeal should also identify anything in the Statement of Case the veteran disagrees with. In addition to VA Form 9, any additional evidence, such as records from recent medical treatments or evaluations may be included as part of the appeal.

In most instances, a veteran can obtain civilian medical records and other non-government documents supporting his or her case by calling or writing directly to the office that keeps those records. VA regional office personnel and VSO representatives are experienced in locating many items that can support your case, such as service medical records, VA treatment records, and other government records. The VA does have a duty to assist veterans in the developing of their cases. However, individual veterans need to assist the VA in identifying the evidence that can prove the case.

If new information or evidence is included with VA Form 9, the regional office will prepare a Supplemental Statement of the Case (SSOC). The SSOC is similar to the Statement of the Case, but addresses the new information or evidence. If a veteran is not satisfied with the SSOC, a written statement must be mailed to the regional office within 60 days from the mailing date of the SSOC.

It is important to realize the importance of submitting the VA Form 9-Substantive Appeal on a timely basis, otherwise, the right to appeal may be lost. Remember, the VA Form 9 is due the later of:

1 year from Regional Office determination mailing date

or

60 days from Statement of Case (SOC) mailing date

An extension of the 60-day period for filing VA Form 9-Substantive Appeal or the 60-day period following a Supplemental Statement of the Case **may** be approved if a written request is filed with the local VA office handling the appeal. An extension will only be approved if the veteran can show "good cause" (can offer a valid reason why the extra time is needed).

DOCKET

A veteran's VA Form 9-Substantive Appeal becomes part of his or her claims folder, and is the basis for adding the appeal to the Board's *docket.*

The Board's docket is the record of all appeals awaiting review by the Board, listed in the order that appeals (VA Form 9) are received.

When an appeal is placed on the Board's docket, it is assigned the next higher number than the one received before it. The Board reviews appeals in the order in which they were placed on the docket. Thus, the lower the docket number, the sooner the appeal will be reviewed.

LAWYERS AND OTHER REPRESENTATIVES

A veteran may represent himself or herself. However, over 90% of all people who appeal to the Board of Veterans' Appeals obtain representation. The majority choose to be represented by Veterans' Service Organizations (VSOs) or their state's veterans department.

A lawyer may also be hired for representation. There are strict guidelines about what a lawyer may charge for services, as well as restrictions on fees that a lawyer may charge for work performed prior to issuance of the Board's final decision.

In addition to VSOs and attorneys, some other agents are recognized by VA to represent appellants.

To authorize a VSO for representation, VA Form 21-22 must be completed. To authorize an attorney or recognized agent for representation, VA Form 22a must be completed. Both forms are available at all VA offices.

LENGTH OF APPEAL PROCESS

No one can determine exactly how long it will take form the time an appeal is filed until receipt of the Board's decision. However, veterans can expect an average of two years from the time an appeal is placed on the Board's docket until issuance of a BVA decision.

If a veteran believes his or her case should be decided sooner than others filed earlier, a *motion to advance on the docket* can be submitted. The motion should explain why the appeal should be moved ahead. Because most appeals involve some type of hardship, before a case can be advanced, there needs to be convincing proof of exceptional circumstances (i.e. terminal illness, danger of bankruptcy or foreclosure, or an error by VA that caused a significant delay in the docketing of an appeal. Veterans should be aware that, on average, fewer than 3 out of every 20 requests for advancement on the docket are granted.

To file a motion to advance on the docket, a written request should be sent to:

Board of Veterans' Appeals (014)
Department of Veterans Affairs
810 Vermont Avenue, NW
Washington, DC 20420

PERSONAL HEARINGS

A personal hearing is a meeting between the veteran (and his/her representative) and an official from VA who will decide the case. During the hearing, the veteran presents testimony and other evidence supporting the case. There are two types of personal hearings:

- Regional office hearings (also called RO hearing or local office hearings); and
- BVA hearings.

A regional office hearing is a meeting held at a local VA office with a "hearing officer" from the local office's staff. To arrange a regional office hearing, a veteran should contact the local VA office or appeal representative as early in the appeal process as possible.

In a BVA hearing, the veteran presents his or her case in person to a member of the Board. Appellants in most areas of the country can choose whether to hold the BVA hearing at the local VA regional office, called a "Travel Board Hearing," or at the BVA office in Washington, D.C. Some regional offices are also equipped to hold BVA hearings by videoconference. (Check with the regional office for availability.)

The VA cannot pay for any lodging or travel expenses incurred in connection with a hearing.

The VA Form 9-SubstantiveAppeal has a section for requesting a BVA hearing. VA Form 9 is not used, however, to request a local office hearing. Even if a BVA hearing is not requested on the VA Form 9, a request can still be requested by writing directly to the Board. If a BVA hearing is requested, the request must clearly state where the hearing is requested – at the VA regional office, or at the Board's office in Washington, D.C. A BVA hearing cannot be held in both places. (Travel Board hearings may not be available at regional offices located near Washington, D.C.)

The requested type and location of the hearing determines when it will be held. Generally, regional office hearings are held as soon as they can be scheduled on the hearing officer's calendar.

The scheduling of BVA hearings held at regional offices (Travel Board hearings) is more complicated, since Board members must travel from Washington, D.C. to the regional office. BVA video-conferenced hearings are less complicated to arrange, and can be scheduled more frequently than Travel Board hearings.

Hearings held at the Board's offices in Washington, D.C. will be scheduled for a time close to when BVA will consider the case – approximately three months before the case is reviewed by the BVA.

LOCATION OF CLAIMS FOLDER

If a BVA hearing is not requested, the claims folder remains at the local VA office until shortly before the BVA begins its review, at which time it is transferred to the BVA.

If a Travel Board hearing is requested, the claims folder remains at the local VA office until the hearing is completed, at which time it is transferred to the BVA.

If a video-conferenced BVA hearing or a hearing held at the Board's office in Washington, D.C. is requested, the claims folder remains at the local VA office until shortly before the BVA hearing is held. It is transferred to the BVA in time for the hearing and the Board's review.

When a claims folder is transferred from the local VA office to Washington, D.C., the local VA office will send the claimant a letter advising that he or she has 90 days remaining (from the date of that letter) during which more evidence can be added to a file, a hearing can be requested, or a representative can be selected (or changed).

The BVA cannot accept items submitted after the 90-day period has expired, unless a written explanation (called a "motion") is also submit, explaining why the item is late and showing why the BVA should accept it (called "showing good cause"). A motion to accept items after the 90-day period will be reviewed by a Board member who will issue a ruling either allowing or denying the motion.

CHECKING ON THE STATUS OF AN APPEAL

To check on the status of an appeal, veterans or their representatives should contact the office where the claims folder is located (see previous section).

If a claims file is at the Board, veterans or their representatives may call (202) 565-5436 to check on its status (be sure to have the claim number available).

THE BOARD REVIEW PROCESS

When the VBA receives an appeal from a local VA office, the veteran and/or representative will be notified in writing. The Board will then examine the claims folder for completeness, and will provide an opportunity to submit additional written arguments. The case is then assigned to a Board member for review. If a BVA hearing was requested, the Board member assigned the case will conduct the hearing prior to reaching a decision.

When the docket number for an appeal is reached, the file will be reviewed by a Board member and a staff attorney, who will check for completeness, review all evidence and arguments, as well as the regional office's Statement of the Case (and Supplement Statement of the Case, if applicable), the transcript of the hearing (if applicable), the statement of any representative, and any other information included in the claims folder. The staff attorney, if directed to do so by the Board member, may also conduct additional research and prepare recommendations for the Board member's review.

When, in the judgment of the Board member, expert medical opinion, in addition to that available within the VA, is warranted by the medical complexity or controversy involved in an appeal, the Board may secure an advisory medical opinion from one or more independent medical experts who are not employees of the VA.

The VA shall make necessary arrangements with recognized medical schools, universities, or clinics to furnish such advisory medical opinions at the request of the Chairman of the Board. Any such arrangement shall provide that the actual selection of the expert or experts to give the advisory opinion in an individual case shall be made by an appropriate official of such institution.

The Board shall furnish a claimant with notice that an advisory medical opinion has been requested, and shall furnish the claimant with a copy of such opinion when it is received by the Board.

Prior to reaching a decision, the Board member must thoroughly review all materials and recommendations. The Board member will then issue a decision.

The Board member's decision will be mailed to the home address that the Board has on file, so it is extremely important that the VA be kept informed of any address changes.

The BVA must attempt to make its decisions as understandable as possible. However, due to the nature of legal documents, laws, court cases, and medical discussions, decisions can be confusing. If an appeal is denied , the Board will send a "Notice of Appellate Rights" that describes additional actions that can be taken.

The Board annually produces a CD-ROM with the text of its decisions. Most VA regional offices have these CD-ROMS available for review, or the CD-Rom may be purchased from the Government Printing Office. For further information, contact:

Department of Veterans Affairs
Board of Veterans' Appeals (01B)
Washington, D.C. 20420

REMANDS

Sometimes when reviewing a claims folder, the Board member determines additional development of the case is necessary. The appeal is then returned to the local VA office. This is called a "remand." After performing the additional work, the regional office may issue a new decision. If the claim is still denied, the case is returned to the Board for a final decision. (The case keeps its original place on the Board's docket, so it is reviewed soon after it is returned to the Board.)

Depending on the reason for the remand, the regional office may provide the veteran with a Supplement Statement of the Case (SSOC). The claimant then has 60 days from the date the local VA office mails the SSOC to comment on it.APPEALING THE BOARD OF VETERANS' AFFAIRS DECISION

MOTION FOR RECONSIDERATION

If it can be demonstrated that the Board made an obvious error of fact or law in its decision, a written "motion to reconsider" can be filed. Any such motions should be sent directed to the Board, not to the local VA office. A motion to reconsider should not be submitted simply because of disagreement with the BVA's decision. The claimant must be able to show that the Board made a mistake, and that the Board's decision would have been different if the mistake had not been made. A motion to reconsider should be sent directly to the Board, not to the local VA office.

REOPENING

If a claimant has "new and material evidence," he or she can request that the case be re-opened. To be considered "new and material," the evidence submitted must be information related to the case that was not included in the claims folder when the case was decided.

To re-open an appeal, the claimant must submit the new evidence directly to the local VA office that handled the claim.

CUE MOTION

The law was amended in 1997 to provide one more way to challenge a Board decision. A Board decision can be reversed or revised if the claimant is able to show that the decision contained "clear and unmistakable error" (CUE).

The written request for the Board to review its decision for CUE is called a "motion." CUE motions should be filed directly with the Board, and not with the local VA office.

Because CUE is a very complicated area of law, most claimants seek help from a representative to file a CUE motion.

A motion for CUE review of a prior Board decision must meet some very specific requirements, described in the Board's *Rules of Practice*. If the motion is denied a claimant can't ask for another CUE review of the way the Board decided the issues raised in the first CUE motion, so it is very important that the motion be prepared properly the first time out.

Not many CUE motions are successful, because CUE is a very rare kind of error, the kind that compels a conclusion that the Board would have decided the claimant's case differently but for the error. A difference of opinion is not enough.

A motion to review a Board decision for CUE can be filed at any time, but if it is filed after filing a timely Notice of Appeal with the Court, the Board will not be able to rule on your CUE motion.

UNITED STATES COURT OF VETERANS' APPEALS

The United States Court of Veterans' Appeals was created under *Public Law 100-687*, on November 18, 1988. The Court has seven judges, appointed by the President and confirmed by the Senate. Judges are appointed for a 15-year term.

If a claimant is not satisfied with the Board of Veterans' Appeals decision, an appeal can be filed with the United States Court of Veterans Appeals.

If a claimant is not satisfied with the Board of Veterans' Appeals decision, an appeal can be filed with the United States Court of Veterans Appeals (referred to as the "Court"). The Court is an independent court that is not part of the Department of Veterans Affairs. The Court does not hold trials, receive new evidence, or hear witnesses. It reviews the BVA decision, the written record, and the briefs of the parties. Claimants do not need to appear in Washington, D.C. for an appeal. (In approximately 1% of decided cases, the Court holds oral arguments in its Washington courtroom, or occasionally, by telephone conference call.)

A claimant may represent himself or herself, but may want to get advice from an attorney or from a service officer in a veterans organization or a state or county veterans' affairs office. The VA will be represented by its attorney, and a claimant's case may be better presented if he or she is represented.

The Court does not recommend or appoint attorneys to represent claimants. However, the Court does have a *Public List of Practitioners* which shows who is allowed to represent appellants in the Court, and have said that they are available. Most attorneys charge a fee.

To appeal a Board of Veterans' Appeals decision, a claimant must file a "Notice of Appeal" with the Court within 120 days from the date the Board's decision is mailed. (The first day of the 120 days a claimant has to file an appeal to the Court is the day the BVA's decision is postmarked, not the day the decision is signed.)

If a claimant filed a motion to reconsider with the Board of Veterans' Appeals within the 120 day time-frame, and that motion was denied, the claimant has an additional 120 days to file the "Notice of Appeal" with the Court. (This 120 day period begins on the date the Board mails a notification that it has denied the motion to reconsider.) If the Board denies the motion to reconsider, a "Notice of Appellate Rights" will be mailed to the claimant.

In addition to the above 120 day limit, in order for the Court to consider an appeal, a Notice of Disagreement must have been filed with the VA regional office handling the case on or after November 18, 1988.

An original "Notice of Appeal" must be filed directed with the Court at:

United States Court of Veterans Appeals
625 Indiana Avenue, NW, Suite 900
Washington, D.C. 20004
Fax: (202) 501-5848
(Appeals cannot be filed by e-mail)

The fee for an appeal is $50.00, and should be included with the "Notice of Appeal." If a claimant is unable to pay this fee, a "Motion to Waive Filing Fee" form must be completed and returned with the "Notice of Appeal."

If a claimant appeals to the Court, a copy of the "Notice of Appeal" must also be filed with the VA General Counsel at:

Office of the General Counsel (027)
Department of Veterans Affairs
810 Vermont Avenue, NW
Washington, D.C. 20420

Please note that the *original* "Notice of Appeal" that is filed with the Court is the only document that protects a claimants right to appeal a BVA decision. The copy sent to the VA General Counsel does not protect that right, or serve as an official filing.

If the Court accepts an appeal, it will send a printed copy of the rules of practice and procedure to the claimant and his/her representative, if applicable.

To obtain more specific information about the "Notice of Appeal," the methods for filing with the Court, Court filing fees, and other matters covered by the Court's rules, a claimant should contact the Court directly at:

United States Court of Veterans Appeals
625 Indiana Avenue, NW, Suite 900
Washington, D.C. 20004
(800) 869-8654

If either party disagrees with the Court's ruling, an appeal may be filed with the U.S. Court of Appeals for the Federal Circuit, and, thereafter, may seek review in the Supreme Court of the United States.

DEATH OF APPELLANT

According to the law, the death of an appellant generally ends the appellant's appeal, and the Board normally dismisses the appeal without issuing a decision. The rights of a deceased appellant's survivors are not affected by this action. Survivors may still file a claim at the regional office for any benefits to which they may be entitled.

GENERAL GUIDELINES FOR EFFICIENT PROCESSING OF CLAIMS

The following guidelines may help ensure that an appeal is not unnecessarily delayed:

- Consider having an appeal representative assist with the filing of the appeal.

- File the Notice of Disagreement and VA Form 9-Substantive Appeal as soon as possible
- Be as specific as possible when identifying the issues the Board should consider.
- Be as specific as possible when identifying sources of evidence for the VA to obtain. (For example, provide the full names and addresses of physicians, along with dates of treatment, and reasons for treatment.)
- Keep VA informed of current address, phone number, and number of dependents.
- When possible, provide clinical treatment records, rather than simply a statement from a physician.
- Include the claim number on any correspondence with the VA.
- Do not submit material that is not pertinent to the claim. This will only delay the process.
- Do not use the VA Form 9 to raise new claims for the first time. (VA Form 9 is only to be used to appeal decisions on previously submitted claims.)
- Do not use the VA Form 9 to request a local office hearing.
- Do not raise additional issues for the Board's review late in the appeal process. This may cause the appeal to be sent back to the regional office for additional work, and may result in a longer delay.
- Do not submit evidence directly to the Board unless a written or typed statement is included, stating that consideration by the regional office is waived. The statement must clearly indicate that the Board is to review the evidence, even though the regional office has not seen it. If a waiver is not included with any additional evidence submitted directly to the Board, the case may be remanded to the regional office for review, and may result in further delays.
- Do not submit a last minute request for a hearing or a last minute change to the type or location of a hearing unless it is unavoidable. Such a request will likely result in a delay in reaching a final decision.
- Do not miss a scheduled VA examination or hearing.

CHAPTER 35

VA REGIONAL OFFICES & BENEFITS OFFICES

Department of Veterans Affairs Headquarters
810 Vermont Avenue NW
Washington, DC 20420
(202) 273-5400

Alabama (SDN 5)
Montgomery Regional Office
345 Perry Hill Road
Montgomery, AL 36109

Alaska (SDN 8)
Anchorage Regional Office
1201 North Muldoon Road
Anchorage, AK 99504

Arizona (SDN 9)
Phoenix Regional Office
3333 North Central Avenue
Phoenix, AZ 85012

Arkansas (SDN 7)
North Little Rock Regional Office
2200 Fort Roots Drive
Building 65
North Little Rock, AR 72114

California (SDN 9)
Los Angeles Regional Office
Federal Building
11000 Wilshire Boulevard
Los Angeles, CA 90024

Oakland Regional Office
1301 Clay Street
Room 1400 North
Oakland, CA 94612

San Diego Regional Office
8810 Rio San Diego Drive
San Diego, CA 92108

Colorado (SDN 8)
Denver Regional Office
155 Van Gordon Street
Lakewood, CO 80228

Connecticut (SDN 1)
Hartford Regional Office
555 Willard Avenue
Newington, CT 06111

Mailing Address:
P.O. Box 310909
Newington , CT 06131

Delaware (SDN 3)
Wilmington Regional Office
1601 Kirkwood Highway
Wilmington, DE 19805

Florida (SDN 5)
St. Petersburg Regional Office
9500 Bay Pines Boulevard
Bay Pines, FL 33708

Mailing Address:
P.O. Box 1437
St. Petersburg , FL 33731

Georgia (SDN 4)
Atlanta Regional Office
1700 Clairmont Road
Decatur, GA 30033

Mailing Address:
P.O. BOX 100026
Decatur, GA 30031-7026

Hawaii (SDN 9)
Honolulu Regional Office
459 Patterson Road
E-Wing
Honolulu, HI 96819-1522

Idaho (SDN 8)
Boise Regional Office
444 W. Fort Street
Boise, ID 83702-4531

Illinois (SDN 6)
Chicago Regional Office
2122 West Taylor Street
Chicago, IL 60612

Indiana (SDN 2)
Indianapolis Regional Office
575 North Pennsylvania Street
Indianapolis, IN 46204

Iowa (SDN 6)
Des Moines Regional Office
210 Walnut Street
Des Moines, IA 50309

Kansas (SDN 6)
Wichita Regional Office
5500 East Kellogg
Wichita, KS 67211

Kentucky (SDN 3)
Louisville Regional Office
321 West Main Street, Suite 390
Louisville, KY 40202

Louisiana (SDN 7)
New Orleans Regional Office
1250 Poydras Street
New Orleans, LA 70113

Maine (SDN 1)
Togus VA Med/Regional Office
1 VA Center
Augusta, ME 04330

Maryland (SDN 3)
Baltimore Regional Office
31 Hopkins Plaza Federal Bldg
Baltimore, MD 21201

Massachusetts (SDN 1)
Boston VA Regional Office
JFK Federal Building
15 New Sudbury St. Government Center
Boston, MA 02114

Michigan (SDN 2)
Detroit Regional Office
Federal Building
477 Michigan Avenue
Detroit, MI 48226

Minnesota (SDN 6)
St. Paul Regional Office
1 Federal Drive
Fort Snelling
St. Paul, MN 55111-4050

Mississippi (SDN 5)
Jackson Regional Office
1600 East Woodrow Wilson Ave.
Jackson, MS 39216

Missouri (SDN 6)
St. Louis Regional Office
Federal Building
400 South, 18th Street
St. Louis, MO 63103

Montana (SDN 8)
Fort Harrison Regional Office
3633 Veterans Drive
Fort Harrison, MT 59636-0188

Nebraska (SDN 6)
Lincoln Regional Office
3800 Village Drive
Lincoln, NE 68516

Mailing Address:
PO Box 85816
Lincoln, NE 68501-5816

New Hampshire (SDN 1)
Manchester Regional Office
Norris Cotton Federal Bldg
275 Chestnut Street
Manchester, NH 03101

New Jersey (SDN 2)
Newark Regional Office
20 Washington Place
Newark, NJ 07102

New Mexico (SDN 8)
Albuquerque Regional Office
Dennis Chavez Federal Building
500 Gold Avenue, S.W.
Albuquerque, NM 87102

Nevada (SDN 9)
Reno Regional Office
5460 Reno Corporate Dr.
Reno, NV 89511-2250

New York (SDN1)
Buffalo Regional Office
130 South Elmwood Avenue
Buffalo, NY 14202

New York Regional Office
245 West Houston Street
New York, NY 10014

North Carolina (SDN 4)
Winston-Salem Regional Office
Federal Building
251 North Main Street
Winston-Salem, NC 27155

North Dakota (SDN 6)
Fargo Regional Office
2101 Elm Street
Fargo, ND 58102

Ohio (SDN 2)
Cleveland Regional Office
A.J. Celebrezze Federal Building
1240 East 9th Street
Cleveland, OH 44199

Oklahoma (SDN 7)
Muskogee Regional Office
125 South Main Street
Muskogee, OK 74401

Oregon (SDN 8)
Portland Regional Office
100 SW Main Street, Floor 2
Portland, OR 97204

Mailing Address:
100 SW Main St FL 2
Portland, OR 97204

Pennsylvania (SDN 2)
Philadelphia Regional Office
5000 Wissahickon Avenue
Philadelphia, PA 19101

Pittsburgh Regional Office
1000 Liberty Avenue
Pittsburgh, PA 15222

Rhode Island (SDN 1)
Providence Regional Office
380 Westminster St.
Providence, RI 02903

South Carolina (SDN 4)
Columbia Regional Office
6437 Garners Ferry Road
Columbia, SC 29209

South Dakota (SDN 6)
Sioux Falls Regional Office
2501 West 22nd Street
Sioux Falls, SD 57117

Tennessee (SDN 4)
Nashville Regional Office
110 9th Avenue South
Nashville, TN 37203

Southern Area Office
3322 West End, Suite 408
Nashville, TN 37203

Texas (SDN 7)
Houston Regional Office
6900 Almeda Road
Houston, TX 77030

Waco Regional Office
1 Veterans Plaza
701 Clay Avenue
Waco, TX 76799

Utah (SDN 8)
Salt Lake City Regional Office
550 Foothill Drive
Salt Lake City, UT 84158

Vermont (SDN 1)
White River Junction
Regional Office
215 N. Main St.
White River Junction, VT 05009

Virginia (SDN 3)
Roanoke Regional Office
116 N. Jefferson St.
Roanoke, VA 24016

Washington (SDN 8)
Seattle Regional Office
Federal Building
915 2nd Avenue
Seattle, WA 98174

West Virginia (SDN 3)
Huntington Regional Office
640 Fourth Avenue
Huntington, WV 25701

Wisconsin (SDN 6)
Milwaukee Regional Office
5400 West National Avenue
Milwaukee, WI 53214

Wyoming (SDN 8)
Cheyenne Regional Office
2360 East Pershing Blvd.
Cheyenne, WY 82001

District of Columbia (SDN 3)
Washington DC Regional Office
1722 I Street N.W.
Washington, DC 20421

Puerto Rico (SDN 5)
San Juan Regional Office
50 Carr 165
Guaynabo, PR 00968-8024

Philippines (SDN 9)
Manila Regional Office
1501 Roxas Boulevard
Pasay City, PI 1302

Note: SDN = Service Delivery Network

CHAPTER 36

STATE BENEFITS

Many states offer services and benefits to veterans in addition to those offered by the Department of Veterans' Affairs. To find out more about a particular state's programs, individuals should contact the following:

Alabama Department of Veterans' Affairs
RZA Plaza
770 Washington Ave, Suite 530
Montgomery, AL 36102-1509
(334) 242-5077

Alaska Department of Veterans' Affairs
P.O. Box 5800
Fort Richardson, AK 99505-5800
(907) 428-6031

Arizona Department of Veterans' Services
3839 North Third Street, Suite 209
Phoenix, AZ 85012
(602) 248-1554

Arkansas Department of Veterans' Affairs
2200 Fort Roots Drive
Room 119 – Bldg 65
North Little Rock, AR 72114
(501) 370-3820

California Department of Veterans' Affairs
1227 O Street, Suite 300
Sacramento, CA 95814
(800) 952-5626

Colorado Division of Veterans' Affairs
6848 South Revere Parkway
Centennial, CO 80112
(720) 250-1500

Connecticut Department of Veterans' Affairs
287 West Street
Rocky Hill, CT 06067
(860) 616-3603

Delaware Commission of Veterans' Affairs
Robbins Building
802 Silverlake Blvd, Suite 100
Dover, DE 19904
(302) 739-2792
(800) 344-9900 (in state only)

Florida Department of Veterans' Affairs
Mary Grizzle Building, Room 311-K
11351 Ulmerton Road
Largo, FL 33778
(727) 518-3202

Georgia Department of Veterans' Affairs
Floyd Veterans Memorial Building
Suite E-970
Atlanta, GA 30334
(404) 656-2300

Hawaii Office of Veterans' Services
Mailing Address:
459 Patterson Road
E-Wing, Room 1-A103
Honolulu, HI 96819

Location:
Tripler Army Med Center (Ward Road)
VAMROC, E-Wing, Room 1-A103
Honolulu, HI 96819
(808) 433-0420

Idaho Division of Veterans' Affairs
351 Collins Road
Boise, ID 83702
(208) 577-2310

Illinois Department of Veterans' Affairs
362 North Linwood Rd.
Galesburg, IL 61401
(309) 343-2510

Indiana Department of Veterans' Affairs
302 West Washington, Room E120
Indianapolis, IN 46204-2738
(317) 232-3910

Iowa Commission of Veterans' Affairs
7105 N.W. 70th Avenue
Camp Dodge - Building 3663
Johnston, IA 50131-1824
(515) 242-5331

Kansas Commission on Veterans' Affairs
Jayhawk Towers
Suite 1004
700 S.W. Jackson Street
Topeka, KS 66603-3714
(785) 296-3976

Kentucky Department of Veterans' Affairs
1111 Louisville Road
NGAKY Building
Frankfort, KY 40601
(502) 564-9203

Louisiana Department of Veterans' Affairs
P.O. Box 94095
Capitol Station
1885 Wooddale Blvd.
10th Floor, Room 1013
Baton Rouge, LA 70806
(225) 219-5000

Maine Bureau of Veterans' Services
117 State House Station
Camp Keyes Building 7, Room 115
Augusta, ME 04333
(207) 430-6035

Maryland Department of Veterans' Affairs
16 Francis St. 4th Floor
Annapolis, MD 21401
(410) 260-3838

Massachusetts Department of Veterans' Services
600 Washington Street, Suite 1100
Boston, MA 02111
(617) 210-5480

Michigan Department of Veterans' Affairs
7109 W. Saginaw
Lansing, MI 48913
(517) 335-6523

Minnesota Department of Veterans' Affairs
State Veterans Service Building
20 West 12th Street, 2nd Floor Rm. 206
St. Paul, MN 55155-2079
(651) 296-2562

Mississippi State Veterans' Affairs Board
3466 Highway 80 East
P.O. Box 5947
Pearl, MS 39288-5947
(601) 576-4850

Missouri Veterans' Commission
Mailing Address:
205 Jefferson Street
12th Floor Jefferson Building
P.O. Drawer 147
Jefferson City, MO 65102
(573) 751-3779

Montana Veterans' Affairs Division
P.O. Box 5715
1900 Williams Street
Helena, MT 59604
(406) 324-3740

Nebraska Department of Veterans' Affairs
State Office Building
301 Centennial Mall South
P.O. Box 95083
Lincoln, NE 68509-5083
(402) 471-2458

Nevada Commission for Veterans' Affairs
5460 Reno Corporate Dr. Suite 131
Reno, NV 89511
(775) 688-1656

New Hampshire Office of Veterans' Service
275 Chestnut Street
Room 517
Manchester, NH 03101-2411
(603) 624-9230
1-800-622-9230 (in state only)

New Jersey Department of Veterans' Affairs
Eggert Crossing Road
PO Box 340
Trenton, NJ 08625-0508
(800) 624-0508

New Mexico Veterans' Service Commission
Bataan Memorial Building
407 Galisteo St. Rm. 142
Santa Fe, NM 87504
(866) 433-8387

New York Division of Veterans' Affairs
2 Empire State Plaza
17th Floor
Albany, NY 12223-1551
(518) 474-6114

North Carolina Division of Veterans' Affairs
325 N. Salisbury Street
Raleigh, NC 27601
(919) 807-4250

North Dakota Department of Veterans' Affairs
4201 38th St S # 104
Fargo, ND 58104
(701) 239-7165

Ohio Governor's Office of Veterans' Affairs
77 South High Street
Columbus, OH 43215
(614) 644-0898

Oklahoma Department of Veterans' Affairs
2311 N. Central Avenue
Oklahoma City, OK 73105
(405) 521-3684

Oregon Department of Veterans' Affairs
100 South Main St.
Portland, OR 97204
(503) 412-4777

Pennsylvania Department of Veterans' Affairs
Fort Indiantown Gap
Building S-O-47
Annville, PA 17003-5002
(717) 861-2000

Rhode Island Division of Veterans' Affairs
480 Metacom Avenue
Bristol, RI 02809
(401) 462-0324

South Carolina Office of Veterans' Affairs
1205 Pendleton Street, Suite 463
Columbia, SC 29201
(803) 734-0200

South Dakota Division of Veterans' Affairs
425 East Capitol Avenue
c/o 500 East Capitol Avenue
Pierre, SD 57501
(605) 773-3269

Tennessee Department of Veterans' Affairs
312 Rosa Parks Ave.
Nashville, TN 37243-1010
(615) 741-2931

Texas Veterans' Commission
1700 Congress Ave.
Austin, TX 78701
(512) 463-5538

Utah Division of Veterans' Affairs
550 Foothill Blvd, Room 202
Salt Lake City, UT 84113
(801) 326-2372

Vermont State Veterans' Affairs
118 State Street
Montpelier, VT 05602
(802) 828-3379

Virginia Department of Veterans' Affairs
900 East Main Street
Richmond, VA 23219
(804) 786-0286

Washington Department of Veterans' Affairs
P.O. Box 41150
1011 Plum Street
Olympia, WA 98504-1150
(800) 562-0132

West Virginia Division of Veterans' Affairs
1514-B Kanawha Blvd., East
Charleston, WV 25311
(304) 558-3661

Wisconsin Department of Veterans' Affairs
201 West Washington Avenue
Madison, WI 53703
(800) 947-8387

Wyoming Veterans' Affairs Commission
Wyoming ANG Armory
5905 CY Avenue - Room 101
Casper, WY 82604
(307) 265-7372

American Samoa Veterans' Affairs
P.O. Box 982942
Pago Pago
American Samoa 96799
(001) 684-633-4206

Guam Veterans' Affairs Office
Mailing Address:
P.O. Box 3279
Agana, Guam 96932
(671) 475-4222
Location:
"M" Street
HSE #105
Tiyan, Guam

Puerto Rico Public Advocate for Veterans' Affairs
Mailing Address:
Apartado 11737
Fernandez Juncos Station
San Juan, PR 00910-1737
Location:
Mercantile Plaza Bldg,
Fourth Floor, Suite 4021
Hato Rey, PR 00918-1625
(787) 758-5760

Government of the Virgin Islands
Division of Veterans' Affairs
1013 Estate Richmond
Christiansted, St. Croix VI
00820-4349
(340) 773-6663

CHAPTER 37

MILITARY PERSONNEL RECORDS

The U.S. Department of Veterans Affairs does not maintain veterans' military service records.

The personnel records of individuals currently in the military service, in the reserve forces, and those completely separated from military service are located in different offices. A nominal fee is charged for certain types of service. In most instances service fees cannot be determined in advance. If your request involves a service fee you will be notified as soon as that determination is made.

A veteran and spouse should be aware of the location of the veteran's discharge and separation papers. If a veteran cannot locate discharge and separation papers, duplicate copies may be obtained (further information regarding who to contact is included later in this chapter).

Use "Standard Form 180, Request Pertaining To Military Records," which is available from VA offices and veterans organizations. Specify that a duplicate separation document or discharge is needed. The veteran's full name should be printed or typed so that it can be read clearly, but the request must also contain the signature of the veteran or the signature of the next of kin, if the veteran is deceased. Include branch of service, service number or Social Security number and exact or approximate date and years of service.

It is not necessary to request a duplicate copy of a veteran's discharge or separation papers solely for the purpose of filing a claim for VA benefits. If complete information about the veteran's service is furnished on the application, VA will obtain verification of service from the National Personnel Records Center or the service department concerned.

WHO TO CONTACT

The various categories of military personnel records are described in the tables below. Please read the following notes carefully, to make sure an inquiry is sent to the right address. Please note especially that the record is not sent to the National Personnel Records Center as long as the person retains any sort of reserve obligation, whether drilling or non-drilling.

SPECIAL NOTES FOR FOLLOWING TABLES:

- **Records at the National Personnel Records Center:** Note that it takes at least 3 months, and often 6 or 7, for the file to reach the National Personnel Records Center after the military obligation has ended (such as by discharge). If only a short time has passed, please send the inquiry to the address shown for active or current reserve members. Also, if the person has only been released from active duty, but is still in a reserve status, the personnel record will stay at the location specified for reservists. A person can retain a reserve obligation for several years, even without attending meetings or receiving annual training.

- If there were two or more periods of service within the same branch, send your request (only one is necessary) to the office having the records for the LAST PERIOD OF SERVICE.)

LOCATION OF AIR FORCE MILITARY PERSONNEL & HEALTH RECORDS

Status of Service Member or Veteran	Location of Personnel Record	Location of Health Record
Discharged, deceased, or retired before 5/1/1994	National Personnel Records Center 1 Archives Drive St. Louis, MO 63138 (314) 801-0800 Note: Personnel records are Archival 62 years after the service member's separation	National Personnel Records Center 1 Archives Drive St. Louis, MO 63138 (314) 801-0800
May 1, 1994 to September 30, 2004	National Personnel Records Center 1 Archives Drive St. Louis, MO 63138 (314) 801-0800	Department of Veterans Affairs Records Management Center PO Box 5020 St Louis MO 63115 (314) 538-4500
Discharged, deceased or retired from active duty on or after October 1, 2004	Air Force Personnel Center HQ AFPC/DPSSRP 550 C Street West, Suite 19 Randolph AFB, TX 78150-4721 (800) 525-0102	Department of Veterans Affairs Records Management Center P.O. Box 5020 St. Louis, MO 63115-5020 1-800-827-1000

Status of Service Member or Veteran	Location of Personnel Record	Location of Health Record
Active (including National Guard on active duty in the Air Force), TDRL, or general officers retired with pay	AIR FORCE PERSONNEL CENTER HQ AFPC/DPSRP 550 C Street West Suite 19 Randolph AFB, TX 78150 (800) 616-3775	
Reserve, retired reserve in nonpay status, current National Guard officers not on active duty in the Air Force, or National Guard released from active duty in the Air Force	Air Reserve Personnel Center /DSMR HQ ARPC/DPSSA/B 6760 E. Irvington Place, Suite 4600 Denver, CO 80280-4600 (800) 525-0102	
Current Air National Guard enlisted not on active duty in the Air Force	Adjutant General of your state	

LOCATION OF ARMY MILITARY PERSONNEL & HEALTH RECORDS

Status of Service Member or Veteran	Location of Personnel Record	Location of Health Record
Discharged, deceased, or retired (Enlisted) before 11/1/1912	Old Military and Civil Records (NWCTB-Military) Textual Services Division 700 Pennsylvania Ave., N.W. Washington, DC 20408-0001 (202) 357-5000	
Discharged, deceased, or retired (Officer) before 7/1/1917	Old Military and Civil Records (NWCTB-Military) Textual Services Division 700 Pennsylvania Ave., N.W. Washington, DC 20408-0001	

Status of Service Member or Veteran	Location of Personnel Record	Location of Health Record
	(202) 357-5000	
Discharged, deceased, or retired (Enlisted) 11/1/1912 – 10/15/1992	National Personnel Records Center 1 Archives Drive St. Louis, MO 63138 (314) 801-0800	National Personnel Records Center 1 Archives Drive St. Louis, MO 63138 (314) 801-0800
Discharged, deceased, or retired (Officer) 7/1/1917 – 10/15/1992	National Personnel Records Center Military Personnel Records 9700 Page Avenue St. Louis, MO 63132 (314) 801-0800	National Personnel Records Center Military Personnel Records 9700 Page Avenue St. Louis, MO 63132 (314) 801-0800
Discharged, deceased, or retired on or after 10/16/1992	National Personnel Records Center 1 Archives Drive St. Louis, MO 63138 (314) 801-0800	Department of Veterans Affairs Records Management Center PO Box 5020 St Louis MO 63115-5020 (314) 538-4500
Reserve; or active duty records of current National Guard members who performed service in the U.S. Army before 7/1/1972	Commander U.S. Army Personnel Command ATTN: ARPC-ZCC-B 1 Reserve Way St. Louis, MO 62132-5200	
October 16, 1992 to September 30, 2002 (All Personnel)	National Personnel Records Center, NARA 1 Archives Drive St. Louis, MO 63138 (314) 801-0800	Department of Veterans Affairs Records Management Center P.O. Box 5020 St. Louis, MO 63115-50 (800) 827-1000
Discharged, deceased or retired on or after October 1, 2002 (All Personnel)	Note: records are stored electronically at AHRC but requests are serviced by: 1 Archives Drive St. Louis, MO 63138 (314) 801-0800	Department of Veterans Affairs Records Management Center P.O. Box 5020 St. Louis, MO 63115-5020 (800) 827-1000

Status of Service Member or Veteran	Location of Personnel Record	Location of Health Record
Active enlisted (including National Guard on active duty in the U.S. Army) or TDRL enlisted	U.S. Army Human Resources Command AHRC-PDR-VIB 1600 Spearhead Division Avenue Dept 420 Fort Knox, KY 40122-5402 (800) 318-5298	
Active officers (including National Guard on active duty in the U.S. Army) or TDRL officers	U.S. Army Human Resources Command Attn: AHRC-PDR-VIB 1600 Spearhead Division Avenue Dept 420 Fort Knox, KY 40122-5402 (800) 318-5298	

LOCATION OF COAST GUARD MILITARY PERSONNEL & HEALTH RECORDS

Status of Service Member or Veteran	Location of Personnel Record	Location of Health Record
Discharged, deceased, or retired before 1/1/1897	The National Archive's Old Military and Civil Records Branch (NWCTB-Military) Textual Services Division 700 Pennsylvania Ave., N.W. Washington, DC 20408 (202) 357-5000	
Discharged, deceased, or retired: 1/1/1898 – 3/31/1998	National Personnel Records Center Military Personnel Records National Personnel Records Center, NARA 1 Archives Drive St. Louis, MO 63138 (314) 801-0800	National Personnel Records Center Military Personnel Records National Personnel Records Center, NARA 1 Archives Drive St. Louis, MO 63138 (314) 801-0800
Discharged, deceased, or retired on or after: 4/1/1998	National Personnel Records Center Military Personnel Records	Department of Veterans Affairs Records Management

Status of Service Member or Veteran	Location of Personnel Record	Location of Health Record
	Records Center, NARA 1 Archives Drive St. Louis, MO 63138 (314) 801-0800	Center 1 Archives Drive St. Louis, MO 63138 (314) 801-0800
Active, reserve, or TDRL	Commander, CGPC-adm-3 USCG Personnel Command 4200 Wilson Blvd. Suite 1100 Arlington, VA 22203-1804 (866) 634-0574	

LOCATION OF MARINE CORPS MILITARY PERSONNEL & HEALTH RECORDS

Status of Service Member or Veteran	Location of Personnel Record	Location of Health Record
Discharged, deceased, or retired before 1/1/1905	National Archives & Records Administration Old Military and Civil Records (NWCTB-Military) Textual Services Division 700 Pennsylvania Ave., N.W. Washington, DC 20408-0001 (202) 357-5000	
Discharged, deceased, or retired (Enlisted): 1906 – 9/8/1939	National Personnel Records Center, NARA 1 Archives Drive St. Louis, MO 63138 (314) 801-0800	National Personnel Records Center, NARA 1 Archives Drive St. Louis, MO 63138 (314) 801-0800
Discharged, deceased, or retired (All Personnel): 1/1/1905 – 4/30/1994	National Personnel Records Center Military Personnel Records 9700 Page Avenue St. Louis, MO 63132-5100 (314) 801-0800	National Personnel Records Center Military Personnel Records 9700 Page Avenue St. Louis, MO 63132-5100 (314) 801-0800
Discharged, deceased, or retired from May 1, 1994 to December 31, 1998	National Personnel Records Center Military Personnel Records 9700 Page Avenue St. Louis, MO 63132-5100 (314) 801-0800	Department of Veterans Affairs Records Management Center PO Box 5020 St Louis MO 63115-5020 (314) 538-4500

Status of Service Member or Veteran	Location of Personnel Record	Location of Health Record
Discharged, deceased or retired on or after January 1, 1999	Headquarters U.S. Marine Corps Personnel Management Support Branch (MMSB) 2008 Elliot Road Quantico, VA 22134-5030 Phone: (800) 268-3710	Department of Veterans Affairs Records Management P.O. Box 5020 St. Louis, MO 63115-5020 (800) 827-1000
Individual Ready Reserve or Fleet Marine Corps Reserve	Headquarters U.S. Marine Corps Personnel Management Support Branch (MMSB) 2008 Elliot Road Quantico, VA 22134-5030 Phone: (800) 268-3710	

LOCATION OF NAVY MILITARY PERSONNEL & HEALTH RECORDS

Status of Service Member or Veteran	Location of Personnel Record	Location of Health Record
Discharged, deceased, or retired (Enlisted) before 1/1/1885	National Archives & Records Administration Old Military and Civil Records (NWCTB-Military) Textual Services Division 700 Pennsylvania Ave., N.W. Washington, DC 20408-0001 (202) 357-5000	
Discharged, deceased, or retired (Officer) before 1/1/1903	National Archives & Records Administration Old Military and Civil Records (NWCTB-Military) Textual Services Division 700 Pennsylvania Ave., N.W. Washington, DC 20408-0001 (202) 357-5000	

Status of Service Member or Veteran	Location of Personnel Record	Location of Health Record
Discharged, deceased, or retired (Enlisted): 1885 – 1/30/1994	National Personnel Records Center, NARA 1 Archives Drive St. Louis, MO 63138 (314) 801-0800	National Personnel Records Center, NARA 1 Archives Drive St. Louis, MO 63138 (314) 801-0800
Discharged, deceased, or retired (Officer) 1902– 1/30/1994	National Personnel Records Center, NARA 1 Archives Drive St. Louis, MO 63138 (314) 801-0800	National Personnel Records Center Military Personnel Records 9700 Page Avenue St. Louis, MO 63132-5100 (314) 801-0800
January 31, 1994 to December 31, 1994 (All Personnel)	National Personnel Records Center, NARA 1 Archives Drive St. Louis, MO 63138 (314) 801-0800	
Discharged, deceased, or retired on or after: 1/1/1995 (* see note on Navy Records from 1995 on)	Navy Personnel Command (PERS-312E) 5720 Integrity Drive Millington, TN 38055-3120 (901) 874-4885	Department of Veterans Affairs Records Management Center PO Box 5020 St Louis MO 63115-5020 (314) 538-4500
Active, reserve, or TDRL	Navy Personnel Command (PERS-313C1) 5720 Integrity Drive Millington, TN 38055 (901) 874-4885	

NOTE: Beginning in 1995, the United States Navy no longer retires military personnel records to the NPRC (MPR). For the conversion period between 1995 and 1997, either the NPRC or the Navy may hold the record, but it is recommended that all requests relating to Navy personnel discharged, deceased, or retired from 1995 to the present contact:

Navy Personnel Command
PERS-313C1, 5720 Integrity Drive
Millington, TN 38055-3130.

FACTS ABOUT THE 1973 ST. LOUIS FIRE AND LOST RECORDS

A fire at the NPRC in St. Louis on July 12, 1973, destroyed about 80 percent of the records for Army personnel discharged between November 1, 1912, and January 1, 1960. About 75 percent of the records for Air Force personnel with surnames from "Hubbard" through "Z" discharged between September 25, 1947, and January 1, 1964, were also destroyed.

What Was Lost

It is hard to determine exactly what was lost in the fire, because:

- There were no indices to the blocks of records involved. The records were merely filed in alphabetical order for the following groups:
- World War I: Army November 1, 1912 - September 7, 1939
- World War II: Army September 8, 1939 - December 31, 1946
- Post World War II: Army January 1, 1947 - December 31, 1959
- Air Force September 25, 1947 - December 31, 1963
- Millions of records, especially medical records, had been withdrawn from all three groups and loaned to the Department of Veterans Affairs (VA) before the fire. The fact that one's records are not in NPRC files at a particular time does not mean the records were destroyed in the fire.

Reconstruction of Lost Records

If veterans learn that their records may have been lost in the fire, they may send photocopies of any documents they possess -- especially separation documents -- to the NPRC at:

National Personnel Records Center
Military Personnel Records
9700 Page Blvd.
St. Louis, MO 63132-5100.

Alternate Sources of Military Service Data

When veterans don't have copies of their military records and their NPRC files may have been lost in the St. Louis fire, essential information about their military service may be available from a number of other sources, including:

- The Department of Veterans Affairs (VA) maintains records on veterans whose military records were affected by the fire if the veteran or a beneficiary filed a claim before July 1973.
- Service information may also be found in various kinds of "organizational" records such as unit morning reports, payrolls and military orders on file at the NPRC or other National Archives and Records Administration facilities.
- There also is a great deal of information available in records of the State Adjutants General, and other state "veterans services" offices.

By using alternate sources, NPRC often can reconstruct a veteran's beginning and ending dates of active service, the character of service, rank, time lost on active duty, and periods of hospitalization. NPRC can issue NA Form 13038, "Certification of Military Service," considered the equivalent of a Form DD-214, "Report of Separation From Active Duty," to use in establishing eligibility for veterans benefits.

Necessary Information for File Reconstruction

The key to reconstructing military data is to give the NPRC enough specific information so the staff can properly search the various sources. The following information is normally required:

- Full name used during military service;
- Place of entry into service;
- Branch of service;
- Last unit of assignment;
- Approximate dates of service;
- Place of discharge;
- Service number or Social Security number.

CHAPTER 38

CORRECTION OF RECORDS BY CORRECTION BOARDS

Retirees may feel that their records need correcting or amending for any number of reasons. Correction boards consider formal applications for corrections of military records.

Each service department has a permanent Board for Correction of Military (Naval) records, composed of civilians, to act on applications for correction of records.

In order to justify correction of a military record, the applicant must prove to a Corrections Board that the alleged entry or omission in the record was in error or unjust. This board considers all applications and makes recommendations to the appropriate branch Secretary.

An application for correction of record must be filed within three years after discovering the error or injustice.

An application for correction of record must be filed within three years after discovering the error or injustice. If filed after the three-year deadline, the applicant must include in the application reasons the board should find it in the interest of justice to accept the late application.

Evidence may include affidavits or signed testimony executed under oath, and a brief of arguments supporting the application. All evidence not already included in one's record must be submitted. The responsibility for securing new evidence rests with the applicant.

To justify any correction, it is necessary to show to the satisfaction of the board that the alleged entry or omission in the records was in error or unjust. Applications should include all available evidence, such as signed statements of witnesses or a brief of arguments supporting the requested correction. Application is made with DD Form 149, available at VA offices, from veterans organizations or from the Internet

Each of the military services maintains a discharge review board with authority to change, correct or modify discharges or dismissals that are not issued by a sentence of a general courts-martial. The board has no authority to address medical discharges. The veteran or, if the veteran is deceased or incompetent, the surviving spouse, next of kin or legal representative may apply for a review of discharge by writing to the military department concerned, using DoD Form 293. This form may be obtained at a VA regional office, from veterans organizations or from the Internet. However, if the discharge was more than 15 years ago, a veteran must petition the appropriate service Board for Correction of Military Records using DoD Form 149, which is discussed in the "Correction of Military Records" section of this booklet. A discharge review is conducted by a review of an applicant's record and, if requested, by a hearing before the board.

Discharges awarded as a result of a continuous period of unauthorized absence in excess of 180 days make persons ineligible for VA benefits regardless of action taken by discharge review boards, unless VA determines there were compelling circumstances for the absence. Boards for the correction of military records also may consider such cases.

Veterans with disabilities incurred or aggravated during active military service may qualify for medical or related benefits regardless of separation and characterization of service. Veterans separated administratively under other than honorable conditions may request that their discharge be reviewed for possible recharacterization, provided they file their appeal within 15 years of the date of separation. Questions regarding the review of a discharge should be addressed to the appropriate discharge review board at the address listed on DoD Form 293.

JURISDICTION

Correction boards are empowered to deal with all matters relating to error or injustice in official records. The boards cannot act until all other administrative avenues of relief have been exhausted. Discharges by sentence of Special Court-Martial and administrative discharges cannot be considered by correction boards unless:

- Application to the appropriate Discharge Review Board has been denied and rehearing is barred; or
- Application cannot be made to the Discharge review Board because the time limit has expired.

APPLICATION

DD Form 149, Application for Correction of Military or Naval record, must be used to apply for correction of military records. It should be submitted, along with supporting evidence, to one of the review boards listed below:

Army
Army Review Boards Agency (ARBA)
ATTN: Client Information and Quality Assurance
251 18th Street South, Suite 385
Arlington, VA 22202

Navy & Marine Corps
Board for Correction of Naval Records
701 S. Courthouse Road
Bldg 12, Suite 1001
Arlington, VA 22204-2490
(703) 604-6884

Coast Guard
DHS Office of the General Counsel
Board for Correction of Military Records
Mailstop # 485
245 Murray Lane
Washington, DC 20528
(202) 447-4099

Air Force
Air Force Board for Correction of Military Records
1535 Command Drive
EE Wing 3rd Floor
Andrews AFB DC 20331-7002

DECISIONS

In the absence of new and material evidence the decision of a correction board, as approved or modified by the Secretary of the Service Department, is final. Adverse decisions are subject to judicial review in a U.S. District Court. Decisions of the Boards for Correction of Military or Naval Records must be made available for public inspection. Copies of the decisional documents will be provided on request.

CHAPTER 39

DISCHARGE REVIEW

DISCHARGE REVIEW BOARDS

Each branch of service has discharge review boards to review the discharge or dismissal of former service members. (The Navy Board considers Marine Corps cases.)

AUTHORITY

Initial application to a discharge review board must be made within 15 years after the date of discharge.

Discharge review boards can, based on the official records and such other evidence as may be presented, upgrade a discharge or change the reason and authority for discharge. Discharge review boards cannot grant disability retirement, revoke a discharge, reinstate any person in the service, recall any person to active duty, act on requests for re-enlistment code changes or review a discharge issued by sentence of a general court-martial. Discharge review boards have no authority to address medical discharges.

Discharges awarded as a result of a continuous period of unauthorized absence in excess of 180 days make persons ineligible for VA benefits regardless of action taken by discharge review boards, unless VA determines there were compelling circumstances for the absence. Boards for the correction of military records also may consider such cases.

APPLICATION

DD Form 293, "Application for Review of Discharge or Dismissal from the Armed Forces of the United States," is used to apply for review of discharge. (If more than 15 years have passed since discharge, DD Form 149 should be used.) The individual or, if legal proof of death is provided, the surviving spouse, next-of-kin, or legal representative can apply. If the individual is mentally incompetent, the spouse, next-of-kin, or legal representative can sign the application, but must provide legal proof of incompetence. The instruction for completing DD Form 293 must be read and complied with.

Time Limitation

Initial application to a discharge review board must be made within 15 years after the date of discharge.

Personal Appearance

A personal appearance before the Discharge Review Board is a legal right. A minimum 30-day notice of the scheduled hearing date is given unless the applicant waives the advance notice in writing. Reasonable postponements can be arranged if circumstances preclude appearance on the scheduled date. All expenses of appearing before the board must be paid by the applicant. If no postponement of a scheduled hearing date is requested and the applicant does not appear on the date scheduled, the right to a personal hearing is forfeited and the case will be considered on the evidence of record.

Hearings

Discharge review boards conduct hearings at various locations in the U.S. Information concerning hearing locations and availability of counsel can be obtained by writing to the appropriate board at the address shown on DD Form 293. Those addresses are listed at the end of this chapter.

Published Uniform Standards For Discharge Review

A review of discharge is conducted to determine if an individual was properly and equitably discharged. Each case is considered on its own merits.

- A discharge is considered to have been proper unless the discharge review determines:
  - That there is an error of fact, law, procedures, or discretion which prejudiced the rights of the individual, or
  - That there has been a change of policy which requires a change of discharge.
- A discharge is considered to have been equitable unless the discharge review determines:
  - That the policies and procedures under which the individual was discharged are materially different from current policies and procedures and that the individual probably would have received a better discharge if the current policies and procedures had been in effect at the time of discharge; or
  - That the discharge was inconsistent with the standards of discipline; or
  - That the overall evidence before the review board warrants a change of discharge. In arriving at this determination, the discharge review board will consider the quality and the length of the service performed, the individual's physical and mental capability to serve satisfactorily, abuses of

authority which may have contributed to the character of the discharge issued, and documented discriminatory acts against the individual.

DECISIONS

An authenticated decisional document is prepared and a copy provided to each applicant and council.

- A copy of each decisional document, with identifying details of the applicant and other persons deleted to protect personal privacy, must be made available for public inspection and copying. These are located in a reading room in the Pentagon, Washington, DC.
- To provide access to the documents by persons outside the Washington, D.C. area, the documents have been indexed. The index includes case number of each case; the date, authority and reason for, and character if the discharge, and the issues addressed in the statement of findings, conclusions and reasons.
- Interested parties may contact the DVARO or the State veterans Agency for the location of an index. A copy of the index will be made available at the sites of traveling board hearings during the period the board is present.
- An individual can go through the index and identify cases in which the circumstances leading to discharge are similar to those in the individual's case. A copy of these case decisional documents can be requested by writing to:

DA Military Review Boards Agency
ATTN: SFBA (Reading Room)
Room 1E520
The Pentagon
Washington, D.C. 20310.

Examination of decisional documents may help to identify the kind of evidence that was used in the case, and may indicate why relief was granted or denied. Decisional documents do not set precedence - each case is considered on its own merits.

RECONSIDERATION

An application that has been denied can be reopened if:

- The applicant submits newly discovered evidence that was not available at the time of the original consideration.
- The applicant did not request a personal hearing in the original application and now desires to appear before the board. If the applicant fails to appear at the hearings, the case will be closed with no further action.
- The applicant was not represented by counsel in the original consideration and now desires counsel and the application for reconsideration is submitted within 15 years following the date of discharge.

- Changes in policy, law or regulations have occurred or federal court orders have been issued which substantially enhance the rights of the applicant.

SERVICE DEPARTMENT DISCHARGE REVIEW BOARD ADDRESSES

ARMY

Army Discharge Review Board
Attention: SFMR-RBB
251 18th St. South
Suite 385
Arlington, VA 22202-4508

NAVY & USMC

Secretary of the Navy Council of Review Boards
720 Kennon St. SE Suite 309
Washington, DC 20374

AIR FORCE

Air Force Military Personnel Center
Attention: DP-MDOA1
Randolph AFB, TX 78150-6001

COAST GUARD

DHS Office of the General Counsel
Board for Correction of Military Records
Mailstop # 485
245 Murray Lane
Washington, DC 20528

CHAPTER 40

PENAL AND FORFEITURE PROVISIONS

The first section of this chapter outlines basic information for veterans with questions concerning the effect of incarceration on VA benefits. The later sections of this chapter provide detailed information regarding misappropriation by fiduciaries, fraudulent acceptance of payments, forfeiture for fraud, forfeiture for treason, and forfeiture for subversive activities.

> *VA benefits are restricted if a veteran, surviving spouse, child, or dependent parent is convicted of a felony and imprisoned for more than 60 days.*

BASIC INFORMATION

VA benefits are restricted if a veteran, surviving spouse, child, or dependent parent is convicted of a felony and imprisoned for more than 60 days. VA may still pay certain benefits, however, the amount paid depends on the type of benefit and reason for imprisonment. Following is information about the benefits most commonly affected by imprisonment.

Please note that overpayments due to failure to notify VA of a veteran's incarceration results in the loss of all financial benefits until the overpayment is recovered.

VA DISABILITY COMPENSATION

VA disability compensation payments are reduced if a veteran is convicted of a felony and imprisoned for more than 60 days. Veterans rated 20 percent or more are limited to the 10 percent disability rate. For a veteran whose disability rating is 10 percent, the payment is reduced by one-half. Once a veteran is released from prison, compensation payments may be reinstated based upon the severity of the service connected disability(ies) at that time.

The disability compensation paid to a veteran incarcerated because of a felony is limited to the 10% disability rate, beginning with the 61st day of imprisonment. For a surviving spouse, child, dependent parent or veteran whose disability rating is 10%, the payment is at the 5% rate. This means that if a veteran was receiving $188 or more prior to incarceration, the new payment amount will be $98. If a veteran was receiving $98 before incarceration, the new payment amount will be $49.

If a veteran resides in a halfway house, participates in a work release program, or is on parole, compensation payments will not be reduced.

*Increased compensation during incarceration - the amount of any increased compensation awarded to an incarcerated veteran that results from other than a statutory rate increase may be subject to reduction due to incarceration

VA DISABILITY PENSION

VA will stop a veteran's pension payments beginning on the 61st day of imprisonment for conviction of either a felony or misdemeanor. Payments may be resumed upon release from prison if the veteran meets VA eligibility requirements.

VA MEDICAL CARE

While incarcerated veterans do not forfeit their eligibility for medical care, current regulations restrict VA from providing hospital and outpatient care to an incarcerated veteran who is an inmate in an institution of another government agency when that agency has a duty to give the care or services.

However, VA may provide care once the veteran has been unconditionally released from the penal institution. Veterans interested in applying for enrollment into the VA health care system should contact the nearest VA health care facility upon their release.

EDUCATIONAL ASSISTANCE / SUBSISTENCE ALLOWANCE

Beneficiaries incarcerated for other than a felony can receive full monthly benefits, if otherwise entitled. Convicted felons residing in halfway houses (also known as "residential re-entry centers"), or participating in work-release programs also can receive full monthly benefits.

- Claimants incarcerated for a felony conviction can be paid only the costs of tuition, fees, and necessary books, equipment, and supplies.
- VA cannot make payments for tuition, fees, books, equipment, or supplies if another Federal State, or local program pays these costs in full.
- If another government program pays only a part of the cost of tuition, fees, books, equipment, or supplies, VA can authorize the incarcerated claimant payment for the remaining part of the costs.

CLOTHING ALLOWANCE

In the case of a veteran who is incarcerated in a Federal, State, or local penal institution for a period in excess of 60 days and who is furnished clothing without charge by the institution, the amount of any annual clothing allowance payable to the veteran shall be reduced by an amount equal to 1/365 of the amount of the allowance otherwise payable under that section for each day on which the veteran was so incarcerated during the 12-month period preceding the date on which payment of the allowance would be due.

PAYMENT TO DEPENDENTS

VA may be able to take part of the amount that the incarcerated veteran is not receiving and pay it to his or her dependents, if they can show need. Interested dependents should contact the nearest VA regional office for details on how to apply. They will be asked to provide income information as part of the application process.

- VA will inform a veteran whose benefits are subject to reduction of the right of the veteran's dependents to an apportionment while the veteran is incarcerated, and the conditions under which payments to the veteran may be resumed upon release from incarceration.
- VA will also notify the dependents of their right to an apportionment if the VA is aware of their existence and can obtain their addresses.
- No apportionment may be made to or on behalf of any person who is incarcerated in a Federal, State, or local penal institution for conviction of a felony.
- An apportionment of an incarcerated veteran's VA benefits is not granted automatically to the veteran's dependents. The dependent(s) must file a claim for an apportionment.

RESTORATION OF BENEFITS

When a veteran is released from prison, his or her compensation or pension benefits may be restored. Depending on the type of disability, the VA may schedule a medical examination to see if the veteran's disability has improved or worsened.

MISAPPROPRIATION BY FIDUCIARIES

Whoever, being a guardian, curator, conservator, committee, or person legally vested with the responsibility or care of a claimant or a claimant's estate, or any other person having charge and custody in a fiduciary capacity of money heretofore or hereafter paid under any of the laws administered by the VA for the benefit of any minor, incompetent, or other beneficiary, shall lend, borrow, pledge, hypothecate, use, or exchange for other funds or property, except as authorized by law, or embezzle or in any manner misappropriate any such money or property derived wherefrom in whole or in part, and coming into such fiduciary's control in any matter whatever in the execution of such fiduciary's trust, or under color of such fiduciary's office or service as such fiduciary, shall be fined in accordance with Title 18, or imprisoned not more than 5 years, or both.

Any willful neglect or refusal to make and file proper accountings or reports concerning such money or property as required by law shall be taken to be sufficient evidence prima facie of such embezzlement or misappropriation.

FRAUDULENT ACCEPTANCE OF PAYMENTS

Any person entitled to monetary benefits under any of the laws administered by the VA whose right to payment ceases upon the happening of any contingency, who thereafter fraudulently accepts any such payment, shall be fined in accordance with Title 18, or imprisoned not more than one year, or both.
Whoever obtains or receives any money or check under any of the laws administered by the VA without being entitled to it, and with intent to defraud the United States or any beneficiary of the United States, shall be fined in accordance with Title 18, or imprisoned not more than one year, or both.

FORFEITURE FOR FRAUD

Whoever knowingly makes or causes to be made or conspires, combines, aids, or assists in, agrees to, arranges for, or in any way procures the making or presentation of a false or fraudulent affidavit, declaration, certificate, statement, voucher, or paper, concerning any claim for benefits under any of the laws administered by the VA (except laws pertaining to insurance benefits) shall forfeit all rights, claims, and benefits under all laws administered by the VA (except laws pertaining to insurance benefits).

Whenever a veteran entitled to disability compensation has forfeited the right to such compensation under this chapter, the compensation payable but for the forfeiture shall thereafter be paid to the veteran's spouse, children, and parents. Payments made to a spouse, children, and parents under the preceding sentence shall not exceed the amounts payable to each if the veteran had died from service-connected disability. No spouse, child, or parent who participated in the fraud for which forfeiture was imposed shall receive any payment by reason of this subsection. Any apportionment award under this subsection may not be made in any case after September 1, 1959.

Forfeiture of benefits by a veteran shall not prohibit payment of the burial allowance, death compensation, dependency and indemnity compensation, or death pension in the event of the veteran's death.

After September 1, 1959, no forfeiture of benefits may be imposed under the rules outlined in this chapter upon any individual who was a resident of, or domiciled in, a State at the time the act or acts occurred on account of which benefits would, but not for this subsection, be forfeited unless such individual ceases to be a resident of, or domiciled in, a State before the expiration of the period during which criminal prosecution could be instituted. The paragraph shall not apply with respect to:

- Any forfeiture occurring before September 1, 1959; or
- An act or acts that occurred in the Philippine Islands before July 4, 1946.

The VA is authorized and directed to review all cases in which, because of a false or fraudulent affidavit, declaration, certificate, statement, voucher, or paper, a forfeiture of gratuitous benefits under laws administered by the VA was imposed, pursuant to this section or prior provisions of the law, on or before September 1, 1959. In any such case in which the VA determines that the forfeiture would not have been imposed under the provisions of this section in effect after September 1, 1959, the VA shall remit the forfeiture, effective June 30, 1972. Benefits to which the individual concerned becomes eligible by virtue of any such remission may be awarded, upon application for, and the effective date of any award of compensation, dependency and indemnity compensation, or pension made in such a case shall be fixed in accordance with the facts found, but shall not be earlier than the effective date of the Act or administrative issue. In no event shall such award or increase be retroactive for more than one year from the date of application, or the date of administrative determination of entitlement, whichever is earlier.

FORFEITURE FOR TREASON

Any person shown by evidence satisfactory to the VA to be guilty of mutiny, treason, sabotage, or rendering assistance to an enemy of the United States or its allies shall forfeit all accrued or future gratuitous benefits under laws administered by the VA.

The VA, in its discretion, may apportion and pay any part of benefits forfeited under the preceding paragraph to the dependents of the person forfeiting such benefits. No dependent of any person shall receive benefits by reason of this subsection in excess of the amount to which the dependent would be entitled if such person were dead.

In the case of any forfeiture under this chapter, there shall be no authority after September 1, 1959 to:

- Make an apportionment award pursuant to the preceding paragraph; or
- Make an award to any person of gratuitous benefits based on any period of military, naval, or air service commencing before the date of commission of the offense.

FORFEITURE FOR SUBVERSIVE ACTIVITIES

Any individual who is convicted after September 1, 1959, of any offense listed below shall, from and after the date of commission of such offense, have no right to gratuitous benefits (including the right to burial in a national cemetery) under laws administered by the VA based on periods of military, naval, or air service commencing before the date of commission of such offense, and no other person shall be entitled to such benefits on account of such individual. After receipt of notice of the return of an indictment for such an offense, the VA shall suspend payment of such gratuitous benefits pending disposition of the criminal proceedings. If any individual whose rights to benefits has been terminated pursuant to this section, is granted a pardon of the offense by the President of the United States, the right to such benefits shall be restored as of the date of such pardon.

The offenses referred to in the previous paragraph are:

- Sections 894, 904 and 906 of Title 10 (articles 94, 104, and 106 of the Uniform Code of Military Justice);
- Sections 792, 793, 794, 798, 2381, 2382, 2383, 2384, 2385, 2387, 2388, 2389, 2390, and chapter 105 of Title 18;
- Sections 222, 223, 224, 225 and 226 of the Atomic Energy Act of 1954 (42 U.S.C. 2272, 2273, 2274, 2275, and 2276);
- Section 4 of the Internal Security Act of 1950 (50 U.S.C. 783).

The Secretary of Defense, the Secretary of Transportation, or the Attorney General, as appropriate, shall notify the VA in each case in which an individual is convicted of an offense mentioned in this chapter.

CHAPTER 41

PERIODS OF WAR

Military service is classified either as wartime or peacetime service. This is important because there are significant advantages specifically accruing only to veterans with wartime service.

The following list sets out the periods of wartime designated by Congress for pension purposes. To be considered by the VA to have served during wartime, a veteran need not have served in a combat zone, but simply during one of these designated periods.

Indian Wars:
The period January 1, 1817 through December 31, 1898. Service must have been rendered with the United States military forces against Indian tribes or nations.

Spanish-American War:
The period April 21, 1898 through July 4, 1902. In the case of a veteran who served with the United States military forces engaged in hostilities in the Moro Province the ending date is July 15, 1903.

Mexican Border Period:
The period May 9, 1916 through April 5, 1917, in the case of a veteran who during such period served in Mexico, on the borders thereof, or in the waters adjacent thereto.

World War I:
The period April 6, 1917, through November 11, 1918. In the case of a veteran who served with the United States military forces in Russia, the ending date is April 1, 1920. Service after November 11, 1918 and before July 2, 1921 is considered World War I for compensation or pension purposes, if the veteran served in the active military, naval, or air service after April 5, 1917 and before November 12, 1918.

World War II:
The period December 7, 1941 through December 31, 1946. If the veteran was in service on December 31, 1946, continuous service before July 26, 1947 is considered World War II service.

Korean Conflict:
The period June 27, 1950 through January 31, 1955.

Vietnam Era:
The period August 5, 1964 (February 28, 1961 for Veterans who served "in country" before August 5, 1964), and ending May 7, 1975.

Persian Gulf War:
The period August 2, 1990 through a date to be set by law or Presidential Proclamation.

Future Dates:
The period beginning on the date of any future declaration of war by the Congress, and ending on a date prescribed by Presidential Proclamation or concurrent resolution of the Congress. (Title U.S.C. 10)

CHAPTER 42

COMMON FORMS

General Administration Forms	
Form #	***Purpose***
20-572	Request For Change Of Address / Cancellation Of Direct Deposit
Compensation and Pension Forms	
Form #	***Purpose***
21-22	Appointment Of Veterans Service Organization As Claimant's Representative
21-0304	Application For Spina Bifida Benefits
21-0510	Eligibility Verification Report Instructions
21-0514-1	Parent's DIC Eligibility Verification Report
21-526	Veteran's Application For Compensation Or Pension
21-527	Income-Net Worth And Employment Statement
21-530	Application For Burial Benefits
21-534	Application For DIC, Death Pension, And Accrued Benefits By A Surviving Spouse Or Child
21-535	Application For DIC By Parents
21-601	Application For Reimbursement From Accrued Amounts Due A Deceased Beneficiary
21-674	Request For Approval Of School Attendance
21-686c	Declaration Of Status Of Dependents
21-4138	Statement In Support Of Claim
21-4142	Authorization And Consent To Release Information To The Department Of Veterans Affairs
21-4502	Application For Automobile Or Other Conveyance And Adaptive Equipment
21P-4706c	Fiduciary Agreement
21-6753	Original Or Amended DIC Award
21-8416	Medical Expense Report
21-8678	Application For Annual Clothing Allowance
21-8940	Veteran's Application For Increased Compensation Based On Unemployability
21-0958	Notice of Disagreement

Vocational Rehabilitation and Employment Forms	
Form #	**Purpose**
28-1900	Disabled Veterans Application For Vocational Rehabilitation
28-1902	Counseling Record – Personal Information
28-1902n	Counseling Record – Narrative Report
28-8872	Rehabilitation Plan
28-8872a	Rehabilitation Plan – Continuation Sheet
28-8890	Important Information About Rehabilitation

VA Insurance Forms	
Form #	**Purpose**
29-336	Designation Of Beneficiary – Government Life Insurance
29-1546	Application For Cash Surrender Value / Application For Policy Loan
29-4125	Claim For One Sum Payment
29-4364	Application For Service-Disabled Insurance

Finance and Budget Forms	
Form #	**Purpose**
24-0296	Direct Deposit Enrollment
24-5281	Application For Refund Of Education Contributions - VEAP

Miscellaneous Forms	
Form #	**Purpose**
DD 149	Application For Correction Of Military Record
DD 214	Report of Separation From Active Duty
DD 293	Application For The Review Of Discharge OR Dismissal From The Armed Forces Of The United States
SF 15	Application For 10-Point Veteran's Preference
SF 180	Request Pertaining To Military Records
SGLV8283	Claim For Death Benefits – Form Returned To Office Of Servicemembers' Group Life Insurance
SGLV8285	Request For Insurance (Servicemembers' Group Life Insurance)
SGLV8286	Servicemembers' Group Life Insurance Election And Certificate
SGLV8714	Application For Veterans' Group Life Insurance
SGLF8721	Beneficiary Designation for Veterans Group Life Insurance
VAF 8	Certification To Appeal
VAF 9	Appeal To Board Of Veterans' Appeals
VAF 10 –10ez	Instructions For Completing Application For Health Benefits
VAF 3288	Request For And Consent To Release Of Information From Claimant's Records
VAF 4107	Notice Of Procedural And Appellate Rights
VAF 4107b	Notice Of Procedural And Appellate Rights (Spanish Version)
40-1330	Application For Standard Government Headstone Or Marker For Installation In A Private Or State Veterans' Cemetery

INDEX

Would You Like Additional Copies Of
What Every Veteran Should Know?

Simply tear out this form, and:

Phone 309-757-7760 or Fax 309-278-5304

Mail To: VETERANS INFORMATION SERVICE
P.O. Box 111
East Moline, IL 61244-0111

ORDER ONLINE AT: www.vetsinfoservice.com

☐ Yes! Send me _____ copies of "*What Every Veteran Should Know*", at $25.00 each (shipping & handling included). I request the _______ (specify: current already released 2015, or pre-reserve 2016) edition. New annual books are published every March 1st.

☐ Yes! I would like to subscribe to "*What Every Veteran Should Know*" monthly supplement (an 8-page newsletter which keeps your book up-to-date), and receive ______ copies of all 12 monthly issues (1 year) for $35.00 per subscription (shipping & handling included).

☐ Yes! I want to save money, and receive both the book and the monthly supplement. I would like ______ sets, at $55 per set (shipping & handling included).

Name ______ Current Customer ID?

Address ______

City / State / Zip Code ______

Telephone Number ______ E-mail Address

Amount Enclosed ______ Daytime Phone # (including area code)

Method of Payment:

☐ Check ☐ Visa ☐ MasterCard ☐ Money Order

Credit Card # ______ Expiration Date (Month/Year)

Signature ______

Thank you for your order!
If you have any questions, feel free to contact us at
(309) 757-7760
www.vetsinfoservice.com - Email: help@vetsinfoservice.com

Would You Like Additional Copies Of
<u>What Every Veteran Should Know?</u>

Simply tear out this form, and:

Phone 309-757-7760 or Fax 309-278-5304

Mail To: VETERANS INFORMATION SERVICE
P.O. Box 111
East Moline, IL 61244-0111

ORDER ONLINE AT: www.vetsinfoservice.com

☐ Yes! Send me _____ copies of "*What Every Veteran Should Know*", at $25.00 each (shipping & handling included). I request the _______ (specify: current already released 2015, or pre-reserve 2016) edition. New annual books are published every March 1st.

☐ Yes! I would like to subscribe to "*What Every Veteran Should Know*" monthly supplement (an 8-page newsletter which keeps your book up-to-date), and receive ______ copies of all 12 monthly issues (1 year) for $35.00 per subscription (shipping & handling included).

☐ Yes! I want to save money, and receive both the book and the monthly supplement. I would like ______ sets, at $55 per set (shipping & handling included).

Name Current Customer ID?

Address

City / State / Zip Code

Telephone Number E-mail Address

Amount Enclosed Daytime Phone # (including area code)

Method of Payment:

☐ Check ☐ Visa ☐ MasterCard ☐ Money Order

Credit Card # Expiration Date (Month/Year)

Signature

Thank you for your order!
If you have any questions, feel free to contact us at
(309) 757-7760
www.vetsinfoservice.com - Email: help@vetsinfoservice.com

Would You Like Additional Copies Of
What Every Veteran Should Know?

Simply tear out this form, and:

Phone 309-757-7760 or Fax 309-278-5304

Mail To: VETERANS INFORMATION SERVICE
P.O. Box 111
East Moline, IL 61244-0111

ORDER ONLINE AT: www.vetsinfoservice.com

☐ Yes! Send me _____ copies of "*What Every Veteran Should Know*", at $25.00 each (shipping & handling included). I request the _______ (specify: current already released 2015, or pre-reserve 2016) edition. New annual books are published every March 1st.

☐ Yes! I would like to subscribe to "*What Every Veteran Should Know*" monthly supplement (an 8-page newsletter which keeps your book up-to-date), and receive ______ copies of all 12 monthly issues (1 year) for $35.00 per subscription (shipping & handling included).

☐ Yes! I want to save money, and receive both the book and the monthly supplement. I would like ______ sets, at $55 per set (shipping & handling included).

Name | Current Customer ID?

Address

City / State / Zip Code

Telephone Number | E-mail Address

Amount Enclosed | Daytime Phone # (including area code)

Method of Payment:

☐ Check ☐ Visa ☐ MasterCard ☐ Money Order

Credit Card # | Expiration Date (Month/Year)

Signature

Thank you for your order!
If you have any questions, feel free to contact us at
(309) 757-7760
www.vetsinfoservice.com - Email: help@vetsinfoservice.com

Would You Like Additional Copies Of
What Every Veteran Should Know?

Simply tear out this form, and:

Phone 309-757-7760 or Fax 309-278-5304

Mail To: VETERANS INFORMATION SERVICE
P.O. Box 111
East Moline, IL 61244-0111

ORDER ONLINE AT: www.vetsinfoservice.com

☐ Yes! Send me _____ copies of "*What Every Veteran Should Know*", at $25.00 each (shipping & handling included). I request the _______ (specify: current already released 2015, or pre-reserve 2016) edition. New annual books are published every March 1st.

☐ Yes! I would like to subscribe to "*What Every Veteran Should Know*" monthly supplement (an 8-page newsletter which keeps your book up-to-date), and receive ______ copies of all 12 monthly issues (1 year) for $35.00 per subscription (shipping & handling included).

☐ Yes! I want to save money, and receive both the book and the monthly supplement. I would like ______ sets, at $55 per set (shipping & handling included).

Name   Current Customer ID?

Address

City / State / Zip Code

Telephone Number   E-mail Address

Amount Enclosed   Daytime Phone # (including area code)

Method of Payment:

☐ Check   ☐ Visa   ☐ MasterCard   ☐ Money Order

Credit Card #   Expiration Date (Month/Year)

Signature

Thank you for your order!
If you have any questions, feel free to contact us at
(309) 757-7760
www.vetsinfoservice.com - Email: help@vetsinfoservice.com